W9-ALZ-757

CROWN OF
SLAVES

BAEN BOOKS by DAVID WEBER

Honor Harrington:
On Basilisk Station
The Honor of the Queen
The Short Victorious War
Field of Dishonor
Flag in Exile
Honor Among Enemies
In Enemy Hands
Echoes of Honor
Ashes of Victory
War of Honor

edited by David Weber:
More than Honor
Worlds of Honor
Changer of Worlds
The Service of the Sword

Empire From the Ashes (omnibus)
Mutineers' Moon
The Armageddon Inheritance
Heirs of Empire

Path of the Fury

The Apocalypse Troll

The Excalibur Alternative

Oath of Swords
The War God's Own

with Steve White:
Insurrection
Crusade
In Death Ground
The Shiva Option

with John Ringo:
March Upcountry
March to the Sea
March to the Stars

with Eric Flint:
1633

BAEN BOOKS BY ERIC FLINT

Joe's World series:
The Philosophical Strangler
Forward the Mage (with Richard Roach)

1632

Mother of Demons

Rats, Bats, and Vats (with Dave Freer)

Pyramid Scheme (with Dave Freer)

Course of Empire (with K.D. Wentworth)

The Shadow of the Lion (with Mercedes Lackey & Dave Freer)
This Rough Magic (with Mercedes Lackey & Dave Freer) *(upcoming)*

The General series, with David Drake:
The Tyrant

The Belisarius series, with David Drake:
An Oblique Approach
In the Heart of Darkness
Destiny's Shield
Fortune's Stroke
The Tide of Victory

DAVID WEBER
& ERIC FLINT

Crown of Slaves

This is a work of fiction. All the characters and events portrayed in this book are fictional, and any resemblance to real people or incidents is purely coincidental.

A Baen Books Original

Baen Publishing Enterprises
P.O. Box 1403
Riverdale, NY 10471
www.baen.com

ISBN: 0-7434-7148-2

Cover art by David Mattingly

First printing, September 2003

Library of Congress Cataloging-in-Publication Data

Weber, David, 1952-
Crown of slaves / David Weber & Eric Flint.
p. cm.
ISBN 0-7434-7148-2 (hardcover)
1. Life on other planets—Fiction. I. Flint, Eric. II. Title.

PS3573.E217C76 2003
813'.54—dc22

2003014257

Distributed by Simon & Schuster
1230 Avenue of the Americas
New York, NY 10020

Production by Windhaven Press, Auburn, NH
Printed in the United States of America

10 9 8 7 6 5 4 3 2 1

To Andre Norton—

Andre, you proved long ago that being a giant
has nothing to do with physical stature. You've been
taking giant steps and teaching the art of story-telling
for over half a century, and we are among those—
those many—who have been privileged to be your
students. It's time we told the teacher thank you.

PART I:
MANTICORE

CHAPTER 1

"I'M REALLY NERVOUS, DADDY," whispered Berry, glancing almost furtively at the resplendently uniformed soldiers who seemed to line the entire length of the hallway leading to Queen Elizabeth's private audience chamber.

"No reason to be," gruffed Anton Zilwicki, continuing to advance stolidly toward the great double doors at the end of the hallway. The doors, like much of the furniture in Mount Royal Palace, were made of ferran. Even at the still-considerable distance, Anton could easily recognize the distinctive grain of the wood, as well as the traditional designs which had been carved into it. Ferran was native to the highlands of his home planet of Gryphon, and he'd done quite a bit of work with the stuff in his youth. Most Gryphon highlanders did, at one time or another.

Part of him—the rational, calculating side which was so prominent a feature of his personality—was pleased to see the wood. The wooden doors, and the carvings on them even more so, were a subtle reminder to everyone by the Winton dynasty that they valued their Gryphon highlander subjects as much as Manticorans proper. But Anton couldn't help remembering how much he'd hated working with the stuff as a boy. The root of the word "ferran" was a none-too-subtle indicator of its most outstanding property other than the attractive grain and rich color.

The enormous muscles in Anton's forearms were the product of his weight-lifting regimen as an adult; but, already as a boy, those muscles had been hard and powerful. Ferran could not be worked by weaklings. The stuff was almost as hard as iron, and just as easy to shape with hand tools.

Anton's lips twitched. The same accusation—or its kin, at any rate—had been leveled at him, and quite a bit more often than once. *Damn you, Zilwicki! Hard as a rock and just as easy to move!*

That very morning, in fact, and by his lover Cathy Montaigne.

"I think Mommy was right," whispered Berry. "You *should* have worn your uniform."

"They put me on half-pay," he growled. "I'm supposed to wear that silly dress uniform—most uncomfortable thing I own—afterward? Like a poodle sitting up to beg forgiveness?"

Berry's nervous glances at the guards in the hallway were now definitely furtive, especially the glance she cast at the four soldiers following them a few steps behind. Clearly enough, the teenage girl was half-expecting the Queen's Own Regiment to arrest them on the spot for . . .

Whatever fancy legal phrase covered: *charged with being the stubborn disrespectful lout Anton Zilwicki and his adopted daughter.*

"The *Queen* didn't put you on the beach," she hissed hastily, as if that disclaimer might possibly establish her own innocence. "That's what Mommy kept saying to you this morning. I heard her. She was pretty loud."

The thing that flashed immediately through Anton's mind was a soft pleasure at Berry's use of the term *Mommy* to refer to Cathy Montaigne. Technically, of course, she wasn't. Berry and her brother Lars had been adopted by Anton, and since he and Cathy were not married the most that Cathy could officially be called was . . .

Again, his lips twitched. *Daddy's girlfriend*, maybe. *Paramour*, if you wanted to be fancy about it. "Anton's squeeze" was the term Cathy herself enjoyed using in proper company. The former Countess of the Tor took a childish pleasure in seeing pained expressions on the faces of polite society.

For Berry and Lars, born and raised in the hellhole of the Old Quarter on Earth's capital city of Chicago, the legalities were meaningless. Since Anton's daughter Helen had found and rescued them from the catacombs, Berry and Lars had found the first real family they'd ever had. And Anton was glad to see the ease with which that knowledge now came to them.

But pleasure was for a later time. This was a moment for a father's stern instructions. So Anton removed the smile, came to an abrupt halt, and half-glowered at his daughter. He ignored the four soldiers who abruptly found themselves coming to an unexpected halt, almost stumbling into their charges.

"And so what?" he demanded. He made no attempt to keep his basso voice from rumbling down the hallway, although the thickening Gryphon highlander accent probably made the words unrecognizable by the time they reached the ears of the majordomo standing by the far doorway.

"The monarch stands at the center of things, girl. For that, the Crown gets my allegiance. Unconditional allegiance, too, so long as the dynasty respects the rights of their subjects. But the reverse stands true as well. I do not condemn Her Majesty for the actions of 'her' government, mind. It's a constitutional monarchy, and as things stand at the moment, that would be silly. But she gets no praise for it, either."

He almost laughed, seeing Berry swallowing. To the former urchin of Chicago's underworld, power was power and "the laws" be damned. No laws nor lawmen had prevented her from suffering the horrors she'd lived through. Nor would they have, ever, in the world she'd come from. All that had ended it was the naked violence of Anton's daughter Helen, a young Havenite intelligence officer named Victor Cachat, and a dozen ex-slave killers from the Audubon Ballroom led by Jeremy X.

Yet a father's job is to educate his children, and Anton would no more shirk that duty than any other.

He heard one of the soldiers standing behind him clear his throat in a none-too-polite reminder. *The Queen is waiting, you fool!*

A splendid opportunity to continue the lesson, he decided. Anton gave the soldier—the sergeant commanding their little four-man escort—his most intimidating stare.

And quite intimidating it was, too. Anton was a short man, but so wide and extravagantly muscled that he looked like something out of a legend of dwarven kings. The blocky head and dark eyes—hard as agates, at times like these—only heightened the effect. The soldiers staring at him would no doubt be wondering if Anton could bend steel bars with his bare hands.

He could, in fact. And the soldiers were probably also suddenly remembering that the grotesquely built man glowering at them had, in younger days, been the Star Kingdom's champion wrestler in his weight class.

All four of them took a half-step back. The sergeant's right hand even twitched ever so slightly toward the sidearm holstered at his side.

Good enough. Anton wasn't actually seeking an incident, after all. He let his eyes slide away from the soldiery and come back to his daughter.

"I'm no damn nobleman, girl. Neither are you. So we ask no courtier favors—nor do we bend our knees. They put me on the beach, and the Queen said nothing. So she can live with it as well as they or I can. That's why that uniform is in the closet and will stay there. Understand?"

Berry was still nervous. "Shouldn't I, maybe, bow or something?"

Anton rumbled a laugh. "Do you even know how to 'bow'?"

Berry nodded. "Mommy showed me."

Anton's glower was coming back in full force. Hastily, Berry added: "But not the way she does it—or used to do it, anyway, before she became a commoner."

Anton shook his head. "Bowing is for formal occasions, girl. This is an informal audience. Just stand quietly and be polite, that's good enough." He turned and resumed his progress toward the doors leading to the Royal Presence. "Besides, I wouldn't trust you to do it right anyway. Sure as certain not if Cathy showed you how, with all of a noblewoman's flourish and twirls."

His lips twitched again, his good humor returning. "When she's in the mood—not often, I admit—she can make any duchess turn green with envy with that fancy bow of hers."

If nothing else, by the time they reached the doors and a glaring majordomo began swinging them open, Anton's display of highlander contrariness seemed to have relaxed Berry a bit. No doubt she'd reached the conclusion that the Royal Displeasure soon to descend on her father would be so thoroughly focused on *him* that she might emerge unscathed.

In the event, however, the Queen of the Star Kingdom greeted them with a smile so wide it might almost be called a grin. Against Elizabeth's mahogany skin, the white teeth gleamed brightly. From what Anton could determine, the sharp-toothed gape on the face of the Queen's companion Ariel seemed even more cheerful. Anton was no expert on treecats, but he knew they usually reflected the emotions of the human to whom they were bonded. And if that vaguely feline shape lounging casually across the thickly upholstered backrest of the Queen's chair was offended or angry, there was no sign of it.

Despite his contrariness of the moment, Anton could not keep himself from warming toward the Queen. He was still a Crown Loyalist, when all was said and done, even if that once-simple political philosophy had developed a lot of curlicues and embroidery in the years since he'd met Catherine Montaigne. And he approved of this particular monarch, from all that he'd been able to see of her since she came to the throne.

The knowledge was all from a distance, however. He'd never

actually met Queen Elizabeth, other than seeing her at a handful of large official gatherings.

He caught a glimpse of the young woman seated next to the Queen making an almost-furtive motion at the small console attached to her own chair. Glancing quickly to the side, Anton spotted a discreetly recessed viewscreen in the near wall of the small chamber. The display was dark now, but he suspected that the Queen and her companion had been observing him as he approached down the hallway—in which case, they would have heard his little exchange with Berry. Every word of it, unless the audio pickups were a lot worse than you'd expect in the palace of the galaxy's most electronically advanced realm.

He was not offended by the notion. In his days as a Navy yard dog, he might have been. But Anton's many years since as an intelligence officer—which he still basically was, even if in private practice—had given him a blasé attitude toward surveillance. So long as people respected his privacy, which he defined as *his* home and hearth, he didn't much care who snooped on him in public places. Whatever his other faults, Anton Zilwicki was not a hypocrite, and it wasn't as if he didn't do the same himself.

Besides, it was obvious from her smile the Queen wasn't offended. If anything, she seemed amused. He could sense Berry's relaxation as that knowledge came to her also.

But Anton wasn't paying much attention to Berry. As they continued to advance slowly toward the elaborate chairs which served Elizabeth and her companion as informal thrones, Anton's attention was given to the young woman seated next to the Queen.

At first, he thought he'd never seen the woman before, not even in file imagery or a holograph. As he drew nearer, however, he began connecting her features with those he'd seen in a few images taken when the girl was considerably younger. Soon enough, Anton had deduced her identity.

The age was the final giveaway. Anton was no expert on couture, but it was obvious even to him that the young woman's apparel was extremely expensive. The kind of clothing that would be worn by a noblewoman serving as the Queen's adviser. But this woman was much too young for that. Granted, prolong made gauging age rather difficult, but Anton was sure this woman was almost as young as the teenager she looked to be.

That meant a member of the royal family itself, or close kin, and there was only one such who fit the bill. The fact that the girl's complexion was so much paler than the standard Winton skin color just added the icing to the cake.

Ruth Winton, then, the daughter of the Queen's sister-in-law Judith Winton. Ruth had been sired by a Masadan privateer but adopted by the Queen's younger brother Michael when he married Judith after her escape from captivity. If Anton remembered correctly—and his memory was phenomenal—the girl had been born after Judith's escape, so Michael was the only father Ruth had ever known. She'd be about twenty-three years old now.

Because of the awkwardness of the girl's paternity she was officially not part of the line of succession to the throne. Other than that, however, she was in effect Queen Elizabeth's niece. Anton wondered what she was doing here, but he gave the matter no more than a fleeting thought. He had no idea what *he* was doing here, after all, since the Queen's summons had come as a surprise to him. He was quite sure he would discover the answer soon enough.

He and Berry reached a point on the floor which Anton decided marked a proper distance from The Royal Person. He stopped and bowed politely. Next to him, Berry did a hasty and nervous version of the same.

Hasty, yes—but still *far* too elaborate for Anton's taste. However much of his rustic background Anton might have abandoned when he left Gryphon many years earlier, he still retained in full measure a highlander's belligerent plebeianism. Kneeling and scraping and kowtowing and fancy flourishes before royalty were aristocratic vices. Anton would give the Crown his loyalty and respect, and that was damn well *all*.

He must have scowled a bit. The Queen laughed and exclaimed: "Oh, please, Captain Zilwicki! The girl has a splendid bow. Still a bit awkward, perhaps, but I recognize Cathy's touch in it. Can't miss that style, as much trouble as Cathy got me into about it, the time she and I infuriated our trainer by doing what amounted to a ballet instead of an exercise. It was all her idea, of course. Not that I wasn't willing to go along."

Anton had heard about the incident, as it happened. Cathy had mentioned it to him once. Although Cathy rarely spoke of the matter, as girls she and the Queen had been very close friends before their developing political differences ruptured the relationship. But, even then, there'd been no personal animosity involved. And Anton had not been the only one who'd noticed that, after Cathy's return from exile, there was always an undertone of warmth on those occasions when she and Queen Elizabeth encountered each other.

True, the encounters were still relatively few and far between, because the Queen faced an awkward political situation. While Elizabeth herself shared Cathy's hostility to genetic slavery—as did, for that matter, the government of Manticore itself, on the official record—Cathy's multitude of political enemies never missed an opportunity to hammer at Cathy's well-known if formally denied ties with the Audubon Ballroom. Despite Manticore's position on slavery, the Ballroom remained proscribed in the Star Kingdom as a "terrorist" organization, and its leader Jeremy X was routinely reviled as the galaxy's most ruthless assassin.

That was not how either Cathy or Anton looked at the matter—nor the Queen herself, Anton was pretty sure—but private opinions were one thing, public policy another. Whether or not Elizabeth agreed with the stance taken toward the Ballroom by her government, that *was* the official stance. So, however friendly might be the personal relations between her and Cathy whenever they "accidentally" encountered each other at social gatherings, the Queen was careful not to give Cathy any formal political recognition. Even though—of this, Anton was positive—no one would be more delighted than Queen Elizabeth to see Cathy displace New Kiev as the leader of the Liberal Party.

Elizabeth laughed again. "The things she got me into! One scrape after another. My favorite escapade—the one that got her banned from the Palace for months, my mother was so furious—was the time—"

She broke off abruptly. The grin faded, becoming almost strained, but didn't vanish entirely.

"Yes, I know, Captain Zilwicki. And now she's banned from the Palace again—politically, if not personally—and by my order, not the Queen Mother's. Which, as it happens, is why I asked you here. In a complicated sort of way."

The Queen made a little motion to the majordomo. Obviously expecting it, the man and one of the soldiers standing guard brought up two of the chairs against a wall and positioned them in front of the Queen and her companion.

"Do have a seat, Captain, please. Both of you."

Interesting, thought Anton. He was not familiar with royal protocol from personal experience, but he knew a lot about it. Anton knew a lot about most things which bore in any way upon his concerns. He was sure he lacked knowledge of some of the fine points, but the matter of seating etiquette was fairly straightforward. When one was summoned before the monarch, one normally was either presented with chairs as one came into the room, or one stood throughout the audience. The distinction was rather sharp, and indicated either one's status or one's favor with the monarch, or both.

This half-and-half arrangement, he suspected, was the Queen's way of signaling a half-and-half sort of business. What anyone not encumbered by the necessary burden of royal protocol would have indicated by just saying: "Let's see if we can make a deal."

Anton's sense of humor was far more restrained than that of his lover Cathy Montaigne, but it was by no means absent. So, as he took his seat, he found himself fighting off the impulse to respond with "you shuffle the cards and I'll cut 'em."

As soon as he was seated, Elizabeth gestured toward the young woman sitting next to her. "This is my niece Ruth, as I imagine you've already deduced."

Anton nodded; first at the Queen, to acknowledge her guess, and then at the royal niece.

"You would have rarely seen a picture of her—and none in the last four years—because we've always kept her out of the limelight." A bit stiffly: "That is *not*, incidentally—whatever the 'faxes may have speculated about—because the House of Winton is in the least bit concerned about Ruth's parentage, much less ashamed of it. In her early years, it was to protect her from possible harm. Her father—her mother's rapist, I should say—along with many of those Masadan fanatics, escaped after Earl White Haven captured the planet following their attack on Grayson. We've been looking for them ever since, but as I'm sure you know even better than I, we haven't had much success finding them."

The Queen grimaced, and Zilwicki nodded mentally. A hard, disciplined core of the Masadan version of the Church of Humanity Unchained had managed to go deep underground and stay there. The fact that they were still hidden after over fifteen T-years of Manticoran occupation of the planet said things no intelligence professional really wanted to contemplate. Especially since the plot to assassinate both the Queen and the Protector of Grayson which had come within centimeters of success only four years earlier.

"Who knows what those maniacs might have done?" the Queen continued, confirming that her thoughts matched his own. "That was a long time ago, of course, and we don't worry about it much any longer. But since then—"

Elizabeth cocked her head a bit and gave Ruth a wry little smile. "Since then, we've maintained the secrecy at Ruth's own request.

My niece, as it turns out—it's all a bit shocking, really—has a most-un-Wintonesque desire to do her service in some capacity other than following the usual military or foreign service or religious careers."

Anton gave the girl a careful scrutiny, considering everything he already knew about her, as he chewed on Elizabeth's words.

There'd been some furor, especially among the more reactionary aristocracy, at then-Prince and Heir Michael Winton's choice of a bride. As Heir, he was legally required to marry a commoner if he married at all, but the expectation had been that he would simply wait until his nephew replaced him as Heir, then marry someone of his own station. Certainly no one had ever contemplated the possibility that he would marry a *foreign* commoner. Particularly not a penniless refugee commoner from someplace like Grayson. And especially not a pregnant commoner who'd escaped her Masadan captors only by committing multiple murders and stealing a starship along the way.

Michael, however, possessed the stubbornness of the House of Winton in full measure. More important even than that, perhaps, he'd enjoyed his sister's full-blooded support. So, whether anyone liked it or not, he'd married Judith and adopted Ruth.

Not without certain special provisions, of course. Michael was no longer Heir or Prince Michael since his nephew Roger had gotten old enough to be declared his mother's Heir, and they'd postponed the formal marriage until after Roger had replaced him. He was now the Duke of Winton-Serisburg, which had made Judith a duchess, although it was only a life title and would not pass to Ruth. Nonetheless, his adoption of Judith's daughter had included the specific proviso that Ruth would not stand in the succession to the Crown of Manticore. The title of "Princess" normally bestowed upon her was simply a courtesy, although Anton strongly suspected that Elizabeth intended to create a title in the girl's own right when the moment seemed ripe.

But whatever the circumstance of her parentage might be, Ruth Winton *was* a Winton, and the House of Winton, like most capable and intelligent royal dynasties in history, had a long tradition that its young scions went into public service. The normal career course was either the foreign office or the military; in the latter case, with a heavy emphasis upon the Navy, that being Manticore's senior service. Some, those with an inclination for it, chose instead a career in the clergy, however. The Star Kingdom had no established church, as such, but the House of Winton were and had always been members of the Second Reformation Catholic Church. Any number of Wintons, over the centuries, had become clergymen. A few had even gone so far as to adopt the celibacy which was optional for Second Reformed Catholic clergy, but more or less expected for those of them who attained the rank of bishop.

A lot of things came together in Anton's mind. "She wants to be a spy—you're right, Your Majesty, it's a bit shocking—and she wants me to train her. Makes sense, that last, even if the rest of it borders on lunacy. No way she could learn the trade properly through official channels. The Naval Academy would choke on the idea, and the Special Intelligence Service would probably have outright apoplexy. You could force them to it, of course, but they'd be so twitchy about security they'd scramble her brains for sure and certain."

The blank look on Queen Elizabeth's face indicated her suppressed astonishment. Next to her, young Ruth whispered: "I *told* you he was the best."

Anton plowed on. "It's still a crazy idea. Mind you, Your Majesty—meaning no disrespect—the dynasty could use a close member who was proficient at the spying business. Not so much for its own sake as to enable you to detect the trash and garbage which is probably all the so-called 'intelligence' you're getting, after four years of High Ridge's regime. From either ONI or the SIS. Meaning no disrespect. To Your Majesty, that is."

He paused briefly; then: "But that still leaves the matter of security. Not so much of a problem here on Manticore, true, but my work takes me off-planet as often as not. And sometimes to places I wouldn't want to take an alley mutt, much less a princess. A few days from now, in fact—"

Elizabeth interrupted him. "I know about your upcoming trip, Captain. In point of fact, that trip is what sparked this little meeting."

Again, Anton's mind raced; and, again, many things fell into place. At times like this, people who didn't know him found his thought processes almost superhumanly quick. In reality, Anton thought he was a rather slow thinker, with nothing like the quicksilver mind of his lover Cathy. But he was so methodical and thorough about the way he considered everything ahead of time, that once the final key facts started coming in he was able to make sense out of complexity in a way that few people could. The Queen's summons the day before had been completely unexpected, and Anton had reacted the way he always did at such times—by spending hours chewing on all the possible variables which might be involved.

He couldn't keep a little grin from showing. "Decided to stick your thumb in High Ridge's eye, eh? Good for you, Your Majesty." Out of the corner of his eye he saw the majordomo and both of the officers in the room glaring at him. A bit belatedly, he realized it was probably a breach of royal protocol for a commoner spy to congratulate the Queen on her Machiavellian cunning.

Um. Probably a severe breach, in fact. But Anton found he didn't care much, and saw no reason not to widen it.

"An excellent move, if you want my opinion, and on at least three fronts. Remind everyone that the Wintons despise slavery, and Solarian-style neocolonialism just about as much; help counteract some unfavorable publicity about the Star Kingdom in the minds of Solarian commoners—who number in the untold trillions, though people seem to forget that—and give Montaigne a subtle boost in her election campaign without either officially endorsing her or even—oh, yes, it's shrewd; good for you, Your Majesty—having to officially rescind her banning from the royal presence and the House of Lords."

The next words came rumbling like a freight train: "Not to mention that sticking a thumb in High Ridge's eye is an act of grace in its own right. Not sure about the fine points of Second Reformed theology, but in my creed that alone 'ud get you ushered into Heaven."

He cleared his throat. "Meaning no disrespect to Your Majesty."

For a moment, the room was frozen. Both the Queen and her niece were sitting rigid, staring at him. The majordomo appeared to be on the verge of apoplexy, and the two officers likewise. For their part, the soldiers standing guard seemed to be considering the likelihood they'd shortly be carrying out an arrest on the spot. Next to him, Anton's daughter Berry was obviously torn between the urge to hide under her chair and flee the room outright.

And then Elizabeth burst into laughter. No soft and genteel thing, either, but the kind of raucous hilarity more appropriate to a vaudeville theater than a royal palace.

"God, you're good!" she exclaimed, when the laughter subsided. "It took me two solid days to hammer the same notions into the heads of my—ah—inner circle." She gave her niece's forearm an affectionate little squeeze. "Except Ruth, of course."

Mention of Ruth brought Anton's mind to bear on that variable, and it took him no more than two or three seconds to figure out the rest of it. In broad outline, at least. The thing that had puzzled him the most about the Queen's summons was her reason for requesting Berry's presence as well.

"It's probably not a good idea, Your Majesty," he said abruptly. "The part involving your niece and Berry, I mean. I admit the notion has a certain charm, being about as antique a maneuver as there is in the books. Still—"

Forcing himself to remember that he was addressing his monarch, Anton managed to keep a scowl from showing on his face. "Charming or not, and whether it'd work or not—and meaning no disrespect to Your Majesty—there's no way I'm going to agree to it. I was a father before I was an intelligence officer, and I've never had any trouble keeping my priorities straight."

Again, the majordomo and the officers got stiff-faced. But Elizabeth simply gave Anton a long and considering look. "No, that you haven't," she said. "Someday you'll have to tell me all the details of what happened in Chicago, but I know enough about the affair to understand the heart of it. Two swine gave you a choice between being a father and having a career, and you shoved the choice right down their throats."

It was not, Anton reflected, normally considered appropriate for a monarch to refer to her ambassador to the most powerful star nation in the galaxy and to one of her more senior admirals as "swine." Not that Elizabeth seemed concerned by the thought.

"Did you hesitate at all?" she asked.

"Not for a second." He moved his massive shoulders in a little shrug. "Being a beachcomber's not so bad, when you get down to it."

"Good. I believe I can trust a man who isn't afraid of being on the beach when he has to."

Again, he shrugged. This time, as if shifting off a load. "Be that as it may, Your Majesty, I'm still not going to agree to it. It might not be all that dangerous—probably wouldn't, in fact—but it's still my daughter we're talking about here. And—"

He got no further. Anton had forgotten that Berry had a quick brain of her own. She might not have Anton's habit of systematically examining every situation, but she too had wondered why she'd been specifically included in the summons.

"Oh, that's crap!" She flushed. "Uh, sorry, Daddy—and, uh, *really* sorry, Your Majesty. I mean about the bad language."

There was no trace now of the girl's earlier nervousness. "But it's still cra—uh, nonsense. It's *my* life, Daddy, even if I am only seventeen—but I didn't get prolong as early as Ruth—uh, Princess Ruth—did, so I actually probably even look a bit older than she does, if anything, and who'd know the difference anyway, because you've never let anybody get a public image of me either, on account of you're a professional paranoi—uh, very extremely cautious."

For a moment, Anton thought she might actually stick her tongue out at him. She'd done it before, now and then. But Berry managed to recall her circumstances, drew herself up as graciously as a seventeen year old could, and ended with a little sniff.

"I think I'd make a splendid double for the Princess. It'd be exciting for me, that's for sure, and it'd allow her to get out in the world for once."

She and Ruth exchanged admiring smiles. Anton looked to the Queen for help, but Elizabeth was practically smirking.

His shoulders slumped. "Damn," he growled.

CHAPTER 2

BERRY WAS FAR LESS PLEASED with the situation the next day, when she had to return to Mount Royal Palace in order to present herself to the royal clinic.

Anton had insisted from the beginning, and had finally convinced Elizabeth, that the Queen's original idea of having Berry serve as Ruth's double was unworkable. Or, more precisely, would only work for a short time and would likely result in very negative political repercussions.

"You just can't pull it off, in this day and age," he'd argued. "All someone has to do is get a scrap of DNA from either one of the girls to expose the switch, and sooner or later someone will manage that. With modern technology, you can manage it from traces of sweat left on a doorknob. Yes, sure, Berry was born on Earth so her DNA will be as much of a mélange as any human's in the galaxy. But Ruth's of Grayson-Masadan stock, and that genetic variation has far too many distinct traits not to be spotted easily."

The Queen frowned. "I thought you'd agreed, Captain?"

He shook his head. "You're thinking too directly. You don't need an actual *double,* Your Majesty. All you need is misdirection. At no point—ever—will you or I or anyone else directly involved in the affair ever come right out and say 'this girl is Ruth Winton and that one is Berry Zilwicki.' All you need to do is announce that Ruth Winton will be accompanying Captain Anton Zilwicki and Professor W.E.B. Du Havel on their voyage to pay the Anti-Slavery League's respects to the family and associates of the martyr Hieronymus Stein. She'll be coming along to pay the personal respects of the House of Winton. That is *it.* Somewhere along the line—but not in a communiqué from the dynasty—we'll drop a casual mention that Captain Zilwicki's daughter Berry will be coming along also."

He gave the girls each a glance. "We dress Berry up in the fanciest clothing we can find, and have Ruth wear the sloppy teenage stuff Berry usually wears when she's not trying to impress royalty. I'd call it rags except it costs me twice as much to buy the stuff as good clothing would." He ignored his daughter's little choke of protest. "Then, let slip the word before we leave—just in time to let the paparazzi show up. Berry will walk beside me as we pass through the gates into the boarding area, dressed like a princess, with the royal guards acting as if they were protecting *her*. Ruth will tag along behind, looking nonchalant."

Elizabeth's face cleared. "Ah. I see. We don't *tell* them—anyone—that Berry is Ruth and vice versa. We just let them jump to that conclusion on their own."

"Exactly. That'll serve the purpose from the security angle. But it also allows you to slide off the hook later when the confusion eventually gets cleared up—which it will, don't doubt it for a moment—and people start throwing around accusations that the Crown of Manticore was engaging in duplicity. You just shrug your shoulders and say it isn't your fault if the newsies couldn't get their story straight."

The Queen shook her head. "I agree with your logic, Captain, but you're missing the real political problem. Charges of being shrewd and cunning and sneaky, the Crown of Manticore can live with. Frankly, I'd bathe in it. The charge that would *really* hurt is that we were willing to risk the life of a commoner to protect royalty. That's the one thing I can't afford, now of all times. More than ever, these days, the strength of the Crown rests in the allegiance of the commonalty."

Anton bowed his head slightly, acknowledging the truth of her remark.

"I'm curious, Captain," Elizabeth continued. "Yes, your variant will let me slip off the hook when the time comes. But the fact remains that both of us know that we are in fact using a commoner to protect a princess. Doesn't that bother you? I'd think it would, coming from Gryphon. Some of the Manticore Crown Loyalists would undoubtedly do it cheerfully, but you highlanders are a . . . cantankerous lot."

Anton grinned. "Are we not, indeed? The reason it doesn't bother me, Your Majesty, is because my *daughter* insisted on it." He gave Ruth another glance. The girl had been sired upon her mother by a husband who viewed his wives as chattel. "I said I was a father, not a stinking Masadan patriarch. Be damned to the rest of it."

Ruth's cheeks seemed to glow a bit, although her expression remained still. Anton hadn't made the remark for any ulterior purpose, but he realized in that moment that he'd cemented his position as one of the princess' heroes, and he felt his heart sink slightly. Another man might have taken pleasure at the thought of acquiring favor from royalty. Anton Zilwicki—"Daddy Dour," his daughter Helen sometimes called him—saw only the problems and complications involved.

And to think I used to have such a simple life. An unattached widower and an obscure intelligence officer in the RMN, that's all. Now look at me! My lover's the most notorious political figure in the Star Kingdom, and now I've added royal intrigue to the brew!

"There's one other thing we could do to enhance the chances of keeping the switch unnoticed for as long as possible," he added. He studied the two girls for a moment. "Assuming that they're willing to do it, of course—and, meaning no offense, Your Majesty, that you're willing to pay for it."

Queen Elizabeth chuckled. "A nanotech transformation? You're certainly free with the royal purse, Captain Zilwicki!"

Anton made no reply beyond a thin smile. That seemed like a better response than: *sure, it'll cost a small fortune—but for you, that's pocket change.*

Elizabeth studied the two girls herself. She seemed a bit uncertain, although Anton was quite sure the hesitation was not because of the expense involved. Biosculpt would have been cheaper, but biosculpt was—literally—only skin deep, and they needed more than that in this case. Although Berry and Ruth were very similar physical types, aside from Berry's dark brown hair and Ruth's golden blond, they weren't quite the same height. And while neither of them would ever be called stocky, Ruth was noticeably finer-boned than Berry. It wasn't anything which would be hugely apparent to a casual observer, but it would show up instantly if anyone decided to run a side-by-side comparison of their HD images.

Unless, of course, the differences were reversed before the HD cameras ever saw them.

There were drawbacks to that approach, however, and Elizabeth was clearly aware of them. Even leaving aside the fact that doing the procedures in the short time they had available would be uncomfortable at the very least, nanotech body transformations were unsettling in the best of circumstances. Although the changes were easily reversible, it was still disturbing to most people to have their bodies start changing shape on them. All the more so, when the two people involved were very young women, their physical aging furthered retarded by prolong, who were still getting accustomed to the bodies they had.

"It's your decision, Ruth—and yours too, of course, Berry," said the Queen. "I warn you, it won't be any fun."

"Sure we'll do it!" the princess piped up immediately.

Berry herself, noticing that Ruth Winton's expression didn't look nearly as confident as the words themselves, had hesitated a moment. She really knew very little about nanotech, especially as applied to human physiology. But the look of silent appeal the princess gave her settled the issue.

"'Course we will," she'd agreed, trying her best for a tone of confidence. And hoping that her own expression wasn't as transparent as Ruth's.

To Berry's relief, the "clinic" proved to be a fully equipped and up-to-date mini-hospital. Not entirely to her relief, the doctor who appeared upon her arrival to take charge of her proved to be a very friendly but disquietingly youthful person. Judging from appearance, Berry wouldn't have thought the woman was old enough to have graduated from medical school yet.

To her complete chagrin, the doctor lacked the most basic rudiments of a proper bedside manner.

"Is this going to hurt?" she asked nervously, following the doctor down a corridor which seemed excessively sterile and undecorated.

"Probably," Dr. Schwartz replied breezily. She gave Berry a smile that was less sympathetic than Berry thought it could have been. "What do you expect? A full nanotech body transformation in four days!" Schwartz shook her head, as if bemused by the folly of it all. "We're adding almost a full centimeter to your height, you know. And reducing the Princess' the same amount."

The smile was *definitely* not as sympathetic as it should have been, Berry thought crossly. Especially when she heard the doctor's next words.

"There's bound to be a fair amount of discomfort when we start taking your bones apart and putting them back together again," Schwartz said. "Soft tissue changes aren't that bad, but bone alterations are an entirely different matter. Still, I imagine you'll spend a lot of the time sleeping."

Five seconds later, Dr. Schwartz ushered Berry into a deceptively unremarkable looking private hospital room.

Ruth already occupied one of the room's two beds. She looked a little calmer than Berry felt, but not very much, and Berry felt obscurely comforted as she recognized the other girl's matching nervousness.

"All right, now, Ms. Zilwicki," Dr. Schwartz said briskly. "If you'll just climb into your gown and hop into bed, we can get started with the workup."

"Uh, just how much *is* this going to hurt?" Berry asked as she began to obey. It was, she admitted to herself, a bit late to be asking that particular question, but Dr. Schwartz didn't seem to mind.

"As I already said," the doctor told her, "there's always a degree of discomfort involved with bone modifications. Of course, I realize that we doctors tend to make patients a bit nervous when we throw around words like 'discomfort,' but you really shouldn't look at it that way. Pain is one of the body's most effective ways to communicate with us."

"If it's all the same to you," Berry said, "I'd just as soon not be communicated with that way anymore than I have to."

"I'll second that," Ruth put in from her bed.

"Well, we'll do what we can to minimize it, of course," Dr. Schwartz assured both of them. "Actually, the procedure itself isn't particularly difficult. The trick in something like this is in properly programming the nannies, and since we had complete access to both of your medical records, that was fairly straightforward this time. I remember once, when we were doing a rush job for the SIS, and we didn't have access to the med file of the fellow we were supposed to be matching our agent to. Now *that* was a challenge! In this case though—"

She made an airy, dismissive gesture, then frowned at Berry, who obviously wasn't getting out of her own clothes and into the waiting gown rapidly enough to suit her. Berry took the hint, and the doctor nodded in obvious satisfaction as she quickened her pace.

"In this instance, we had all the information we needed, of course," Schwartz continued. "It's the time factor that's the problem. As soon as we've completed the final workups on both of you, we'll fine-tune the nannies' programming and inject them. After that," she said with what Berry privately thought was appalling cheerfulness, "the nannies will start taking you apart and putting you back together again. If we had a couple of weeks to work with, it probably wouldn't feel much worse than, say, a moderately severe case of the flu. In the time frame that we have, I'm afraid it's going to be a bit more taxing than that."

She shrugged.

"As I said, I expect you'll both spend quite a bit of time sleeping over the next few days. A nanny transformation does tend to use up a lot of your energy. We'll provide some meds against the discomfort, but we're going to have to be able to monitor your responses to the modifications, and we can't afford to blur those with anything really potent. That's especially true when we're making the changes so rapidly. So I'm afraid that any time you *don't* spend sleeping is unlikely to be among your fondest memories."

She smiled again, with that same maddening lack of sympathy, and Berry sighed glumly. This had all seemed *so* much simpler when she blithely volunteered for it.

She finished buttoning the gown, then paused. It wasn't really hesitation. She told herself that quite firmly. But it was something uncomfortably akin to it, and an amazing number of butterflies seemed to be hovering in the vicinity of her midsection.

"Ah, you're ready, I see! Good!" Dr. Schwartz approved, smiling more cheerfully than ever, and Berry's butterfly population expanded exponentially. "In that case, let's get started, shall we?"

The next few days were considerably more miserable than the doctor's breezy assurances would have led an unsuspecting soul to believe. But it wasn't really *that* bad—nowhere near as bad as some of Berry's experiences had been. Besides, that same life experience had made Berry about as suspecting a soul, in a friendly and benign sort of way, as anyone she knew.

Well . . . except Princess Ruth.

Berry got to know the Manticoran royal fairly well during those days, since they'd nothing else to do but talk whenever they weren't sleeping. And while Berry soon came to the conclusion that Ruth was a woman she was going to like—a lot, in fact—she also found the contrast between their two personalities more than a little amusing.

Some of the differences were obvious—Berry tended to be quiet, Ruth exuberant. But an even deeper difference, if not an immediately obvious one, was their different outlook on life. True, Berry's life had left precious little in the way of childlike innocence, but she still tended to take a cheery view of the universe and its inhabitants. Ruth, on the other hand . . .

"Paranoid" was not the right term, Berry finally decided. The connotations of that word involved fear, worry, fretfulness—whereas the princess had about as sanguine a temperament as possible. But if the expression "optimistic paranoiac" hadn't been a ridiculous oxymoron, it would have described Ruth fairly well. She seemed to take it for granted that half the human race was up to no good, even if the knowledge didn't particularly worry her much—because she was just as certain that she'd be able to deal with the sorry blighters if they tried to mess around with *her*.

"How in the world did the Queen manage to keep a lid on you for twenty-three years?" Berry finally asked.

Ruth grinned. "I was her accomplice. I figured out by the time I was six that I'd be better off staying out of the limelight." She stuck out her tongue. "Not to mention—*bleah*—that it saved me about a million hours of tedious sitting still and trying to look properly princessy—that means 'about as bright as a donkey'—at official royal events."

"Is that why all the details of your mother's escape were kept out of the public eye for so long?"

"Oh, no." Ruth shook her head firmly. Ruth's gestures were usually done firmly—when they weren't done vehemently. "Don't blame me for that idiocy! If they'd asked my opinion—they didn't, I was only a few years old, but they should have—I would have told them to shout it from the rooftops. As it was, the truth didn't become public knowledge until after Yeltsin's Star had joined the Manticoran Alliance, at which point the Manticoran public reacted by making my mother a national hero. Ha! The same thing would have happened right from the start, even before the treaty was signed! You can be damn sure that releasing the naked, unvarnished truth about the brutality with which Masada treated its women would have made the choice of an alliance with Grayson rather than Masada a no-brainer."

She scowled fiercely. "Which, of course, is exactly why the cretins *didn't* do it. 'Reasons of state.' Ha! The truth is that until the Foreign Office made up its mind once and for all to pursue the relationship with Grayson, the bureaucrats had to 'keep their options open'—there's another weasel phrase for you—with the benighted barbarians who ran Masada! So of course the entire episode had to be swept under the rug."

Berry chuckled. "My father says that 'reasons of state' has been used to cover more sheer stupidity than any other pious phrase in existence. And whenever Mommy—uh, that's Cathy Montaigne—tries to get him to do something he doesn't want to, he immediately says he wants to keep his options open."

"And what does she say?"

"Oh, she tells him he's being a weasel again. And always tries to get me and—if she's home from the Academy—Helen to agree with her."

Berry added piously: "I always do, of course. Daddy can weasel with the best of 'em. Helen usually tries to claim the Academy Code of Honor prevents her from taking a stance, whereupon Mommy immediately accuses her of being a weasel."

Now, Berry looked positively saintly. "And, of course, I always agree with her again."

Ruth was eyeing her oddly. "Hey, look," Berry said defensively, "the truth's the truth."

She realized, then, that she'd misunderstood the meaning of the Princess' scrutiny.

"We're going to be friends," Ruth said abruptly. "Close friends."

It was said firmly, even vehemently. But Berry didn't miss the depths of loneliness and uncertainty that lurked beneath the words. Ruth, she was now certain, was not a woman who'd known very much in the way of close friendship in her life.

Berry smiled. "Of course we are."

She meant it, too. Berry was good at making friends. Especially close ones.

"Sir, *please* tell me you're pulling my leg," Platoon Sergeant Laura Hofschulte, Queen's Own Regiment, begged plaintively.

"I wish I were, Laura," Lieutenant Ahmed Griggs sighed, and leaned back in his chair to run his fingers through his thick, reddish hair. It was his platoon Sergeant Hofschulte managed, and the two of them had served together for almost two T-years. During that time, they'd come to know one another well, and a powerful sense of mutual respect had deepened between them. Which probably helped explain the pained, disbelieving look of—well, betrayal wasn't quite the right word, but it was close— Hofschulte gave him now.

"I'm not sure whose idea it was," Griggs went on after a moment. "My impression from Colonel Reynolds is that it was Her Majesty herself, but it sounds to me more like something the Princess would have come up with."

"Her, or maybe Zilwicki," Hofschulte said darkly. "The man's a professional spook, Sir. God only knows how twisty his mind's gotten over the years!"

"No, I don't think it was him," Griggs disagreed. "As you say, he's a *professional* spook. And a father. I don't see a man as protective as he's supposed to be exposing his daughter to risk this way. Not if it was his own idea, that is.

"Not that it matters who thought it up," he continued more briskly. "What matters is that it's up to us to make it work."

"Let me get this straight, Sir," Hofschulte said. "We're haring off to Erewhon as the Princess' protective detail, but we're supposed to *look* like we're protecting Berry Zilwicki, who everyone else is going to think is the Princess?"

"Yep." Griggs smiled crookedly at her expression. "And don't forget how sensitive relations with Erewhon are at the moment. I'm sure they'll cooperate with our needs, but they're so pissed off with the Government at the moment that that cooperation's likely to be pretty grudging. And they aren't going to be impressed by our concerns about our proximity to Haven, either. Not after the way half of their voters figure the Star Kingdom was willing to throw away the entire Alliance for purely domestic political advantages."

Hofschulte nodded, but her expression was a bit uncomfortable. True, the Queen's Own's loyalty was to the Crown and the Constitution, not to the office of the Prime Minister or to the current government of the Star Kingdom. The regiment's personnel were charged with keeping the monarch and the members of her family alive, at any cost, and they were expected to discuss the parameters of their mission with complete frankness and thoroughness. Which included calling a spade a spade when the stupidity of the government of the day's policies threatened to complicate the primary mission. Still . . .

"Do you seriously expect them to drag their feet, Sir?" she asked more seriously, and Griggs shrugged.

"Not really," he said. "What I do expect, though, is that they're not going to go out of their way to extend *additional* cooperation the way they did when Princess Ruth's father visited Erewhon during the war." He shrugged again. "Hard to blame them, really. Even leaving aside the way we've stomped all over their toes in the last three or four T-years, the Princess is a lot less likely a target than the Duke was, and the threat environment should be a lot less extreme than it was then."

He and Hofschulte looked at one another grimly, remembering

the many friends and colleagues who'd died aboard the royal yacht during the attempt to assassinate the Queen on her state visit to Grayson.

"Well, that's true enough, anyway, Sir," Hofschulte agreed after a moment. "On the other hand, the Duke wasn't the Princess, if you'll pardon my saying so. He was a hell of a lot easier to protect than she's likely to be."

"I know," Griggs agreed glumly. Actually, Ruth was normally quite popular with the royal family's protective details. Everyone liked her a great deal, and she was always cheerful and—like most Wintons, whether by birth or adoption—never snotty to the uniformed people responsible for keeping her alive. Unfortunately, the detail also knew all about the princess' ambition to pursue a career in espionage. Anton Zilwicki's presence gave a certain added emphasis to that ambition, and hobnobbing with Anti-Slavery League activists in a situation as politically complex as the Stein funeral was likely to prove was *not* something any sane bodyguard commander wanted to contemplate. Worse yet—

"How old did you say Ms. Zilwicki is, Sir?" Hofschulte asked, and Griggs chuckled sourly at the proof that her thoughts were paralleling his own.

"Seventeen, actually," he said, and watched the sergeant wince.

"Wonderful . . . Sir," she muttered. "I'd kind of hoped she might, ah, exercise a restraining influence on the Princess," she added rather forlornly.

"It would be nice if someone would," Griggs agreed. Ruth Winton was a perfectly nice young woman, with an exquisite innate sense of courtesy. She had also, by dint of the way the royal family had closed ranks to protect her and her own intense concentration on the subjects of special interest to her, led a very sheltered existence. She was, in many ways, what an earlier age would have called a nerd. A brilliant, talented, well educated, incredibly competent and well-adjusted nerd, but a nerd and—also in many ways—unusually young for her age.

And no one who knew her could possibly doubt even for a moment that she was already busily plotting and scheming to make the most of her escape from Mount Royal Palace to someplace as . . . interesting as Erewhon.

The only real difference between her and the Zilwicki girl is that the extra six T-years have probably only made her even sneakier and more cunning when it comes to evading restrictions, he thought glumly. *They certainly haven't done anything to dull her sense of adventure. Damn it.*

"Well, at least we'll have Zilwicki along to help ride herd on both of them," he observed in a voice of determined cheer.

"Oh, that makes me feel *lots* better, Sir," Hofschulte snorted. "Correct me if I'm wrong, but wasn't he the guy who went out and hunted up the Audubon Ballroom when he needed a little extracurricular muscle?"

"Well, yes," Griggs admitted.

"Wonderful," Hofschulte repeated, and shook her head. But then, suddenly, she grinned.

"At least it won't be boring, Sir."

"Boredom is certainly one thing we won't have to worry about," Griggs agreed with another chuckle. "Actually, I think we're all going to deserve the Spitting Kitty for this one, Sergeant. Riding herd on the Princess, a seventeen-year-old *pretending* to be the Princess, an ASL intellectual, and the Star Kingdom's most notorious ex-spook, all in the middle of a three-ring circle like the Stein funeral on a planet like *Erewhon*?" He shook his head. "Spitting Kitty time for sure."

"I hope not, Sir!" Hofschulte replied with a laugh.

The "Spitting Kitty" was the Queen's Own's nickname for the Adrienne Cross. The medal had been created by Roger II to honor members of the Queen's Own who risked—or lost—their own lives to save the life of a member of the royal family other than the monarch herself. The cross bore the snarling image of a treecat (rumor said that then-Crown Princess Adrienne's own 'cat, Dianchect, had sat as the model), and eleven people had won it in the two hundred and fifty T-years since it was created. Nine of the awards had been posthumous. Of course, the lieutenant reflected, this trip wasn't *really* going to kill them all. It was just going to make them feel that way.

"Oh, well," he said finally. "I guess it could be worse. We could be taking Princess Joanna along, as well. Think what *that* would be like."

They looked at one another, each envisioning what the inclusion of the Queen's younger daughter would have done to the already frightening mix, and shuddered in perfect unison.

CHAPTER 3

"CAPTAIN OVERSTEEGEN IS HERE, Admiral Draskovic."

The dark-haired, dark-eyed woman in the uniform of an admiral of the red looked up from the paperwork on her terminal at the yeoman's announcement.

"Thank you, Chief," she said, with perhaps just a trace more enthusiasm than the Fifth Space Lord of the Royal Manticoran Navy might normally be expected to show over the arrival of a mere captain. "Please show him in," she added.

"Yes, Ma'am."

The yeoman withdrew, and the admiral quickly saved the document she'd been perusing. Then she stood and walked around her desk to the conversational nook arranged around the expensive coffee table. The door to her office opened once more, and the yeoman ushered in a man in the black-and-gold of an RMN senior-grade captain.

"Captain Oversteegen, Ma'am," he murmured.

"Thank you, Chief." The admiral held out a hand and smiled at her visitor in welcome. "That will be all," she added, never looking away from the newcomer.

Her yeoman withdrew once more, and she gripped the captain's hand firmly.

"Good to see you, Captain," she said warmly, and waved at one of the waiting chairs with her free hand. "Please, have a seat."

"Thank you, Ma'am," Oversteegen said, and if it occurred to him that a full admiral of the red did not normally greet the commander of a mere heavy cruiser quite so enthusiastically, no sign of it showed in his expression or manner as he availed himself of the offer. He settled into the indicated chair, crossed his legs, and regarded his superior with polite attentiveness.

"I don't believe that I've had the opportunity yet to congratulate you, Captain," the admiral said as she sat in another chair, facing him across the coffee table. "That was quite a show you put on in Tiberian."

"I had a bit more luck than a man should get into the habit of expectin'," he replied in calm, even tones. "And, even more importantly, the best crew and officers it's ever been my good fortune t' serve with."

For just a moment, Draskovic seemed a bit taken aback. Then she smiled.

"I'm quite certain that you did. On the other hand, even with good luck and an excellent crew, it took a captain a cut or two above the average to polish off four Solarian heavy cruisers. Even," she added, raising a hand to stop him as he began to open his mouth, "when the cruisers in question had Silesian crews. You did us proud, Captain. You *and* your people."

"Thank you, Ma'am," he said again. There was, after all, very little else he could have said under the circumstances.

"You're very welcome," she told him. "After all, God knows the Navy needs all the good press it can get these days!" She shook her head. "It never ceases to amaze me how quickly everyone seems to forget everything else we've accomplished. I suppose it's one more example of 'Yes, but what have you done for us *recently*?' "

"It's always that way, isn't it, Ma'am?" Oversteegen replied, and smiled ever so slightly. "I suppose it's not unreasonable for the man in the street t' be just a tad confused over exactly what the Navy's doin' for him these days." One of Draskovic's eyebrows arched, and he smiled again, more broadly. "I mean," he explained, "in light of the current debate between the Government and the Opposition over what the Navy *ought* t' be doin'."

"I see your point," Admiral Draskovic said, and sat back in her chair to regard him with carefully disguised thoughtfulness. There was something about him that baffled her. No, not baffled—confused, perhaps. He said all the right things, yet she had a sense that he didn't mean exactly what she thought he did. A part of her almost suspected that he was laughing at her from behind his respectful expression and aristocratic accent, but that was ridiculous, and she knew it.

If the captain felt the least discomfort under her regard, he disguised it admirably. No doubt he'd had plenty of practice at that. Unlike Draskovic, he not only came from a traditional naval family, but boasted connections to the most rarefied heights of the Manticoran nobility. He'd probably attended more formal dinners and met more senior officers and peers of the realm than

Draskovic ever had, despite the half-T-century difference in their ages. Or the gulf between their ranks.

For just a moment, Josette Draskovic felt a stab of sheer, unadulterated resentment as she took in his superbly tailored, not-quite-regulation uniform and complete self-assurance. She'd worked hard all of her life to attain her present rank and authority; he'd been born into an elite world of privilege and advantage that had raised him to his current position with the inevitability of gravity.

She started to speak again, then stopped and gave herself a stern mental shake. How he'd gotten to where he was was really beside the point, wasn't it? He'd certainly demonstrated his fitness to command a Queen's ship at Tiberian last year, after all. And whatever some might have suspected about the connection between his birth and his career prior to Tiberian, the Navy had universally approved the promotion to captain senior-grade—and the Manticoran Cross—which that battle had earned him.

"The . . . 'debate' between the Government and the Opposition is probably enough to confuse anyone," she acknowledged. "Especially when we're having to make so many hard decisions about the Navy budget. That's one reason why what you accomplished out there has such implications for our domestic public opinion. It was so black-and-white, an example of the suppression of piracy and murder which has always been the Navy's primary peacetime job."

"As you say, Ma'am," he agreed. "At the same time, however, I think it's fair t' point out that the pirates and murderers in question *had* managed t' get their hands on modern Solarian warships. It seems t' me that the question of just how they managed t' pull that off deserves some careful consideration."

"Oh, I certainly agree with you there, Captain. Admiral Jurgensen has ONI working on that very question, I assure you."

"May I ask if they've come up with any theories, Ma'am?"

"Several," she said wryly. "Most of them mutually contradictory, of course."

"Of course," he agreed with another small smile.

"Obviously, the Sollies didn't just 'lose' four modern cruisers, whatever their government's official 'we don't have any idea what happened' position may be," Draskovic continued. "On the other hand, the Solarian League is huge, and we all know how little genuine control over its internal bureaucracies—including its *military* bureaucracies—its government really has. One theory is that some Frontier Fleet admiral decided to provide for her retirement by putting some of her ships up for sale rather than mothballing them. Which would be a neat trick, if she could do it. Personally, I don't see it. In the first place, those ships were too modern for anyone to be disposing of them on any pretext, including mothballing, *I* can think of. And even if they hadn't been, I can't quite convince myself that even the Sollies' logistics people wouldn't notice the complete disappearance of a million and a half tons worth of warships sooner or later!"

"Unless it was someone a lot more senior than any Frontier Fleet commander," Oversteegen said thoughtfully. "Someone with the reach and authority t' make embarrassin' paperwork vanish at its destination, instead of its origin point."

"That's more or less the thought that had occurred to me. I've spent enough time wrestling with our own paperwork to realize how much easier it would be for some bureaucratic chip-pusher at the top to arrange for their disappearance. Especially someplace like the League." She shrugged. "My personal theory is that somebody very senior in their equivalent of BuShips probably has a bank account somewhere with a very high credit balance."

"I'd be inclined t' agree with you, Ma'am," Oversteegen said. "But I still have t' wonder how someone like that made connections with a batch of Silesian pirates in the first place."

"I doubt that she ever did—directly, at least," Draskovic replied with another shrug. "God only knows how many middlemen may have been involved in the deal! Whoever first took them off the books probably disposed of them to a fence somewhere, who finally brokered the deal at third or fourth hand to the scum you and your people took out."

"You're probably correct," Oversteegen said after a moment, although his tone suggested that he wasn't totally convinced that she was. "But however they got their hands on them, they were operatin' an awful long way from Silesia at Tiberian. And that's not exactly an area noted for rich pickin's for pirates, either."

"No, Captain, it isn't," she acknowledged, allowing just a trace of coolness to color her own tone. "Those same thoughts have occurred to Admiral Jurgensen and his analysts, I assure you. As has the point that they deliberately chose to engage you. That's not typical pirate behavior, even at four-to-one odds."

"As you say, Ma'am." Oversteegen shifted ever so slightly in his chair. "I hope I don't appear t' be belaborin' the obvious, Admiral. It's just that no one seems t' have come up with answers t' the questions which bother me most. Or, at least, no one's mentioned any of those answers t' me if they *have* come up with them." He shrugged. "Given the casualties my people took, I'm afraid I have more than a passin' interest in them."

"I can certainly understand that," Draskovic assured him more sympathetically. "Unfortunately, until and unless ONI can get its hands on some solid leads, I don't think anyone is going to be able to provide those answers."

Oversteegen nodded, and a brief silence descended upon the office. Draskovic allowed it to hover for a moment, then drew a sharp breath and straightened in her own chair.

"Obviously, Captain Oversteegen, what happened in Tiberian is one of the reasons we're redeploying *Gauntlet* to Erewhon now that she's completed her repairs."

Oversteegen regarded her with polite attentiveness, and she shrugged.

"You've demonstrated that you have a good general awareness of the situation in the Erewhon area. That's a major plus. And the fact that you found and took out the pirates who'd ambushed one of Erewhon's own destroyers and killed its entire crew is another one, especially in light of the current . . . strain in our treaty relationship with Erewhon." *And*, she did not add, *so is the fact that your mother is the Prime Minister's second cousin.*

Oversteegen's expression didn't even flicker, but something about his eyes suggested to Draskovic that he'd heard what she carefully hadn't said. Well, no one but a complete political idiot could have been unaware of that consideration in his place. But that was all right. In fact, it was considerably more than all right. Too many of the officers who'd earned reputations in combat against the People's Republic of Haven had made their disagreement with the current Government's policies abundantly clear. Having one of their own demonstrate that he was just as capable—at least!—as the Government's detractors had been a godsend.

"From what you've just said, Ma'am," Oversteegen said after a moment, "I gather that *Gauntlet* will be operatin' solo again?"

"In light of our current naval posture and the fact that Erewhon is—or certainly ought to be—capable of looking after its own security interests, I'm afraid that it's impossible to justify a larger Manticoran naval presence in the area." Draskovic waved one hand and pursed her lips slightly. "I don't know how much a larger naval presence would actually help, under the circumstances," she admitted. "I don't claim to have any special expertise where

Erewhon is concerned, but my own read of the situation is that the present tension in our relationship didn't develop overnight. Which suggests that it's not going to go *away* overnight, whatever we do.

"On the other hand," she continued, "you, Captain, currently enjoy a very high reputation in Erewhonese circles. If we can't send them a battle squadron or two, we can at least send them what the newsies used to call 'an officer of renown.' "

"I see." Oversteegen obviously wasn't the sort to let flattery go to his head, Draskovic noted with a trace of amusement. "Should I assume, then, that my ship's presence will be largely symbolic?"

"To be perfectly honest," Draskovic replied, "any deployment of a single heavy cruiser to an area which is already as well patrolled as Erewhon's neighborhood has to be mostly symbolic. By the same token, however, the fact that you'll be the only Queen's ship on station will mean that you'll face serious and extensive responsibilities. For all intents and purposes, Captain, you will *be* the Royal Manticoran Navy. As the senior officer present, you'll be responsible for protecting and overseeing our commerce, cooperating with Her Majesty's diplomatic representatives to Erewhon, and representing not only the Navy, but the Government and the Crown, as well. In fact, you'll be just as responsible for implementing—or, if it's required, modifying—naval policy as any flag officer commanding a full fleet or task force station."

She paused for a moment, wondering if perhaps she was laying it on just a bit thick. What she'd said was true enough, but any mere captain of the list who took it upon herself to actually "modify" naval policy under any circumstances would require more guts—or gall—than even someone of Oversteegen's exalted connections was likely to possess.

On the other hand, she reflected, *those same connections probably justify at least that much stroking.*

"I imagine that you'll find more than enough things to keep you busy," she concluded.

"No doubt we will, Ma'am," Oversteegen agreed. "I suspect, though, that one of the questions I'm goin' t' be asked is what the Star Kingdom thinks was actually goin' on in Tiberian. That's another reason I raised the point earlier, and I'd appreciate it if ONI could arrange t' brief me directly on our current information about that entire episode." He smiled again, easily. "I'd hate for the Erewhonese t' decide that our 'officer of renown' doesn't have a clue about just how and why he came t' enjoy that renown!"

"Point taken, Captain," Draskovic acknowledged. "I'll have Chief Dautrey put in a priority request to Admiral Jurgensen's office for you."

"Thank you, Ma'am. In addition, however, and in light of what you just said about the responsibilities which are goin' t' devolve upon *Gauntlet*, I'd like t' request the assignment of an additional officer t' assist me in analyzin' situations which may arise."

"Another officer?" Draskovic's eyebrows arched. "What sort of officer? I was under the impression that your table of organization was complete, now that your executive officer has returned to duty."

"Indeed it is, Ma'am," Oversteegen agreed. "That's why I requested an *additional* officer. I realize it's a mite irregular, but I feel that under the circumstances, *Gauntlet* is likely t' require someone with a better background knowledge of Erewhonese affairs and attitudes. And, t' be perfectly blunt, it's entirely possible that circumstances will arise under which it would be most beneficial t' have our own in-house 'spook' available for consultation."

"You're right—that is an irregular request," Draskovic said. She frowned slightly, but her expression and voice were both more thoughtful than condemning. An officer of Oversteegen's accomplishments—and connections, she reminded herself—was entitled to the occasional irregular request. "We don't normally assign intelligence specialists below the squadron level."

"I'm aware of that, Ma'am." Oversteegen, Draskovic noted, did not comment on the blindingly obvious nature of her own last remark. "That's normally the tactical officer's responsibility for a single-ship deployment. Commander Blumenthal, my TO, is an excellent officer, and I have complete confidence in him, both as a tac officer and for normal intelligence functions. But my impression of Erewhon's current attitude towards the Star Kingdom suggests that the situation isn't exactly normal. Under the circumstances, I feel it would be advisable t' assign someone more thoroughly versed in Erewhonese politics and naval capabilities t' *Gauntlet*. Indeed, with your permission, I have a specific officer in mind."

"You do?" Draskovic said, and Oversteegen nodded. "Well, Captain, as you know, it's always been the Navy's policy to accommodate the personnel requests of commanding officers whenever possible. May I assume that you have reason to believe that the officer you're thinking of would be available for assignment to your ship?"

"I do, Ma'am."

"And who might that be?"

"Lieutenant Betty Gohr," Oversteegen said, and Draskovic frowned again, a bit more darkly as the name rang some distant bell in her memory. "She's a bit of an odd duck," the captain continued. "She started as a tactical officer herself, then moved over t' add intelligence work t' her résumé. At the time of the cease-fire, she was assigned t' our intelligence liaison with the Erewhonese navy."

"Gohr," Draskovic repeated, her eyes sharpening suddenly. "Would that be the Lieutenant Gohr who wrote that article about interrogation techniques for the *Proceedings*?"

"Actually, it would," Oversteegen acknowledged, and Draskovic's frown deepened. She couldn't recall the details of the article, but she remembered the gist of it quite clearly, given the furor it had engendered in certain quarters.

"I'm not certain that assigning an officer who has publicly advocated the use of torture to obtain information to a politically sensitive position would be wise, Captain," she said after a moment, her tone decidedly on the frosty side.

"Actually, Admiral, Lieutenant Gohr never advocated the use of physical coercion," Oversteegen corrected politely. "What she said was that the proliferation of military conditionin' programs and drug protocols t' resist conventional interrogation techniques has substantially restricted the options available t' intelligence gatherin' officers. She discussed torture as one possible solution, and noted that under certain circumstances, it *might* be an effective one. She also observed, however, that torture is often and notoriously unreliable under *most* circumstances, in addition t' its morally objectionable nature, and proceeded t' examine other options available t' an interrogator at considerable length. Her phrasin' was, perhaps, unfortunate, since certain casual readers failed t' grasp that she was analyzin' and dismissin' certain techniques, not recommendin' them. The outcry and hysteria her article provoked resulted, in my opinion, entirely from the manner in which both her purpose and her arguments were misconstrued, however."

Draskovic regarded him with hard eyes. He might very well be correct, she thought, admitting to herself that she'd never personally read the offending article. But whatever Lieutenant Gohr might actually have *said*, the "outcry and hysteria" Oversteegen had just mentioned had been . . . severe. The allegation that the lieutenant had specifically suggested the use of torture by Queen's officers, in direct contravention of at least a dozen interstellar treaties to which the Star Kingdom was a signatory, had hit the newsfaxes like a laser head. Collateral damage had threatened to splash all over the lieutenant's superiors, which was why Second Space Lord Jurgensen had declined to defend her. Personally, Draskovic didn't much care one way or the other; the entire debacle had been Jurgensen's problem over at ONI, not hers. But the spectacular fashion in which Gohr's career had nosedived would make assigning her to *Gauntlet* a tricky proposition. The potential public relations drawbacks were obvious enough, but if Jurgensen decided that Draskovic was going behind his back to rehabilitate an officer he'd personally cut adrift . . .

"However her arguments may have been misconstrued, Captain," the admiral said finally, "the fact remains that, if I recall correctly, Lieutenant Gohr is currently on half-pay status specifically because of the controversy her article stirred."

"That's correct, Ma'am," Oversteegen agreed calmly, and actually smiled at her. "That's also how I can be positive that Lieutenant Gohr is available at the moment."

"I see." Draskovic considered him through narrow eyes. He was pushing her, she thought. Definitely pushing her . . . damn him.

"You are aware, I trust," she said after a moment, "that returning an ONI officer to active duty as an analyst without Admiral Jurgensen's approval after she's been placed on half-pay status in the wake of a controversy like this would be far more than 'a mite irregular.'"

"It certainly would be under most circumstances, Ma'am," Oversteegen acknowledged, tacitly accepting Draskovic's implication that Jurgensen would never approve Gohr's return to duty. "However, Lieutenant Gohr isn't really an ONI officer. She's a tactical officer, with a secondary specialization in combat psychology, who was assigned t' London Point t' work with the Marines on specific means t' *resist* strenuous interrogation techniques . . . like torture. She was seconded t' ONI after Admiral Givens reviewed several of her articles on that subject."

"Which doesn't change the fact that she was assigned to ONI when the fallout of her last article hit the fan," Draskovic pointed out.

"That wasn't exactly my point, Ma'am," Oversteegen said. "What I was suggestin' was that she be assigned—officially, at least—t' *Gauntlet* as a tactical officer, not an intelligence specialist. As I say, I'm completely satisfied with Commander Blumenthal, but my assistant tactical officer is due for promotion. What I'd like t' request is that he be relieved from duty aboard *Gauntlet* and assigned t' a slot elsewhere, better suited t' his seniority, and that Lieutenant Gohr be assigned t' *Gauntlet* in his place."

"I see." Draskovic considered him in silence for several more seconds while she considered the patently transparent fig leaf he was proposing. It was remotely possible that he actually believed she was stupid enough not to recognize the quagmire into which he was inviting her to step. It wasn't very likely, though, since no officer could have accomplished what he'd pulled off in Tiberian without a functioning brain of his own.

She began to open her mouth to refuse his suggestion point-blank, then paused. If Jurgensen found out about this, he would be livid. It was unlikely that he would confront her about it openly, of course. He was too old and experienced a hand at bureaucratic infighting for something that crass and crude. Oh no. He'd find his own, far more subtle way to get his own back. But Josette Draskovic had never been particularly fond of Francis Jurgensen at the best of times. And there was the fact that Oversteegen was currently the entire Navy's golden boy. Not to mention a close family connection of the Prime Minister, himself.

Besides, she thought, *given the fact that* Gauntlet *is headed for Erewhon, it's entirely possible the idiot* won't *find out about it. Or, at least, not until it's too late for him to convince even Janacek that Oversteegen wasn't entirely justified asking for her in the first place. . . .*

"All right, Captain," she said at last. "I'll look into it and see what can be arranged."

"Thank you, Admiral," Michael Oversteegen murmured, and he smiled.

CHAPTER 4

"I FEEL RIDICULOUS WEARING THIS GET-UP," grumbled W.E.B. Du Havel, as Cathy Montaigne led him down a wide corridor of her townhouse toward the even wider staircase which swept down to the main floor.

"Don't get pigheaded on me, Web." Cathy gave his portly figure a look that was just barely this side of sarcastic. "You'd look *really* ridiculous trying to pull off the Mahatma Gandhi routine."

Du Havel chuckled. "'Minus fours,' didn't he call it? When he showed up in London wearing nothing much more than a glorified loincloth?"

He glanced down at his ample belly, encased in a costume whose expensive fabric seemed wasted, as brightly colored as it was. Red, basically, but with ample splashes of orange and black—all of it set off by a royal blue cummerbund, parallel white and gold diagonal sashes running from left shoulder to right hip, and a slightly narrower set of the same colors serving as pinstripes for his trousers. The trousers were also blue; but, for no discernable reason Du Havel could make out, were at least two shades darker than the cummerbund.

The shoes, needless to say, were gold. And, just to make the ensemble as ludicrous as possible, ended in slightly upturned, pointed tips festooned with royal blue tassels.

"I feel like the court jester," he muttered. "Or a beach ball."

He gave Cathy a skeptical glance. "You're not playing some sort of practical joke on me?"

"How fucking paranoid can you get, anyway?"

"Well, at least your language hasn't changed since Terra. That's something, I suppose."

They were almost at the top of the stairs, entering an area where the left wall of the corridor gave way to an open vista over a balustrade, looking down upon a huge foyer which seemed packed with people. Du Havel's steps began to lag.

Cathy reached back, grabbed his elbow, and hauled him forward. "Relax, will you? Neo-Comedia is all the rage this year. I had that outfit made up special for you, just for this occasion, by the second best tailor in Landing City."

No help for it, then. Du Havel decided to make the best of a bad situation. They began walking slowly down the stairs, Cathy at his side acting as if she were escorting visiting royalty.

Du Havel, his curious mind active as ever, whispered: "Why the *second* best?"

He was amused to see the smile on Cathy's face. Her *be a nice girl at formal occasions* smile, that was. Not one she often wore, for sure, but she was as good at it as Cathy was at most anything she put her mind to. She even managed to hiss back a reply without once breaking the smile.

"I'm trying to get along with Elizabeth, these days. She'd be pissed if she thought I was trying to swipe her favorite tailor."

He chewed on that, for the few seconds it took them to parade down the long and sweeping staircase. By the time they neared the bottom, it seemed as if all eyes in the foyer were on him—as well as those of many people spilling into the multitude of adjacent rooms. For all that he'd now been resident for two weeks in the Montaigne townhouse—"pocket Versailles" would be a better word for it—Du Havel was still bewildered by the architecture of the place. For some odd reason, his prodigious intellect had never been more than middling-stupid when it came to spatial reckoning.

"Surely the Queen of Manticore can't be *that* petty?"

On the next to last riser, Cathy came to a halt; with a subtle hand on his elbow, bringing Du Havel to a halt also. He realized that she was doing it deliberately, to give the entire crowd a moment to admire the evening's special guest.

Still, her formal smile never wavered. "Don't be silly. Elizabeth's not petty at all. It's not the principle of the thing, it's the sport of it. She and I used to swipe things from each other all the time, when we were kids. It was something of a contest."

"Who won?" he whispered.

"I was *way* ahead on points, when the Queen Mother—she was still the Queen, back then—banned me from the Palace altogether. Elizabeth's still holding a bit of a grudge, I think. So I saw no reason to rub her nose in it again, all these many years later."

The majordomo stepped forward. In a bellowing voice:

"*Catherine Montaigne, former Countess of the Tor! And her guest, the Right Honorable W.E.B. Du Havel, Ph.D.!*"

A voice piped up from the back of the room. A youthful feminine voice which Du Havel recognized. His eyes immediately spotted the tall figure of Anton Zilwicki's daughter Helen.

"You're slacking, Herbert! How *many* Ph.D.s?"

A quick laugh rippled through the crowd. The majordomo let the laughter subside before booming onward.

"*Too many to count, Midshipwoman Zilwicki! My feeble mind is not up to the effort! I can recall only—*"

He began reeling off the list of Du Havel's academic degrees and awards—not missing many, Du Havel noted—and ended with the inevitable: "*Nobel-Shakhra Prize for Human Aspiration, and the Solarian Medallion!*"

"You two hussies orchestrated this," Du Havel muttered. Cathy's smile just widened a bit.

But, despite himself, Du Havel couldn't help but feel genuine pride at hearing the long list recited. Granted, a number of those degrees were honorary. But most of them weren't—and even the ones which were, never would have been bestowed upon him had it not been for his own accomplishments.

Not bad, really, for a man who'd come into the universe in a Manpower Unlimited slave pit, with the birth name of J-16b-79-2/3.

Within a half hour, Du Havel had managed to relax. Fortunately, Cathy proved to have been correct about his preposterous costume. If anything, it was quite a bit more subdued than those worn by many people at the soirée. And while Du Havel was not accustomed to being the official guest of honor at a huge social gathering of a star nation's *haute monde*, he was by no means a shy wallflower. Like any experienced and accomplished university don, he was a past master at the art of making conversation.

Besides, as he'd realized almost at once, the jocular interplay between the majordomo and Helen Zilwicki had given his introduction to Manticore's high society just the right touch of good humor. He was quite sure Cathy had planned it for the purpose.

He was rather impressed, in fact. He'd known for a long time that Cathy had the makings of a superb politician. But, in those long years of her exile on Terra, when he'd first met the woman, she'd never really exercised them. He'd suspected then—and thought the suspicion was confirmed now—that the ultimate reason was her own shock at being expelled from Manticore's aristocracy. No matter how much she might have denied caring about it, few people can easily handle being rejected by the society they'd been raised in. Even if subtly, their self-confidence would take a beating on a level below that of conscious thought.

Watching her now, the ease and grace with which she moved through the crowd, he knew that she'd gotten it all back. Back—and then some, because the years of exile had not been wasted either. This was no headstrong young woman, any longer, sneering at tactics from the lofty mount of principle. This was a woman in her early middle age, entering the prime of her life, with her confidence restored and armed by years of study and political struggle.

Look out, Manticore, he thought with amusement.

He brought his attention back to the conversation he was having with an elderly gentleman and his two female companions. His sisters, if Du Havel remembered their introduction correctly.

He wasn't quite sure. All three of them were prattling half-baked nonsense, and he hadn't paid much heed to most of it. Just enough, with the experience of years at academic social gatherings, to be able to make the necessary sage nods and judicious noises at the proper intervals.

Fortunately, Du Havel had trained himself to be patient at these things. Not easy, that. By nature, he was not given to suffering fools gladly.

He heard the majordomo booming another introduction.

"*Captain Michael Oversteegen, MC, CGM, GS, OCN, commanding officer, Her Majesty's Starship* Gauntlet*!*"

A tall, slender man in a Manticoran naval uniform had entered the room. Du Havel didn't pay much attention, until he noticed a definite lessening in the volume of noise produced by the crowd. As if most conversations had either faltered momentarily, or the speakers had lowered their voices.

That included, thankfully, the three siblings. Du Havel spotted Helen Zilwicki not far away, and disengaged himself from the Babbling Trio with a smooth and meaningless polite phrase.

"Who's he?" he murmured into Helen's ear, when he came alongside her. The young woman hadn't noticed him until then, because her own eyes were riveted on the Manticoran officer. Just about everyone's seemed to be—and Du Havel had already spotted Cathy making her way through the crowd toward the newly arrived guest.

"Oh. Hi, Web. That's Oversteegen. *The* Oversteegen. Cathy invited him, but she never once thought he'd show up. Neither did I."

Du Havel smiled. "Let's start back at the beginning, shall we? 'The' Oversteegen may mean something to you. But as someone who just arrived in the Star Kingdom two weeks ago from Terra, I'm afraid it means nothing to me."

Helen's eyes widened, as a youngster's will when she stumbles across the shocking discovery that not *everybody* shares her own particular interests.

"He's the captain who won the Battle of Tiberian," she replied, and shook her head at his uncomprehending expression. "The one where his ship took out four other cruisers single-handedly," she added in a tone that was half-protesting, as if leaving unspoken: *How can ANYONE not know about it?*

"Oh, yes. I recall reading about the incident at the time. A year or so ago, wasn't it? But I got the impression his opponents were merely pirates, not a naval force."

Helen's eyes widened still further. Du Havel had to fight to keep from grinning. The nineteen-year-old girl was too polite to come right out and say it, but it was obvious to him that her thoughts were running along the lines of: *How can ANYONE be such an idiot?*

She managed, however, to keep most of the outrage out of her ensuing reply. She only spluttered twice.

"Those were *Gladiator*-class cruisers, for Chr—" She suppressed the splutter, and continued in a calmer tone of voice. Much the way a mother restrains her indignation at the folly of a toddler. "*Gauntlet*'s sensor records proved that beyond a shadow of a doubt."

Du Havel raised a questioning eyebrow. Helen Zilwicki had to suppress another splutter.

"How can any—?" Cough. "The *Gauntlet* was the name of Oversteegen's ship. Still is, I should say." The next words were spoken a bit slowly, as a mother might speak to a child, introducing simple concepts.

"*Gladiators,* Web. The Solarian League Navy's most recent class of heavy cruisers. They've got completely up-to-date weaponry and EW capability, probably as good as anything we've got. Solarian ships of the wall are nothing much—leaving aside the sheer number of them—because the League hasn't fought a real war in centuries. But their lighter warships always stay a lot closer to cutting edge, since those are the ones that do the SLN's real work."

Her eyes grew a bit unfocused, as if she was thinking far back—or far ahead. "Nobody's defeated a Solarian heavy cruiser in open battle in over half a century, Web. And nobody's *ever* beaten four of them at once, with a single vessel of any kind short of a dreadnought—much less another cruiser. Not, at least, that there's any record of, in the Academy's data banks. I know. I did a post-action study of *Gauntlet*'s engagement for a course I just finished. Part of the assignment was to do a comparative analysis."

She bestowed a look of deep reproof upon Du Havel. "So what difference does it make if they were 'pirates'? Even chimps would be dangerous in *Gladiators*, if they knew how to operate the vessels in the first place."

"How did pirates ever get their hands on them?"

Helen scowled. "Good question—and don't think everybody isn't asking it, too. Unfortunately, the only pirates who survived were low-level muscle, who didn't know anything."

She hesitated a moment. "I guess I probably shouldn't say this, but . . . what the hell, it's nothing that hasn't been speculated on in the news media. There's really only one way they could have gotten them, Web. For whatever reason, somebody in the League with big money and just as much influence must have been behind that 'pirate operation.' Nobody that I know has any idea what they were up to, but just about everybody—me included—thinks that Manpower must have been behind it. Or maybe even Mesa as a whole."

Her scowl was now pronounced. "If we could *prove* it—"

Du Havel shifted his gaze back to the Manticoran captain under discussion. With far greater interest, now. However much distance there might be between him and most, in terms of intellectual achievements and public renown, there was one thing which Web Du Havel shared with any former genetic slave.

He hated Manpower Unlimited with a bone-deep passion. And though, for political reasons, he disagreed with the violent tactics used by the Audubon Ballroom, he'd never once had so much as a qualm about the violence itself. There was not a single responsible figure in that evil galactic corporation—not a single one, for that matter, on the entire planet of Mesa—whom Web Du Havel would not himself have lowered into a vat of boiling oil.

Capering and singing hosannas all the while—if he thought it would accomplish anything.

He took a deep breath, controlling the sudden spike of rage. And reminding himself, for perhaps the millionth time in his life, that if sheer righteous fury could accomplish anything worthwhile, wolverines would have inherited the galaxy long ago.

"Introduce me, would—" He broke off, suddenly realizing the request was moot. Cathy Montaigne was already leading Captain Oversteegen toward him.

It would be a while before they got there, however, given the press of the crowd and the fact that several people were stepping forward to offer their hands to the captain. Hastily, he whispered: "Just so I don't commit any social gaffes, why are you—and Cathy—so surprised to see him here? He was invited, was he not?"

He heard Helen make a little snorting sound. As if, once again, the well-mannered girl had suppressed another outburst of derision.

"Just *look* at him, Web. He's the spitting image of a younger Baron High Ridge."

Du Havel's face must have registered his incomprehension. Not at the name itself—he knew enough about Manticoran politics to know that Helen was referring to the current Prime Minister—but at the subtleties which lay beneath.

Helen pursed her lips. "I thought you were supposed to be the galaxy's expert—okay, one of maybe ten—on political theory? So how come you don't know your ass from— Uh. Sorry, didn't mean to be rude."

He grinned, enjoying the girl's lapse from social manners. Given Du Havel's slave origins and present exalted status, most people were excessively polite around him. Obviously petrified lest they trigger off some buried resentment, of which they apparently assumed he harbored a multitude.

As it happened, Web Du Havel was thick-skinned by nature—and enjoyed few things so much as a sleeves-rolled-up, hair-hanging-down, intellectual brawl in which quarter was neither asked nor given. Which was the reason he and Catherine Montaigne had become very close, many years earlier. That had happened the first time they met, within an hour of being introduced at a social event put on by the Anti-Slavery League on Terra.

The argument rolling properly, Cathy had informed him, in her usual loud and profane manner, that he was a damned bootlicker with the mindset of a house slave. He, for his part, had explained to the assembled crowd—just as loudly, if not as profanely—that she was a typical upper class dimwit, slumming with the chic downtrodden of the day, who couldn't bake a loaf of bread without romanticizing the distress of the flour and the noble savage qualities of the yeast.

It had gone rapidly downhill from there. By the end of the evening, a lifetime's friendship had been sealed. Like Du Havel himself, Cathy Montaigne was one of those ferocious intellectuals who took their ideas seriously—and never trusted another intellectual until they'd done the equivalent of a barbarian ritual. Matching intellectual wound to wound, sharing ideas—and derision—the way ancient warriors, meeting for the first time, mixed their actual blood from self-inflicted wounds.

"Give me a break, Helen," he said, chuckling. "The real problem here is *your* provincialism, not mine. The ins-and-outs of the political fine points here on Manticore only seem of galaxy-shaking importance to you because you were born here. Your backyard looks like half a universe, because you have no idea how big the universe really is. Abstractly, you do—but the knowledge has never really sunk into your bones."

He paused, giving the slowly approaching captain another glance. Still plenty of time, he decided, to continue the girl's education.

"The Star Kingdom is a polity of five whole settled planets in only three star systems, since Trevor's Star's annexation—and assuming you can call Medusa a 'settled planet' in the first place. Even with San Martin added, your total population does not exceed six billion. There are five times that many people living in the Solar System alone—or Centauri, or Tau Delta, or Mithra, or any one of several dozen of the Solarian League's inner systems. The 'Old League,' as it's popularly known. The Solarian League as a whole has an official membership of 1,784 planets—that's not counting the hundreds more under Solarian rule in the Protectorates—which exist in a volume of galactic space measuring between three and four hundred light-years in diameter. Within that enormous volume, there are literally more stars than you can see here at night with the naked eye. No one has any idea what the total population might be. The Old League alone has a registered population of almost three trillion people, according to the last census—and that census grossly undercounted the population. No serious analyst even tries to claim they know how many more trillions of people live in the so-called 'Shell Worlds' or the Protectorates. I leave aside entirely the untold thousands—millions, rather—of artificial habitats scattered across thousands of solar systems. Each and every one of which star polities has its own history, and its own complex politics and social and economic variations."

The captain and Cathy were getting close, now. It was time to break off the impromptu lecture, since he still needed to know the reasons for Helen's bemusement at Oversteegen's appearance at the event.

"Let me just leave you with the following thought, Helen: It's only been since the human race spread across thousands of worlds that political science has really deserved the term 'science'—and it's still a rough-and-ready science at that. Sometimes, it reminds me of paleontology back in the wild and woolly days of Cope and Marsh, battling it out over dinosaur bones. If nothing else, the preponderance of the League in human affairs skews all the data. But at least now we have a range of experience that allows us to do serious comparative studies, which was never possible in pre-Diaspora days. But that's really what someone like me does. I look for patterns and repetitions, if you will. The number of individual star systems whose political details I'm familiar with is just a tiny percentage of the whole. The truth is, I know a lot more about ancient Terran history than I do about the history of most of today's inhabited worlds. Because that's still, more often than not, the common history we use as our initial crude yardstick."

Suitably abashed, the girl nodded.

"And you *still* haven't explained—in terms I can understand—why you and Cathy are so surprised that Captain Oversteegen showed up. Or, for that matter—given the surprise—why she invited him in the first place."

"Oh. It's because he doesn't look like High Ridge by accident. He's part of that whole Conservative Association bunch of lousy—well. The crowd I don't like, let's put it that way. Cathy hates them with a passion. He's related to the Queen—distantly—on his father's side, but his mother is High Ridge's second cousin. As his looks ought to tell anyone who lays eyes on him!"

Du Havel nodded, the picture becoming clearer in his mind. He was more familiar with Manticore's politics than that of most star systems, naturally. Even leaving Catherine Montaigne aside, Manticore played a far more prominent role in the Anti-Slavery League than its sheer weight of population would account for. He understood the nature and logic of the Conservative Association well enough, certainly. It was an old and familiar phenomenon, after all, as ancient as any political formation in human affairs. A clique of people with a very prestigious and luxurious position in a given society, who reacted to anything which might conceivably discommode them with outrage and indignation—as if their own privileges and creature comforts resulted from laws of nature equal in stature to the principles of physics. Very fat pigs in a very plentifully supplied trough, basically, who attempted to dignify their full stomachs by oinking the word "conservative."

Given that W.E.B. Du Havel considered himself, by and large, to be a conservative political theorist—using the term "conservative" loosely—he found the phenomenon not only understandable but detestable.

"Bunch of lousy swine will do nicely, Helen. But you can't confuse the individual with the group. Does Oversteegen *himself* belong to the Conservative Association? And, if so, why did Cathy invite him? And, if so—and having invited him nonetheless—why did he choose to come?" He gave the large crowd a quick overview. Diehard members of the Liberal Party, for the most part—and the ones who weren't, with not more than a handful of exceptions, departed from the Liberals to the left of the political spectrum. "I'd have thought that as likely as a Puritan agreeing to attend a witches' Sabbath."

"What's a 'Puritan'?" she asked. "And why would witches—silly notion, that—hold a soirée on— Never mind." Cathy and the captain were almost there. Quickly, Helen whispered: "I don't think he's in the CA. Truth is, I don't know much about his own personal opinions. Not sure many people do. But—"

A last, quick, hissed few words: "Sorry. You'll have to find out the rest from him, I guess."

A moment later, Cathy was making the introductions. And Web Du Havel began getting his answers.

He was delighted, of course. Except that, within a few minutes, he was back to silently cursing his ridiculous costume.

There was no way to roll up the sleeves!

CHAPTER 5

"BEEN WANTIN' T' MEET YOU FOR YEARS," the captain stated, speaking in a drawl which Du Havel immediately recognized. Not specifically, of course—the galaxy had easily ten times as many dialects and verbal mannerisms as it did languages and inhabited worlds. But he knew the phenomenon for what it was, since it, too, was as ancient as privilege. Members of an elite group—"elite," at least, in their own minds—almost invariably developed a distinctive style of speech to separate themselves from the common herd.

Oversteegen, smiling thinly, gave the crowd his own quick overview. "Only reason I agreed t' come t' this Walpurgis Night of prattlin' political heathens."

He bestowed the smile on Cathy, widening it a bit. "Present company excepted, of course. I've long had a grudgin' admiration for the Countess here—former Countess, I suppose I should say. Ever since the speech she gave at the House of Lords which got her pitched out on her ear. I was there in person, as it happens, observin' as a member of the family since my mother was indisposed. And I'll tell you right now that I would have voted for her expulsion from the Lords myself, had I been old enough at the time, on the simple grounds that she had, in point of fact, violated long established protocol. Even though, mind you, I agreed with perhaps ninety percent of what she'd said. Still, rules are rules."

Cathy smiled back. "Rules were meant to be broken."

"Don't disagree," Oversteegen replied immediately. "Indeed they are. Providin', however, that the one breakin' the rules is willin' t' pay the price for it, and the price gets charged in full."

He gave Cathy a deep nod, almost a bow. "Which you were, Lady Catherine. I saluted you for it then—at the family dinner table that night, in fact. My mother was infinitely more indisposed thereafter; tottered back t' her sick bed cursin' me for an ingrate. My father was none too pleased, either. I salute you for it, again."

Turning back to Du Havel: "Otherwise, breakin' rules becomes the province of brats instead of heroes. Fastest way I can think of t' turn serious political affairs int' a playpen. A civilized society needs a conscience, and conscience can't be developed without martyrs—real ones—against which a nation can measure its crimes and sins."

Du Havel's interest perked up sharply. He understood the logic of Oversteegen's argument, naturally. It would have been surprising if he hadn't, since it was a paraphrase—not a bad one either, given the compression involved—of the basic argument Du Havel had advanced in one of his books.

Oversteegen immediately confirmed his guess. "I should tell you that I consider *The Political Value of Sacrifice* one of the finest statements of conservative principle in the modern universe. Havin' said that, I also feel obliged t' inform you that I consider the arguments you advanced in *Scales of Justice: Feathers Against Stones* t' be—at best!—a sad lapse int' liberal maudlinism. Principles are principles, Doctor Du Havel. You, of all people, should know that. So it was sad t' see you maunderin' from one compromise t' another, tradin' away clarity for the sake of immediate benefit. Sad, sad. Practically gave social engineerin' your blessin', you did."

Hallelujah! Du Havel began plucking at his sleeves, in a vain attempt to find the buttons so he could roll them up.

"Social engineering, is it? Ha! Explain to me, Captain Oversteegen, why it is that so-called 'conversatives'—nothing of the sort, mind you; just dinosaurs with pretensions—only object to social engineering when it threatens to hang over into their own—invariably lush and well-kept—front gardens? Yet never have the slightest objection to social engineering when it created those palatial grounds in the first place?"

Oversteegen drew himself up a bit, looming even taller than ever. Cheerfully—except for the problem with the sleeves; dammit, where were the buttons?—Du Havel plunged on.

"Consider your own aristocratic system here on Manticore, if you would. Blatant social engineering, Captain. As crude as it gets. A pack of rich people, creating a constitution deliberately designed—with greed aforethought, if not malice—to keep themselves and their descendants in a blessed state of privilege. Or are you going to try to argue that the principles of aristocracy arose from the native soil of what was then an alien planet? Like weeds, as it were—which, by the way, is a pretty apt analogy for any variety of caste system. Weeds, preening like roses."

Oversteegen grinned, acknowledging the hit. A splendid intellectual warrior, Du Havel noted gleefully, not fazed in the least by a mere dash of blood. He was practically clawing at the sleeves, now.

"You'll get no argument from me on *that* issue, Doctor. Indeed true. Can't even argue that my ancestors were better murderers and robbers and rapists than anyone else, I'm afraid, the way a proper Norman baron could. Just bigger moneybags and an earlier arrival date, that's all. Lamentable, isn't it, the lengths to which modern nobility is driven by the advance of social conscience? Still, I'll argue in favor of an aristocracy."

A high-pitched, derisive snort issued from his long and bony nose. "Not because I believe for an instant that Conservative Association babble about good breedin', much less their downright superstitions on the subject of so-called good birth. No, the issue isn't the worth of the *individuals* in any given aristocracy. It's simply the social advantage which havin' *any* aristocracy gives a nation. Pick 'em by lottery, for all I care. But just the fact it exists gives the nation manifold benefits."

Cathy interrupted. "Web, those sleeves *can't* be rolled up. The style doesn't allow for it."

He glared at her. "Is that so? Hmph. Watch this."

Du Havel had been bred a J-line by Manpower. That was—supposedly; as usual, their claims fell wide of reality—a breed designed for technical work. Thus, an emphasis on mental capability, at least of a low and mechanical variety. But also, since J-lines were designed basically for engineering work, a breed which was physically quite sturdy. Web wasn't particularly tall, and his long years of sedentary intellectual activity had put thirty kilos of fat on his frame. But the frame beneath was still square and solid.

So were the muscles which went with it.

Riiip. Riiip.

"Ah. That's better. Let me begin, Captain, by pointing out that you're paraphrasing—not badly at all, either—Jutta's argument in her *Barriers Needed for Progress.* Good for you. An excellent book, overall, even if I think Angelina's too prone to rigidity. But let me go on to point out that those barriers—I prefer to think of them as 'limits' or 'frames'—are themselves the product of social engineering. Goes all the way back to the original program which Jutta praises so highly—yet she never mentions was itself a deliberate project to engineer the society its founders wanted. I refer, of course, to the Constitution of the ancient United States. The thing was practically an architect's dream. A carefully balanced allotment of powers; limitations on democracy which were absurd on the face of it—just to give one example, why in God's name should the members of small provinces be given the same power as those in larger and more important ones? and if so, why only in *one* house instead of all?—you name it, and if it was possible to engineer, they did it. Tried, I should say, since naturally half of their schemes came unraveled within a few generations. Their sanction of slavery, for instance."

By now, naturally, a large crowd had gathered around. Naturally, also, it contained the inevitable know-it-all-who-didn't.

"That's not possible," the man proclaimed firmly, frowning. "I know my ancient history, and the United States—you *are* referring to the American one, yes?—arose long before genetic slavery." He half-sneered. "Long before they even knew anything about DNA, for that matter. Bunch of primitives."

Du Havel closed his eyes briefly. *God, give me the patience to suffer fools gladly.*

Alas, he was an atheist.

"Who said anything about *genetic* slavery? Slavery's been around since the dawn of civilization, you—you—"

Fortunately, a woman cut him off before he could begin alienating the crowd.

"But—on what *basis*?"

He stared at her. "I mean," she continued brightly, "they certainly couldn't just enslave *anyone.* There had to be *some* genetic basis for it."

He recognized her now. Susan—or Suzanne, he couldn't remember—Zekich. One of the Liberal Party's provincial leaders, formerly in the orbit of the Countess of New Kiev, who'd lately been gravitating toward Cathy Montaigne. Not out of principle, but simply because the woman seemed to have a good nose for detecting which way the wind was starting to blow.

Cathy was polite to her, even gracious. The long years of exile had at least given her tactical sense. Even if, in private, she referred to her as "the Zekich slut."

Web Du Havel took a deep breath. Fools, especially snotty twits like the man who had superciliously informed him that slavery could not possibly antedate genetic science, he did not suffer gladly. But he knew the difference—had always known, since the slave pits—between an irritating jackass and an enemy.

This woman was an enemy, not simply a fool. In the future, for a certainty, if not today. Exactly the kind of "forward-looking progressive" who would denounce genetic slavery in the abstract—but would share all the prejudices against the slaves themselves. And, with those slaves once risen to their feet and rattling the bars of the cage, would demand stridently that discipline be restored to the zoo.

"Indeed," he said, smiling thinly. "Indeed, Ma'am, they did. Mind you, slavery as a social institution is ancient, and long antedated the era I'm discussing, which was only a few centuries pre-Diaspora. Originally, slavery had no particular connection to genetic variation. But by the time we reach the era in question, people based their slave system of the time on genetics as they understood it. The key concept, in those days, went by the term of 'race.' "

A number of people in the surrounding crowd, those who apparently had some knowledge of either genetics or history, frowned thoughtfully. Trying, obviously, to figure out how such a vague ethnological term as "race" could be coupled to a political system. Most of the people, however, simply looked puzzled.

"You have to remember," Du Havel explained, "that this was long before the Diaspora. Several centuries before, in fact. In those days, genetic variation within the human race was not only relatively simple, but largely allotropic. Longstanding genetic pools, most of them sharing a few simple and obviously visible somatic traits, only recently brought into systematic and regular contact with each other. As a result, those of them who shared a recent mutation which favored albinism and a few other superficial features, and who happened to be the predominant 'race' at the time, set about enslaving others. One in particular was favored for the purpose. A genetic variation which had settled into a temporary somatic mold in the continent of Africa. 'Black' people, they were called. It was assumed, based on the genetic pseudo-science of the time, that they were particularly suited for a servile existence. An assumption which, stripping away the superstitious claptrap, was based on nothing much more than the fact that they had dark skins, which were usually coupled with—"

He proceeded to give a quick sketch of the phenotype generally to be found among Africans of that ancient time. When he was done, most of the people in the crowd had a rather strained look on their faces. The Zekich woman herself had taken a full step away from him, as if trying to distance herself from the suddenly revealed regicide in their midst.

Well. Not "regicide," precisely speaking. Du Havel tried to dredge up his very rusty Latin. *Hm. What would be the proper jargon for someone who advocated enslaving royalty?*

Oversteegen, on the other hand, had listened to his entire impromptu lecture with a steadily growing smile and no sign at all of confusion. The captain was obviously a man of many parts, Du Havel decided. Too many of those interested in political theory had no matching interest in the history which set the frame and reference for that theory, much less in something as ancient as pre-Diaspora Terra's barbaric, pretechnic social institutions. Oversteegen clearly did. Because, unlike most of the expressions about him, his expression was one of pure and simple humor.

"What fun!" he exclaimed. "I'd love to have been there when you discussed it with Elizabeth!" Shaking his head, grinning. "You did have an audience with her, as I recall. Two days ago, I think it was—and quite a long one, if the news accounts were accurate. Surely the subject came up."

Most of the crowd looked even more pained. Several of them were even glaring at Oversteegen. Du Havel found that interesting, but not surprising. For all their often vociferous public disputes with the Queen of the Star Kingdom, even the members of the Liberal Party shared the general cultural attitudes of most Manticorans. Even the members of the *left* wing of that Party, who made up most of the crowd, shared them.

Yes, the Queen was sadly misguided by her advisers. Especially those warmongering imperialists in the Centrist and Crown Loyalist crowds.

Still.

She *was* the Queen!

"I can't *believe* it," gasped a woman nearby. She was quite literally clutching her throat with distress. "Why . . . that would describe Queen Elizabeth!"

"Most of the House of Winton, going all the way back," growled a man standing next to her. He glanced around. "Not to mention a considerable number of the people in this room. I knew the ancients were full of insane superstitions, but—" He gave Du Havel a look which fell just short of a glare. "Are you sure about this?"

Du Havel shrugged. "That would be simplifying too much. You really must understand what two thousand years of the Diaspora has done to human genetic variation. The combination of a gigantic population explosion—less than ten billion humans, all told, at the time the Diaspora began, to how many trillions today—spread across thousands of planetary environments instead of a relative handful of regional ones, many of them far more extreme than anything the human race encountered on Earth itself. Then, factor in the endless cross-mixing of the species, not to mention intentional genetic alterations . . ."

He shrugged again. "Your Queen Elizabeth bears, at best, an approximate somatic match to the ancient Africans—and that, only if you restrict the comparison to superficial features like skin color. I'm quite sure, for instance, that if you matched her blood characteristics against that recorded for ancient so-called 'races' that they would have little resemblance to the blood characteristics of most Africans of the day. Skin color is especially meaningless, as a genetic indicator, since that's a superficial feature which adapts rapidly to a change in environment. Consider, for instance, the extreme albinism found today on one of the two Mfecane planets—Ndebele, if I recall correctly—despite the fact that the population's ancestors were Bantu."

He brought up his memories of the Queen, from his recent meeting with her. The memories were quite extensive, since the captain was right—it *had* been a long audience. He and Elizabeth Winton had hit it right off.

"Her hair's not really right, for starters. Very wavy, true, but not much like the tightly kinked hair found in ancient times among most of the tropical ethnic variants. Then, her facial features—especially the nose—are much closer to those which our ancestors would have labeled by the term 'Caucasian' than the term 'Negroid.' And while her skin color is indeed quite lustrous, it's really not the tone you would have found among Africans of the day. It's too light, for one thing, and for another, that definite mahogany tinge is really closer to that of a dark-skinned 'Amerindian'—that was a term used for North American indigenes—than an African."

The crowd seemed to relax. All except Cathy, that is, who was watching him closely. Cathy, unlike the rest, knew exactly how much fury was roiling beneath the surface.

For people who have never experienced it—or never really thought about it—"slavery" is an *abstract* injustice.

"Not that it would have mattered in the least," he continued, trying to keep from snarling. "Except in the specific abuses she would have suffered. She's quite close enough, I assure you. Except that, with her appearance, she would have been considered what was called a 'mulatto.' Coupled with her youth and good looks, that would most likely have resulted in her being been made the concubine of a slave master, assigned to his bed instead of the fields. That was a common fate for those women known as 'mulattos' at the time. Those of them who weren't sold to brothels and made outright prostitutes."

The strained looks were back. Du Havel favored them with a grin which, alas, he was quite sure was several degrees too savage for proper decorum at such an event. But he couldn't help doing so. It was only with the greatest difficulty that he managed to restrain himself from sticking out his tongue, as the Ballroom killers did when they'd cornered their slaver prey, to show the crowd the genetic markers which Manpower's gengineers had given him while still an embryo.

"Oh, yes. Be sure of it. To see a proper reflection of the phenotype which would have been assigned to a life of back breaking labor, you need to consider the Queen's—what is she, Captain? you're a relative of the royal family, I think—some sort of cousin, I believe. Michelle Henke, I'm referring to. I was introduced to her also, at the audience. I didn't quite catch her military rank—sorry, but I'm just not familiar enough with Manticoran tables of organization to understand the fine points—but I believe it was quite prestigious. And got the feeling, I might add, that the rank resulted from her own accomplishments instead of family pressure or influence."

Oversteegen grunted. "First cousin. Michelle's the daughter of the Queen's aunt. Fifth in line t' the throne, now that her father and brother were assassinated. She's a commodore." He grunted again. In its own way, the sound was as savage as Du Havel's grin. "And I don't know a single naval officer—no servin' line officer, for sure—who thinks she got the rank by pull."

"Yes, her. If I'm not mistaken, her phenotype is much more typical of the House of Winton than the Queen's. Very dark skin, almost a true black. And in her case, the hair is right. Not the facial bone structure, perhaps, although it comes fairly close. But it wouldn't have mattered at all, not with that color of skin. Today's universe assigns her to command navies, and doesn't even think about it. The ancients would have had her doing menial unskilled labor. And, if she was unable to avoid the attentions of the overseer, she would have been raped in a shack instead of a plantation manor house."

Silence, for a moment. Du Havel took a deep breath, bringing his anger under control.

The captain helped. "Pity the poor bastard who tried t' rape Mike Henke!" he snorted. "Or Elizabeth herself, for that matter. With her temper? Ha! The bastard might manage it, but he'd find his throat cut within a day. As well keep an angry hexapuma in your bed."

A titter went through the crowd. Oversteegen's crude but accurate observations served to remind them all that these were *not,* after all, ancient times riddled with savage superstitions.

Still—much to Du Havel's relief—the tension had been enough to cause most of the crowd to drift away. Honored guest or not, many of them had clearly come to the conclusion that being in close proximity to W.E.B. Du Havel was also a bit too much like being near a panther. Granted, a panther with a long and impressive list of academic credentials and prestigious honors attached to his tail. But, still a panther—and one who, if not precisely angry, seemed to have an uncertain temper.

"Bit thinned out, hasn't it?" said the captain, smiling slyly. "Good. I dare say there'll be fewer silly interruptions." He rubbed his hands. "T' get back t' the point, Doctor Du Havel—"

" 'Web,' if you would, Captain. Academic titles are tediously long-winded."

Oversteegen nodded. " 'Web,' then." His brow furrowed. "Come t' think of it— Pardon my askin', but what *does* 'W.E.B.' stand for, anyway? I just realized I've never seen anythin' but the bare initials."

Du Havel shook his head. "That's because it doesn't stand for anything except the initials themselves. I didn't know what they stood for myself, when the immigration officer on Nasser insisted I give him a name for their records. I'd only escaped a few months earlier, so my knowledge of history was still pretty limited." He shrugged. "I just combined what I remembered from two names of ancient men I'd read about, briefly, and who'd struck me as righteous fellows. W.E.B. Du Bois and Vaclav Havel. When it finally dawned on me—that night, as it happened, when my fellow escapees demanded to know what they were supposed to call me, now that 'Kami' was out of bounds—I couldn't think of anything except 'Web.' "

The rest of the soirée went splendidly. The captain kept Du Havel monopolized throughout, much to Du Havel's delight. For a man who'd spent most of his adult life mastering the elaborate and often arcane skills of a naval officer, Oversteegen had an impressive grasp of the galaxy's political theory.

Granted, Oversteegen was far too biased in favor of his own views. Granted, he tended to read far too little of the thinking of those he disagreed with, and dismissed them much too quickly and easily. Granted also, his entire outlook was somewhat warped; first, by the inevitable prejudices of his social background; second—Du Havel thought this was much more important—by the equally inevitable prejudices of a man whose active life had been shaped by the immediate demands of a long and savage war.

Still, all in all, a very fine fellow indeed. And, when the soirée ended, Du Havel parted company with the captain with considerable reluctance.

"If I could, I'd propose we meet again sometime soon," he said, shaking Oversteegen's hand. "Alas, I'm afraid I'll be heading off for Erewhon within the week. I'll be accompanying Captain Zilwicki on his voyage there, in order to pay my respects to the family of Hieronymus Stein and his surviving colleagues in the Renaissance Association."

There seemed to be an odd little gleam in Oversteegen's eye. "So I understand. I have t' leave the system myself, in any event. Tomorrow morning, in fact. But, who knows? As fate might have it, Web, we may meet again."

He gave Du Havel a stiff little bow; then, to Cathy Montaigne, one which was neither stiff nor little. "Doctor Du Havel, Lady Catherine, s'been a pleasure." And off he went.

"What's so funny?" he asked Helen Zilwicki, who'd kept well within the orbit of his long conversation with Oversteegen throughout the evening, even if she'd never said a word herself. Web suspected the midshipwoman had a quiet case of hero worship for the captain, even if she'd be caught dead before admitting it.

Helen grinned. "You know, Web, every now and then you might tear yourself away from your scholarly tomes to look at the daily news. It was just announced today, in the naval section. Captain Oversteegen and *Gauntlet* have been reassigned to Erewhon. Anti-piracy patrol, they're calling it. The ship's leaving orbit tomorrow."

"Oh." A bit embarrassed, Web's eyes dropped. Encountering the sight of torn sleeves, his embarrassment deepened.

"Oh. Hm. I'm afraid your guests must have thought me quite the barbarian, Cathy."

Cathy's grin was even wider than Helen's. "And so what if they did? This wasn't *really* my crowd tonight, Web. Not most of them, anyway. It was mainly made up of Liberal Party bellwethers, trying to test the shifting winds at an event they could attend without having to openly thumb their nose at New Kiev."

"Yes, I know. That's why I'm a bit concerned I made the wrong impression."

She shrugged. "That depends on how you define 'wrong,' doesn't it? I'll tell you what, Web. I'll leave the theory to you, as long as you leave the sordid tactics to me. It won't hurt me one bit to have lots of aristocratic Liberal Party hacks convinced that I'm the only one who knows how to get along with lower class barbarians."

As they were climbing back up the stairs, heading toward the townhouse's elaborate set of bedrooms—fortunately, Cathy would guide him to his own—Du Havel asked another question.

"Where was Anton tonight, by the way? And Berry, for that matter?"

Seeing the expression on Cathy's face, he grunted. "What? Another case where I should have read the news reports?"

"Hardly! Not unless—"

She shook her head. "Never mind, Web. 'Need to know,' and all that. You'll find out soon enough. For the moment, you can go to your rest in the serene confidence that before too long you'll be able to offend somebody else from the upper crust."

"Oh, splendid," he said. "I do so enjoy that, as long as I'm not fouling something up for you."

"In this case, I doubt it. First, from what Anton tells me, because the upper crustee in question probably doesn't offend all that easily. Secondly, because I don't give a fuck anyway."

"You really should watch your language. Especially now that you're a politician instead of a rabble-rouser."

"Don't be silly, Web. It's part of my charm. Persona, if you will. Who else can the Liberals turn to when the mob gets unruly, except someone who can cuss like a deep-space cargo-walloper?"

"You have a devious mind, Catherine Montaigne. I'd fear for your soul, except I don't believe in souls. Not a shred of evidence to support the notion, I'm afraid."

They'd reached the door to his bedroom. He began to open it, but paused.

"Well. I admit your daughter Berry could be considered a piece of evidence in favor. Hard to explain otherwise how she turned out, really."

"Isn't she a gem?" agreed Catherine enthusiastically. "I sometimes think she's the most levelheaded person I've ever known. Most of the time, I'm sure of it."

"Well put." He shook his head sadly. "I'll miss her, when I leave. I surely will."

As he entered the bedroom and closed the door, he caught a glimpse of Cathy, still standing in the corridor. There seemed to be an odd gleam in her eyes. Maternal pride, perhaps.

CHAPTER 6

GETTING TO HIS SHIP A FEW DAYS LATER was a madhouse for Anton. Queen Elizabeth had waited until the last minute to leak the news, but the Star Kingdom's paparazzi had the same lightning reflexes possessed by that breed throughout the galaxy. By the time Anton and his entourage reached the gate to the landing field where the orbital shuttle awaited them, the area was mobbed with journalists.

For all that he'd planned for it, Anton still found the whole situation a bit infuriating. For one thing, he'd become so accustomed to working in the shadows that he'd overlooked how much *he* would be an item of avid interest. As many of the paparazzi seemed interested in getting holopics of him as they were of the Princess.

Glumly, he could imagine the tabloid headlines.

Disgraced officer on mystery trip with royalty!

Captain Zilwicki tosses over the Countess for the Princess!

Catherine Montaigne heartbroken! "My lover left me for a younger woman!"

Another scandal in a scandalous career!

It didn't help any when Berry, filled with excitement at the occasion, planted a sloppy impromptu kiss on his cheek right in front of the journalist mob. That it was a daughter's kiss and not a lover's should have been blindingly obvious to anyone nearby. But the paparazzi were kept at a distance by the police, and all their carefully cropped holopics would show was the sight of a pretty young woman dressed up like a princess apparently slobbering over a much older man.

Something of his unease must have shown. Behind him, he heard Princess Ruth murmur with amusement: "Oh, stop worrying, Captain. The proper news media will carry the official version of the story, and who pays any attention to the scandal sheet tabloids anyway?"

About two-thirds of the population of Manticore, thought Anton sourly. *Ninety percent, on Gryphon. I'll never be able to show my face in the highlands again.*

Despite the sourness of the moment, he was pleased with Ruth herself. The young royal was playing her part in the charade to perfection. She was ambling casually along a few paces behind, engrossed in a conversation with Web Du Havel except when making wisecracks to her purported "father." The spitting image of a bright and none-too-respectful daughter.

Nevertheless, he couldn't help wincing at the sheer number of paparazzi present at the landing field. Like locusts swarming over ripe grain.

Great, just great. And now I'll be an item myself. The notorious Cap'n Zilwicki, rogue of the spaceways.

Modern holopic technology did not involve the dramatic flashbulbs of ancient times. But, at that moment, Anton felt as if every spotlight in the universe was focused on him.

He didn't feel any better once they reached orbit and transferred from the shuttle into *Pottawatomie Creek*, the ship the Anti-Slavery League had provided for the voyage. There hadn't been any physical problem getting through the landing gate, of course. Paparazzi took scuffling with police for granted, in order to get closer to their targets, but not even they were crazy enough to meddle with royal bodyguards from the Queen's Own Regiment. Lieutenant Griggs and the other troopers in Griggs' unit detached from the regiment as an escort for the Princess in her trip were heavily armed, scowling as ferociously as such well-trained and disciplined soldiers ever did, and making absolutely clear with their body language alone that they would instantly gun down any paparazzi who managed to break through the police line. Gun them down and probably gut the corpse for good measure.

The problem lay elsewhere. Princess Ruth was as much of a political junkie as Anton had expected she'd be, given her fascination with intelligence work. So, the moment they'd entered the ship, she'd made a beeline for the wardroom's HD and turned it on. Even after the ship left orbit, there'd be time to catch the evening news broadcasts before they were out of reception range.

Not to Anton's surprise, the show Ruth turned to was the prestigious talk show *The Star Kingdom Today.* The show's moderator, Yael Underwood, had a flair for presenting serious news in a manner which captured popular interest. Personally, Anton thought Underwood was a much shallower thinker than he managed to project. But he'd readily admit the man was an expert showman, and his news did have more substance than the usual fire-and-a-freak fare.

He caught the last part of a question posed by Underwood to his panel of guests.

"—think there's no truth, then, to the rumors regarding a romantic tie between Captain Zilwicki and Princess Ruth?"

"Oh, for God's sake!" exclaimed one of the guests. Anton recognized her as one of Underwood's regulars. A woman named Harriet Jilla, who'd once been some kind of academic specialist in who-can-remember-what but had long since traded that in for a more lucrative career as a Professional Talking Head.

"Not even the tabloids are going to push that for more than a day or two," she jibed. "If for no other reason than that they're going to suffer from schizophrenia, seeing as how they'll also want to run all the holopics they got from Montaigne's townhouse. I'm told the paparazzi were almost as thick on the ground there as they were at the landing field."

Underwood gave the audience his patented knowing smile. It was quite a superb thing, combining shrewd intelligence and *savoir-faire* with just the right touch of slightly sardonic humor.

"I'd say you're right, Harriet. In fact—" He glanced away for a moment, as if checking something with an off-stage technician. "Yes. Let's run a little footage of our own from that scene."

Anton had time to wonder about the origin of the peculiar term *footage,* used throughout the news industry to refer to imagery despite its apparent meaninglessness, before the scene itself came on.

"Goddamit," he growled. "Is there *any* privacy left?"

"That's a little rich coming from you, Daddy," retorted Berry. "Mr. Supersnoop."

Anton silently admitted the justice of her remark. But it still didn't make him feel any better seeing his parting embrace—kiss, too, and a damn passionate one, as usual with Cathy, public spectacle be damned, when did she ever care?—from the former Countess of the Tor and current candidate for Parliament. Now plastered all over Manticore's news media for untold millions to watch.

Still . . .

From a *professional* point of view, now that he could see it from a distance, Cathy had performed perfectly. He took a certain personal comfort, as well, in the fact that the embrace and kiss she'd given him at the doorway of their house would certainly put paid to any notions that Anton was lusting after another woman.

Objectively speaking, true, Catherine Montaigne wasn't perhaps all that physically attractive. Anton thought otherwise, but he was dispassionately willing to admit that was his own emotional involvement speaking. Cathy was far too slender, for one thing, and if her face had an open pleasantness about it, it was hardly the sort of face most people would associate with female beauty.

But none of it mattered, as Anton could see for himself watching the newscast. Cathy's kiss was a *kiss,* and the long leg half-looped around his thigh as part of the embrace made clear to umpteen million Manticoran viewers that whatever problems Captain Anton Zilwicki might have, getting laid—well, and often—was not one of them.

"Gosh, Berry, your mother is so *sexy,*" murmured Ruth. "I bet she just got another twenty thousand votes."

Anton ignored the first part of the remark, in a properly aloof fatherly manner. As for the second . . .

He wasn't sure. Cathy Montaigne's let-it-all-hang-out-and-damn-the-bluenoses style, in her personal life as well as her political one, was a two edged-sword. It could easily slice her up—as, indeed, years before it had led to her expulsion from the House of Lords. On the other hand, if it caught the mood of the public . . .

Yeah, maybe. God knows she's a breath of fresh air in Manticore's politics. Nobody's going to believe Countess New Kiev balls her husband's brains out. And if New Kiev's political partner Baron High Ridge has any balls at all, he's keeping them well under wraps.

The professional side of him, however, was primarily interested in the rest of it. Following Cathy's farewell embrace of Anton, she bestowed one just as energetically upon Princess Ruth. In this case, of course, a maternal embrace rather than a romantic one. But Anton was certain that not one of the tens of millions of people watching would suspect for an instant that the casually dressed apparent teenager upon whom Cathy bestowed that hug was anyone other than her quasi-adopted daughter Berry. Just as they wouldn't suspect that the warm but far more reserved handshake which she then gave to Berry herself was the salutation given to a royal princess.

"Perfect!" exclaimed Ruth, clapping her hands. She grinned at Anton. "It's going to work just like you said it would."

Even Anton was not impervious to that intense a degree of

admiration. But he allowed himself only a moment's pleasure, because a slight frown was beginning to gather on his brow. Or, at least, gather in his mind.

Belatedly, Anton was realizing that there was something not quite right about the way Underwood was covering this issue. Granted, Underwood was not above dipping into items of popular interest for the sake of keeping up the ratings for *The Star Kingdom Today.* Still, the man was always careful to link such an item to something of deeper significance. Or, at least, provide depth to the item itself.

In this instance . . .

For a moment, the view in the display moved back and Anton was able for the first time to see all the panelists on the show that night. His eyes were immediately drawn to the man sitting on the far right. Snapped to him, more properly.

His daughter was sitting next to him, and her eyes followed his. "Who's he?" Berry asked.

"I have no idea," replied Anton, shaking his head. "But I can tell you this. He's no Talking Head. And, unless I miss my guess . . ."

Damn—damn—damn—

"He's in the trade himself. First cousin, anyway."

Sure enough. After spending a minute or so polling his panel to get a general consensus that whatever was involved with Captain Zilwicki and Princess Ruth's voyage to Erewhon, it was not a romantic escapade, Underwood allowed the well-oiled-and-practiced panel to segue into a learned (but not *too* learned) analysis of the political subtleties involved in the affair.

Nothing there surprised Anton. It was all much as Queen Elizabeth had foreseen and, with Anton's advice, schemed and plotted for.

—think it's scandalous myself, the way the Government is officially ignoring Stein's funeral. What in God's name is New Kiev thinking? If you ask me, she should have broken with the Cabinet on the issue and at least spoken out in public. Stein's been one of the idols of the Liberal Party for decades now, and if she doesn't think—

—can't say I agree with you, Harriet, unless you think New Kiev's ready to resign outright. Which I don't think there's the proverbial snowball's chance in Hell of happening. You're right, of course, that she's going to take a beating from Montaigne on the issue.

—more interested, myself, in the way the Queen's sending a lot

of messages at once. First—this one's as blunt as it gets—by choosing Catherine Montaigne's live-in lover as Princess Ruth's unofficial escort—

—agree completely! I mean, really, does anyone think the Queen couldn't round up a ship of her own for a trip to Erewhon?

Exactly! Sure, the former Countess of the Tor is still officially *in the Royal Black Book, but I'd say that pretense is getting threadbare. For all their famous public clashes—which are a lot more famous than they were frequent, I might add; don't forget how many issues the Queen and Montaigne agree about—does anyone with half a brain think Elizabeth wouldn't jump for joy if Montaigne displaced New Kiev as—*

—not going to happen any time soon, though. New Kiev's still got a lock on the leadership of the Liberal Party, I don't care how many rank and file Liberals she's ticked off by her silence on the Stein issue. What I think is more interesting is the way the Queen's also using the issue to send a message to the Solarians themselves. Nobody's come forward to take credit—if you can call it that—for Stein's murder even now, but the general opinion everywhere seems to be that Mesa, or at least Manpower, was behind it. How else explain the refusal of the Solarians themselves to launch a serious investigation? That sector of the Solarian League is in Mesa's pocket, and everybody knows it. So Stein's family had to flee to Erewhon for the funeral, and who does the Queen of the Star Kingdom send to escort Princess Ruth to pay her respects? The same guy who's literally in bed every night with the most famous Manticoran leader of the Anti-Slavery League, that's who. You ask me, the Queen is—

Anton had been holding his breath throughout. All of this he could live with, easily enough, if not comfortably. But who *was* the out-of-place panelist sitting on the right? The man hadn't spoken yet, and Anton was wondering why Underwood had included him at all. He had a gnawing feeling he would find out sooner than he wanted to.

Smoothly, Underwood interjected himself into the panel's jabber-jabber. Just as smoothly, like the well-trained seals they were, the Learned Ones slid into silence. (Slid, not fell. There was nothing uncouth or openly servile about the way they accommodated their meal ticket.)

"It seems to me that in all the endless talk about Captain Zilwicki which this affair has sparked, what's most absent is any serious examination of the central figure involved. And that's

Zilwicki himself. Everybody talks about him only as he relates to someone else."

And that's just the way I want it, thought Anton grimly. *I've got a bad feeling about this.*

"Cathy Montaigne's lover, Princess Ruth's escort, and so on and so forth," continued Underwood. "But who is *he*? Where does he come from? What produced him? What is it about the man named Anton Zilwicki that leads one of Manticore's thirty richest women to trust him with her fortune as well as her affections, and leads the *richest* woman in the Star Kingdom to trust him with her niece?"

Underwood's well-coiffed head swiveled toward the Unknown Panelist, like a suave cannon might bring itself to bear on its target. Or, rather, its ammunition.

"You haven't spoken up yet, Mr. Wright. If I'm not mistaken, though, I think you have some relevant expertise on the subject."

The Unknown Panelist cleared his throat.

"Who's 'Mr. Wright'?" demanded Berry. "Have you ever heard of him, Daddy?"

"No," growled Anton. "And if 'Mr. Wright' is his real name, I'll eat the sofa we're sitting on." He took a deep breath and let it out in something of a sigh. "But I'm pretty sure that *what* he is . . ." He paused briefly, eyeing the sallow-faced man on the screen. "He's some kind of former intelligence analyst, dollars for donuts, now in private practice. Probably from the SIS. The Office of Naval Intelligence types tend to make a fetish out of physical fitness, whereas this guy has the struggle-to-lift-a-martini air about him that the civilian spooks seem to think is especially suave."

He fell silent. "Mr. Wright" was finally speaking.

What followed was a nightmare, and before it was over Anton had condemned Yael Underwood to a thousand horrible deaths. This was worse—far worse—than Anton had imagined. He'd been expecting, at the most, that "Mr. Wright" would trot out some hitherto-unknown facts about Anton's involvement with the now-famous Manpower Incident on Terra some years back. Instead, it soon became obvious that Wright was part of a thorough and well-planned news scoop that Underwood must have been working on for *months.* The recent flap involving Princess Ruth had just given him the handle to tie it on.

What the audience got, in essence, was *The Life of the Mysterious Captain Zilwicki.*

All of it. From his boyhood in Gryphon's highlands on up. His early career in the Navy. His athletic prowess as a wrestler, culminating in multiple championships. His marriage to Helen . . .

That part brought a lump to his throat. Underwood was making no effort to smear Zilwicki. If anything, the biography leaned toward excessive praise. And Underwood, ever the master showman behind the sophisticated veneer, knew a good show when he saw one. So the audience got a full dose of Helen Zilwicki herself, all the way to an extensive analysis of the battle in which she lost her life defending the convoy carrying her husband Anton and their daughter Helen from an overwhelming force of Peep raiders.

That part of the show ended with a drawn-out shot of the Parliamentary Medal of Valor, which Helen had been given posthumously, fading away into darkness. The lump in Anton's throat seemed the size of a fist.

Dimly, he sensed Berry's hand sliding into his. When the viewscreen reemerged, a man was sitting there being interviewed by Underwood. The footage had evidently been taken some time before.

Anton recognized the man, vaguely, though he could no longer remember his name. He'd been one of the bridge officers on *Carnarvon,* the ship carrying Zilwicki and his daughter when his wife Helen was killed.

"Oh, yeah, I'll never forget it. The kid was sobbing her heart out, sitting on his lap. Zilwicki himself . . ." The officer shook his head. "When the screen showed that his wife's ship had been destroyed—no chance of any survivors—I saw the look on his face. If ever a man turned to stone, it happened to Anton Zilwicki that moment."

"Oh, bullshit!" snapped Berry. Her small hand gave Anton's very powerful one a firm squeeze. "Daddy, these people are *stupid.*"

Oddly enough, Berry's words snapped Anton out of his black mood. Far enough, at least, that he was able to watch the rest of the show with his usual analytical and objective detachment.

Most of it, of course, was devoted to the Manpower Incident. By the time it was halfway through, Anton was able to relax a bit.

"How true is all this?" asked the Princess, half-whispering, her eyes glued to the holodisplay. "We got some of it in the Palace, sure, but only the sketchiest summaries."

Anton waggled his head. "Some of it's pretty close. Quite a bit, actually. But it's got all the usual weaknesses of an analysis done by a tech weenie. To *really* understand something, there's no substitute for HUMINT."

What the hell, he thought whimsically. *Since my career as a spy is pretty well on the rocks after this, I may as well start on my new one as Royal Spy Trainer.*

"Don't ever forget that, Ruth. The Queen tells me you're a whiz with computers, and that's good. I'm no slouch myself. But spying is like whoring. They're the two oldest professions, and both of them are ultimately fleshy in nature. You can't have sex without a partner, and you can't spy worth talking about without real live *spies.*"

Web Du Havel chuckled. The princess, sitting next to him, did likewise. "I'll remember that."

Anton gave his attention back to the show. Mr. Wright was finally wrapping it up.

"—never know, I imagine, exactly how Zilwicki put it together. The murkiest part of it remains the involvement of the Peeps. That they *were* involved, somehow, is beyond question. But exactly how—"

Underwood interrupted. "You don't think, then, that the rumors the Peeps were behind the kidnapping of Zilwicki's daughter are accurate."

Wright shook his head firmly. "Not a chance. Oh, don't get me wrong. Some other time, some other place, I wouldn't have put it past the old Peep regime to pull a stunt like that. But on *Terra?* That year? Not a chance. The key thing, you see, is that—"

One of the other panelists, evidently frustrated by long silence, was bold enough to interrupt.

"Parnell, of course. With him arriving to testify to the Solarian League about Peep atrocities . . ."

Her voice fell off, the slightly pained look on her face indicating a sudden realization that she'd committed a Major Talking Head Goof. The smug expression on the faces of both Wright and Underwood were enough to indicate that her Learned Insight was about to be trumped.

"Parnell was a factor, of course. But, *as I was saying,* the key factor is the identity of the man who, at the time, was the commander in charge of the Peep embassy's Marine detachment. The same man, I might add, who was clearly just as responsible for the havoc wreaked on Manpower as the Ballroom trigger-pullers."

He paused for dramatic effect. "The Peeps—the new Republic of Haven, I should say—have done a good job of covering it up. But with a lot of digging, it's now clear that the obscure Peep colonel involved was none other than *Kevin Usher.* Today, as I needn't remind this panel of guests, the head of the Republic of Haven's highest police body. A former Aprilist himself, and possibly the closest personal friend of President Eloise Pritchart."

This *was* news, and the oh-so-sophisticated panel of Talking Heads wasn't dumb enough to pretend it wasn't. After a moment's silence, Harriet Jilla tossed her head as if to clear it and barked: "No way! Give the devil his due. No way Kevin Usher—any real Aprilist—would have been involved with that."

"Except as the wrecking crew," said one of the other panelists grimly. A former Marine general, that one. He gave "Mr. Wright" a level stare. "What you're saying, in short, is that two corrupt Manticoran officials in cahoots with Manpower—"

For a moment, the screen flashed images of former Ambassador Hendricks and Admiral Young, at one time Anton's superiors on Terra. He was pleased to see that they were wearing their new prison uniforms.

"—to use Zilwicki's daughter in some scheme of their own—God knows what insanity that was, I don't think we'll ever know—and Zilwicki tore out their lungs. Cut out on his own, put together an informal alliance of Peep Aprilists and Ballroom gunmen, wrecked Manpower on Terra, and put the two bastards behind bars. And, of course, got his daughter out safe and sound. All of his kids, actually, since he wound up adopting the boy and girl his daughter Helen rescued in the course of the whole thing."

Mr. Wright nodded sagely. "That about sums it up." With a thin smile: "And I guess we can all figure out more or less how Catherine Montaigne got those famous and mysterious files of hers that have since then put dozens of other people behind bars for trafficking in slavery."

Anton glanced at his watch. *The Star Kingdom Today* had only a short while to run. It was about time, as usual, for the host to sum up the night's proceedings.

The screen moved to Underwood. His smile was as suave as ever, but this time it seemed to have a slightly wicked gleam to it.

"Well, you've all heard it. Here's what *I* think is happening. Yes, the Queen's sending a lot of messages to a lot of people. But I think the biggest message of all is the one she's sending to those people—whoever they might be—who murdered Hieronymus Stein. You want to play it rough, do you? Fine. I'm sending you a serious hardcase."

The screen faded to an advertisement.

Anton winced. "God, that's corny. Not to mention sandbox stupid."

Berry clapped her hands. "Well, it's about *time* you got some credit!"

Princess Ruth clearly shared Berry's glee, but made an effort to be analytical about it all. "Of course, it *has* pretty well ruined the Captain's career as a spy. After this, he's going to be one of the most famous people in the Star Kingdom."

"I don't *care,*" insisted Berry.

"It also," grumbled Zilwicki, "plays merry hell with our plans for *this* trip. How am I supposed to—"

He was interrupted by the appearance in the lounge of the lieutenant in charge of Ruth's guards. The man was scowling at Anton ferociously.

"Is there a problem with the ship, Lieutenant Griggs? I thought the liftoff was as smooth as you could ask for."

"The *ship* is fine, Captain Zilwicki. I came to express my deepest concerns over the *crew.* My people and I have been making a reconnaissance, and it is our firm conviction that possibly a good third of this crew is composed of Audubon Ballroom terrorists."

Du Havel was obviously trying to keep from grinning. Anton sighed and rubbed his face.

To his surprise, Ruth piped up. "Seventy-three percent, actually. At least, I think so. Sixty-eight percent, for sure. I'm not positive about a few of them. Just about everybody except the department heads and the most skilled ratings. I'm pretty sure the Captain's doing the same thing with this ship he is with all seven of the Anti-Slavery League's armed vessels. Using them as training grounds for Ballroom privateers-to-be."

Anton's hand dropped. So did his jaw. For one of the few times in his life, he was genuinely astonished.

The princess gave him a nervous, apologetic smile. "I hacked into your data banks yesterday. Well. Not your *personal* data banks. I'm not sure anybody could hack into those. I bounced like a rubber ball. But the ASL itself is a lot sloppier about its security than you are."

"I will be *damned,* Sir," the lieutenant began to roar, "if—"

The princess cut him off. "Don't be stupid, Lieutenant Griggs! There's not a chance in the universe that Ballroom members would hurt me—quite the contrary, and you know it perfectly well. So why waste everyone's time with official huffing and puffing?" Sharply: "You have your orders. Go about them."

Griggs snapped his mouth shut, goggled at her for an instant, and then hurried out of the ship's lounge. Anton was impressed. The girl might not have any Winton genes, but clearly enough she'd picked up the Winton knack for authority. Of course, given the way her mother had come to be a Manticoran in the first place . . .

He was more impressed, however—quite a bit more—by Ruth's other talents. Even given the quality of training he was sure she'd gotten, and even allowing for the fact that hacking was often a youngster's forte, the fact that she'd been able to get into the ASL's data banks was remarkable for anyone, much less a twenty-three-year-old. True, Anton didn't manage that system himself, and he knew the ASL's specialists tended to be a bit slack about security. Still . . .

"I'm curious," he said. "Did you tell the Queen about your findings?"

"'Course not! Aunt Elizabeth's a frightful worrywart." Ruth gave him that little nervous, apologetic smile again. "You know how it is. If I'd told her most of the crew of the ship I was going on were a bunch of bloody-handed terrorists, she'd probably have made a fuss about it. Might even have grounded me."

"This might just work," he murmured. *Cap'n Zilwicki, retired rogue of the spaceways. Now a tutor to the royal house. One of whose princesses has the makings of a rogue herself. Good start on it, anyway. She's got breaking and entering down pat, that's for sure.*

PART II: EREWHON

CHAPTER 7

THE TRIP FROM MANTICORE TO EREWHON was complicated but not all that difficult. There was no direct junction terminus connecting the Star Kingdom to Erewhon's solar system, but there was a connection via the Phoenix Cluster, the rather inaccurate name given to a three-star system republic (of sorts) which was home to the Phoenix Wormhole Junction. Compared to the Manticoran Junction, the Phoenix Junction scarcely deserved the term. The Phoenix terminus of the Manticoran Junction was associated with the Hennesy System, but the Phoenix "Junction"—which boasted only two termini and linked the Cluster to Erewhon—lay in the Terra Haute System. To get there, the *Pottawatomie Creek* had to first go to Hennesy via the Manticoran Junction and then make a five-day-long trip through hyper across the intervening twenty-five light-years to Terra Haute. Since junction transits were effectively instantaneous, it was the Hennesy-Terra Haute leg which accounted for virtually the entire length of the journey.

Of course, if Phoenix had been inclined to be sticky about it, the *Pottawatomie* would have been unable to use the Phoenix Junction at all up to less than six T-months before. The cluster had closed its wormhole to all military traffic the moment war broke out between the Star Kingdom (and its Erewhonese allies) and the late, unlamented People's Republic of Haven. In the absence of a formal peace treaty between Manticore and Haven, Phoenix had declined to rescind the prohibition until quite recently. Rumor said that the initiative in dropping it had come from Erewhon, not Phoenix, but not even Zilwicki's sources were positive about that.

Still, Anton's ship *might* have been allowed to transit even before the change in policy. She *was* a private vessel, after all, not a warship in the service of the Crown. But that didn't change the fact that she was also the equivalent of a frigate—in fact, she *was* a frigate in all but name, designed and built by one of the Manticoran yards which did a lot of naval construction. The Tor fortune made Cathy one of the few private individuals able to finance *Pottawatomie*'s construction. Actually, not even she could have afforded such a project, but she'd been able to advance enough seed money to begin a subscription campaign which had rapidly tapped into a deep well of Manticoran opposition to genetic slavery—a well made deeper than ever by widespread public anger over the way High Ridge had been able to contain the damage done by Montaigne's files.

Among that opposition, oddly enough, had been Klaus Hauptman. By far the wealthiest man in the Star Kingdom, Hauptman was not normally the sort who would have had any sort of truck with "terrorists," however noble their particular cause might be. But the man was a quirky individual, and one of his quirks was a detestation of genetic slavery. He'd made support for its extirpation one of the major philanthropic commitments of the Hauptman Foundation his father had endowed seventy T-years before and whose board his daughter Stacey now chaired. Hauptman himself had not actually participated directly in the subscription campaign, although Stacey had done so rather discreetly. But what he *had* done was even more valuable: he owned the shipyard which built the Anti-Slavery League's frigates, and he did the work at cost, with no profit and none of the usual padding which went into military projects.

For all their expense, frigates were too small in this day and age to be really suitable for the navies of star nations. On the other hand, the vessels were very well designed and equipped to deal with the slavers and pirates who were their natural prey.

Thus, one of the *Pottawatomie*'s features was speed. But, given the passengers he was carrying, Anton saw no need to push any higher than the Zeta bands of hyper, so she made the trip in what was, for her, a rather leisurely amble.

The three courier boats which were also on their way to Erewhon, on the other hand, were under no such compunction. In fact, although they'd departed from Manticore several hours after *Pottawatomie,* two of them were specifically determined to get to Erewhon ahead of Anton, and they were well-equipped for the task. Effectively nothing but a hyper generator, a pair of Warshawski sails, and an impeller drive, they were designed to ride the ragged edge of the Theta bands, which gave them the next best thing to a forty percent speed advantage over *Pottawatomie.* So, although they actually made transit from Manticore to Hennesy after Anton's ship, they quickly overtook and passed her on the Hennesy-Terra Haute leg of the journey.

The people on the third courier ship didn't even know about Anton's situation. But that vessel was making the entire trip in hyper-space directly from Haven, and the natural habits of a Havenite courier crew moving through what was technically hostile space—Manticore and the Republic were officially still at war, even if hostilities had been suspended—meant they weren't dawdling.

As a result, by the time Anton Zilwicki and his companions arrived at Erewhon, the news of his impending arrival had preceded him—along with copies of Underwood's program—and several interested parties were studying the material.

The Havenites had known nothing about it until they arrived the day before. Having made the trip directly from the Republic to Erewhon, they hadn't passed through the Manticore Junction and therefore hadn't picked up the broadcast. But they were no less interested than others.

To put it mildly. Victor Cachat was even driven to a rare use of profanity.

"What a fucking mess," he snarled, after Ginny turned off the recording. "Anton Zilwicki! The *last* person we want to see here."

Virginia Usher eased back into the couch in their hotel room, crossed her very shapely legs and shrugged her very shapely shoulders—all the more shapely in that the sari she was wearing was designed to show them off. The garment bore only a passing resemblance to the ancestral style which had originated millennia before in south Asia. Ginny's sari wasn't quite as revealing as the version of it she'd worn in years past, when she'd worked as a prostitute after escaping from Manpower, but it skirted the very outer edges of anything which might be called suitable dress for polite company.

Victor eyed the garment sourly. "And why are you putting on the act, anyway? There's nobody here but the two of us."

Ginny gave him her patented grin. Like the sari, the expression wasn't quite as salacious as the one she'd once bestowed on prospective customers, but it came close.

"Oh, stop sulking. Kevin would have a fit if he found out I broke cover on assignment. What if somebody should come knocking on the door—room service, maybe? Seeing me in the sweats I usually wear at home would play merry hell with my image as a slut. And after all the trouble Kevin's gone through to establish it! Me too, for that matter."

Victor shook his head. There were things about his boss and mentor he'd never understand. The cheerful way Kevin Usher had his wife pretend to be a tramp was one of them. Part of it could be accounted for by Kevin's phenomenal self-assurance, true; but most of it, Victor was convinced, was due to the man's quirky sense of humor. Who else but Kevin Usher would get a chuckle out of the way most people derided his personal life? (In private, of course, not to his face.)

When Kevin Usher had emerged from the shadows after the Theisman coup, to accept the Pritchart Administration's request that he take over Haven's new internal police agency, he'd been faced with the problem of what to do about his wife. Heretofore, he'd seen to it that no one but a handful of anti-Pierre Aprilist conspirators had even known of her existence. Now . . .

There'd been no way to keep her a secret any longer, given the public exposure Kevin would have as head of the new Federal Investigation Agency. And that made Kevin very nervous. Granted, Eloise Pritchart was one of Kevin's oldest and closest friends—although not even she had known about Ginny, since there'd been no need for her to know—and she was now President of the new Republic. He trusted her completely, and was inclined to feel the same way about Thomas Theisman, the admiral who'd led the coup d'etat which had put her in power. And he shared their commitment to reestablishing the rule of law and a tradition of peaceful transfers of power in the Republic. But if Kevin Usher's whole life had taught him one thing, it was that political power in the Republic of Haven was a treacherous beast. You never knew when it might turn on you, and until it was safely muzzled, he had no intention of trusting it.

So, Kevin had solved the problem in the way the man did everything—combining directness with cunning, and with not a smidgeon of concern for his own reputation. He assumed the public role of a cuckold the same way, in times past, he'd accepted the public role of a drunk. If worse came to worst and Usher underwent one of the dramatic falls from grace so common in Havenite politics—which, judging from the history of the past two centuries, might well end up with him before a firing squad—at least Ginny would likely be able to avoid it. Nobody viewed a promiscuous cheating wife as a threat, after all, to anyone but her husband.

Victor could appreciate the professional artistry involved. The "Usher flair," as he thought of it. What he *didn't* appreciate—not in the least—was that Kevin and Ginny had immediately (and rather gleefully) appointed Victor as the cuckolder-in-chief. The young subordinate and protégé who was repaying his trusting boss by having an affair with his mentor's wife.

"It's a classic," Ginny had pronounced.

"It makes me look like a complete swine!"

"Well, true," Kevin had allowed, grinning at Victor. "Just think of it as part of your training, wonderboy. What kind of silly amateur spy worries about his 'image,' anyway?"

"We're not 'spies' any longer," Victor groused.

"Don't be so sure about that." Kevin shrugged. "Who knows what we'll be facing, in the years to come?"

Victor might still have refused, except that Ginny cornered him. "Please, Victor," she'd pleaded, in that inimitable half-comic/half-serious way of hers, "it'll make my life *so* much easier. You're the one man I know that I won't have to be fending off in private after making eyes at him in public."

That had been true enough. Victor was by no means immune to the temptations of the flesh, and there were times he found being in such close and intimate proximity with Ginny immensely frustrating. But his emotional relationship with her, in the time since they'd met on Earth, had settled into something very close to that of a younger brother and his older sister. He wasn't oblivious to Ginny's often well-exposed female figure. But it wasn't really much different from his life as a boy, growing up in the cramped slums of the Dolist quarters of Nouveau Paris, when he'd also been frequently exposed to the half-naked forms of his mother and three sisters.

To be sure, neither his mother nor his sisters had been gorgeous, the way Ginny was, and they'd possessed none of her subtle skills at tantalizing a man—which Ginny, damn her black heart, *insisted* on practicing on Victor.

Still . . .

Victor would admit that, in its own grotesque way, the gambit worked like a charm. By fitting himself, Ginny and Victor into flamboyant and well-established roles—older husband, besotted and foolish; young nymphomaniac wife, cheating on him right under his nose; unscrupulous and treacherous underling—Kevin had provided his wife and his protégé with a real measure of protection in case political life went sour again in the Republic of Haven.

And since Kevin had never been a man who'd miss the chance to kill two birds with one stone, the same gambit allowed him to use Victor and Ginny as his special and informal investigating team. He could send them anywhere, at any time, to do anything—and all but a handful of people in the know would simply observe the phenomenon with a smirk.

That explained why they were sitting in a hotel room in Erewhon's capital city of Maytag. The assassination of Hieronymus Stein had presented Haven's new president with a very awkward political situation, and, as often in her history, Eloise Pritchart had turned to Kevin Usher for aid and assistance.

"Let's send Ginny and Victor," he'd immediately proposed. "Ginny's got a perfectly believable public excuse for going to pay her respects, since she's a former Manpower slave herself."

Eloise interrupted. "What do you think, Kevin? Do you agree that Manpower was behind the killing? That seems to be the accepted wisdom, but my antennae aren't quite convinced of it."

He shrugged. "Who knows? The odds are that it was Manpower, yes. If I had to put money down on it, that's the way I'd bet also. On the other hand . . ."

He shifted in his chair across from the President's desk, as if uncomfortable. "Your instincts might just have something, Eloise. The whole operation was a bit too . . . flamboyant for me to be entirely happy with the notion, myself. Manpower Unlimited—the whole planet of Mesa, for that matter—is so convenient for so many powerful forces in the Solarian League that it's been able to thrive for a long time just by keeping slightly under the public horizon. Why run the risk of shaking up that well-established profitable situation with something as guaranteed to cause a huge public stir among Solarians as murdering the leader of the Renaissance Association?"

"*You're* asking that question?" Eloise chuckled. "Kevin, in case you hadn't noticed, Manpower's been taking some hard hits lately—one of them being the hit you landed on them in Chicago during the Manpower Incident. Even cold-blooded slavers can lose their temper, you know."

Kevin shrugged. "Sure. But why take it out on Stein and the Renaissance Association?" Eloise opened her mouth but Kevin forestalled her retort with a raised hand. "Yes, yes, I know Stein and the RA have been the main public voice denouncing genetic slavery in the Solarian League, other than the Anti-Slavery League itself. So what? Stein's been doing that for decades, and Manpower just shrugged it off. They know just as well as you or me or anyone with half a brain that the so-called 'democracy' of the Solarian League is a pure fiction, at least above the level of some of its planetary affiliates. The League is run—lock, stock and barrel—by its bureaucrats and commercial combines, and by and large those pigs-in-a-trough think Manpower and Mesa are just dandy things to have around. And since they've always been smart enough not to step too hard on the personal liberties of Solarian citizens on Earth and the older, well-established colony planets, the moral preachments of the Renaissance Association and the Anti-Slavery League have never made a dent in Solarian policy."

Eloise eyed him for a moment. "What about you? Are you worried they might take out their irritation on you personally?"

Kevin grinned. "Not after the way Zilwicki turned their strike force against Cathy Montaigne on Manticore last year into so much hamburger."

Pritchart snorted. The sound combined sarcasm with something very close to pure glee. Like any old-style Aprilist, Eloise detested Manpower and all it represented. Granted, she had sharp differences and animosities with the Star Kingdom, but whatever else divided Pritchart and Manticore's Queen Elizabeth, hatred of genetic slavery was not part of it.

So Eloise had been savagely amused herself when Manpower's attempted retaliation on Montaigne had backfired so badly. In the years since Montaigne had returned to Manticore from Earth with her new-found lover, Captain Anton Zilwicki had spent his time and energy after his dismissal from service in the Star Kingdom's Navy building what was publicly passed off as a "security agency." The depiction had been accepted readily enough, given Zilwicki's skill at deception. He'd even managed to keep it intact after foiling the assassination attempt on Montaigne.

Which had been . . . difficult, given that the grounds of the Tor estate had been littered with the corpses of would-be assassins. Not a single member of the large and well-organized assassination team had survived.

Rumor had it that their bodies—pieces of them, anyway—had wound up being delivered by freight shipping to several of the large recruiting halls on Manpower's home planet of Mesa. Slavery was not Mesa's only profitable business. The planet was also the galaxy's largest center for free-lance mercenary outfits.

The whole episode had been successfully passed off for public consumption as a murky and mysterious business. After a few days, it had faded out of public notice in the Star Kingdom; and had never been noticed much at all in the Solarian League, since Solarians always tended to be oblivious to anything happening outside of their own gigantic borders. Manpower Unlimited had not, obviously, accepted any public responsibility for the affair. And, for different reasons, neither "Zilwicki Security" and Catherine Montaigne nor—certainly!—the High Ridge Government had wanted the thing scrutinized carefully. But, soon enough, every serious intelligence agency in the settled portion of the galaxy had figured out the truth. Catherine Montaigne was now using her fortune and the talents of her new lover to finally give the Anti-Slavery League some real teeth—and Anton Zilwicki had just bared them, dripping with blood.

Since then, from all anyone could determine, Manpower had kept a distance from Montaigne. If nothing else, after seeing two task forces shredded by Zilwicki—one in Chicago, and now another on Manticore—the sort of professional mercenaries who provided Manpower with their muscle would be demanding astronomical prices for any further such projects.

Eloise smiled. "Am I to infer, Kevin, that you've set your own little mantrap in case Manpower ever decides to go after you? I'm not sure that isn't bending the spirit of the law which governs your Federal Investigation Agency, you know."

"Bends it into a pretzel," agreed Kevin. "On the other hand, it keeps my people on their toes—and keeps Manpower off my back."

Eloise didn't pursue the matter. She knew perfectly well that there was no way Kevin Usher wouldn't wander into gray legal areas in his new post. His current profession as Haven's chief cop was a set of clothing worn by an old and experienced conspirator, after all. But so long as he didn't break the new laws outright and refrained from "black ops," she'd look the other way.

So, she brought the discussion back to the subject directly at hand.

"I've got a problem here, Kevin."

"That's one way of putting it," he chuckled humorlessly. "The Renaissance Association invited the Republic of Haven to send official representatives to the funeral, just like they did every other government in the galaxy. If we don't show up, all our preachments about political wickedness are going to look like so much self-serving prattle. But if we *do* show up, we're guaranteed to irritate—at best—most of the forces in the Solarian League that we're still relying on for tech transfer."

Pritchart scowled. "God *damn* High Ridge. If the Manticorans would just sign a peace treaty with us, I'd cheerfully tell those Solarian scumbags to take a hike." She sighed heavily. "I don't suppose Foraker could . . ."

"You'd have to ask Tom Theisman about that," replied Usher. "But I doubt very much if even Shannon Foraker can keep upgrading our military capability without a fair amount of tech transfer from the Sollies."

He cocked his head and regarded Eloise. "That's why I'm proposing we send Ginny. Sure, it'd still be a 'private response,' not an official one. But . . ." He trailed off, thinking for a moment.

"Might do the trick. Well enough, anyway. Everybody knows you and I are personally close, and since Ginny's my wife it won't take any brains at all for people to understand that you're making your own feelings clear in the matter—without doing it in a way that forces the Solarians to take public umbrage."

"There's more to it than that, Kevin. We've been getting some odd—and very interesting—feelers from the Erewhonese lately. Both through Giancola's people and the Federal Intelligence Service."

It was her turn to cock her head. "I see that doesn't surprise you any. Ha! Old habits die hard and all that." Mock-sternly: "Kevin Usher, you are *not* supposed to be in the foreign intelligence business any longer. You're a cop now, remember?"

He didn't bother to respond to the half-accusation with anything more than a flashing smile. "So I am. But this here honest cop doesn't trust your Secretary of State Arnold Giancola any farther than I can throw him—neither do you, Eloise—and while I don't dis-*trust* Wilhelm Trajan, he's—ah, what's the word—"

"He's a plodder," said Pritchart bluntly. "No dummy, mind you, but I wanted him in charge of the Federal Intelligence Service mainly because I knew he wouldn't use that post to start the usual kind of old-style Havenite political scheming. The way Giancola's been doing with the State Department, damn him."

She ran fingers through her long platinum hair in a gesture that combined aggravation and weariness. "You and I both know that you'd have been ten times better than Wilhelm at running the FIS, Kevin. But what I really needed, more than anything, was someone

I trusted completely on top of our new *domestic* police agency. A person can scheme all he wants, as head of the FIS, but he can't organize a coup d'etat. For that, you need the internal security forces."

Kevin understood the logic. He'd understood it from the moment Eloise had first offered him the job. Nor did he disagree with Pritchart. Still, it left Haven with an intelligence service which was . . . under par. One of the first things Thomas Theisman had done after the coup d'etat he'd carried out against Oscar Saint-Just was smash into pieces the old State Security which had served the Pierre/Ransom/Saint-Just dictatorship and the Legislaturalist regime before them. However beneficial that might have been to Haven's political hygiene, it had wreaked real havoc in its intelligence service. If they were lucky, any members of StateSec even slightly tarred with Saint-Just's brush who'd survived the initial fighting which had toppled their master had been summarily dismissed from service. Some of the worst of them had been executed anyway, after scrupulously fair trials and only after being convicted of actually breaking even StateSec's own "laws." But by far the larger number of those who'd been arrested were now serving long prison terms. The only reason Theisman hadn't executed more of them outright was his concern that the new regime not give everyone the same bloodthirsty and brutal image that previous Havenite governments had done.

"A pity, really," murmured Kevin, half to himself. "I can think of at least seven of those clowns sitting behind bars that I'd happily shoot myself."

Eloise had no trouble following his skewed little train of thought. Her face lit up with a smile. "Only seven? God, did you lead a sheltered life! I'm sure I could list at least thirty without even trying."

For a moment, the two longtime Aprilist comrades shared a look of pure satisfaction. They could live, easily enough, without sheer revenge. The fact remained that the bastards *were* finally behind bars.

"Where they belong," growled Eloise. "And where they'll *stay* for the next sixty T-years . . . unless we get overthrown."

Usher managed to keep his mouth shut. That was difficult, with Eloise Pritchart, in a way it wouldn't have been with almost anyone else. Their friendship was a very close and very long-standing one.

But . . .

Eloise, he knew, had a fierce determination to keep the new Haven regime of which she was President from committing the errors and crimes of previous ones. A determination so fierce, in fact, that Kevin thought she made mistakes because of it. Not many, but some. So, here and there, privately and without telling her, Kevin had quietly taken care of what was needed.

Have no fear, Eloise. One of things the FIA is in charge of is running the maximum security prisons. Whatever happens, I've seen to it that the only way those StateSec ringleaders will ever get out of prison until they've served their sentence is in body bags. Every single one of their cells comes equipped with concealed poison gas containers.

He shook off the grim satisfaction of that knowledge. Eloise would be upset if he told her. Strictly speaking, after all, those secret execution mechanisms were in violation of the law she was sworn to uphold.

So, he kept his mouth shut. And pressed on with the subject at hand.

"I know about the Erewhonese . . . 'feelers,' as you call them. And don't bother telling me I shouldn't know. You're not *that* much of a tight-ass, Eloise." He ran fingers through his own hair, dark where hers was platinum blond. "And I think what I suspect is exactly what you're thinking. High Ridge has been treating them like servants, the Erewhonese are having second thoughts about their alliance with Manticore, and now that Haven has a new government they're giving us a second look."

She nodded. Kevin pursed his lips. "Guthrie's our ambassador on Erewhon, and that's not good. He's a second-rater at best. Nothing *wrong* with him, exactly, but not much really right either. A ticket-puncher, basically. The kind of guy who'd react to a tricky opportunity like this by worrying about how it might screw up his career."

Pritchart nodded again. "And the officer in charge of the FIS mission there—Jacqueline Pallier, I don't believe you know her—is no better, trust me. Even Wilhelm Trajan is frustrated with her, and Wilhelm's not exactly possessed of lightning reflexes himself. Between the two of them, from what I can tell, Guthrie and Pallier have managed to dodge every feeler sent our way as if they were virgins dodging a lecher's gropes. By now, the Erewhonese probably think we're all a bunch of imbeciles."

Usher grinned. "Odd you should use that term. I'll send Victor along with Ginny, of course, and I sometimes wonder if *he's* still a virgin."

"You and your clever schemes! I'll give you this much, Kevin Usher, you're just about the only man I know who doesn't give a flying damn about the public image of your masculinity." A fond little smile touched her lips. "Not that you need to, I'll be the first to admit."

For a moment, Usher shared that smile. Off and on, over the many years they'd known each other, Kevin and Eloise's relationship had included quite a bit of time spent in bed together. It had been a friendly sort of thing, not especially romantic, and was now all in the past since both of them had fallen in love with other people. But it did give their friendship an extra something; the kind of easy relaxation of people who have few secrets from each other.

They savored the moment, but didn't dwell on it. Within seconds, Eloise was sitting upright at her desk again and her beautiful face was creased with a small frown.

"Do you think Cachat's up to it? I know he's your favorite, Kevin, but he's awfully young for something like this."

Kevin shrugged. "'Young' and 'incapable' are two different things. I grant you the kid still seems tied up in knots about sex, but on anything which involves his professional skills . . . He's *good,* Eloise. He's thoughtful in a way that damn few 'ops' ever are, but when he needs to be he can be as decisive and ruthless as anyone in the galaxy. Don't forget how beautifully he handled the situation in La Martine, and he's had several years experience since then. Sure, he's still young—and so what? Every fighter's 'too young' until he steps into the championship ring. Victor's ready for it. I can't think of anyone who'd do any better, and he has the advantage of providing us with a ready-made cover."

Pritchart spread her hands on the desk and leaned her weight on them. Kevin recognized the characteristic gesture. Eloise was a champ herself when it came to being decisive.

"Good enough. We'll go with Cachat. But—!"

Now she was shaking a forefinger at him. "You make sure he understands—and that starts with *you,* Kevin—that I don't want any loose warheads here. None of your wild and woolly Usher tactics, you hear? And since you brought up La Martine, let me remind you that Cachat's tactics there were about as wild and woolly as it gets. I want this done by the rule book."

Kevin gave her a submissive smile.

He hoped it looked submissive, anyway. Since he was pretty sure he'd be disobeying her and leaving the rule book in tatters.

"Dammit, Ginny," grumbled Victor as he climbed into bed, "I don't see why you're so blasé about Anton Zilwicki being here on

Erewhon. That man is too smart by half. He's got more brains in his over-muscled big toe than the whole Manticoran embassy here has put together."

Ginny chucked him under the chin. "I'm not *blasé* about it, I just don't see the point in losing sleep over something we've got no control over." She yawned lazily, reached an arm across and drew him close. "Tomorrow'll be soon enough to worry about it. You need some rest, lover boy."

"And that's another thing! How am I supposed to get any sleep with you draped all over me? Especially wearing that—what do you call it, anyway? That handkerchief-masquerading-as-a-night-gown."

"S'a 'teddy,'" she murmured against his chest. "And don't you make wisecracks about it, either. It cost Kevin plenty, since I bought it just before we left at one of the fanciest boutiques in Nouveau Paris." Happily: "I'm sure there were at least two spies in the place, and God only knows how many remote spy-eyes. Just like there probably are in this room. You can't be too careful."

Not likely, thought Victor. *Not with the equipment I brought with me. By now, any spy-eyes in this room are so much fried junk.*

Just to prove her point, Ginny slid a bare and very shapely leg over his thighs. Which, Victor sighed, were covered by nothing more than the thinnest pair of pajamas he owned. Ginny wouldn't let him get away with anything else.

Yet he didn't insist that Ginny sleep on her side of the bed. There was a carefully walled-away part of him that found the feel of her body against his . . . disturbing. But he was accustomed to it, by now. This was hardly the first time he and Ginny had shared a bed, after all, nor was it the first time Ginny had worn a "night-gown" that bore more resemblance to a stripper's outfit than anything else.

What was more important was that Victor had long since come to understand why Ginny insisted on this somewhat silly routine. True, there was neither romance nor sex between them, and never had been. But Victor understood that in some peculiar way he'd come to be for Ginny the family she'd never had growing up in Manpower's slave quarters. The young brother she'd never been able to cuddle through that long darkness, come to her at last.

It was a very warm thought, and, not for the first time, Victor drew strength and determination from it. He cupped his hand around her head, drew her closer still and gently kissed her hair.

Within a few minutes, he was able to shed his frets and worries, and fell asleep himself. Wondering, as he drifted off, whether he'd ever find a woman of his own he cared for as much as he did for Ginny.

Probably not, he concluded. Victor was pretty sure romance was something that was going to be absent from his life. In truth, he'd been pretty sure of that since he was fourteen years old and dedicated himself to the revolution. The only thing that had changed, since he'd met Ginny, was that now the knowledge bothered him.

CHAPTER 8

OTHER PEOPLE FOUND GETTING TO SLEEP that night far more difficult. A room full of naval officers in a hotel not far from the one Victor and Ginny were staying at erupted in a bouillabaisse of curses and imprecations. The officers had just finished watching the recording of Underwood's show brought by the first courier ship to land.

"Just what we needed," complained one of them, an officer wearing the uniform of a commander in the Solarian League's navy. "God *damn* so-called 'special ops.' Why do they even bother distinguishing between 'gray' and 'black' ops, anyway? It all stinks the same."

The foul-tempered remark was aimed at the officer's superior, a captain in the same navy. The captain, a trimly built man on the small side, smiled lazily in response.

"It's an imperfect universe, Edie. Do you want me to make it worse by trotting out obnoxious old saws? 'You eat what's set on your plate.' 'Play the hand you're dealt.' I warn you, I can go on for hours. My father was addicted to the blasted things."

The captain spoke loudly enough to be heard by everyone, and the mood in the room lightened visibly as a result. A large part of Captain Luiz Rozsak's charisma was his easy and relaxed sense of humor. Without it, the man's fierce ambition would have driven people off instead of drawing them like a magnet. As it was, Rozsak's unusually rapid rise in the Solarian League Navy—all the more unusual in that he came from one of the outlying systems instead of the old colonies which provided the SLN with most of its senior officers—had been greatly aided by his talent for drawing a capable and loyal staff around him. Instead of resenting his superior abilities, his subordinates found working with the man both pleasant and rewarding. Rozsak repaid loyalty in kind, and as he'd moved up the promotion ladder he'd seen to it that his followers did likewise.

To be sure, in so doing he was simply following the time-honored traditions of the Solarian League Navy, for which favoritism and empire-building were viewed almost as a law of nature. That did not offset the fact that Rozsak did it with the same superb skill he did everything else. No ambitious officer was going to rise in the SLN without developing a network of patronage, civilian as well as military. That was a given. But only a very unusual officer could have overcome Rozsak's handicaps thoroughly enough to have created the network he had. Perhaps best of all, he did it without constantly rubbing his followers' noses in their subordinate status—which was also a tradition in the SLN, but one which Rozsak seemed to have no difficulty eschewing.

He'd even proved to be talented at "special operations," something which still half-astonished his own followers. As a rule, the talents and skills required for that line of work fit a military man about as well as gloves would fit a horse.

So, while all of Rozsak's subordinates in the hotel room were disgruntled by what they'd seen in the broadcast, none of them were really downcast about it, much less panicky. Yes, it was an unfortunate turn of events. But they were quite sure Rozsak would figure out a way to make a silk purse out of a sow's ear. They'd seen him do it before, and more than once.

"It's not as bad as it looks, Edie. Of course, we'll have to figure a way to get Zilwicki out of the picture. And damn quickly, too."

"Is he really as good as all that?" asked Lieutenant Karen Georgos. She pointed a slender finger at the now-dark HV. "What I mean is, that had all the earmarks of a *show.* Nobody as slick as Yael Underwood is going to spend that much time boring everyone with drab and dreary reality."

Captain Rozsak cocked an eye at another officer in the room, signaling him to provide the answer.

Lieutenant Commander Jiri Watanapongse levered himself out of a slouch in an armchair across the room. He'd been the most disgruntled of them all, watching the broadcast, and was still clearly trying to fight off a dark mood.

"He's that good, yes." He gave the holoviewer a sardonic glance. "Oh, sure, they milked the romantic angles for all they were worth. Heroic dead wife, stoic widower, plucky daughter, new love found in unlikely places, twaddledeedee, twaddledeedum. Beauty and the Beast, you name it, Underwood hauled it all out. But don't kid yourself. I can guarantee you that right this very moment—"

He cast another sardonic glance at the window. Somewhere beyond it, behind the curtains and the electronic shields Rozsak's people had erected as soon as they took possession of the hotel suite, rose the towering structure of Suds Emporium, the oldest and still tallest edifice in Erewhon's capital city of Maytag. The Suds, as the Erewhonese called it, was an odd sort of building. It combined the functions of Maytag's most prestigious hotel, its largest commercial exchange, its most expensive boutiques—and, in practice if not in theory, was the real center of Erewhon's political life.

Most people assumed that the "Suds" of the title, as with the name of the planet's capital city itself, were testimonials to obscure figures from Erewhon's early history. Intrepid pioneers, no doubt, Erewhon's equivalent of Lewis and Clark.

Watanapongse, Rozsak's intelligence specialist, had done his research and knew the truth. The people who'd founded the colony of Erewhon, centuries earlier, had apparently had a wry sense of humor. So, digging up long-forgotten terms from the ancient history of Earth, they'd bestowed names which tweaked the respectable Solarian society they'd left behind, without that society even realizing it.

Today, Erewhon was as respectable a planet as any in the galaxy, even if it still retained some odd customs deriving from its origins. But it had been founded by a consortium of successful figures in organized crime, looking for a way to—the expression was still in use, although very few people in modern times understood its etymology—"launder the money."

The sardonicism in Watanapongse's glance, however, was not due to that. It came from the fact that he knew which odd collection of people was having a meeting simultaneously with this one, except—damn fools—they'd insisted on doing it in plush surroundings instead of, as he and Rozsak had opted, choosing a modest and less well-known hotel.

"Leave it to the Mesans," he sneered, "to insist on crapping in a gold toilet."

A harsh little laugh swept the room. By normal standards, none of the men and women gathered in that hotel room were especially burdened by finicky moral sentiments. But the contempt they held for Mesa and all its works was not simply that of hard-boiled military officers of a hard-boiled society. Even for them, Mesa was a byword for foulness.

"Our courier ship overtook theirs along the way. And since we had military-grade sensors and we got here first, we were able to catch them right after their junction translation and verify that it was the same Jessyk Combine vessel which left Manticore ahead of us."

He let that item get digested for a moment. The Jessyk Combine was one of the giant commercial enterprises which dominated the Mesa System. Manpower Unlimited, the galaxy's premier trafficker in genetic slavery, was another, and by far the most publicly notorious. None of them, however, were what could be called "ethical enterprises," and Jessyk in particular had close if informal connections with Manpower. The connections were distant enough—obscure enough, rather—that Jessyk had never been outlawed in the Star Kingdom, as Manpower had. But no one in the know doubted for a moment that wherever you found a Jessyk courier carrying information, Manpower would be getting it just as quickly as Jessyk.

"I can guarantee you," Watanapongse continued, "that the people gathered over there took even less pleasure than we did watching that recording. A lot less. They've run into Zilwicki in the trenches, which we haven't."

"And won't, if all goes well," added Captain Rozsak firmly. His eyes swept the room, his gaze harder than usual. "I trust that's understood by everyone. We've got no bone to pick with Anton Zilwicki, and only a fool—judging from all evidence—would pick a bone with him just for the hell of it."

Relaxed and normally good-humored he might be, but Luiz Rozsak was also *the boss*, and nobody doubted it. His brown eyes swept back across the room again, and were met by a little wave of nods.

"Good," he grunted. Then, more easily: "I admit he's a headache for us, so we'll have to figure out how to ease the pain. But nothing direct, people. The last thing we want is to draw that man's attention *our* way."

For a moment, his face assumed some of the sour expression that had earlier been on the face of Commander Edie Habib. In truth, Captain Rozsak was no fonder of "black ops" than any of his subordinates, for all that he was much better at it than most military officers. It was ultimately a filthy business, no matter how much perfume you sprayed over it. And while Luiz Rozsak was perfectly prepared to get his hands dirty in the pursuit of his ambitions, he preferred the dirt to be soil instead of sewer muck.

He swivelled his head and brought the most junior officer in the room under his gaze. Thandi Palane was the only Marine lieutenant in the group, and, even after a year, she still seemed a bit dazed at having been selected by Captain Rozsak to be one of his inner circle. As a junior officer from a backward frontier system, she'd assumed her career would be slow at best, and would soon enough stall out completely. She'd been resigned to that prospect, since even early retirement from the Solarian Marines was vastly superior to any life she'd have had if she'd stayed on her home planet. Ndebele was still under the control of the Office of Frontier Security, which meant—in practice, if not in the official theory of the Solarian League—that she would have remained the serf of Solarian bureaucrats and their allied conglomerates.

The last thing Thandi Palane had expected was an invitation to join the staff of one of the SLN's better-known fast-track captains. True, there was a trace—more than just a trace, in fact—of the "outsider" about Luiz Rozsak himself. But there was also the smell about him of an up-and-comer, too. Rozsak had already punched several tickets as a ship commander, and was now enjoying the prestigious status of a Central Staff officer detached for duty to one of the Solarian League's important sector provinces. Rank be damned. Above the junior levels, civilian connections counted for at least as much in an officer's prospects for advancement as official rank did, and Luiz Rozsak was now officially the second ranking officer in the Maya sector. He might not hold flag rank—yet—but most commodores in the SLN and not a few of its admirals would have given their eye teeth to be on his close terms with System Governor Oravil Barregos and his political chief-of-staff and Lieutenant Governor Ingemar Cassetti.

Rozsak was amused at the way Palane so obviously had to fight to meet his eyes. Sooner or later, he knew, he'd have to overcome that shyness. He needed followers who were self-confident in their own right, not simply obedient to him. He'd even considered the tactic of seducing the young woman, something he normally avoided with his subordinates, in the hopes that an affair with her much-idolized patron might rub away some of her social awkwardness. That he'd succeed in the seduction, he didn't doubt at all. Rozsak was a physically handsome man as well as a charismatic one, and the lieutenant had all the signs of a young woman with a crush on her glamorous boss. But he'd come to the conclusion such a course would be far more likely to do harm than good for Palane's development, even leaving aside the obvious dangers it posed for overall discipline.

He'd come to that conclusion with some regrets, to be sure. The lieutenant was a very attractive woman, all the more so in that the genetic strain which had produced her was far enough outside the usual parameters of the now much-mixed human species to appeal to Rozsak's taste for the exotic. But one of the reasons for Luiz Rozsak's rapid rise was his iron self-discipline. He let nothing get in the way of ambition, neither his distaste for black ops nor the prospect of pleasure with a beautiful young woman.

"What about your Amazons, Thandi? They might do the trick."

He recognized her hesitation for what it was, and had to suppress a sigh. Even after working in close proximity with Rozsak for months, Lieutenant Palane still wasn't comfortable with the idea of contradicting her superior.

Fortunately, Edie Habib had all the instincts and skills of the superb executive officer she'd been when Rozsak had had a ship command.

"C'mon, Thandi, spit it out. I promise the Captain won't bite your head off."

Another little laugh swept the room, though it was not a harsh one. Most of the men and women in that room had at one time been in Thandi's position, and they were not unsympathetic to her plight. Rozsak's style of leadership was rather unusual in the Solarian League's armed forces, most of whose senior officers did not take kindly to subordinates who argued with them. It took some getting used to.

Her hesitation was only brief, however. This much Lieutenant Palane had learned: the one thing which was guaranteed to bring the Captain's wrath down on your head was to dance around him or try to feed him whatever line you thought he wanted to hear.

"It's not a good idea, Sir. In my opinion, that is," she added hastily.

Rozsak inclined his head, urging her to elaborate.

"The thing is, my—uh, 'Amazons,' as you call them—really don't know their ass from their elbow, when you get right down to it." She flashed a smile which, for all its quick nervousness, was dazzling enough to make Rozsak regret again that he'd decided to maintain his personal distance from her. "They remind me a lot of me, that way."

Again, some laughter, which Rozsak joined in. Now obviously more relaxed, Thandi continued.

"So the problem is that while I don't doubt if we waved them under Zilwicki's nose we'd draw his attention—especially with one of his daughters along for the trip—"

"No kidding!" exclaimed one of the Navy lieutenants lounging against a wall. Jerry Manson, that was. "Let Zilwicki get a whiff of some Scrags on Erewhon, he'll have his hackles up like a dog in an alley."

Rozsak caught the sudden frown on Thandi's face and cleared his throat. Manson was a problem, and Rozsak decided that slapping him down would be all to the good.

"Lieutenant Palane has already requested once that we avoid that term when referring to her special unit. As you may recall, I agreed with her. A leader who sneers at his own troops—or lets anyone else do it—hasn't got a pot to piss in when he needs it, people."

The flush on Manson's face, combined with the look of thanks on Thandi's, made it clear that Rozsak had made his point. Several points, actually, not the least of which was to remind everyone that while the captain was relaxed and easy-going, he *was* the Captain.

The point being made, Rozsak saw no reason to rub salt into the wounds. "I don't mean to bite your head off, Jerry. It's an easy slip to make, but we still need to watch it." He gave Palane a friendly smile. "For that matter, I suppose I should stop calling them 'Amazons.'"

Thandi shook her head. "I don't think that would bother them at all, Sir. In fact, if they knew what it meant, it'd probably tickle them pink. It's just that . . ."

Watching the young woman struggle with her thoughts, trying to find a way to express them properly, Rozsak decided to do it for her. In truth, he was quite pleased with Palane's instinctive defense of her unit, and understood where it came from perfectly well. Unlike a lot of the SLN's officers—most of them, in fact—Rozsak had combat experience. He also had high hopes for the Marine lieutenant. Where Rozsak was going in the years ahead, he was going to need good combat officers around him. Staff officers, even capable ones like Manson, he could buy by the dozen.

"It goes all the way back, Lieutenant Palane. *Esprit de corps,* if you want to get fancy and antique about it. There's never been an army in history worth a damn that was ashamed of itself. So, given where they're coming from, I can well understand why your—ah, ladies—"

Another laugh, and this a loud one—loudest of all, from the lieutenant herself.

"—don't want to be called Scrags." His eyes swept the room, hard as stones. "And that's an end to it. Please continue, Lieutenant."

When his gaze came back to meet Thandi's, he saw the gleam in her eyes. And, once again, had to firmly suppress the treacherous urge. The young officer really *was* extraordinarily attractive. Those gleaming eyes—the dazzling smile even more so—would look splendid against a pillow.

"The thing is, Sir, I don't see any chance they could keep the maneuver going. A direct assault, sure, that's one thing. But this kind of tricky dancing . . . If Zilwicki's half as smart as he's made out to be, he'd smell a red herring. And then he'd start wondering what the red herring was supposed to distract him *from.*"

Rozsak decided she was probably right. In fact, the girl seemed to have more of a knack for the kind of twisted thinking black ops required than he'd expected.

Definitely someone to keep an eye on. So just keep your pants sealed, Luiz. You can buy sex, too, when it comes down to it.

"All right, that makes sense," he concurred. Now his eyes moved to Manson.

Whatever reservations Rozsak had about Manson, the lieutenant was as smooth a staff officer as you could find. He'd been expecting the glance, and moved right up to the challenge.

"We might be able to do it with the Komandorski tidbit, Sir, yes." For a fleeting instant, Rozsak could see contradictory impulses warring on the lieutenant's face. The desire to please his boss—stronger than ever, right after being admonished—fighting with his own reservations.

The fight didn't last more than a split second, however, and resolved itself to Rozsak's satisfaction. So, once again, he decided to keep Manson around instead of cutting him loose. Granted, the lieutenant was too obsequious toward him, and too quick to take swipes at other members of the team. But as long as he kept it under control and put Rozsak's ambitions ahead of his own, the captain would live with it. As he'd told Habib, it was an imperfect universe.

"To be honest, though, I'm reluctant to do it. Yes, it would probably distract Zilwicki long enough—what the hell, that's a trip all the way to Smoking Frog and back again, even leaving aside the time he'd have to spend there finding his way through the thicket. But . . ."

Rozsak barked a laugh. "God help us, we're all starting to think like spooks. But you hate to waste a so-called 'asset,' right? Even though neither you nor I nor anyone in this room has any idea right now what else we'd do with it."

The jocular tone made it clear the words were not a barb. So Manson just smiled and nodded his head, acknowledging a friendly hit.

"That's pretty much it, Sir. As you said, I have no idea what *we'd* do with that tantalizing tidbit. I just hate to give it up, just for the sake of taking someone out of the picture we'd never counted on being there in the first place. Seems a waste, somehow."

For the first time that night, the other Marine officer in the room spoke up. "I swear to God," growled Lieutenant Colonel Huang, "—any god, too, I don't much care—I wish we were all back on Boniface. Even thirty percent casualties is better than this . . ."

His thick hands made a swimming motion in front of his face. "This stinking murky muddled mess."

No one laughed in response, although quite a few faces were twisted with grimaces. Not smiles, exactly. Too many of those people had been with Rozsak when he'd led the final assault on the rebel stronghold on Boniface. It was a well-known episode in the recent history of the Solarian League Navy, which had put Rozsak on the captains' list several years ahead of the normal career track. The reason it was well-known, however, was because the rebels had been far better armed than frontier rebels usually were as well as more fanatical. Thirty percent casualties suffered by the Solarian forces, and . . .

One hundred percent, all fatalities, suffered by the rebels. The rebellion had been triggered off by the depredations of the conglomerate in control of Boniface—the Jessyk Combine, as it happened—which had gone far beyond even the loose limits which such conglomerates normally set for themselves in areas under OFS authority. Since the OFS District Officer had been appointed his direct superior in the campaign, the Frontier Security forces having already been chewed up by the rebels, Rozsak had had no choice but to obey the man's commands.

I want them all dead, Rozsak. Down to the cats and dogs.

Rozsak didn't think for a moment that the DO's command had been issued in the heat of anger. The greedy swine had surely been taking a huge payoff from Jessyk, and was determined to have any eyewitnesses to their practices on Boniface removed forever.

Boniface had been sheer slaughter, at the end. But Rozsak had been with his troops throughout the campaign, even after the fighting moved dirtside, and had carried out his orders faithfully. He'd even done that with flair, and as much in the way of mercy as could be managed. At his orders, the last surviving pet in the city had been brought to him and Rozsak had personally blown the cat's brains out, after having the little beast tied to an execution post. That too had become part of the Boniface legend, especially favored by the Marines who did most of the fighting and dying. Here was a commander who'd get his hands dirty, and manage to sneer at the bureaucrats at the same time he did their bidding. *Worth keeping an eye on, boys and girls. This one's . . . different.*

Rozsak let the memory of Boniface linger in the room, but not for long. His people had a right to be proud of the way they'd fought, yes. But it was still a foul memory, when all was said and done. Not a taste you wanted to leave lingering in your mouth.

"I can't really say I agree with you, Kao." With a quick smile: "Not that I don't sympathize with your attitude. But let's look on the bright side, for a moment."

It was about time to wrap up the meeting anyway, since the matter involving the Komandorski "tidbit" was best pursued privately with Lieutenant Manson. So Rozsak sat up straight and issued another of the many little pep talks with which he usually ended these semi-informal staff meetings.

"Yes, we've been given the worst assignment by the Governor. By Cassetti, I should say. I doubt very much if Governor Barregos knows about any of it. But the best units always get the worst assignments. It's been that way since the days of Ashurbanipal, people, so there's no point complaining about it. The only thing that's changed is that we get to ride to battle in faster air-conditioned chariots. So we're going to do this *well,* the way the best units always do everything. Understood?"

The wave of nods came quickly, but they also came easy and relaxed. Rozsak thought he had the best staff—inner circle, to call things by their right name—in the entire Solarian League Navy. And, clearly enough, his staff shared that assessment.

"Meantime, like I said, look on the bright side. At least this time, if all goes the way it should, we'll wind up butchering hogs instead of cattle." The smile that came with those words had no humor in it worth talking about.

"Amen," murmured Huang. The stocky lieutenant colonel of Marines was not smiling at all. As was true of a disproportionate number of Rozsak's inner circle—and most of the actual combat units in the Solarian League's armed forces—Huang came from a frontier planet himself. More than once, in his career, he'd heard the sneering word "sepoys" fall from the lips of superior officers from the inner planets of the League.

Never from Rozsak, of course. The captain was not exactly a "sepoy," since he came from a planet which was at least not under OFS jurisdiction. But he was close enough; and, more to the point, a student of history. It had been the captain who, on the day he recruited Huang to his staff, had told him about something in ancient history called the Indian Mutiny. *Except this time, we'll do it right.*

"Amen," he repeated.

After the private meetings which followed, Rozsak ended the long day with a short and final conference with Habib. The commander had been with Rozsak almost from the beginning of his career, and whatever specific title the woman had held since, she was always "the XO."

"What do you think, Edie? Is there a chance in hell that Cassetti's oh-so-clever scheme isn't going to come off its wheels before we get halfway there?"

Habib shrugged. "That mostly depends on how well we do our job. And look on the bright side, if you'll allow me to swipe one of your favorite expressions. We don't *want* the complicated contraption to get all the way there. Just far enough to grind Cassetti under the wheels when it all comes apart. We can walk the rest of the way, easily enough. After that wreck, the Governor'll greet us with open arms."

Rozsak grinned coldly. "You have a way with words, XO. Did I ever tell you that?"

"No. Maybe I could get a career as a poet, after you go down in flames."

They shared a chuckle. There was indeed quite a good chance that Rozsak would wind up going down in flames, sooner or later. But if he did, it was as sure as anything that Habib would go down with him.

"Butchering hogs instead of cattle," Habib murmured. "You have a way with words yourself, Luiz. I like the sound of that."

"I thought you would." Rozsak looked at the window beyond whose curtains lay the Suds Emporium. "For that matter, we'll be killing off a fair number of snakes and scorpions while we're at it."

"Amen to that."

CHAPTER 9

AS SHE WALKED INTO THE SUITE in the hotel where her special unit was quartered, Lieutenant Thandi Palane was also thinking about snakes and scorpions. Walking into that suite reminded her of walking into a nest of the dangerous creatures.

But, as she closed the door behind her, she forced the analogy out of her mind. It was unfair, she knew, and more a reflection of her own dark mood than anything about her . . .

Ah, "ladies."

Rozsak's clever quip brought a little smile to her face at the same time that it darkened her mood still further. One of the many things she liked about the Captain was his sense of humor.

Oh, give it up, Thandi. You could spend an hour listing all of Luiz Rozsak's fine qualities, come to the conclusion—again—that he's the sexiest man around, and wind up going to bed—again—alone and frustrated.

The worst of it was that she knew Luiz Rozsak found her sexually attractive also. The captain was very good at keeping it under wraps, and the Marine lieutenant was pretty sure that no one else, except possibly the XO, had noticed. But Thandi had no doubt at all that she aroused the man. She was not what anyone would call an experienced femme fatale, but neither was she a naïve virgin. Such creatures did not exist on her home planet of Ndebele.

After closing the door and making sure it was locked, she leaned back against it, crossed her arms, and sighed heavily.

Actually, that *wasn't* the worst of it. The real worst of it was that she also understood—was fairly certain she did, anyway—why Rozsak was making no attempt to pursue her. Which only increased her attraction to the man; since, in essence, he was looking out for her own best interests.

His too, of course. Thandi knew perfectly well that Rozsak was extremely ambitious and quite capable of being as ruthless as need be to advance that ambition. Some other young woman—probably most other young women—would have found that knowledge repellent. But those young women hadn't been born and raised on one of the worst hellholes in OFS territory. Men on Ndebele were either cold-bloodedly ambitious or, as was true of ninety percent of them, they were beaten into a lifetime of what amounted to serfdom. The same was true for women, except the percentages were even worse. By the time she was sixteen, Thandi had come to the conclusion that whatever else happened to her, she would not settle for being an OFS helot.

So, seeing no other option, she'd enlisted in the armed forces. The *Solarian* armed forces, not one of the auxiliary military units the League maintained, like the Frontier Forces. She wanted no part of OFS, despite their easier entrance requirements. Besides, Thandi was smarter than average and had applied herself in school, so she was angling for a career as an officer, not simply a grunt. The Solarian League's regular armed forces would accept officer candidates from protectorate planets readily enough, even if they rarely enjoyed much of a career. In the OFS, that would be impossible.

Even with her intelligence and grades, that hadn't been easy to swing, for someone coming from her background. Not to her surprise, she'd had to settle for the Marines rather than the regular Navy she'd have personally preferred. Not to her surprise also, she'd had to provide sex for the SLN recruiting officer during the weeks the process had required, before he'd agreed to make sure the thing went through.

She hadn't minded, particularly. It wasn't the first time she'd had to perform that service, since it was a common practice on many of the protectorate worlds under OFS jurisdiction. Certainly on Ndebele. And at least the recruiting officer had been a fairly pleasant man, who'd tried to be gentlemanly about the whole thing—quite unlike the brutish factory manager who'd made her one of his concubines as a teenager in exchange for allowing her to attend school at night instead of working. He'd also had her boyfriend beaten senseless when he tried to object.

Remembering that old boyfriend, Thandi's crossed arms tightened and, with an effort, she pushed the memory away. He'd been a sweet kid, true enough. And, by the time he was eighteen, had been hammered into proper helotry.

She'd left all that behind her along with everything else. There was no way a man like Luiz Rozsak could be described as "sweet," whatever his other fine qualities. By the same token, he was neither beaten down nor bore any resemblance to a helot. Thandi could accept the man's cold-blooded ruthlessness easily enough, since the alternative was far worse.

The problem was that the captain wasn't simply ruthless, he was also *smart.* And smart in a way that—at least in Thandi's admittedly limited experience—few ruthless men were. He could think like a chess player, not simply like a human shark. And for all his obvious self-assurance, he was even smart enough to understand that he could only rise so far on his own. So, he was one of those very rare people who could apply ruthlessness to himself as well as others, and made sure that he built a strong team around him instead of lessening them for his own narrow and immediate purposes.

And so it was, she sighed, that she'd spend another night alone. It was too bad, but . . .

Grow up, girl. It's just a crush, so forget it. If you're that frustrated, it's not as if you can't find other outlets.

Plenty of them, for that matter. The captain was by no means the only man in her vicinity who'd found her tall and athletic self very enticing. He was just the only one who didn't make any advances—and, alas, the only one she was interested in herself.

"Moping again, are we? Must be man trouble, comrades."

"Stupid, then. If you want a man, kaja, just take him."

"If you need help, we'll hold him down till you're finished."

Thandi looked up, scowling. Sometimes she appreciated the rough humor of her charges. Other times—this being one of them—she didn't. Not in the least.

Seeing the fierce scowl, the women who'd entered the suite's central room from their sleeping chambers backed up a step or so. The quickness with which they did so brought some good cheer back to Lieutenant Palane. Partly, because the grace of those steps illustrated their own athleticism, which was something any ground combat officer liked to see in her troops. Mostly, however, it was because the quickness of those steps was proof positive that none of those women had any doubts, any longer, that if she wanted to Thandi Palane was quite capable of hammering them into dog food.

Superhumans or not. They'd still be dog food when she was done.

"Just joking, kaja," apologized one of them.

Thandi uncrossed her arms and waved the apology away. "Never mind, Lara. Man trouble indeed, as you say. But since when are men really worth troubling about?"

They grinned at her. Despite herself, Thandi had always liked those grins. At least, after a few sessions in the full-contact court—and several broken bones—had removed the underlying smirks. Those weren't the expressions worn by snakes and scorpions, after all.

"My very own half-tame wolf pack," she murmured to herself. Then, struck by a thought, asked aloud: "Is there such a word as 'wolfess'?"

As Lt. Commander Watanopognse had forseen, the Mesans staying in the Suds Emporium were even more disgruntled by the news of Zilwicki's arrival than the Solarians had been.

"They're a pack of wolves, Unser, what do you expect?" Haicheng Ringstorff motioned toward the closed door through which they'd come. "Except wolves don't tell lies in their sleep. So . . ."

Ringstorff's lieutenant, George Lithgow, was already slouched in a chair. Ringstorff moved to another chair and did likewise. "Are they telling the truth? How am I supposed to know? All I can tell you is that *I* certainly didn't order Stein scragged."

Unser Diem glared down at his nominal subordinate. "A poor choice of words, Haicheng. What the hell are you doing anyway, letting Scrags into Security? We've always been careful to keep them at arms' length."

Ringstorff didn't quite sneer, but his facial expression made clear that he understood just as well as Diem did that his subordinate status was mostly fiction. Leaving aside a meaningless title, Ringstorff was essentially in charge of all Mesan security operations in and around Erewhonese space. He answered to Mesa's Council of Coordinators, not to any of the specific corporations represented on that council. And while Unser Diem's position as the Jessyk Combine's representative on Erewhon—roving troubleshooter would be a more precise term—meant he couldn't be openly ignored or shrugged off, his actual authority over Ringstorff was effectively nil. The more so since Ringstorff had Manpower's nod of approval, and Jessyk was in fact if not in name what amounted to a subsidiary of Manpower Unlimited. The ownership records were a closely held secret, of course, and the two corporations were officially unconnected. In practice, Jessyk served as a convenient way for Manpower to keep a large portion of its revenues hidden from public scrutiny.

"I don't much like it either, Unser. But in case you hadn't noticed"—here, his lip did curl a bit—"I'm not operating inside the Solarian League. Which means, on the good side, that I don't have to be as twitchy about appearances; but, on the bad side, means I have to take what I can get. You know as well as I do that most of the security contractors on Mesa won't sign up for extended duty outside League territory or the Silesian Confederacy. Sure as hell not after that fiasco we had with *Gauntlet*."

Diem made a face, and slid into a chair across from Ringstorff. "Yeah, I know. Still . . . Scrags, for God's sake! Word gets out . . ."

"Gets out to *who*?" demanded Ringstorff. "We're far enough outside the League here that damn few people remember any of Earth's ancient history. The 'Final War' is just a phrase they pick up out of history textbooks in school. It doesn't mean anything to them, really, much less the details. There aren't more than a handful who'd even recognize the term 'Scrag' to begin with."

He snorted sarcastically. "The truth is that we're running a lot more of a risk by having Masadans on our payroll. Those fanatics *have* pissed off people in this neck of the galaxy—and not more than a few years ago. Since it's the Masadans who want the Scrags, the only way to get rid of them is to get rid of the Masadans. Which—trust me!—I'd be glad to do in a heartbeat, if the Council tells me to. It was their idea to hire them in the first place, not mine."

Diem scowled. He felt, as did the Council, that the services of the Masadans were too valuable to give up. The religious fanatics were willing to take on jobs that no regular security contractor would even look at. In the final analysis, the Masadans weren't mercenaries. Not exactly, at any rate.

Which was also why Ringstorff had argued against hiring them, of course. The Masadans were a double-edged sword, since their employer could never be quite certain when the zealots would step beyond the limits officially set for any operation. Which was a problem with which, in another guise, Ringstorff had recently had personal, painful experience in this very neck of the galaxy.

The whole thing was a mess. Diem rubbed his face and sighed. "All right, fine. So tell me what *you* think. Who killed Stein? Or had him killed, I should say."

Ringstorff shrugged. "I have no idea. I sure didn't authorize it. Why would I? Stein's been squalling for decades, big deal. If it's hurt business any, nobody's ever noticed."

"Who else, then?"

"How the hell should I know? It's a big galaxy! A self-righteous loudmouth like Stein makes enemies right and left—and he had half a century to pile them up. Could have been almost anybody."

"We're getting blamed for it!"

Ringstorff sat up straight. "Were you born yesterday? Mesa gets blamed for *everything,* Unser. And so what? If you want my opinion, it just adds to the romance of the planet. We're too useful to too many people with real power and influence for anyone to ever do anything. In the meantime, our reputation just draws more business our way."

Diem glared at him and spoke through gritted teeth: "For someone who's supposed to be a 'security expert,' you've got the brains of an insect. *Somebody* killed Stein, Ringstorff, and *we're* getting blamed for it. Has it ever occurred to you—even once!—that maybe that was the whole point of the exercise?"

Ringstorff's sneer was now open and full-spread. "Stick to what you know, Diem. That kind of fancy maneuver doesn't exist outside the holovids. Security Rule Number One: Don't ascribe to clever conspiracy what can be explained by stupidity. Stein was killed because somebody finally blew their stack at the jerk. Good riddance. They'll put up some shrines and ten years from now nobody'll remember and we'll still be raking in the cash."

Diem rose. "There's no point in continuing this. I'll register my objection with the Council when I get back."

Ringstorff shrugged. "Do whatever you want."

"Right. In the meantime, can I trust you to at least keep those wolves of yours on a leash?"

"For Christ sake, Diem, you were standing right there when I gave them the order! 'Nobody touches Anton Zilwicki. He's off limits.' And you heard them swear they wouldn't. Swear on their own God, too, when I insisted. That's one good thing about the maniacs. They won't break *that* oath."

In the nearby common room of the suite in the Suds Emporium where Ringstorff's special security unit had retired after their meeting with the Security Chief and Diem, their leader paused the replay.

"Will you all recognize her?" he demanded.

A wave of nods went around the room. One of the Scrags who'd attached himself to the Masadans tossed his head in the direction of the door. "Do we obey them?"

Gideon Templeton had been about to resume the recording, but the question caused him to delay. With some difficulty, he managed to keep a scowl off his face. Most of the new converts to the Church of Humanity Unchained (Defiant) still had a shaky grasp of theology. Gideon was honest enough to admit—in private, to himself, if no one else—that part of the problem lay in the fact that his sect of the church was a new one, founded by his father Ephraim not so many years earlier, after Ephraim had been forced to flee persecution on Masada itself. As a result, the doctrine of the new church was not always clear, since Ephraim had not spoken on all subjects before his death.

Still . . . fighting off the scowl was difficult. *This* question, after all, ought to be obvious. Not for the first time, Gideon was faced with the problem that the new converts had certain ingrained attitudes which made their conversion an uncertain proposition. Even Gideon, at times, found it hard not to think of them as "Scrags," though he himself had been the one to forbid the term in the ranks of the Select.

"We gave our oath in the name of the Lord," he said curtly, almost snapping out the words. "Such an oath cannot be violated."

If the Scrag—Gideon shook off the term; the "Select from the War Against Unholiness"—was in the least bit abashed by the admonishment, he gave no sign of it. With all the casual arrogance of his genetically enhanced breed, he simply grinned at Gideon and made a slight shrug. The gesture was aimed at his fellow converts, obviously enough. As if to say: *it's kind of silly, if you ask me, but we'll not argue the point.*

Gideon decided to let the matter slide. For all that they frequently annoyed him with their slack attitude toward doctrine, the new converts were simply too valuable to risk alienating them with overly harsh and frequent instruction. Once again, he resigned himself to patience.

"We will obey the order to stay away from Zilwicki," he repeated. "That oath is binding upon us. But—but!—like all binding oaths, it is also specific. Since we are not heathens, we will accept that the limit applies to all Zilwickis. Even including his bastard daughter." He bestowed a glare on all the occupants of the crowded room, being careful not to single out the new converts. "Is that understood?"

One of his men—an old Faithful, this one, not a new convert—got a pained look on his face. Understanding the meaning of that expression, Gideon smiled coldly.

"Given that we did not *specifically* mention her by name, I think we can allow ourselves some latitude here if the tactical needs of the moment require it. She may not be *harmed*—not seriously, at least—"

One of the new converts had a sly smile on his face. Understanding the meaning of that also, Gideon scowled at him. "That includes possession, Zyngram!"

The Scrag—it was *so* hard to avoid the term, especially in one's private thoughts—responded with that same casual shrug. This time, Gideon decided the issue needed to be pressed. He was willing to be patient about doctrine, but not slack.

"Do not trifle with me," he growled. "We do not recognize the heathen notion of 'rape,' to be sure. But since the heathens do, and we gave this oath to a heathen, we will respect that boundary. Not because we respect the heathen, but because we do not cavil with God. Do you understand?"

He waited until the new convert nodded. "Good. The girl may therefore neither be seriously harmed nor possessed. Beyond that, however, I see no reason we are obliged to stay away from her entirely as we must Anton Zilwicki. If she happens to be present when the time comes, I'm sure it will not be difficult to simply thrust her aside. If she suffers a few bruises in the process, so be it."

He picked up the remote control for the HV. "For the moment, concentrate on what is important." The images from the recording sprang back into life. Gideon's glaring eyes focused on one of the figures.

"My sister," he hissed, "conceived in female deceit, born and raised in whore-worshiping apostasy. The moment Zilwicki is not around . . ."

CHAPTER 10

"*GALAXY CARAVAN*, WE'RE NOT GOING to tell you again," the harsh voice said over the com. "Cut your drive and open your hatches, or we'll blow your ass out of space!"

"Are there actually people this stupid in the galaxy?" Lieutenant Betty Gohr demanded under her breath as she watched her display.

"It would appear so," someone replied, and she looked up quickly. Apparently, she hadn't spoken quite as softly as she'd thought she had, and Commander Joel Blumenthal, *Gauntlet*'s tactical officer, gave her a crooked smile.

"I'm sorry, Sir," she said. "It just . . . I don't know, offends my sense of professionalism, I suppose, to see even a pirate do something this stupid. I like to think that it takes at least a modicum of intelligence to be able to figure out what buttons to push on the bridge."

"He does seem just a tad less than brilliant," Blumenthal acknowledged. "On the other hand, we *are* doing our best to encourage him to screw up by the numbers."

"I know," Gohr said. "But still, Sir . . ."

Her voice trailed off, but Blumenthal understood exactly what she meant.

HMS *Gauntlet* wasn't even coming close to setting a passage record for the voyage from Manticore to Erewhon. Exactly whose idea it had been to assign the cruiser to ride herd on the unofficial convoy was something the captain hadn't discussed with any of his officers. For all Blumenthal knew, Oversteegen might have arranged it himself. After all the casualties they'd taken in Tiberian, not to mention the routine transfers which always afflicted a ship's company when she was put into yard hands for major repairs or a refit, they needed all the exercise and drill time they could get. So it would have made sense for the captain to arrange—or at least to cheerfully accept orders—for *Gauntlet* to make this long, slow, circuitous trip, trundling along with half a dozen lumbering freighters. It had certainly given them plenty of time to train!

And he might just have seen the merchies as bait in a trap, Blumenthal thought privately. *Especially if he still has as many questions as I do about what happened the* last *time we were out this way.*

If that was what the captain had been thinking, it seemed to have worked . . . sort of. At least they appeared to have caught a pirate of sorts, although judging from the emissions signature Blumenthal's tracking section was picking up, whoever this was certainly wasn't whoever sent out heavy cruisers to do his dirty work.

"We're getting a better read on them, Sir," he said, turning his chair to face the command chair at the center of *Gauntlet*'s bridge. "Judging from the impeller signature, CIC makes her tonnage around eighty to ninety-five thousand tons. Her active emissions seem to fit fairly well with something that size, too. From what we're picking up, her sensor fit is pretty close to completely obsolete, though."

"How close?" Captain Oversteegen asked.

"It's almost certainly inferior to prewar Peep hardware," Blumenthal replied.

"In that case, Sir," Commander Watson put in, "calling it 'obsolete' is entirely too kind."

"I'm inclined t' agree." Oversteegen studied his own repeater plot for a handful of seconds, then shrugged. "If his sensors are that bad, then I suppose we really shouldn't blame him for fallin' for our little ruse. On the other hand, even the worst sensors in space are goin' t' see through our EW if he gets much closer."

"Sir," the com officer said, "whoever it is is hailing us again. Basically the same demand as before. Should I keep stringing him along?"

"Still no identification from his end?" Oversteegen's tone seemed almost disinterested, but his eyes never left the red icon on his plot.

"No, Sir."

"Well, that certainly seems t' establish that he's not anyone with official standin', doesn't it?" the captain murmured.

Which it did, Lieutenant Gohr conceded. Of course, the fact that *Gauntlet*—*Galaxy Caravan*, as far as the other ship knew—had so far refused to obey its orders ought to have suggested to anyone with the brains of a rutabaga that she wasn't exactly what *she* seemed to be, either. The pirate vessel had been within its missile range of *Gauntlet* for well over twenty minutes, during which time Oversteegen had steadfastly declined to cooperate. Instead, he'd continued to "run" deeper into the Shadwell System's gravity well, drawing the other ship steadily farther and farther away from the G5 system's twenty-light-minute hyper limit. Any genuine merchant skipper would have been trying to break back out *across* the hyper limit, since her only possible hope of outrunning the smaller, handier vessel would have been to escape back into hyper. But the legitimate merchantmen under Oversteegen's escort had crossed the hyper limit a half hour after *Gauntlet*, and the warship's apparently suicidal course was designed to suck the pirate after her, instead of them, while Lieutenant Cheney, her com officer, did an excellent imitation of a frightened merchant skipper doing her very best to talk herself out of trouble.

If Gohr had been in command of the pirate, she would either have gone ahead and fired into *Gauntlet* long since, to show she meant business, or else have broken off entirely on the assumption that only a warship trolling for pirates would deliberately court a missile attack by refusing to comply with instructions. Of course, *Gauntlet*'s EW was undoubtedly better than anything the pirate had ever imagined might exist, which helped to explain how he could be so unwary, but even so . . .

"All right, Guns," Captain Oversteegen said finally. "I believe it's time we convinced this gentleman of the error of his ways."

"Aye, aye, Sir!" Blumenthal said with considerably more enthusiasm, and Oversteegen smiled thinly. But then the captain shook his head.

"Under the circumstances," he said, "I think this might be an appropriate time for our Assistant Tac Officer t' try her hand at pirate swattin'. We've already established your own bona fides in that regard, I believe."

"As you say, Sir," Blumenthal allowed only a trace of disappointment to color his tone, and Lieutenant Gohr felt herself sitting suddenly straighter in her own chair as she sensed the captain's eyes on her back.

"All right, Lieutenant," he said calmly, "I want this fellow discouraged from harassin' legitimate merchant ships. I intend t' give him an opportunity t' surrender. If he declines, however, I want him discouraged as permanently as possible. How would you recommend we accomplish that?"

"Are we interested in capturing or examining his vessel if he declines, Sir?" she heard herself ask in an equally calm voice.

"I think not," the captain replied. "It's unlikely the Admiralty would be interested in buyin' her into service, and it's even less likely that we'd learn anythin' useful from her records."

"In that case, Sir, I recommend we make it short and sweet. With your permission, I'll set up a double broadside. At this range, and given the crappy hardware he seems to have, that ought to do the trick in a single launch. We may waste a few birds on overkill, but it certainly ought to discourage him as permanently as anyone could ask."

"Very well, Lieutenant," Oversteegen said. "Set it up and prepare t' launch on my command."

"Aye, aye, Sir." Gohr's fingers flew as she punched commands into her console. The weight of the captain's eyes urged her to hurry, but she took the time to make sure she did it right. She tapped in the final targeting code, then ran her gaze rapidly over the entire set up. It looked good, she decided, and punched the "commit" key.

"Firing sequence programmed and locked, Sir," she reported.

Oversteegen didn't say anything for just a second, and she realized that he was reviewing her commands. There was a brief silence, and then she heard a soft grunt of approval from the captain's chair as he reached the end. It was, she decided, a good thing she had included not only the enablement of *Gauntlet*'s point defense against the possibility that the pirate might actually get a few missiles of his own away, but also had a dozen follow-up salvos programmed to cover the highly improbable chance that the other ship would survive *Gauntlet*'s opening broadsides.

"Very good, Lieutenant," Oversteegen approved. "Stand by t' engage as programmed on my command."

"Standing by, aye, Sir," she confirmed, and the captain glanced at Lieutenant Cheney.

"Live mike, Com," he said.

"You're live . . . now, Sir," Cheney replied, and Oversteegen smiled unpleasantly.

"Pirate vessel," he said flatly, "this is Captain Michael Oversteegen, of Her Majesty's heavy cruiser *Gauntlet*. Strike your wedge immediately and surrender, or be destroyed!"

At such a short range, the communications lag was negligible, and every eye on *Gauntlet*'s bridge watched the tactical display while they awaited the pirate's response. Then, abruptly, the red icon altered course, clawing frantically away from *Gauntlet* even as it rolled in a feeble effort to interpose its wedge between it and the cruiser.

"Pirate vessel," Oversteegen's harsh voice was as unyielding as battle steel, "strike your wedge *now*. This is the only warnin' you will receive."

The pirate's only response was to push his acceleration still higher. He must be riding the very brink of compensator failure, Gohr thought, watching her display with a sort of icy detachment. Another twenty heart beats sped into infinity.

"Lieutenant Gohr," Captain Oversteegen said formally, "open fire."

"Actually, I think she's working out quite well, Sir," Commander Watson said. Michael Oversteegen leaned back in his chair in his day cabin aboard *Gauntlet*, his expression an invitation for his executive officer to continue, and Watson smiled.

"All right, I'll admit it," the dark-haired exec said, with a chuckle which few of Oversteegen's officers would have been comfortable emitting in his presence. "When you first came up with the notion of asking for a 'spook' as an ATO, I thought it was . . . not one of your best ideas. But Lieutenant Gohr doesn't seem to have forgotten which end of the tube the missile comes out of, after all."

A bit of an understatement, that, she thought. *Of course, that poor shmuck was hardly up to our weight, to begin with, but Gohr was certainly right about how many broadsides it would take to blow him out of space.*

"I'm pleased you approve," Oversteegen murmured, and Watson's startlingly light-blue eyes glinted with amusement. The captain was glad to see it. The exec had been critically wounded at Tiberian, and he'd frankly doubted, at first, that Lieutenant Commander Westman, the ship's surgeon, would be able to save her. Even though Westman had managed to pull that off, it had taken even longer for the Manticoran medical establishment to repair Watson than it had for the Navy to repair *Gauntlet*. They'd managed it in the end, and they'd even been able to save the exec's left leg, but Oversteegen had nursed carefully concealed concerns over how well she would actually come back. Watson had been trapped in the wreckage of *Gauntlet*'s auxiliary command deck for over forty-five minutes before the medical and rescue parties could reach her. Forty-five minutes with no anesthetic while she slowly bled to death.

Oversteegen had expected to see at least some ghosts hiding in her eyes when she returned to duty. God knew an experience like hers would have been more than enough to finish off the combat career of many an officer. But if Linda Watson was haunted by any nightmares or inner terrors, she hid them well. Well enough that not even someone like Oversteegen, who'd known her literally since the Academy, could see them.

"I'm sure you are—pleased, I mean," she told him now. "Not that it would have fazed you if I hadn't."

"Well, of course it wouldn't have," he agreed. "On the other hand, keepin' the XO happy is always high on the list of any captain with his wits about him. There are so many little ways she can make her displeasure felt if he doesn't, aren't there?"

"I'm sure I wouldn't know about that," Watson assured him.

"It's been my observation that Sphinxians, for some reason, aren't very good liars," Oversteegen told her. "Not as sophisticated as we native Manticorans, I suppose. Still, it's somethin' you might want t' work on."

"I'll bear that in mind," she promised.

"Good." He gave her the smile which she'd always thought it was a pity he was willing to show to so few people, then tossed his head in the mannerism which indicated a mental change of gears on his part.

"Now that we've disposed of the good lieutenant," he said, "and now that you've had time t' digest our mission brief, what do you think?"

"I think that, with all due respect, your esteemed relative's Government must have worked long and hard to gather so many idiots into one place," she replied, and Oversteegen barely managed to swallow his laughter. None of his other officers would have dared to express themselves quite so frankly about the High Ridge Government's shortcomings, he thought affectionately. Not even Blumenthal.

"Should I assume that you're referrin' t' the composition of the current Government's ministers, rather than t' the quality of the personnel assigned t' *Gauntlet*?" he asked after a brief pause to be sure the laughter remained swallowed.

"Oh, of course! After all, it was the Admiralty who arranged our peerless crew's roster. The Government never got a real chance to screw that bit up."

"I see." He regarded her severely. "And just which of my esteemed cousin's ministers provoked that comment?"

"All of them," she said bluntly. "In this case, however, I'll admit that I was thinking particularly of Descroix and Janacek. She obviously doesn't have the least damned clue of how rickety a handbasket our relations with Erewhon are already in, and Janacek is cheerfully helping her push them the rest of the way to Hell." She shook her head. "Frankly, your cousin is completely tone deaf when it comes to diplomacy, and picking someone like Descroix as Foreign Secretary only made it worse."

"Scarcely the proper way for a servin' officer t' describe her political superiors," Oversteegen observed dryly, and she snorted.

"Tell me you approve of our current policy—naval or diplomatic," she challenged, and he shrugged.

"Of course I do. On the other hand, I believe I just mentioned how much better we native Manticorans are at lyin', didn't I?"

"Yes, I believe you did," she agreed. Then she leaned forward slightly in her chair, and her expression grew more serious.

"All kidding aside, Michael," she said, allowing herself to use his given name, since no one else was present to hear it, "we ought to be moving Heaven and Earth to get back onto the Erewhonese's good side, and you know it. We've managed to piss off effectively every other member of the Manticoran Alliance over the last couple of T-years, and Erewhon is probably the only one of them who's madder at us than *Grayson* is! But does anyone in the Government seem even remotely aware of that? If they were, they'd have sent at least an SD(P) division out here to show the flag—and a little respect—instead of a single heavy cruiser. And they'd have replaced Fraser as Ambassador long before this!"

"I might point out that Countess Fraser is another of my apparently endless supply of cousins," Oversteegen said.

"Is she?" Watson grimaced. "Well, I stand by my original opinion. I suppose every family has to have its share of idiots."

"True. It's just my misfortune that at the moment a majority of my family's idiots appear t' have found their ways into positions of power."

"Maybe. But to be fair to Descroix, I think she may actually have made a fairly accurate estimate of Fraser's abilities. Which only makes the fact that she's assigned her to Erewhon an even worse indictment of the Government's failure to grasp just how bad the situation out here is. Obviously, Descroix figures this is a sufficiently unimportant slot that she can use it to find makework for a well-connected total incompetent."

"And Cousin High Ridge agrees with her," Oversteegen acknowledged.

"What bothers me the most about this entire situation from our own selfish perspective," Watson said, "is the fact that we're going to be expected to back Fraser up as the Star Kingdom's official representative and spokesperson. And, frankly, you aren't going to be in as strong a position to . . . help shape her policy as someone with flag rank would. Which means we're likely to find ourselves with no choice but to help her make things still worse if—or when—something goes wrong. And you know as well as I do, that *something* always goes wrong. And that the Foreign Office always blames the Navy when it does."

"Accordin' t' Admiral Draskovic, I'm the senior officer in Erewhon," Oversteegen pointed out. "And accordin' t' regulations, the SO is required t' *coordinate* with Her Majesty's ambassador. Doesn't say anythin' about whether or not the SO in question is an admiral of the green or an ensign."

"Oh, that will make things ever so much better!" Watson snorted again, harder. "I know you, Michael Oversteegen. The only thing I haven't figured out is how in the universe Janacek and the Prime Minister have failed to realize just how stupid you think their policies are."

"I must have forgotten somehow t' send them the memo," Oversteegen said. "Although, t' be totally honest, Linda, I don't have any fundamental quarrel with their basic domestic objective."

She looked at him with something like incredulity, and he shook his head.

"I said their *basic* domestic objective. Which, boiled down t' the bare bones is t' preserve the House of Lords' current constitutional position. In that respect, I am a Conservative, after all." He grinned at her expression, then sobered. "It's the way they're tryin' t' *accomplish* that objective that I disagree with. Well, that and the outright graft and corruption they're willing t' accept or even encourage along the way. However important preservin' the existin' constitutional balance of power may be, the Government's overridin' responsibility—both morally and pragmatically speakin'—has t' be t' preserve the entire Star Kingdom and its citizens, first. And I'd like t' think that we could do the job with a modicum of integrity, as well."

Watson regarded him across his desk for a few seconds. She'd always known that, despite all of his sophistication and deliberately affected world-weary cynicism, there was more than a trace of a romantic idealist hiding inside Michael Oversteegen. She knew how intensely irritating his mannerisms could be—they'd irritated *her*, often enough, and she knew him far better than most ever would—yet behind them was a man who truly believed that the privileges of aristocratic power carried with them responsibility. It was that belief which had sent him into the Queen's uniform so many years before, and somehow it still survived, despite his proximity by birth and blood to powermongers like High Ridge. And someday, she feared, despite that same proximity, his belief that duty overrode self-preservation and responsibility overrode pragmatism would destroy his career. The ensuing brouhaha was also likely to splash onto his senior officers, of course, but—

Well, if it does, I could be in worse company, she thought.

"I'm not too sure that 'integrity' is a word I'd associate with Countess Fraser," she said aloud. "Which brings me back to your original question about our mission brief. I think this has the potential to be a very rocky deployment—from a lot of perspectives. To be honest, though, I don't see much we can do to prepare for any potential diplomatic furor. So I suppose we should be concentrating on more pragmatic problems."

"Agreed. Obviously, our primary mission is goin' t' be t' show the flag, but as part of that, I'll want us t' do all we can t' repair our relationship with the Erewhonese navy. Or t' minimize additional damage, at least. Since *Gauntlet* seems t' enjoy a certain reputation as a result of our endeavors at Tiberian, let's plan on takin' advantage of that. I want a full round of port visits and mess invitations laid on. And I want all of our people—enlisted, as well as commissioned—t' be well aware that I will . . . take it amiss if they should happen t' do anythin' t' *exacerbate* the situation."

"Oh, I think I can take care of that, Sir," Watson assured him.

"My confidence in you is boundless. In addition, however, let's not forget *Gauntlet* is a Queen's ship. We may be the only Manticoran vessel in Erewhonese space, but that makes it more likely, not less, that when something finally goes wrong, we're goin' t' find ourselves in it, right up t' our necks. So I want t' continue our drill schedule as we'd previously discussed. But I'd also like t' add a bit more emphasis on less conventional operations. In particular, I think we need t' be thinkin' in terms of the police function."

"Of course, Sir," Watson said when he paused, but she was a bit puzzled. Obviously they needed to concern themselves with the police function—that was the entire reason they were here in what was ostensibly, at least, peacetime.

"I mean," he clarified, "that I want Major Hill t' be thinkin' in terms of more than routine customs boardin' details. And," his eyes sharpened, "I particularly want us t' develop our own contacts—on every level possible—instead of relyin' solely on the intelligence input of our Embassy. Whatever ONI may think, there's somethin' very peculiar goin' on out here, Linda. It may be that swattin' those 'pirate cruisers' put an end t' it, but somehow, I don't think so. And, like you, I don't have the most lively respect in the universe for Countess Fraser or the sorts of intelligence appreciations someone like her is likely t' be encouragin' her people t' put together."

"I see," she said, and nodded. "I'll sit down with Hill to discuss that ASAP. And I'll see if I can't involve Lieutenant Gohr in the conversation, as well."

"Good, Linda. I knew I could rely on you," he murmured.

CHAPTER 11

"THIS IS A *FUNERAL*?" BERRY ASKED DUBIOUSLY. "If I didn't know better, I'd think it was a carnival."

"It is, in a way," Anton replied, his eyes slowly scanning the huge crowd. "It's been months since Stein died, so even his family has had time to work through most of the grief. Now . . ."

"It's time to do business," concluded Ruth. "I imagine that's what Stein would have wanted himself, when you get right down to it."

Anton nodded. "Milk it for all it's worth. Whether or not Stein was a saint, I'll leave for others to decide. What I know for sure is that the man was a slick politician and a superb showman." He glanced up at the ceiling far above and smiled. "He'd have loved it. A big top and everything."

Berry was scrutinizing the ceiling herself. "Did they really use to make these things out of cloth?"

"They did, indeed, if you go back far enough. Circuses are an ancient form of entertainment, you know. Nowadays, we put up temporary edifices like this using contra grav instead of tent poles, but the original 'big tops' were just gigantic tents, essentially."

Berry was still dubious. "How did they hold up the trapezes and highwires and stuff?" She paused for a moment, watching an acrobat making his way gingerly across a highwire suspended far above. "And how would you even use them anyway, back in the days before contragravity?"

Anton told her. Her eyes grew very wide.

"That's *sick*."

He shrugged. "People still gawk at accidents, you know. And speaking of gawking, I think we've done enough." He nodded toward a cluster of people gathered on a large dais across the crowded floor. "It's time to pay our respects."

Berry and Ruth immediately sidled behind him. A moment later, so did Web Du Havel. "You lead the way," commanded his daughter.

"You're the widest. Besides, your best scowl will probably part most of the crowd all by itself."

Zilwicki looked back at the soldiers from the Queen's Own, momentarily tempted to order *them* to clear a path. But he dismissed the idea immediately. Lieutenant Griggs' squad wasn't even paying attention to him, their eyes continually scanning the crowd looking for threats. They were charged with guarding the princess—which they couldn't do marching ahead of her.

No help for it, then. Anton scowled. Three people standing near him edged away. "How come I *always* get the Moses assignment?"

From a different edge of the mob, Victor and Ginny were facing the same problem.

More precisely, Victor was.

"I still think you'd do better at this," he groused, trying to nudge someone else aside without precipitating an actual brawl.

"Don't be silly," countered Ginny, pressed close against his back. "I'm way too small and—more to the point—my outfit's way too demure. If you'd let me wear the sari I *wanted* to wear—"

"We'd have both gotten arrested—you for soliciting and me for being a pimp." His scowl bid fair to rival Anton's. "In that outfit, you don't have to say a word and you're being obscene."

"Oh, pfui." Victor jumped a little as Ginny tickled him. "You're just a hopeless prude. Back in the Solarian League, that outfit barely gets a glance. Well, maybe two."

With a deft maneuver, Victor managed to get them past a small clump of people chattering away. Another few meters forward.

"And you're so *good* at this, anyway. I'll make sure to tell Kevin so he can add that to your dossier."

"Thanks a lot, Ginny. Thank you so very much."

"Thank God we got here early," whispered Naomi to her uncle, leaning over in her chair to do so. "I'd hate to be fighting my way through that mob to greet the royal family, instead of already being here on the dais."

Walter Imbesi let no trace of humor show on his solemn face, when he whispered back. "Gives you a whole different perspective on Brownian motion, doesn't it? But *do* try to keep the witticisms under control, if you would." He made a miniscule nod in the direction of Jessica Stein and her entourage. "I don't think they'd much appreciate being referred to as the 'royal family.'"

His niece didn't have quite the degree of control Walter did, so a faint trace of distaste was evident on her face. Evident, at least, to someone who knew her well.

"I'm sure they wouldn't, the damn poseurs. Hieronymus Stein may have been a modest saint and an ascetic—I have my doubts, but I admit I'm something of a cynic—but his daughter bears no resemblance to that description." She cast a quick glance at the woman in question and the people around her. "Much less her hangers-on."

"Be charitable, Naomi. They've been patient a long time."

"No credit to them. As long as Stein was alive, they *had* to be patient. Now . . ." She cast another glance, this time at a man leaning over and exchanging some witticism with Jessica Stein. "I don't *like* him. Even less than I like her."

Imbesi's shrug was as minimalist a gesture as his nod had been. "Neither do I. In fact, since I know a lot more about the man than you do, I'm sure I like him a lot less. But whether you or I like him is neither here nor there. Ingemar Cassetti is the right-hand man of the governor of the nearest Solarian League sector province. That makes him just another rock we've got to deal with."

"Poor little Erewhon. 'Between a rock and a hard place,' except we've got so *many* rocks."

Again, Imbesi made that little nod. "Many indeed. With Manticore's current government as the hard place allotted to us by the Lord Almighty, for whatever inscrutable reasons He might have."

He would have sighed, except that Walter Imbesi hadn't sighed in public since he was eight years old. The thrashing he'd received from his father afterward had made sure of that. The informal regimen which the youngsters of Erewhon's central families underwent was severe, for all that it wasn't concerned with the trivial matters that obsessed most of the galaxy's elites.

Sexual mores being one such triviality, as Naomi immediately demonstrated.

"So which one of these clowns do you want me to seduce?" she asked. The very faint smile on her face indicated that the question was asked partly in jest.

Partly.

"I assume your normal rules apply?"

"They certainly do. Rocks and a hard place or not, Erewhon isn't *that* desperate. I don't insist on Adonis or Venus, but the seducee has to have *some* appeal to me."

Imbesi allowed himself a little smile. Naomi's free-wheeling ways tended to irk most members of the family, but he was not one of them. Possibly that was because he was the recognized head of the family, and couldn't afford to overlook any asset. "In that case, I suspect you'll be enjoying—or not—a very chaste funeral. If there's any man here worth seducing that you'd *like* to sleep with, I can't think of who it might be. Nor any woman, for that matter."

Naomi's eyes wandered for a moment. Seeing the direction of her gaze, Imbesi gave his niece a very curtailed—but very abrupt—shake of his head.

"Whatever you do, girl, stay the hell away from Luiz Rozsak. I don't care how pretty he is. You might as well bed with a cobra."

Naomi's eyes widened just a bit. "That seems a little rough, Uncle. My impression is that he's less vile—quite a bit less, in fact—than the rest of that Solarian crowd."

"Who said anything about 'vile'? Cobras aren't vile. They're just deadly." All trace of banter left his voice. "Just take my word for it, young lady. Stay away from Luiz Rozsak. That's an order."

"Okay, okay. You don't have to go all *paterfamilias* on me about it."

Her eyes moved slowly across the rest of the small crowd assembled on the dais, narrowing as they went. "Yuck. I think you're right. I may as well enter a nunnery now and be done with it."

A little motion off to the side—an eddy in the mob surrounding the dais—drew her eyes in that direction. The eyes began to widen again. Then another eddy, almost on the opposite side, drew her gaze that way.

"But what's this? *Two* very interesting looking gentlemen, all of a sudden. Please, Uncle—don't tell me they're out of bounds also."

Imbesi looked one way, then the other. This time, he really had to struggle to keep from smiling. From grinning outright, in fact.

"Good luck, you vamp. To the left, you see Anton Zilwicki, formerly a captain in the Manticoran Navy. I'll admit you're way better looking than his girlfriend—a lot younger, too—but your entire savings wouldn't match her pocket change. Besides, he's supposed to be fidelity incarnate, according to all reports."

His eyes moved in the other direction and narrowed a little. "On the other side . . . Hm. Not sure. The name's Victor Cachat, and we don't know much about him. He's evidently the favored special agent of Haven's director of their federal police force. That's Kevin Usher, which means Cachat must be awfully good to have his approval, as young as he is. On the other hand—"

He didn't need to finish the caveat. Naomi had already caught sight of the woman following Cachat. Following him very closely indeed.

"Oh, life is so unfair. How am I supposed to compete with *that*?"

Imbesi started to make a quip in response, but the witticism died a-borning. Now that he thought about it . . .

"Kevin Usher is *really* good, Naomi."

He spoke even more softly than before, even though Walter had great confidence that the scrambling devices he and Naomi were wearing made their conversation impossible to pick up beyond a range of one meter. Nor did he think that any of the forces gathered at that public event were all that interested in the doings of the Imbesi family. Certainly not interested enough to have focused very rare and expensive spying equipment on them.

The Imbesis were officially part of the Erewhonese political opposition, not one of the families represented in the existing government. To almost all non-Erewhonese, that made them not much of a factor in the political equation. The informal methods by which Erewhon's dominant families governed were simply too alien to other polities which lacked Erewhon's history and traditions. Not so much because it was informal—the croneyism of the Solarian League's elites was notorious, after all—but because it was *honorable.* True enough, Erewhon had been founded by a pack of thieves. But those thieves had become as wealthy and successful as they were because, whatever their other sins, their word had been their bond—and they'd *never* made the mistake of forgetting the ancient saw: "One day you're up, the next day you're down."

All of which meant that the families which currently ruled Erewhon were careful to retain close ties with the Imbesi family. And they made just as sure that if the Imbesis should come back into power, which was not at all unlikely, that at no point had anyone mortally offended them. Or even irritated them, for that matter. "Mortality" among Erewhonese was not an abstract concept.

Naomi was able to follow her uncle's unspoken thoughts quite well. "Enough said," she murmured. She gave Victor Cachat one last glance; just enough to make sure she'd recognize him anywhere in the crowd, but nothing more than that. Naomi wasn't quite as accomplished a seductress as she liked to think she was, but she'd long since learned the basics. And one look at that stiff young face was enough to make clear to her that seducing Victor Cachat was going to require adroitness.

"My motto. Nothing gauche."

Imbesi decided he could venture a public laugh. Too much stiffness, after all, was a mistake in its own right.

"Since when? What about that time—don't try to claim you've forgotten the pool before the statue in Sears—what I had to go through to cover *that* one up—"

"Don't you be gauche, Uncle. I was young and foolish then. Besides, I'm not drunk now—haven't touched a drop. Besides besides, this fellow is a challenge and Freddie Havlicek was just *cute.*" Firmly: "So it doesn't count."

Other Erewhonese notables sitting on the dais were not being so careful. They, too, had spotted Victor as soon as he emerged from the mob. Had spotted Ginny, more precisely, and were following her with their eyes as she approached. In the case of both the men as well as the woman, Ginny's figure had something to do with their interest. But not much, in truth. The three families which currently dominated Erewhonese politics had been trying for months to establish a private liaison with the new government of Haven, and they were all wondering if . . .

They didn't wonder for long. "That's Virginia Usher's toyboy," whispered Jack Fuentes to Alessandra Havlicek.

She maintained the usual Erewhonese sangfroid in public, but her returning whisper bore traces of scorn. "No accounting for taste, and there's the proof of it. I'd give her a lot better time than that . . . God in heaven, from the looks of him I bet he sits at attention on the toilet."

Next to her, on her other side, the third of the trio who more or less governed the planet did a fair imitation of sitting at attention himself. Tomas Hall gave a little meaningful glance at one of the Solarian officers clustered around Cassetti. Spotting the glance, the Navy lieutenant detached himself and sidled over.

With another glance, Hall led the lieutenant's gaze to Ginny and Victor. Seeing them, Lieutenant Manson's lips curled a bit with derision.

"Ha! I guess that's one way for a slut to give herself a holiday with her boyfriend. Just call it a visit to pay personal respects to a saint's memory."

"You're sure?"

Manson shrugged. Like the sneer, the gesture seemed expansive to Erewhonese. "We did some investigating of our own. Whatever Usher's skills may be—I'm not as impressed as most—they sure as hell don't extend to his personal life. His wife's been making a fool of him everywhere they go."

Hall nodded, and Manson sidled away. The lieutenant's

movements, at least, were subtle enough. To anyone watching, he would have simply been a Solarian officer exchanging a casual pleasantry with an Erewhonese notable at a public event. If nothing else, Manson was careful not to let anyone realize he was taking money from the Erewhonese on the side.

Which made the Erewhonese trust him not at all. Still—so far, at least—Manson's information had proven reliable enough.

"What do you think?" asked Fuentes softly. Like Imbesi, all three of the Erewhonese sitting together had full confidence in their scrambling equipment. But caution was a habit with them, and had been since their childhood.

"Take it at face value," stated Havlicek.

"I'm inclined to agree," said Hall. Privately, he didn't fully share Havlicek's assurance. Alessandra was normally very sharp, but her sexual orientation did sometimes lead her to hasty conclusions. In particular, he'd noticed before, she tended to resent beautiful women who were too overtly heterosexual and dismiss them as bimbos. Still . . .

He observed the none-too-subtle way Virginia Usher was casually fondling her male companion as they approached the dais. If it was an act, it was certainly a good one.

"I'm inclined to agree," he repeated. Then, and just as easily as Imbesi had done, he repressed a sigh. "Isn't there *anyone* in Haven's new government who has the brains of a termite?"

"What an idiot," hissed Henri Guthrie. Haven's ambassador to Erewhon was making no attempt to hide his glare at Virginia Usher.

"Which one?" snorted Jacqueline Pallier. "Her or her husband?"

"Both. Her for screwing around in a situation that's already messy enough—and him for being stupid enough to let her do it." Virginia Usher had now reached the steps leading onto the dais, and Guthrie looked away. He decided to pretend he hadn't noticed her, which was plausible enough given that they'd never actually met. He only knew what she looked like from holographs brought by the same courier which had brought the idiot woman. Ambassador Guthrie was *damned* if he was going to let a tramp's shenanigans get in the way of his duty.

"For God's sake," he muttered, "the Manticorans are already making a fuss over every stupid jot and tittle of everything we do. Let them get word that the wife of *Kevin Usher* is here . . ."

Pallier shrugged. "I think you're worrying too much. First, because the Manticoran staff here are dimbulbs; second, because even dimbulbs can figure out that there's nothing more involved here than an old whore proving she can't learn any new tricks."

"I see Lieutenant Manson is up to his tricks again," murmured Rozsak. The captain had just casually detached himself and Habib from the crowd gathered around Jessica Stein.

"Yeah, I noticed," said Habib sourly. The commander was making no particular effort to speak softly. Habib had great confidence in the scrambling equipment she and Rozsak were carrying, since it was the very best available in the Solarian League. It was probably even as good as anything Manticore could produce.

"You want me to finally lower the boom? It'd be my pleasure, believe me."

Rozsak shook his head. "No, no. There's bound to be a treacherous little grifter somewhere in our midst. As long as we know who it is, we can control the damage—even take advantage of it. What I'm wondering is why the Erewhonese are so interested in Virginia Usher?"

"We already went over that, Luiz. At this point, I think they'd grab any straw Haven tossed their way. Although describing Usher's wife as a 'straw' is probably an insult to honest straw."

Again, Rozsak shook his head. "I think we're jumping to conclusions. Now that I've actually seen him in the flesh."

Habib frowned. "What 'him'?"

Somehow, without either looking in their direction or making any sign toward them, Rozsak made clear he was talking about Virginia Usher and her companion. "The boyfriend, Edie. The *so-called* 'boyfriend,' rather. When you get a chance—not now—take a really close look at him. That kid's a young wolf if I ever saw one, not a gigolo."

Habib didn't have Rozsak's skills at this miserably non-military "special ops" work, but she was neither stupid nor slow. So, she didn't so much as glance at the couple now climbing onto the dais. Her frown simply deepened as she tried to remember what little she'd seen of the young FIA officer's face.

"Can't remember," she confessed. "I'll give him a look-see later, once the festivities get rolling. Is there anything you want me to do in the meantime?"

Rozsak hesitated for a moment. Then: "Yes. Tell Lieutenant Palane to sidle over to me. Make sure she understands to keep it all casual."

✧ ✧ ✧

"You wanted to speak to me, Sir?"

Rozsak was impressed by the lieutenant's subtlety. Most young officers, told to "appear casual," would have erred on the side of exaggeration. Thandi Palane, on the other hand, managed to make it all seem genuinely casual—as if she'd just bumped into her commander by happenstance and was making idle chitchat at a social gathering.

He'd always known Ndebele was a hellhole, even by OFS standards. The young woman's ease with subterfuge, he suspected, was one of the side effects.

"I want to ask you to do something, Thandi, but before I start let me make clear that this is entirely voluntary. If you find it distasteful, just say so. I won't hold it against you in any way. That's a promise."

The tall young officer gazed down at him for a moment. Then, not quite able to suppress a sigh, looked away.

"The answer's 'yes,' Captain, whatever it is. I can guess. I just wish—" She gave her head a little shake. "Never mind."

When she turned her head back to face him, her expression was composed. "What is it, Sir? Or 'who' is it, I suppose I should say."

He gaze her a wry little smile. "If I've never mentioned before that I think you're smart as a whip, Lieutenant Palane, let me correct the oversight here and now." He made a little nod in the direction of the couple now chatting with Jessica Stein.

"Him. The young man accompanying Virginia Usher."

Palane gave the man in question a quick glance. "Tough looking little bastard," she murmured.

"I'm not asking you to sleep with him, Thandi. Do or don't, that's entirely your business. If you don't feel like it, then don't. What I want to know is simply whether you *could*."

She seemed a bit startled. "What—"

"Let's just say we're testing a cover story, how's that?"

Palane gave the couple in question another glance. A longer one, this time, since it was clear neither of them was looking her way. Certainly long enough not to miss the way the woman was stroking the young man's back.

"Word is that he's her toyboy. Find out for me if it's true."

Thandi's eyes widened. Then, for the first time since the conversation began, her expression grew humorous.

"Oh, bullshit. Pardon my language, Sir. Except for the complexion and features, that—what'd I call him?—tough-looking little bastard might have come right off the streets of Mzilikazi. And no helot, either. The kind of guy nobody in their right mind plays games with, no matter how much bigger they are."

She gave the tough-looking little bastard another glance. This one was definitely longer and more lingering. Then, her quick gleaming smile appeared.

"Sure, Captain. Be my pleasure."

After she left, the captain gave the man in question a lingering glance of his own. One of envy, in his case.

"Discipline, Rozsak," he muttered to himself. "The sacrifices of command, and all that."

He made no attempt to suppress his own sigh. Like Habib, he had full confidence in his scrambling equipment.

CHAPTER 12

THERE WAS SOMETHING VAGUELY UNPLEASANT about Jessica Stein. Anton wasn't quite sure what it was. Some of his reaction, he was sure, was simply due to the people who surrounded her. Stein's own coterie of Renaissance Association leaders were no more repellent than such people ever were: self-righteousness and moral loftiness serving as a none-too-thick patina over ambition. But the Solarian who made it a point to stay at her elbow the entire time set Anton's teeth on edge.

Not that the man wasn't polite and cordial. Anton was quite certain that no one had ever accused Lieutenant Governor Cassetti of being crude or uncouth. But since the same could be said for any suave reptile, Anton was not impressed. And, in Ingemar Cassetti's case, he knew more than enough about the man to be certain that his emotional reaction was well founded.

Still, there was also something about Stein herself that made Anton uneasy. Perhaps it was the subtle sense that her grief at her father's death was more than offset by the elation of newfound power and influence. Jessica Stein wasn't *simply* the daughter; for at least twenty years, she'd served as Hieronymus Stein's closest aide and confidante. Now that the founder of the RA was gone, she'd quickly and surely seized the mantle of leadership.

And . . .

Anton had a pretty good idea where she intended to go with that new authority. Whatever doubts he might have had were dispelled by seeing the obvious rapport between Jessica Stein and Ingemar Cassetti. The Renaissance Association, for years, had been riven by an internal faction fight which was none the less savage for all that it had been conducted without violence. It could be described, loosely, as a quarrel between doves and hawks—or, perhaps more accurately, between those people who preferred a long, patient, educational and moral campaign to transform all of Solarian society, versus those who looked to settle for something less sweeping but faster and surer. Soft and slow, versus quick and hard.

The most obvious route for such a "quick and hard" campaign to take was for the RA to gain the support—and return it in kind—from one of the Solarian League's powerful sector governors. *Voila . . .*

Ingemar Cassetti, political hatchet-man for one Oravil Barregos, governor of the smallish but highly industrialized and wealthy Maya Sector. And also one of the sector governors more famous than most—less infamous, it might be better to say—for his comparatively high ethical standards and lack of venality. Of all the sector governors of the Solarian League, Barregos had been the friendliest toward the Renaissance League and at least paid lip service to the RA's program, the so-called "Six Pillars."

With how much sincerity, of course, remained open to question. Anton was quite sure that Barregos had little if any use for the first through the third of the Six Pillars: the RA's calls for a genuinely federal structure to the Solarian League's government, anti-trust legislation, and the establishment of mass-based organs for popular control of the bureaucracy. His appointment of Cassetti as his lieutenant governor said quite a lot about his own ambitions, and a man of his stripe was unlikely to genuinely favor anything which would have reduced his own power. On the other hand, he probably was favorably inclined toward the other three pillars: the removal of all grades of citizenship, abolition of the Office of Frontier Security, and the eradication of genetic slavery.

The Maya Sector was an anomaly in the Solarian League. The sector's central planet of Smoking Frog was as highly industrialized and economically advanced as any in the galaxy, and most of its other settled worlds not much less so. From the standpoint of its social structure, the sector resembled the autonomous inner worlds of the League rather than the outer colonies. It had little in common with most of the sectors still under the control of governors appointed by the Office of Frontier Security. For the Maya Sector, the harsh social stratification which characterized most of the League outside of the inner worlds was neither necessary nor economically advantageous—and the political restrictions were extremely irksome.

Despite having been originally appointed by the OFS, for a number of years now Governor Barregos had been championing the growing demand for a change in Maya Sector's status. The OFS had resisted that demand with its usual heavy-handedness—but had not (so far, at least) quite dared to remove the very popular governor. Doing so might possibly trigger off an outright revolt. And while the OFS normally didn't worry about provincial rebellions, because the backward planets where they usually occurred could be easily suppressed, a revolt in the Maya Sector could be . . .

Dangerous. Unless the revolt was crushed quickly, Smoking Frog alone had enough resources to create a fairly impressive naval force. Not one which could possibly stand off a fully mobilized Solarian League Navy, but a powerful enough one to raise such a ruckus as to draw the spotlight of Solarian League public attention onto the policies of the OFS which had led to such a fiasco.

By its nature, the OFS was a nocturnal predator. The last thing the bureaucrats who ran it wanted—much less the commercial combines who were their unofficial partners—was to be examined in the light of day.

So, Barregos stayed; so, the demand for independent status for Maya kept growing; so, the OFS kept reacting like a Mesozoic dinosaur. It was a situation which reminded Anton of water coming to boil in a pressure cooker.

As he'd been ruminating, the steady stream of visitors come to pay their official respects had gently but steadily pushed him toward the edge of the dais after he'd presented his own respects. Now that they were out of hearing range of Jessica Stein and her inner circle, Ruth put into words what Anton was thinking.

"Sun Yat-sen is dead. Long live Chiang Kai-shek."

Anton was startled. He hadn't expected that kind of sophisticated historical knowledge from such a young woman. Once again, he reminded himself not to underestimate the Princess.

Du Havel was nodding. "Like all historical analogies," he said, "you can't push it too far. But . . . yes. That's about what I was thinking myself, although I was reminded more of India's history. Gandhi and what followed. But the Kuomintang's a good analogy too. Maybe a better one, in fact. Like the RA, the KMT started off as a society of idealists. And then, after Sun Yat-sen died, became essentially a front group for warlords. Within a generation, it was every bit as brutal and corrupt as the imperial mandarinate—and a whole lot less educated."

Anton started to add something; but, sensing the presence of an approaching person, broke off and glanced up. And froze.

Froze so abruptly, in fact, that both Berry and Ruth bumped

into him. Curious, the two girls peered around his shoulders at the odd apparition who'd caused this highly unusual state of affairs. Captain Zilwicki, to put it mildly, was not known for being easily taken aback.

The young man standing in front of Anton cleared his throat. "Good evening, Captain Zilwicki. I hadn't expected to meet you here."

Anton's throat-clearing was a lot noisier. "Good evening, Citiz—ah . . . what *is* your title these days?"

The smile on the young man's face was much like the face itself: on the square side, a bit gaunt, and mostly made up of angles and edges. "Just 'Special Officer Cachat,'" he said. "I'm no longer in the, ah, foreign security side of things. These days I'm a cop instead of a spy."

Anton's self-possession was back. "I see. Usher took you along with him, then."

Cachat nodded. "But I'm forgetting my manners. Ginny—" The young Havenite officer turned half around and more or less hauled a shortish woman away from her conversation with one of the guests. "Captain Zilwicki, may I present Virginia Usher, the wife of our new director of the Federal Investigation Agency. Virginia, Captain Anton Zilwicki, formerly of the Royal Manticoran Navy."

The woman in question was shapely, beautiful, and possessed of a smile that was even more dazzling than her costume.

"Oh, Victor!" she laughed, extending her hand to Anton. "I'm quite sure Captain Zilwicki knows exactly who I am. Even if I did manage to stay out of his sight while we were all having our little adventure on Terra."

The last remark caused Berry and Ruth's eyes to widen.

"Oh!" Berry gasped, staring at Cachat. "*You're the one*—"

She broke off, fumbling for the words. Anton, despite the fact that most of his brain was simultaneously cursing fate and listening to alarm bells going off, decided that straight-forwardness was called for.

"Yes, he's the one. Saved my daughter Helen's life—and Berry's, most likely." He gave Cachat a deep nod, almost a bow. "I never really had the chance to thank you properly at the time. Please allow me to do so now."

Cachat looked uncomfortable. Virginia Usher laughed again. "Look at him blush! It still amazes me, as many times as I've seen it. S'about the only thing Victor does that makes him look his age instead of"—here she poked his rib cage playfully with a finger—"a crazed cold-blooded assassin."

Now, Victor's expression was pained. "Ginny, 'crazed cold-blooded assassin' is the silliest oxymoron I've ever heard."

"Nonsense!" She grinned at Anton. "You were *there,* Captain. So what's *your* opinion?"

For a moment, Anton's memory flashed back to a weirdly lit grotto in the subterranean depths beneath Chicago's ancient ruins. He'd come to the scene just a bit too late to witness it himself, but Jeremy X had described it to him afterward. Seeing the carnage, Anton had had no difficulty believing him. The way a young State Security officer named Victor Cachat, driven by a semi-madness Anton thought he could understand—more or less—had stood his ground at point blank range and methodically slaughtered a dozen Scrags and StateSec goons hunting Anton's daughter Helen. It had been a sheerly suicidal act on Cachat's part; even if, amazingly enough, Cachat had come out at the end covered with blood and gore—none of which was his.

"Victor Cachat is not an assassin," he said abruptly. "Of that, I'm as sure as anything. On the other hand . . ."

He shrugged. "Sorry, Special Officer Cachat. I think if there's anyone who's ever done something simultaneously cold-blooded and crazy, it's you. Oxymoron or not."

"See?" demanded Virginia triumphantly. She wagged a finger in front of Cachat's nose. "And you won't find a more expert opinion than Captain Zilwicki's, let me tell you! Speaking of which—"

In that quick and indescribably charming way the woman had about her, Virginia was now facing Anton again. The grin was as infectious as ever.

"—what are you doing here, Captain? I mean, besides pretending to be paying your respects to the not-so-grieving daughter, like we're pretending to be doing."

"Ginny!" Cachat choked.

"Oh, pfui. Captain Zilwicki is *certainly* not going to believe our cover story—what a ridiculous notion—so why bother with the rigmarole? We're here on some kind of desperate and dangerous secret mission—when are you going to tell me what it is, anyway?—and you can be sure the Captain is doing the same." She bestowed a look of great sympathy on Ruth and Berry. "I'm sure he hasn't told you either. Aren't men a pain in the butt?"

Berry and Ruth made little sounds that bore a suspicious resemblance to suppressed laughter. Anton scowled. Tried to, anyway; he was fighting down a laugh himself. He started to make noises about loose lips in public places but Usher's wife drove right over it.

"Oh, don't be silly. Manticoran scrambling equipment is the best in the galaxy, like almost all your electronics. That's why Victor and I are wearing it ourselves. My husband—bless the man—swiped it somewhere or other."

Finally, she fell silent, just gazing up at Anton and smiling cheerfully. Still waiting for the answer.

He couldn't stop a laugh from coming out. "Damnation, Ms. Usher—"

"Call me Ginny."

"Ginny, then. Manticore and Haven are still officially at war. So I am *not* going to tell the wife of the Republic of Haven's chief of police what my secret mission is." He cleared his throat again, noisily; and sounding, even to himself, like an idiot. "*If* I were on a secret mission in the first place. Which I'm not, much less a desperate and dangerous one."

He placed a fatherly hand on each of the girl's shoulders. "Would I have brought my own daughter and one of the royal princesses with me if I were?"

"Sure," came the instant response. "Makes a great cover." Again, her lithe finger flew to Cachat's rib cage; tickling him, this time. "Just like me and Victor are pretending to be hot and heavy lovers. Works like a charm."

Cachat tried to fend off the finger. For a moment, he and Anton exchanged a look of sheer sympathy. Then, failing to see any other workable tactic, Anton fell back on pell-mell retreat.

"'Fraid it's past the girls' bedtime." Ruth and Berry scowled. "Okay, then—it's past *my* bedtime. We gotta go. Nice meeting you again, Special Offi—ah, Victor. And you too, Ms. Ush—ah, Ginny. S'been a pleasure, really has."

Once they got outside, Berry started laughing aloud. So did Du Havel. "I don't think I've *ever* seen you move that fast, Daddy."

"That woman makes my bones ache," rumbled Anton.

Berry cast a glance back at the big top. "Well, what do you think? Is she telling the truth, or is she making Victor Cachat's bones ache? With her energy, I bet a man would be doing well to get out of bed alive."

Anton took a slow breath. He'd been wondering that himself, with part of his mind.

Again, Ruth gave voice to his own tentative estimate.

"No. She's telling the truth. Those rumors about her and her so-called 'lover' are so widespread that someone *has* to be spreading them on purpose. We've only just gotten here, and I've already overheard it from three separate sources. Not even gossip's that fast—and nasty little minds are too lazy to be that systematic."

Anton nodded. "What I think, too. Besides—"

He broke off and gave Ruth a sharp look. "You *are* good at this, young lady. So let's see how good. What's the *other* reason the rumors don't make a lot of sense?"

Princess Ruth's eyes narrowed and her lips pursed a little with thought. "Well . . . I'm not sure, because I don't know enough about Usher. But if he's as sharp as he's supposed to be . . ."

"He is," said Anton. "On Terra, he managed—well, never mind. Just take it as good coin that Kevin Usher ranks at the top in this screwy trade."

"Okay, then. The *other* reason it doesn't make sense is because there's no way Usher wouldn't know that his wife is cheating on him. Which leaves us with only two options: It isn't happening at all, or he's got exotic tastes when it comes to sex. Voyeurism, whatever." She shrugged. "That last is always possible, of course, but if so—why wouldn't he take advantage of it for professional reasons, since it doesn't bother him emotionally? If he's really that smart, that is."

"Dead on the money," said Anton softly. "Dead on the money. So what *is* their desperate and dangerous secret mission here on Erewhon?"

He and Ruth exchanged a knowing look. Berry made a face. "Why do I feel like the only dimwit in the crowd?" she complained.

"Don't feel bad," Du Havel said, smiling. "I don't understand what they're smirking about, either—and I've got the Nobel-Shakhra Prize, which says I'm supposed to be a genius at political theory."

Ruth gave her a serene smile. "S'okay, Berry. You're just not nasty-minded, that's all. And Web doesn't know the particulars. But I've got to tell you that for those of us who are and do, the answer is a no-brainer."

"A real 'duh,' " agreed Anton sourly. "High Ridge's arrogant policies toward Manticore's allies have aggravated all of them. Erewhon probably more than any besides Grayson—and the Erewhonese have a long history of practicing what used to be called *Realpolitik*. So, to cut to the heart of it, Victor Cachat—Usher's wife, too, I don't believe for a minute she's in the dark—are here to play the devil's advocate."

He sighed. "Tomorrow I'll go and try to talk to our Ambassador here." He sighed again, more heavily. "And when she fails to pay any attention, I'll waste my time talking to the chief of station of the SIS."

"That's Countess Fraser and Charles Wrangel you're talking about," said Ruth. "Waste of your time."

Anton nodded. "Fraser and Wrangel, versus Cachat and Usher. Talk about a mismatch."

"Well, look on the bright side," pointed out Berry cheerily. "At least Ms. Usher—Ginny, I mean, and boy did I really like *her*—got one thing wrong. *We're* not here on any secret and desperate and dangerous mission."

They'd reached the outskirts of the immediate area around the big top, by now. The lighting here, in what amounted to a huge impromptu parking lot in a field somewhere just outside Maytag's city limits, was noticeably dimmer. In response, the soldiers from the Queen's Own had moved closer—and now, seeing a man appear out of the darkness, moved closer still.

The man spread his hands a little, just a subtle motion to demonstrate that he was unarmed. That, and the Solarian League Navy uniform he was wearing caused the guards to relax a little.

"Captain Zilwicki," he said, in a soft and pleasant voice. "Lieutenant Manson here, attached to Captain Rozsak's staff. I wonder if I might have a word with you in private?"

"Why do I feel like I'm on the verge of a nightmare?" Anton muttered under his breath.

But all he said aloud was: "Certainly, Lieutenant. Web, Berry, Princess Ruth"—deliberately nodding to the wrong girl each time he addressed them—"please wait here for a moment."

When Anton re-emerged from the shadows, he forestalled Ruth's question with: "Later."

CHAPTER 13

ALTHOUGH HE HAD NO WAY OF COMPARING notes with him, Victor Cachat's reaction to Jessica Stein was about the same as Anton Zilwicki's.

"Something about that woman gives me the creeps," he muttered to Ginny, after they'd presented their respects to The Grieving Daughter and Close Associates of the Martyred One, and quietly eased themselves off the dais.

"What was it, exactly?" chuckled Ginny. "The way she gauged the political value of our respects in an eyeblink, down to the last millimeter? The way she brushed us off not a nanosecond too late? The way she fawned all over Cassetti's not-so-witticisms? Or is just the fact that when she laughs at his stupid jokes her front teeth are too big?"

Ginny took Victor by the elbow and steered him firmly toward an approaching robotray. "I need a drink. Me, it was her sandals did it. Call me old-fashioned if you will, but I do not think high-heeled sandals are proper attire for a funeral."

Victor glanced down at Ginny's feet. "And what do you call *those* things?"

"I'm not the grieving daughter," Ginny responded firmly, snatching two cocktails from the passing robotray and handing one to Victor. "Here, try this. I have no idea what it is, but it's bound to be bad for you."

Dubiously, Victor tried the beverage. "Yuck. Tastes like—"

"Alcohol. Of course. What it is, mostly. You don't like *any* drinks, Victor, except that Nouveau Paris slum-brewery so-called ale you and Kevin swill down. How do you expect to be a galaxy-famous great spy if you don't pick up a little suave along the way?"

Victor took a second gingerly sip. "First, 'galaxy-famous great spy' is another oxymoron. Great spies are never famous. Second, I'm not a spy anyway. I'm a cop these days, remember?"

"Victor, give it a generation or so, and the distinction between 'spy' and 'cop' may mean something in the Republic of Haven. Today, it's like insisting on the difference between a mutt and a mongrel."

"Don't ever let President Pritchart hear you say that." Victor held the cocktail further away, as if it contained some toxic substance. "This stuff is really bad, whatever it is. Is there somewhere I can dump it without being crass?"

The last two sentences had been spoken a bit loudly. To his surprise, a voice came in from over his left shoulder.

"Sure. Give it to me." A moment later, a female arm appeared and deftly removed the glass from his hand. The arm was bare, lightly freckled, and quite nicely formed if a bit on the plump side. The hand attached to it, likewise.

Victor turned and saw a young woman smiling at him. Her face was of a piece with the arm and hand: pretty, in a slightly full and snub-nosed way; green-eyed; coppery-haired; peaches-and-cream complexion; and with a very appealing sprinkle of freckles across the cheeks and bridge of the nose.

In another deft motion, the woman drained the glass.

"Yuck. This is that godawful crap they concocted as a 'special punch' for the festivities—uh, sorry, solemn occasion. I think they even had the nerve to call it a 'Stein memorial martini,' which'd have Stein spinning in his grave if he had one, which he doesn't because they never found more than a few pieces of the body."

Despite himself, Victor found the professional interest irresistible. "I'd heard he was murdered with a bomb. But my impression was that it was a fairly narrow-focus device."

The woman didn't sneer, exactly. The lip-curling expression simply had too much relaxed humor to qualify for the term. But she came close.

"That's what the RA said for public consumption. I'm not sure why, exactly. Been me, I would have broadcast the fact that whoever killed Stein was callous enough to plant a bomb which not only turned Stein into molecules and scattered him across a city block, but also killed three of his aides, two secretaries, and"—here the trace of good humor vanished—"two five-year-old kids playing on the street outside the RA's office. Blind luck all the people living in the building next door managed to get out alive."

By the time she'd finished, Victor's interest in the woman had gone from *Casual Accidental Encounter* to *Full Professional Alert.* He could tell from subtle signs in her posture that the same was true for Ginny.

Ginny launched a probe. "At a guess, I'd say the RA wanted to keep the focus entirely on Stein. There's a difference—a subtle one, true, but still there—between an *assassination* and an indiscriminate attack. From the viewpoint of public relations, the first has a clearer edge to it."

"Yes, there is," said the woman, "and, yes, I think you're probably right." She nodded toward the dais. "I take it you were no more overwhelmed by the grief of the occasion than I've been."

Now, her smile widened and her eyes crinkled. Even with his professional caution aroused, Victor found himself warming to her.

"I'm Naomi Imbesi, by the way. As I'm sure you've figured out by now, our meeting was about as coincidental as a rigged lottery. But I *do* think I pulled it off rather nicely, for public consumption."

Ginny's responding smile was just as wide and just as cheerful. "I thought you were great. And the outfit's perfect. That—what is it, anyway? some kind of riding apparel variation?—sets off your figure perfectly. The bust alone ought to be bronzed. Same for the hips and ass."

"I'd call it jodhpurs and vest, except I'd die laughing—and don't think I wouldn't, the way I'm built, wearing this thing." Rather complacently, she gazed down upon herself.

It was a self which Victor was trying his best not to ogle. Naomi Imbesi had the kind of lush figure modern society officially frowned upon as "overweight," and a good percentage of that society privately had fantasies about.

Ginny's sharp elbow caught him in the ribs. "You lout! After all the trouble this poor woman's put herself through, you're not even going to *look*? You have to excuse him, Naomi. He's really a sweet guy—honest—but he's as sophisticated as a turtle. No *savoir-faire* at all."

Ginny raised her glass and drained the drink. Then, looked around. "But who am I to talk? Speaking of *savoir-faire*, I'd better get started on my own job for the evening."

Victor must have been frowning a little, trying to follow Ginny's train of thought. Seeing the expression, she smiled sweetly.

"Getting pie-faced drunk, dimwit. Falling-down comatose. How else are we going to get the awkward paramour out of the way so business can proceed?"

She transferred the smile to Naomi. "Won't take long. I can't handle liquor at all." A moment later, she was making a beeline for a nearby robotray.

When Victor looked back at Naomi, he saw that she was studying him. Still smiling, true, but there was more in the way of calculation than good humor in her eyes.

Yet, whatever she saw must have reassured her, for the humor came back soon enough. "Don't worry, Victor. It won't hurt."

Finally understanding, he flushed a little, suppressing the impulse to say aloud: *I have been seduced before, you know.* He had a moment's desperate wish for a mug of slum-brewery Nouveau Paris ale. *Okay, once, when I was sixteen years old and one of my sister's friends . . . ah, never mind.*

Ginny was plowing her way back toward them, triumphantly holding four glasses aloft. "Three for me and one for Naomi," she announced upon arrival. "You don't get any, Victor, 'cause you can't hold your liquor all that well, either, and we can't afford to blow the opportunity." She handed one of the glasses to Naomi. "Um. Possibly a poor choice of words."

Naomi and Ginny burst into laughter. Victor flushed again and resigned himself to . . .

Well, possibly a very pleasant night, true enough. But, he was darkly certain, an endless period of ridicule thereafter.

As Naomi and Ginny continued to chatter away, he fell deeper and deeper into a gloomy assessment of just how long and constant that ridicule would be. Ginny was bad enough on her own, when it came to teasing him. Now that she seemed to have found a like-minded female with whom to share her low-minded sense of humor . . .

He was far enough into his morose ruminations that the jarring collision took him completely by surprise. All that kept him from toppling to the floor was a hard and very powerful hand holding him by the arm.

The reflexes of constant hours of training kicked in. Over the past few years, under Kevin Usher's ruthless regimen, Victor had become quite a good—if not naturally adept—martial artist. His forearm twisted out of the grip, turning into an elbow strike, while his foot lashed back and—

The kick was blocked by a foot on the calf and the unseen hand was now on his wrist, holding it in a grip which Victor was dead certain was about to result in a broken elbow.

His. And his calf *hurt.* The foot blocking his strike had been as hard as the hand.

But he was thinking again now, not just reacting. And if Victor wasn't especially adept at the martial arts, he *was* a quick thinker. So, within a split second, he realized that the grip on his wrist was just there to immobilize him, and the strike on his calf, as painful as it might have been for a moment, had caused no real damage. Which he was quite sure whatever still-unseen person had delivered it could have easily done.

He pictured an ogre in his mind. Had to be. That grip was *powerful.* So he was quite surprised to hear the monster speak in a mezzo-soprano.

"Hey, take it easy, will you?" There was an undertone of laughter in the voice. "It was just an accident."

The hand left his wrist and he could sense the monster moving back a bit. Victor took a step away and turned around.

Facing him was another woman, this one wearing a Solarian League Navy uniform. A Marine uniform, actually, Victor corrected himself. The uniform fit her . . . very well. Some part of Victor's brain went through wild gyrations, finding weird amusement in the fact that he was surrounded by three women, each of whom in a different way was an archetype of female pulchritude. Not often that happened to him!

Ginny was petite and shapely; Naomi was voluptuous; and this woman was . . .

What's the word, anyway? "Statuesque" doesn't quite do it. Statues don't move, and I'll bet this woman moves like a lioness.

She was a good ten centimeters taller than Victor, had broader hips and shoulders, longer legs and a narrower waist—all of which the gaudy Marine uniform accented—and *still* managed to look completely feminine. Which was something of a mystery, given that Victor was dead certain her percentage of body fat fell way outside the normal parameters for human females.

She held up her hands in a pacific gesture. "I come in peace. Actually, I didn't *come* here at all. I stumbled over some jerk in a hurry who got in my way."

Victor didn't believe her for an instant. That a jerk in a hurry might have gotten in her way, sure. Said jerk would have discovered himself sprawled on the floor while the Marine lieutenant went on her way as unperturbed as a lioness brushing past a mouse.

Apparently, Ginny shared his assessment. "Oh Lord," she muttered. "Glad I'm going to be out of it." She guzzled one of the three drinks she was holding—the one in her right hand—plopped the empty glass on another passing robotray, did a quick shift of the other two glasses and started working on the next. "You may not survive the night," she whispered to Victor. "I'll see to it that Kevin puts up a plaque in your name in FIA headquarters. Died heroically in the line of, um, duty."

Ginny's version of a whisper was what Victor thought was called "*sotto voce*." For about the millionth time in his life, he knew he was flushing and hated the fact of it.

Fortunately, neither of the other two women seemed to notice. They were too busy eyeing each other like prizefighters stepping into the ring.

Somewhat to his surprise, the new woman broke it off first. She brought her gaze back to Victor and smiled.

The smile transformed her completely. She seemed much younger—Victor suddenly realized she was not much older than he was—and less of a two-legged tigress than an impish young woman. It was a very wide smile, for starters. Victor found himself wondering what her actual grin would look like—and hoping he'd find out. The smile bordered on dazzling. The woman had skin so pale it was almost pure white—which went a bit oddly with the broad features and very full lips. Her short hair was an odd combination also: kinky, densely matted, but so blond it was almost silvery. Her eyes were a very pale hazel color, except the smile seemed to warm them to a darker hue.

The complexion, combined with the woman's physique and her very distinctive hair and facial features, started ringing a bell in Victor's mind. But before he could bring the thought into focus, Ginny spoke up.

"You're from one of the Mfecane worlds, aren't you?"

The woman nodded. "Ndebele, the worse of the two. That was true even before the OFS took over." She bowed slightly to Ginny. "Name's Thandi Palane. First Lieutenant in the SLN Marine Corps, currently attached to the staff of Captain Luiz Rozsak. I'm surprised you're familiar with the worlds. They're pretty obscure."

In that casual way she had about it which still tended to unsettle Victor, Ginny stuck out her tongue and displayed the Manpower genetic markers. Seeing them, Palane stiffened.

Victor began to bridle, until he realized the lieutenant's stiffness was due to anger, not revulsion.

"Stinking swine," she hissed. Her lips pursed, as if she'd tasted something foul.

Ginny extended one of her drinks. "Here, guzzle this. It'll taste about as bad, but it's just booze."

Palane took the drink and knocked back half of it in one quick gulp. Victor noticed, however, the way that her eyes remained level throughout; at no point—which was hard to do, guzzling a drink—exposing her to attack. That confirmed his tentative estimate that the Marine officer was a master of the martial arts. Young be damned; this woman was *dangerous.*

After lowering the drink, she said to Ginny: "You'd have seen a fair number of us, then. I've been told Manpower favors the stock."

"Not exactly. They haven't engaged in outright slave catching for several generations now, so the original Mfecane stock has been diluted. But, yes, they started with a lot of it. They favor those genetic strains for the combat and heavy labor varieties of their product."

"Yeah, they would." Again, Palane's lips made that foul-taste purse. "I'm not sure which were worse. The founders of Manpower Unlimited or my ancestors. 'Second Great Bantu Migration,' ha. Can you believe the cretins *selected* high-gravity worlds to settle? In order, they said, to 'improve the pure true original human stock.' Between the child mortality rate, the mortality rate in general, the lack of resources common to most high-gravity planets—not to mention that they didn't have squat to begin with for all their pretensions—by the time our worlds were rediscovered we were a basket case."

She raised her hand and glanced down at it. The faint tracing of the veins could be seen under the ivory skin. "Just to finish the irony, on Ndebele—not so much on Zulu—the weak sunlight selected for melanin deficiency. Bantus paler than Vikings, no less! But it did produce a genetic variant that's at the edge of current human physical performance. Big deal. Just made us prime meat for the OFS grinder, that's all."

Victor was a bit surprised to hear an SLN officer express her hostility to the OFS so openly, but not much. He knew the Solarian Marines had a particularly high recruitment rate in the protectorate worlds, which explained why the OFS used them only as a last resort. He knew of at least one incident where an OFS Security Battalion had been mangled during a pacification campaign by Solarian Marines supposedly backing them up. *An unfortunate "friendly fire" mishap* had been the official explanation, never mind explaining how a "friendly fire mishap" could produce sixty percent casualty rates for an entire battalion.

Palane transferred her gaze from Ginny to Victor. "You're Victor Cachat, if I'm not mistaken. I can't remember your title, but you're attached to Kevin Usher's staff." Her eyes moved back to Ginny. "Which, if I'm right, would make you Virginia Usher."

For the first time since Palane had inserted herself into their little circle, Naomi Imbesi spoke up.

"Your simple soldier routine is slipping, Lieutenant," she murmured. There was more than a trace of malice in the words, which annoyed Victor. It was pure cattiness, and even though he understood that he was the cause of it himself—not often that happened to him, either—he still found it distasteful. He'd never particularly liked the fact that women generally ignored him. He was now discovering that he liked being fought over by them even less.

Fortunately, Palane seemed inclined to avoid the fight. "No secret," she said pleasantly, taking another sip of her drink. "I'm assigned to Captain Rozsak's intelligence unit, so it's my job to know these things." For an instant, she glanced down at the drink in her hand. "Can't say I like it any more than I do this stuff, but duty is duty and beggars can't be choosers. And you'd be Naomi Imbesi, I believe, one of Walter Imbesi's kin. Niece, as I recall."

There was something vaguely triumphant about Palane's last words, as if she were playing a trump card. Victor noted the fact that she managed to convey the sentiment *your cattiness identifies you* without saying it in so many words. It would appear the imposing Marine lieutenant had a subtle streak also.

He found himself *really* wanting to see Palane's outright grin. Strongly enough, in fact, to wonder about it. To ponder over it, rather, the way Victor was prone to do with his own emotional reactions.

He didn't have to ponder for long, this time. The reason he felt such a stronger attraction to the Solarian officer than to the Erewhonese socialite was obvious enough to him, and had nothing to do with their respective physical attractions.

For an instant, his eyes met Palane's. There was no expression on her face beyond pleasant amusement, but Victor understood the meaning of that glance. They came from the same kind of place—generically, at least—and they both knew it. Plebes among patricians; respectable plebes, now, but still plebes.

Palane polished off the rest of her drink. "And I think I've interrupted your conversation long enough, so I'll be off." She gave Ginny a little nod; did not give one to Naomi; and gave Victor simply another glance. "Have a pleasant evening."

She was off, striding away. After taking a few steps, one of the many inebriates now sprinkled through the crowd stumbled in front of her. Without breaking stride, Palane seized him under the armpits and set him back on his feet as easily as a woman handling a child. A moment later, her tall form had disappeared into the mob.

"Accident, my foot," muttered Naomi. Again, the words held an undertone of malice; and, again, Victor found it annoying.

CHAPTER 14

ONCE THEY REACHED THEIR HOTEL SUITE, Anton lowered himself into an armchair and took a long and slow breath.

"Didn't mean to be rude. But for this, I'm not relying on any portable scrambling equipment small enough to carry on your person." He glanced toward the corner where the suite's scrambling device was located, checking the green light to make sure it was operating. The double-check was more a matter of habit than anything else. *That* equipment, paid for out of Cathy's fortune, was the very best available anywhere in the galaxy.

"So what's up?" asked Ruth brightly.

The dubious expression on Berry's face amused Anton. Unlike Ruth, she was *not* a princess in training to be a spy and, clearly, was not at all sure she wanted to hear whatever it was Anton had learned from the Solarian officer. Berry still hadn't decided what career she wanted to pursue, but the one thing it was not going to be was espionage.

"One in the family is *enough,*" as she'd put it once over the dinner table. "If you added another, we'd all go crazy." To which Cathy had immediately added: "Amen to that," and his daughter Helen—sharp as a serpent's tooth is the ingratitude of children—had chimed in with: "Not sure we haven't all gone crazy already. No, Daddy, that's just my dog wagging his tail in the corner, hoping I'll toss him some food; he's not a robot sabo-toor, honest. So don't you dare dissect him."

Anton still wasn't sure what career course Berry would finally settle on. The girl suffered from a mental condition which, though probably excellent from the standpoint of her own sanity, was a severe handicap in a modern society: she was interested in everything, but not obsessively interested in any particular thing. A generalist rather than a specialist, by temperament. Someone whose emotional stability continued to privately amaze Anton—the more so, given the horrors the girl had gone through in her childhood—but who showed no special talent for any given occupation.

Berry herself made jokes about it, now and then. He smiled, remembering another conversation which had once taken place over the dinner table. Just a few months ago, in fact, over the end-of-form holidays, when Helen was enjoying her first extended leave from the Naval Academy on Saganami Island.

"It's obvious, Daddy," Berry pronounced. "There are only two things I'd be good at. First, being a housewife—talk about an obsolete profession—or, second, being a queen." Berry pursed her lips thoughtfully: "A constitutional monarchy would be best, I think. I'm sure I'd be a flop as a despot. Too easy-going."

"Be a lawyer," Helen chimed in between mouthfuls. "There's no opening for queens anywhere that I know about, and at least as a lawyer you'd be able to meddle in everything."

"I don't *meddle*," Berry said, a bit crossly.

"Nope, you sure don't," came Helen's reply, "even though everybody's always confiding in you. Which means you'd make a *great* lawyer."

Anton's natural daughter broke off for a moment, shoveling food into her mouth at a rate Anton was certain was anatomically impossible. There *had* to be a demon residing somewhere in the girl's belly.

Helen's metabolism was a little scary. At the age of fourteen, she'd been on the smallish size. Four years later, she was already over a hundred and seventy-five centimeters tall and still probably hadn't reached her full adult size. The girl had gotten her musculature from Anton, but clearly enough she'd inherited the height which was normal in her mother's family—even if her mother herself hadn't shared it.

"I don't *want* to be a lawyer."

"'Course not. So what? You don't much want to be a housewife or a queen, either. Besides, the first one would bore you to death—you're too sensible to slobber all over babies—and, like I said, there's no opening for the second. So," Helen concluded triumphantly, finishing her plate and scooping on seconds, "lawyer it is. Process of elimination."

Scoop, scoop. Anton began to fear for the structural integrity of the table.

"I learned about it this semester, at the Academy, in my course in introductory logic." *Scoop, scoop.* Like most of the furniture in Cathy's mansion, the table was an antique. Gorgeous thing, sure.

But with Helen around, Anton would have preferred an industrial strength assembly bench. "My prof was fond of quoting some ancient philosopher. 'Once you eliminate the impossible, whatever remains, however . . . um, how'd he put it?"

Helen broke off for a moment, in order to feed the demon. "Can't remember, exactly. 'However implausible,' I think. Anyway—" She broke off again. The demon was apparently still rampaging in full fury. "Whatever's left, however screwy, has got to be the right answer. So lawyer it is, Berry. Mark my words."

Judging from the little smile on her lips, Anton suspected that Berry was remembering the same conversation.

"I'd rather you did hear it, Berry," he said. "Whatever decision I make—we make—you'll be involved." He looked at Du Havel, adding: "I'd like to get your reactions, too."

Du Havel nodded. "For what they're worth. I warn you, Anton, I'm a theorist—not a practical-minded spy."

By now, Ruth was perched on the edge of her chair. She, clearly enough, did not share any of Berry's misgivings. Nor, for that matter, any of Web Du Havel's easy relaxation. The princess seemed on the verge of bouncing up and down with impatience.

"What that Solarian lieutenant had to tell me was that he could provide me with the link to track down—try to, anyway—the origins of the mysterious Elaine Komandorski."

The name obviously meant nothing to the two girls or Web. Anton would have been surprised if it had. So far as he was aware, even the woman's name was known only to a small number of Landing City's police force. And none of them had found out, as Anton had, what eventually happened to her.

"She doesn't use that name any longer. She changed identities quite some time ago. Nowadays, she's known as Lady Georgia Young, formerly Georgia Sakristos."

Both girls knew *that* name, even if Du Havel didn't. Berry's eyes were wide; Ruth's, as wide as saucers.

"The wife of the Earl of North Hollow," Anton continued. "And the person who is considered by many people, me included, to be the gray eminence—at least when it comes to the dirty work—behind the current government of the Star Kingdom." He gave the princess a glance. "You can add her name to Kevin Usher's on that little list of the galaxy's top spies."

Ruth stroked her throat. "She controls North Hollow's black files, doesn't she?"

Anton nodded grimly. "Yes, she does. For all practical purposes, anyway. Those damned files assembled by the old Earl North Hollow, which have been used to blackmail more of Manticore's politicians than I want to think about. And, I don't have any doubt, were all that enabled High Ridge and his cohorts to contain the damage which *should* have ensued after Cathy and I released the files we brought back from the Manpower Incident on Terra."

"Who was 'Komandorski'?" asked Berry.

"Elaine Komandorski, in her heyday, was one of the most notorious criminals in Landing City—among the police, at any rate, even if her name wouldn't have meant anything to most Manticoran citizens. She was no crude armed robber, you understand. She specialized in things like industrial espionage, swindling; financial crimes, essentially. Except that the police are sure she was responsible for the murder of at least two people, and had something to do with the 'suicide' of yet another, in order to cover her tracks."

"But—" Berry shook her head. "If you could prove that the current Lady Young was—"

Anton shook his head. "Not good enough. Yes, with DNA evidence it could be proved that Georgia Young and Elaine Komandorski were one and the same person. But Komandorski was never convicted of anything, despite being the subject of an amazing number of police investigations. The cops are morally certain that she committed most of the crimes she was suspected of, but they couldn't prove it.

"So"—shrugging—"the most we could get out of it, as it stands, would be publicly embarrassing the High Ridge regime. Big deal. As long as High Ridge has his hands on those black files, he can put enough pressure where it matters to keep a lid on it. Just like he did with the Manpower investigation."

Ruth's quick mind had already raced ahead. "The police, I take it, were never able to find out where Komandorski came from."

"No. Neither have I. She just . . . appeared one day, in Landing City, and with enough of a bankroll to start her scams. And they weren't piker scams, either."

"So if you could track down her origins, you might be able to break the thing wide open."

"Sure. But—"

Ruth cut him off. "Yes, I know, the question's obvious. *Why* did a Solarian junior officer hand you this juicy little tidbit? And who's he acting for? You can be dead sure—okay, ninety-nine percent dead sure—that altruism wasn't the motive. Which means, so far as I can see, only one of three alternatives."

Anton leaned back. He was curious to see how far the girl could work the chain of logic.

The princess started ticking off her fingers. "The first alternative—the best one, from our point of view—is that someone else has a grudge against Komandorski but, for whatever reason, isn't in a position to act on it. So they're setting up Captain Zilwicki as their hatchet man."

"Good," grunted Anton. "Now tell me what's wrong with that picture."

Ruth frowned. The expression made her thin face—well, *Berry's* thin face, if Anton wanted to be precise—look more intense than ever. Hunched over in her chair as she was, elbows on knees, her blue eyes peering intently at the floor, with her long dark hair spilling over her shoulders, she made Anton think of a young witch pondering her first major incantation. A very young witch, and a rather pretty one, true; but a witch sure and certain.

Anton, as he had many times since the nanotech transformation, found himself more than a little disconcerted. The fact that Ruth now looked like Berry, and Berry looked like Ruth, he could handle. But their *personalities* hadn't been transformed, a fact which often left him feeling confused. An intense—almost high-strung—"Berry" was a contradiction in terms.

"It's still . . . possible," Ruth said after a few seconds' thought. "But probably not very likely. I'd think it would be even harder to track whoever Komandorski used to be *forward* in time than it is to track Komandorski backward. Which was so hard to do—the latter, I mean—that neither you nor the LCPD was able to do it."

Still with her head lowered, she cocked a questioning eye at Anton. He nodded approvingly.

"Yes. As long as someone's got the money—which Komandorski did, judging from the size of the war chest she had when she popped up in Landing City—it's very easy to break off an old life and create a new one, with almost no tracks left at all. It's a big galaxy, even the little part of it humans have explored and settled."

"That's what I thought. And if that's the case, then anyone who was tracking her because *they* had a grudge to settle, presumably had plenty of resources of their own. Plenty enough, you'd think, to handle their own hatchet work." She paused briefly, again.

"Which means that it's far more likely that whoever did spot the connection stumbled across it by accident."

"Not necessarily 'by accident,'" countered Anton. "For their own reasons, they might have been investigating something Komandorski was involved in. Still, I agree with your main point. It's not at all likely that they were specifically looking for *her*."

He made a little motion with his hand. "Continue. What's the next alternative?"

"Well, that one's obvious. Whoever it is has a grudge against *you*, and is using Komandorski to bait the trap." This time, when she looked at Anton she raised her head. "And you'd be hard pressed not to take it, wouldn't you?"

Anton's jaws were set. "There is no way in hell I would *not* take it, unless I was dead certain it was nothing but a trap. Getting rid of Georgia Young and those stinking North Hollow files would be the best political hygiene the Star Kingdom could possibly enjoy."

Now it was Berry's turn to clutch her throat. "But—Daddy—you can't—"

Anton shook his head. "Relax, Berry. As it happens, I think that's the least likely variant. Not impossible, sure, but . . ."

Again, he waved his hand at Ruth. "You explain, if you can."

The princess didn't hesitate. "It's not likely just because it's too convoluted. The problem with hacking up the Captain"—she gave Anton a smile—"is that there's so little you can hack *at* except himself. Most political dirty work involves ruining someone's reputation, and . . . ah . . ."

Anton grinned. "My reputation is a great shambling pile of ruins to begin with. What are you going to threaten me with? Wrecking my naval career? Been done. Exposing my extramarital affair with a notorious countess? Been done. Accuse me of consorting with dangerous radicals? Been done."

Berry was chuckling now. "Can't even accuse you of adopting wayward orphans from God-knows-where. Been done."

"Which only leaves attacking the Captain directly," concluded the princess. "And that's more than a bit dicey, as a certain Manpower-financed raiding party discovered not too long ago. Although if you were going to try again, I suppose it'd make sense to finagle him out from behind his normal security. Draw him into unknown territory."

Anton shook his head. "Not all that much sense. Outside of Manticore itself—or Terra, where I still have lots of contacts—

Smoking Frog is the *last* place you'd want to try to pull any stunts with me."

The blank look on the girls' faces made Anton realize he'd left something unsaid.

"Oh, sorry. Forgot. The lieutenant's link leads to Smoking Frog, in the Solarian League's Maya Sector. That's where whoever Lady North Hollow was then had her Komandorski identity created. Makes sense, when you think about it. Smoking Frog's a technically advanced planet. Their bio-sculptors are as good as any in the galaxy, except possibly those on Terra itself or Beowulf."

Ruth was still puzzled. "But I still don't see why it wouldn't make a good place to ambush you."

Du Havel chuckled. Anton glanced at him and said: "You explain it to her, Web."

The academic's smile had a grim feel to it. "It would make a terrible place to try to get rough with Anton—given his close ties with the Audubon Ballroom. There's no planet in the galaxy that has more Ballroom members living on it than Smoking Frog. Not even Terra, since Barregos became governor. The moment Anton arrives, he can provide himself with a bodyguard that nobody will want to fool with."

He shrugged. "Escaped slaves need somewhere to go, and there's always someplace that—for its own reasons—makes itself a refuge. Partly out of ideological commitment, but as much as anything simply to stick it to whichever establishment has irritated them. Barregos and Mesa are public enemies, so Barregos has nothing to lose by turning Maya Sector in general and Smoking Frog in particular into the modern equivalent of Boston at the end of the Underground Railroad."

"What's a Boston?" asked Berry. She pressed hands to her temples. "My head hurts."

Anton saw the princess hesitate, and realized that she'd seen the next variant quite clearly.

"Well, yes," he said, his deep voice harsher than usual. "The most likely alternative—this'll be Ruth's 'third'—is that someone is trying to lure someone *with* me to Smoking Frog. It wouldn't be as easy for me to protect a companion as it is to protect myself."

Still holding her head in her hands, Berry began to shake it. "That doesn't make *sense*, Daddy. Sure, I'm your daughter now, but nobody's got a grudge—oh."

Her head popped up; her face turning to Ruth. "It's *you* they're after!"

The princess shrugged. "Who knows? But—yes—I think that's the most logical explanation." She turned to Anton. "Am I right?"

"Yes and no." His hand motion, this time, consisted of wiggling fingers. "You're right as far as it goes. But . . ."

He tried to figure out the best way to explain it. "You're good, Princess. Very good. But you're still young and suffer from the classic young agent's syndrome. Things make too much sense to you. You trust logic too much, which means you'll wind up oversimplifying in order to *make* things make sense. If you see what I mean."

He almost laughed. A young witch, frowning; wondering why her old crone of a mentor *insisted* on using messy bat's ears and toad's blood when the *grimoire* plainly said—

"Just trust me on this one, girl. The universe is a lot messier and murkier than you think it is. Logic's a good habit to develop, but don't trust it too far. It's a wild and dangerous animal, unless it's muzzled and leashed by *facts*. Of which—"

He planted hands on knees and sat up straight. "Of which, we don't have enough yet. So here's what we're going to do: I *will* go to Smoking Frog—this lead is just too potentially valuable to pass up—but you, both of you, will stay here on Erewhon." He glanced at the door, beyond which the Queen's Own stood guard. "Between them, and Erewhon's own security forces, you should be safe enough. Unless someone is prepared to risk a major diplomatic incident—and I can't see why anyone would—you ought to be safe enough until I get back."

Berry and Ruth exchanged looks. Clearly enough, warring impulses were at work. On the one hand, no youngsters with any spunk at all wouldn't enjoy the prospect of being on their own for a time. On the other hand . . .

"How long will you be gone?" asked Berry in a small voice.

"Maybe a month. Depends on what I have to do when I get there. I'll take the frigate, of course. It's only about fifty light-years from here to the Maya Sector—call it a week's travel in the Eta bands, if we push it a little—and Smoking Frog's five-point-five light-years or so inside the sector line. Call that another day or so. So, figure sixteen days' travel and two weeks there to dig up whatever I have to dig up. A T-month, more or less."

"Oh. Four weeks aren't so bad." The look which Berry and Ruth now exchanged had no warring impulses at all.

"No wild parties," growled Anton. "No orgies. Especially no *wild* orgies. If this hotel isn't still standing—no wreckage at all, mind!—when I get back—"

Berry had never been as feisty as Anton's natural daughter, Helen, true enough. She didn't have the same temperament. On the other hand, having Helen for a sister these past four years hadn't gone to waste either.

"That's nonsense, Daddy! *Me?!* And Ruth—a *princess of the realm?*" Somehow, she managed to flounce with indignation while sitting in a chair. "I never heard such a ridiculous—"

On and on. Needless to say, Ruth added her own flounces and indignation. On and on. Anton got gloomier by the moment.

Du Havel didn't help any. "That's *it*," he said, grinning. "The clever scheme unveiled, Anton. You're being lured off Erewhon so that the folly of young women can be proven to the galaxy at last."

"I'm counting on *you* to keep them steady, Web," Anton growled.

"Don't be absurd. I'm an absent-minded professor. They'll outwit me right and left."

CHAPTER 15

BY THE TIME VICTOR AND NAOMI managed to get Ginny settled in bed, Victor's annoyance with the Erewhonese woman had eased a lot. Catty and nastily competitive Walter Imbesi's niece might have been earlier, in the presence of the Solarian League Marine lieutenant. But Naomi had been charming and good-humored thereafter—never more so than when Victor had been faced with the awkwardness of having to drag a thoroughly plastered Virginia Usher away from the crowd before she committed sheer mayhem in the way of social embarrassment and public scandal.

Ginny had not been kidding when she'd said she couldn't handle liquor well. Victor had never seen her get drunk before, and, now that he had, hoped fervently that he'd never witness the event again.

It wasn't the puking he minded, in and of itself. Although he still retained a certain stiffness of demeanor, despite all of Kevin and Ginny Usher's efforts to rub it away these past few years, Victor was far removed from a prude. The Dolist slums of Nouveau Paris which had produced him were a poor culture medium for prissiness, after all. It wasn't as if he'd never seen anyone heave their guts, or been through the experience himself.

But he'd never seen anyone do it with Ginny's single-minded target selection. The moment her face had suddenly turned a shade of green and her eyes had widened—Victor had immediately recognized that unmistakable *can't-hold-it-down* sign—Ginny had started feverishly scanning the crowd.

Naomi had recognized the signs as fast as he had. "Here," she said to Ginny laughingly, "hold on to my arm. I know where the nearest women's lavatory is."

Ginny shook her head. "S'a waste," she muttered through tight teeth, her eyes sweeping back and forth until they fixed on something.

Somebody, rather. "There—s'perfect!" Despite the so-obvious nausea of the moment, there was something gleeful in the words. A moment later, Ginny was tottering off with great determination, somehow managing the oxymoron of "lurching steadily forward." She even managed—barely—to stay on her feet when, at one point, she stumbled out of one of her high-heeled sandals. But only by kicking off the other, forcing Victor to delay a moment while he scooped up the abandoned footwear.

That moment's delay prevented him from stopping Ginny before she could commit her Major Diplomatic Incident of the Minor Variety. Naomi was still more-or-less holding Ginny by the arm. But, not knowing Ginny as well as he did, didn't realize what she intended until the deed was done.

"Oh, Christ," hissed Victor, on one knee as he picked up the pair of sandals. He'd just lifted his head and seen where Ginny was headed.

A table toward the side, where the official delegation from the Solarian League was sitting. Minor diplomatic officials, all of them, identifiable by their distinctive consular outfits and the fact that they were obviously trying to maintain as low a profile as possible. They'd clearly been instructed to Make An Appearance For The Record—and nothing more than that. Victor had kept an eye on them, from time to time, and had seen that at no point had any of them so much as glanced in the direction of Jessica Stein, much less gone to pay their respects.

For all that he didn't much care for Stein himself, the studied insult angered him. He'd always found the Renaissance Association's preachments somewhat holier-than-thou and vacuous, true. But at least Hieronymus Stein *had* denounced the multitude of evils committed under the name of "Solarian League democracy and social justice," which was more than could be said of anyone in the Solarian League's own government, outside of a few figures like Oravil Barregos. Ginny herself having been one of the victims of that official indifference, Victor knew she had strong feelings on the subject of the League.

He lunged to his feet and made a desperate attempt to divert her. None of which availed any purpose except to bring him close enough to witness the entire ensuing scene in—quite literally—visceral detail.

Ginny staggered up to the table, bumped against it, braced herself on spread hands, and bestowed a green-faced smile on the six diplomats assembled at the table.

They all stared back at her, frowning slightly as diplomats will do when in the presence of gaucherie.

"Don't believe 've been introduced," Ginny blurted out. Words were at a premium now, running out like water on a beach before the tidal wave hits. "You people really make me sick."

The tsunami arrived, then, washing across five of the six before it was done. Some portion of Victor's brain decided he was witnessing a miracle. Two miracles, in fact—first, that *any* of the six diplomats had emerged unscathed, given the volume of the torrent and its volcanic energy; second, that a woman as small as Ginny could produce such a volume in the first place.

Startled, Naomi released Ginny's arm and stepped back. Startled beyond compare, the diplomats lurched to their feet and did likewise, tipping over their chairs in the process.

Not startled at all, Victor grabbed Ginny by an elbow, swung her around, and began marching her off. "Sorry 'bout that," he said over his shoulder to the now-very-distinctively-outfitted Solarian diplomats. "She's a bit under the weather," he added lamely, to the staring crowd around them—a statement which he privately thought was ludicrous. Like announcing the weather had turned iffy during a cyclone.

"See here!" he heard one of the diplomats cry out angrily.

"Sure," hissed Ginny. "Did I miss one?" She began struggling in Victor's grip, apparently determined to return and rectify the oversight.

For all her petite size, Ginny was no weakling. So even with Naomi now holding her other arm, Victor knew he was in for a struggle. He was about to let the pair of sandals drop, to free himself for desperate action, when a familiar mezzo-soprano voice intervened.

"Outrageous! You'll have to leave!"

An instant later, two powerful hands had his collar and the back of Ginny's sari firmly in their grip. Inexorably, they were propelled . . .

Away from the diplomats. Victor cocked his head around and saw that the lieutenant's grin was every bit as dazzling as he'd thought it would be.

"I wouldn't have missed that for anything," whispered Thandi Palane. "But we'd better get you out of here quick, before she starts an actual shooting war."

✧ ✧ ✧

Once they were safely out of the big top and into the relative darkness beyond, the lieutenant released her grip on them and stepped away. Naomi was standing a few feet to one side, frowning. Now that Palane was back, Imbesi's good humor seemed to have vanished.

For a moment, Victor was afraid that the earlier catty unpleasantness would return. But Palane forestalled that by, once again, removing herself from the scene.

She came to attention, facing Ginny. Then snapped a very crisp salute. "Madam Usher, I salute you. The Solarian Marines salute you."

She flashed Victor that quick gleaming smile, said: "But you'd better make yourself scarce now," turned precisely on her heel and marched back into the big top. Her broad shoulders seemed to be quivering a bit, as if she were trying to suppress a laugh.

Fortunately, Ginny didn't make much of a scene during the taxi ride back to their hotel. Even more fortunately, the ride was short enough that she was able to refrain from vomiting again until they reached their own room. Then, all the earlier whimsy gone, she spent the requisite miserable time hunched over the lavatory bowl.

Victor gave her what help he could. But, for situations like this, if not female-competitive ones, Naomi proved to be a marvel. The Imbesi scion, clearly enough, was no stranger to the effects of wild partying and excessive alcohol consumption. More important, she had a relaxed and tolerant humor about the situation, which did Ginny a lot more good than Victor's fastidiousness.

"Okay, girl," Naomi concluded, hefting Ginny to her feet after there couldn't *possibly* be anything left. "You're off to bed."

Naomi was taller than Ginny and quite a bit heavier, so she had no trouble half-carrying her the few steps needed without Victor's assistance. But as they neared the door to the bedroom, Ginny began to struggle again.

"No! Put me onna couch."

Naomi hesitated. Twisting in her grip, Ginny grinned back and up at her. "Y'll need th'bedroom, dummy. 'Sides, never been used right anyway and whatsa point of *that*, inna swanky hotel."

She jerked in the arms enfolding her, motioning toward the couch. "I'll be fine over there."

Naomi cocked an eye at Victor. Shrugging, he waved at the couch. "Might as well. In case you hadn't figure it out already, she's stubborn as a mule."

A few seconds later, Ginny was stretched out on the couch. A few seconds after that, she was fast asleep. But, in the intervening time, she managed a few more slurring words.

There was no humor in these, none at all. One eye closed, she gave Naomi a cold stare with the other. "You be nice to him, hear? I love Vic-*hic*-tor. Kill you if you're not, swear I will."

The basilisk eye closed, and Ginny was out cold.

By the time Palane found Captain Rozsak, Stein and her associates were no longer even trying to maintain the pretense that the event was anything other than a political one. The liquor was flowing freely, and a large portion of the space under the big top had been turned into a dance floor. So it took the lieutenant a while to track down the whereabouts of Rozsak and his staff.

Not that long, however, once she realized that another portion of the floor had been set aside for tables. She just started looking for the biggest table. Rozsak's staff was efficient about everything.

Rozsak himself wasn't at the table. He was standing nearby, sequestered in a conversation with Lieutenant Manson.

Thandi hesitated. She didn't want to intrude on the captain when he was in the midst of a private discussion. Nor, for that matter, did she much care for Lieutenant Manson. But the captain must have spotted her, for Palane saw him cock an eye at her. The subtle expression made clear he wouldn't object to an interruption.

Trying not to smile, Thandi headed toward him. Not the least of Manson's obnoxious habits was his tendency to fawn on his superiors. Palane suspected that the "private discussion" between Rozsak and Manson had already degenerated into unwanted flattery.

Rozsak wasn't immune to flattery. More precisely, he didn't object to it—provided it was kept to a reasonable minimum. But he was one of those supremely self-confident men who didn't need an underling to assure him that he was the greatest. He knew that already.

When Thandi came up, Manson broke off and gave her an unfriendly glance. The sort of quick hostile look one rival gives another—which Thandi thought was a little absurd, since she and Manson were in completely different career tracks. He was a naval staff officer, she a Marine combat leader. Outside of staff meetings, their paths hardly crossed at all.

But it was inevitable, she supposed. Manson's constant petty attempts to undermine his "rivals" was as much of a reflex as his compulsive toadying to superiors. It was more a matter of instinct than logic.

Rozsak cleared his throat. "Lieutenant Palane's been doing some work for me, Lieutenant Manson."

The hostile look immediately vanished from Manson's face, replaced by smooth politesse.

"Ah. I'll be on my way, then."

"No, actually, stick around. This probably involves you."

Palane was a little surprised to hear that, but not much. Manson did handle much of the captain's intelligence work, after all, although Rozsak usually assigned the more delicate parts to Edie Habib or Watanapongse.

"Well, Thandi? What's your assessment? Oh, sorry. I'm being rude. There are refreshments on the table."

She shook her head. "No thanks, Captain. Right now the last thing I want is booze. Having just seen a spectacular demonstration of its ill effects."

Rozsak cocked his eye again. Palane took the invitation and gave him a quick summary of the recent episode involving Virginia Usher.

When she finished, Rozsak was smiling and Manson was frowning.

"The woman's an idiot," Manson pronounced. "The last thing Haven can afford—"

Thandi decided she'd had enough of Manson. "Don't be silly," she interrupted. "The Havenites get their tech transfer through private dealings with industrial combines. What does Trommp Enterprises—just to name one—care if a bunch of minor officials got barfed on? Besides, if the Solarian League's consular staff here is as deaf-dumb-and-blind as usual, they don't even know who she is."

Manson's face tightened. Thandi realized she'd just made an enemy out of someone who'd previously been competitive with her simply out of habit. After thinking about it for a second or two longer, she also realized she didn't care in the least. After a year in Rozsak's service, Thandi was no longer as insecure in her status as she had been.

And Manson genuinely annoyed her. She'd *liked* Virginia Usher. Liked her quite a bit, in fact, from the little she'd seen of her.

Rozsak, smooth as always, defused the tension. Smooth as always, by making clear to Manson what was what.

"Have to say I agree with Lieutenant Palane here, Jerry."

If she hadn't seen it before, Thandi would have been amazed at the instantaneous manner in which Manson veered from anger to bonhomie. She was quite sure he'd been on the verge of dressing her down for disrespect to a senior officer. Instead, he chuckled and shook his head ruefully.

"Well . . . true. If there's a League consular staff anywhere in the galaxy that can find its ass with both hands, I've yet to encounter them."

Thandi decided it wouldn't hurt to ease things a bit herself. "I agree that she shouldn't have done it, Lieutenant Manson. But . . . she's a former Manpower slave, you know. Those consular officials are lucky the only thing she sprayed on them was vomit."

It was clear from the startled look on his face that Manson *hadn't* known. Startled—then stiff. Apparently the Navy lieutenant shared the common prejudice against genetic slaves.

"Interesting," mused Rozsak. "I hadn't been aware of that fact myself. It certainly explains a great deal, though, doesn't it?"

The last was addressed at Thandi, excluding Manson altogether, despite the fact the words had been addressed to both of them. Manson nodded sagely, of course, but it was blindingly obvious he didn't have any idea what the Captain was talking about.

"Yes, it does," replied Thandi. Since Rozsak had invited Manson to remain, and was making no effort now to ease him out of the conversation, Thandi decided he was privy to the information.

She raised a thumb. "First, it helps explain why Kevin Usher would go to such lengths to establish a cover for her, in case things go sour again in the Republic. Oh—yes, Sir, it *is* a cover. Whatever the relationship is between Virginia Usher and Victor Cachat, it's close but not adulterous. I'm sure of that. Second, it tells us something about Kevin Usher." She didn't so much as glance at Manson, but she was sure Rozsak understood what she meant. *Unlike some people, Usher isn't a stupid bigot.* "Third, it enables Haven's President to send a private sign of support to the RA, since you can be sure *they* know about Virginia Usher's origins. Fourth—"

"I think we can leave the rest for later, Lieutenant Palane," said Rozsak easily. He turned toward Manson, all business now.

"If the Havenites are here on business and not a private dilly-dally—which it seems they are, from what Lieutenant Palane says—that changes the equation a bit. It seems to me, at least."

Manson's nod of agreement was something genuine, this time,

not simply obsequiousness. Thandi reminded herself that underneath it all Manson *was* generally a quite capable intelligence officer.

"I agree, Sir. For starters, it adds another complication to what was already a mare's nest. But what's probably more important is that it might provide us with an alternate way . . ."

He hesitated, glancing at Thandi.

Rozsak chuckled drily. "A bit pointless to keep it a secret from her, wouldn't you say? Who do you think is going to wind up leading the charge, assuming it happens?"

Again, Manson nodded. And, again, it was a genuine sort of thing.

"True enough." He smiled thinly. "Close-quarters assault is certainly not my line of work."

Close-quarters assault? What are they talking about?

Thandi's interest peaked sharply. She'd been under the assumption that the "special ops" assignment Rozsak had been given here—most of which was still mysterious and murky to her—was simply a matter of espionage and double-dealing. That it might involve unit action was news to her.

Seeing her obvious interest, Rozsak grinned. "Did you really think I'd assigned you those Amazons just for the sake of social rehabilitation, Thandi?"

She *had* wondered a bit, but . . . There were any number of reasons, after all, that Rozsak might have use for an unofficial strike force sooner or later.

"But later for that too," said Rozsak firmly. "It may not happen anyway. With the Havenites added to the brew, there's at least one other possible variant." He rubbed his hands together briskly. "For the moment, let's concentrate on the immediate business."

All traces of social informality were gone now. The Captain started handing down his orders.

"Lieutenant Manson, I'm afraid I'll have to ask you to leave us, now. Need to know and all that."

Manson nodded and walked off immediately. As much as Thandi was sure the ambitious lieutenant hated to do so, he'd been working for Rozsak long enough to know better than to resist.

As soon as he was out of scrambler range, Rozsak turned to Thandi. Now, his voice grew harsh.

"All right, Lieutenant. I think it's time I brought you into the center of things. We can start with the fact that Lieutenant Manson is a treacherous bastard who's been selling information to—hell, who knows? The Erewhonese, for one."

Thandi stiffened, fighting the urge to glance after Manson's departing figure. "D'you want me to—?"

"No, no. Not yet, anyway." Rozsak's smile was completely mirthless. "A traitor you know about can be an asset, Lieutenant. The reason I told you was to bring you to full alert. Because the *other* thing a traitor usually is, is a damn fool. And what's bothering me now is that I'm no longer as confident as I was that Manson is on top of what he's *supposed* to be on top of."

Thandi waited. She was completely at a loss, now, but was quite sure Rozsak would clear it up. Enough, at least.

The captain's smile widened and developed a bit of warmth. "Good, good. Those Masadans you've been keeping an eye on, at a distance. Close up the distance, Lieutenant. Manson's supposed to take care of this himself, but I don't trust him any longer not to screw it up. When the time comes—and that'll be mostly your own judgment on the spot, I'm warning you—"

Ten minutes later, Thandi was in something of a state of shock. Not that she didn't understand what Rozsak wanted from her, but simply because . . .

It took her another four hours to absorb the shock. By the time she'd done so, she'd long since returned to her room in the hotel and was staring out the window at the now-sleeping city of Maytag.

Shock had given way to . . . not sadness, exactly. More like simple bleakness. She'd known since an early age that the universe was a cold and uncaring place. But there was still some small part of her, apparently—some young and girlish part—which was capable of being hurt when reminded.

She did her best to look on the bright side. At least, if nothing else, she knew she wouldn't be plagued at night any longer by frustrated thoughts concerning the captain. Luiz Rozsak was still a most appealing and charismatic leader, true enough. But as a man, up close and bare . . .

It would be like having fantasies about a cobra. She found herself remembering the face of a young Havenite officer. Stiff and somewhat solemn, true; but she'd sensed the good humor somewhere underneath. More important, she'd seen Virginia Usher caress him. The adultery was a cover, she was sure of that; but the warmth of those caresses had still been genuine.

Thandi was able to laugh softly then. The universe was whimsical as well as cruel. It was perhaps odd that she should find comfort in the memory of a woman vomiting, but she did. That spoke well of the woman's instincts, after all. Thandi was pretty sure that a woman who could puke that unerringly probably didn't make too many mistakes when it came to aiming her affections either.

When Thandi woke up the next morning, she was in a much better mood. She was a morning person by temperament, so she'd expected to be. Sunlight was always good for her.

Even better, perhaps, were the sunny expressions on the faces of her special unit after she explained their new assignment. Almost despite herself, Thandi had grown fond of those women. Yes, they were often callous and brutal in their attitudes; yes, they still tended to be infected by an unthinking assumption of superiority; yes, yes, yes—their faults were legion.

But they were *trying,* weren't they? In a universe whose overall temperature was but three degrees above absolute zero, that counted for quite a bit in Thandi Palane's book.

Besides, those wolfess grins were *so* infectious.

"Be our pleasure, kaja," said one of them. "You want them quartered also, or just drawn?"

CHAPTER 16

STARING UP AT THE CEILING OF HIS HOTEL bedroom, Victor Cachat was trying to decide what mood he was in. He didn't trust the sensations produced by the sunny warmth spilling across him from the lightly shaded window. Sunlight was a treacherous thing, apt to confuse a man and make his brains woolly.

But, try as he might, he couldn't help himself. He felt good. Very good indeed. Not elated, just . . . the kind of self-satisfaction that a man feels when, against all instinct, he has Done The Right Thing.

Of course, he also felt incredibly stupid. And was quite sure that, the moment Ginny showed up, she'd be rubbing salt into that wound.

Sure enough.

The door opened and Ginny bustled in, carrying a tray laden with food. Victor avoided looking at her.

There was perhaps three seconds of blessed silence. Just enough time for Ginny to size up the situation. Victor *on* the bed, and still fully clothed. Naomi Imbesi sleeping in the same bed, and no longer wearing her outfit of the night before. But, still, wearing a robe. And, still—it was blindingly obvious—not having spent the time engaged in carnal activity.

"Victor, you're *hopeless,*" he heard her growl. "I can't believe I wasted a night's drunkenness just to give you the opening and—you! It's disgraceful!"

"I feel great," countered Victor, still avoiding her eyes. "And you should talk, anyway. In fact, I'm surprised you can talk at all, the hangover you must have, Ms. Comatose-After-Causing-A-Scandal."

Repartee with Ginny was usually a lost cause. "Aren't you the barbarian? D'you think we're still in the dark ages?" She set the tray on a nearby table and beamed approvingly down on Naomi. Who, for her part, was lazily raising her head and smiling back.

"Great stuff, Naomi. Works way better than the junk I brought with me ever does."

"Best hangover-preventative I've ever found," agreed Naomi sleepily. With a soft laugh: "And I tried a lot of them, believe me."

She raised herself up in bed, making no attempt to cover her breasts as her robe fell open. Victor felt uncomfortable for a moment, in the way that a young man caught in flagrante delicto by his older sister will. But the sensation didn't last long. Ginny was neither a prude nor given to hypocrisy, even leaving aside the fact that she'd connived in the whole affair herself.

The whole affair . . .

Victor found himself wondering if this still-to-happen episode could even be given the name of "affair." He had no doubt at all that Naomi's attempt to seduce him came from ulterior motives. That was part of the reason he'd gotten mulish, at the end.

Only part of it, though—and, being honest, only a trivial part. Like many of the young cadre who'd joined State Security from the Dolist slums, Victor had something of a puritanical streak. But that was more in the way of a reaction to the slovenliness of Dolist life than anything driven by hard ideology, much less religious conviction. Victor had no religious convictions, beyond a hard agnosticism and the certainty that even if something which could be labeled "God" did exist, it cared not in the least about the sexual habits of a minor species inhabiting a tiny portion of one galaxy among untold billions.

No, the real reason he'd gotten stubborn the night before wasn't because of any self-prohibition against casual sex. It was simply due to Victor's natural contrariness. He didn't necessarily object to a woman attempting to seduce him for ulterior motives—not that it had ever happened much in his life. He was just damned if he was going to be *easy.*

Naomi, clearly enough, hadn't been fooled by his claims of not feeling well. To his relief, she hadn't tried to push the issue. But, she'd insisted on sleeping in the same bed, because for her to leave the suite altogether—at that hour—would undo her carefully crafted work of providing them with an excuse to be seen together. And she'd made something of a production about getting undressed and into a robe.

"And how about *you,* Victor?" Naomi asked slyly. "Are you feeling better this morning? Or do you need some of my stuff to counter the effects of your—ah, what was it?—one drink? Two?"

Grinning, Ginny picked up the food tray and handed it to Naomi. The Erewhonese woman perched it on her lap and started eating with enthusiasm. She offered some to Victor, but he settled for a couple of the fruits. Erewhon's notion of what constituted a proper breakfast nauseated him a little. He was accustomed to the typical Nouveau Parisian's breakfast, which ran heavily toward grains instead of . . .

"What *is* that, anyway?"

"Blood pudding, Erewhon style," said Naomi cheerfully. "They make it by—"

"Never mind! I can probably guess, not that I want to."

Naomi and Ginny exchanged the sort of glances which culinary sophisticates exchange in the presence of stick-in-the-mud louts.

By the time Naomi was finished, Ginny was perched on the foot of the bed, sitting cross-legged. She was wearing a version of a kimono, this morning, which was every bit as immodest as her usual wear. Victor was puzzled by the choice, in fact, since maintaining the cover seemed singularly useless under the circumstances.

He said as much; and, once again, found Naomi and Ginny exchanging the same irritating glance.

"And what are you two being so superior about *now*?"

Ginny shook her head. "I worry about you sometimes, Victor. All this travel you've done, these past few years—and it hasn't broadened your horizons one single bit. We're about to start a *ménage à trois,* dummy. How else are you going to have Naomi keep hanging around, with me in tow?" She made a face. "I am *not* getting drunk every night just to keep a cover going, especially when you insist on wasting the opportunity."

Victor's eyes widened. Naomi chuckled throatily. "Great minds think alike, obviously. Mine and Ginny's, that is. It'll work just fine, Victor. I'm well-known in Erewhon's *haute monde* for being bisexual—not that that's anything unusual here, this planet's almost as easygoing that way as Beowulf—and by now anybody will believe anything about Ginny's preferences. So the three of us can keep seeing each other, anywhere and any time, and nobody will wonder about it. In fact—"

She cocked an inquisitive eye at Ginny. Ginny smiled and shook her head. "No thanks. I don't actually sleep around on Kevin, despite the act. It's not even because he'd get jealous. To be honest, I'm not sure he would, he's such an oddball. It's just . . ." Her face lost all expression.

"Um." Naomi winced. "Yeah, I can imagine. If I'd been brought up in Manpower's slave quarters, I probably wouldn't have any interest in sex at all."

Ginny shrugged. "It's not that bad. Still, if I ever had any notion that the grass is greener on the other side of the fence, I lost it long ago."

Naomi rose, holding the tray, and padded over to the table where she set it down. Completely oblivious, so far as Victor could tell, to the fact that her lush figure was half-spilling out of the hotel robe. He found it somewhat unsettling. For all that he knew his relationship with Naomi was fundamentally political, Victor still found it impossible to be that casual about intimacy. Not for the first time in his life, he felt like a country bumpkin.

Having set down the tray, Naomi turned around. She was smiling.

"Not that I'd actually mind—you're pretty cute, Victor—but I hope I'm right in assuming that the two of you are here to establish a private liaison with Erewhon. Or else I'll be wasting a lot of sweat, politically speaking."

Ginny cocked her head. "Yes, we are. But—who exactly is 'Erewhon,' Naomi? Or am I wrong in assuming that you're . . . ah, working, on behalf of your uncle?"

"No, you're right. But don't assume that because Walter's got no official position that he won't get listened to."

Now that they'd moved onto political ground, Victor felt more at ease. He understood the way Erewhon's government worked better than Ginny did. Between her own sharp wits and the fact that she was Kevin Usher's wife, Ginny's grasp of interstellar politics was acute. But she rarely spent the time in study that Victor did as a matter of routine. In the end, when all was said and done, Ginny was an amateur at this business and he was a professional.

"I understand that," he said. "What I don't understand is why the families in power didn't send someone to, ah—"

"They're not as smart as my uncle, for starters. But even if they were, they'd have hesitated. Everybody on Erewhon is furious with the Star Kingdom—its government, at least—for the way they've been treating us the past few years. Just about anywhere you go, now, you'll hear the same wisecrack: 'With Manticorans as allies, who needs enemies?' But the families running things at the moment are noted for being cautious. So even if they'd figured out what you're really doing here, they'd probably have privately asked my uncle to serve as the go-between anyway. 'Plausible deniability,' and all that."

Victor nodded. Then, decided he had no choice but to stretch the truth a bit. "That's about our position. We're not here officially representing President Pritchart, either." *To put it mildly; she'd have kittens if she knew what Kevin was doing.* "But it's fair to say she'd listen carefully to anything we said to her." *She* would, *too. Then she'd skin Kevin alive.*

Naomi was all business, now, moving over to a nearby armchair and easing into it. She even managed, in some weird manner Victor couldn't begin to fathom, to wear her robe like formal business wear.

"That's good enough for a start. Unlike the ruling families, my uncle *has* made up his mind. He thinks Erewhon's alliance with the Star Kingdom is a losing proposition and that—given the change of government you've had—we'd do a lot better in alliance with the Republic of Haven. But I'll give you fair warning—he'll drive a hard bargain. If Erewhon comes over to Haven, we're in position to give you a lot more in the way of tech transfer than anything you'll get from the Solarians for years to come."

Victor heard Ginny's sharply indrawn breath. In a way, that was odd, since this possibility was one he and Kevin had discussed in Ginny's presence. But even Victor was feeling a bit light-headed. Naomi had just bluntly put on the table what would, without a doubt, be the greatest intelligence coup Haven had had in years, if it happened. Because of its position as a member of Manticore's alliance, Erewhon had . . .

EVERYTHING. Well . . . not quite. But we're pretty sure they've got their hands on the latest Manty compensators and FTL com, just for starters. They aren't as fully up to speed as the Graysons are, but that's only because they had too much infrastructure in place when they signed on with Manticore. They haven't been as aggressive about rebuilding from the ground up, and their hardware was already good enough to get by—better than anything we *had, at any rate! But they've still got at least eighty percent of the total Manty package, and that means—*

Sweet Jesus. Practically overnight, we'd make up almost all of Manticore's tech edge.

He shook his head, trying to focus on immediate questions. "What do you mean by a 'hard bargain'?"

Naomi shrugged. With her bosom, wearing a robe that was too small for her, the gesture was . . . distracting. "I don't know. You'd have to work that out with my uncle. And then—assuming he was satisfied—he'd have to work it out with the families in power. I can tell you for sure that at the very least they'd insist that the Republic of Haven help us deal with the Congo problem."

"Deal with it in what way?"

"How about carpet nuclear bombardment?" Ginny snarled. "For starters."

Victor grimaced. "Ginny, most of the people living on Congo are slaves."

Ginny started to snap a reply; then, took in another breath and nodded abruptly. "Okay. I take it back. How about a simple war of conquest? Then we shoot everybody except the slaves. Better yet, leave them stranded in that jungle with nothing more than a loincloth and let them die slowly."

Victor sighed and rubbed his face. "Congo" wasn't even the name of the planet they were talking about. Not officially, at least. The star manuals listed it simply under a catalog number, and the Mesan corporation whose private property the planet essentially was called it "Verdant Vista."

But for everyone else in this portion of the galaxy, the place was called Congo. Victor even knew the obscure historical reference from which the name had derived, a place on ancient Earth called "King Leopold's Congo." A colonial hellhole, reborn—and often cited by the Anti-Slavery League and the Renaissance Association as a prime example of the horrors unleashed by the galaxy's toleration of Manpower and Mesa.

Manpower, as it happened, was the Mesan corporation in question and maintained a slave-breeding center there. But the main product of the jungle planet was a variety of pharmaceuticals which were both valuable and difficult to duplicate artificially—and which Congo's owners extracted by using the most savage forms of forced labor imaginable. One study commissioned by the Renaissance Association claimed that the life expectancy of the average slave laborer once they began working on the plantations was not more than six years.

"Please, Ginny," he said softly. "Anger will get us nowhere." He cocked an eye at Naomi. "I assume Erewhon has considered the possibility and ruled it out."

Again, Naomi shrugged. Victor had to repress the urge to shout: *Put real clothes on, woman! I'm trying to think!*

"You'd have to get the details from my uncle. But, yes, I know we've considered the option of a straight-up military campaign and decided it just wasn't feasible. For starters, while we could defeat Mesa's private fleets, there's the distinct possibility that their

OFS cronies could bring in official SLN intervention, as well. Wouldn't fit in very well at all with the League's *official* position on genetic slavery, but that's never kept Frontier Security from finding justifications to assist non-Solly polities or commercial development in the name of 'frontier stability.' Granted, that's unlikely in this case. But it's certainly not impossible, and no Erewhonese government is going to risk the possibility of an open breach with the League. Besides, even leaving that entirely aside, we simply don't have the ground forces to occupy the planet. We're essentially a commercial power, not a military one. And any ground campaign on Congo . . ."

She let the sentence trail off. Something like sixty percent of Congo's land surface, if Victor remembered correctly, was classified as rain forest. And the other forty percent was mostly worse: swamps, marshy lowlands, bayous—every conceivable form of terrain guaranteed to make life miserable for ground troops.

The solution was immediately obvious to Victor, but he was quite sure no Erewhonese had ever thought of it. And he wasn't at all sure they'd accept the idea once he proposed it. It would be a radical solution, sure to rub the wrong way against the cautious businessmen and merchants who dominated Erewhon's oligarchical society.

If he even proposed the idea in the first place, he reminded himself, exercising his own caution. His tentative scheme would only work if . . .

There were at least two big "ifs" he could think of, right offhand. Before he could take the idea any further, he'd have to establish his own liaisons with the relevant parties involved. One of whom—

That last thought came with an odd combination of emotions. A bit of guilt, mingled with quite a bit more in the way of anticipation. It wasn't as if Naomi was actually his *girlfriend,* after all. Nor was it Victor's fault if the only direct liaison he could think of with the Solarian League's most capable military officer in the region just happened to go through a dazzling smile.

"Let's pursue this later," he said, clearing his throat. "For the moment, I assume that Erewhon is furious with the Manties because they won't lift a finger to deal with Congo."

Naomi's face was tight. "Congo poses a constant threat to us. We weren't too concerned until a few years ago, when the Mesans discovered the system had its own wormhole junction. But that changed everything. Sure, Mesa wouldn't attack Erewhon directly—but who's to say whom else those scumbags might allow through the junction? It's like having a gangster for a neighbor, with the combination to your back door. We were assured by the Star Kingdom that after the war with Haven was successfully prosecuted and peace was made, they'd give us whatever help we needed to deal with Congo. Including the promise to put their diplomatic clout into making damned sure that any OFS bureaucrat's temptation to rent Mesa an SLN task force or two was firmly dissuaded. Those assurances were given by the Cromarty Government, of course."

Victor felt the need to play the devil's advocate. Not out of perversity, but because his political instincts told him that he needed to appear objective to the Erewhonese. "In all fairness, Cromarty probably *would* have kept the promise."

"Yes, probably. Instead, however, Cromarty was assassinated and High Ridge took over, and the new regime has made it crystal clear that they don't feel bound by any commitments made by the previous administration." Harshly: "The dishonorable bastards."

Victor understood the anger lurking under the last sentence, and knew as well that no Manticoran in the current regime would. The informal style of Erewhonese politics came with a cultural background that was just foreign to such people as Baron High Ridge. On Erewhon, a person's word was considered his bond—and the bond was assumed by the families involved. If a man made a promise, and was unable to keep it for any reason, it was expected that his relatives would do so.

Probably the most common popular saw on Erewhon was: *a deal's a deal.* The Erewhonese were notorious throughout the galaxy—their own portion of it, at least, as well as those sectors of the Solarian League which had regular contact with them—for being inveterate hagglers and bargainers. But they were also just as well-known for being trustworthy once a bargain was made. It was no accident that Erewhon had the lowest percentage of lawyers relative to the general population of any industrialized world in the human-settled galaxy. The Erewhonese just didn't think in terms of "lawyering"—whereas a long-standing joke in the Solarian League had a man suing his mother for the trauma inflicted upon him by childbirth.

"Okay, then. I think I've got the basic parameters of the problem clear enough. For the moment, at least. I need to—ah—investigate a few things. When and where can we meet with your uncle?"

Naomi grinned. "*The Wages of Sin,* where else?"

Ginny clapped her hands. "Oh, I've *always* wanted to see that place!" She sprang to her feet and flung herself upon her closet with what struck Victor as excessive enthusiasm. "Wait'll you see the outfit I'm going to wear! Victor's gonna look like a lobster, he'll be so embarrassed!"

Five minutes later she was parading around, showing off the outfit. Victor looked pretty much like a lobster, all the way down to the way his back was hunched. When Naomi announced she was going to match Ginny and go her one better, an impartial observer would have said he bore a closer resemblance to a hermit crab, desperately looking for a shell to crawl into.

To his relief, Victor discovered that the rendezvous with Walter Imbesi couldn't happen immediately, because of the Erewhonese magnate's other pressing business. He'd have a least a day or two of relative tranquility, before he had to board the shuttle for the space station which was Erewhon's most notorious tourist attraction, accompanied by two women both of whom seemed determined to kill him by public embarrassment.

Of course, Victor's definition of "tranquility" would have puzzled most people, who didn't associate the term with scheming and plotting and scurrying in the shadows. But that was a world which Victor had grown comfortable in, during the past several years.

Comfortable enough, even, to feel no particular qualms about entering a Manticoran-officered warship disguised as a customs official, early the following afternoon. And why should he? It wasn't *technically* a Manticoran warship, after all, and while Victor himself wasn't *technically* a customs official, the subterfuge had been approved by the niece of an Erewhonese magnate who, even though neither she nor he were *technically* officials in the Erewhonese government, didn't seem to have any trouble finding the necessary documents on very short notice.

Besides, Victor did know the basic procedures and lingo of customs officials; and, besides again, he wasn't in the least bit interested in either the Manticoran officers of the warship or the warship itself. Just one of the members of the crew. Any one of seventy-three percent of the members of the crew, for that matter.

And, in the event, his skulking mission proved simpler than Victor had dared hope. There was even a member of the crew who recognized him.

"Fancy meeting you here," drawled Donald X. "I won't bother to ask if Captain Zilwicki invited you aboard." He glanced at the far exit to the small mess compartment where he'd been sitting at a table. "Can you wait long enough to let me get out before you start blowing apart whoever it is you came here to blow apart?" After another quick glance around the compartment: "Which must be ethereal spirits, I guess." There was no one else in the compartment.

Victor was probably flushing, as much from irritation as embarrassment. Donald had been one of the Ballroom gunmen who'd observed Victor's berserk massacre of the StateSec squad and the Scrags searching for Helen Zilwicki in Chicago's underground ruins.

"Why are you complaining? I saved you some work."

"True enough," grunted Donald, smiling faintly. He clasped thick hands on the table before him, fingers intertwined. The hands and fingers were so thick that the resultant double fist looked almost the size of a ham. Donald X had come into the universe in Manpower's slave-breeding vats, bearing only the name—breeding number, more precisely—of F-67d-8455-2/5. The "F" prefix indicated a slave bred for a life of heavy manual labor. Donald had decided otherwise, years later, but his adult body still bore the imprint of that original intention. He was not excessively tall, but thick and muscular in every dimension.

"What can I do for you, Victor Cachat?"

"You remembered my name?"

Donald's thin smile widened a bit. "You're a very hard man to forget. And now, I ask again—" He unclasped his hands and raised one of them in a pacific gesture. "Easy, comrades, there's no problem."

Victor turned and saw that two other crewmen were standing in the hatchway he'd come through to enter the mess compartment. Also members of the Audubon Ballroom, obviously. Victor hadn't even heard them arrive, and reminded himself that he was dealing with people who were generally accounted the most dangerous terrorists in the galaxy.

Or "freedom fighters," depending on how you looked at the question.

Freedom fighters, Victor told himself firmly. He turned back to Donald and said: "I need to talk to Jeremy."

Donald shrugged. "Be difficult, that. Jeremy's somewhere else."

Victor wasn't surprised. It would have been blind luck to have found the head of the Ballroom conveniently located on Erewhon.

"I still need to talk to him, as soon as he can get here."

"Just like that, eh? And what, exactly, gives you the right to summon Jeremy?"

" 'Right' has nothing to do with it. The word is 'opportunity.' " He hesitated for an instant. But, then, remembering that Donald was close to Jeremy, added:

"How would you like a planet of your very own?"

CHAPTER 17

"COMMANDER, IT LOOKS LIKE *Pottawatomie Creek* is leaving her parking orbit."

Linda Watson turned towards the tactical section at Lieutenant Gohr's report. At least the lieutenant came closer to pronouncing the ship's outlandish name more or less correctly than most of *Gauntlet*'s crew managed. That was Watson's first thought. Her second was to wonder just where Anton Zilwicki might be going.

Gauntlet's CIC had been keeping an unobtrusive eye on Zilwicki's frigate ever since the cruiser's arrival in-system. Not that anyone had asked them to. Officially, Ambassador Fraser had taken no notice whatsoever of the small warship. Perhaps she felt that if the Queen chose to put a thumb so publicly into the High Ridge Government's eye, then it was only tit for tat for her to give the back of her hand to Ruth Winton's taxi. Or, more probably, to the taxi driver, given how . . . unpopular one Anton Zilwicki had managed to make himself with the Government.

Captain Oversteegen, however, had taken it upon himself to stay quietly current on both the vessel and her passengers' itineraries. Neither of which had suggested that *Pottawatomie Creek* might be going anywhere.

Zilwicki was under no requirement to keep *Gauntlet* apprised of his schedule. As a private citizen of Star Kingdom, he was free to come and go as he chose. Moreover, although *Pottawatomie Creek* might be Manticoran-built, she was officially registered in the Alizon System. It was only a legal fiction, perhaps, but appearances had to be maintained where what amounted to a vest-pocket privateer was concerned.

Given who one of *Pottawatomie Creek*'s passengers was, however . . .

She touched a com stud on the arm of her command chair.

"Captain speakin'," a voice said almost instantly in her ear bug.

"It's the exec, Sir. Sorry to disturb you, but our friend with the unpronounceable name appears to be leaving orbit."

"She does, does she?" There were perhaps three seconds of silence, then: "Have Lieutenant Cheney hail her, Linda. Tell her t' ask—politely, mind you—if I might have a few moments of Captain Zilwicki's time. If he accepts the request, put it through t' my quarters, please."

"Yes, Sir." Commander Watson released the communications stud and turned towards *Gauntlet*'s com officer with the rather wistful thought that she wished she could be a fly on the captain's bulkhead during *that* conversation.

Abraham Templeton listened for a few seconds to the voice murmuring in his earbug. Then, nodding, turned to his cousin Gideon.

"Ezekiel is reporting back from the spaceport. He was able to bribe someone and get a look at Zilwicki's dispatch to Traffic Central. There's no final destination listed, but Zilwicki did inform Erewhon's traffic control that he was going to be leaving orbit. That's definite. And he didn't ask for a new one anywhere else, either."

Gideon pursed his lips, staring at one of the walls of the suite in the Suds occupied by himself and his unit of Masadan and Scrag mercenaries.

"He's leaving the system entirely, then." He cocked his head toward Abraham, without moving his eyes from the wall. "And it's also definite—yes?—that Zilwicki's daughter and my sister have remained behind."

"Yes, Gideon. I just got another report from Jacob on that, not ten minutes ago. The bitches are still in their rooms."

Gideon concentrated on the wall. It was just a blank wall, without any decorations on it. But it seemed, at that moment, like a vista opening up before him.

"Thank you for agreein' t' speak t' me, Captain Zilwicki."

It was difficult, even for one of Anton Zilwicki's formidable self-discipline, to remember that the face on his com screen did not, in fact, belong to the Prime Minister of Manticore. It looked so *damned* much like Michael Janvier that Zilwicki couldn't help expecting to hear Baron High Ridge's indescribably irritating voice.

But at least this *one's voice is irritating for another reason*, he reminded himself. *It's not what he says, just the way he says it. And be honest. Even that probably wouldn't set my teeth so much on edge if I weren't a Gryphon Highlander.*

"I try to observe at least the bare fundamentals of courtesy, Captain Oversteegen," he said, and Oversteegen smiled ever so slightly at the edge Zilwicki couldn't quite keep out of his deep, rumbling voice.

"Spoken like a true Highlander, Captain," he replied, and his eyes actually seemed to twinkle. "I had a most enjoyable debate with your friend Web Du Havel at one of Ms. Montaigne's soirees. I feel certain, somehow, that your own discussions with him tend t' be . . . interestin', Sir."

"As a matter of fact," Zilwicki admitted with a faint smile of his own, "they are. Not least because Professor Du Havel takes a certain natural delight in assuming a contrarian position, just to see where the conversation will go. Unlike myself, of course."

"I can well believe that statement is accurate . . . at least in so far as Professor Du Havel is concerned," Oversteegen said genially.

"Oh, it is," Zilwicki assured him. Then, courtesy and pleasantries dealt with, he got down to business. "May I ask just why you did want to speak with me, Captain?"

"According t' my sensors, Captain Zilwicki, *Pottawatomie Creek* is currently headed for the hyper limit."

"Yes, she is," Zilwicki said with no inflection whatsoever.

"Captain, it's not my intention t' interfere in your business or your movements, I assure you," Oversteegen said with just a touch of patience. "I am aware, however, that a member of the Royal Family traveled to Erewhon aboard your vessel. As the one and only magnificent unit of Her Majesty's Navy currently in Erewhonese space, I feel a certain responsibility t' keep myself abreast of Princess Ruth's whereabouts."

A spark ignited in Zilwicki's eye, and Oversteegen raised one hand in a soothing gesture.

"Please, Captain. Should the princess be aboard your vessel, I will have no qualms about her safety. I'm reasonably well informed about both your own reputation and the capabilities of your ship. In particular, I was fascinated t' read ONI's report on her class' electronic warfare suite. Apparently, the Hauptman Cartel pulled out all the stops for the Ballroom. Ah, I mean the Anti-Slavery League, of course."

Zilwicki sat back in his chair. Oddly enough, Oversteegen seemed genuinely amused, rather than outraged, by the fact that *Pottawatomie Creek* and her sisters had been specifically built for the galaxy's most notorious "terrorist organization," whatever the official record might say. It was not the attitude he would have anticipated from someone so closely related to High Ridge.

There you go again, Anton! He shook his head mentally. *You know this man's record. Whatever else he may be, he* can't *be an idiot. And it's obvious that he's not exactly on the same wavelength as his cousin.*

"It's amazing how many people who should know better seem to make that same mistake, Captain Oversteegen," he said with a straight face. "I suppose it's natural enough. Although the Anti-Slavery League strongly supports a political and legal process, its goal *is* the eradication of genetic slavery throughout the civilized galaxy. As such, we do find ourselves sometimes in agreement with, or at least understanding, the Ballroom's position, however much we may decry their choice of tactics from time to time."

"Oh, I'm sure," Oversteegen said with exquisite politeness, which was somewhat spoiled by the toothy, unmistakable grin which accompanied the words. "On the other hand, Captain, if you honestly expect anyone t' believe a word of that, you might want t' consider renaming your vessel. Admittedly, very few people are likely t' take the time t' track down the reference, but it rather leaps t' the eye for any student of the history of slavery, genetic or otherwise. A name like, oh, *Tubman*, let's say, would sound ever so much more 'process-oriented.' "

"Really?" A circuit seemed to close somewhere inside Zilwicki with an almost audible click as he saw that grin. Whatever this man might look like, he most assuredly was *not* a High Ridge clone. "I argued for *Buxton*, myself. Or possibly *Wilberforce*. But Cathy overruled me."

That was a fib. Cathy would have preferred a different name also—or, at the very least, simply *John Brown*, rather than the name of one of his two most notorious acts of violence. But Jeremy X had insisted the first two frigates be named *Harper's Ferry* and *Pottawatomie Creek*—primarily, Anton knew, because he was placating the more fanatical members of the Ballroom at the same time he was quietly moderating his actual tactics. It had been a compromise, in the end. Cathy had extracted concessions from the Ballroom in exchange for letting them have the names they wanted. But, for public consumption she had to take responsibility for the names themselves.

From the toothy grin which remained on his face, Anton

suspected that Oversteegen wasn't taken in by the little subterfuge. But all the Manticoran captain said was:

"Well, I can see how John Brown of Pottawatomie Creek and Harper's Ferry might well appeal t' the Ballroom. Not exactly someone *I* would care t' meet, and probably at least as murderous and fanatical as any of his opponents, of course. But direct—very direct. And I don't suppose there was ever very much doubt as t' which side of the question he was on."

"No, there wasn't," Zilwicki agreed. "But we seem to have drifted a bit from your original question, Captain."

"Yes, we have." Oversteegen nodded. "As I say, Captain Zilwicki, my concern is solely t' keep myself informed as t' Princess Ruth's location in case it should become possible or desirable for *Gauntlet* or myself t' offer her any assistance in your own absence."

"As you seem to have already deduced, Captain," Zilwicki, "I'm leaving the princess—and my daughter, Berry—here in Erewhon. Professor Du Havel has agreed to stand in as a surrogate parent, and Lieutenant Griggs, the commander of the princess' security team, has been kept fully informed of my plans. I won't say I'm entirely pleased to be letting two such, ah . . . high-spirited young ladies out of my sight. Unfortunately, I don't have much choice. My present errand is as pressing as it was unexpected."

"I see." Oversteegen nodded slowly from the com screen. He did not, Zilwicki noted, press for any details about that "unexpected" errand of his.

"Have you informed the ambassador that you've unleashed the princess?" the captain asked politely.

"No." Zilwicki suppressed a chuckle at Oversteegen's word selection and shook his head. "First, it is my pious, if rather optimistic, hope that Web will be able to exercise sufficient moderating influence for 'unleashed' to be a somewhat exaggerated choice of verb. Second, in the much more likely event that my hopes are disappointed and 'unleashed' becomes exactly the correct choice, it's not really any of Countess Fraser's business."

"Deborah isn't the sharpest stylus in the box, Captain," Oversteegen conceded. "She is—unfortunately, and God help us all—Her Majesty's official ambassador t' Erewhon. So if your daughter and Princess Ruth should accidentally burn down the Suds or somethin' of the sort, she's also the one who'll be officially expected t' sort out the ensuin' hullabaloo. I suppose one might argue under the circumstances that it would be courteous t' alert her t' the Sword of Damocles you've just suspended above her head."

"It probably would. On the other hand, and with all due respect, Countess Fraser has never done anything in her entire life to cause me to feel any concern about any little surprises which might come her way."

"Hmmmmm." Oversteegen rubbed his chin thoughtfully for a moment, then shrugged with something suspiciously like a chuckle. "Come t' think of it, I can't actually recall anythin' she's ever done t' instill a great concern for her in *me,* either."

"There you are, then," Zilwicki said with a shrug of his own. His expression sobered slightly. "Still, Captain, I think I may sleep a little better knowing that Lieutenant Griggs—and Web—have you for backup while I'm gone."

"Flattered, I'm sure," Oversteegen murmured. "Very well, Captain Zilwicki. I have no intention of involvin' myself in the princess' affairs, but I will try t' keep at least a distant eye on them."

"I appreciate that," Zilwicki told the aristocratic face on his com with a sincerity he found distantly surprising. Perhaps the most ironic thing about the situation was that Anton realized he was telling the truth: he *would* feel better leaving Erewhon knowing that Oversteegen was on the scene. Mannerisms aside, the captain was extremely competent and . . . even someone Zilwicki was finding it hard not to like. "Thank you."

"Oh, you're quite welcome, Captain," Oversteegen told him with another faint smile. "Oversteegen, clear."

Gideon Templeton came to a decision and rose to his feet. "Double—or triple, whatever it takes—the watch on my sister. With Zilwicki out of the scene, we should get an opportunity to strike soon. The best chance we'll get."

His second-in-command Abraham looked a bit dubious. "She still has those bodyguards, cousin. Zilwicki left them behind."

Gideon shrugged, his lips half-sneering. "That's just muscle. The brains are gone now."

The half-sneer grew into a full one. "If such a term as 'brains' can be applied to someone who just did something as stupid as Zilwicki. Leaving women to their own devices! You watch, Abraham: sooner than you know it, the whores will turn to whoring. It's in the nature of the beasts. And since the Manticorans were cretins enough to bestow the title of 'princess' on my sister, she'll be able to override the objections of her guard detail."

He went back to staring at the wall, as if finding certitude in its blankness. "They'll be out in the open, then. That's when we'll strike."

CHAPTER 18

THANDI STUDIED THE RENDEZVOUS location for fifteen minutes before finally deciding it wasn't a trap.

Actually, she'd determined that much within two minutes, insofar as the word "trap" held a military connotation. The other thirteen minutes she spent trying to determine her own emotional state. That represented a different sort of trap. She found it disturbing as well as interesting that the prospect of a lunch engagement with Victor Cachat was causing her a considerable degree of anticipation, even excitement.

Why? she wondered, as she examined the young man sitting at a table in a small restaurant in one of Maytag's less reputable neighborhoods. Thandi had a good view of Cachat, peering at him through an electronic haze-curtain which shielded her booth from the dining room as a whole. She'd chosen this restaurant for their meeting because of that feature. It gave her a chance to arrive early and reconnoiter the situation before committing herself. Lieutenant Commander Watanapongse had given her the option of simply backing out of the meeting if she found anything struck her wrong. If she decided not to follow through, she could just slide out the rear exit without ever being spotted.

Maybe. She was beginning to wonder if she wasn't completely outclassed in this cursed secret-agent business. Thandi was an amateur, when all was said and done. A gifted amateur, perhaps, and one with the advantage of extensive military training. But she knew that Victor Cachat was a professional at it—and quite possibly one at the top of the trade.

The first thing she'd noticed about Cachat was that *he* had arrived early also. In fact, he'd already been sitting at the table when Thandi eased herself into the booth. So much for cleverness.

The second thing she'd noticed about him was that he seemed to spend no time at all examining his surroundings. He hadn't left the table once, or seemed to do more than glance around the main dining room. He'd ordered one of the rich coffee drinks for which Erewhonese restaurants were famous and spent the time slowly savoring it while he proceeded to read something on the table's built-in display screen. To all appearances, a man simply whiling away a long lunch break while he waited for his companion to arrive. Yet she sensed that, within a minute of his arrival, Cachat had assessed his surroundings thoroughly.

At one point, Thandi had seen him exchange some sort of jest with the waiter. She had a dark suspicion the jest was at her expense; some variation on the ancient theme of women and their concepts of punctuality. Which, if true, was ironic as well as irritating. In point of fact, Thandi was a bit obsessive about being punctual—not to mention the fact that she'd arrived early to this engagement. For all the good it had done her.

The waiter ignored Victor thereafter, being no more energetic than he had to be. The restaurant was not particularly noted for its food or service, so its clientele was fairly sparse. Victor was certainly not tying up a table. And since Thandi had been let in the back way by the restaurant's owner, the waiter himself didn't realize there was a woman waiting in one of the special booths. The existence of those booths was the restaurant's real stock in trade, and only the owner handled their clientele. Lieutenant Commander Watanapongse had discovered the restaurant shortly after Rozsak and his team set up their operations on Erewhon, and the SLN officers had wound up using it often for clandestine meetings.

Pfah! She was growing to detest so-called "special operations." She felt like an idiot sitting in a clever secret booth while a man awaiting her company simply browsed through what she was sure was nothing more exotic than the local news. What made the whole situation particularly aggravating was that Thandi had realized soon enough that the real reason for her hesitation was personal, not professional. She could see no signs of an ambush, nor was there any logical reason for one, anyway. She was just nervous because of her emotional reaction to the man.

Why? she asked herself again. Cachat wasn't particularly attractive, at first glance. True, his figure was well-shaped, and probably a lot more muscular than it appeared. But Thandi didn't find that particularly impressive. Why should she? Thandi routinely made men blanch in the local gym she used for her exercise routines. She'd once gotten rid of a man pestering her in that gym by bench-pressing a hundred and fifty kilos. Not once, either—a full set of ten. She hadn't even been sweating hard when she was done.

People who'd never encountered the human variation which had evolved on the Mfecane hell-planets were often aghast once they realized they'd encountered someone with the strength of an ogre—but without an ogre's clumsy reflexes. Thandi considered her ancestors a pack of racist idiots, but there was no denying that at least on a physical level their project had been a successful one. Her special team had been shocked when they discovered that their "superhuman" phenotypes didn't begin to match her own.

Nor was Cachat a handsome man. He wasn't ugly, to be sure. But his square face, with its severe lines, was hardly something that would cause advertising agencies to come looking for his services. Except, possibly, someone wanting to recruit for a missionary sect. *Zealots needed. Must be young, clean-cut, grim-looking. Pretty boys need not apply.*

And . . . that was it, she knew. Cachat had a *purpose* to his life. It was obvious to her in everything he said and did; just the way he carried himself. The purpose might be right or wrong—Thandi was in no position to judge—but it gave Cachat the same assurance that Luiz Rozsak possessed. Even a greater one, perhaps. Rozsak's self-confidence was purely a personal matter, whereas Cachat's came as much from his sense of belonging to something larger than himself.

Thandi found that immensely appealing in a man. She was self-analytical—sometimes to the point of brooding, she often thought—and knew that her reaction was the product of her upbringing. And, therefore, not to be trusted at all. But she still couldn't help the emotional reaction itself.

As she continued studying Cachat, she found herself wondering what would have happened on Ndebele if *this* man had been her boyfriend. She didn't wonder for very long. She'd have gotten her education without having to pay a price on the side. The plant manager would have been too terrified of Cachat to do otherwise. There was something . . . indefinable, maybe, but still there about the young Havenite. He was quietly intimidating, pure and simple.

Oh, enough! She rose abruptly from her table and passed through the screen-haze into the main dining room.

Cachat spotted her immediately. His dark eyes followed her calmly as she strode toward his table, his face bearing no expression at all. Thandi had an uncomfortable feeling that he'd known she was there all along.

She asked, as soon as she sat down.

Cachat shrugged, very slightly. "Did I *know* you were there? No. But I suspected you'd be in one of those odd little booths. You picked the restaurant, after all—and why else would you have done so? The food's lousy."

"How do you know?" she asked, a bit belligerently. "Have you ever eaten here?"

He smiled, warming his expression considerably. The subtle impression of ruthlessness remained, but he suddenly seemed like a very nice man underneath it all. Thandi found herself warming to him a *lot,* and cursed the reaction. She had no business getting attracted to this man, under these circumstances. She still had no idea what Cachat was after. Neither had Watanapongse, when she raised the message she'd received the night before with him. But neither Thandi nor Rozsak's chief intelligence officer thought the matter was a personal one. The Republic of Haven was trolling in some very troubled waters here, and Victor Cachat was presumably the bait. If he was asking for a private meeting with an officer on Rozsak's staff—he'd specifically requested it be Lieutenant Palane—then it was presumably for political reasons. And, most likely, reasons which would not mesh particularly well with Rozsak's own plans.

"I asked," he replied. Again, he made that modest little shrug. "I suspect I have better local connections than you do. At least, when it comes to knowing which of the city's restaurants are good for eating, and which are good for fooling around."

Thandi's lips tightened. She hadn't liked Imbesi's niece any more than the woman had liked her. But most of her reaction—disturbing, this—was due to the fact that she *really* didn't like the idea of Victor having pillow talk with the woman.

And now you're jealous, too! What other idiot fancies are you going to indulge in?

But she said nothing. And something subtle in Cachat's expression made it clear to her that he appreciated her ability to refrain from making the catty remark which she was tempted to make.

She covered the personal awkwardness with political awkwardness.

"So what's this about, Officer Cachat? Why all the secret agent rigmarole?"

The smile was still on his face. "As I recall, *I* simply sent a message over to your hotel asking for a lunch date. Nothing spy-ish about it. Wasn't even written in secret code. *You* were the one who insisted on meeting here."

Thandi was a bit embarrassed. She was tempted to tell him that Watanapongse had insisted on the location. But, again, she didn't. Thandi was no more capable of being catty about a fellow officer than another woman. She'd agreed, after all.

"Okay, maybe it was foolish. But . . . what *do* you want? And don't bother telling me it was just the pleasure of my company."

"As a matter of fact, that *is* the reason I specifically asked for you," he said. The words came out a bit stiffly. Thandi suspected Cachat was as uncomfortable with personal emotions as she was. And, again, felt herself warming toward him still more; and—*again*—felt like an idiot for having the reaction. She was a professional military officer trying to advance her career, damnation, not a schoolgirl with a sudden crush on a man who was essentially a complete stranger.

Fortunately, Cachat hurried past the moment. "What this is about, however, is the political situation in Erewhon. It seems to me that the Republic of Haven and certain officers of the Solarian League Navy with close connections to Governor Barregos have certain interests in common. And, if I'm right, there's a way we could both advance those interests."

Her eyes narrowed a little. "You're suggesting a distance exists between the Governor and . . . ah, what you call 'certain officers' in the SLN. For the record—"

"Cut it out, Lieutenant Palane. 'For the record,' all officers of the SLN are disinterested and apolitical military figures whose personal and political loyalties are identical. 'For the record,' the Office of Frontier Security is an organization devoted to the advancement of backward planets. 'For the record,' while we're indulging in this game, a brothel is a clinical center for the study of human sexual behavior. Of those three statements, which do you think is the least absurd?"

She snorted. "The one about the brothel."

"My opinion also." He leaned forward in his chair. "Look, Lieutenant, I don't care in the least what personal ambitions Captain Rozsak might have. Or how those ambitions might—or might not—clash eventually with those of Governor Barregos. It's none of my business. Nor is it the Republic of Haven's business, except insofar as any changes in the Solarian League's political setup might affect the none-too-secret tech transfer we get from certain Solarian commercial interests."

"I'd think that would be your major concern."

He waggled a hand. "Yes and no. Yes, it's always out major concern about the Solarian League. We avoid irritating them over minor matters, which is the reason that Ginny and I were sent here to pay Haven's respects to the Stein family instead of an official delegation. But—no—we don't lose a lot of sleep over it, if it involves something important enough to make it worth our while to annoy the Solarians. Push comes to shove, as long as we can keep coming up with the cash, somebody in the Solarian League will sell us what we need. The only difference between a major SL commercial combine and a whore is that a whore is more selective and a lot less mercenary."

Thandi couldn't find any fault with that characterization. Certainly not with any of the Solarian combines which maintained operations in OFS territory. So, with a little waggle of her own fingers, she indicated her agreement.

"Keep talking."

Cachat planted his hands on the table. Then, after a short pause, began moving the utensils around. The sight reminded Thandi that she was getting hungry.

"Let's call the salt shaker 'Erewhon.' The spoon shows the wormhole connecting Erewhon with the Solarian League. This is the only terminus the Erewhonese have, except for the one to Phoenix, which means that they're commercially more tied to the Solarians than they'd like to be. Okay, now let's call the pepper shaker—"

"I need to eat," she said abruptly.

He paused, scrutinizing her. "Sorry. I'm always forgetting to eat, myself. I'm overlooking the price you'd have to pay for your physique. You must have a metabolism like a furnace."

He turned and motioned at the waiter. The man began slouching over. A bit disgruntled, obviously, that he was going to have to do some work.

After she and Victor gave the waiter their orders, Thandi cocked her head. "And what would you know about my metabolism?"

"I study things. Ginny tells me I'm compulsive about it. So after I met you, I did some research on the Mfecane worlds. Ndebele, in particular."

"And?"

He made a face. "If you'll pardon my saying so, your ancestors were a bunch of lunatics."

"Tell me something I don't know."

"Still, there was a method to their madness. At least, once you get past the initial premise that the African genotype is the purest human stock. It's actually the most variegated, since it's the oldest. However, in an odd sort of way, that initial racialist obsession worked to their advantage. Because it meant that they had the widest genetic variation to start applying natural selection to, not to mention—"

"Their own grotesque genetic manipulations." Harshly: "Tell me something I *don't* know."

He shrugged. "What I suspect you don't know—fully realize, anyway—is that the combined effect of the whole process made the Mfecane worlds an even greater experiment in human development than the Ukrainian laboratories which produced the so-called 'supersoldiers' of the Final War, whose modern descendants we call 'Scrags.' About the only thing comparable is the slave breeding laboratories run by Manpower Unlimited. Except that Manpower is deliberately trying to contain development within narrow limits, whereas your ancestors were trying to exceed all limits. Which they certainly did, as far as most physical characteristics are concerned."

"Yeah, great," she said sourly. "That explains why we're all serfs today."

"Well, I *did* say they were a bunch of lunatics. I know this will sound cold-blooded, but I actually find the fact that neither the Ukrainians nor the Mfecane founders succeeded in their aims to be profoundly satisfying. Philosophically, if you will." A bit stiffly: "I've detested elitism my entire life. That much hasn't changed, whatever else I've changed my mind about."

Thandi smiled crookedly. "Shrimps of the world, unite, is that it?"

His own smile was just as crooked. "What can I say? I'm not much good at it myself, but the crude and simple fact is that the main way the human race gets ahead is by being lovers, not fighters. Mix it all up, and let the devil take the foremost. If nothing else, the supermen will starve quicker."

She burst into laughter. And since, fortunately, the waiter had just plopped down bowls of soup, didn't find the humor of the moment undermined by famine.

She more or less inhaled the soup. The waiter appeared with a basket of rolls, and she began mopping up what was left of the soup. Victor was trying not to stare at her.

"S'true," she mumbled, after more or less inhaling her third roll.

"I have to eat—lots—at least four times a day. If I don't, I start suffering starvation symptoms way, way faster than most people."

There was a fourth, and last, roll left. She eyed Victor and he gestured politely.

After inhaling the fourth roll, she'd taken the edge off. "It's something of a problem for me, actually. On campaign, I need to carry a lot of extra rations. Luckily, the weight's not a big deal for me. As it is, my field kit's about twice as heavy as that of most Marines."

"Do you like being a Marine?"

She considered the question for a moment. "Not . . . exactly. I like the status, yes. I also like the training and skills." Coldly: "Wish I'd had them when I was a kid. There's a few bastards—ah, never mind. Ancient history. But—overall? I don't know. It's something to do, and I don't know what else I'd do instead."

She shook her head. "Enough of me." Pointing to the pepper shaker: "Continue, please."

Victor started moving things around again. "Actually, now that it's available, let me use this big empty roll basket instead to represent the Solarian League. Okay, now we'll use the pepper shaker—"

He positioned it not far away from the salt shaker which marked Erewhon.

"—to indicate the location of Congo. And now—"

Quickly, he positioned his knife and fork, and the knife he borrowed from Thandi's side of the table.

"—we can see the whole thing. Through hyper-space, Congo's not more than three days travel from Erewhon. And now it's been discovered that Congo's system has a wormhole junction with no fewer than *three* termini. Since the wormhole was first found by Mesan interests only a short while ago, the presumption is that at least one of them connects to the Solarian League. But nobody really *knows* where its termini lead to, except the Mesans." He wiggled one of the knives to indicate that its actual line of connection was uncertain.

Thandi studied the arrangement. "And your point is?" Before Victor could answer, she added: "I'm not being sarcastic. Astrography is not my strong suit. I'm a foot soldier, remember?"

"My point is that since the junction was discovered, Congo has been simultaneously a giant headache and a giant opportunity for Erewhon. A headache, because so long as it's controlled by Mesan interests, the system acts as a potential attack route."

"Who'd want to attack Erewhon?"

Victor shrugged. "Who knows? At the moment, Erewhon's allied with Manticore, and the only official enemy they have is us. The Republic of Haven. But we're not a threat—not through Congo, anyway—because we're located"—he balled up his napkin and planted it toward the edge of the table—"way over here. I suppose it's possible that one of those termini leads to Havenite space, but if it does the Republic certainly doesn't know about it. I admit, the Erewhonese would have to take our word for that, but it does happen to be true."

He studied the arrangement for a moment. Then, softly: "The Erewhonese are big believers in cold-blooded politics, Lieutenant Palane. What's sometimes called by the old name of '*Realpolitik*.' No different, in that respect, from the Andermani. So the question of 'who' really doesn't matter to them. What matters to them is that Congo will always pose a potential danger, so long as it's in unfriendly hands."

"In what sense is Mesa 'unfriendly hands'? Yeah, sure, they're stinking rotten scum. But they're a pack of commercial combines, not a star nation."

Victor cocked one eyebrow quizzically, and she shrugged irritably.

"All right, so Mesa *is* an independent star nation, but you know what I mean. Since we're being so blunt and frank here, let's both go ahead and admit that for all its independence, the system is encysted right in the middle of the Solarian League. Sure, officially it enjoys sovereignty and the right to pursue its own diplomatic and military policy, but do you really think even League bureaucrats would put up with a loose warhead in the middle of their own territory? Puh-leeze!" She rolled her eyes. "The one thing no bureaucrat will ever tolerate is anything that threatens to destabilize her personal patch of turf."

"True," Victor agreed mildly. "But as you just pointed out, Mesa is at least technically independent and also perhaps the galaxy's most shining example of just how nasty pure unbridled capitalism can be when coupled to total amorality."

"So? There still wouldn't be any point I can think of in their attacking Erewhon. The League sure as hell wouldn't thank them for it, so why should Erewhon be worried about . . . ?"

The question trailed off, as Thandi realized the answer herself.

Victor put it in words. "Exactly. You're right that Mesa itself probably would never attack Erewhon. But they'd *sell* the attack route in a heartbeat, to anyone who came up with the price, especially if they can distance themselves from the entire operation. 'Oh, *we* didn't have anything to do with those nasty pirates raiding Erewhon space. No, not us! All we did was open our junction to legitimate merchantmen. Surely you don't think any of them were *pirates,* do you?' "

He snorted, and the two of them exchanged bitter, cynical smiles. Then he shrugged and continued.

"It's not quite like having the combination to your back door in the hands of a thief. It's more like having it in the hands of the neighborhood's biggest fence. Comforting, eh? In some ways it's even worse, because a big fence knows a lot of thieves, and is always happy to drum up new business."

"All right, point taken," Thandi agreed, and it was her turn to shrug. "Hell, I can even see a few scenarios under which our hypothetical League bureaucrat would actually encourage an operation like that. After all, one way to whack an uppity minor power—especially a commercial one—would be to permit plausibly deniable pirates to do the dirty deed for you. So now that we've agreed on the potential negatives for Erewhon, where's this 'big opportunity'? The Erewhonese already have a wormhole junction connecting it to the Solarian League. Why do they need more?"

"The 'Solarian League' covers a huge chunk of the galactic neighborhood, Lieutenant. I'm afraid my little jury-rigged setup—"

"Call me Thandi."

She said it very abruptly. Almost harshly. As if—which was probably true—she wanted to force Victor Cachat as much as herself toward a personal involvement. In that direction, at least.

Cachat hesitated, while he took a deep breath. Then, to her surprise, murmured: "It's always hard for people like us, isn't it? Never been sure if that's a curse or a blessing."

For a long moment, their eyes met. Now that she was seeing them straight on, in good light, Thandi was surprised. She'd thought Cachat's eyes had been very dark brown, almost black. But, they weren't. More like the color of a wood on Ndebele derived from teak; a color, she knew, which varied a lot depending on the grain of the time or the mood of the moment. Sometimes, a brown which was astonishingly light and warm.

This was such a time. She felt a certain smile spreading across her face, in response. *That smile.* The involuntary one that sometimes came upon her, and made men forget her metabolism.

Cachat took another deep breath, and looked away. "I wish . . ."

He shook his head. "Lieutenant—Thandi—this little setup of mine doesn't begin to capture the reality. The Solarian League is *enormous.* Even compared to the Republic of Haven, much less star nations like Manticore or Erewhon. Having more wormhole termini connecting to different parts of the League—assuming that's where at least one of them leads—would be a blessing for Erewhon's trade. But it hardly matters. If there's one clear and consistent pattern in history since the advent of star travel, it's that a discovery of a new wormhole junction *always* leads to economic expansion. All of which—looking at it from an Erewhonese viewpoint—means both expanded business possibilities as well as expanded threats. Either way, Erewhon wants to make sure that Congo is . . . what's the right way to put it? Let's just say 'locked up.' Secure, if you will."

Thandi examined the arrangement on the table, trying to visualize the actual three-dimensional reality it represented.

"Okay. So why don't the Erewhonese just grab it themselves? They're a star nation, with a real fleet. Even got state-of-the-art ships of the wall."

"Well . . . Let me put it this way. The Erewhonese, like the Andermani, believe in *Realpolitik.* But there's a subtle difference. Gustav Anderman founded the Empire, and he thought like a military man. So the Andermani version of *Realpolitik* has a definite militarist flavor to it. The Andermani probably *would* just grab Congo in a shooting war. But Erewhon was founded by a consortium of successful gangsters. And the thing about gangsters—this much hasn't changed on Erewhon, for sure—is that they're basically a cautious and conservative lot. Cold-blooded business people, really. Getting too rough is more likely to bring down the police on your head, or other gangsters, and that's especially true when the potential troublemaker is someone like Mesa. So they tend naturally to think in terms of 'arrangements.' Rather than try to act like a cop, they'll prefer simply to put the cop on their payroll."

He smiled suddenly, the expression wry. "I sometimes think that's one reason they haven't been as fanatical about building up their navy—even in the middle of a war—as the Graysons. Because one thing Graysons *don't* think in terms of is 'arrangements.' "

"That might work with a local cop," Thandi agreed. "But it strikes me as a risky proposition dealing with a star nation. What's the old saying? 'An honest cop is one who stays bribed'? How do you make sure a star nation stays bribed? What's the secret?"

He pondered the thought for a few moments, then shook his head. "Well, I wouldn't say there's any general catch-all secret. But in this instance, I happen to think there *is* a clear solution to Erewhon's problem. And one which would also suit the Republic of Haven, and—I think, anyway—the man you're working for."

Smiling, he wiggled his fingers. "I will leave it unsaid, who that man might be. The captain or the governor, or both, I really don't care." The smile faded away. "And would also have the advantage of hammering Mesa and Manpower, who are truly the scum of the universe. *And*—this matters to me, even if it doesn't to anyone else—would start to correct a real injustice."

Thandi's eyes widened. "Ambitious, aren't you? Okay, Victor. Tell me what it is."

After Victor told her, Thandi's eyes were even wider. "You are clinically insane. Why in the world would Captain Rozsak—you didn't hear me say that name—go along with this?"

He told her. Now, Thandi's eyes were narrow.

"I'll give you this, Victor Cachat. You're gutsy as well as sharp. What makes you think you can say something like that and not get assassinated? Nothing personal, mind."

"By you?" He shrugged. "You'd never get out of this restaurant alive—well, not more than ten meters from it—and why would you do it anyway? You're certainly not personally offended. Neither will Rozsak be, when you tell him. I'm not accusing him of being anything but shrewd and ambitious, after all. That's hardly an insult, in Solarian circles."

Thandi's eyes quickly ranged around the room, looking for the implied threat and not finding it. "Being *very* shrewd and *very* ambitious is an insult, Victor," she muttered. *Never get out alive—not more than ten meters—what did he mean by that?* There was no one she could detect in the restaurant who posed any real threat to her. "Well, okay. Not an insult, exactly. Just dangerous."

She dismissed the waiter immediately. She'd already gauged and dismissed the restaurant owner when she came in. One of the patrons, maybe? But she couldn't see any of them who'd—

"Relax, Thandi. It's nobody *in* the restaurant."

She'd already reached that conclusion. "Who's outside, then? Havenites? Can't be. We examined the Republic's assets here on Erewhon early on. They aren't much, even leaving aside the fact that your ambassador and FIS chief-of-station are incompetent. The best you could come up with on such short notice would be local goons. And—no offense, Victor, but I'm not bragging, either—I'd go through them like I went through the rolls and soup."

He shook his head. "Use your brains, Thandi. I already told you I always do my research ahead of time. Do you really think I'd be advancing this proposal if I hadn't gotten the agreement of the key players involved? I have and they did. In fact, early signs are that they are wildly enthusiastic about it. Enthusiastic enough, anyway, to provide me with an armed guard. And I can guarantee you that you wouldn't go through *them* easily, if at all."

Thandi sucked in a long breath. "Oh, Jesus. Victor, you are out of your mind to fool around with those people."

"I am not 'fooling around' with them, for starters. And I already know them anyway, from . . ." He waved his hand vaguely. "Back when. And spare me the lectures, given the people you and Rozsak are willing to work with. You look stupid, frankly, perched way up there on your moral high horse."

She nodded, acknowledging the hit. "Still . . ."

"Just raise it with Rozsak, will you? I think you might be surprised how he'll react."

Thandi did, and she *was* surprised.

"We'll certainly pursue it," Rozsak said instantly, as soon as she'd finished. He cocked an eye at Watanapongse. "Jiri?"

"I agree. If it worked, in fact, it'd be ideal. Mind you, I think it's probably too tricky to pull off, but . . ."

They were meeting in the lieutenant commander's hotel room. Watanapongse looked at the computer in the corner desk. "Then again, maybe not. I've been doing some research myself, for the past couple of days. Victor Cachat is . . . an interesting fellow. His record is completely murky, except for these odd little flashes of lightning here and there. The Manpower Incident on Terra, early in his career. Then, whatever he did in La Martine to keep that sector from rebelling against the new Pritchart regime. A couple of other episodes it's hard to make any sense out of, except that he was centrally involved."

Watanapongse swung back to face Rozsak and Palane. "Add it all up? The only reason for a record that murky is because Haven's been making strenuous efforts to keep Cachat out of the limelight. And why would they bother, if he was just a run-of-the-mill agent?"

"He's not even an 'agent' at all, Sir," Thandi half-protested. "Nowadays he's supposed to be a cop."

Captain and lieutenant commander, simultaneously, bestowed a certain look upon the most junior lieutenant on Rozsak's staff.

"Okay, you don't have to rub it in," she grumbled. "Sir and Sir. I *was* born yesterday, almost."

Rozsak chuckled. "We'll keep pursuing Cachat's option, for the moment. So stay in touch with him, Thandi."

PART III:
THE WAGES OF SIN

CHAPTER 19

"THEY'RE MOVING, KAJA. All of them, it looks like."

The soft voice in her earbug caused Thandi to sit up straight in her chair. She lowered her palm reader, staring unfocused at the wall of her room.

"Where?"

"Don't know yet. They're breaking into separate groups as they pass through the hotel. Three groups, one large, two small." Before Thandi could ask, the woman on the other end answered her next question: *"We've got them covered. The men in the big group are all carrying overnight bags. Too small to shield any weapons from detection."*

"Maybe." Thandi didn't share the former Scrag's confidence that modern search devices could really detect small weapons. Normal ones, to be sure. But leaving aside special high-priced weapons, Thandi simply knew too many ways that effective weapons could be jury-rigged. Of course, how "effective" they'd be would obviously depend on their purpose. But if this was an assassination attempt getting underway . . . it was really awfully easy to kill a human being, when you got right down to it.

Still, an assassination attempt didn't seem too likely to her. Why involve the entire group, for one thing? There were over forty men in Gideon Templeton's special Masadan-Scrag task force. Mobilizing all of them for a straightforward assassination seemed like overkill. Besides, who'd be the target? Any target Thandi could think of on Erewhon would either require far fewer men—or couldn't be done at all with anything smaller than a battalion of professional assault troops.

"Numbers, please."

"Thirty-five of them in the big group. That includes Templeton himself. Three in the smallest group. That includes his lieutenant,

Flairty. Six in the third group. That includes the two pilots of their spacecraft."

The words in Thandi's ear came quickly and easily. That was Hanna speaking, with her usual relaxed nonchalance. Thandi's special unit were all self-confident. And had reason to be, in truth, even if Thandi thought they tended to overdo it. They were all extremely capable by nature, and Thandi's own training had brought that to a high gloss. She didn't doubt they'd be able to monitor Templeton's movements without being spotted themselves. Which was impressive, given that they were personally known to all of the male Scrags who'd joined forces with the Masadans. Ex-boyfriends, some of them.

Thandi's lips quirked in a thin, somewhat bitter smile. "Ex" was the word for it, too. It had been the decision of the male Scrags in their band to convert to Masada's brand of the Church of Humanity Unchained which had finally shaken the female Scrags loose from their lingering attachment to Manpower. None of them were in the least bit interested in becoming female chattel, which was the only role that religion gave to women. It had been pure luck that Watanapongse had run across them looking for a new employer. On their own, as disoriented as they'd been, Thandi didn't think they would have survived for very long as an independent mercenary unit. As it was, they'd thrived under Thandi's regimen—at least, once they overcame their initial skepticism.

Thandi tried to imagine what Templeton was up to. But she didn't make the mistake of jumping to any conclusions until she'd gotten more data. So she waited, and in the meantime gave some thought to whether or not she should alert Watanapongse.

She decided against it. Rozsak's orders had been crystal clear, after all—including his stress on maintaining the necessary cutout in case the operation went sour. Translated into simple terms, "cutout" meant that Thandi was the one slated to take the fall, if necessary. Neither Rozsak nor Watanapongse would appreciate it in the least if she tried to inform them of what she was up to on the eve of the operation. That would inevitably erode their "plausible deniability," and for no reason other than nervousness on the part of a junior officer.

"The operation." The term left a sour taste in her mouth. As straightforward as he normally was, even Rozsak had a tendency to slip into the sanitized jargon of black ops.

Kill them. Every last one, if you can, but make sure of Templeton and his lieutenants. First chance you get.

He hadn't told her the reason, but Thandi hadn't had much difficulty guessing what it was. That guess left a *really* sour taste in her mouth.

So much for the simple and straightforward life of the Marine officer she'd signed up to be.

She shook her head, to clear away the extraneous thoughts. This was no time for that. If Templeton was finally pulling all of his people out of the Suds Emporium, Thandi was being given her first chance to complete the operation. She didn't much like the assignment, true—not that she had any qualms about killing Masadans and Scrags. But if it was going to be done at all, she'd just as soon get it over with.

"They're all out of the hotel, now. But Flairty and his little group just went into the restaurant on the corner. They look to be ordering a big lunch. The others . . . I think they're all headed for the shuttle grounds, kaja. Almost sure of it, with the pilots. They just got into a private jitney, and the cabbie had that pleased look that comes from a fat fare. Templeton and his mob all piled into the subway. They skipped the first station, and took the second one. That line leads to the shuttle grounds."

Hanna was guessing, of course, but Thandi thought the guess made sense. Could Templeton simply be planning to leave Erewhon altogether?

Possibly. It would make sense for the pilots to take the earliest shuttle, even at the cost of a private jitney. That way they'd have Templeton's ship ready for departure when Templeton arrived.

But why wouldn't Templeton himself go with them? Why was he remaining with the large group? From Thandi's observations of the man, he struck her as the type who was very much insistent on command prerogatives. She found it hard to imagine someone who was, after all, a known and wanted terrorist throughout the Manticoran Alliance subjecting himself to the inconvenience—and potential exposure—of a trip in a crowded, start-and-stop mag-train. Not when he could have enjoyed the relative comfort and security of a jitney and made the entire trip in one uninterrupted bound.

Unless . . .

"No." Unthinkingly, she spoke the word aloud with the throat mike still activated.

"'No' what, kaja? You don't want us to keep tracking them?"

"Sorry. I was thinking to myself. Keep them under observation, Hanna. But I think you're right—so don't bother trying to follow them through the subway. Too much risk of being spotted. Just assume they're all going to the shuttle grounds and get there ahead of them. Take jitneys yourselves."

"It's your expense account. What about the three in the restaurant?"

"Leave Inge to cover them. And Lara."

"Poor bastards. Flairty's trio, I mean."

Thandi understood the harsh wisecrack, and smiled thinly. Inge and Lara were perhaps the two most murderous in her team—and the whole team was a murderous bunch. But that was, indeed, why she was leaving them there.

Leaving them behind, rather. Thandi was the most murderous of them all, and she'd be leading the rest of the operation.

She'd made up her mind, and sprang to her feet. She was now convinced that, whatever the reason, Templeton *was* leaving the planet. If so, that gave her the best possible opportunity to finish the job.

Perhaps not herself, of course. At the moment, she could see no straightforward way to kill Templeton on a shuttle, much less all the others. But it hardly mattered. Rozsak had prepared for the possibility that Templeton might try to leave Erewhon. That was why he'd instructed two of the destroyers in his orbiting flotilla to do whatever Thandi told them to do. Both of them were *War Harvest*-class ships, as large and powerful as many a light cruiser, too. Templeton's ship, for all its artfully concealed weaponry, would never have been a match for even one of them, far less both.

Quickly, she stripped off her robe and put on what she thought of as her civilian war gear. It was expensive stuff, provided for her by Rozsak, designed as much as possible to provide the same protection and assets as a Marine skinsuit while still being able to pass as a civilian outfit. It wasn't *quite* as well armored as a skinny, since it had to make do with anti-ballistic fabric rather than hard-skin anti-kinetic armor. And it certainly couldn't function as an all-up vac suit. But she could walk right through almost any sensor net without tripping any "Marine Armed to the Canines!" alarms, and it was more than adequate for fending off most civilian-grade weaponry.

Dressed, she opened the locker where she kept her weapons. Then, after hesitating a moment, simply closed it and reset the combination lock. Her weapons, like those carried by her team, were military-grade hardware. There was no possibility that she'd be able to smuggle them through the notoriously rigorous security measures maintained by Erewhon's authorities when it came to public transport. All she'd accomplish by attempting to do so would be to get detained and questioned for hours, at the very least. And time was now at a premium.

She'd have to take a jitney herself, in fact, if she was going to reach the shuttle grounds at the same time as her team. One of the express jitneys, to boot. The cost of which, for a single person, made her wince even though none of it was coming out of her own pocket. But not even her realization of Rozsak's seemingly bottomless war chest could overcome the ingrained habits of a childhood spent in abject poverty.

"I'm leaving now," she said, as she passed through the door into the hotel corridor.

"We're already in a jitney ourselves. Two of them, actually. What orders for Inge and Lara?"

"They're to keep observing Flairty's group until I tell them otherwise."

"You won't be able to reach them once we're in orbit."

Thandi was already chewing on that problem as she moved down the corridor as fast as she could, without making it obvious that she was racing. Fortunately, with her long legs, a brisk stride covered ground quickly.

"I know that. We'll just have to play it by ear for the moment. Until we're sure that the rest of them are all leaving the planet, I don't want to precipitate any action."

"Understood. Inge and Lara are going to grumble."

"They can grumble all they want, so long as they follow orders."

"Not to worry. Lara says her arm still hurts, even though the doctor swears the bone's healed."

"I broke it pretty good. She irked me."

Thandi was going out the hotel's front door now, waving over one of the jitneys lined up at the curb. The imperious hand gesture, coupled with the grin on her face, got her instant service.

The gesture was the product of her impatience. The grin, the product of Hanna's response.

"Great kaja, you are. Orders will be obeyed."

That much, she had accomplished. Given their origins and the peculiar subculture they'd developed in the long centuries after the Final War, the Scrags had nothing resembling normal human families. Their social organization was more like that of certain pack predators. The term "kaja" was slang, and hard to translate directly. It carried some of the connotations of "mother," though more those of "big sister." But Thandi thought the closest equivalent was probably the status of the biggest, toughest, meanest she-wolf in a pack.

Great Alpha Female, as it were.

"Orders *will* be obeyed," she muttered.

She'd forgotten the pick-up mikes in the jitney. The driver gave her an aggrieved look in the rearview screen.

"I heard you the first time, lady. I'm pushing the express limit as it is. Any faster and we'll get shut down by central traffic." He pointed a finger at the speed indicator. "They'll do it in a heartbeat too, don't think they won't."

"Sorry. Wasn't talking to you."

Scowling a little, Thandi pondered one of the universe's small mysteries. How did it happen that a planet founded by gangsters had the inhabited galaxy's strictest traffic laws?

Halfway to the shuttle grounds, she remembered something.

Damn. I was looking forward to it, too.

She reached out and flicked off the cab's pick-up mikes, to give herself privacy. Then, quickly murmured the connection she needed. A moment later, a pleasant male voice came into her ear.

"*Victor Cachat, here. I assume that's you, Thandi. Nobody else I know is twitchy enough about security to scramble an incoming number.*"

"Sorry. I didn't even realize the scrambler was on. It's set for default. Look, Victor, I won't be able to make our lunch date. Something's come up."

The pleasant tone in the voice faded a bit. "*So you spotted Templeton moving too, huh? I'd ask why that requires you to move quickly, but . . . never mind. I can make at least three guesses, and all of them lead me to the conclusion that I'll be meeting you on* The Wages of Sin. *Perhaps for dinner, eh?*"

Cachat's quick thoughts had left Thandi behind. "Why *The Wages of Sin?* All I know—" She hesitated, then decided that playing security games with Victor Cachat bore too close a resemblance to a mouse trying to play tag with a cat.

"Okay, screw it. Yes, I'm following Templeton. But all I know—and I'm still guessing about that—is that he and his crew are headed for the shuttle grounds. I've been assuming they're most likely heading for their own ship. Why would religious fanatics be heading for a place like *The Wages of Sin*?"

An obvious possibility occurred to her. "Oh, Christ. You don't think—"

"No, I don't. Indiscriminate terrorism against random sinners isn't Templeton's style. He's looking for a specific target."

"Who?"

"You know anything about the Manticoran royal family?"

Dumbfounded, Thandi stared out the window. They'd left the limits of Maytag, and the Erewhonese countryside was rushing past them below. Traveling as low as jitneys were required to by law, the landscape was a blur. So was her mind.

"Not much. It's a constitutional monarchy, and the current Queen is an Elizabeth, of one number or another." Like most Solarians, Thandi tended to be oblivious to the political curlicues of the galaxy's multitude of miniature star nations. Only a specialist would try to keep track of such minutia as the royal family of a "star kingdom" with no more than a handful of planets. There were well over two thousand star systems in the Solarian League, counting the hundreds who were effectively under SL dominion in the Protectorates.

Then, suddenly, she remembered the broadcast recording she'd watched a few days earlier. *Anton Zilwicki and a certain—*

"Are you talking about 'Princess Ruth'? What the hell would she mean to Templeton?"

"She's his sister. Half-sister, rather. And by his lights, a renegade and a traitor and a whore. And she and her companions—Anton Zilwicki's daughter and Professor Du Havel—just left for The Wages of Sin *last night. Shortly after Zilwicki himself left Erewhon for parts unknown."*

"Oh. Shit."

"'Oh, shit' is right. As in: it's all about to hit the circulation system. I'll see you there, Thandi."

"What are *you* going to be doing?"

"Playing it by ear, of course. What else? But this is a lucky break, I can smell it."

He broke off the connection. Thandi sniffed. She couldn't smell anything, herself, beyond the scent of old upholstery kept freshly scrubbed by Erewhon's fanatically strict sanitation codes.

"Oh, great," she grumbled. "I'm about to get caught in a three-way shoot-out with a bunch of lunatics and the galaxy's number one Junior Superspy. All of it under the nose of gangsters-cum-saints, who've got the zeal of converts when it comes to lawbreaking."

She flipped the mikes back on. "Out of idle curiosity, do you have a death penalty here on Erewhon?"

The cabbie gave her a very aggrieved look. "Of course not, lady! Erewhon's a civilized planet, y'know."

She started to relax. Not much, though, as the cabbie expanded on the theme.

"Worst you can get is life without parole. In solitary confinement. For really nasty cases they tack on 'sensory deprivation,' too. That means your cell is maybe two meters by three meters, with no windows, and the only exercise you get is in a stimulation tank."

He was apparently an enthusiast on the subject. "Yup. No sunlight for your top felons. We don't go easy on criminals here on Erewhon, you betcha. Not one single day, for the rest of their stinking existence. Live like vampires. Not only that—"

CHAPTER 20

IN THE PLUSH REAR SEAT OF HER PRIVATE runabout as it left atmosphere Naomi turned toward Victor, sitting next to her. He could see the earbug which she'd been using to talk to Walter Imbesi.

"My uncle wants to know if you think he should meet us once we arrive."

"In public?" Victor shook his head. "That'll run the risk of wrecking his plausible deniability. So I'd advise against it—unless he wants to bring Erewhon security down on Templeton and his crew, before they make their move. Which—"

Victor shrugged. "It's his decision, of course, but I'd strongly urge him to let things unfold some more. If we stop Templeton before he strikes, we lose most of our political leverage. But if we don't, and people find out Walter Imbesi *could* have stopped Templeton before then—but didn't—there'll be all hell to pay."

Naomi nodded and began muttering under her breath, in the easy manner of someone accustomed to using hidden throat mikes. Then she fell silent, listening to whatever her uncle was saying.

She glanced at Victor. "Walter says that could get very rough on the girls."

Victor could feel his face tighten. He could also, out of the corner of his eye, see the little frown on Ginny's face. She was sitting on the seat across from them, looking out the viewport at the receding surface of Erewhon. From this distance—they'd just about reached the orbit of *The Wages of Sin*—the planet was a gorgeous blue-and-white ball. The sight didn't seem to be pleasing Ginny, though.

"I realize that," he replied. "But I'm not in the business of rescuing Zilwicki's daughters and Manticoran royalty. If we can manage it, I'll certainly do my best to protect them. But . . ."

Ginny's frown was deepening. Victor's face tightened still further. "Look, it's your uncle's decision. But the best way to handle this, from a purely political viewpoint, is not to worry about collateral damage."

Again, Naomi nodded and began speaking to Imbesi.

"'Collateral damage,'" Victor heard Ginny muttering. "I hate that damn phrase."

Victor tried to figure out something to say, but Ginny just waved a hand without looking at him. "Never mind, Victor. I understand, and I'm not faulting you. I just don't like it, that's all."

Neither do I. The faces of the two young women he'd met at the Stein funeral floated into his mind. *Damn Zilwicki, anyway. Does he* always *wind up losing his daughters? I just hope this one's as tough as the other one. I'll do what I can, but . . .*

That wouldn't be much, being realistic about it. Victor was throwing this operation together as he went along. Zilwicki's frigate was by now well into hyper-space on its way to Maya Sector. Along with him had gone most of the Ballroom that Victor had any contact with beyond Donald, who'd stayed behind on Erewhon after faking an illness, and seven others. Victor had been moving so fast that Donald and the three men with him were scrambling to catch a shuttle to *The Wages of Sin* using public transportation. Which meant that unless Victor or Imbesi notified the resort's own security force, Templeton would have to be handled by Victor, a few Ballroom members, and Thandi and her unit—who were outnumbered something like three-to-one.

So be it. Zilwicki's daughter and Princess Ruth would either be protected by their escort from the Queen's Own Regiment, or they wouldn't. Presumably, the Manticoran soldiers who'd been selected for this detail were proficient in close quarter combat. And Victor was sure that the Erewhonese had allowed them to retain their sidearms, waiving the usual draconian security measures protecting *The Wages of Sin.*

That wouldn't be true for anyone else involved. The space station's security scanners were reputed to be as good as any in the galaxy. Like Victor and his people, Thandi and her team would have left their weapons behind; they weren't even going to try to smuggle arms into the space station. Neither would Templeton, unless he was a lot less expert than Victor thought he was. The Masadan zealots had not managed to evade Manticore's efforts to catch them for years by being ignorant or overconfident about modern security measures.

Sooner or later, of course—and probably very quickly—Templeton would be obtaining weapons from overwhelmed security guards. But those would be light-powered side arms, not the kind of powerful weapons which could wreak general havoc in a firefight on a space station. Even caught by surprise, the princess' guards should have a good chance to get the girls somewhere to safety.

Well. A chance, anyway. But even if they failed . . .

Victor chewed on the problem. He wasn't positive, but he suspected this was a kidnapping attempt rather than an assassination under way. And if so, a new possibility raised itself.

"Oh, *wow*," whispered Berry, staring out over the main gaming hall of *The Wages of Sin*. She and Ruth, followed by their guards, had just emerged through the entrance. Web Du Havel had remained behind in their suite, claiming that his age and sedentary habits would leave him exhausted if he tried to tag along with two youngsters enjoying their first romp through one of the galaxy's premier gambling casinos.

Even the princess, accustomed as she was to the splendor of the Star Kingdom's royal palaces, was impressed. " 'Oh wow' is right. Although—I'd say it was garish, except the word 'garish' doesn't begin to do it justice."

Berry chuckled. Leaving aside the flashy gaming tables and machines themselves, everything about the main hall seemed designed to overwhelm the senses of anyone standing in it. She was particularly taken by the holograph images spreading across the entire ceiling, some thirty meters or so above the floor. Right now, the gaming hall seemed to be racing through the center of a galaxy, with the coruscating side effects of an invisible black hole ahead of it. A moment later, the holographic image swept aside and they were back out in intergalactic space, with the Sombrero Galaxy looming in the rear of the hall.

"*Wow*," Berry repeated.

Seeing the expressions on the faces of her special unit as they stared at the space station looming ahead of them, Thandi had to keep from smiling. For all their superior airs, the truth was that the ex-Scrags were the equivalent of country hicks. Their whole lives had been spent either in the slums of Terra's major cities, or skulking through other interstices of the inhabited galaxy. Their education was as spotty as Thandi's had been, when she'd left Ndebele years earlier—but, unlike her, they hadn't spent the intervening years in a determined effort to remedy the lack. Secure in their own subculture's superstitions—*what do supermen need to learn from sub-humans?*—they'd only begun resuming a program of study since encountering Thandi herself. She'd enforced that just as firmly as she had everything else. But, her program hadn't placed any great priority on teaching her new charges the curlicues which galactic luxury could create.

"Luxury" was only part of it. The shuttle, designed specifically for the transport of prospective sheep to their fleecing place, had a huge viewing port. All the better to whet the appetite of the sheep when they got their first sight of the place where they thought they'd be munching the greenest grass in the universe. Which, indeed, they would be—while being fleeced in the process.

The space station wasn't simply dazzling and impressive, it was also *huge.* Huge, and incredibly complex in its design. Roughly speaking, it was the shape of a sphere—but not a solid so much as a construct of interlocking tubes and passageways and, here and there, much larger chambers. Thandi was fond of a type of food which still went by an ancient term referring to its origins—*Italian,* it was called—and *The Wages of Sin* reminded her of nothing so much as what a bowl of spaghetti might look like in zero G. Keeping in mind that the pasta and the meatballs were colored in every shade of the rainbow, lit throughout by a dazzling display of modern fluorescence and holographic technology—and somewhere in the vicinity of eighteen kilometers in diameter. The shuttles she could see in its vicinity, here and there, looked like specks beside it.

A gleam from reflected sunlight on what was apparently a large ship not far away caught Thandi's eye. She suddenly realized that the merchant ship the shuttle had passed very recently was not more than six or seven hundred kilometers from the space station—the space-going equivalent of being within mooring distance.

"Excuse me a moment," she muttered, going over to the viewport controls and turning up the magnification. One of the passengers in the shuttle glared at her, but said nothing. The combination of her imposing height and figure and the fact she'd been polite, was, as usual, enough to deter anything more vehement.

Yes. That gleaming sunlight *did* come from the same freighter they'd passed. A fairly standard commercial design, massing perhaps five million tons.

Thandi returned the magnification to its normal setting and turned away from the viewscreen, frowning. She wondered what the ship was doing there. There was no particular reason for a freighter to be riding in orbit that close to a pleasure resort, after all. A liner, certainly. *The Wages of Sin* was Erewhon's principal tourist attraction. But not a freighter.

She hesitated, and then decided it was time anyway to alert Rozsak's destroyers that they might soon be needed.

One of the other luxuries afforded by *Wages of Sin*'s transportation was a complete communications suite, with a plentiful supply of encrypted channels whose privacy the government guaranteed. *Which*, she reflected as she plugged her personal com into one of them, *means a bit more here than it might somewhere else, doesn't it?*

Not that it prevented her from bringing her own encryption software on line.

"Horatius, *Lieutenant Carlson speaking*," the voice of the duty com officer said into her earbug. "*What can I do for you, Lieutenant Palane?*"

Her personal encrypt had identified her, just as it had automatically routed her to the watch officer instead of one of the duty ratings. But it was still reassuring—and satisfying—to be part of an operation where Navy senior-grade lieutenants (the equivalent of a Marine captain) not only knew which end was up but actually sounded like they wanted to help her do her own job.

"Mainly, I'm just checking in, Ma'am," Thandi informed her, speaking very quietly into her privacy mike. "My unit and I are about to make rendezvous with *Wages of Sin*—we're aboard their shuttle *Diamond*."

"*Half a sec, Lieutenant*," Carlson replied. Thandi could hear her saying something to someone else, then she came back on the line. "*Tracking has you, Lieutenant. We make your ETA about eighteen minutes.*"

"Confirm, Ma'am. As far as I can tell at this point, everything's under control, but I'm declaring Code Maguire."

"*Acknowledged*," Carlson said. The Navy officer had no idea in the universe what Code Maguire was all about, but it was on her priority list as an operational ID. "*I'll inform the captain. Anything else we can do for you at this point, Lieutenant?*"

"Just one other thing," Thandi said. "Do we have any idea what that big freighter is doing riding in orbit so close to the space station?"

"*Hold on, and I'll check.*" After half a minute or so, Carlson's voice came back in her ear. "*It's the* Felicia III, *a combined freighter and personnel transport. Registered as an independent carrier out of Yarrow—that's a system in Grafton Sector—but our records show it's really owned by the Jessyk Combine. According to the manifest they filed with Erewhon's orbital monitors, they're carrying about three thousand economy-rate passengers and are making a short stop—four days—to let their customers enjoy the resort.*"

Thandi stared at the space station. It was gigantic, now, filling the entire viewport.

She didn't believe it for an instant. True, there were freighters who provided comfortable if slow passage for people who couldn't afford the top rates charged by cruise liners. But Jessyk Combine's hybrid freighters specialized in transporting the galaxy's poorest residents. People who'd barely been able to scrape up the money to afford a single trip, almost always a voyage to settle as colonists in a new world somewhere. The one thing they wouldn't have was extra money to splurge on a four-day stop at a pleasure resort. Certainly not on a Jessyk vessel—the Combine was notorious for being able to squeeze blood out of a stone.

But there was no point in asking anything further from Lieutenant Carlson. A Solarian destroyer wouldn't have access to the records she needed.

"Thank you, Ma'am," she murmured. "Lieutenant Palane, out."

Again, she hesitated. Then she pulled her personal com out of the shuttle's communications systems and switched to a dedicated channel it hadn't had when she first arrived in Erewhon.

"Victor, can you hear me?"

His voice came into her earbug immediately. Still, the same pleasant tenor; but, this time, with the slightly detached flavor which Thandi recognized as the tone of an experienced fighter heading into combat.

"*I'm here, Thandi. We just docked a few minutes ago.*"

"Can you talk to anyone in a position of authority on that space station?"

There was a moment's pause. Then: "*Yes. But I've got to be careful about it. Cutout.*"

She understood the meaning of the last terse phrase. Thandi wasn't positive, but she suspected Victor was in communication with Walter Imbesi. Quickly, she considered the parameters of the situation, and came to the conclusion that Victor had decided it would be best to let Templeton's scheme unfold a bit before taking action. If so, it was obvious why he'd be chary of involving Imbesi unless it was absolutely necessary. The political repercussions if it became publicly known that Imbesi had delayed informing the Erewhon authorities would be fairly catastrophic.

"I think it's important, Victor."

Immediately the tenor voice came back. Calm, relaxed, detached—supremely self-confident without making any effort to show it. Thandi felt some primitive part of herself heating up—and another part of herself, that self-analytical faculty she'd had as long as she could remember, almost jeering.

Oh good, Thandi. You and your fixation on alpha males. Kinky, kinky, kinky. When are you going to learn?

She drove the thought away. This was no time for another morose self-examination of the fact that the only men who ever really excited her were precisely the ones she trusted the least. Or the irony that a woman who could break most men in half without working up a sweat had such a wide submissive streak running deep under the surface—which she never let out because she trusted it even less.

"Good enough, Thandi. What is it?"

She explained quickly. As soon as she was done, the assured tenor told her he'd get back to her as soon as possible. She had no doubt he would. When they broke contact, she was feeling a bit flushed.

Damn you, Victor Cachat. I don't need this!

His voice was back within five minutes. By now, her shuttle was nearing the boat bay, and most of the space station had spread out of sight beyond the viewport's edges. The sight reminded her of a small fish on the verge of being swallowed by one of the enormous sea beasts native to her home planet. As was common on heavy gravity worlds, Ndebele's surface was largely covered by oceans.

"I think you're on to something. According to their records, the only people from the Felicia III *who've come across to* The Wages *are a dozen or so officers and crew. They've been splurging in the ritzier casinos."*

"That's what I suspected. Jessyk's crews are notorious for slack discipline. They're making an unauthorized stop for their own entertainment. Which means that whatever passengers might be on that ship are being kept quarantined. There's no way to know without boarding them, but I think that ship is a slaver on its way to Congo masquerading as a combined freighter and cheap transport vessel."

"That would fit the facts, certainly. Do you think this is tied in with Templeton?"

"No way to tell yet. But I think . . . I think they're tied in because *Templeton's* planning to tie them in somehow. I don't think it's prearranged. You say they've been here two days? That would be just about right for Templeton to find out and launch whatever scheme he's had in mind."

She'd lost track of the two smaller groups detached from Templeton's main group. The members of her team who'd been tracking the half dozen men apparently headed for Templeton's own ship had broken off once the Masadan pilots had entered the spaceport. They'd rejoined Thandi and were accompanying her on the shuttle. And, unfortunately, the low-powered transmitters she was using were no longer able to stay in touch with her two women tracking Templeton's lieutenant, Flairty.

And why *had* Flairty and two others remained behind on the planet?

Victor's voice came into her ear. *"Anything else, Thandi?"*

It was a little hard to believe that that relaxed and supremely self-confident voice belonged to a man no older than she was. Two or three years younger, in fact. As usual, Thandi felt herself shying away from the attraction—and then brought herself up sharply.

Grow up! Forget your damn Hormone Anxieties. The man's good *at this, girl, he's not putting on an act to impress you.*

She felt herself relax. Captain Rozsak *had* given her the authority to make her own decisions, after all. Bringing Cachat into her full confidence was within her parameters.

"Yes, there is." Quickly, she filled Cachat in on the situation with Flairty. "Do you have any idea why he'd have been left behind?"

"Give me a moment to think about it."

There was silence for perhaps ten seconds. When Victor's voice came back, there was for the first time a slight trace of excitement in it.

"Yes. It all fits, now. This is a kidnaping attempt, Thandi, not an assassination. Templeton's planning to grab the princess—don't ask me what for, exactly. At a guess, they'll try to use her as a hostage for a prisoner exchange with Manticore and Grayson. There are hundreds—hell, thousands—of Masadan fanatics being held in prison there."

She was trying to catch up with Victor's thinking. "But . . . There's no way Templeton can escape Erewhon with a captive. Not in that ship of his. Oh, sure, it's got a couple of heavy weapons mounts, but no armor, and its sidewalls are a joke. It's not really a *warship* at all. Anything bigger than a LAC could blow it out of space without even breaking a sweat. Hell, it'd be easy enough to just *board* the damned thing! Okay, sure, keeping the princess alive would be difficult as hell, but— Oh."

"Yeah. 'Oh.' Erewhon might or might not be willing to risk the life of Princess Ruth. They might, actually. Manticore has a long-standing tradition of being willing to sacrifice members of the royal family if need be. But there's no way even cold-blooded Erewhonese would risk the slaughter that would ensue on a ship carrying thousands of innocent people. Templeton can't threaten too many people on The Wages *itself with whatever side arms he'll pick up there, but once he gets aboard that freighter all bets are off. If nothing else, he can just blow it up by kicking out the governors on the fusion bottle. He's a religious fanatic, so he won't have the usual fear of suicide."*

Thandi stared out the viewport. The freighter was barely visible in one corner for a moment, and then vanished from sight as the shuttle entered the docking bay of the space station.

She came to an instant decision. "I should board that ship *now,* before they're alerted."

"Yes, I agree. I'm willing to bet the reason Flairty was left behind—eating in a restaurant so close to the Suds—is because at the proper time he's going to march back into the hotel and inform Mesa's supposed overseers that their flunkeys just carried out a little rebellion and Mesa will, thank you, provide them with transport out of the Erewhon System, whether Mesa likes it or not. Probably to Congo—where, thank you, Mesa will provide them with protection, whether Mesa likes it or not. Which, if I'm right, means that you have not more than a couple of hours to make your move. Keep in mind that the third Masadan group—the one with the two pilots—is almost certainly going to be boarding that freighter ahead of you and will have taken control of it. You won't just be coming up against a sleepy freighter crew."

She shook her head. As capable as he might be otherwise, Cachat was no expert on boarding operations. Thandi was.

"It's not that simple, Victor. Without knowing the entry codes, the only way to board a ship is to blow your way in. I don't have the equipment to do that. Templeton might, on his own ship, but I sure don't. I'm not even carrying sidearms. Holodramas be damned, you don't punch your way into a modern starship—not even a freighter—using a prybar."

There was a pause at the other end. Then: *"You're the expert. All right, then, here's what I propose. We'll have your people trailing Flairty grab him right after he meets the Mesan bigshots. Then bring all of them up here. I'm sure I can get Imbesi to provide private transport for that."*

She winced. "Victor, my two girls are good but that's asking a lot of them. Flairty—and up to half a dozen other men? They might be able to manage that, but—"

"O ye of little faith. You keep forgetting who I'm working with, Thandi. The four of them on their way up here aren't the only ones on Erewhon. As soon as I can pass the word through Imbesi, your ladies will have the help they need. Just tell them to wait somewhere outside the restaurant. My people will know how to spot them. After all, they've been hunting them for decades."

Thandi almost choked. "Victor, ah . . . Jesus. Talk about supping with the devil—looked at from either side."

The amusement was obvious in his voice, even if it was a subtle thing. *"True enough. But the oldest wise saw of all is probably 'the enemy of my enemy is my friend.' I'd say it applies in this case, don't you?"*

"Hard to argue the point. How do you propose to get me over there?"

"We'll worry about that when the time comes. I'm putting this together on the run, Thandi. Just get me Flairty—those Mesans he'll be with, rather—and I'll get the codes out of them."

His words had begun with a bit of warmth, under the calm and relaxed tone. By the time he finished speaking, they sounded like cubes of ice. Thandi didn't think to ask how Cachat was so confident he could get the information. As well ask a tiger why he was complacent about his prey.

"All right. But you'll have to get in touch with my women yourself, Victor. They're carrying military coms designed for planetary ranges and covert communications, so they're not tied into the system-wide net. They can't pick me up from here, and even the shuttle's systems can't hit them from here without a bucket receiver."

"No problem. I'm sure my contact here can do it."

A gentle chime sounded through the passenger compartment of the shuttle. The vehicle lurched a bit, and then settled down into that steady state which indicated: *We have arrived.* Other passengers were already beginning to get to their feet, carrying their luggage, and heading toward the entry doors.

"I'm at the station now, Victor. Where and how will we meet?"

"Who knows? I haven't been here long myself. Just follow your nose, Thandi—most of all, your ears. Things are going to be getting a little noisy around here. I still need a code word—something—to get in touch with your two ladies."

As she rose and headed toward the entry doors, followed by her team—none of them were carrying luggage, of course—Thandi's lips twisted a little. "Just have your people say *great kaja* sent them. And that if they don't follow orders, I'll break Lara's other arm and beat Inge to a pulp. That'll do the trick."

She could hear Victor's little chuckle in her ear. *"Remind me never to enlist in any boot camp you're running. All right, Thandi. Good luck."*

CHAPTER 21

GIDEON TEMPLETON LET THE NEW CONVERTS do the killing. For all that their slack attitudes toward doctrine often annoyed him, there was no question that as sheer physical specimens any of them were more capable than the Faithful-since-birth. Certainly in unarmed combat, if not with sophisticated weaponry and equipment they had little experience with.

Fortunately, Gideon's old Faithful were extremely competent with high-tech gadgetry—such, at least, as bore directly on their sacred duties. Templeton gave Jacob a glance. Three of the Masadan party were lined up against a wall of the security lounge, as if posing for a portrait. Jacob, standing in front of them, seemed to be fiddling with the holorecorder with which he was about to record their image for posterity.

Jacob was waiting for Templeton's glance, and responded with a slight nod. The "holorecorder" Jacob was holding was actually a white-noise generator designed by a Solarian firm which specialized in security equipment. Very expensive, as such state-of-the-art electronic devices always were. But Gideon's successful activities of the past fifteen T-years had left him with very large financial resources, to add to the considerable war chest which his father Ephraim had managed to assemble before he fled Masada.

Jacob's nod told Gideon that most security devices in the lounge were temporarily disabled, in one way or another. The audio pickups would be blanketed in silence as soon as the noise suppressor kicked in, and the video recorders interrupted with what would appear to be a malfunction of some sort. There was no way, even with that equipment, to blanket the energy sensors designed to pick up the discharge of power weapons. But Gideon was not concerned with that, since, if all went as planned, there would be no weapon discharges taking place. Not here and now, at any rate.

The noise suppressor would be activated by a timer within a

few seconds. Gideon looked away, and made the same minimal head gesture. He was careful not to look at anyone in particular when he did so, certain that the individuals for whom that nod was intended would be watching him. Whatever their other faults, the new converts were dependable enough in these matters.

"That'll be it then, gentlemen," said the attendant, smiling as he emerged from the side room in the security lounge where he'd stored their personal weapons. He closed the door, turned, and his finger lifted to punch in the security code. "You'll be able to retrieve them when—"

The timing kicked in on the noise suppressor. The attendant's mouth kept moving for a second or two, until he began to realize he wasn't making any sound at all.

But, by then, his eyes were widening for more pressing reasons than unexplained speechlessness. Moving with the grace and speed provided by his genes and training, one of the new converts—Stash, that was, short for Stanislav—vaulted the counter with liquid ease. The attendant tried to shout something, but no sound emerged. He had no time for anything further. What would have been a cough of agony exploded silently from his lungs as Stash's fist went into his kidney like a piston-driven club, hammering the attendant against the still-unlocked door. The second blow of the same fist to the same kidney followed within a split-second, finishing the work. Stash tossed him aside and piled through the door into the weapons room.

Two other new converts had also vaulted the counter. One of them took the time—casually, contemptuously—to grab the dazed attendant and smash the side of his skull against the edge of the counter. Again, the genetically engineered musculature and reflexes proved their worth. In his mind if not his ears, Gideon could hear the sound of the thin temple bone shattering, driving portions into the brain. The new convert let the attendant's body slip lifeless to the floor and followed his two comrades into the weapons room.

Gideon was already turning away, sure that the rest of the immediate work was being done to the same degree of perfection.

Indeed so. The three guards who'd accompanied Templeton and his people down the corridor from the shuttle docking bay to the security lounge were already immobilized. They'd been physically silenced too, which was quite unnecessary—but probably inevitable, given the ingrained fighting habits of the new converts. They weren't really accustomed to working with the advantages of the Masadans' high-tech gadgetry, such as the noise suppressor.

In the case of two, the method of silencing—throats collapsed by hard-edged hand blows—would complete the task of killing them. As Templeton watched, the third had his neck snapped by a sudden and powerful movement by the new convert holding his head. Imre, that was, perhaps the strongest of the lot.

Aside from Templeton's crew, there had been three other visitors to *The Wages of Sin* on the same shuttle who had also been brought by the guards to check in their personal weapons. They all died within seconds, never overcoming their shock at the sudden eruption of murderous action long enough to put up any resistance at all beyond raising their hands in futile protest. And, as with the guards and the attendant, the noise suppressor kept any auditory warning they might have issued from being able to carry to the shuttle docking bay where two of the space station's guards had remained.

Gideon grunted—silently.

Some of that grunt was due to his satisfaction at the success of this stage of his plans. He'd decided to take the risk of retrieving their weapons rather than attempt an immediate firefight in the docking bay. To some extent, that was simply to reduce the number of his immediate opponents. Primarily, however, it had been due to Gideon's calculation that the guards would have lost their initial edge of alertness after escorting a seemingly docile new group of visitors to the security lounge. They would have done this innumerable times by now, since possession of personal weapons was commonplace in this portion of the galaxy. Most of what problems they'd faced in the past would have come from visitors unfamiliar with the draconian security policies of the space station. But those would have protested immediately, while still in the docking bay. Templeton and his men had acted casually, as if they'd already been aware of the station's policy—which they had been, of course—and took it as a given.

For the most part, however, Gideon's grunt was an expression of piety. He'd sometimes wondered why the Lord had saddled him with the often-thankless and always-exasperating task of welcoming the new converts into his flock. Now he was sure he was catching a glimpse of the Almighty's great design. On their own, he was fairly confident that his old Faithful could have managed this work. But . . . not so easily, nor so surely. Whatever else, the new converts were the sharpest of blades placed into his hands by Providence.

Stash was already emerging from the weapons room, carrying

several of the side arms they'd brought with them to *The Wages of Sin.* He spread them on the counter and turned back to retrieve more. Between him and his two comrades, all of the weapons which Templeton and his men had brought to the station were quickly back in their hands, along with others they'd found to arm the rest of the crew and serve them for spares if needed.

Everyone was moving quickly, especially Jacob, who was already working at the security console on the counter next to the weapons check-in room. Gideon had stressed the importance of not leaving the white-noise scrambler running for any longer than absolutely necessary. Even the type of slackers who could normally be found working in low-wage security jobs would get suspicious if a "video malfunction" continued for long enough.

But, within seconds, Jacob was smiling. He lifted his head and gave Gideon a firm nod. Then, confirming the news, turned off the noise suppressor.

"All set. The scrambler's hooked into the security computer. It'll keep the scanners—audio and video both—looping back through the previous half hour's recordings. They're a lot of sinners, Solarians, but I will say their electronics are good."

Gideon grunted his satisfaction. To any security guard in the station's central security room who glanced at the monitors covering this lounge, it would appear to be empty again—as if, the weapons having been checked, all the passengers had left and the guards had returned to their posts. Until and unless somebody noticed that the same security guards were still moving around in the docking bay, long after their shift ended, they should be fine. They still couldn't use weapons, of course, without setting off alarms all over the station.

Stash was scowling a bit. As the former leader of the new converts—most dominant figure, more precisely—he tended to question Gideon more often than any of them.

Stash gestured back at the still-open weapons room. "There's better stuff in there. A hand-tooled side-arm flechette gun—beautiful thing, don't want to think what it cost—three military-grade pulsers, and even a tri-barrel. Ha! What idiot would have brought *that* to a place like this? I guess he was thinking he might go on safari if he got bored. Add the head of a Giant Faro Dealer to his trophy collection."

"*No.*" Gideon growled the word, but managed not to snarl it. "I've made this clear before, Stash. We've still got a long way to go—we don't even know where she is—to find my sister. This vile place won't have the same extensive security scanners in the interior of the station, but they *will* have them. As it is, I'm gambling that we can carry these low-powered guns without being spotted, because some of the guards within are bound to be carrying similar weapons. They can't very well have alarms going off constantly, simply because guards are doing their duty. But there'd be no reason for military-grade or powerful weapons to be loose in the station, and I'm sure the scanners are set to detect those. Unless we had special registers indicating that these were authorized—and there's no way to get those codes—it'd be too much of a risk."

He let it go at that, since Stash was clearly not going to press the issue. And, truth be told, Gideon wasn't very happy with the situation himself. He was quite sure that his sister's bodyguards *had* been given the codes necessary to register their military-grade weapons with the station's security scanners. Diplomatic strains or not, there was no way Erewhon would run the risk of having a Manticoran royal successfully attacked because her Manticoran bodyguards had been disarmed. In fact, Gideon was quite sure that security for *The Wages of Sin* had been beefed up all the way around. Somewhere in the station, there'd even be a heavy-weapons unit on standby.

Templeton wasn't too concerned about a possible—probable, rather—heavy-weapons unit. They wouldn't be directly positioned to cover his sister, in any event. Princess Ruth was not making an official state visit following a carefully planned route. Since there would be no way to predict the movements of an empty-headed sinner at her play, the management of the station would not want to alarm all their other guests by having a highly visible armored unit trampling through the gaming areas in her wake. Instead, they'd simply have them on standby at some central location. Deadly enough, when they arrived—but if Templeton's project went as planned, they'd get there too late.

That still left the problem of his sister's immediate bodyguards, and those *were* a matter of great concern. Leaving aside the fact that they were much better trained and motivated than a pleasure resort's security guards, they'd also have weapons considerably superior to the ones in the hands of Templeton and his men. Hand pulsers, to be sure, not heavier equipment. But military-grade sidearms, in the hands of elite soldiers, were nothing to sneer at.

Templeton had even considered bringing chemical-powered weapons with him, instead of the puny personal use and sporting hand pulsers they'd brought. For all their primitive design, the right sort of chemical-powered guns could be far more lethal. But . . .

Not possible. Such weapons were very rare, which was exactly why Templeton was well-nigh certain the station's internal scanners wouldn't pick them up, since they had no power source. But that would not have been true for the more extensive security devices in the docking bay. The guards there would have been instantly suspicious to discover that so many men in the same party all had a burning passion for antique weaponry. As it was, Gideon had had to do a bit of explaining to account for the fact that most of his party were armed. Fortunately, the fact that he'd ordered over a third of his men to arrive unarmed had done the trick. That, and a vague reference to the ingrained frontier customs of their supposed planet of origin.

Again, he congratulated himself for the shrewdness of his scheme. He'd calculated—correctly—that there would be enough hand weapons in the check-in room left by earlier passengers to arm the rest of his party. His scheme had been all the more shrewd, in that he'd been forced to improvise most of it the moment he discovered his sister was traveling to *The Wages of Sin.*

But, ever mindful of the sin of pride, Gideon didn't dwell on the self-satisfaction. Nor did he overlook the fact that there'd been an element of carelessness on his part involved also. Given the foul nature of his sister, he should have known from the very beginning that the whore would fly to such a den of iniquity at the first opportunity, like a moth to a flame. So, if he'd done an excellent job of planning hastily, some of the hastiness itself had been the result of his own slackness.

He broke off the rumination. Everyone in the party was armed now—many with an extra weapon—and they were ready to begin the next stage. His men had dragged the bodies and tossed them into the weapons check-in room. One of them had even found a cloth somewhere and was beginning to wipe up the blood which one of their victims had coughed onto the floor.

"Don't bother," said Gideon. "By the time anyone else comes in here, it will all be a moot point."

His cousin and chief lieutenant, Abraham Templeton, cocked an eye at him.

"You've decided, then, to kill the guards still in the docking bay?"

"Yes. You heard what that one guard told me, when I inquired casually. There's not another shuttle scheduled to arrive at that dock for hours."

Abraham nodded. The gesture was as much one of respect as agreement. Gideon had planned for that, as well, deliberately taking a shuttle which would arrive at the tail end of the station's peak business hours for the day. That would most likely have them docking at one of the bays used only to handle overflow traffic—as, indeed, had proved true.

"That's enough time for us to do the rest," Templeton continued, "as much of it as will set off all alarms, anyway. And it'd be safer to leave no one behind who might wander over here and set off a premature warning."

Abraham nodded and gave the assembled team a quick inspection. His eyes lingered for a bit longer on the new converts. Although they were generally unaccustomed to more elaborate weaponry, the new converts were just as proficient with simple hand weapons as they were with unarmed combat.

Stash returned Abraham's gaze with a lazy smile. "Be like butchering sheep."

Indeed, it was so. And Gideon felt his piety strengthened as a result. *The Lord moves in mysterious ways,* after all. And if it suited Him to provide Gideon with otherwise-flawed instruments for His work, Gideon Templeton was not a man to question God's will.

Templeton had been very concerned himself, about this stage of the plan. Concerned enough, in fact, that he'd almost decided to follow Abraham's advice to leave the two remaining guards in the docking bay untouched. The problem, in a nutshell, was that they did not dare attack the guards while still in the bay. No matter how slack, not even low-paid security guards could be taken down by a direct assault without managing to set off at least some of the alarms. And since the white noise generator couldn't suppress actual weapons discharges, there would be the added risk of one of the guards managing to fire his pulser.

Stash had assured Templeton that he could handle the problem through misdirection. Or—if Stash didn't match the physique of one of the guards well enough—one of the other new converts could do so.

So it proved. Gideon was able to observe the events indirectly, using a tiny holobug set up by Jacob.

The docking bay was attached to the security lounge by a short corridor. Unlike the bay or the lounge, there were no audio-video monitors set to cover that corridor. There would undoubtedly be energy sensors, but those were of no concern.

Gideon found it hard not to suppress a sneer—and did suppress it, only because of his constant vigilance for the sin of pride. Heathen sinners could always be counted on to let avarice override caution. Had Godly men been in charge of security for *The Wages of Sin,* there would have been audio-video sensors everywhere—with keen-eyed Faithful to monitor them in the station's central security room. But the greedy management of the sinful place had naturally avoided the expense, and placed them only in critical areas.

Gideon watched Stash, now dressed in a uniform taken from one of the dead security guards who had approximately his size and build, amble down the corridor. "Amble" was the right word, too. No old Faithful could have managed that slovenly shuffle—nor the equally slack manner in which Stash leaned around the corner where the corridor debouched into the docking bay and waved an arm at the two remaining security guards.

The arm-wave, too, was perfect. *It's done, boys. Shift's over—so let's get us a beer.* All of it conveyed without Stash having to say a word—or give the two guards more than a glimpse of him.

But . . . it was the glimpse they'd been expecting. Indeed, awaiting. So, within seconds, the two men appeared in the corridor, walking in the easy manner of sinners looking forward to their sins. Not "ambling," exactly—they were moving too quickly for that term to apply—but with nothing at all in the way of alertness or caution.

Stash was facing away from them, down on one knee, apparently adjusting the fit of one of his boots. His face was obscured by the bill of the cap on his head. As the two security guards came alongside, one of them said something. A jest, apparently, judging from the grin on his face. Templeton couldn't hear the actual words, because the miniature transmitter Jacob had set up alongside the corridor's wall was not able to pick up audio signals.

It didn't matter, anyway. Stash was moving again, and this time there was nothing either slovenly or shuffling about it. He came up like a tiger out of its crouch, striking once—twice—

Then, quickly, finishing the work once the guards were on the floor. It was all over in a manner of seconds. And Gideon had heard not a sound coming around the bend of the corridor where he and the others waited in the security lounge.

One of the new converts went to help Stash carry the two bodies into the security lounge. It was the work of a few more seconds to stuff them into the weapons room with the other corpses.

Then, all was done except the final strike on the princess.

Gideon's initial plans had worked to perfection. They departed the security lounge, filing down the corridor leading to the halls of the Devil's playground where the whore sister would surely be found.

First Lieutenant Ahmed Griggs was not a happy man. To put it mildly.

Not because of anything to do with his own people, of course. He and Laura Hofschulte had chosen Sergeant Christina Bulanchik's squad from Griggs' own platoon for the detail for several reasons. The biggest one was Bulanchik herself, a long-service noncom who, like Griggs, held the Sphinx Cross. Several of the other members of her squad had been decorated for valor also, but that wasn't particularly uncommon in the Queen's Own Regiment. Almost all of its personnel were on at least their second term of enlistment in the Royal Manticoran Army (those who hadn't been cross-transferred from the Marines, as Griggs himself had been), and the Queen's Own was able to pick and choose only the very best. But Bulanchik had two other points in her favor. One was that she had always scored very high in public place training scenarios, and the other was that Ruth Winton liked her. It wasn't essential for a protectee to have a friendly personal relationship with one of her protectors, but it never hurt. Especially when it came to guarding Princess Ruth in such a crowded, busy, distracting, security nightmare of a place like *The Wages of Sin*.

Since they'd entered the pleasure resort, a part of Griggs' mind had never stopped cursing. Some of those silent curses, needless to say, had been visited on the princess herself. But not many. No one expects a headstrong young woman to be sensible about security, after all, especially the people assigned to protect her.

More of his curses were visited on the now-absent head of Anton Zilwicki. Haring off on a mysterious mission for a month, leaving his daughter and the princess to manage their own affairs!

But . . . the lieutenant didn't curse Anton much more than he did the girls. He knew the man's reputation, and if Anton Zilwicki thought something was important enough for him to leave for a month, Griggs didn't really doubt it was true.

No, most of the lieutenant's curses were visited on a man far distant from Erewhon: the Star Kingdom's Prime Minister, whose arrogant and stupid policies had so thoroughly alienated the people and government of Erewhon and made the princess' "informal" voyage to Erewhon necessary in the first place.

The Queen had not, needless to say, explained her purpose in sending Princess Ruth to Lieutenant Griggs personally. But there'd been no need. Like all officers assigned to the Queen's Own, Griggs was quite well aware of the political situation in the Star Kingdom. In times past, when Manticore's foreign relations had been in the hands of Prime Minister Cromarty and people of his choosing, Queen Elizabeth herself might have made the trip to Erewhon—or, if not she, someone representing her officially. On such occasions, Lieutenant Griggs would have been able to take all the added security measures which were taken for granted during such elaborate events.

Now, however . . .

Griggs had no quarrel with the Erewhonese themselves. As soon as he informed them of the princess' proposed visit to *The Wages of Sin,* without even being asked, the Erewhonese had volunteered to waive the usual security rules and allow Griggs and his men to retain their sidearms. They'd also immediately informed him that they would beef up the station's normal security by assembling their special weapons unit and keeping it on standby.

And that was, realistically, as much as he could ask for. There was simply no way that security for an informal jaunt by a member of the royal family could come close to the level of security which was possible for official visits of state. Especially when the member in question wasn't even in the line of succession. Such elaborate security measures were extremely disruptive for the normal course of business, after all. If Griggs had tried to push the issue, the Erewhonese would have simply declared the space station off limits for the princess—and he would have had to face Ruth's wrath. That, by itself, he would have been willing enough to do. But he knew perfectly well the princess would simply have overruled him—he was her bodyguard, not her keeper—and he would have wound up facing the same situation anyway, with disgruntled Erewhonese to deal with instead of cooperative ones.

As they wandered through the gaming halls of the pleasure resort, the princess and her companion were gazing awestruck at the holographic displays on the ceiling whenever they weren't distracted by one or another of the equally dazzling displays at the gaming tables themselves. Griggs ignored it all. Most of his mind was given to the task of studying all the people in the vicinity, looking for any possible danger. The rest was wallowing in tradition. His family treasured the ancient art of the curse.

—to the third generation. As for High Ridge's great-grandchildren, may each and every one be born with genetic defects—not much to ask, given THAT gene pool—and suffer a protracted and agonizing death. May their corpses be dismembered by wild animals. May their body parts—

As soon as Thandi and her team got off the shuttle and past the initial screen of security guards and scanners, she called Victor again.

"This place is a maze, and I don't know it at all. I don't see any point to wandering around looking for the Princess. You and Imbesi and your—ah, bodyguards—will have to do whatever you can at the point of initial contact. I think it makes a lot more sense for me to get into position to intercept Templeton after he makes his strike."

There was a slight pause; then Victor's calm voice came back. *"Agreed. I should have thought of that myself. Naomi's been with me since I arrived and she knows this place backwards and forwards."*

"I bet she does," Thandi snorted. But she didn't have the throat mike activated when she said it.

"So I didn't think to consider what it would be like coming into it cold. What do you need?"

"I need to know where I am in relation to the most likely area—or areas—where Templeton would make his move. Even more important, where he'd be most likely to make his exit from the station—and the fastest way for me to place myself across that route. Or routes, if there'd be more than one."

"You'll need to give me some time. Five minutes, at least, probably more. Neither Naomi nor Walter will have that information, so we'll have to check with someone else."

Seeing no point to wandering around any further with no goal in mind, Thandi halted her team with a little gesture. They'd drawn alongside one of the resort station's multitude of little refreshment areas recessed from the corridor, and Thandi led the way into it. Her metabolism was starting to make warning signals, so since she had a bit of time she'd take care of that problem. Quickly, she and her team ordered food and began more or less gulping it down. Thandi's women grinned at her as they did so. Their metabolisms were more ferocious than average also, of course, but nothing compared to hers.

✧ ✧ ✧

Templeton also found the space station a maze, but he'd had time to prepare for it. So, guided by the holo-guides one of his men had obtained the day before, he and his team passed quickly enough through the corridors toward the main gaming halls at the center of the station.

He was quite sure his sister would be found there. A moth to the flame. And once he got close enough to begin picking up her chemical traces, the very expensive tracking equipment he'd brought with him would do the rest.

Thandi had just finished wolfing down her food when Victor's voice returned.

"All right. Here's the best I can come up with. Templeton arrived at one of the more isolated docking bays. Good luck for him, unless he planned it that way—which he very likely did. But he won't return by that route. He's more likely to use one of the maintenance docks—either in Tube Gamma or Epsilon—and seize two or three of the shuttles which are always stationed there for routine work. Those bays aren't guarded since there's no way to enter them from the outside without security codes. Leaving them, of course, is a different matter. That requires codes also, but I'm sure he'll get the codes from the employees working there. They're not trained to stand up under torture."

"Okay. Where's—"

"Patience, patience." A trace of easy humor filtered into the relaxed, confident voice. Thandi felt a little stab of passion and suffocated it ruthlessly. No time for that—even if she knew the man!

"I was just about to tell you," Cachat continued. *"Right now, you're in Tube Beta. A bit of good luck for us, since you're much closer to Epsilon or Gamma than Templeton will be when he makes his move."*

"Which will be where?"

"In the main gaming hall at the center of the station. The Manticoran women are already there, and I'm sure that's where Templeton's headed. I'm heading down there myself, as soon as this conversation is finished."

"All right. I'll find my way, easily enough. There are holo-guides all over the place." She hesitated a moment. "Take care, Victor. By now, they'll almost certainly be armed."

"There's no question they are, I don't think. Imbesi just made a call to the docking bay where they arrived, and got no answer. I'm sure they've slaughtered the guards and taken their weapons. Along

with whatever they brought themselves. Hopefully, they won't have any military-grade equipment."

Thandi hesitated again. She'd already considered the methods available for arming her team. They'd brought no weapons at all, since she'd known there was no way the station's security would have allowed them to enter with their weaponry.

Victor anticipated her thoughts. "*Take what you need from the station's guards, when the time comes. But if you can, try not to kill any of them.*"

"That'd be hard to do, to be honest. Besides . . . we'll see, once I get a look at the fighting ground. I might be able to get the weapons from Templeton's men themselves."

It was Cachat's turn to hesitate. "*That could be . . . ah,* really *dangerous, Thandi.*"

"Yes, it could. On the other hand"—her lips quirked a little—"I'm really that good, too. We'll make a deal. I won't tell you how to do cloak-and-dagger stuff; you don't tell me how to do mayhem."

She heard his soft chuckle. "*Fair enough. Good luck, Thandi. When I hear anything more, I'll pass it along.*"

Thandi rose from the table. The women in her team, scattered at three other tables as well as her own, were on their feet instantly. Glancing around, Thandi saw that they were alone in the little room.

"We've been warned to be careful," she said cheerfully. "It seems Templeton is dangerous and my—ah, gentleman friend—is a bit concerned for my health."

That got the reaction she'd expected. All of the women were scowling.

"Men!" snapped one of them. "Great kaja, you are. Eat them alive."

CHAPTER 22

"THAT'S IT, THEN," SAID VICTOR SOFTLY, turning to face Naomi and her uncle. The two were sitting in what looked like superbly comfortable armchairs. So Victor assumed, at any rate. All the furniture he'd seen so far in the Imbesi family's private suite in *The Wages of Sin* looked—there was no other term for it—sinfully expensive and luxurious. That was part of the reason Victor hadn't availed himself of the comfort personally, aside from the fact that he was too full of energy to sit down anyway. For someone of his background and ideological convictions, there was something vaguely distasteful about using a piece of furniture whose price could have fed a poor family for months. It was an irrational reaction on his part, of course—but he was still the person who lived inside the skin of "Victor Cachat."

"Do you really think this will work?" Walter asked, frowning a little. "It seems excessively complicated."

"It *is* excessively complicated. But I can't see any other way to squeeze the opening we want out of the situation. Just smashing Templeton won't do it. We need to use him like a prybar."

Naomi's frown was more pronounced than her uncle's. "What I don't understand is why you're so confident that Templeton will even *find* his sister." She glanced at the door which opened into one of the space station's public corridors. "Victor, I'm not sure you have any real idea just how convoluted those passageways are. Sure, there are holo-guides. But those aren't really all that easy to use, especially for someone who's never been here before—which I'd be astonished if Templeton has, given his theology."

"She's got a point, Victor," chimed in Walter. "Templeton's more likely to just blunder about. And within two hours or so the alarms are going to go up all over the station. At that point, he'll just get smashed anyway. So why not do it now—and possibly save quite a few lives?"

"I'm *counting* on that theology, Walter. At a guess, how many people from either Grayson or Masada do you think ever visit *The Wages of Sin*?"

Imbesi chuckled. "Maybe a dozen. Possibly a few more . . . but not many of them, that's for sure. The Graysons don't share the Masadans' more fanatical effusions of 'morality,' of course. They don't have any prohibitions against gambling—within limits, at least—but even for them, this place is pretty much a synonym for 'wickedness.'" He grinned. "I think it has something to do with the female entertainers' costumes. Or lack thereof. Hm. Come to that, most of them are probably just as uncomfortable with the *male* entertainer's outfits!" he added, transferring his grin to his niece.

"Exactly," Victor nodded. "And the Grayson-Masadan genetic variant is quite distinct. The equipment needed to pick it up out of stray molecules suspended in the air is extremely costly, true. But the Masadans have piled up a lot of loot from their piracies over the past fifteen years—on top of a pile which was very substantial to begin with. Templeton's not stupid. I can't imagine he would have tried this stunt if he didn't have such a chemotracker."

Naomi's eyes widened. "I've heard of that sort of equipment. But is it really *that* good?"

"Yes," replied Victor firmly. "I've seen the gear in action. In the hands of someone who knows how to use it, it's almost like magic. Mind you, if they were trying to track Zilwicki's daughter in this crowded madhouse, it wouldn't do them any good except at close range. But that's because she's Terran, and her DNA traces would be impossible to distinguish from most people's until they got within a few meters of her. But with the princess, it's a different matter altogether. Especially since Templeton's crew is all male, so they can set the readings to filter out anything but a female from their genetic stock. Closer than that, in fact, since she's Templeton's half-sister and he can use his own DNA to key the settings."

"All right," said Walter, "that makes sense. But I still don't see why you're so confident you can bring Templeton to ground after he strikes."

"Genetics again." He eyed the Imbesis for a moment, hesitant to offend them. One of the prominent characteristics of Erewhonese culture—one which Victor himself appreciated, in fact—was that they were ferociously egalitarian. That aspect of their culture was not evident to most foreigners, who saw only the very stratified nature of Erewhon's power structure. But a structure and the individuals who filled its niches were not the same thing. Yes, the Erewhonese had little use for what most people would called "genuine democracy." But they had even less use for the notion that any *individual* could not aspire to anything he or she could manage. It was standard practice for Erewhon's great families to adopt promising youngsters, with no regard for class or genetic background. In fact, one of the worst insinuations which could be made of a prominent and influential family was that it was too selective in its mating habits—"screwing in-round," to use the crude Erewhonese expression.

Still, facts were facts, and he didn't think either of the Imbesis—Walter, especially—was all that blinkered by custom. "I don't think you really appreciate how much difference it can make, especially in a hand-to-hand melee, to have people on your side with the genetic make-up of Lieutenant Palane and her Amazon wrecking crew. Especially Palane."

Naomi made a little face. "Female weight-lifter," she muttered.

With some difficulty, Victor suppressed his annoyance. Leaving aside his own feelings for Lieutenant Palane, which still confused as well as unsettled him, what made Naomi's cattiness so irritating was that Victor knew there was nothing personal about it in the sense of jealousy about *him.* It was just the Imbesi woman's ingrained competitiveness toward other females at work.

"That's the least of it," he said, almost snapping. "Physical superiority by itself doesn't necessarily mean that much. In fact, it can be a handicap if it leads to overconfidence. I once—" He shook his head. "Never mind. Just take my word for it—or don't, as you choose. Palane didn't claw her way out of where she came from simply by using her muscles. She's smart, disciplined, and very well-trained. And while I think the Solarian Navy is over-rated—they haven't fought a real war against a serious opponent in centuries—the Solarian Marines are a different story altogether. Given all the brushfires they're constantly being called on to stamp out, they probably have at least as much combat experience—their best units, anyway—as even Republican or Mantie Marines. So when the time comes, I'll put my money on her."

Walter Imbesi had been studying Victor in the course of his little sermon. Now, he shrugged and spread his hands wide on the armrests. "And I'm putting my money on you. I've got my doubts, but . . . I learned a lot time ago not to second-guess myself. Okay, Victor, we'll do it your way. And now what?"

Victor glanced at his watch. "And now I'd say it's time for me and mine to set forth for the fray."

"What do you plan to do?"

"Have you ever seen holorecordings of that rather brutal ancient Terran sport called 'bull-fighting'? Or the variant of it they still play in the Solarian League's Nueva Oaxaca sector, using native animals?"

Walter's eyes widened. "I've seen the Nueva Oaxacan sport you're talking about, though not in person. If you can call that bloody business a 'sport.' "

"Can't say I approve myself," agreed Victor. "But it's a nice little analogy. I'm counting on Thandi—Lieutenant Palane—to drive in the sword. But the beast needs to be bloodied and weakened first."

"I can't get you weapons, Victor," warned Imbesi. "Not without tipping off my own place in this scheme of yours—which I can't afford to do. I've stretched my 'plausible deniability' far enough as it is."

"I wasn't asking you to," replied Victor mildly. He loosened his wide belt and palmed an object nestled into the ornate buckle. "This'll be enough to get me started."

Naomi stared at the object. "I've never heard of a palm pulser accurate at more than a few meters. I hope—"

"A few meters will be plenty. And it isn't a pulser. No pulser, no matter how small, could have made it through the security scanners in this place. It's a nonlethal stunning device, inertly powered, and you don't want to know how much it cost to make it detection-proof."

"But what—"

Walter was almost scowling. "I certainly *hope* it's nonlethal. If you start killing security guards yourself, it's going to be impossible to keep you sorted out from the bad guys when the dust settles." He glanced at the four men who were leaning casually against a nearby wall. "Especially given the nature of your own wrecking crew. We're cold-blooded on Erewhon, but not *that* cold-blooded."

One of the four men was Donald X. The thickset ex-slave gave Imbesi a thin smile. "Not to worry. Victor's aged a bit since the last time we encountered him. I'm sure he won't run amok the way he did on— Well. Let's hope, at any rate."

Imbesi sighed. "Damn High Ridge, anyway. Damn him and his children and their children. May—"

✧ ✧ ✧

Outside, in the corridor, Donald's smile widened. "Hadn't realized the Erewhonese were masters of the curse."

"They aren't, really," said Victor, now hurrying. "It's just that they have a serious grievance—and they're not a folk who take grievances lightly."

"Wheeeee!! Way to go, Princess!"

Lieutenant Griggs winced at the piercing feminine squeal in his ear. He normally found Princess Ruth's voice pleasant enough, but when she was excited like this . . .

Not, perhaps, all *that* excited. He noticed that she'd still had the presence of mind to call Berry Zilwicki "Princess" when her companion managed to strike the jackpot again. Of course, from the vantage point of someone born and raised in the Manticoran royal family, the amount of money involved in the "jackpot" would hardly be overwhelming.

Even Berry didn't seemed overwhelmed, actually. The girl was smiling widely, to be sure, but Ahmed thought that was more due to the pleasure of the game itself rather to any great glee over sudden fortune. Griggs didn't think he'd plumbed the depths of the Zilwicki girl's character on such a relatively short acquaintance. But one thing was already clear to him—Berry Zilwicki just didn't seem to care all that much for any of the small measures of triumph by which so many people gauged their lives. She seemed far more mature than her seventeen T-years would have led him to expect.

But he didn't spend much time pondering the matter. His eyes were moving steadily across the crowd, checking for any possible sign of danger and making sure his people were maintaining good positions.

Fat lot of good that'll do them, as much of a madhouse as this place is. With these milling crowds, a damned army could sneak up on us before we'd spot them.

But the thought was only middling-sour. In truth, Griggs was not really expecting any trouble here that he and his troopers couldn't handle readily enough. There was this much to be said for the space station's persnickety security policies: any assailant would presumably have been disarmed. The worst trouble he'd encountered thus far was an inebriated fellow who'd apparently found "Princess" Berry stunningly attractive. But the girl had fended him off with a couple of witty phrases—and the lieutenant's glare had been enough to send the man stumbling off in search of easier if less nubile prey.

Berry Zilwicki hit the jackpot again.

"*Wheeeee!!!*"

Ahmed Griggs resigned himself to a long night.

"I've got her now," murmured Gideon, studying the readouts on the chemotracker's display. He moved the device in his hand back and forth, selecting between three corridors. Then, nodded to the left. "The whore's scent comes from there."

His cousin Abraham gave the display no more than a perfunctory glance. The readouts were far too complex to be read casually, and their leader was the only one who'd mastered the art. Of course, that was mostly because he'd never let anyone else do more than look at the incredibly costly gadget.

"To the left," said Abraham softly, passing along Gideon's command to the men trailing behind. He did not have to speak loudly. Since there was no way to disguise the fact that the large group was traveling together, Gideon Templeton had decided to turn a minus into a plus. His strike force was lined up double file, each man carrying the hand luggage which contained their weapons, as if they constituted a well-organized tour.

A moment later, Templeton and his three dozen killers were moving down the corridor. Once again, Gideon was awed by the subtlety of the Lord. On their own, he doubted very much if the old Faithful could have maintained the image of being simple tourists. Some, yes—but most had expressions on their faces which were so pinched and hostile that a solid body of them would have been rather alarming. Almost half of his crew were new converts, however, and those men made up for it by their cheerful swagger and open ogling at the sights around them. Practically the image of "brash tourists," they were.

Within a few minutes, they could hear the sound of revelry coming from ahead. Clearly, they were nearing the gaming halls. One young female voice sounded particularly loud and excited.

"Whores born," hissed Gideon, "each and every one. A place like this brings out the truth of it for all the universe to see, if the faithless had eyes."

By the time Thandi neared her destination, she'd been able to make enough sense of the holo-guide she'd purchased to decide on a battle plan. She was basically an infantry officer, with a specialization in ship-boarding, so she had a very good sense for "ground." Provided that the air circulation ducts were wide enough . . .

There was no way to tell until they tried them, but she was betting they would be. Like any enclosed pleasure resort trying to please as wide a range of customers as possible, *The Wages of Sin* needed to keep the air in the station fresh and frequently scrubbed. The easiest and cheapest way to provide for that would be with wide air ducts. Wide enough, she was almost sure, to allow even someone as big as she was to pass through them. Not standing, to be sure, but Thandi had spent enough time crawling during training exercises that she wasn't concerned about being able to maneuver quickly through something as straightforward as a circulation duct.

And they had one *big* advantage: Epsilon and Gamma corridors ran more or less parallel to each other for a quarter of a loop around the space station. Unless the Erewhonese designers of the place had opted for some exotic alternative, the two corridors were almost bound to be connected frequently to the same air circulation system. If so, she could essentially cover both of Templeton's possible escape routes without dividing most of her forces.

"Most of her forces." *Ha! All ten of them—eleven, counting herself. And none of them armed except for the weapons provided by nature.*

Which . . .

She glanced back at her team and smiled coldly. Amazons, indeed.

. . . ain't no small thing, when you get right down to it.

As they'd planned ahead of time, Ginny was waiting for Victor and his men in a small salon not far from one of the entrances to the main gaming hall. The salon was one of many such scattered about *The Wages of Sin*, in order to provide patrons a place to rest in some peace and quiet before launching themselves back into the fray. Victor and Ginny had chosen that salon because it was tucked away around a corner and went largely unnoticed by the public patrons—for which reason, it was favored by the resort's employees whenever they found the chance to catch a quick break.

Especially the security guards. Sure enough, when Victor walked into the salon he found Ginny seated on an upholstered stool, wearing a skimpy outfit which showed off her bare legs to perfection. Sitting around her in a semicircle were three of the station's security guards. From the intent expressions on their faces, all of them seemed to be finding Ginny's cheerful prattle the most profound philosophical insights they'd ever heard.

Victor managed not to smile. Ginny in Full Charm Mode was something of a shock to men who weren't familiar with her.

He glanced about, first checking the door in the corner which led to a small supply closet. The door was security coded, but Victor had already examined it earlier and was sure he could crack the code in a matter of seconds. It was a purely perfunctory lock, simply designed to keep out idly curious patrons. Then his eyes swept the rest of the salon, noting the two food-service employees sitting at a small table against a far corner. That was a bit unfortunate, but it would have been blind luck to have found the salon empty of anyone except the ones he wanted.

Donald and one of the other Ballroom members wandered in a few seconds later. Paying Victor no attention, they ambled lazily over to a table next to the one where the two food-service women were enjoying their break.

So much for that. Victor was quite confident they'd handle that end of the business. The remaining two Ballroom people would stay outside in the corridor to keep watch for anyone else.

Let's do it, then.

He moved toward Ginny and her admirers. Seeing him come, Ginny gave him her most inviting smile. "*Edward!*" she called out happily, and started to rise.

The three guards, needless to say, were by no means so delighted to see him. All of them glanced sourly at Victor; one of them was scowling outright. As their attention was distracted, Ginny gave out a little cry of distress. A moment later—she'd apparently gotten her feet tangled in the stool as she rose—she was spilling over backward.

Thump. Fortunately the floor of the salon was well-carpeted. Ginny landed on her back, her now-completely-bare legs flailing haplessly in midair. Except for her underwear—which was every bit as skimpy as the rest of her outfit—all was, as the expression went, "completely exposed."

It was an irresistible sight, especially for men who'd been momentarily distracted already. All three guards were gawking at her. One of them began to rise to give her a gentlemanly hand.

Thtt. He collapsed back onto his own stool and then slid to the floor unconscious. *Thtt. Thtt.* The other two guards, likewise.

As Ginny scrambled lithely to her feet, grinning, Victor turned toward the small scuffling sounds in the far corner. Donald and his comrade had seized the food-service workers and hauled them to their feet. With one hand clamped over their mouths to keep them silent, they were forcing the two women toward Victor.

He gauged their body weight and adjusted the settings on the tranquilizer gun accordingly. The drug used in the needles could be dangerous, even fatal, if used in too great a dosage.

Fortunately, since he was in a hurry, the settings were not really all that critical. He passed over the woman in Donald's grip, since Donald was so powerful she was completely helpless, and shot the other woman first. Then, Donald's. *Thtt, thtt,* and it was all over. There had been hardly any noise beyond a bit of scuffling and soft thumping and the thin sound of the compressed gas firing the needles. A nice, quick operation.

By the time Donald and his comrade Hendryk had deposited the two unconscious women next to the supply locker door and carried over the three guards, Victor had broken the security code. It was the work of a minute to place all five people in the closet in as comfortable a position as possible, given the cramped quarters, but they'd survive the experience with nothing worse than mild bruises and cramped muscles. The needles themselves wouldn't even have to be surgically removed. They were made from organic compounds which, once exposed to blood, would disolve harmlessly within a few hours.

Fortunately—this had been Victor's one big worry—the supply closet had its own ventilation ducts. There was no danger of suffocation.

"How long does that stuff last?" Hendryk asked.

Victor closed the door behind him and set a different combination for the lock. That would add a further delay if another employee should happen to need something in it. "Hard to say, exactly. It varies from one person to the next based on resistance and body weight. But they'll all be out for at least four hours, more likely six to eight."

"Long enough," Donald grunted. "I will say your technique has gotten a lot smoother since Chicago."

Victor handed the guns they'd taken from the guards to three of the Ballroom members. According to Donald, they were the best shots with handguns. Victor and Donald himself would just have to make do.

So would Ginny, but Victor was bound and determined to keep her out of the coming fray. Fortunately, despite her self-confident personality, Ginny was not a gunhandler at all and was not prone to useless heroics.

She was, however, prone to useless wisecracks.

"I told you!" she scolded Donald. "It's all due to my feminine influence. Soothes the savage male, all that. Otherwise he'd have hacked them up with an ax, or something."

Victor forbore reply. Always the safest course, dealing with Ginny.

"Let's do it, then. We're not three minutes from the gaming hall. Remember: unless it looks like they're planning to kill her, we'll let them take the princess before we intervene."

Ginny shook her head. "On the other hand, it'll take me *years* before I've got him shaped up as what you'd call a bona fide Knight in Shining Armor."

CHAPTER 23

WHEN TEMPLETON SPOTTED the two young women standing at one of the gaming tables, he turned away in order to conceal his glare of fury from the very alert-looking officer standing a few paces from them. The officer was out of uniform, but Templeton had no doubt at all he was in the Manticoran military.

He spent the few seconds he needed to bring his sudden flare of rage under control studying the readings on the chemotracker in his palm, turning still further aside in order to prevent the Manticoran officer from getting a real glimpse of the device. From a distance of more than five meters, cupped in a man's hand, the chemotracker would be indistinguishable from a holo-guide.

The readings matched perfectly. They practically screamed: *The whore is here! And very close!*

"That's her, isn't it?" murmured Abraham. "The one in the fancy apparel?"

Gideon nodded. "Don't seem to be staring. Have the men spread out and find all the security people in the area, as well as the slut's own bodyguards. Do nothing before reporting back to me."

A moment later, Abraham was passing along the orders. Gideon was careful to keep his eyes on a nearby gaming table, as if gauging his chances at it, but he was able to follow the progress of his men well enough. Again, he gave thanks to the Lord. The old Faithful were moving a bit stiffly and awkwardly. As experienced as they were in such affairs, they were much like Templeton himself—too angry and outraged by the environment of this nest of evil to be able to act really casually. The new converts, on the other hand, handled the matter to perfection. They were spreading out easily and moving through the crowd looking for guards as if they were nothing more than avid thrill-seekers. Which, in a way, Templeton suspected they were.

Within a minute, reports began coming in. Fortunately,

Templeton had been able to afford the best and most discreet personal communicators, so he wasn't worried that the security staff might pick up the transmissions. He'd be able to maintain tight information, control and command throughout, something which was not always possible in such operations. And if he fell in the service of the Lord, Abraham would be able to replace him immediately. He also had a full-link command communicator, as did his own lieutenant Jacob, who would be next in command if Abraham was struck down.

"The bitch has seven personal bodyguards, all of them looking like nervous rodents. Their leader is standing near their perimeter, on the right side. The one with the red hair. All of them are carrying sidearms only."

"Three security guards at each of the four main entrances to the hall, including the gate we need to pass through once we've got the slut. Their weapons are holstered and they don't seem particularly alert."

"Two guards in tandem drifting through the crowd. I'm following them. They're armed but their weapons are holstered."

"A guard gabbing with a customer by one of the tables. I've got him when the signal goes up."

"A guard practically draped all over a whore at a table not far from the princess." That was a new convert speaking; no old Faithful would have had that undertone of concupiscence. *"Her husband doesn't look any too happy about it either."*

Victor *wasn't* happy about it, but only because the guard's holster had a buttoned-down flap that would take too long to get open and retrieve the weapon. He'd spotted the Scrag several seconds earlier, since the man was acting as carelessly as Scrags tended to do. The "superman's" version of "undercover work" was almost laughable. Victor hoped that Thandi had at least managed to beat that habit out of her own crew.

He decided to turn the Scrag's arrogance to advantage.

"Do you see them all?" he murmured into his communicator.

Donald was standing at the same gaming table, not more than ten feet away, appearing to be studying the game under progress. His voice was full of amusement.

"It's a bit like spotting wild animals swaggering through a coffee house, isn't it? The Scrags, I mean. The Masadans look like they've all eaten a jar full of pickles. I count fifteen, in my viewing range."

Victor had counted about the same number, including Gideon Templeton—who was standing with two men he presumed to be his lieutenants not more than thirty meters away from the princess. He was sure the remaining men were somewhere out of sight in the crowd. Many of them would be positioned to take out the security guards by the entrances to the gaming hall.

There was nothing he could do about those, anyway, even leaving aside the fact that he had no intention of stopping the fanatics from kidnapping the princess and making their escape. Some of them, rather. He intended to kill at least half of the Masadans, including Templeton if at all possible. Bleed the beasts so Thandi could spring the trap.

The security guard was now casually placing his hand on Ginny's arm. Ginny herself, to all apparent purposes, seemed to be enjoying the attention. Victor decided the circumstances allowed him to scowl openly.

He didn't have to fake the scowl, either. He *hated* complicated operations which depended on coordinated timing, but he hadn't seen where he had any choice. Glumly, he knew that Kevin Usher would have sarcastic remarks to make when he got a full report—even assuming the fancy maneuver came off properly.

For a moment, he was tempted to call Thandi again, just to reassure himself that her people still on the planet were up to the task of grabbing Flairty and the Mesans and getting them up to *The Wages of Sin* in time for the rest of the operation to go as planned. Imbesi already had a private shuttle waiting for them at the shuttle grounds, but . . .

He pushed the worry aside. Thandi's people would either manage it or they wouldn't. At this point, there was nothing either he or Lieutenant Palane herself could do about it. So he turned back to the business at hand.

"I'll have to take the Scrag watching Ginny," he murmured. "You get the guard's gun."

Donald made no reply beyond: *"Okay."*

Out of the corner of his eye, Victor studied the Scrag again. The man was perhaps five meters away, now. A bit too distant for the short-range accuracy of the tranquilizer gun.

Speaking of which . . . turning slightly away, he palmed it into his hand.

"*Are you utterly insane?*" Unser Diem shrieked. The Jessyk Combine's troubleshooter had shot out of his chair before

Templeton's Lieutenant Flairty had completed the third sentence of his terse statement.

"What do you madmen think you're doing?" he bellowed.

Haicheng Ringstorff was furious himself, but he didn't waste time in pointless harangues. Still sitting, he exchanged looks with George Lithgow. His lieutenant's eyes were slitted with anger, and his hands were clenched on the armrests of his own chair, but Lithgow was no more prone than Ringstorff himself to useless displays of rage.

What do you think, Unser? They're religious fanatics, you idiot. You were expecting reason and logic?

For a moment—and not for the first time—Ringstorff reflected gloomily that this whole protracted operation in Erewhonese territory was pure folly. The Mesans had gotten their way for so long that they'd grown arrogant, sloppy and careless.

And now . . .

It was time for one Haicheng Ringstorff to extricate himself from what was rapidly becoming the worst fiasco he'd ever encountered in his life. True, the Mesans paid well. But no amount of money in the galaxy was worth the grief and risks they'd been putting him through for the past couple of years. Bad enough they'd gotten him tangled up last year with a Mantie cruiser captained by an apparent naval wizard. That had already cost Ringstorff and the Mesans four destroyed cruisers of their own. Now, by insisting that Ringstorff rely on maniacs like Masadans and Scrags for a "security team," the Mesans were about to bring the entire wrath of the Star Kingdom upon on his head.

The Mesans could be as cocksure as they chose. One Haicheng Ringstorff had had far more experience than they had when it came to the grief Manties could ring down.

Unser was still screaming invective at a passive-faced Flairty.

"I want out," Ringstorff muttered, "pure and simple."

He started to rise. So did Lithgow.

The door to the Mesan suite erupted in a flash. The concussion knocked Ringstorff off his feet. In a daze, he saw Diem and Lithgow and Flairty hammered to the floor as well. Fortunately, the two Masadans who'd remained standing next to the door absorbed most of the force of the explosion. Their shattered bodies went flying across the room.

Ringstorff knew he needed to act immediately, but his brain and nervous system were still responding sluggishly. So he wasn't able to do much more than lurch to his knees and gurgle an inarticulate protest before people started pouring through the ruptured doorway.

He was a bit surprised to see two women coming through first. Then, recognizing their distinctive phenotypes and facial structure, understood the reason. *Scrags.* Faster, probably, than the two Mesan security guards fumbling at their weapons. Since they'd been the farthest from the door, they'd managed to remain on their feet.

Fat lot of good it did them. The first woman through the door had a pulser in her hand and fired two quick and expert bursts. The two guards went down, dead before they landed.

The second woman strode over to Flairty, who was still lying prone on the floor, her gun pointed at the back of the Masadan's head.

And good riddance, thought Ringstorff. At least he wouldn't die without seeing the bastard zealot sent to his grave first.

But, to his surprise, the woman didn't fire. At the last moment, she swiveled the gun aside and just kicked Flairty in the back of the head. It was a powerful kick but not the lethal one she could have so obviously delivered. Just enough to daze Flairty completely.

Four men had now entered the room, moving a bit more slowly than the women. One of them remained standing near the door, a pulser in his fist but pointing at no one in particular. One of them came toward Ringstorff, another headed toward Diem, the third toward Lithgow. Lithgow, like Ringstorff himself, was now up on his knees. Diem was still flat on the floor, apparently unconscious.

The approaching men were carrying hand pulsers but, like the one by the door, didn't seem to be planning to use them. Not immediately, at least. Ringstorff decided he and Lithgow still had a chance—a piss-poor one, true—and tried to gather himself for a sudden lunge.

Then the man coming toward Ringstorff stuck out his tongue—stuck it *way* out—and Ringstorff froze. The genetic markers were easily visible and . . . unmistakable.

"Shall we dance?" the man jeered. "I don't recommend it though, Ringstorff. I really doubt you're up to being my partner."

Audubon Ballroom. More fanatics. *I'm dead meat.*

"My name's Saburo X, by the by. Give me any shit and I'll blow off your arms and legs, cut off your nose and feed it to you. Be a good boy, and you'll live. Maybe a long time, who knows?"

Mutely, Ringstorff gave him a nod. Then, without being asked, clasped his hands behind his head. Out of the corner of his eye, he saw Lithgow do the same. Nobody in their right mind—certainly not anyone on Mesa's payroll—was going to doubt a Ballroom fanatic's threats of mayhem.

Apparently satisfied, Saburo X glanced at the woman who'd kicked Flairty.

"It was well done," he said. The words sounded a bit grudging.

"Of course it was," she replied. But there was no heat in the response. True, she was frowning. But it seemed more like a frown of concentration than displeasure.

"Do that again," she said abruptly.

"Do what?"

She stuck out her tongue. Saburo goggled at the sight. Then, his jaws tightened.

"Please," said the woman, as if the word didn't come easily to her.

Saburo suppressed whatever angry words he'd been about to speak; hesitated; shrugged; and stuck out his tongue again.

The woman examined it for an instant.

"I can live with that," she pronounced. "In fact, it looks kind of intriguing. I'm Lara. Have you got a woman?"

The Ballroom member was back to goggling. "Not recently," he choked. "Why?"

"You do now," Lara stated, as casually as if she were announcing the time of day. "I don't like being without a man, and the one I had isn't going to live out the day. The stinking pig."

She reached down with her left hand, seized Flairty by the scruff of his blouse, and yanked him easily to his feet. Flairty wobbled, his eyes still dazed, held up only by Lara's grip.

"You can take a while to get used to the idea," she announced. "But don't take too long. I'm horny."

She began muscling Flairty toward the door, carrying him more than guiding him. On the way, she gave Ringstorff a cold glance.

"Give my new man any trouble and you'll be lucky if you die before he's done. I'll—"

By the time she had Flairty through the door, Ringstorff felt sick to his stomach. The ex-Scrag female's vivid description of the mayhem *she'd* inflict on him made Saburo seem like a saint.

"She's crazy," Saburo choked.

"I dunno," said the Ballroom terrorist who was now manhandling Lithgow to his feet. "I thought the last bit had a certain charm."

"Not *that,* Johann," replied Saburo, shaking his head. "The other part."

Johann grinned. "I dunno," he repeated. "I'm not sure I'd argue the point with a woman like that, myself. Besides, you were complaining the other day that your life was too boring."

"Especially his sex life," chimed in the Ballroom member by the door. "Bored me to death about it, he did, just yesterday." He, too, was grinning. And by the time he finished, was looking at the other ex-Scrag female still in the room.

"And what's your name?" he asked.

She grinned back. "Inge. But don't push it. I want to get a report from Lara first."

Less than five minutes later, the four Mesans had been bundled into an expensive private air-car waiting by a service entrance behind the Suds. By then, Ringstorff had gotten over his astonishment at the ease with which the abduction had been managed—there had been *no one* along their way through the huge edifice, not even so much as a janitor—and was now grimly certain that his life hung by a thread. This was obviously not just an Audubon Ballroom operation. Somebody high up in the Erewhon hierarchy must have run interference for them.

As he was half-thrown into the back seat of the luxurious vehicle, piling on top of Diem, he caught a glimpse of the monogram on the controls.

Imbesi. Oh, what a nightmare.

By the time Imbesi's private shuttle launched, carrying Flairty and the three Mesans up to *The Wages of Sin,* the major families who ruled Erewhon had their representatives already inspecting the damage.

"We can live with this," pronounced Tomas Hall, as his eyes ranged through the Mesan suite in the Suds.

"Barely," hissed Alessandra Havlicek.

The third member of the planet's triumvirate shrugged. "It's really not a problem, Alessandra. Four dead, all flunkies—two of them Masadans, from the look of the bodies. Big deal. The wrecked door's got the management of the Suds more upset than anything."

Havlicek was not mollified. "I don't like Walter Imbesi's high-handed ways. He's really pushing it, in my opinion."

Hall shrugged again. In private, the gesture was less restrained than it would have been in front of a public audience. But there was no one in the room beyond themselves, three bodyguards—and, of course, the representatives of the press.

Hall turned toward one of the reporters. His third cousin, as it happened. Like everything else on Erewhon, "freedom of the press" was refracted through a family prism.

"Keep it quiet for now, would you?" For all the politeness of the question, it was really a command.

The third cousin understood how it worked. Perfectly, in fact, or he wouldn't have enjoyed his position.

"No sweat. An unfortunate accident. We'll have to run a little vague on that, or the Suds management will get upset at the suggestion of incompetence."

"Blame it on the Mesans themselves," suggested a second reporter. An adopted member of the Havlicek clan, she was. "Fiddling with dangerous psychedelic drugs, no chemists they, an open flame presumed to have been present—*boom.*" She chuckled harshly. "That'll do it. Nowadays, anybody will believe anything about Mesans."

Her harsh chuckle was echoed through the room.

"Done," said Fuentes. He cocked an eye at Alessandra.

Grudgingly, she nodded. "As you said, we can live with it. For now. But Imbesi better damn well have a good reason—and explain it to us fully, too, none of his usual caviling."

"What is he up to, anyway?" asked Hall. The question was addressed to Fuentes, who'd been the one to receive Walter Imbesi's hurried call.

"Don't really know. But I don't share Alessandra's skepticism. Not fully, at least. Yes, Walter can be a pain in the neck with his daredevil ways. He's also as shrewd as they come. So I'm for letting him have the reins for a bit. Let's see what happens."

Since all three were in agreement, Fuentes brought out his communicator. This was no delicate hidden device, but a full-powered one easily able to reach the space station.

"All right, Walter," he spoke into it. "We'll cover you from this end. But that's it. You're on your own for the rest—and you're the cutout. If whatever you're doing goes sour, you take the fall."

The response came immediately. *"Of course. Thanks, Jack. I'll be in touch."*

"Sooner than you think," was Fuentes' curt reply. "We're on our way up there ourselves, Walter. Leaving now."

Everyone was in place, finally, everything set. Gideon Templeton took a moment for quick prayer. Then spoke the battle cry of the Church of Humanity Unchained, Defiant.

"The Lord's will be done."

CHAPTER 24

VICTOR HAD GAMBLED THAT WHEN the time came, the Scrag would do it casually, so as not to alert anyone with a sudden motion.

"Casually," in these circumstances, meant slowly. Before the Scrag had even gotten the hidden pulser out of his bag, Victor had already taken two quick strides toward him and was within three meters. Fine range for his special palm gun.

The Scrag's eyes widened. Thinking and moving as quickly as that genetically enhanced breed could do, he realized he couldn't get out the gun in time and tried to hurl the entire handbag at Victor.

But Victor, though no "superman," was highly conditioned by training and exercise. If he wasn't as fast or as coordinated as the Scrag, he was close enough.

Thtt, thtt, thtt. Victor was taking no chances with a Scrag. If he died from an overdose, good riddance.

The Scrag was down, Victor's hand already plunging into the handbag. He groped for the gun by feel alone, however. His eyes were elsewhere, ranging the gaming hall to find the Manticoran princess.

Donald X was too thick and muscular to move that quickly. But speed was really not essential when dealing with a man bedazzled by Ginny's flirtation. The security guard never even noticed him coming until Donald's arm went round his chest, pinning his own arms. A couple of seconds later, Donald had the guard's pulser in his hand and sent the man flying with a powerful heave.

Donald took two steps to get shelter behind the gaming table. Then, like Victor, looked to find the princess. The center of the action would be on her. He paid no attention to Ginny. Usher's wife was no fool and her part in the affair was over for the moment. Donald caught a quick glimpse of bare legs squiggling under the gaming table, and grinned thinly.

Part of the grin was because his three comrades had arrived. One of them positioned himself next to Donald, while the other two went to ground in flanking positions which would allow them the best possible field of fire. Their guns were out and ready to cover the area where Templeton's main crew would make the attack. Mostly, though, he was grinning because he knew that with Ginny safely out of the way, Victor Cachat would be able to devote his full concentration to murder and massacre.

Donald X had seen Victor in action, once. *Pity Templeton!*

Sergeant Christina Bulanchik and Corporal Darrin Howell, assigned as Ruth and Berry's close escorts, were also alert. Their attentive eyes swept the crowded chamber endlessly, and the brains behind those eyes reacted with professional paranoia the moment the random drifting of the crowd in the gaming hall was interrupted by sudden purposeful movement. Highly trained instincts reacted with instantly enhanced attention, and their eyes narrowed as at least a dozen men separated themselves from the crowd by the simple act of moving in coordinated unison. The troopers understood they were under attack even before they spotted the guns in the hands of their assailants.

Howell's left hand darted out, catching Berry by the shoulder and spinning her away and to the floor with far more haste than care, even as his right hand flashed towards his pulser. Bulanchik reacted with matching quickness, sweeping Ruth behind her and sending her tumbling towards the floor, as well, as the sergeant went for her own holster. Both troopers managed to draw their weapons, but the time they'd taken to get their charges out of the line of fire had cost them precious fractions of a second. Before either of them could fire, they were dead in a hurricane of pulser darts.

"*Werewolf!*" Christina Bulanchik's warning cracked like an old-fashioned pistol shot over the Queen's Own's com net. That single code word was the most terrifying thing any member of a Manticoran protective detail could hear, and Lieutenant Ahmed Griggs reacted to it instantly.

He hadn't been facing the same direction as Howell and Bulanchik, and so he'd missed the initial swirls in the crowd which had alerted them. But Bulanchik's warning snapped his pulser into his hand with the serpent quickness of trained muscle memory. The safety came off in the same fluid movement, even as his brain dropped into the ice-cold, detached mode of a trained bodyguard who was also a highly decorated combat veteran. His eyes swept the crowd before him, seeking threat sources, and the pulser came up smoothly, so smoothly, as the first assailant identified himself. Griggs couldn't have explained exactly how the man had done that. It was something about his stance, the way he moved against the crowd, the expression in his eyes or the tenseness in his shoulders. It was *something* that shouted the truth to the lieutenant's trained senses, and his pulser hissed in a precise, three-dart burst that blew the terrorist's chest apart.

Ahmed Griggs was a crack shot with any hand weapon, and his entire being was focused on the crowd before him as people began to scream in terror. The quicker-witted were already flinging themselves towards the floor, and a tiny corner of his brain felt a flicker of gratitude as the innocent took themselves out of the line of his fire. Another corner realized that personally shooting attackers was the worst thing he could be doing. That his job was to command his entire detachment, to enforce order and coordination upon his people's response.

But there was no time to worry about what he *ought* to be doing. All he could do was respond, and his succeeding quick bursts took down three more men—all dead—before he was struck by the first return fire. A pulser dart mangled his shooting arm at the elbow in the split second before several more darts ripped into his legs. They lacked the full velocity of military-grade weapons, but even civilian-grade darts attained a velocity no chemical-powered firearm could have hoped to match. The darts were more than sufficient to reduce bone to splinters and rupture flesh. Griggs went down hard, his entire body screaming with agony, and his pulser landed on the floor beside him.

By then, the four other troopers in Griggs' unit had taken down an additional six men—and, again, all of them from fatal wounds. Ten assailants down—half again their own number, despite having suffered the loss of two troopers before they could fire even a single round.

Three of them were down, as well, and Laura Hofschulte was the only one still in action. She'd gone to one knee behind the dealer's console—pausing only to grab Ruth and throw her forcefully under the gaming table as the princess tried to climb back up onto her own hands and knees. Now her left hand stabbed the panic button on her belt com pack, alerting the detachment's supporting Erewhonese heavy-weapons squad, even as her right hand tracked onto a fresh target. She squeezed her trigger, taking down yet another attacker, but there were too many threat sources, too much background clutter to hide them from her, and she knew it.

She spotted another weapon coming at her from the left flank and twisted, bring her pulser across her body, tracking into the threat. The man's eyes met hers at a range of less than four meters. Strange eyes, a flashing thought told her, and a memory trace shouted the word "*Scrag!*" at her. There was shock in those eyes, as well. Disbelief at how rapidly and lethally the outnumbered detail had responded to the threat, mingled with hatred and predator arrogance that turned ever so fleetingly into something else as the muzzle of her weapon found him.

They squeezed their triggers in the same heartbeat of time.

It was as splendid a response as anyone could have asked from the soldiers of the Queen's Own, fighting in the worst conceivable circumstances: a stand-up gunfight at point-blank range in the middle of a huge mob, reacting to a surprise attack in greatly superior numbers from every direction. The names of the detail's troopers would be duly recorded on the Wall of Honor in the Queen's Own's Permanent Mess in Mount Royal Palace, along with the Adrienne Crosses each of them received for his or her actions that day.

All of them posthumous. In the end, they were simply overwhelmed.

Through the haze of the shock, Griggs could hear screaming erupt throughout the huge gaming hall. Unlike his own people, who'd taken pains to avoid hitting innocent bystanders, the attackers had been careless. Not even the Queen's Own could have avoided hitting any bystanders in a fight like this one. Anyone who thought they could have was dreaming . . . or completely ignorant of the realities of high-powered weapons. No, there would have been innocent civilian casualties, whatever happened and even leaving aside the security guards, with their much lower standard of training, elsewhere in the hall. But the Masadan terrorists' complete indifference to those casualties made them far, far worse. Blood and bodies were everywhere, in a whirlwind of carnage, and the sheer number of attackers told Griggs this was a major operation. He was sure whoever had planned this attack would see to it that every possible danger to them was cleared aside.

His brain worked no further than that, other than to register his own mortality. If nothing else, he'd bleed to death from the wounds he'd already received long before any medical assistance could reach him.

He did manage to turn his head enough to see that both of the girls were under the gaming table. Zilwicki's daughter seemed unusually composed, given the circumstances. The real princess, in her much less fine apparel, seemed a bit stunned. But that could have been simply from the bruise on her forehead. Ahmed suspected that Christina or Laura must have thrown her down roughly. He noted that much, then felt a stab of fresh agony that had nothing at all to do with his own wounds as he saw Laura Hofschulte go down in a spray of blood and tissue.

Then, he faded out.

The Manticoran soldiers were all dead now. Templeton was shocked at the effectiveness of the resistance they'd put up. In the space of seconds, before being finally brought down, the Queen's Own had managed to kill more than a quarter of his entire strike force—and over forty percent of the ones directly participating in the assault on the princess. He'd known he was facing elite troops, but he hadn't expected such an instantly murderous response. Not with the advantages he'd had of a surprise attack on favorable ground, led by men as lethal themselves as his new converts.

For a moment, Gideon was so shaken that he was unable to move. But then, after a quick inspection of the corpses littering the area, he settled down. Once again, he could see the Hand of God at work. Most of his casualties—eight out of twelve—had been new converts. Stash, the most obstreperous of the lot, was among them. The Lord provideth—and, when the time comes, the Lord taketh away.

Through his earbug Templeton was now getting reports from the teams throughout the gaming hall. They were also reporting success in taking down the security guards. Much easier success, needless to say, than Templeton had had coming up against elite soldiers.

All except one of his team, who failed to report at all. That was the man who'd been covering the guard dallying with a whore. A new convert, that one. Slack, as always. Gideon had no doubt he'd succeeded in his mission, but had simply failed to report.

Templeton and the other surviving men of his main detachment had reached the large gaming table now, their eyes searching for the princess. There were sixteen of the Masadans left, more than enough to search the immediate area. The bodies of the dealer and two customers, killed by stray shots from Templeton's fusillade, were draped over the table. Two more customers lay dead on the ground nearby. Once the corpses had been tossed aside, it took Templeton no more than two seconds to figure out what had happened. His sister and the Zilwicki bitch must be hiding under the table. It was more than large enough to conceal two women—and Templeton now saw that the area beneath was shielded from view by a fringe of fabric. Fancy and cheerfully decorated fabric, once, designed to please and stimulate customers. Now, half of it was soaked in gore. Blood was beginning to drip from the tassels onto the floor.

"Surround the table!" he shouted. "Get her when she comes out." Templeton was holding the chemotracker in his left hand, his gun in the right. He stooped across the body of a fallen Manticoran bodyguard and lifted the fringe with the chemotracker, taking care to point the pulser away. In his fury and excitement, he still had enough self-control not to risk killing the slut with an accidental shot.

"Okay," said Victor softly into his throat mike, "it's definitely a kidnaping, not an assassination. So hold your fire for a moment. If they'd just wanted to kill her, they'd already be aiming under the table. Get ready. Remember—Templeton stays alive. The one next to him also, the man wearing the blue embroidered jacket. He's the lieutenant. Abraham's his name, some sort of relative. Leave one other alive, so they can get the girl out easily."

"*Which one?*" murmured Donald's voice in his ear.

There was no time for anything fancy. Victor picked the one with the gaudiest clothing. "The Scrag wearing that irridescent yellow outfit. Those three stay alive. Kill the rest."

As soon as he stooped low enough, Templeton spotted the two figures huddled in the shadowy gloom under the table.

"Come out, sister mine," he hissed at the woman in the royal finery. He went down on one knee to get a better angle and aimed the pulser at his sister's companion. "Come out at once. Or I'll kill the Zilwicki bitch."

That much he would give his sister credit for. She didn't hesitate for more than a split-second before beginning to crawl toward him. Craven and cowardly, at least, the whore was not. That would be the male parentage at work. Gideon's father had been famous for his courage, and he'd sired Ruth as well.

The Zilwicki girl seemed dazed. Templeton decided that was good enough for his purposes. He'd leave her be, as he'd sworn on the Lord's oath. She made a feeble attempt to restrain the princess, but her groping hand fell short as Templeton's sister crawled resolutely toward him.

Everything was going well, finally. From the sounds of the screaming all over the gaming hall, Templeton was certain the entire room was a madhouse, with everyone now simply trying to escape. He and his men would just join the mob, unnoticed in the chaos and confusion.

When his sister reached him, Templeton shoved the pulser into the back of his pants and grabbed her by the hair. Then, jerked her out from under the table and hauled her to her feet.

He still had the chemotracker in his left hand, and he glanced at it. It was a casual glance, really. Nothing more than a last-minute check.

The readings were . . . meaningless.

He froze; then, struck by a guess, moved the tracker's sensors toward the girl still under the table.

Fury seized him, and he shook the woman's head by the hair in his hand.

"You bitches! I'll—"

Ahmed Griggs faded back in. He was staring at a man's boots, not a meter away. A girl's expensive slippers fell off her feet, as if they'd been shaken loose.

What was happening?

Confused, the lieutenant's eyes shifted and spotted his pulser, lying on the floor within reach of his left hand. The sight of the familiar weapon blew the confusion out of his brain like a strong wind. The reflexes of a combat veteran took over.

Ignoring the agony streaking through the rest of his body, Griggs had the pulser in his hand and ranging upward, seeking his target. He couldn't shoot as well left-handed as right, but at this range it hardly mattered.

As soon as the body mass loomed over the sights, Ahmed began firing. The pulser darts shredded Gideon Templeton's groin and abdomen, and the Masadan leader's body exploded like a volcano of blood, shredded tissue, and splintered bone.

The religious fanatic never had time to finish explaining his final purpose, before his God gathered him to whatever place might be his destiny.

Watching Templeton almost cut in half, Victor restrained a curse. There was no help for it, after all, and he was not a man to swear at another brave man for doing his duty even from the brink of the grave. And not when the Manticoran lieutenant was now being shredded by a tornado of darts from Templeton's enraged comrades.

That rage would work to his advantage, Victor realized. He waited until the princess, flung aside by Templeton's last convulsive movement, hit the floor and was out of the line of fire. Zilwicki's daughter would be safe enough, he thought, still sheltered under the table. And the sudden killing of their leader had both confused and distracted his followers.

He spoke quickly, but calmly. "Keep your shots waist high, no lower. Remember, Abraham and the yellow-jacket stay alive. Kill the others. *Now.*"

Donald and his three Ballroom comrades began firing with the single, deadly precise shots of expert gunmen, and the fifteen Masadans still on their feet around the gaming table began falling like scythed grain. With, somehow, as if by a miracle, Abraham and one other remaining unharmed. As Victor had anticipated, the sudden attack from the side had caught the Masadans completely by surprise. Standing up, without the cover of the mob to conceal them and confuse the marksmen, they were like so many targets in a shooting gallery.

Victor made no attempt to add his own fire to the carnage. He was a good marksman, but not an expert one—and never would be. And while the range was easy for pistoleros like the Ballroom gunmen, it was long enough that Victor didn't think he'd add much to their efforts. He was more concerned that his stray shots might kill or injure one of the bystanders still trying to flee the area. There weren't many left anywhere near the gaming table, of course—not standing, at least. But there were still half a dozen people desperately trying to crawl away, and perhaps the same number lying about wounded. It was essential for Victor's plan to have no innocent casualties laid at his own feet.

Besides, speaking of the plan, it was time to start on the next stage of it. Victor began trotting through the gaming hall, weaving in and around the tables, heading toward the exit which

Abraham Templeton would use to take away the Manticoran princess.

On the way, he took the time to call Lieutenant Palane.

"They'll be coming soon, Thandi. Gideon Templeton's dead, so his cousin Abraham will be leading them. Abraham, one other, and whoever else they pick up from the rest of the hall. I'll try to give you a count when I spot them myself."

"*Good enough,*" came her voice in his ear. "*We'll just have to hope Abraham was privy to all of Gideon's plans. Any word from the planet?*"

"Yes. Walter called me not two minutes ago. They've got the Mesans and Flairty and are bringing them up. Everything went perfectly, it seems."

"*Good.*" There was a short pause. Then: "*One thing, Victor. This is my part of the deal. I need Flairty dead. I don't care about the others. But Flairty goes down.*"

Victor's mind raced, even while his eyes kept ranging the hall looking for more of Templeton's men. Within ten seconds, he'd spotted seven of them making their way toward the exit. Those would have been among the ones assigned by Templeton to take out the perimeter guards.

He estimated there'd been nine of them. Victor and Donald had taken out one. That left one still missing. Where was he?

But most of Victor's brain was occupied with analyzing Thandi's forceful request. By the time he spotted the last man, straggling far behind, he'd figured it all out.

"Sweet boss you've got, Thandi. But I won't argue the point. Flairty goes down. I assume you'll do Abraham yourself. Eliminate anyone who'd know the truth."

He spoke the words calmly, but there was enough of a foul taste in his mouth to condemn a man to death. As soon as Victor came within range of the Masadan straggler—who'd been so concerned with trying to find his way out that he hadn't noticed the man stalking him—Victor stopped, brought up his pulser in a two-handed grip, and cut the man down.

He'd planned to let him live long enough to join the others in the trap, but . . .

It was a really *foul* taste. And since Masadan fanatics were just as foul, Victor took out his anger by killing him immediately.

Though it didn't really seem to help much.

"All right, Thandi. I've got a full count now. I'm pretty sure it's accurate—close enough, anyway. You should be facing Abraham Templeton and eight others."

"Cut 'em down by almost three-fourths, did you? Thanks. But you might want to consider those numbers, before you condemn others for being too ruthless."

He took a long, deep breath. "The Manticoran soldiers accounted for a dozen of them. But there's a difference anyway, Thandi, and you know it. For me, there's a purpose. For your precious captain, just his own ambition."

She said nothing in response. What could she say, really?

Victor didn't know the full story yet—though he'd make sure to find out—but at least one mystery had been cleared up. Hieronymus Stein had not been murdered by Manpower, after all. He'd been murdered by Templeton and his religious goons working on the side. Not for their own purposes, but simply because they'd been hired to do so by Captain Luiz Rozsak—and now Rozsak had ordered Thandi to eliminate the witnesses.

Why? Victor was quite sure it was part of a scheme by Rozsak to advance his career. Probably by displacing Cassetti as Governor Barregos' indispensable man, because Victor was fairly certain that the order had been given by Cassetti. The governor himself probably knew nothing about it. By all accounts, Cassetti was utterly unscrupulous—and just the sort of man to come up with an elaborate scheme like this one. Kill Stein, throw the blame on Manpower—and then use that to drive forward Maya Sector's growing alienation from the Solarian League. Get the Renaissance Association's political backing as a result of Stein's murder, and . . .

Yes, it all made sense to him. Cassetti would have been the one. Cassetti, dreaming of the days when he could be the right-hand man—and possibly the successor—to the leader of an independent star nation richer and more powerful than any in the galaxy except the Solarian League itself. With the Solarians half-paralyzed by the fact that it had been Manpower's overweening arrogance and brutality which seemed to have been the final straw to lead to the revolt.

A clever scheme—and, like almost all such, too clever. Cassetti had overlooked the possibility that the man he'd chosen to do the "wet work" might turn it against him, when the time came.

Victor slowed down a bit. He was nearing the exit, and didn't want to be spotted by Abraham Templeton and his men as they left the gaming hall. Hiding was going to be more difficult now, because most of the panicked mob had managed to flee from the hall. He spotted a particularly elaborate gaming table with a central tower of some kind, and trotted over to stand behind it. The tower's flamboyant, coruscating lights would hide him from sight.

There, as he waited, he completed his calculations. It all came easily enough, since he'd already understood that Rozsak's ambitions would probably lead him to have a favorable response to Victor's overture. All that was really new was that Victor now understood that Rozsak had been responsible for the Stein assassination. Which . . .

Yes, yes, shocking. But Victor had overcome his initial surge of anger, and was thinking cold-bloodedly again. The truth was that Rozsak's actions would make him all the more willing to go along with Victor's scheme. Nor would Cassetti interfere. For both of them, Victor's plans for Congo would work splendidly. Giving them—whichever won out in their own internecine conflict—an even greater moral luster to drape over their personal ambitions.

So be it. Victor could live with foul tastes. He'd lived with Oscar Saint-Just for years, hadn't he? What the revolution required of him, Victor would give.

Flairty would go down, then. Victor swallowed the taste and ignored it thereafter.

He found himself now wondering what it all tasted like for Thandi Palane. Just as foul, he suspected. He hoped so. The woman was coming to occupy more and more of his thoughts, whether he wanted it or not.

On the planet below, other people were dealing with the taste of things.

"*What the hell is going on?*" Cassetti's voice was practically screaming in Captain Rozsak's earbug.

Luiz glanced at Lieutenant Commander Watanapongse, who gave him a little thumbs up. The recording was being made.

The Solarian Navy captain eased back in the armchair in his suite. "I don't know, exactly. From the garbled reports I've been getting, Sir, it sounds like the Masadans have run amok. I warned you, if you recall, that it was dangerous using them."

"*They were all supposed to be taken out afterward!*"

"And I *also* told you that 'taking out' over forty armed and dangerous men was no picnic, unless you wanted me to bring down the fleet and level half of Erewhon's capital. Assuming I could have fought my way through the Erewhonese Navy—which I couldn't possibly have done, anyway. All I've got is what amounts to a commodore's flotilla. They've got ships of the wall in orbit here, Ingemar. They'd have swatted me like a fly."

The lieutenant governor was silent. What could he say, after all? The entire scheme depended, among other things, on maintaining public approval for the high moral stature of Governor Barregos. Starting a war with a neighboring star nation would undo all the gains of the Stein killing—and then some.

When Cassetti's voice came back, it was in its normal cold and calculating tone. *"All right. Point taken. Spilt milk and all that. But what do you suggest we do now?"*

"I may have it taken care of already, Sir. The one good thing about Templeton's rampage is that it got him off the planet. It'll be a lot easier to take him out where he is, without too much in the way of collateral damage. And whatever such damage there is, Templeton's own actions will be blamed for it anyway."

"True enough. I hope you've got somebody good handling the thing."

"The best, Sir, when it comes to that kind of operation. The very best."

Cassetti cut off the transmission without so much as a final word of salutation.

"Rude bastard," muttered Rozsak. He studied the very fancy looking recording machine on the center table. The thing made him a bit nervous, as any such state-of-the-art electronic equipment tended to do. Rozsak had been burned too many times by the promises of research tech weenies, whose "miraculous" new designs so often failed the test in actual combat.

But he'd had no choice. Not surprisingly, Cassetti had insisted on using the very best communication devices for this *very* black operation—and such devices were extremely difficult to unscramble for a recording.

Watanapongse didn't share the captain's skepticism. "Damn, I love this gadget," the intelligence officer practically crooned. "Worth all that we paid for it. Listen to this."

He pressed a control and the conversation came back, the words as clear as anyone could ask for.

Captain Rozsak grunted. "Add it to the other recordings, then."

Watanapongse grinned. "Governor Barregos will have a fit when he finally finds out what his precious lieutenant governor has been doing in his name. Word of it ever gets out, Barregos is ruined. And—if you'll pardon the flattery, Sir—I think you've done a brilliant job of making it clear to anyone who listens that you tried to talk Cassetti out of it."

Rozsak smiled. "I didn't try *too* hard, of course. But, yes, I did. And I also made it clear enough in those recordings that I was assuming all along that the governor had given Cassetti the go ahead."

He clasped his hands over his midriff and gazed complacently at the device. Yes, it was too fancy. But, on the other hand, sometimes "too fancy" worked.

"And I will be shocked, naturally—*shocked,* I tell you—when I finally discover that Cassetti was operating all on his own. I'll have no recourse but to make a full report to the governor—call it a confession, if you will, since everyone trusts a man who confesses—of the entire sad affair. Also pointing out, needless to say, the best way to make a silk purse out of a sow's ear."

Edie Habib was sitting on another chair around the table. For the first time since Cassetti's call came in, she spoke. "First thing you do, you kill the sow."

CHAPTER 25

"THEY'RE TAKING TUBE EPSILON," Victor's voice said. *"Abraham's in the lead. The princess is at the rear, with just one man holding her."*

"Thanks, Victor." Crouched in a ventilation duct connecting Epsilon and Gamma tubes, Thandi considered the situation for a moment. Most of her thoughts involved the ventilation ducts themselves, which she and her women had been exploring a bit while they waited for the action to reach them.

As Thandi had hoped, the tubes were more than big enough to crawl through, even for someone her size. And . . . they were a maze. None of the ducts were charted in the holo-guide she'd purchased. Like most such, that holo-guide was for tourists, who would have simply been confused by the added layer of unnecessary complexity. Even the public portions of the space station were complicated enough.

She turned to one of her women. "Raisha, go down Tube Epsilon maybe twenty meters or so—just around the bend out of sight of this ventilation duct. Remove the cover from the first duct you see, and leave it lying beside the open vent."

Thandi turned and opened the tool box next to her. That tool box had been left behind by a mechanic, who must have fled like a rabbit the moment he'd heard the sounds of gunshots and screams echoing down the tube from the main gaming hall. The man had been apparently been about to start working on one of the ventilation ducts, but the only thing he'd done was remove the cover. Thandi had hauled the tool box into the duct and out of sight, more out of reflex than anything else. Now . . .

She pulled out one of the tools designed to easily detach the duct covers and handed it to Raisha. "Use this. Go. Quickly."

Raisha took the tool, nodded, and sped off as fast as a crawl could take her. Thandi removed two more of the little tools and slid the tool box toward another woman, extending the tools in her hand at the same time.

"Yana, you and Olga take the box and the tools. You carry the box to the duct Raisha will open and leave it next to the opening. Then, the two of you and Raisha open every other outlet all down the tube, working backward toward us. The ceiling vents as well as the side vents. Understand?"

They nodded and were gone, Yana hauling the heavy tool box behind her with no real effort. Thandi reflected, not for the first time, that despite their often irritating attitudes there were real advantages to having former Scrags as her special action unit.

The immediate necessities done, she gave thought to the best disposition of her troops. It didn't take her long to plan it all out, since there was really only one of them with the speed and strength to launch an unarmed frontal assault. She'd use the rest of them in a rear attack.

Quickly, she outlined her plan. The women seemed doubtful. Judging from the scowls on their faces, at least—none of them actually tried to argue the point.

"Don't be stupid," she hissed. "Even for me, it'll be hard. Just do as you're told."

The last sentence was spoken in full *kaja* tone. An instant later, her women were crawling off toward the nearest junction in the maze of ventilator ducts. They'd use that to position themselves where they could drop into Tube Epsilon and attack the Templeton crew from the rear after they'd passed by. And they wouldn't be slowed by having to open the duct covers, nor—Thandi hoped—would Templeton and his men think it odd to see so many open ducts. The tool box in plain sight should be enough for that.

Thandi hoped so, anyway. She consoled herself with the thought that even if Templeton's men got suspicious, the light hand pulsers they'd be carrying probably couldn't punch darts through the metal walls of the corridors. If worse came to worst, her women could simply retreat back into the ducts.

That'd be hard on the princess, of course. And even harder on Thandi herself.

So be it. This was what she'd signed up for. She could always have stayed on Ndebele, and spent her life as a serf.

That thought was angry enough to send her scrambling down the duct toward the opening into Tube Epsilon. By the time she got there, the duct cover had already been removed. This was a ceiling vent, and she could see the duct cover lying on the side of the tube below her.

As good a place as any. Thandi rested on her haunches, like a great predator in a tree.

Berry Zilwicki had been blessed with steady nerves as far back as she could remember. She was glad to see they weren't failing her now.

Why should they, really? Yes, she was in what most people would consider a very bad spot—kidnaped by religious fanatics apparently under the assumption they'd kidnaped the actual princess. If they found out the truth, they'd kill her at once. And even if she was able to maintain the pretense, she doubted if her fate would be much better. The savagery of Masadan zealots—especially toward women—was a byword in this part of the galaxy.

But it wasn't the worst situation Berry had ever found herself in, after all. Not born and raised as she'd been, in the lawless underground warrens of Terra's capital city of Chicago. With no father she could remember until Anton Zilwicki entered her life, and a mother who was a prostitute and a drug addict and gone half the time anyway, even before she disappeared completely when Berry was only twelve years old.

Steady, girl, she told herself. *What doesn't kill you, makes you strong. Just keep an eye out for an opening.*

Seconds later, the opening appeared—and in the literal sense of the term.

Abraham and his crew came around yet another bend in the confusing tube—confusing, mostly, because the station's internal gravity field made it seem as if they were circumnavigating a tiny planet made up of nothing but corridors. Always seeming to climb up a hill, even if the gravity remained constant, with a new vista spreading out before them as they reached a continually receding crest.

Around—or over—this bend in the tube, the vista actually *was* new. Nothing all that exciting, really, just the scene of what was apparently a maintenance project. Instead of being flush with the walls and ceiling, the ventilation duct covers had been removed and were lying on the floor. From her position at the rear of the little group, Berry could see a dull red tool box lying next to one of the openings.

She fixed on the color as her goal. *That one.* The ventilation duct was waist-high, and quite large enough for someone of her size to scamper into.

First, of course, she had to get loose. But she was only being held by one of her captors, and that one—*typical Scrag carelessness,* she thought derisively—was satisfied with merely holding her by the scruff of her fancy jacket.

Idiot. By now, Berry had already surreptitiously loosened all the tabs of the jacket, just in case. . . .

"The last one just passed below us, kaja. He's got the girl by the neck."

Thandi said nothing. In her mind, she reviewed her estimate of the distances, gauging the right time to make her drop.

Six seconds. She began counting off.

Now. Berry wriggled out of the jacket and dove headfirst into the duct. The moment she was inside, her spirits soared. This wasn't Terra, no, but she'd grown up in the underground. She felt the same way about tunnels and warrens that any small animal did. Safety from the predators.

She scrambled down the duct like a mouse running from cats.

"That fucking bitch!"

"Get her, you idiot!"

The moment Thandi heard the shouts, she understood what must have happened. She discarded her count-off.

Now.

She was through the duct, holding the edge with her hands and swinging down gracefully in a half-somersault; then, a short drop to the floor of the tube, landing silently on her toes.

Abraham Templeton and all of his men were facing away from her, staring at the open duct next to the tool box which the princess must have used for her escape. Several of them were still shouting, with Abraham's furious voice overriding the rest. Thandi could see the feet of a man disappearing into the vent as he set off in pursuit.

Bless you, girl. You may have just saved my life.

One-two-three strides, moving like a ghost. Abraham Templeton died without ever seeing it come. Thandi's fist crushed the back of his skull like an egg. Her ensuing kick drove his corpse into his followers, sending half of them sprawling.

The nearest one left standing swivelled his gun hand toward her.

A Scrag, he was, with the fast reflexes and the sneer to go with it. The sneer didn't fade even when her hand closed over his wrist. The Scrag, well-trained, simply began a standard disengagement maneuver.

Thandi knew the counter, but saw no reason to bother with it. She just slammed the Scrag against the wall of the duct, using his wrist to hurl him as if he were a toddler. Almost as an afterthought, she broke the wrist.

He slumped, stunned, his gun falling to the floor. Thandi ignored the pulser. Speed and sheer force would be her best weapons in the here and now.

One and a half long strides put her in the middle of them. They were still confused, several just getting back onto their feet. The stride ended in another kick, which caved in a rib cage. An elbow strike shattered a face and broke the man's neck in the bargain. An open palm strike did the same for another. A spinning side kick broke a thigh; the follow-on kick dislocated the shoulder.

Now, a Scrag, quicker and stronger. For the first time, she had to block a blow. And did so with such violence the man's forearm was broken. An instant later, Thandi's fist shattered his sternum, driving bone into his heart. The Scrag fell back, dying, a look of sheer astonishment on his face. The expression of a man who'd thought to face a woman in battle, only to find a monster in disguise.

She danced back, poised, ready—

No need. Her women were there, now, and Thandi had only left two of Templeton's men intact. The fact that they were both Scrags didn't help them in the least. Made it worse, in fact, since the women had a score to settle. Which they did, bare-handed, so savagely that Thandi was almost appalled.

Almost, not quite.

That still left the man who'd gone into the duct after the princess. As well as three of the men whom Thandi had taken down, but not killed.

She hesitated, but only for a second or two. Captain Rozsak had specified Templeton and his lieutenants, but he'd made it clear he'd be even happier if Thandi removed all of them from the equation. The man was paying the freight, after all—and, besides, Thandi wasn't really sure who among Templeton's men might have been taken into his confidence.

So, again, death danced through the corridor, stamping out lives under pitiless and iron-hard heel strikes. It took but a few seconds.

Then, Thandi studied the duct into which the princess and her pursuer had plunged. She'd lose almost all her advantages in there, but . . .

No help for it. That was part of the deal she'd made with Victor Cachat. They needed the Manticoran princess—alive—in order to keep the trap unfolding. Thandi's job was done, almost. But she knew that Victor was trolling for much bigger fish.

Her lips quirked for a moment. *A deal's a deal. When in Erewhon, do as the Erewhonese do. And I really don't think I want to piss off Victor Cachat anyway.*

Her women, seeing the little smile, grinned back. The expressions made them seem more like she-wolves than ever.

"You lead, great kaja. We'll follow."

For once, there was not even an undertone of mockery in the words. Studying their faces, Thandi understood that she'd sealed their loyalty completely. The exercise hall was one thing, and even broken bones knit soon enough. Whereas this—

Great Kaja, indeed. Death on two feet. The fact that they'd seen those same two feet, now and then, wearing elegant sandals and looking very feminine, only added to their satisfaction.

"Make *us* their chattel, would they?" snarled one of the women. She glared down at the corpse of one of the Scrags; then, just for good measure, stamped its face into a pulpier mess.

Since Thandi couldn't think of a fancier battle plan than—*after them! follow me!*—she said nothing. Just stooped, retrieved a pulser from the floor, and wriggled her way into the ventilation duct.

It wasn't until she'd gotten maybe twenty yards in, that the obvious problem occurred to her. She keyed to Cachat's channel, feeling obscurely unhappy that the man was proving to have feet of clay, after all.

"This isn't going to work, Victor. Templeton—both of them, Abraham as well as Gideon—was certainly staying in contact with his men on the *Felicia III*. It's not as if we're the only ones in the galaxy who have personal communicators."

"Don't worry about it," he replied immediately. *"How are things at your end?"*

"Oh. Uh, forgot to tell you. Everything's fine. We just took out Abraham and his men. All except one, who went into the ventilation ducts after the princess escaped."

She could hear him chuckle. *"Why am I not surprised? And on two counts, I might add. The first count being that you're just as murderous as you claimed to be. But it's like you said: I won't tell you how to do mayhem, you don't tell me how to do scheming. I'm* counting *on Templeton's men in the* Felicia *knowing that things have all gone wrong, Thandi. But the key is that they won't know exactly why or how or what. Am I safe in presuming that you didn't give Abraham time to make coherent reports?"*

Thandi felt simultaneously embarrassed and pleased. Embarrassed by herself; pleased that the man of her increasingly frequent fantasies—one of them flashed through her mind that very moment, in fact—didn't have feet of clay, after all.

And crawling through a duct in pursuit of a desperate criminal is no time to be having fantasies. You idiot.

"All right," she said gruffly, covering her embarrassment. "What's the second count?"

"Anton Zilwicki up to his tricks. The other girl—the one Templeton left behind in the gaming hall—has gotten over the shock. Mild concussion, maybe, nothing worse. But she's coherent now, I can assure you. And it turns out that she's *the Manticoran princess. The one you're chasing after is Berry Zilwicki."*

Again, she could hear Victor chuckle. *"And let me tell you—I speak from experience—Zilwicki girls can play merry hell in a tunnel. Good luck, Thandi."*

And so Lieutenant Palane crawled on, resolute, determined, hand pulser clenched in her fist. No one watching would have imagined that she did so while being distracted by a veritable cascade of florid fantasies.

Except, possibly, for Victor Cachat—who was increasingly uneasy at the effect that mezzo-soprano voice was having on his nervous system. But he had the advantage, at the moment, of facing something quite a bit livelier than a dull, gray-painted ventilation duct. A Manticoran princess, no less, and one in full and fine fury.

"Don't tell me you couldn't have stopped them! I'm not an idiot, whoever-you-are, and if you could drop all of those bastards around this table like you did—I was under it, you know, watching 'em fall like flies—and quit trying to tell me I'm concussed!—I just banged my head a little!—then you could have taken them all out! Before they killed my soldiers! Before they grabbed Berry!" The next words came in a wail: *"The best friend I've ever had!"*

Victor decided that diplomacy was pointless. The young woman was practically hopping with rage.

"Sure, I could have. But why should I?" he asked bluntly. Then, nodding stiff-necked: "Introductions are in order again, perhaps. Since you seem to have forgotten—"

"Oh."

The princess' little gasp of shock drained all the anger from her face. "Oh. You're Victor Cachat. I didn't recognize you. You seem . . . a lot different than you did at the Stein, uh, funeral."

Clearly, though, the princess recovered from shock quickly. Anger seeped back into her expression.

"To be more precise," she snapped, "you seemed a *lot* nicer man. Than you do now. You cold lousy fish."

Fortunately for Victor, Ginny arrived at that moment. She'd disappeared for a bit, to try to repair as much of the damage as she could to her costume. The outfit, needless to say, had never been designed for use on a battlefield.

"He's the same guy," she announced, smiling. "He just suffers from a bit of a split personality. There's Victor the Sweetie, who's as cute as a teddy bear. And then . . ."

The smile vanished and Ginny was now inspecting Victor as if he were, indeed, a cold lousy fish.

"Then there's this guy. Machiavelli's Nightmare. The Fifth Horseman of the Apocalypse. Face like a stone and a heart that's harder still."

She shrugged. Then, in one of her inimitable lightning changes of mood, smiled sweetly and gave his ribs a little tickle with a forefinger. "What would he do without me?"

She transferred the sweet smile to the princess. "You might want to keep your voice down a little, though. Chew the cold lousy fish out quietly to your heart's content. But if word gets out that the girl in Templeton's hands *isn't* really you . . ."

"Omigod!" Princess Ruth's hand flew to her mouth. "I'm a moron. The captain'll wring my neck. If they find out . . . they'll kill Berry!"

Victor shook his head. "Relax, will you? Your Highness, or whatever people like you get called. In polite society, which I'm not. I *do* have a plan, you know—and, so far, it seems to be working pretty damn well, for something slapped together at the last minute. Besides, your friend Berry's not a captive any longer." He tapped his earbug. "I just got the word. She escaped from Templeton and his gang and made it into the ventilation ducts. And there's only one of them left to chase after her, because . . . uh, well. Let's just say the others have been dealt with."

"A plan?" Ruth glared at him, but she did lower her voice. "What kind of idiot *plan* justifies allowing the murder of my security people? Or letting those murdering bastards get their hands on Berry? You—"

"A plan," Victor broke into her half-hissed tirade with flat, hard-edged assurance, "which will get your friend Berry back alive. And which will take out—once and for all—a crew of Masadan terrorists *your* intelligence people haven't been able to catch up with in over a decade. *And*," he finished as her eyes widened in surprise, "one which will hit Manpower and the entire genetic slave trade where it really counts."

The eyes which had widened narrowed suddenly, with what was obviously mingled suspicion and hard, intense speculation overcoming anger. They didn't displace that emotion, but even though Victor had hoped for a reaction along those lines, he was a bit taken aback by how quickly and powerfully it occurred. He didn't even try to follow the thoughts flashing through her brain, but he could actually see the moment at which the sums suddenly came together for her.

Ginny wasn't the only female around capable of instantaneous mood switches, it seemed. Princess Ruth's face went from anger to keen interest in a split second.

"A plan?" she repeated in an entirely different tone. "Hmph." She thought again for a moment, then nodded sharply. "So you're working with Erewhon, are you? Well, of course. You'd have to be to be standing around hip-deep in bodies without being arrested. So that means . . ." She grimaced. "If you're talking about hurting Manpower, then you've got to be thinking about Congo. I can see a couple of angles, I think. But if you want my opinion—"

Which she proceeded to give, at some length, despite knowing virtually nothing about the situation. The worst of it, from Victor's point of view, was how uncannily close she often came and how genuinely expert her opinion often was. Anton Zilwicki's influence and training there, Victor was sure of it.

Great. A Manticoran enemy princess with aspirations to being a spy—and some real talent for it, too. Just what I need. Like a hole in the head.

On the other hand . . .

Victor pondered *the other hand* for a bit, as Ruth kept talking. He would have labeled it "chatter" and "prattle" and "babble," except it wasn't. In fact, the girl was giving him some ideas.

The clincher came when the security guards who'd rallied to

the scene finally started letting in the press. The Manticoran princess, it seemed, could also be a fine actress when she wanted to be.

"Oh!" she cried, half-sobbing into the holorecorders. "It was horrible! They took the princess away!" She clutched Victor's arm. "Would have gotten me too, if this gentleman hadn't come along."

Now it was pure chatter and prattle and babble. Which was exactly what the situation required. When the Erewhonese press, well-trained as always, finally let themselves be led away, Victor whispered into Ruth's ear.

"All right, fine. You want in?"

"Try and keep me out, you cold lousy fish."

CHAPTER 26

BERRY WAS GETTING A LITTLE DESPERATE. She'd been certain she could elude her captors, once she got into the ventilation ducts. She knew very little about air circulation systems on large space stations, and nothing at all about the specifics of this one. But the man who'd adopted her had once been a yard dog for the Manticoran Navy. Since Berry found everything interesting, she'd managed on several occasions to get the normally taciturn Anton Zilwicki to talk about his experiences. And she could remember him telling her that, second only to the electrical network, there was nothing as convoluted in a large space habitat as the ventilation system.

Unfortunately, she was discovering, abstract knowledge was not the same as concrete familiarity. She realized now that she'd been too quick to assume that the ventilation system of *The Wages of Sin* would be like her well-remembered Chicago underworld. The difference was that she *knew* that underworld and its passageways, and *didn't* know this one.

So, she'd lost time, guessing at which route to take and—twice!—finding herself in a cul-de-sac and forced to retrace her steps. Retrace her crawls, rather. And frustrated, over and again, by the fact that the ventilation covers in the space station had not been designed to be easily opened from the *inside* of the ducts. So, time after time, she'd had to pass by inviting but impossible avenues of escape back into the main corridors of the station.

She could hear the scuffling sounds of her pursuer not far behind her. *Piss-poor design philosophy, anybody wants my opinion,* she thought crossly. *They should have taken into account the possibility that somebody masquerading as a princess might someday be crawling through these ducts trying to escape a slavering maniac.*

The humorous edge to the thought reassured her, though. She

was still steady, still calm. She couldn't really remember a time in her life when she hadn't been. Berry had little of the sheer athleticism of her sister Helen, and none of the martial arts training. But she could remember Helen once telling her: *If I ever met anyone with nerves of steel, Berry, it's you.*

Maybe it was true. All Berry knew was that she was an expert on only one subject in the universe—*survival*—and you didn't survive by getting rattled.

So, she crawled on, using her smaller size and relaxed ease in cramped passageways to offset the fact that her pursuer—she'd caught a glimpse of him, once—had the superior reflexes and agility of a Scrag. Even if she hadn't been able to find an actual escape, she seemed to be able to stay ahead of him. And she remembered something else her father Anton had told her:

A stern chase is a long chase.

Staring at the carnage in Tube Epsilon, the two Imbesis appeared to have lost some of their usual composure. Naomi's freckles stood out in sharper relief than ever, against a skin that seemed drained of blood. And even Walter, with his many more years of experience, had a grim expression on his face. Victor couldn't see the faces of the six armored guards from the space station's special weapons unit—they'd finally arrived, too late to do any good—but from what he could sense of their body language, they were just as shocked as anyone. Coming on top of the gruesome scene in the main gaming hall, this latest scene of mayhem was probably overwhelming them a bit. Even well-trained security guards don't expect to see their place of employment turned into a slaughterhouse.

Web Du Havel was less visibly shocked, but he did appear subdued. He'd arrived in the gaming hall just as Victor and the Imbesis had started to leave, looking for the spot where the special weapons unit had reported finding Templeton's body. Du Havel had insisted on accompanying them, once he was assured Ruth Winton was safe. Web was not only very fond of Berry herself, but was obviously feeling guilty that he'd been resting in his room when the attack was launched. Not that he would have made the slightest difference if he'd been there, other than to have probably gotten murdered himself.

"For the love of God," Walter muttered, "what did she use on them? A sledgehammer?"

Victor was able to study the scene with more in the way of

clinical detachment. But even he was a little shaken. It was a bit odd, perhaps, since the gore and blood left in the main gaming hall was actually far worse than this. But one expects to see gore and blood when pulsers come into play.

He looked, again, at the corpse of Abraham Templeton, lying prone on the floor. The back of his head had literally been caved in; the occiput not simply broken but splintered—and then the pieces driven a centimeter or more into the brain.

"Just her hands and feet and elbows," he said quietly. "I really don't think you understand what she is, Walter."

"She's a freak," hissed Naomi.

I have had enough of you! Victor began to snarl something in reply, but Walter cut him off.

"Shut up, Naomi," her uncle snapped. "There's no such thing as a 'freak,' when it comes to human beings. Except an actual sport of nature, like a mutant. But those are just objects of pity, and almost always die young anyway. This is . . . something else. Explain, Victor."

Victor decided to ignore Naomi's sullen expression. Whatever attraction the woman had once had for him was gone now, anyway.

"The thing is, Walter, that if the Mfecane worlds had remained isolated from the rest of the human race—say, maybe twenty more generations—they probably wouldn't have been part of the human species any longer. Not, at least, in the precise biological sense of the term 'species.' "

The scions of Erewhon's great families were highly educated, so Walter understood the point immediately. "Part of the same gene pool, able to interbreed. The variation had diverged *that* much? In such a short space of time? Those worlds were only isolated for a few centuries, as I recall."

As usual, an intellectual problem was enough to settle down Du Havel.

"Over a full millennium, actually," he said. "Their ancestors were almost as lunatic as the original Graysons, if for somewhat different reasons, and they set out about the same time and had less distance to travel."

The professor glanced around at the carnage, wincing. "Natural selection on those two planets was ferocious, Mr. Imbesi. I know a fair amount about the Mfecane worlds, as it happens, because they're one of the standard extreme cases used by theorists when we calculate the effects of genetic variation on political processes.

The child mortality rate in the first few generations approached eighty percent. Worse than that, on Lieutenant Palane's home planet of Ndebele, which was the more extreme of the two environments. Combined with an isolated population, those are the classic conditions for rapid speciation. Plenty long enough, even leaving aside the genetic manipulations of the founding colonists. In fact, if the population had been one of simple animals, they probably *would* have become a separate gene pool. But that's always harder to manage, when the animals involved are intelligent. A lot harder. It's—ah—" He smiled, perhaps a bit ruefully. "The final step in speciation is always the development of a distinct set of mating rituals, and that's *very* hard to do with humans. We're just too bright not to be able to figure out how to screw around."

He examined Templeton's corpse again. "So, she's still human, in all that matters. Still part of the same gene pool—as Manpower proved by incorporating so much of the Mfecane genotype into some of their breeding stock. For that matter, I'm sure you've heard of Duchess Harrington?"

Both his listeners nodded, and he grinned crookedly. "The Salamander" was one of the very few Manties whose name had not become "Mud" in Erewhonese ears.

"Well, she's not as extreme a case as Lieutenant Palane, but that's probably only because her ancestors managed to avoid an environment quite as extreme as Ndebele."

Victor chimed in here. "When the Navy captured her—back before she escaped from Cerberus and blacked both of StateSec's eyes in the process—we were . . . motivated to assemble even more data on her. That's when we found out that she's descended from a genetic modification program which has a *lot* in common with Thandi's ancestors.

"But Thandi's ancestral environment's taken it quite a bit further. For instance, her bones are much denser than those of most people's. Harrington apparently really enjoys swimming, but someone like Thandi Palane would have a hard time doing that without artificial aids, because her body won't float. For any distance, that is, although she could certainly sprint faster than most people. But, per unit volume, even with her lungs full of air, she's heavier than water. Her muscles aren't simply harder and stronger; like Harrington's, they have a different composition. A higher percentage of quick-firing cells, a—"

He broke off. This was not the time for an extended lecture on human physiological variation. "It's a mixed bag, of course. These things always are. Gain here, lose there, there's no magic involved. She can break most people in half, including strong men—but put her in a concentration camp on starvation rations with a bunch of withered crones, and she'd be the first to die."

"No endurance, you're saying?"

Victor shook his head. "No, that's not it. As long as she's *fed*, her endurance will be phenomenal. Way better than yours or mine."

Walter nodded, looked about at the bodies lying all over the floor of Tube Epsilon, and then glanced at Naomi. His niece's face was still tight with anger.

"There will be no breeding in-round in *my* family, girl," he said in a low, cold tone. He turned back to Victor.

"What are the possibilities for encouraging emigration from those worlds? Here to Erewhon, I mean. Unless I miss my guess, we're all in for 'interesting times' in the years to come."

Victor grinned, like a wolf. "As it happens, that's just what I've been thinking about. It'll depend on the Ballroom, of course, but if they get their own planet . . ."

Du Havel started. This was the first time he would have heard anything about Victor's long-range plans. His interest was obviously acute, but he managed to keep silent and simply listen.

Walter matched the grin. "They'll have one of two choices. Keep it an exclusive little club—surest way in the universe to sink like a stone—or make it a beacon for the galaxy's despised and unwanted. With Erewhon—and its comforts—just a hop, skip and a jump away."

Victor started to frown—so did Du Havel—but Walter pressed on. "No, no, I understand. We Erewhonese have our faults, but we're no lousy Solarian League, bleeding its colonies like a leech. There'd be no 'brain drain,' Victor. We'd have to devote a fair amount of our own resources to make Congo livable and attractive. Incentives for people to go *back*, after they got an education here. Still—"

Du Havel grunted. "It'd work, Walter. If you're smart and think in the long term, anyway, instead of being stupid-greedy. And it's not just the Mfecane worlds, either. There are still Scrags scattered here and there all over the galaxy. Most of them are attached to Mesa, sure, but Lieutenant Palane's already shown that some of them can be broken loose. Another group of outcasts—and there are still others. Plenty of them. It's a big galaxy."

The head of the Imbesi family turned his head away slightly, eyeing Victor out of the corners of his eyes. The way a man will, trying to gauge every side of a thing.

"And that's what you've been angling for, isn't it?"

Victor shrugged. "Mostly—no surprise—I'm trying to break Erewhon's allegiance to Manticore." He snorted. "From what she's said, Princess Ruth has certainly figured that much out by now! And, if possible, I want to lay the basis for an alliance with my own star nation, of course. But nobody—certainly nobody on Erewhon—is going to make that kind of decision simply based on a little secret-agent razzle-dazzle. The thing has to end—*has got to end*—with an objective situation that satisfies everybody. You don't just need a Congo that's been pried loose from Mesa, Walter. You need a Congo that's three other things as well."

He gave Du Havel a long, considering look. "I'd be interested to hear your opinion, Professor." Then, Victor began counting off on his fingers.

"First, strong. Or, at least, tough as a nut to crack. A system that will fight tooth and nail on its own against any possible would-be conqueror."

"Agreed," said Du Havel.

"Second, prosperous and stable on its own terms—or that wormhole junction won't do Erewhon much good at all. Nobody wants to depend on a shipping route that passes through an area that's not only dirt-poor but, as usually happens, rife with instability and piracy."

"Correct," said Du Havel. "Keep going, young man."

"Third—this follows from the first two—a system that is an *independent* star nation. On close and friendly terms with Erewhon, of course, and with lots of objective reasons to stay that way. But not an Erewhonese colony or puppet. That has the further advantage, by the way, of making those wormholes an even less attractive attack route to Erewhon—because any enemy of yours would have to violate Congo's neutrality."

"That's been done before," countered Walter, "often enough in history." But there wasn't much force to the words. The tone was more that of a man playing devil's advocate.

Du Havel shook his head. "No, Cachat's got it right. Of course, it's certainly true that small and neutral nations have been trampled. Poor little Belgium, to use an example from ancient history. But—" Du Havel's grin was almost as wolfish as Victor's. "Belgium wasn't a nation founded by the Audubon Ballroom, much less with a heavy influx of immigrants from places like the Mfecane hell-worlds and the leftovers from Ukrainian bio-labs."

Imbesi grunted, acknowledging the point. He was as well educated in ancient history as biology. "More like Switzerland, then. A neutral nation with strong natural borders—Congo's swamps and jungles to the Swiss mountains—and whose men had been Europe's most feared mercenary soldiers for centuries. So nobody messed with them, because it just wasn't worth the grief."

Victor nodded. "There are other examples, and no historical analogy can be stretched too far in any event. But . . . yes. That's the deal, Walter." He gave Du Havel another long, considering look. "And I think you'd better start applying your mind to the matter also."

Imbesi smiled thinly. "I'm not running the show here on Erewhon, Victor."

"You will be soon enough, unless I miss my guess. Back in the middle of things, anyway. But it doesn't matter—and you know it. If you make the deal, Walter, and I come through with my end of it, then the families that are running the show won't renege."

It was the perfect place for a stiletto, and Victor didn't miss it. "Sure, they're a little too cautious. But they aren't the Baron of High Ridge and Elaine Descroix and the Countess of New Kiev, either."

Walter scowled. "Pack of scoundrels. A deal's a deal, dammit. It binds a whole family—a whole people—even if the one who made it was a screwball and you have to slap him down hard in private."

He and Victor studied each other for a moment. Then, Walter struck out his hand. Victor clasped it, and the deal was made.

When their hands fell away, Walter smiled. It was a sardonic expression.

"Of course, all of this depends on whether your Amazon can keep the, uh, not-princess alive. I'm only guessing, but I'm pretty sure your whole scheme depends on that."

Victor's returning smile was on the pained side. "More than just my scheme, actually. Probably my life. Sooner or later, you know, Anton Zilwicki is going to be back. And if he finds out I got his daughter killed in the course of a political maneuver . . ."

Victor glanced down at Abraham Templeton's shattered skull and grimaced. "Did you know that Anton Zilwicki still holds the record in the Manticoran Games—in his weight class, anyway, which is plenty big enough—for almost all the weight-lifting events? Leaving aside the fact that he was their champion wrestler, three games running."

Du Havel chuckled. But the sound was more gloomy than humorous. "Oh, yes, I've been thinking about it myself—given that Anton Zilwicki will be none too pleased with *me* either. Not more than a day after he left the girls in my so-called 'care'—ha! But you neglected to mention the rest, Mr. Cachat. *And* he's got the brain of a Machiavelli himself, *and* he's got the soul of a Gryphon highlander vendettist. If his girl dies—even gets badly hurt—our ass is grass."

At the moment, Lieutenant Thandi Palane was feeling more like a fish in a can than an "Amazon." Yes, the ventilation ducts were big enough—just barely—for her to crawl through. No, she didn't exactly suffer from claustrophobia. But the whole experience was still enough to leave her exceedingly unhappy.

So were the women behind her, judging from their grumbles.

"Shut up," she hissed. "You'll warn the Scrag we're after him."

The moment the term left her mouth, she regretted it. She could sense, in the sudden silence behind her, hurt feelings as well as obedience.

She sighed. Then, decided to break her own command.

"All right, I'm sorry." Then, after a pause, hissing: "No, dammit, I'm *not* sorry. The pig *is* nothing but a 'Scrag.' That doesn't mean you are, but it does mean we need to come up with a different name. For you, I mean. I can't keep thinking of you just as 'my Amazons.' "

Yana's voice drifted up from behind her. "What does 'Amazon' mean, anyway? You used the word once before."

Thandi explained. When she was done, she could hear a low rumbling chuckle in the duct, coming from several throats.

" 'Amazon' it is, then," pronounced Yana firmly.

Thandi frowned. "Not sure," she whispered. "There might be a decent male ex-Scrag coming along one of these days, you know. Decent enough, anyway."

"So what?" replied Yana. "No problem. He can be an Amazonette."

"Amazonix," countered Raisha.

"Amazon-boy," offered Olga.

The burst of laughter which echoed down the tube then would have been enough to waken the dead, much less alert a Scrag. But Thandi discovered that she didn't really care, any more.

Yeah, that's right, superman. The super-bitches are hot on your tail. Which means you are dog food.

✧ ✧ ✧

The Scrag did hear the noise, in fact, but he'd already known he was being pursued by someone. His hearing was very acute, and he'd picked up the sound of bodies scuffling their way down the ventilation duct behind him some time earlier. At first, he'd assumed that was his own people coming to his assistance. But eventually, from subtle details in the soft sounds which he couldn't analyze consciously, he'd understood that the people behind him were women.

That could only mean that, somehow, Abraham Templeton had been brought down. And that, whoever the women were following behind him, they were no friends of his. The fact that the recent loud burst of laughter had contained a confident edge—even a savage one—made him certain they were bitter enemies.

So, as he continued his pursuit of the princess, he began thinking about his own options. He was almost certain there was really no point, any longer, to continuing that pursuit. He'd never really known what the Templetons had in mind when they planned this operation—this utter fiasco—but whatever their scheme had been, it was all a moot point now.

For a minute or so, he considered breaking off the pursuit and simply trying to make his own escape. He was almost sure he could do so, at least as far as breaking through one of the duct covers and getting back into the main corridors of the space station. The princess had passed them by, because she wasn't strong enough to just kick the covers loose. But he was sure he could, with his genetically enhanced muscles.

Whether he could then manage to escape the station itself . . .

Probably not. But he found that he didn't really care, anyway. Like so many Scrags, the one crawling through the ducts of *The Wages of Sin* was not entirely sane. Or, it might be better to say, the twisted history of his subculture gave him a death wish which resembled those of the ancient Norse berserks or the hardcore Nazis. Better to die heroically, in a glorious final battle, than to whimper away into oblivion in a universe ruled by sub-humans.

All the more so if he could flaunt his contempt for the sub-humans before he died. Templeton and his religious fetishes be damned. Here at the end, the Scrag would return to his own faith. He'd raped women before, but never a princess. He could think of no better way, under the circumstances, to make the appropriate obscene gesture from his funeral pyre.

✧ ✧ ✧

Ahead of him, but no longer far ahead, Berry was beginning to despair. Not of her will, but simply of her body. She was young, true, but the unnatural and unaccustomed effort of crawling rapidly through the ducts had drained her strength. It had been years since she'd scurried like a mouse in Chicago's underworld passages—and, unlike her sister Helen, Berry had never been much attracted by physical exercise.

If I survive this, she told herself firmly, *I'll have Daddy get me a whole set of gym equipment.*

Victor's voice was back. *"I need this one alive, Thandi. Don't argue with me, either. He's a Scrag, so Templeton wouldn't have let him know more than the minimum. And you've left enough dead bodies lying around here to satisfy even your precious captain."*

The last two words had a slightly different taste to them, Thandi thought. An actual flavor, instead of Victor's usual calm, relaxed, self-confident tone.

Thandi savored the taste, for a moment. Savored it, because she recognized the flavor immediately. She'd tasted it herself, not so long ago.

My, how interesting. I do believe Victor is feeling a bit jealous.

It was a cheery thought. Also not a very sane one, since a romance between a Solarian Marine officer and a Havenite spy would be a picture perfect illustration of the phrase "star-crossed lovers." Still, Thandi was cheered by it. And why not? She'd never found the universe to be all that sane a place to begin with.

"Sure, Victor. But you'll need to define 'alive' for me. I warn you, my own definition is pretty stringent."

Victor's chuckle, like his voice, was that of a tenor. Nothing boyish about it, though, just the same melodious male sound that had thrilled so many women through the centuries. Thandi being one of them, in this instance. Again, she forced a sudden florid fantasy out of her mind.

"I can live with 'stringent,' Thandi. Just so long as he can talk. A croak will do, in fact."

"Consider him croaked."

When Berry turned the corner, she knew it was the end. She'd had to guess, at the last T-intersection, and she'd guessed wrong. This branch of the duct simply ended in a vent. There was no way she could break through the cover, even if she weren't exhausted.

So be it. Now her only thought was to get out of the ducts.

Whatever else, she didn't want to be captured like a mouse in a hole. The T-intersection behind her, like several she'd passed, was an actual *room*. Not a big one, no, but it would be better to face capture there than anywhere else.

Summoning her last strength, she backed out as quickly as she could and, sighing with relief, slid out of the duct and plopped onto the floor of the little ventilation room. It was a tiny room, not more than three meters cubed—just enough to hold the air-circulation fans which filled a third of it, and still provide enough space for maintenance people to work. But, at the moment, it seemed like a glorious vista.

The vista seemed just as glorious to the Scrag, a few seconds later, when he slid into the room from the duct he'd been following her down. The princess was a pretty girl, and looked well-shaped—all the more so with her fancy royal apparel torn and dirty and ragged, and her face flushed and sweaty.

Lust came easily to the Scrag, never more than now. He didn't have much time, but not much would be needed. He wouldn't even bother to undress. He grinned down at the girl and opened the front of his trousers. He was already erect.

Then, hearing a slight sound behind him, he began to turn. But the girl's voice cut his caution down, fluttering, like a knife cutting down a banner.

"You're going to rape me with *that*? Ha! Do I *look* like a chicken? Good luck, you pathetic shithead! Maybe you can dig up a pair of tweezers around here someplace. You'll need a magnifying glass, too, just to find it."

Rage came to the Scrag even more easily than lust. He took a step forward, raising his hand to strike her senseless.

An iron vise closed over his wrist.

"Not a chance." It was the voice of an ogre.

Mezzo-soprano, oddly enough.

CHAPTER 27

THANDI HAD INTENDED TO JUST SHOOT the Scrag in the leg. But when she emerged from the duct and saw what he intended to do, that cold-blooded plan went flying. She left the pulser in the duct and slid easily and almost silently to the floor of the ventilation room.

She'd been raped herself, as a girl, in fact if not in name. In that moment, the Scrag in front of her was the embodiment of a childhood's serfdom.

As soon as Berry caught a glimpse of the shape looming in the duct behind the Scrag, her quick mind came up with the taunts she'd used to distract him. She'd intended to continue, but . . .

The tall figure now coming up behind the Scrag, having flowed into the room like liquid menace, was enough to silence anyone. Berry was vaguely astonished to realize that the thing was female, it looked so much like a demon. Taller than the Scrag, as wide in the shoulders—the creature just shrieked silent *power.*

Like an ogress, except for the human clothing. And except—

The ogress seized the Scrag's wrist, hissed something—Berry didn't catch the words—and slammed him into the metal housing of the air fans. Hard enough to put a dent in the thin covering deep enough to interfere with the fan blades. What followed was accompanied by the screeching of tortured metal as well as the screeching of the Scrag himself.

Except I think she'd actually be kind of gorgeous, if her face wasn't so distorted with fury.

The ogress now broke the Scrag's elbow; then, the other. About as easily as a person twisting off chicken wings. The Scrag was howling with agony. The howl was cut off by a forearm strike which broke his collarbone and sent him smashing into another wall.

Is there such a thing as a beautiful ogress?

The ogress stepped forward, her fist cocked and ready for a strike which would surely be fatal. Would crush the man's skull, wherever it landed. The ogress was obviously skilled in hand-fighting, but the skill was almost superfluous. Does an ogress need to be a martial artist? The fist itself, for all that Berry could see it belonged to a woman, looked as big and deadly as the head of a mace.

But, she stopped the strike. Barely, thought Berry, just barely. Then, a second later, the ogress shook herself like a dog shaking off water. Clearing away the rage, satisfied now with just letting the Scrag slump unconscious to the floor.

When she turned away and looked down at Berry, her face went through a transformation. The glittering pale eyes softened, the hard face even more. Rage faded from the cheeks, leaving them their natural color—very pale flesh slightly tinged with pink, almost a pure albino. It was a somewhat exotic skin color, coupled with those facial features.

Within seconds, the ogress was gone. Gone completely. Just a big woman remained. Very big, and easily the most powerful-looking woman Berry had ever seen in her life. And—in that moment, at least—easily the most beautiful.

"Damn," she said. "Princess Charming, to the rescue. If I weren't heterosexual, I'd be demanding a kiss." She started giggling, a little out-of-control. Then, staring down at her ruined clothing, giggled even louder. "The hell with a kiss. If you were a guy, I'd be tearing what's left of this off myself. See if I wouldn't."

The woman smiled—gorgeous smile—and reached down to take Berry's hand.

"Sorry, but we're both out of luck. I've got my kinks, but they're fixated on men."

She lifted Berry easily to her feet. "One man in particular," she muttered.

"Which one?" asked Berry. "I'll put in a word for you."

The woman's lips quirked in a wry little smile. She started to make some sort of riposte, but stopped. Then, to Berry's further surprise, her face softened still more. Berry suddenly realized that the woman was not really that much older than she was. In her late twenties, perhaps, no older than her early thirties—and in that moment, she looked even younger.

"Would you?" she asked softly. "My name's Thandi Palane. I'm a lieutenant in the Solarian Marines and . . ." Now she looked downright shy. "I've got a really bad crush—really bad—on a spy.

Not even a Solarian one. And I've got no idea what to do about it."

"Let's see what we can manage."

Berry was feeling better and better. She'd often been approached for help whenever someone had a difficult personal situation to deal with. Despite her youth, people just naturally seemed to trust her—and her judgment—and she enjoyed helping them out. "Whose spy is he?"

"Republic of Haven."

"Oh." Berry would have shied away, then, but the challenge appealed to her. "We'll probably have to keep it quiet from my father, mind. Whatever help I can give you. He finds out . . . Anton Zilwicki generally detests Peeps almost as much as he does slavers—*oh*."

She'd suddenly remembered that she was supposed to be "Princess Ruth." *Her* father was Michael Winton.

Lieutenant Palane's grin was just as dazzling as her smile. "Your secret's out, Berry. In selected circles, at least."

Instead of being relieved, Berry was suddenly swept with anxiety. "Oh, hell—I forgot. How's Ruth? Did she—"

"She's fine. A bit bruised, apparently, but nothing worse."

A voice came from the entrance of the duct. "How much longer this chit-chat, kaja? It's cramped in here."

Berry turned . . . and froze. The features of the person in the duct opening were those of another woman, true. But Berry could also recognize the rather distinctive features in that face. She'd seen them before, skulking in Chicago's warrens.

Scrag!

Anton had told her, once, that the Ukrainian biologists who'd shaped the original genotype for the so-called "Final War" had possessed their own version of racialist fanaticism. A type of pan-Slavism which was really no different, except for the specific template, from the Nordic obsessions of the Hitler gang of an earlier century. So they'd selected, among other things, for facial features which matched their image of the "ideal Slavic type." And then, like the fanatics they were, had locked that appearance into the genetic code. The end result was a breed of people who, centuries later, could usually still be recognized by someone who knew what to look for.

"Relax," said Palane. "She's not a Scrag, any more. She's—ah—an Amazon."

The Scrag—former Scrag, whatever—flowed into the room with almost as much ease and grace as Palane had done earlier. The

Amazon planted hands on hips, beamed down at the bloody and battered Scrag, beamed at Berry.

"All is well, yes? So now, kaja, can we please *go*? We're all sick of these miserable ducts."

On their way out, crawling through the ducts and dragging the Scrag behind them, Berry—interested, as always, in anything—asked one of the Amazons what the word "kaja" meant.

Yana, that was. Berry had learned all of their names within a short time, without giving it any thought. She had a knack for getting people on her good side, and you simply couldn't do that if they remained nameless. The ultimate rudeness was the expression: *Hey, you.*

After Yana explained, Berry chewed on it for a while. Then, said to her:

"You're going to have to come up with a different way of handling things. With other people, I mean. Appearances to the contrary—often enough, I admit—human beings really aren't wolves."

"Hard to tell the difference," muttered Yana. "Why didn't the idiots design these duct vents to open from the *inside,* anyway? But, yes, I know you're right. We all do. But . . . so far, our kaja is the only other human being we trust. It's been hard enough for us to even accept other people as really human in the first place. So what else can we do?"

A moment later, apparently, Lieutenant Palane had had enough. Berry heard her snarling voice from up ahead in the ducts. "Damn these idiots! Give me some leg room. They can pay for fixing it themselves, since they were too stupid to build it right in the first place."

WHAM! There followed the tinny sound of a vent cover—much the worse for the experience, no doubt—clattering on the floor of a main corridor. Berry winced a little. Her mind had no trouble imagining a powerful ogress' foot hammering right through thin metal, shearing away bolts like so many pins.

"Kaja!" grunted Yana, with deep approval.

"There's more than one kind of strength," Berry said quietly.

Yana grunted again. "Prove it."

"I have no idea where we are, Victor. Could even be Tube Epsilon, for all I know."

"All right, then. Just stay put, Thandi. We've got the security guards reorganized, and there are teams searching all of the tubes you could have reached. They'll find you within a few minutes. Unless you've got some medical emergency—?"

"Nothing that can't wait. Scrapes on everybody, especially Berry—ah, the Princess. And the Scrag's in piss-poor shape, of course. But he won't bleed to death, and for the rest, who cares? Let the bastard suffer."

"She's still 'the Princess' for public consumption, Thandi. Let her know that too, would you? If she wants approval from someone other than me—which would hardly be surprising, seeing as how Manticore and Haven are still technically at war—I can have her talk to Ruth Winton herself." He glanced at the young woman standing next to him. "She's right here, in fact."

"Hold on a second." A bit of time went by. *"No need. Berry—ah, the Princess—says your reputation precedes you. I'm not sure she meant that as a compliment, mind, but she's not going to argue the matter. 'The Princess,' she stays."*

"Good. We'll talk later. Right now . . ." He could see Walter Imbesi coming through the door of the suite in the space station which they'd turned into an impromptu command center. Not the Imbesi suite—Walter had felt that would be impolitic—but one of the luxurious suites reserved for special guests of *The Wages of Sin.* Luxurious enough, certainly, to make Victor uncomfortable.

Walter gave him the thumbs up.

"Okay, Thandi, I've got to go. I just heard that the Mesans and Flairty have arrived at the station."

"This, I want to see. I hope I get there in time."

Victor disconnected, feeling suddenly empty and sad. *And I hope you don't get there in time, Thandi. It's . . . not going to be something I'd want you to remember me by.*

But the sadness faded quickly, leaving only the emptiness. And the cold, icy soul of a man who would carry through his purpose, whatever that took. Victor recognized the iciness, since it had come over him before, and more than once. As before, never sure whether to welcome it or fear it.

"Bring them to the main gaming hall, since it's still cleared of people," he commanded. And it *was* a command, not a request. Time and place and proper lines of authority be damned. In the here and now, Victor Cachat was running the show.

Imbesi didn't seem in the least inclined to argue.

"You're calling the shots."

Victor wasn't surprised, really. He found it hard to accept himself, but he knew just how intimidating he could be when he put on what he thought of as "the act."

Or was it an "act"? he sometimes wondered. Never sure if he really wanted an answer.

He rose. "Princess, I'd appreciate it if you and Professor Du Havel would remain here. As we discussed, you need to be ready to talk to Captain Oversteegen as soon as he arrives."

Ruth nodded. Victor headed for the door, picking up the hand pulser lying on a side table. "Have them all tied in chairs, Walter, in a semicircle. I want all of them to be able to see each other."

"That's not normal interrogation technique." But before he'd even finished the sentence, Walter's eyes were sliding away. "Never mind," he added quietly. "As I said, you're calling the shots." He began murmuring the orders into his throat mike.

On their way—the gaming hall was some distance—Walter added a note of caution. "The three ruling families are all here now, Victor, and they'll be present at the scene. Not just representatives, either. Jack Fuentes, Alessandra Havlicek, Tomas Hall—they took their own shuttle to get up here."

Victor ignored the implied warning. "What's the news been, down on the planet?"

"Biggest headlines in years, of course. *Princess of Manticore Abducted! Manpower Suspected! Slaughter in the Gaming Halls! A Manhunt in The Wages of Sin!* What you'd expect."

"That's fine. Perfect, actually—as long as there's no awkward specific details."

"No, nothing." A bit defensively: "We've got a free press here, but 'free' and 'careless' aren't the same thing."

Victor's face twisted into a little grimace. He could remember a time when Cordelia Ransom, the former head of the Peoples' Republic of Haven's so-called Public Information Service, would have said something quite similar. Today, under President Pritchart's lean-over-backwards methods of rule, the Havenite press was starting to look downright "yellow-journalish." Victor wasn't sure if the new press was any more truthful and accurate than the old one, truth be told. But, at least, it no longer marched to the beat of a single drummer.

One of his mentor Kevin Usher's favorite little saws came to him. *It's not a perfect universe, Victor. That doesn't absolve us from the responsibility of making it better. Just remember that it'll never be perfect—and, if you're not careful how you do it, trying to make it so just makes it worse.*

"I wasn't criticizing, Walter," he said softly. "Really, I wasn't."

If the Erewhonese press on the planet below was being somewhat constrained, no such constraints were being placed on the ambassadors of either Manticore or Haven.

"What do you mean—you don't know if she's still alive? She's the niece of Queen Elizabeth, for the sake of God! If she dies . . . All diplomatic hell will break lose, you morons! Let me talk to either Fuentes or Hall or Havlicek!"

The trio being mysteriously unavailable, the further shrieks and threats of Manticore's ambassador to Erewhon, Countess Fraser, were inflicted upon one of the government's lesser officials. But he bore up under the strain fairly easily. Like all Erewhonese, he'd grown sick and tired of the arrogance and contempt with which the High Ridge regime dealt with their "allies."

Sick and tired enough, finally, to just break off the conversation. Which was easy to do, since the Manticoran ambassador hadn't even bothered with the courtesy of a personal visit. Just called him up, as she might to berate a servant.

"The fact that she's a princess doesn't make her immortal," he said bluntly. "As for the rest, we're doing the best we can. And I will remind you—how many times has it been, now?—that so long as Congo remains in Mesan hands, you can expect the worst. Good day."

The ambassador from the Republic of Haven did make a personal visit—and even had enough sense to come to the suites in the Suds where Erewhon's real power elite was to be found, rather than call on the pack of officials in the far more modest-looking "Palace of State." But he, too, was sent packing—just as quickly, if more politely—by one of Jack Fuentes' close associates. One of his adopted brothers, as it happened.

"Sorry, we don't know anything yet."

"Sorry, but neither President Fuentes nor Alessandra Havlicek nor Tomas Hall are available."

"Sorry, we don't know where they are." Here, a modest clearing of the throat. "Havlicek and Hall, you know, are simply private citizens—who don't have to account to the government for their whereabouts. Erewhon *is* a free star nation, after all."

"Sorry, yes, I know it's all very inconvenient."

"Sorry."

Jabber, jabber, jabber. The long-suffering adopted brother reflected that Haven's Ambassador Guthrie, while he was less arrogant than Countess Fraser, was also a lot more long-winded and given to pointless verbiage.

Finally, though, even Guthrie managed to get to the point.

"Yes, Ambassador, I understand that. Whatever might be the involvement of certain citizens of Haven by the names of Victor Cachat and Virginia Usher—and all I know is what you do, what's in the press, that they seem to have somehow been caught up in the mayhem in orbit—they are simply here as private individuals and their actions do not in any way reflect upon, or reflect—or even refract, if that will make you happy—the policies of the government of the Republic of Haven. And now, we still have a crisis on our hands. So, good day."

On the bridge of HMS *Gauntlet,* Captain Michael Oversteegen was having a face-off of his own with Erewhon's authorities. But, in his case, the exchange was at least civil. Partly, because Oversteegen wasn't being arrogant and overbearing; but, mostly, because—polite or not—Oversteegen had considerably more power at his immediate disposal than did Countess Fraser.

All the power of a heavy cruiser, to be precise. And one which, though hopelessly outweighed by the sheer mass of the Erewhonese fleet in orbit around the planet, had a well-deserved reputation in that part of the galaxy for being deadly in naval combat. True, in the encounter which had earned her that reputation she hadn't triumphed without suffering horrendous casualties of her own. But that fact, far from reassuring the Erewhonese, simply added extra caution. Michael Oversteegen had already proven once that he would not flinch from what he perceived as his duty simply because of a ruinous butcher's bill.

"I say again, Sir," Oversteegen stated firmly at the image of the Erewhonese admiral in the bridge's display screen, "that I am not questionin' Erewhon's jurisdiction in the matter. But I will also be damned if I intend t' stay here simply twiddlin' my thumbs." He gave a cold glance at another display, this one showing the tactical situation in the vicinity of *The Wages of Sin*. "If that so-called 'freighter' so much as starts warmin' up its impellers, I shall see t' it that it's so much vapor. Be sure of it, Sir. You may choose to play the fools, but I shall not."

The admiral began to say something, but Oversteegen—the first time he'd been a bit rude—chose to override him. "Enough, Sir. All due respect, you know and I know—anyone but a complete imbecile knows, and I do hope you fire the imbeciles you've had workin' on your so-called 'orbital security'—that that 'freighter' has no business bein' there. It's part of the plot, whatever the plot may be. What is certain, is that Manticore will be no part of it. If the Princess dies, such be fortune. The Star Kingdom and the House of Winton will grieve, but they will not fall, or even shake. Indeed, Sir—I know the woman personally, she's a relative of mine—Queen Elizabeth would be the first t' condemn me for allowin' her house t' be used as a hostage against her nation."

Again, the admiral began to speak, and, again, was over-ridden—but, this time, not by Oversteegen. Someone—someone with impressive authority—had simply overridden the Navy's broadcast with their own.

Oversteegen found himself staring at a man he didn't know. Which didn't necessarily mean very much, since—again, he cursed them silently—the High Ridge Government had not seen fit to provide him with the in-depth political background he'd requested when he'd been sent him on this deployment.

Fortunately, Oversteegen had very good Communications and Tactical departments.

"This signal's coming from the space station itself, Sir." Lieutenant Theresa Cheney said. The com officer tapped a query into her panel and shrugged. "It carries their normal Navy protocols and signal encrypt, though, so it's definitely government sponsored."

"Betty here has him IDed, Sir," Commander Blumenthal put in, and nodded to his assistant.

"That's Walter Imbesi, Sir," Lieutenant Gohr said. "He's officially nothing in the government, but he's more-or-less the recognized head of the Opposition. Which, as I told you, works a bit differently here on Erewhon. And since I'm pretty sure Fuentes and Havlicek and Hall were on that shuttle that docked not long ago, I think you can figure he's speaking for all of them. They'd be using him as their 'cutout.' "

Oversteegen absorbed all that with one part of his mind while he listened to Imbesi's opening words with the rest. Imbesi was, thankfully, brief and to the point. Oversteegen's never-too-lengthy patience was by now strained to the breaking point.

"If I'm understandin' your proposal correctly, Mister Imbesi, you want me—me personally, yes?—t' come aboard the space station? I'm sorry, Sir, but I would be derelict in my duty were I t' abandon my command at a time like this, when—pardon my bluntness—we may be on the verge of hostilities."

Imbesi sighed. Then, with a little ironic smile: "Your stubbornness is not simply a matter of reputation, I see. That's a compliment, by the way. All right, Captain Oversteegen. Can you be certain this exchange can't be unscrambled by anyone on that freighter? Or anyone else, for that matter?"

Oversteegen's eyes narrowed, and he glanced at Cheney, who nodded vigorously.

"We're usin' *Alliance* technology here, Mister Imbesi. On both ends," Oversteegan said, turning back to the face on his com . . . and careful to substitute "Alliance" for "Manticoran." Imbesi would probably notice his choice of adjectives, but one had to be polite. Especially with an ally who was already pissed off with one's government.

Again, his eyes moved to the tactical display. And an ironic little smile came to his own lips.

"I imagine those Solarians have an inflated notion of their own technical abilities—and what *is* a Solarian flotilla doin' in this system, anyway?—but I can assure you that not even they stand a chance of eavesdroppin' on this exchange."

Imbesi nodded. "All right, then." His smile widened and became, oddly enough, even more ironic. "Let me introduce you to someone."

A moment later, a young woman's image came into the display.

"Hello, Michael," she said, and Oversteegen frowned. The face on his screen was obviously Berry Zilwicki, yet there was something about that voice . . . something he couldn't quite put his mental finger on.

"Pardon me, Ms. Zilwicki," he said, after a moment, "but I don't believe we've been formally introduced."

"No, you and Berry Zilwicki haven't," that maddeningly familiar voice agreed. "But I'm not her. I'm Ruth Winton, Michael."

Oversteegen stiffened. As a distant relative of the Queen (and one who had been in much better odor at Mount Royal Palace before his relative had become Prime Minister), he was one of the very small number of people who had actually met the reclusive princess. Who didn't look much at all like the young woman on his display. But the voice, now . . . He strained his memory, and his frown deepened.

"That's . . . an interestin' announcement, 'Your Highness,'" he said a bit slowly. "Under the circumstances, however, I trust you will agree that it behooves me t' be certain that you are, indeed, who you claim t' be."

The girl smiled. "Of course I agree. Unfortunately, I don't have any secret code words and—" Her smile faltered abruptly. "—I'm afraid none of my protective detail have survived to verify my story." She inhaled deeply, then shook herself. "All I can offer is that I do remember we were introduced once, though I can't remember anything about the occasion except it was big, and formal, and boring beyond belief."

Oversteegen's memory of the event was far better, naturally, since it wasn't often that a relative as distant as himself was invited to a royal family gathering.

"It was the christenin' of your cousin Robert, Your Highness," he said, and the face on his screen flashed another brilliant smile.

"Oh, very *good,* Michael!" she congratulated. "It most certainly wasn't Robert's christening—I was home with the flu that afternoon. But now that you've jogged my memory, I recall that it *was* my cousin Jessica's christening, wasn't it?"

Oversteegen felt himself relax, and he cleared his throat. "So it was, Your Highness. I take it that reports of your abduction were, ah, somewhat exaggerated, then."

The princess shook her head. "Not all that highly, Captain. They *did,* in fact—yes, it was Masadan fanatics, that part's all true—abduct Berry Zilwicki, whom they *thought* was the princess."

Oversteegen didn't need Lieutenant Gohr to explain what was now obvious to him, but that didn't keep the lieutenant from muttering under her breath. "Zilwicki! Him and his tricks! He must have switched the identities of the girls and—oh."

The captain fought down a smile. It wasn't often that his ATO lagged behind his own calculations.

"Oh," Gohr repeated. "The Queen must have been part of the deception from the beginning. We're swimming in deep waters here, Sir, if you'll pardon my saying so."

"Deep waters, indeed," Oversteegen murmured.

Princess Ruth continued: "But the thing is, you see, they didn't really manage to abduct her either. Because—with some help from—oh, lots of people—she escaped. She's quite safe, at the moment. And now—"

Oversteegen suspected that he was witness to an unusual event. Princess Ruth seemed at a loss for words. Something which, he was almost certain, happened very rarely to the young woman.

Where military protocol seemed no longer quite applicable—

and with Manticoran diplomatic niceties in the complete mess which High Ridge and his crew had left it—Oversteegen decided to fall back on old-fashioned aristocratic chivalry.

"Would you like me t' come and pay a personal visit then, Your Highness?" A quick glance at the tactical display. The freighter was giving no signs of life at all. "So long as you can assure me—"

The princess' loss of words was momentary. Firmly, even regally: "Yes, I would, Captain. And I can assure you there will be no—what did you call it?—outbreak of 'hostilities.'" Her slender jaw set. "Not the kind you meant, anyway. Forget that freighter, Captain. That slaver ship, I should say, because that's what we're sure it really is."

The princess glanced aside, as if studying someone not visible in the display image. Her jaw seemed to tighten further, and she almost hissed the next words.

"I shall be very surprised, Captain, if any guilty party on that ship is alive for very long. If they are alive, they'll certainly be in custody—and might very well *wish* they were dead."

Oversteegen now found himself as curious as he was relieved.

"You must have met some interestin' people lately, Your Highness. I do hope you'll see fit t' introduce me. In any event, I'll be over as soon as my pinnace can bring me. We'll consider the matter a family visit."

He cocked an eye. "Armed, or unarmed, Your Highness? And with or without a military escort? Naturally, I'd normally come unarmed and unescorted into your presence, on such an occasion."

Princess Ruth's smile was now royal graciousness personified. "Oh, I don't think arms will be necessary, Captain, other than your own personal sidearm. As for an escort, I'd simply recommend your ATO. That's Lieutenant Gohr, I believe. Betty Gohr. My—ah, Captain Zilwicki—has a high regard for her."

"Done, Your Highness."

The image vanished, and Oversteegen glanced at Gohr. The lieutenant's face looked simultaneously pleased and—very, very apprehensive.

"I don't *know* Anton Zilwicki, Sir!" she protested. "How the hell—sorry, pardon the language—how would he possibly know *me*?" Almost wailing, now: "I'm just a lieutenant!"

For some peculiar reason, the young officer's distress cheered Oversteegen up immensely.

"Deep waters, indeed, Lieutenant Gohr. Though it's said, y'know—granted, mostly by a lot of disreputable rascals—that Captain Zilwicki is the shrewdest fish in those waters."

CHAPTER 28

AS IT HAPPENED, THANDI DID GET THERE IN TIME. When she entered the main gaming area of the space station, Berry and her women in tow—they'd left the mangled Scrag in the hands of security guards, to be given medical attention—she saw that the huge hall had been almost cleared of people. Except for five people sitting at a table some distance away, everyone was gathered in the center. Two of the gaming tables had been pushed aside to make for an open space perhaps ten meters in diameter.

Thandi couldn't really see who the five people were, at the table to the side. Three men and two women, but beyond that she couldn't make out their faces. The hall was very dark, except for the spotlights shining down in the center.

"It's so *dark,*" Berry whispered, glancing up at the ceiling far above. Thandi couldn't tell exactly how far above, because the ceiling was pitch black.

Four men were sitting on chairs in the center of the hall. More precisely, they were shackled to the chairs: ankles to the chair legs, and their arms cuffed behind the back rests. The chairs were arranged in an arc, covering perhaps a third of a circle. Enough of an arc, Thandi realized at once, to enable them to see each other easily.

She recognized those men, of course. Their faces, unlike those of the people at the table to the side, were brightly lit by the spotlights.

Flairty, who was now one of the few survivors of Templeton's original group of Masadans and Scrags.

Unser Diem, the roving troubleshooter—*ha!* Thandi jeered silently—*talk about trouble!*—for Jessyk Combine; and, effectively, Mesa's chief representative in the Erewhon system.

Haicheng Ringstorff, who was officially a "security consultant" but was, in reality, Mesa's strong-arm specialist in the area.

Thandi studied him for a moment, through slitted eyes. She knew Ringstorff was suspected by Lieutenant Commander Watanapongse of having been responsible for a number of major crimes over the past couple of T-years, including:

—the presumed massacre of two thousand religious colonists headed for the planet Tiberian;

—an upsurge of piracy in general in Erewhon's galactic region;

—the destruction of an Erewhonese destroyer sent to investigate;

—and the ensuing attack on the Manticoran cruiser *Gauntlet* sent to investigate the disappearance of the destroyer.

That last attack had gone awry, mainly because the captain of the Manticoran cruiser had proven to be ferociously more competent at his trade than the pirates who attacked him. It remained unclear exactly how pirates had managed to get their hands on naval cruisers in the first place, but Thandi had heard Watanapongse speculate that they'd probably gotten them from Technodyne Industries of Yildun.

TIY's reputation for shady dealings wasn't quite in the same league as Jessyk's or Manpower's, but it was fairly impressive in its own right. Yildun's location, roughly a hundred and eighty-three light-years from Earth, put the A1 star almost exactly on the boundary between the ultra-civilized core planets of the original League and the more recently settled systems whose attitude towards things commercial (and sometimes military) remained rather more bare-knuckled than the satisfied worlds nearer the League's heart. Yildun was far enough off the main sequence to have no habitable planets, but the system was rich in asteroids and contained the second oldest known wormhole junction in the galaxy. It had only three termini, including the central junction, yet that had been more than enough to turn it into a central hub for shipping. Industry had followed, exploiting the incredible natural wealth of the system's asteroids, and, over the centuries, TIY had become one of the SLN's primary builders, with an in-house R&D division which enjoyed an enviable prestige.

TIY was also one of the trans-stellars which had vociferously protested the technology embargo the League had slapped on the belligerents in the Manticore-Haven War. Which might have had just a bit to do with its habit of occasionally disposing of the odd modern warship under questionable circumstances. It was rumored that the Yildun yards routinely built five to ten percent more hulls than the SLN had ordered and either kept them off the books completely or else "lost" them in a maze of paperwork which eventually deposited them in some very strange places indeed. And it was a demonstrated fact—no rumor, this!—that dozens of warships TIY had purchased "for reclamation" had ended up in the hands of third and fourth-tier navies (and sometimes pirates).

Of course, "losing" four almost-new *Gladiator*-class ships to a single customer would have been something of a new record, even for TIY. But given the whispers that Mesa and Yildun enjoyed a much closer relationship than either was prepared to admit officially, TIY seemed far and away the most likely source of the vessels.

Wherever they'd come from, there'd been very few survivors from the four pirate cruisers. Enough of their personnel had been captured on the surface of the planet Refuge, in the Tiberian System, however, for interrogation. And said interrogations had, apparently, provided evidence which suggested Ringstorff had been in overall charge of the affair. Unfortunately, the evidence hadn't been enough to bring any charges. And since Ringstorff enjoyed the official seal of Mesan approval and protection, he had to be handled with kid gloves, even on Erewhon.

Thandi suppressed a harsh laugh. *Kid gloves!* In point of fact, she noticed, the man who was standing at the very center of the tableau—Victor Cachat, not to her surprise—was putting on a pair of gloves at that very moment. But they weren't kid gloves. Whatever substance they were made of, they were dead black in color; and the slow, careful way Cachat was fitting them on his hands was somehow incredibly menacing. Traditionally, she remembered reading somewhere, executioners always wore gloves to carry out their trade.

The fourth man shackled to a chair was George Lithgow, Ringstorff's chief lieutenant. Also someone suspected of the foulest crimes. And also someone who enjoyed Mesa's approval and protection.

Berry's thoughts must have been running tandem to Thandi's own. The girl whispered again:

"I think Mesa's line of credit just ran out. Who's that guy standing in the middle?"

"Victor Cachat," Thandi whispered back. "He's—well, he's from Haven, although he's supposedly just here on a private visit."

Berry Zilwicki's jaw sagged. "But . . . I *met* him. This guy doesn't look . . . oh. I guess he is the same guy. But he sure doesn't look the same as he did at the funeral."

The girl studied Cachat for a moment longer. Then: "He looks maybe fifteen centimeters taller, fifteen centimeters wider—I don't remember his shoulders being that broad—a lot older, and . . . oh, Jesus." The next words came in a whisper so low they could barely be heard: "I really feel sorry for those guys."

"I don't," hissed Thandi.

Their whispers must have been louder than Thandi thought, because Cachat turned his head to look at them. There was no expression on his face. In fact, Thandi could barely recognize him herself. The pale features under the spotlights were the same, true, but the eyes now seemed like black stones, and the face itself no longer seemed square so much as a block of marble.

Cachat's eyes met hers. Still, there was no expression on his face, no sign of any recognition, or sentiment, or . . . anything. There was nothing. It was like staring into the darkened eyes of a statue—or a golem.

Cachat's head swiveled away, bringing the eyes back to bear on the men shackled to the chairs. Despite their immobilization, the four of them tried to lean away from his gaze. Even the religious fanatic Flairty seemed to shrink like a slowly deflating balloon. Thandi could only imagine how menacing those black eyes must seem at close range, when you were their actual target.

"He's really a pretty scary guy, isn't he?" whispered Berry. "I remember Daddy telling me that once, even though . . . well. He *did* save Helen's life. Mine too, maybe. It's hard to understand."

For a moment, Thandi felt a vast gulf opening between her and the girl beside her. And, boiling out of that gulf, the magma of raw fury. She understood Victor Cachat in a way that Berry Zilwicki never would—no pampered rich bitch ever would—and—

She drove down the rage and sealed the gulf. Forcefully, and feeling profoundly guilty as she did so. For all that Berry was now dressed like a princess and consorted with one, Thandi reminded herself that the girl had *not* been born into privilege. Watanapongse had sketched the girl's biography for her. In most ways, in fact, Berry's life had been even harder than Thandi's own. Or Victor's. Berry had just managed, somehow, to come out of that life with apparently none of the hatred and anger which had played such a role in shaping people like Thandi Palane and Victor Cachat. How'd she'd done so was a mystery to Thandi, but she realized in that moment—it came to her with a genuine sense of shock—just how unusual a person the girl truly was. Like a human diamond, untouched—unscratched, even—by a universe full of cruelty and indifference. As if, where other people specialized in skills and talents, she'd simply specialized in sanity.

She felt Berry's hand sliding into her own, and gave it a little squeeze.

"I'm pretty sure this is going to get ugly, Berry," she whispered. "Do you want us to leave?"

"No," came the soft reply. "There's no point in running from things." The girl's face was creased with a little smile. "Besides, you make one hell of a terrific big sister."

Thandi felt a glow inside. The feeling relaxed her, and she resumed her study of the rest of the scene. Victor Cachat was . . . Victor Cachat. She would deal with that, or she wouldn't, but whatever happened it could be put off for some future time.

Other than Victor and the prisoners, there were eight men and three women at the center of the hall. Those were standing back a bit, facing the prisoners but leaving a space for Cachat. They were a peculiar mix.

The three women, she knew: Inge and Lara, whom she'd left behind to follow Flairty; and Ginny Usher.

Inge had no expression on her face, but Lara seemed very pleased with the whole situation. Thandi couldn't figure out why, until she saw the look which Lara bestowed upon a man standing not far from her. The look combined a sort of hard affection, none-too-veiled lust, and amusement. It bordered on being downright predatory.

The man himself seemed a bit nervous—more than a bit, after he spotted Lara looking at him—and Thandi once again had to stifle a laugh. Her Amazons, she knew, had their own notions of proper courtship ritual—which usually came as a severe shock to the males at the receiving end. Thandi didn't really approve, but . . . it was hard not to find a certain poetic justice in the thing. Thandi had run across some ancient mythology in her studies. She was quite sure that the fellow was feeling like Europa would have felt if she'd been a man named Europe instead, and the great beast whose lustful eyes were upon him was a giant cow named Zeusa.

She was a bit puzzled, at first, by the object of Lara's intentions. Whoever the man was, Thandi was sure he was a member of the Audubon Ballroom. Traditionally, the Ballroom and Scrags were the bitterest of enemies. But . . .

In its own way, she realized, it made sense. Lara's subculture, of which the woman had shed some but not all the attitudes, had always prized a capacity for violence. And however much the Scrags had hated the Ballroom, they'd also feared them. They might sneer at other "sub-humans," but those who were the lowest of the low had demonstrated often enough that they were the equal of any Scrag when it came to sheer mayhem. So it was perhaps not really so strange, that once Lara realized she'd have to find a man from somewhere other than the ranks of the Scrags, she'd find a hard-core Ballroom member . . . quite attractive. Thandi wouldn't be surprised if a number of her Amazons started making similar attachments.

Ginny Usher, on the other hand, seemed unhappy. Ginny's face, so expressive when Thandi had met her before, was now still and cold. Thandi wasn't sure why, at first, since the former Manpower slave would hardly be upset at seeing the four men shackled to chairs come to a bad end. They weren't simply the "representatives" of genetic slavery—they were the direct instruments of the evil itself.

But then, seeing the way Ginny was gazing at Victor, she understood. Ginny Usher didn't give a damn about Mesan goons—had even, if not perhaps to the same extent as Berry, managed to put her past life behind her. But she did care, and deeply, about the young man standing in their midst. And was probably wondering—as Thandi had sometimes wondered, about herself—how often a human being could assume a role before the role itself became the reality. Before a man, or a woman, became the golem of their own creation.

The eight men standing there, Thandi didn't know. But she was almost certain they were all from the Audubon Ballroom. Then, suddenly, she knew for sure. Cachat must have given some unseen signal—or perhaps it had simply been prearranged once he finished donning his black gloves.

All eight of them—with Ginny following suit a second later—stuck out their tongues at the men shackled to the chairs. Stuck their tongues *way* out, exposing the Manpower genetic markers.

The curtain rises. Thandi's thought was more grim than amused. *We begin with the baddies in a very desperate situation. Manpower bigshots and goons, bound and helpless, surrounded by their victims. Eight of whom are killers dedicated to their destruction.*

Victor Cachat lifted the pulser out of its holster.

And a very desperate situation just got worse.

Way, way, way, way worse.

Haicheng Ringstorff didn't doubt it at all. The black eyes staring down at him—then moving slowly across the faces of Diem and Lithgow and Flairty—seemed completely empty. It was like being stared at by a void. The pale, harshly cut face had no expression Ringstorff could detect beyond, perhaps, a certain clinical detachment. They weren't even the eyes of an executioner. Just the eyes of a man conducting an experiment, the end result of which was a matter of indifference to him. Whether positive or negative, it would be simply data to be recorded.

The voice, when it spoke, was the same. Nothing. Just words, sounding like surgical instruments.

"Here's how it will be. I require certain information from you. The information would be useful, but not essential. With the information, I can proceed with my existing plan. Without it, I'll need to develop another one."

The square shoulders shifted a little; it might have been a shrug.

"I'm very good at developing plans. Still, getting the information from you would save me some time and effort. Not much. But perhaps enough to keep you—some of you, or just one of you—alive. We'll see. I can't say I care, one way or the other."

Ringstorff could see Diem's face just as easily as he could the others. Lithgow's face seemed frozen—just as Ringstorff suspected his own did. The fanatic Flairty was glaring, although the glare was a washed-out sort of thing. Diem, on the other hand, was obviously on the verge of sheer panic. His eyes were swiveled as far over as they could be, staring at the five people sitting at the dark table some distance away. Ringstorff had spotted them himself, almost as soon as he'd been hauled into the room and forced into the chairs by security guards, although he'd never been able to recognize any features. The guards had departed, then, leaving it to the Ballroom terrorists to finish the work of shackling them.

"*What the hell are you doing?*" Diem shrieked. "Goddamit, I *know* you're Erewhonese, whoever you are! *Imbesi—are you there?* Why are you letting this maniac—"

There was the sound of a pulser firing, and the side of Diem's head was suddenly shredded. It wasn't a fatal wound—not even an incapacitating one—but his left ear and a goodly chunk of his scalp was now gone. Blood began spilling down his shoulder.

"I require information, not prattle."

Ringstorff's eyes jerked back to the man with the black gloves, and saw him lower the pulser. Perhaps a centimeter or two. The hand holding the weapon seemed as steady as a statue's.

"Prattle again, Unser Diem, and you are a dead man."

Diem stared up at him, his eyes wild and open, his face showing all the signs of shock. Other than being gory and disfiguring, the wound wasn't really a serious one. But Ringstorff knew Diem was a stranger to personal violence. Unlike Ringstorff himself—and Lithgow and Flairty—Diem was a man who committed his violence at one step's remove. He'd certainly never experienced mayhem visited upon *him.*

"Who the hell *are* you?" he whispered.

"Just think of me as the man who will be killing you, and very soon." The pulser in the hand made a little sweeping motion. "You'd do better to give the surroundings a good look, than to ask pointless questions. This is where your life ends, Diem. At the moment, I'd give it a ninety percent probability. If you don't control your panic, the estimate goes to one hundred percent. And the time frame drops to seconds, instead of minutes."

Ringstorff was amazed at the complete indifference in the man's tone of voice. He'd always thought of himself as "hard-boiled," but . . . this guy . . .

What demon's pit did they dredge him up from, anyway?

"First, I require the security codes to the *Felicia III.* It's possible my estimate is wrong, and the *Felicia* is not a slaver in the employ of the Jessyk Combine. In that case, of course, you won't know the security codes and will be useless. All of you will then die immediately. Beyond that—"

Again, he made that minimal shoulder twitch. "But there's no point wasting time with what might come 'beyond that.' We probably won't get there anyway."

He paused, and gave them all that slow, sweeping, empty-eyed examination.

"I have neither the time nor the inclination to use interrogation drugs or torture. Neither is really all that reliable, nor do I see where it's necessary. All that's necessary is for me to establish clearly in your minds that I have no respect at all for your lives, and will kill any of you without a moment's hesitation."

He raised the pulser, aimed, fired. A hole appeared between Flairty's eyes and the back of his head exploded. Flairty's body rocked back and forth for a moment in the heavy chair, and then slumped in the shackles.

"I believe that's now been established." The voice still had no tone at all. "But in case it hasn't—"

The pulser swiveled again, to come to bear on Diem's head. "Do I need to make another demonstration?"

Suddenly, a woman's voice interrupted. Ringstorff found that even more startling than the killing of Flairty. He'd forgotten anyone else in the universe existed except the terrifying monster in front of him.

It was the slave woman. "He *will* do it. Don't ever think he won't. He'll kill every one of you, and never blink an eye." The words were hard and bitter. "God, I hate you bastards. For that, more than anything."

Ringstorff didn't doubt her for a moment—and he was *not* a religious zealot. The words practically spilled from his mouth.

"I don't have the codes—neither does Lithgow—but Diem does." He swiveled his head and glared at the Jessyk Combine's representative. "Give him the codes, you fucking idiot!"

But Diem was already talking—babbling, rather. The man with no name had to quietly threaten him again, in fact, before Diem could slow down enough for the codes to be recognizable. Then he repeated them twice, each time more slowly, while the slave woman made a record.

"It seems you'll all remain alive," the man said. Much as a chemist might record the results of a minor experiment. "For a time. I'll require more information later."

He turned his head and spoke the next words to the Ballroom killers. "Take them out of here—give Diem some medical treatment, nothing beyond the minimum—and lock them up. If any of them gives you any trouble, kill him. The further information they can provide would be useful, but certainly not critical."

Moments later, rough hands were manhandling Ringstorff—still shackled, though no longer to the chair—toward one of the exits. It was all Ringstorff could do not to burst into hysterical laughter. Never in his life, not once, had he imagined he would be grateful to fall into the hands of the Audubon Ballroom. But he'd have welcomed the Devil himself, in that moment, if he'd just get him away from that empty, cold, human-shaped void. That *golem*.

The Ballroom killer who was hauling Ringstorff away was the largest of them. A great hulking brute, showing all the signs of a slave bred for heavy labor. Ringstorff felt like a child in his huge hands.

His voice was of a piece, heavy and hulking. "Quite a fellow, isn't he?" The chuckle which followed was even heavier. "And if you're still wondering if he's really a demon—oh, yes, indeed, he most certainly is. Though I will say he's gotten a bit less maniacal. The last time I saw him do this, he slaughtered a dozen of you swine."

"What's his *name*?" choked Ringstorff. For some reason, he needed to know.

But no answer came. Just another heavy, hulking chuckle. And so Ringstorff, as he was hauled down the corridors toward whatever fate awaited him, had plenty of time to reflect on the fact that falling into the hands of the Audubon Ballroom was really not all *that* much of a blessing.

When the prisoners were gone, and it was all over, Thandi looked down at Berry. The girl's face still seem composed, although the little hand in her own was clutching it rather tightly.

"You okay?" she whispered.

Berry's face made a little whimsical twitch. "I certainly didn't enjoy it. But, yes, I'm okay."

Her eyes came up to meet Thandi's. They were green eyes, but seemed darker in the dim lighting. Thandi was surprised to see what might be a twinkle in them.

"Don't tell me. Is *that* the spy you've got a crush on?"

Thandi didn't say anything, but the answer must have been obvious from her expression. Berry puffed out a breath; then, she made a little shrug. "You are one kinky lady. On the other hand . . ."

The girl studied the figure of Victor Cachat with eyes that seemed much older than her seventeen years of age. "On the other hand . . . yeah. If you could trust him, I could see where you'd feel safe around him." She looked back up at Thandi. "And I can guess that you'd care about that. A lot."

Thandi's returning squeeze of the hand was powerful. Powerful enough, in fact, to make Berry wince.

"Sorry. I forget my own strength. More than that. I hate having to watch it all the time. And, yes, Berry, you're right. It probably is kinky, I don't know. It's not even so much that I need a man I feel safe around, as one that I know feels safe around me." Her dark eyes moved to Cachat, who was still standing silent and still at the center of the room, as if lost in his own thoughts. "Not even a monster woman is going to screw around with *him*."

She was startled to feel Berry's hand jerk out of her own. Even more startled, when Berry reached up and slapped her.

"Don't ever say that again!" The girl was genuinely angry, the first time Thandi had seen her be anything other than calm and composed. "Nobody calls you a monster to my face, not even you. *Is that understood?*"

And that was the most startling moment of all. The way that such a small girl, glaring up at a woman twice her size and many times her strength, could command such instant obedience. As if she were a princess in truth.

"Yes, Ma'am. Uh, Berry."

CHAPTER 29

FROM THE DARK TABLE, JACK FUENTES WATCHED Victor Cachat walk over to the two women who'd entered from the other side of the gaming hall, and observed the recent events from that vantage point. That would be the Solarian officer, and the Manticoran girl she'd rescued.

"This is awfully rough, Walter," he said hesitantly. "I'm not sure—"

To his surprise, Alessandra interrupted. "Oh, piss on it! I think it's time things got rough."

Jack and Tomas Hall both turned to stare at her. Tomas seemed as surprised as Jack was. Of the three of them, Havlicek had always been the most gingerly in her approach to the Mesa-Congo problem. And even more gingerly, in the way they dealt with Manticore.

The woman who headed the powerful Havlicek clan and was one of Erewhon's three triumvirs was scowling. Oddly, perhaps, the harsh expression made her seem more attractive than usual. Jack thought that was probably because it was so rare to see *any* expression on her face. A face which, besides, had been so often reshaped by biosculptors that Fuentes thought of it less as a "face" than a permanent mask.

But there was no mask, now. Alessandra was genuinely angry and determined. "I know I've been urging caution all along. But that was just because I couldn't see a good way to strike them down without exposing ourselves. Don't you see? This kid is *it.* Right out of the old days. *Lei varai barbu.* Sure, he's not of us—he's a Havenite. But this is no time for screwing in-round."

Lei varai barbu. Jack Fuentes thought about it, for a moment. Alessandra was using an ancient slang term, from the hybrid patois of their gangster ancestors. Like most such expressions, the exact translation was rather meaningless—"the true bearded one"—but the connotation was precise. The one you went with, when the family's life or honor was at stake. The one who might die in the doing, to be sure, since fortune was a fickle thing. But would neither flinch, nor hesitate, nor cry in pain or fear. Not ever. And who, even if he failed, would strike such terror in the family's enemies that they would never forget the penalty to be paid.

Jack saw Tomas Hall's expression undergo a change, and knew that further argument was pointless. And, not more than a second later, felt the same change in his own heart and mind anyway.

Alessandra's right—and Walter was right all along.

Piss on it. This is now a matter of honor. Let it go any further, and we might as well just admit we've become Manticore's lackeys. Sitting up like poodles, begging for scraps from the baron's table. Taking a pat on the head for a gesture of respect.

"All right, Walter," he growled. "It's a go. First, tell us what you need. Then—"

He and Havlicek and Hall exchanged quick glances. Clearly enough, they'd let him take the lead.

"Then, give us your terms."

There was always this to be said for Walter Imbesi, Jack thought. He was too reckless in his policies, too much the gambler, but he was never anything other than gracious when it came to the rest.

"Terms can be discussed later, at our leisure. Believe it or not, I feel no burning need—not at the moment, anyway—to turn this into a quadrumvirate." He nodded deeply, almost a bow, and added an ancient expression of his own. "*Maynes uverit, banc etenedu.*"

Tomas grunted, approvingly. "Hands open, table wide." Loosely, that meant: *Let's take care of pressing business, and we'll worry about the divvy later. There'll be plenty to go around.*

"Good enough," said Jack. "And for the moment?"

Imbesi didn't reply immediately, taking the time to study Cachat again. By now, Cachat had reached the two women and was discussing something with them.

"I'm not sure," he replied. "First, we all need to stay in the background." He gave Alessandra a glance of sly approval. "*Lei varai barbu,* indeed—but part of the purpose of such, after all, is to save the family by taking the fall himself. If need be, of course, which we hope it won't. But . . . who knows?

"Beyond that, I think we just ought to keep giving Cachat the reins. He was lying, you know—stretching the truth, at least. He really *isn't* a planner. If he were, this scheme of his would have collapsed already, from the complications. He's just a genius at improvisation. So let him keep improvising."

Havlicek grunted her own approval. "Like I said: *lei varai barbu.* Break in the door and see what that leads to. Good enough for me. If nothing else"—the scowl had faded, and was now replaced by a truly savage smile—"he'll scare the daylights out of Manpower and Mesa and the Manticorans and everybody else who's been shitting on us. You can be sure of that."

After Fuentes, Havlicek, and Hall rose and left the table, sliding out the back still covered by darkness, Walter Imbesi turned to study his niece. Naomi was not looking her usual insouciant self, to put it mildly. In fact, she seemed on the verge of nausea.

"He doesn't seem cute, any longer?"

Naomi's quick headshake was a minimal thing, as if she were afraid that an expansive gesture might trigger off the nausea.

Walter saw no reason to push the issue. He wasn't really surprised. Naomi had led a much more sheltered life than she liked to think she had. An affair with a "foreign secret agent" was romantic, flashy, daring, risqué. Sleeping with a cold-eyed man who could blow out another man's brains with nerveless hands was . . .

Something quite different.

He shrugged mentally. People have their limits, and Imbesi had never seen any reason to push them beyond it. All that usually accomplished was simply ruining them within their limits.

"Go on home, then."

She was gone in a flash, insofar as the term could be used at all in such a great and gloomy hall.

Standing alone now at the center of the hall, Ginny watched her go. She was no more surprised than Walter. But far less charitable about it.

"Go, you worthless bitch," she hissed softly. "Run back to your kennel."

She turned her back on Naomi's departing figure and studied a different woman.

This one, on the other hand . . .

"So what's next, Victor?" Thandi asked. "When do you want me to board the *Felicia*?"

His face still seemed like something made of marble. She was almost surprised to see the lips move.

"Not for a number of hours, yet. At least twelve, maybe eighteen."

Her surprise overrode her concern. "Why that long? I'd think you'd want to keep pushing."

"Keep pushing with *what,* Thandi? Sure, you could probably keep driving ahead. But everyone else—including me—needs some rest. Besides, we've got a lot of groundwork that needs to be laid. It doesn't do us any good to take the *Felicia* before we're ready to do anything with it. The truth is, so far as that goes, we could wait for several weeks."

She was trying to follow his thoughts, and failing completely. "What are you talking about? You've already got the incident you need. Templeton's mania did for that. All you've got left to do is grab the *Felicia* and be able to show the universe that it is in fact a damned slaver and . . ."

Her words trailed off. Victor's face was still expressionless, but there was *something* gleaming in those dark eyes.

Berry spoke up. "You're planning way ahead, aren't you?"

"It'd be more accurate to say that I'm jury-rigging ahead. But, yes. Something the princess said—Ruth, I mean, the real one—made everything fall into place. That's why I asked her to get that Manticoran captain over here. She should be talking to him soon."

However mature she might appear at other times, at that moment Berry looked all of seventeen. She was practically clapping her hands. "Oh, that's nifty! Is there a part for me to play too?"

Thandi saw the gleam in the dark eyes brighten, and felt her own heart sinking.

"Victor, you can't be serious." Almost desperately: "I can take that damn ship alone, if I have to. With the codes—I'm an expert with a skinsuit in open-space maneuvers, and that's not a warship with military-grade sensors. They'll never spot me coming—I can enter through any one of . . . God, it's a *merchant vessel,* there must be dozens of ports. From there—I can take weapons this time, too—I'll only be facing half a dozen Masadans and Scrags and a ship's crew that by now is probably pissing in their pants anyway. They're *meat,* Victor—and I'll plop 'em right on your table. Dressed and boned."

"I don't want *them,*" he said harshly. "We need the *ship,* Thandi. More than that. We need it, to all appearances, still under Masadan control—and for *weeks.* There's no point in having a Trojan Horse if you haven't got the men to fill it with. And that'll take weeks.

The Ballroom is scattered all over the place. Even leaving aside the fact that it's going to take days anyway to talk the Manticorans and your preci—ah, Captain Rozsak—into their end of the deal."

She shook her head, trying to clear the confusion. "What are you *talking* about? And what the hell is a 'Trojan Horse'?"

She'd seen Troy mentioned, in one of the books she'd read. But her knowledge of ancient history and mythology was really pretty spotty.

Apparently, though, the term meant something to Berry. The girl's eyes were very wide. "I get it now," she whispered. "You want me to keep pretending to be the princess, and get over to that ship . . . but then . . . Oh. Of course. It's obvious."

Her own eyes were now gleaming. Thandi's heart sank deeper and deeper.

"It's perfect!" Berry almost squealed. "You'll have a classic 'tense standoff.' God, the press will have a field day! They'll come running from every star nation around, slobbering all the way. The Princess of Manticore, still a hostage even though most of the fanatics died in the attempt—yeah, that'll work, dead bodies will make anything seem plausible and you sure left a lot of dead bodies lying around—but where does Captain Oversteegen . . . ? Oh, sure!"

This time, she did clap her hands. "He's *perfect*! Just the kind of stiff-upper-lip Manticoran nobleman who will be *damned, Sir!* if he'll let a bunch of lousy slavers and pirates hold the Star Kingdom to ransom, but—he *is* my distant relative, after all—well, okay, the real Ruth's—and so he won't *really* want to pull the trigger. So . . ."

At that point she began to falter a bit, but Thandi could see the rest. She didn't have Berry's quickness of thought, perhaps, but she did have a much better grasp of military affairs.

The look she bestowed on Cachat was completely hostile. She had to restrain herself from striking him with her fist.

"You cold-blooded bastard. You'd use this girl—she's *seventeen,* Victor—just to buy you time so you could pack that ship full of your damn Ballroom killers and then—yeah, swell, the deal is made—the *Felicia* is finally allowed to go to Congo where supposedly the 'Princess' finally gets released from captivity. *God damn you, Cachat! They're maniacs!* What'll happen to her in the meantime? *Weeks* she'll be trapped in there with those—"

Cachat's eyes weren't gleaming now. They just seemed . . . pained. And Berry was actually glaring at her.

"Oh," Thandi said.

"Oh," she repeated. She felt like a complete idiot.

But at least Berry wasn't glaring at her any longer. "It's okay, Thandi," she said, patting her arm. It was a bit like a kitten patting the arm of a tigress, granted. But Thandi still appreciated the gesture.

Especially when she saw the pain still in Victor's eyes.

"I am sorry," she said softly. "I wasn't thinking. All you need is to get Berry over to that ship, and for them to let her in." A further realization came to her. "That's why you insisted I keep that one Scrag alive, isn't it? But also told me I could hammer him as hard as I wanted. All the shuttle's viewscreen will show those pirates is the Princess and a mangled but still alive Scrag coming over. Probably with Berry here making the call, desperate because she's alone in a craft she can't handle. They let her in—what else can they do, with a Manticoran cruiser ready to turn them into vapor?—and while they're being distracted . . ."

"You'll be there already," Berry said. "Just like Victor planned. I'm *sure* that was part of his plan, all along. Wasn't it, Victor?"

He didn't reply, but Thandi had no doubt at all that he *had* planned it that way. Why wouldn't he? She knew by now that he was genuinely brilliant at this kind of thing.

There was no reason to keep the pirates alive a second longer after the princess made the crossing. The weeks-long "standoff" which followed could be faked easily, so long as Thandi had gotten onto the ship secretly—which Victor would know, before he let Berry make the crossing. Except for those involved in the plan, no one else would realize that there were no pirates left alive on that ship—and hadn't been, from the moment Berry Zilwicki set foot on it.

It was so obvious—and *would* have been obvious to her, except . . .

Except for the memory of a cold-eyed man shooting another in the head, just to terrify three more into giving him what he wanted. The same man who had, ruthlessly, stood by and watched instead of intervening before Templeton's gang murdered perhaps three dozen Manticoran soldiers and Erewhonese civilians, in order to further his own plans.

Victor nodded, very stiffly. "Walter Imbesi has already seen to it—at my request—that *Felicia* will continue to get garbled news account from this space station indicating that a long-running and desperate struggle has ended with a standoff in one of the tubes. That will keep *Felicia* immobilized, since by now Templeton's men will have established control over there and they certainly won't do anything until they discover what's happened with their leaders and the other fanatics. That buys us the time we need immediately. Other than that, there's nothing more to be done now except convince Captain Oversteegen of his part in the affair. Which I, a citizen of Haven, am hardly the person to do. Hopefully, Princess Ruth will manage the business."

He gave Berry a gaze that was much warmer than the one he'd given Thandi. "I would appreciate it—so would she, I imagine—if you could give Princess Ruth a hand. By all accounts, Captain Oversteegen is a stiff-necked man." He jerked his head backward, pointing to Imbesi. "Walter can show you the way."

He looked back at Thandi. The sense of hurt was gone, replaced by pure iciness. "So I'll get some sleep. I suggest you do the same. We're all likely to need it, in the day ahead."

He started to turn, but paused. Then said, very softly and without looking at her:

"I am indeed cold-blooded, Lieutenant Palane. I make no apologies for that. I wouldn't apologize even to those courageous Mantie soldiers who lost their lives, much less you. I'm sorry they died, but—being blunt—I'm a lot sorrier that ten times as many Manpower slaves die every day, year in and year out, while the universe stands by, clucks its tongue, and does exactly nothing to stop it. That doesn't make me a monster, who would . . ."

He seemed to choke for a moment. "Yes, I'll *risk* her life. But no more—look at her—than she'd risk it on her own. No more than those soldiers were willing to risk their lives when they volunteered for the Queen's Own Regiment. But to think that I'd—I'd—drag her like a sacrifice to an altar and sharpen the blade for the priests . . ."

He said nothing further. Just turned and walked away. Within seconds, he'd left the hall.

"Oh, hell," Thandi muttered, her heart lower than ever. "I really blew it, didn't I?"

"Don't be silly," Berry scolded. "It's just your first lovers' spat. You accused of him of being an inhuman fiend, and he got a little miffed. No big deal."

Berry left then, to have Walter Imbesi show her where to find Princess Ruth, Professor Du Havel, and Captain Oversteegen. Thandi remained behind. Staring at nothing, at first. Then, staring at the only other person left in the huge room. Ginny Usher, who gazed back at her with eyes that didn't seem much less hostile than Victor's.

It took Thandi a minute to make her decision.

Fifty-nine seconds, dithering over a lifetime's disappointments, foul compromises, and crushed hopes. One second, to cast all that experience aside.

She strode over to Ginny. "Show me where he's staying."

"Well, it's about time. I was starting to get worried."

But Ginny was smiling by the time she finished the last sentence, and already tugging Thandi toward the exit.

"He'll be so thrilled to see you! Oh, yes, he will!" Ginny waved a scolding finger. "Don't let that lousy fish-eyed stare of his fool you for a moment, you hear! It's just an act. Well, sort of. But underneath it all—okay, way underneath—he's got the hots for you *way* more than he ever did for that no-good rotten—"

CHAPTER 30

"—HIGHLY DOUBTFUL, PRINCESS RUTH. I grant you, the Cherwell Convention would give me—"

The speaker broke off and cocked an eye, seeing Berry come into the room. The tall, narrowly built officer in the uniform of a captain of the list in the Royal Manticoran Navy looked dismayingly like a much younger, far more athletic version of the Prime Minister of Manticore. His limbs had that look of the Janviers of High Ridge—as if they were somehow too long for the rest of his body—and she felt her heart sink at the very sight. But then she saw his eyes. Dark eyes, yes, but nothing like the half-slitted, perpetually calculating ones the Prime Minister showed the rest of the world. They were the eyes of a man unprepared to take anything from anyone, but they were also clear and thoughtful.

The corner of the captain's mouth ticked with sardonic humor. "And this, I take it, is the supposed 'Princess Ruth.'" He rose and bowed politely, with all the ease and grace of a man born and raised in the highest circles of the Star Kingdom's aristocracy. "Captain Michael Oversteegen, here. Delighted t' see you none the worse for the experience, Ms. Zilwicki. Don't appear t' be, at any rate."

Listening to the man's aristocratic drawl and speech mannerisms, Berry was glad that she'd taken time to quickly change before coming to join Princess Ruth and the captain. She strongly suspected that beneath the suave exterior, Oversteegen had all the unconscious attitudes of a Manticoran nobleman, who simply wouldn't have taken seriously a girl who appeared before him in tattered rags—no matter that the rags were of the most expensive material, and that she had a reasonable excuse for their state of disrepair. Appearances were appearances. Captain Oversteegen's own uniform was immaculate.

The lieutenant had risen also. The tall man turned to her and waved a languid hand. "May I introduce my assistant tac officer, Lieutenant Betty Gohr."

Rather than bowing, Lieutenant Gohr stuck out her hand in a rather abrupt gesture. She was smiling politely, but there seemed to be some sort of uneasy question lurking in her eyes.

"Pleased to make your acquaintance," she said. Then, almost blurting the words: "But I'd like to know how your father knows about me."

Berry's eyes widened. "I have no idea, Lieutenant Gohr. But I'd assume it's because you're either very good—or very bad—at intelligence work. My father makes it a point of keeping track of these things."

Oversteegen chuckled. Although, to Berry's ears, the sound reminded her more of the snort of an aristocratic horse. A high-pitched, sharply ended little neigh, as it were.

"Very good, then," he pronounced. "The lieutenant *certainly* wouldn't fit the alternative description." He bestowed a sly smile on Gohr. "I believe you may rest easy, Lieutenant."

The little question was still in Gohr's eyes, but she no longer seemed uneasy. "Damn snoops," she muttered.

She'd probably not meant the words to be overheard, but Berry had acute hearing. She grinned and said: "Yup. That pretty much describes my father to a tee. Damn snoop."

With as much in the way of sophisticated aplomb as she could manage, Berry slid herself onto the couch next to Ruth. "And don't think I haven't started worrying about what will happen once I get myself a boyfriend. Gah. Bad enough my father's a snoop—he's also a very good one."

Feeling rather proud that she'd managed to seat herself gracefully—not easy, given the fancy clothing she was wearing—Berry segued forward smoothly. "But I believe I interrupted things. You were saying, Captain?"

Oversteegen had resumed his seat. Before continuing, though, he cocked an eye at Ruth.

"Berry is entirely within my confidence, Captain." She nodded toward the man seated on her other side. "As is Professor Du Havel. You may proceed accordingly."

Oversteegen hesitated before he spoke again, but not for more than a second.

"Very well. As I was sayin', Princess, I think it's extremely doubtful that the Manticoran ambassador here would give her sanction to your proposal. Whether I could proceed without it . . ." He shrugged. "Probably. If I were convinced it was the proper course to follow, I would certainly do so. Let the consequences be what they might."

Ruth smiled. "A comment which my aunt Elizabeth made recently might interest you, Captain." She nodded toward Berry. "The comment was made to her father, in fact. 'I believe I can trust a man who isn't afraid of being on the beach when he has to.'"

Oversteegen returned the smile with a wry one of his own. "Indeed. I take your point, Princess—but *you* still have t' convince *me* that it would be a good thing t' do in the first place. The Queen's not here, after all, and whatever decision I make has t' be made quickly or there's no point t' it at all."

Ruth began to open her mouth, but Oversteegen raised his hand slightly, forestalling the words.

"The issue's not the idea itself, Princess. Truth be told, leaving aside the undoubted charm of Congo becomin' a planet run by slaves, I can see at least two other advantages t' it."

He held up his forefinger. "First—bearin' directly on my duties here—it would make anti-piracy work far easier. No pirate in his right mind—much less a slaver—is goin' t' be playin' around in a stellar backyard with ex-slaves on the loose and armed. Especially when—let's not even pretend otherwise, shall we?—those slaves will be largely led and organized by the Audubon Ballroom."

Oversteegen held up a second finger. "Moreover—and *provided* such a slave planet remained politically neutral—it could provide a very useful neutral port in the region." Grimly: "There's no tellin' what armed clashes might erupt in this region in the future, but so long as Congo remained neutral and in ex-slave hands, at least any new outbreak of hostilities wouldn't produce the usual rapid upsurge in piracy."

Ruth was starting to look pleased, but Oversteegen's next words erased that.

"Which brings me t' my chief concern, Princess—and that's the role bein' played in all this by the Havenite secret agent, Victor Cachat."

Berry saw Ruth start to speak, then hesitate. She had no doubt that the princess had been about to argue that Victor Cachat was *not* really a "secret agent," but . . .

Fortunately, Ruth had the good sense not to advance the proposition. Seeing as how, to anyone as obviously knowledgeable as Captain Oversteegen, it would have been absurd.

Instead, Ruth just said, a bit curtly: "Elaborate, please."

"I'd think it was obvious. Cachat is certainly tryin' t' use this episode t' advance the interests of the Republic of Haven in Erewhonese space. Interests which are just as certain t' be inimical t' those of the Star Kingdom."

Ruth nodded. "Yes. Of course he is. Specifically, I'm quite sure—and so are you, I imagine—that he hopes to use the episode as a lever to pry Erewhon loose from its alliance with us. Possibly even to work them into an alliance with the Republic of Haven. Which, as you say, would be very inimical to our own interests. If nothing else, even if the current truce leads to an actual peace treaty, Erewhon could provide the Havenites with a tech transfer of almost everything which now gives us a military edge over them."

"Exactly."

"And so what, Captain?" demanded Ruth. "Whether or not Cachat can manage to pull it off, how do you think we could forestall him by *not* participating in his project? The problem we face, putting it crudely, is that Cachat has effectively boxed us in. He's got us trapped between two jaws of a vise."

Her own jaws tightened for a moment. "You're constrained by military protocol from saying it out loud, but I am not."

It was Ruth's turn to hold up a forefinger. "Jaw number one. Thanks to the idiocy of the High Ridge Government's foreign policies, Manticore's reputation here on Erewhon is now the equivalent of mud."

Her thumb came up. "Jaw number two. Regardless of its possible ramifications, Cachat's proposal with respect to Congo is something which we simply can't oppose on its own merits. If we do so—"

She brought her thumb and forefinger together, like a pincer. "—if we do so, we'll simply look even *worse* than we do at present. Once again, the Star Kingdom will demonstrate to the Erewhonese that we'll roll over *their* interests for the sake of our own—and our own interests, just to make it worse, are really the product of our own stupidity and arrogance."

She dropped her hand and almost—not quite—glared at Oversteegen. "In short, Captain, if we fail to assist the Erewhonese in Cachat's plan, we run the risk of making the political situation even worse. Whereas if we help Cachat . . ."

She let the thought trail off. After a moment, Oversteegen sighed.

"Yes, I understand. Whereas if we help Cachat, we might at least minimize the damage."

Du Havel interjected himself into the discussion for the first time. "More than that, really. Don't forget the need to think in the long term, Captain. Manticore's governments come and go, but what remains is the dynasty. It will be no small thing, I believe, if nothing else, if you demonstrate here and now that the honor of the House of Winton is not made of the same tissue as the unprincipled schemes of Baron High Ridge. That might mean nothing today—or next year—but history is properly measured in decades and centuries. Like prime ministers, alliances come and go as well."

Oversteegen cocked his head, then squinted at Ruth. "Ah. Do I take it, Princess, that you have some proposal for a member of the dynasty t' become *directly* involved in the affair? In the line of fire, as it were?"

Ruth did her best to look innocent, but . . .

Good as she was, Berry thought, she was still only twenty-three years old. Oversteegen wasn't fooled for a moment.

"As I thought," he gruffed, sitting up straight. Any trace of aristocratic languor was quite gone. "Whatever else, Princess Ruth, I can't *possibly* agree t' allowin' a member of the royal house t' put herself at risk. The idea's positively absurd. T' begin with—"

Berry resigned herself to a long evening.

When Ginny entered the suite, Thandi trailing behind her, Victor was sitting in a chair by a table, staring at the suite's display screen. The screen, filling most of the far wall, showed nothing more than a view of the stellar neighborhood looking outward from Erewhon—a view which was grand enough, but as bleak as it was cold.

He didn't turn his head when they entered. Indeed, for all Thandi could tell he was oblivious to the sound of the door opening and closing.

"Figures," muttered Ginny. "Leave it to Victor Cachat to sit in the most uncomfortable chair in a luxury suite."

Still, he didn't look their way. "And why are we *in* this damn thing, anyway? I didn't ask for it."

"I did," stated Ginny forcefully. "And you've got a guest, so stop grousing."

Thandi realized Victor had had no idea anyone had entered with Ginny. Given the man's usual sensitivity to his environment, that alone was enough to make clear that he was immersed in a black depression.

He turned slightly. When his eyes fell on Thandi, they opened a bit. Then, narrowed. And then, within a second, he was staring back at the display.

"What is *she* doing here?" The words were spoken in a tone of voice just about as cold as the interstellar void shown on the screen.

Thandi felt herself shrivel, and started to turn away. But Ginny slapped her arm, as a mother might slap a child, stopping her in mid-turn. And then—to Thandi's utter amazement—marched over to Victor and gave him a gen-u-ine, down home, motherly box on the ears. No affectionate pat, either. This was a real *whap*!

Victor jerked with surprise, his hand flying up to the side of his face.

"Don't act the asshole around *me,*" Ginny growled, her face tight and angry. "She's *your* guest because *I* told her she was. Make me a liar, Victor, and you can figure on using your ears for cauliflower soup."

She turned to Thandi and, in that lightning manner which Thandi still found hard to follow, was all sunshine and good cheer.

"Do come in," she cooed. "Victor is delighted to see you. Aren't you, Victor?" The last sentence was spoken through the same cheerful smile, but the temperature in the words plunged to somewhere not far above zero degrees Kelvin.

"Uh. Yeah, sure. Come in—uh, Lieutenant Palane."

Ginny raised her hand for another box on the ear. Victor hastily amended: "Thandi, I mean."

Hesitantly, Thandi took a few steps forward.

What the hell am I doing here? This is crazy! The man is furious with me—can't say I really blame him—and I ought to just—

"I'll be going then," announced Ginny brightly. "Now that the two of you are off to such a good start."

Matching deed to word, she walked past Thandi and was through the door—closing it behind her—before Thandi could think to protest.

She stared at Victor. He was staring back. After two or three seconds of that, Thandi jerked herself together.

To hell with it. To hell with him, for that matter. Pride and dignity, girl. Well . . . dignity, anyway.

"I apologized once, Victor. I'm not going to do it again. Take it or leave it."

His face was frozen for a moment, set in the same bleak expression it had held when she came in the room. Then, the expression faded into one of simple melancholy and he looked away.

"Never mind, Thandi. Apology accepted—and I should extend you an apology for being such a prick about it. I'm sorry. It's just . . ."

She could feel her warmth toward him coming back. Pouring back, more like.

"Yeah, I know. It's just that you wonder about it yourself." She moved over and perched on the wide armrest of a chair not far from him. "Think I don't? In order to get where I am today—which isn't really such a great place, anyway—I had to do a lot of things I'm not happy about. Some of them still make me a little sick, and all of it makes me wonder about myself. Wonder a lot, sometimes."

He nodded. Still, looking melancholy. Thandi realized that, whatever his other strengths, Victor Cachat wouldn't be very good at handling his own self-doubts. He'd ignore or deny them, most times, and positively wallow in them when he couldn't.

The knowledge warmed her up still further. Quite a bit further, in fact. In that constant self-analytical way of hers, Thandi was simultaneously able to recognize two things. First, she had a serious case of the hots for Victor Cachat. *Serious.* More so than anything she'd felt since her first boyfriend, long years before. Second, she thought she finally understood the reason for the attraction.

The realization made her chuckle, very throatily. *That* chuckle. The one which, like *that* smile, had a rather dazzling impact on men.

Victor was no exception. He was back to staring at her, but this time with an expression which had little resemblance to the barrenness of outer space.

"Leave it to me to save myself for a devil with a heart of gold," she murmured. "Kinky, kinky, kinky."

She rose from the armchair, almost lazily, and began unfastening her tunic.

"Why don't you give your demons a rest, Victor? We've all got demons, you know. What makes us human is how we handle them."

She was starting to come out of her clothing, moving as quickly as she always could when she wanted to. Her voice was husky, throaty—she'd made her decision and was letting the heat of it pour through her.

"So how about helping me with my demons, for the rest of the night? I'm willing to bet this suite has a *huge* bed. We'll need it."

He was very wide-eyed, now. His head was partly turned away, as if he was trying not to stare but . . . couldn't move his eyes, which had a life of their own.

Still, he tried to rally some humor. "I suppose resistance would be futile, huh? How could I stop you from ravishing me?"

She felt like magma; her boots finally off and the rest of it peeling away. Her laugh was huskier and throatier than her voice.

"As it happens, Victor, my inclinations run entirely the opposite direction."

She was completely nude. Two steps and she plucked him out of the chair like a baby. Then, carried him into the bedroom, dropped him on the bed, and more or less poured herself next to him.

"Pardon the role reversal," she gurgled, starting to run her hands over him. She didn't need to help him get out of his own clothing, since Victor was now handling that just about as fast as she'd done.

"Did it ever occur to you that a lady weightlifter might get sick of it?" she whispered, caressing and kissing. He was nude himself, within seconds. His body was hard and muscular, as she'd known it would be. Not as hard as hers, at any moment except this one. But in that moment, finally, she felt completely soft; more than she'd ever been able to feel in her life, and was reveling in it. Soft and open, almost boneless.

Her hand slid down and discovered, to her delight, that every part of Victor was exactly the opposite.

"Oh, God, *yes,*" she hissed. "Just *take* me."

CHAPTER 31

BY THE TIME OVERSTEEGEN LEFT their room, Ruth's face was drawn and haggard. An observer who didn't know the princess as well as Berry did would have assumed the distress resulted from Oversteegen's adamant refusal to agree to Ruth's proposal.

But Berry did know her friend—very well, by now—and was not surprised at all to see her burst into tears the moment the Manticoran captain closed the door behind him. Du Havel was obviously startled, but Berry had been expecting it.

Ruth was one of those people whose initial response to any situation is to *act,* doing whatever is needed *right now*. It was a valuable trait, in a crisis—Berry had it herself, if not to the extreme degree Ruth did—but also one which took its toll thereafter, because acting *now,* decisively, all too often required one to push one's emotions aside. A person could do that . . . for a time. But not forever. In the end, the price of decisiveness had to be paid, and that price could be high. Especially for someone like Ruth, who lacked Berry's capacity for self-analysis.

She put her arm around the princess and hugged her tightly. "S'okay, Ruth."

"It is *not* okay," Ruth half-sobbed. "I feel like such a *traitor.*"

The word "traitor" seemed to burst the dam wide open. Ruth started sobbing uncontrollably, and her own arms slid around Berry, clutching her tightly. Almost desperately.

Berry caught a glimpse of Du Havel's face. The professor's expression had gone from surprise to understanding—*ah, of course; she's finally reacting to the horrible bloodshed*—to, once again, surprise and incomprehension.

"Traitor"? What is she talking about?

Berry was a little annoyed with Web, but not much. In truth, Ruth was such an odd person in so many ways that Berry didn't think anyone but she herself would really understand what the young woman was feeling at the moment.

Well . . . except for one other person, perhaps. By now, as close as their friendship had become, Berry knew a lot about Ruth's history. And that of her family.

"Your mother would have done the same," she murmured. "Don't think she wouldn't have, Ruth."

The princess kept sobbing. "I *liked* Ahmed Griggs," she choked out. "Once—once—he got over being so stuffy. And—and—"

The next words came almost in a wail: "And I *really* liked Laura and Christina! I can't believe they're all dead!"

Berry had been extremely fond of Sergeants Hofschulte and Bulanchik herself. Lieutenant Griggs had been too unbending for Berry to warm up to him much, though she'd had no doubts of his devotion to duty. But Christina Bulanchik had had a warm personality—as had Laura Hofschulte, who'd also possessed a sense of humor as quick and ready as the reflexes which had kept her fighting to the end, after seeing to Ruth's own safety.

Berry's own memory of the savage and terrifying gunfight was mostly one of blurred confusion and sudden terror. But she knew she'd always remember Laura Hofschulte's last moments alive, which Berry had witnessed while crouched under the gaming table.

First, the sight of Hofschulte on one knee, something in the sure set of her stance making clear that the pulser rounds being fired by the sergeant were going home. Then, the stance crumpling, and the horrible sight of Laura's lifeless eyes staring sightlessly at Berry after the sergeant's body fell to the floor—with the body of her last assailant collapsing next to her.

"That *bastard,*" Ruth half-hissed; half-sobbed. "That stinking fucking *murderer.* I can't believe I'm—and I didn't even hesitate!"

It was obvious from the expression on his face that Web was now completely confused. Berry wondered, for an instant, how a man so very intelligent could also be so obtuse.

But she only wondered for an instant. Berry had her own memories of what life was like, when you were one of the universe's unwanted and despised. There were certain inevitable results, one of which was a very stripped-down moral code and precious little in the way of "fine sentiments."

"He's not a 'murderer,' Ruth," she said softly. "That's neither fair nor accurate, and you know it as well as I do."

"He could have stopped them! The lousy bastard!"

Berry said nothing. First, because there was nothing to say—

Cachat *could* have prevented the horrendous loss of life. Most of it, anyway. He could have certainly given enough warning to keep the Queen's Own from dying.

But, mostly, she said nothing because she knew that wasn't what was really upsetting Ruth. The princess would weep over her dead, to be sure, and find a clean anger at the man who had allowed it to happen. But that wasn't what had left her so completely *shaken.* It was the fact that, with no hesitation, she had allied herself with Cachat afterward.

Berry saw Web's face clear up. Finally, he understood.

"Oh."

Yeah, Web, she thought sourly. *"Oh." Ruth may have her mother's genes, but she's been a princess all her life. How did you THINK she'd react, when it finally caught up with her?*

"Oh," Web repeated. He rubbed a hand over his short hair, sighing. "Ruth . . ."

The princess raised bleary eyes toward him. Du Havel sighed again, more heavily. He gave Berry a glance of appeal, but Berry just shook her head. Let Du Havel handle this part of it. Berry's job, for the moment, was just to provide comfort.

"I really wouldn't beat myself too hard," Web said softly. "Given where you're coming from, Ruth, it's to your credit you're having this emotional reaction now. But it's also to your credit—at least from where *I'm* coming from, anyway—that you had the initial one. Right when it all happened."

Now Ruth was the one confused. "Huh?"

Web's normally kind face was set in hard lines. "Look, Princess, I'll be blunt. I understand someone like Victor Cachat a lot better than you do. I had nothing at all against Lieutenant Griggs and his detachment—in fact, I was rather fond of Sergeant Hofschulte myself—but I had nothing *for* them, either."

He gave Berry another glance. "It's Berry's father's attitude toward the Crown. He doesn't blame the Queen of Manticore for the stupid things her ministers do in her name, but neither he nor Cathy Montaigne give her any credit for them, either."

Ruth wiped tears from her eyes and raised her head from Berry's shoulder. Berry was almost amused, really. It was in the nature of Ruth Winton that any kind of challenge would get an immediate rise from her. Emotions, be damned—you can wait!

"Explain that," the princess commanded, almost snapping the words. "I heard Captain Zilwicki say the same thing to Berry the day we met, but I don't understand its bearing on what *you're* saying!"

Web shrugged. "Why am I, or Victor Cachat, supposed to place the life of a Manticoran soldier—or the life of a wealthy Erewhonese tourist—above the life of a slave?"

His face was now hard as stone. "And why, for that matter, should *you*? Do keep in mind that Lieutenant Griggs—and Sergeants Hofschulte and Bulanchik—were at least given the right to *volunteer* for their potentially dangerous assignment. Ask any of Manpower's slaves—like the thousands and thousands on Congo, whose work is almost guaranteed to take their lives within a few years—if anyone ever gave them that right." He nodded toward Berry. "Or ask her if, when she was born, anybody ever asked her to volunteer for a life in Terra's warrens. Or ask your mother if anyone ever asked her to volunteer for a life as a Masadan female chattel."

He snorted derisively. "God, I love the 'fine morality' of the wealthy and powerful. You'll spill tears over your own, in a heartbeat. And then never even look twice at people below you, whose lives are ground under every day, day after day, year after year. Such are beneath your contempt, aren't they?"

Ruth jerked herself out of Berry's embrace and sat up straight, wiping away the last of the tears with a quick, angry hand. "That's not *fair,* Web!"

Du Havel gave her a level gaze. "No, as a matter, it's not fair—applied to *you.* Very unfair, as a matter of fact. And I know that's true because of the way you reacted immediately, once you understood that Cachat was up to something."

Ruth stared at him. Web's stony face suddenly creased into a little smile. "Do keep that in mind, Princess of Manticore. The very same behavior that now has you flagellating yourself for being a 'traitor' is, in fact, the behavior that makes a former slave of Manpower find himself inclined to trust a princess. And it's not often I feel *that* way, I can assure you. I normally trust people in high places about as much as I'd trust a serpent. On that subject—slaves have long and bitter memories—I'm really not much different from Jeremy X, when you get right down to it."

Ruth turned her head and stared at Berry. Berry smiled, and shrugged.

"What he said. And, when you get a chance, I really think you and your mother should have a talk about it."

Ruth's lips quirked. "My mother. Is that the same one my father's been known to refer to as the one member of the dynasty, in some five hundred years, who could teach the House of Winton what 'cold-blooded' *really* means?"

"Yup. Your mother, the murderess."

"Pirate too, I believe," said Du Havel cheerily.

Ruth looked back and forth from Web to Berry. "I still don't feel good about it. And Cachat's still a bastard."

"No one's asking you to feel 'good' about it, Princess," pointed out Du Havel. "As I said—given where you're coming from—the emotional reaction is inevitable. Um. Probably be a little scary if you *didn't* have it, in fact. But don't let that reaction blind you to the reality. Victor Cachat may or may not be a 'bastard.' I don't know the man well enough, frankly, to have an opinion of his personal character one way or the other."

He leaned forward in his chair, hands on his knees. "But here's what I *do* know. While everyone else has spent years pissing and moaning about the horrors of Congo—and doing precisely *nothing* about it—Cachat is willing to kick over the whole stinking mess. So I'm really not too concerned about whether his hands are clean. Seeing as how I'm not impressed at all by the fine velvety gloves everyone else has been wearing."

"And you think this is all because of his fine, high principles and ideals?" Ruth challenged in return. "The man's a Havenite agent, Professor. A *Havenite* agent. As in, an agent of a star nation with which Manticore happens to still be at war." She met his eyes unflinchingly. "He may very well be willing to 'kick over the whole stinking mess,' but I doubt that you're naïve enough to believe that that's why he came to Erewhon in the first place!" She snorted bitterly. "If you are that naïve, I assure you that *I'm* not."

"No, I don't suppose it is," Du Havel conceded. "But does that change the practical consequences of his arrival?"

"From my perspective, it certainly does," Ruth said flatly. "Don't get me wrong, Professor. I hate the notion of slavery about as much as anyone who was never a slave herself possibly could. As you say, my mother had a little experience with the institution, and she never pulled any punches when she described her experiences to me. And, yes, Cachat *is* willing to do something about Congo, which should be counted in his favor. But you heard what Oversteegen and I just finished arguing over. And what if the captain's right to have reservations? What if Cachat does succeed in detaching Erewhon from the Star Kingdom and actually swings it to Haven? And we end up back actively at war with Haven? And Erewhon hands over all the tech advantages which let us win the last round? Do you have any idea how many thousands—how many hundreds of thousands, or even millions—of Manticorans may be killed as a result? How many Graysons? While you're being so morally high and mighty, Professor, and telling me how right I was to support Cachat's crusade against Congo, remember that I have no special, individual responsibility to Congo. Or to *you*, for that matter."

Her eyes were hard, now, and Du Havel reminded himself that whatever her origins, this was a princess of the House of Winton. And that the House of Winton, unlike all too many royal dynasties throughout history, still took its responsibilities as seriously as it did its privileges.

"I do have a responsibility to those Manticorans," she went on now, "just as I did to Lieutenant Griggs, and Laura and Christina. A direct, personal responsibility. And if I were meeting that responsibility, I'd be doing everything I possibly could to stop whatever Cachat is trying to accomplish, not getting behind it and helping the bastard who let my security detachment—*my* detachment, Professor, the people I did have a personal responsibility to—be slaughtered when he could have prevented it. And don't you *dare* tell me that he couldn't have, or suggest that I should put his high and noble anti-slavery principles above the debt I owe my own dead!"

Du Havel opened his mouth, then paused and cocked his head. He considered her thoughtfully for a moment, and a part of his mind noted her anger and decided it was probably a much healthier reaction than her despair had been. But that wasn't why he paused. No, he paused because she was right, he realized.

"Why didn't you oppose him from the beginning, then?" he asked after a moment, instead of what he'd been about to say, and Ruth sighed.

"Because I couldn't," she said, in a tone which mingled bitterness with something else. She gazed down at her hands, examining them as if they were a stranger's. "Because like I told Oversteegen, between him and the damage that idiot High Ridge has already done to our relationship with Haven, the best I can do is try to minimize the consequences of whatever it is he's up to. I certainly can't *stop* him, and if I try, I'll only make the fresh damage worse. So the only pragmatic response available to me is to dig in to *help* him, instead. To salvage what I can in terms of credit for having recognized my Star Kingdom's—or, at least, my family's—moral responsibility to do whatever we can to end the problem of Congo."

"Solely because of *Realpolitik* and pragmatism, Your Highness?"

Du Havel asked softly, and she looked back up quickly. It was odd, really, how such a pudgy man could have such an eagle's gaze.

"Is that all it was for you?" he pressed. "Political calculation? Oh, you're right, of course. My own analysis matches yours almost exactly, although I'm sure you're more intimately familiar with the local political, diplomatic, and military parameters of the entire situation. But is that the only reason you supported him so quickly?"

She looked back at him steadily for several seconds, then shook her head.

"No," she said softly. "I almost wish I could say it were, but it isn't." She inhaled deeply. "As you say, whatever else he may be up to, he *is* willing to do something about Congo. And if he manages that, the consequences for Manpower and the entire institution of genetic slavery . . ."

She shook her head again.

"My people are already dead," she said even more softly. "I can't bring them back. But if Cachat can pull this off, then maybe I can at least make their deaths mean something."

"Precisely," Du Havel said. "And that's my point. A point *you* obviously already understand perfectly—intellectually, at least. I'll even concede all those other points, all those other responsibilities. But the bottom line is that right here and now, you can't do anything about those. You *can* do something about your other responsibilities, though. The ones that everyone has—like the one to do whatever you can to fight something like slavery."

He snorted harshly, and his expression hardened.

"That's the perspective of an ex-slave, Your Highness. Obligation and responsibility weave complicated nets, and your net is as complicated as they come. But, like all Gordian knots, there comes a time when the only alternative is to cut through all the twists and turns and constrictions. And in this instance, the sword doing the cutting is brutally simple. All that remains is for you to look inside and see if you have the guts—and the integrity—to pick it up and swing it.

"So what's it going to be, *Princess*? Are you going to keep flogging yourself over your so-called 'betrayal' of your 'morality,' or are you going to be one of those rare upper crust types who isn't afraid of getting her own hands dirty? Personally, I hope you keep trusting your own instincts."

Ruth looked down at her hands once more, now folded in her lap.

"You two would make really *lousy* psychotherapists," she pronounced. "Aren't you supposed to be . . . you know. At least a *little* sympathetic?"

Berry thought Web's response was exceedingly uncouth. "Why?" he demanded. She herself was already giving Ruth another warm hug.

"Don't be a bastard, Web," she growled, squeezing Ruth more tightly for just an instant.

"Why not? I *am* a bastard." He stuck out his tongue, showing the genetic markers, pointing to them with a stubby forefinger. "Thee? Nod a wegaw pawent in thide."

He withdrew the tongue. "Nope. Neither mother nor father recorded, to give me a proper upbringing. Just 'J-16b-79-2/3.' That's me. A bastard born and bred."

Ruth managed a chuckle, of sorts. "You don't have to be *quite* so smug about it."

"You certainly don't," chimed in Berry firmly. She tightened her arms around Ruth's shoulders. Berry understood Web's attitude, well enough—Cachat's too, for that matter. She even shared it herself, to a degree. But she also thought both of them had a tendency to err in the other direction; a tendency which, pushed too far, could become every bit as ugly as the callous indifference of the high and mighty.

"It's kind of a screwed-up universe," she whispered into Ruth's ear. "We just do the best we can, that's all."

Ruth was back to sobbing again; or, at least, trying to stifle the sobs. But Berry could feel her head nodding. Quite firmly, in fact.

She found that very reassuring. Especially combined with the sobs.

"I really like you a lot," she whispered. "And I know Laura and Christina did too. They told me, once."

There was no stifling the sobs now. Nor should they have been stifled. Berry just maintained the embrace, while giving Web a meaningful glance.

He didn't mistake the meaning of that glance. *Okay, bastard. You've done your job. She'll be fine in a few hours. Now get the hell out of here.*

He was on his feet and heading for the door at once. No professor, not even Du Havel, was *that* absentminded.

CHAPTER 32

COMMANDER WATSON GREETED Oversteegen as he stepped onto *Gauntlet*'s bridge.

"Sorry to disturb you, Sir," the XO said, "but I thought you'd better take a look at this." She gestured at the display screen.

"What is it?" Oversteegen came over.

The XO pressed a button, bringing up a display. "It's a recording of a broadcast made less than an hour ago by Countess Fraser. The first official statement on the kidnaping by our ambassador."

Oversteegen tightened his jaws. From the look on Watson's face, he wasn't going to like what he was about to see.

By the end, in fact, he was downright furious. The first two-thirds of Fraser's statement he could have accepted, more or less, as meaningless diplomatic prattle. But the Manticoran ambassador hadn't been satisfied with just leaving it at that. Instead, at the end, she'd placed the blame squarely on Erewhon:

"*. . . outrageous that the Princess' guards were slaughtered, in the middle of Erewhonese security . . .*"

"She *is* aware that almost two dozen Erewhonese security guards were also murdered by Templeton's gang, isn't she?" grated Oversteegen. The XO, recognizing a rhetorical question—and the seething anger behind it—made no reply.

"*. . . entirely Erewhon's responsibility, and the Star Kingdom of Manticore will hold its authorities responsible for the well-being of the Princess. Furthermore—*"

That was the point at which Oversteegen reached out a long finger and ended the recording. The gesture had something of the finality of an executioner pushing a red button.

"Get me the Manticoran embassy," he said. "I'll take the call in my cabin."

Within seconds after Oversteegen entered his cabin, an embassy official was on the screen. Someone named Joseph Gatri, who apparently bore the resplendent title of Third Consular Assistant, or some such.

"I'm afraid the ambassador isn't available at the moment, Captain. Is there something I—"

"Tell Deborah that if she's not 'available' in—" His lips peeled back in a smile that was indistinguishable from a snarl. "—exactly one minute, there will be royal hell t' pay."

The Third Assistant Whatever stared at him. "But, ah, Captain . . ."

Oversteegen was studying his watch. "Fifty-five seconds. That's also, by the way, a measure of the time left in your probable career. *Get Deborah, you nincompoop!*"

Countess Fraser appeared with less than ten seconds remaining in Oversteegen's deadline. She did not look like a happy woman.

"What is it, Captain Oversteegen? And I *would* appreciate it if you'd stick to the proper formalities."

"Get screwed, Deborah. You're one of my multitude of cousins—God must have been a bit absentminded, there—and every bit as incompetent as your whole branch of the family usually is. What in God's name do you think you're doin'? Our relations with Erewhon were bad enough already, without you addin' a completely gratuitous public insult t' the mix."

She drew back angrily. "You can't—!"

"Talk to you this way? The hell I can't. And answer my question!"

The countess' lips tightened. Then, suddenly, what might have been a sly look came onto her face.

"Oh. I see. You only met her once, as I recall, so you probably don't remember."

"What are you talkin' about?"

It *was* a sly look. "Ha! You've been duped, Michael. The Erewhonese are playing us for fools. Trying to, rather, but I found them out. That so-called 'kidnaped princess' is nothing of the sort. I've *met* Princess Ruth—and she was on broadcast blabbering about her adventures. They must have used nanotech to change their appearances, but the voice was a giveaway. The girl those maniacs grabbed is the other one, the Zilwicki girl."

Oversteegen shook his head. Not in disagreement, simply in order to clear it. The ambassador's thought processes made no sense at all.

"I fail t' see what relevance that has t' the issue—assuming it's true, which I won't argue. What difference does it make, anyway? Regardless of which girl Templeton and his maniacs attacked, we have no business insultin' the Erewhonese over it."

Now, Fraser managed to combined slyness with exasperation. "Oh, for pity's sake, Michael! I didn't make that statement in order to hurt the feelings of your darling little Erewhonese. I did it simply to get us—you, to be precise—out of an impossible situation. If the girl Templeton grabbed *had* been Princess Ruth, we'd have had to get her out no matter what the cost. As it is—"

She shrugged. "Hopefully, of course, no harm will come to the Zilwicki girl. But it's not as if it really matters to the Star Kingdom, does it? And whatever happens—*thanks to my statement*—it will be the Erewhonese and not us who take the blame for it."

Oversteegen stared at her for perhaps five seconds. His sheer anger was gone by the end of that time, replaced by something very close to weariness.

"I will leave out of all this the petty consideration that we're talkin' about the life of a teenage girl. I realize that's a matter beneath your contempt. I will just take the opportunity t' tell you, since I don't believe I've ever done it before at one of our family gatherin's—not precisely, I mean—just how brainless you are, Deborah. Truly brainless. Not simply stupid. *Bar-ain-less.* As in: brains of a carrot."

"You can't—!"

"*You imbecile!* First of all, the entire inhabited galaxy *will* most certainly hold us responsible for our own actions—or inaction—in this episode. But it really doesn't matter, Deborah. It certainly won't matter t' *you,* that's for sure. Because if Anton Zilwicki decides you were responsible for his daughter's death, I can assure you that the man won't be in the least impressed by your official lack of responsibility. He's a rather notorious fellow, don't you know? Not given, so far as I can see, t' much in the way of respect for his betters."

He reached out a finger to the control panel. "This conversation is ended, since it was obviously pointless t' begin with. I will remind you, Madam Ambassador, that as the senior naval officer in the system, I am obliged to 'coordinate' with you but am in no way under your authority. So, Deborah, consider us havin' 'coordinated'—you are a cretin and I told you so—and I will attend t' the Queen's business."

He pushed the button and the display vanished. Then, after

chewing on the matter for perhaps five seconds, Oversteegen got in touch with his com officer. "Lieutenant Cheney, be so good as t' get me Berry Zilwicki. You'll be able t' find her through the station's central com. Put the call through t' me here, please."

Within a minute, Ruth Winton appeared in the display.

"Yes, Captain?"

Oversteegen cleared his throat. "Ah. Ms. Zilwicki. How nice t' see you again. I simply called t' let you know that I've changed my mind. Please feel free t' apply your, ah, special skills t' the task we discussed, and call upon me whenever you find it necessary. Have a good evenin'."

Ruth managed—barely—to refrain from issuing a war whoop. The enthusiastic manner in which she slammed open the door to Berry's bedroom in the suite probably made up for it. Obviously, Berry thought dryly, the princess had come fully to grips with any demons which might have spring from her decision to support Cachat's efforts.

"Let's go!" she hollered. "Oversteegen changed his mind! We're on!"

Fortunately, Berry had just finished changing into casual wear. So Ruth didn't do any actual damage to the tough and practical fabric, as she hauled her companion through the suite toward the door leading to the corridor.

"Okay, okay!" Berry protested. "I'm coming." She glanced at the door to Du Havel's bedroom. "What about the professor?"

"Let him sleep." The princess had her through the outer door. Once Berry closed it, Ruth let her go and started trotting down the corridor. "What happened?" Berry asked.

"Damfino. Somebody must have really pissed off the captain, though, from his expression." She turned her head, giving Berry a cheerful grin. "Don't think I'd particularly want Oversteegen mad at *me,* I can tell you that. He's a throwback, you know. Rumor has it that he's the reincarnation of his great-grandfather—mother's side—Orville Suderbush. Man fought something like fourteen duels. All but three ended fatally. Not a scratch on him."

She was around the corner and piling into an elevator.

"Where are we going?" Berry was starting to pant a little. Again, she made a vow to start an exercise program.

"See Cachat and Palane, what else? They're the ones who'll be running the show, for the next few days."

The elevator deposited them in a slightly less opulent-looking corridor. "I think Cachat's in Suite Klondike 45," Ruth muttered. "Should be right around this bend. . . ."

Her estimate was correct. But the proof of it caused the two girls to draw up short for a moment. Ginny Usher was lying on the corridor floor, right in front of the door to the suite. Sound asleep, apparently.

"Hm," murmured Ruth.

" 'Hm' is right," whispered Berry. "I think we ought to—"

What she thought went unspoken, since Ginny opened her eyes at that moment. Gave them a sharp look, then, apparently satisfied they posed no problem, stretched and sat up. She reminded Berry of a very good-looking cat.

"What's up?" Ginny yawned.

"We need to talk to Victor," replied Ruth.

Ginny shook her head. "Not a chance. He needs some, ah, rest. That's why I'm camping out here, to make sure nobody disturbs him."

She said the words placidly enough, but it was obvious to Berry that she'd be immovable on the subject.

Ruth had apparently reached the same conclusion. "Okay, then. We can probably start with Lieutenant Palane instead. Do you know where we could find her?"

"Sure." Ginny hooked a thumb at the door against which she was now leaning. "She's in there with Victor. Resting. I use the term a bit loosely, you understand."

Ruth and Berry stared at her. Ginny grinned.

"So there's not a cold chance in Hell I'm letting you in there. Forget it. I don't care if you're on a mission to save the galaxy. The galaxy will just have to wait."

Ruth and Berry stared at each other.

"Oh," said Ruth.

Berry was more loquacious. "Oh. Yeah."

Ruth sighed and leaned against the wall of the corridor. Then, sighing more heavily, slid down until she was sprawled on the corridor floor. "Damn."

Berry sat down next to her. "Look on the bright side. At least they'll be in a better mood in the morning than they were just a little while ago. Well. I hope, anyway."

A noise came through the door. There were no distinguishable words. Berry had an image of a tigress in heat, howling mezzo-soprano passion.

"Oh," repeated Ruth.

"Much better mood," said Berry firmly.

Ruth shook her head. "Yeah, sure, but . . . Damnation, we have *got* to start making plans."

Ginny was now giving them a quizzical look. "Plans for what?" She held up her hand. "Never mind. I can figure out the gist of it. Victor Cachat lunacy. That being the case, why wait for the madman? I'm sure the two of you can make up a crazy scheme all on your own."

Ruth and Berry peered at her. Ginny's grin was back.

"Try Grand Suite Sutter's Mill 57," she suggested. "Two floors down. That's where most of Thandi's wrecking crew is spending the night. They could probably serve you as a sounding board. And if they can't, I'm sure the Ballroom maniacs could. By now, I suspect most of them are there too."

Ruth lunged to her feet. "Great idea!"

Berry rose also, but was less sanguine. "Uh. Uh."

"Oh, don't worry about it," said Ginny. "That's a huge interconnected suite, with a central salon about the size of a tennis court. Most of the actual orgying will be taking place in the bedrooms. I'm sure you can find *somebody* who'll talk to you."

Berry was less sanguine than ever. "Uh . . ."

But Ruth had her by the collar and was marching her down the corridor. "Don't be a prude," she said firmly. "They have orgies all the time in Mount Royal Palace."

Berry gaped at her.

"Well." Ruth's face was firmly set, in the way a youngster's will when she's making pronouncements about subjects she knows absolutely nothing about. "Not my *aunt,* of course. But I'm sure the servants do."

"Not like this, I bet," chortled Berry under her breath, after one of Thandi's Amazons let them into the suite. Yana, that was. The two girls were following the woman into the central salon, doing their best to ignore the fact that she was nude and seemed utterly oblivious about it.

"Someone to see you," Yana said lazily, to the two people sprawled on a couch. "I assume it's you they need to talk to, anyway. Sure as hell isn't me, since by now Donald ought to have his energy back."

Yana headed for a nearby door, smiling. It was an odd sort of smile, combining ease with anticipation. As she opened the door and slipped through into the room beyond, Berry caught a glimpse of a large man raising his head from a pillow. She had to stifle a cackle. The man's expression was priceless. Anticipation combined with . . . something not too far from sheer terror.

"What's up, girls?" asked the woman on the couch. That was Lara, also nude, and more or less draped over another man. Berry wasn't sure, but she thought that was the one known as Saburo X. He was wearing exactly as much in the way of clothing as Lara, but seemed much less insouciant about it all.

Berry was at a loss for words. Fortunately—or otherwise—Ruth wasn't. Although Berry noticed that the princess kept her eyes firmly fixed on the opposite wall as she rattled off the nature of their mission.

When she was finished, Lara lifted her head and looked up at Saburo. "You want to deal with this, or not?"

Berry suspected the man was sardonic by nature. His smile on this occasion certainly was.

"Amazing. You're actually *asking* me something?"

Lara grinned. "What are you complaining about? Just think how much scheming and plotting I saved you."

"True enough." Saburo ran a hand over his close-cropped hair. Then, spoke very softly, in words which Berry overheard but were obviously addressed to Lara alone. "I'm not sure this is going to work, but . . . if it does, it'll be because we give each other plenty of room. Agreed?"

Lara's answer amounted to a purr, accompanied by an affectionate stroke along Saburo's thigh. "Sub-human or not, I could really get used to you. Yes. It's agreed."

She rose quickly and padded over toward another door. "We'd better get dressed, then. You want that crap you had on, or will you settle for one of the resort's luxury robes?"

"Robe'll do." Saburo turned his face toward Berry and Ruth. "Give us a moment, will you? Lara could probably manage it—being a superwoman and all—but I'm just not up for first-class plotting and scheming in the raw."

"No problem," stated Ruth firmly. Berry didn't think the little squeak in her voice detracted much from the dignity of the moment.

She herself said nothing. She felt silence would be sufficient. After all, *she* wasn't the member of a royal house perched in the middle of a wild orgy between sub-human terrorists and maniacal superwomen. *She* was just—

"Daddy's gonna kill me," she hissed. "I'm dead. Dead-dead-dead."

"He'll never find out," Ruth whispered back.

"Yes, he will. Anton Zilwicki finds out *everything.*"

"That should do it," Lieutenant Commander Watanapongse said. The Solarian naval officer leaned back in his chair in the space station's central com room and glanced up at Walter Imbesi. "It's your call, of course."

Imbesi stared at him for a moment; then, for a longer moment, stared at the control panel. He was tempted to ask—*very* tempted—how it was that Watanapongse had enough of Abraham Templeton's voice recorded to have put together the message he had. In less than two hours after arriving at *The Wages of Sin.*

For that matter, Imbesi was tempted to ask how Watanapongse had managed *that,* as well. Just about the only way the lieutenant commander could have gotten to the space station that quickly was if he'd been standing by a shuttle down in Maytag.

Walter suspected that he had been, in fact. But . . .

Best to leave the questions unasked. See no evil, hear no evil, etc., etc. If I get the results I want, I'll let the rest of it pass.

"Go ahead," he commanded. "Send it."

Watanapongse nodded and pressed the control. "This will go out on the Masadans' channel. Which—ha!—they think is still secure."

Walter listened carefully, as the recording being sent out was played back in the com room's audio outputs.

It was Abraham Templeton's voice—so, at least, the Solarian officer claimed; Walter himself had never heard the Masadan speak—sounding broken and strained. As if the man saying the words was badly injured and exhausted.

"Hosea. Solomon, whichever's there. [Sharp intake of breath, as if from a stab of pain.] Gideon's . . . dead. Most of us're dead. I'm not long. We've got the bitch. [Long pause, vague sound of gurgling breath. Maybe a sucking chest wound.] It's a stand-off, here. They can't get to us without . . . [Another sharp intake of breath, accompanied by a soft moan.] Killing the slut. Told them I would. They're backing off. [Another pause, shorter. The next words were forced, as if the speaker was running out of energy.] Hold tight. Twelve hours or so. We'll have a deal. Let us go if we keep the bitch alive. [A sudden, low cry, as if Templeton was fighting down agony.] Just hold on. Twelve hours or so. We'll be coming over."

Watanapongse flipped a control, and the voice cut off. "And there it is. That should do it, all by itself. But I'll keep monitoring the channel, and put together something else if it looks like we need it."

The Solarian leaned back in his chair, looking pleased and relaxed. "Piece of cake. All you and I have to do now is just let the—ah, what's the word? The 'wet work specialists,' how's that? Let them do their business. Eighteen hours from now—sooner, probably—it'll all be over except the waiting."

Walter nodded. "That'll be tricky, mind you. Trying to keep something like this secret, for weeks."

Watanapongse was polite enough not to sneer outright. "With the tame press you've got? Piece of cake."

Imbesi scowled. "Not the press I'm worried about. Sooner or later, you know, Anton Zilwicki's going to hear about this and come back. Then—"

"Enlist him in the scheme. Tie him in."

"Well, yes. That's the plan. But what if he doesn't feel like being enlisted?"

Watanapongse said nothing. But Imbesi was pleased to see the smug look vanish from his face.

CHAPTER 33

VICTOR WOKE UP QUICKLY AND EASILY, as he always did, alert to his surroundings. Normally, this would be followed within seconds by him rising from the bed and beginning the day's activities.

This morning, however . . . was unlike any other in his life.

For starters, the moment he stirred, the arm around his chest and the leg draped over his thighs began to tighten. Granted, the motion was gentle, the limbs were supple, and the skin was silky smooth. It was still like being held by a python.

The feel of those anaconda muscles brought back to him in a flash everything that had transpired in the course of the night. The very long night. For a brief moment, Victor gave thanks that Thandi Palane enjoyed being sexually submissive. If she hadn't, he'd probably be a corpse. "Dominating" her had been like a mortal "dominating" a goddess—a feat which was only possible because the goddess willed it herself.

And that, of course—given Victor's capacity for self-reproach—was the main thing which held him paralyzed. As episode after episode from the night before flashed through his mind, he began to plunge into an abyss of guilt and remorse. The problem wasn't that he'd acceded to Thandi's wishes. Deeds were simply deeds, after all. Victor had committed acts far worse—by many orders of magnitude—than anything he'd done the night before and, more or less, shrugged them off afterward.

But that was because he hadn't *enjoyed* them. Whereas . . .

I'm a pervert, he thought bleakly.

He probed his memory, trying to find some particle of distaste; some instant of hesitation; one single point where he'd paused—just for a second!—before wallowing in the sheer pleasure of it all.

Nothing.

Face it, freak. You found the whole thing completely thrilling. Best sex you ever had in your life—ever dreamed of—not that you've had all that much sex to compare it to, but still . . .

Pervert! Admit it, Cachat! You loved every minute of it! Every second!

Gloomily, he started dwelling on this or that remembered moment. Each and every one of which had made him ecstatic. Within seconds, his gloom deepened. He was getting erect again.

And there's the proof of it. You swine.

Thandi was awake herself now. Her lips pressed against the back of his neck, open, her tongue starting to work. The same tongue which figured quite prominently in a number of those remembered flashes. He was completely erect even before her hand found him.

"Dream lover," she murmured. The anaconda body writhed, pulling Victor on top of her. Resistance would have been futile, not that Victor tried. Quite the opposite, in fact—and the gloomiest moment of all came when he saw how avidly he discarded all melancholy and plunged back into rampaging lust.

He did, for an instant, try to tell himself he was just being "very energetically passionate." The instant lasted perhaps a nanosecond.

The worst of it came when it was over. Thandi was a very verbal lover, and once his passion was spent, Victor was able to look past his moral qualms to face the underlying reality. Even more than the goddess body, it was that mezzo-soprano voice which thrilled him. He remembered something his father had once told him, in one of those occasional periods of lucidity when he wasn't drunk.

Son, you'll know you're in love when a woman's voice settles into your spine. Trust me on this one.

Victor had doubted him, at the time. Which seemed wise, given that his father's inebriate advice and observations were usually suspect. He didn't doubt him any longer.

"What are we going to do?" he whispered into her ear. Then, a last shred of his rigid moral code exerted itself, and he tried to leave her a way out. "If we're not careful, this could . . . you know. Get serious."

Thandi's hands slid under his armpits and she lifted him away from her. Not far, just enough to see his face clearly. The ease with which she did so went a long way toward quieting his remorse. Whatever helpless-female, bodice-ripping fantasies Thandi might have—okay, Victor admitted, he had, too—he was reminded that any man who *actually* tried to rape the woman would be lucky if she just maimed him.

Something of those thoughts must have shown in his expression. Thandi chuckled, and a smile spread across her face. *That* smile. The one which, along with her voice, put the goddess body in the shade.

"Don't be silly, Victor. We both enjoyed it—lots and lots—and who cares about the rest? Fine, it's a little kinky. Big deal. I weigh one hundred and fourteen kilos—"

Victor winced. Thandi laughed aloud.

"Good thing I like being on the bottom, huh? And if I say so myself, there isn't a lot of it flab. I once lifted well over twice my body weight—two hundred and fifty kilos—in a clean and jerk. Not to mention that I have black belts in four separate martial arts; I'm an expert with most edged or blunt weapons; and I'm a crack shot with any kind of projectile or energy weapon, as well. So give your tender conscience a rest, will you?"

The smile spread into her pale, hazel eyes. Victor was lost, and he knew it.

"As for the 'serious' business," she continued, "speak for yourself. From my point of view, that advice is maybe, oh, six hours late."

She held the smile, and the warmth in her eyes, allowing Victor to find the exit if he wanted to.

But he didn't—and took comfort in the fact that he never even considered it. A freak and a pervert, he might be, although he was beginning to suspect that Thandi's cheerily amoral view of the matter was probably a lot saner than his own. But he was not a faithless one. Never that.

"I'm crazy about you," he said quietly. "I have no idea what we're going to do about it, but . . . there it is. Crazy or not. There it is."

Her eyes were watery. "Thank you, Victor," she whispered. "Just for saying it. Yes, it's undoubtedly insane. I don't care. For once in my life, I'm going to do something just because I want to."

She lowered him, and the long kiss which followed was a quiet thing. They'd both purged enough passion and lust over the past hours to allow for that. Just . . . quiet. A promise, not a prize.

They were eventually interrupted by someone knocking on the bedroom door. The courtesy was pointless, perhaps, since Ginny barged in less than two seconds later.

"Victor, you look better than I've ever seen you," she pronounced.

"Thandi, you're a gem. And now, I'm afraid, the two of you have to get moving. The whole thing's coming apart."

Victor was up and already starting to dress. Thandi, likewise. "What's happening?"

"The station just got a transmission from the *Felicia.* Your attempt to stall for time didn't work. Templeton's people say they're going to blow it up if we don't transfer the Princess over there within two hours. The transmission was received by every news station on Erewhon, I might add."

Victor pursed his lips. "They moved faster than I expected." He gave Thandi a guilty glance. "I guess we probably shouldn't have—"

"Finish the sentence and you're a dead man," growled Thandi.

"And I'll feed your corpse to the scavengers," Ginny chimed in immediately. "They've got really nasty ones on Erewhon, too, I hear. Some kind of giant worm—more like a centipede—starts by burrowing into your intestines and working its way out."

She shook her head. "Fair warning, Thandi: your new boyfriend's capacity for self-recrimination is just about bottomless."

Thandi smiled, as she began putting on her boots. "I noticed. On the other hand, I believe I can do something about that. Made a good start on it last night, that's for sure." She glanced at Victor, the smile becoming sly. "Look at him, will you? Blushing! The same man who ravished me—again—less than an hour ago. He wasn't blushing then, Ginny, I can tell you that."

Victor was quite sure his face was pink. Beet red, probably. It suddenly dawned on him that Thandi was going to be as bad as Ginny, when it came to teasing.

"There I was, begging for mercy—among other things, I admit—and did he care? Ha!"

No, she was going to be worse.

"Have you had a chance to do any window-shopping here yet, Ginny? I'll bet a place like this has a *great* leather shop."

"Got to," agreed Ginny. "Soon as we get a chance, we'll find out." Thandi was on her feet, now. Ginny cocked her head and examined the tall woman standing in front of her.

"Chains too, I think. You'd look *fantastic* in chains. The barbarian princess, at the mercy of her conqueror."

Thandi grinned. "One of my favorite fantasies. In fact—"

Desperately, Victor tried to change the subject. All the more desperately, because of the sudden vivid image which came to his mind. Thandi; nude; chained; helpless. He was having trouble getting into his pants.

"What was the exact wording of the message—"

Thandi drove right over it. "—I'm thinking I'll have to get Victor some kind of whip. Nothing heavy-duty, of course. I'm not *really* a masochist, I just like to play at it. But I've seen those cute little velvet things. They couldn't do more than sting a bit."

The anaconda body writhed briefly. "Oh—please!" Then, she grinned at Victor. "Something wrong with the pants, sweetheart? Want some help?"

He tried to glare at her. But wound up just laughing.

"I'm ruined," he proclaimed.

"About time," said Ginny. She turned and headed toward the front door to the suite. "You'd better have those pants on in five seconds, Victor, or you'll be ruined in public. I'm letting everybody in."

She gave him ten seconds. Just enough time for Victor and Thandi to emerge from the bedroom and close the door behind them. Victor's pants were on by then—not that it made much difference. Modern styles for men's casual wear ran on the tight side. He might as well have been wearing a codpiece.

Hastily, as Ginny opened the front door, Victor flopped into a nearby armchair and crossed his legs. Moving less hurriedly, chortling all the while, Thandi eased into an armchair next to him.

Princess Ruth was the first one through, already talking as she entered the suite.

"Everything's set." She jerked a thumb over her shoulder. "Even Jiri finally agreed I had to go with you. So don't even bother arguing the point, Thandi. He's your superior officer, after all."

Lieutenant Commander Watanapongse was the next one through, followed closely by Berry. Seeing the frown on Thandi's face, the Solarian intelligence officer shrugged.

"It's not actually an order, Lieutenant Palane. But I've been working with Princess Ruth for the past several hours, and the truth of it is that she's a better hacker than I am. And I probably need to stay behind on the station, anyway, in case anything needs to be coordinated with Captain Rozsak's flotilla."

Thandi shook her head, her frown deepening. "What are you both talking about? You left out a few sentences there."

"Oh." Ruth looked surprised. "Sorry. The assault you'll be leading on the *Felicia.* You're the only one who's really an expert on deep space skinsuit maneuvers, except maybe Jiri, but we figured we could slave everyone else's controls to yours. I probably wouldn't need it, myself, since I've played vacuum polo since I was eleven." She grinned. "One advantage of being out of the succession—Palace Security doesn't have heart failure whenever you want to do something *fun.* But if you want to slave my controls, too, I won't argue the point. Besides, your Amazons are so prickly that if they see me being a good little girl, they'll be easier to handle."

Again, Thandi shook her head. "I'm still panting for breath, trying to catch up. You're proposing a *mass* assault? Me—and you—and my whole unit? I'd just been thinking of a solo operation." A bit stiffly: "I can assure you that I won't need any help against *that* little pack of carrion-eaters."

Watanapongse smiled. "Probably not, Thandi—*if* you could find them, once you got into the ship. But that's not going to be simple, and you know it. The interior layout of any five-million-ton commercial vessel, especially for a hybrid passenger-freighter like this one, is too complex—and *big*—for any boarding party to keep straight without at least a detailed set of plans. But this is a slaver, so it's virtually certain her layout doesn't match the rest of her official classmates anymore. And even if it did, there'll be an elaborate set of internal security measures to penetrate."

He nodded at Victor. "The codes he got are only the general Mesan codes for ship entry. The internal security codes will be specific to each vessel, and there's no way of finding them out without getting on board and hacking into the ship's computer." Now, he nodded toward Ruth. "She can do it, I'm sure she can, and while she's at it, she can pull out a complete schematic of *Felicia*'s blueprints for you, too. The girl—sorry, young woman—is a whiz with security programs. Just to prove it, she cracked the codes of *The Wages of Sin* inside half an hour. The toughest ones of all, in fact, the ones which govern access to the hidden security scanners in all the rooms and suites in the station."

The Solarian officer's smile grew lopsided. "A bit flamboyant, you ask me. *I* certainly wouldn't have violated your privacy that way."

Victor and Thandi both froze. Princess Ruth looked exceedingly uncomfortable. "Look, sorry. It was just the suite number I remembered right off. I switched off after—three seconds, at the most."

Berry giggled. "What a liar. More like three minutes."

Victor rubbed his face. "Ruined," he muttered.

"Don't be silly," Berry stated firmly. "First of all, I made sure Ruth erased everything. Second of all, even if I hadn't, the worst thing you'd face is hordes of female admirers. It was . . . Ah. Impressive."

"Hordes of *dead* female admirers," muttered Thandi. She gave Ruth a look which was not filled with admiration. "You ever do that again, girl, and I will introduce you to a new word: *regicide.*"

Ruth looked suitably abashed. Insofar, at least, as a young woman of her temperament ever could. "Not sure that's right, actually. 'Regicide'—I think—refers to a ruling monarch. But"—she hurried on—"that's okay. I'd just as soon avoid princessicide too. I really didn't mean any harm. I just had to prove to Jiri I wasn't bragging."

Thandi transferred the look-not-filled-with-admiration to the Solarian intelligence specialist. "Superior officer or not, Commander—"

"Have no fear, Lieutenant Palane. My lips are sealed." Watanapongse's smile was now very lopsided. "I've also seen you in a full contact court, remember? And I've never had any problem keeping my priorities straight. Staying alive comes a long way ahead of gossip."

He took two steps and eased into the couch across from Victor and Thandi. "So let's get back to the subject." He tossed his head toward Berry and Ruth. "While the two of you were—ah—indisposed, we fleshed out the plan. Lieutenant Palane, you'll lead the skinsuit assault on the *Felicia,* with the Princess and your Amazons slaved to your controls until you reach the ship. Once you get in, you'll be in command—and you'll have your special unit along, as well as Princess Ruth to provide you with tech assistance. We figure you should be able to reach the bridge within two hours."

He made a face. "We'll just have to hope that's enough time. But I'm afraid there's no way around the fact that Ms. Zilwicki—still posing as the Princess—will have to transfer over to the *Felicia* within the hour. I don't think anybody doubts that Templeton's maniacs will make good on their promise."

Victor scowled fiercely. "That was *not* part of the plan. Like you said, they're maniacs. We can't leave Ms. Zilwicki in their hands for hours before she's rescued. No way."

"It's either that or watch eight thousand people get vaporized," Berry said bluntly. "You do what you want, Victor Cachat. It really doesn't matter, because the decision is mine and I already made it."

Thandi's eyes were wide. "*Eight* thousand?"

"Yup. As part of their broadcast, Templeton's men showed interior scans of the *Felicia.* The bastards have that ship packed to the gills with people. All of them genetic slaves from Manpower's breeding station on Jarrod. Tech and heavy labor varieties, mostly. Congo uses up slaves like firewood."

All that, the seventeen-year-old girl said in a level, even voice. The words which came after seemed to have no tone at all. "They won't kill me, Victor. Not right away, for sure. The worst that'll happen—fairly standard practice for Masadans—is that I'll get raped. I've been raped before. I'll deal with it afterward, well enough. It beats eight thousand people being murdered. So there's nothing to discuss."

Victor stared at her for a few seconds. Then, nodded. The gesture was more of a sign of respect than agreement.

"All right, then. But you're not going alone. I'll go with you."

"Are you nuts?" protested Berry. "What's the point? They'll kill *you* right off."

"No they won't." Victor's face had a little lopsided smile of its own. "Not after I let it drop that I've got critical information for them. Which I'll refuse to divulge, of course. And our anti-drug immunization programs are even better than Manticore's, so they'll have to fall back on torture. That'll have the added advantage of distracting them from you."

"*What* 'critical information'?" demanded Princess Ruth.

Victor shrugged. "Who knows? I'll figure out something in the next hour. Biggest problem I'll have is posing as your . . . tutor, whatever. Somebody who insisted on coming with you. My Nouveau Paris slum accent is hard to disguise."

"Just roll your 'r's a bit," suggested Watanapongse. "And toss in some French words here and there. Havenite patois will work fine, since they won't know the difference anyway. You can pass yourself off as a scholar from Garches."

Seeing Victor's puzzled expression, he added: "It's a planet in Ventane sector. Dirt poor, but settled originally by idiot intellectuals. Their major export crop is half-baked nannies with delusions of grandeur."

Thandi was staring at him, her face tight. "Victor . . . I'll get there as fast as I can, but. . . ."

He gave her a smile. Then, deciding that discretion was pointless anyway—certainly in front of an audience which had been watching them in flagrante delicto, excelsior—turned it into something of a leer. "One of my father's favorite sayings, you know: 'turnabout is fair play.' Although I do hope you get to me before they wear out the leather and start pulling out the iron stuff."

CHAPTER 34

"THIS ISN'T GOING TO WORK," Berry said quietly, as she studied Victor.

The words didn't seem to register on him for a few seconds. Victor just kept staring at the viewscreen, watching the image of the *Felicia III* slowly grow larger. Then, his eyes still seeming a bit unfocused, he swivelled his head toward her. He and Berry were sitting in the first two seats in the small shuttle, with Lieutenant Gohr and three Marines from the *Gauntlet* sitting in the shuttle's four other seats. Because the front row of seats faced backward, Victor and Berry were looking straight at the Manticorans.

"We can still turn back," he said. "All you have to do is say the word."

"I didn't make myself clear. I'm fine. The reason it's not going to work is because of you."

Victor frowned. Berry looked at Betty Gohr.

"I ask you, Lieutenant: does this man bear the slightest resemblance to a tutor for a royal princess?"

Lieutenant Gohr chuckled. "About as much as a falcon resembles a mouse. She's right, Officer Cachat. I was just thinking the same thing myself."

Victor shrugged irritably. "I'm not putting on the act now. Once we get aboard—"

Gohr shook her head. "Not a chance. If you were just going to be playing that role . . . maybe. I don't know how good an actor you are. But not even the best actor in the galaxy can play two parts at once. And the problem is that you're *also* preparing yourself for torture. Steeling yourself enough to stand up to at least two hours of it. Whatever it takes to give Lieutenant Palane the time she needs. And you'll give it to her, won't you? I don't much doubt you're one of those rare people who'll withstand torture until you simply lapse unconscious."

Victor repeated the irritable shrug. "I have a high pain threshold, that's all. Fourth highest ever recorded at the People's Republic's StateSec Academy, in fact." His lips twisted briefly. "Yes, that was part of the training. I understand they've dropped it nowadays, since Saint-Just was overthrown. Not sure if I approve or not, to be honest."

He still didn't understand, Berry realized. She and Gohr exchanged a glance. The Manticoran lieutenant took a breath, and continued.

"Look, Officer Cachat, as it happens—"

"Call me Victor."

"Victor, then. As it happens, I'm something of an expert on combat psychology. I did some research on the subject while I was attending London Point. And also some research on . . . interrogation techniques." Victor's eyes widened slightly.

So did Berry's. She knew that London Point was the promontory of Saganami Island where the Royal Manticoran Marine Corps ran one of the toughest finishing schools for small-unit combat commanders in the known galaxy. Her father Anton had once told her about it. So what, precisely, had a *Navy* officer been doing there?

Gohr obviously recognized their curiosity, but she only shook her head and continued. "I even published a couple of articles in scholarly psych journals. And," her mouth twisted wryly, "one in the Naval *Proceedings*, as well. That one got a bit wider readership, unfortunately."

She shook her head again, and her expression smoothed back to one of professional concentration.

"The important point is that, first, I know what I'm talking about, and, second, that I'm not talking about technical details like pain thresholds. I really don't think you understand what an unusual human being you are, Victor."

He scowled. "I'm not following you. Other than my personality quirks—everyone has them—I'm no different from anyone else." Harshly: "As a Manticoran, you'll probably disagree. But I recognize no distinctions of breeding or birth. There are no supermen in the world—nor any sub-humans, either."

She scowled right back. "Give me a break. And give your Havenite ideology a rest too, while you're at it. I wasn't suggesting you were either 'above' or 'below' the normal standard. But what you *are*—you do recognize the reality of human variation, I hope?—is a very unusual type of person. What's sometimes called a 'natural killer.' "

Victor looked away, not in shame but simply in suppressed anger. His scowl had faded; his mouth turning down in an expression of contempt.

"Thank you very much. I imagine it comes easily to a Manticoran naval officer to sneer at people like me. Not that you haven't turned thousands of people into so much molecular gas. Or won't, if you haven't already, when given the order. My killing is done up close—but it's only measured by the handful. Unlike your mass slaughter. How very ethical of you. Easy enough, when your murdering is done antiseptically, by pushing a button from a distance measured in—"

"*Victor!*" Berry half-shouted, loudly enough to break him off in mid-sentence. When Victor's eyes went to her, she shook her head.

"I don't think that's what she's getting at. And, anyway, it's rude of you to interrupt her."

Victor turned to look at Gohr. The Manticoran intelligence officer had a crooked smile on her face. "Victor, I wasn't making any *moral* distinction. I was just trying to explain that—yes, you're right. It *is* easy, relatively speaking, for people, with some training, to kill other people at a distance. And most people can manage to do it in person if they're in the grip of a powerful emotion like rage or terror. What we do, essentially, when we train infantry soldiers is train them how to harness and discipline those emotions. But the number of people who can kill up close, calmly and cold-bloodedly . . . There aren't very many, Victor, and that's the truth of it."

Victor started to say something, but she pressed on.

"I said I'm not making any moral distinctions—or judgments—and I'm not, because it would be stupid. Not to mention hypocritical as hell. Sure, people like you can be monsters . . . but so can the 'kill at a distance' crowd. It's not a matter of having a *taste* for it; it's simply a matter of being able to *do* it, and from what I've seen of you, you don't seem to enjoy it one bit, even when you know it's completely necessary.

"But the same kind of mentality that lets you do that is also one that can face torture with relative equanimity. What you might call clinical detachment, applied to yourself. Absolutely confident that you can stand up to the pain for quite some time before breaking. Most people can't do that either."

"What's your point, Lieutenant?"

"My point is that being able to do either one can't be

combined with acting the part of an intellectual airhead. There's a direct connection—it's not simply 'psychological,' it's profoundly physiological—between your conscious behavior and your emotional symptoms and behavior. Or, to put it another way, you can't remain steadfast and courageous—or ruthless—while you're trying to act otherwise. Certainly not on your level of capacity. That's why—"

She gave Berry a somewhat apologetic glance. "I know how you got those security codes, Victor. Berry described what happened to me. Do you really think you could have intimidated those men so easily if you'd been *acting*? Not likely. You terrified them because you were exactly what you told them you were—a man who'd kill them instantly and unblinkingly. And it *showed.* If you'd been on medical monitors, I'm sure your pulse rate and blood pressure wouldn't have so much as blipped."

Lieutenant Gohr turned to the view screen. The *Felicia* filled it now, looming over the shuttle like an alloy cliff.

"We're almost there, Victor. There's still time to turn back. But whatever you decide, give up the plan you've got. It'll never work. Within two minutes after we come aboard, the men in that ship will understand—instinctively, if you will—that they just let a wolf into their cage. They'll kill you, Victor. Don't think they won't. Out of fear, if nothing else. They'll never believe a word of your story."

"She's right," chimed in Berry.

Victor took a deep, long breath. Then, to Berry's relief, nodded abruptly. "All right. We'll go with my other plan."

Her eyes widened. "What *other* plan?"

Victor smiled thinly. "The one I just came up with. Three seconds ago."

The shiver and hollow *clang* of the shuttle docking into one of the *Felicia*'s entry bays echoed through the little craft.

"No time to explain now," he said, rising. "Just follow my lead. Say better, my improvisation."

I will never, ever, ever, ever do this again, Thandi thought grimly. For perhaps the twentieth time since they began their EVA, she'd been forced to correct their course due to one of her Amazons. *Goddam stupid so-called "super"-women. Why can't they just act like limp sacks of potatoes? If a princess can do it, they should be able to as well. The idiots!*

Ironically, Ruth Winton—the one Thandi had worried about

ahead of time—was proving to be the only one of her companions who wasn't giving her any trouble. The princess was doing exactly what Thandi had instructed all of them to do—*absolutely nothing.* Just ride along in their skinsuits as if they were comatose, allowing Thandi to control their course with the SUTs' slave circuits.

Alas, her Amazons still had more than a trace of that old Scrag sense of superiority. *Whatever you can do, I can do better.* Hence their continual, aggravating—downright infuriating—attempts to "help" Thandi.

Fortunately, they didn't have any control over their actual thrusters. Thandi had insisted on completely slaving the controls for the Sustained Use Thruster packs strapped over their standard-issue Marine skinsuits, much to their disgust. Good thing she had, too, she now realized, or this entire jury-rigged expedition would have wound up scattered halfway across Erewhon's orbit. But the Amazons were still able to make Thandi's life miserable by their "helpful" assumptions of whatever body positions *they* thought were needed. The end result was a course which consisted of a series of little jerks instead of the smooth, continuous trajectory which Thandi could have easily managed with Ruth Winton alone.

Not for the first time, Thandi regretted the fact that they had no way of knowing exactly what sort of off-the-books sensor capability might have been built into the *Felicia*. The odds were overwhelming that she had the off-the-shelf sensors of most commercial vessels. Which was to say, not a hell of a lot. If that were true, the Erewhonese Navy could have delivered her team to the ship aboard one of its stealthed assault boats without any worries. But if it *wasn't* true, if Mesa had given their slave ship upgraded passive sensors without mentioning it to anyone, they'd be almost certain to spot even a stealthed boat at this absurdly short range. And if the terrorists aboard her did that, there would instantly be eight thousand dead slaves—and two more people who had somehow become enormously important to one Thandi Palane.

Which was why she was essentially towing a long line of pods, all connected with a single, fiber optic-cored tether, instead of using a nice, convenient boat. Which still wouldn't have been that bad, except for the fact that these "pods" were so-called superwomen wearing SUT-equipped skinsuits, each and every one of whom—again, she left Ruth out of her general damnation—insisted on behaving like an intelligent pea in a pod. With just about the vegetable results you'd expect.

Never again!

They were very near the *Felicia,* now. Thandi started to decelerate, wincing at the prospect of trying to control her charges as they "helped" her again. Slowly, one after another of them slid past her, as they maintained their previous velocity. On the plus side, none of them was clumsy, so there was no risk of collision. On the minus side . . .

Fortunately, the fiber optic tether gave her a completely secure link to her team's SUTs, and her gloved fingers flew over the panel on her chest, tapping in commands which overrode the Amazons' assistance before it could cause outright disaster. Equally fortunately, Thandi's com was switched off at the moment. She and her team could have chattered away with complete security, once again because of their connecting tether, but Thandi had insisted on com silence anyway. She did *not* need any distractions while she piloted—*attempted* to pilot—her Amazons to their destination. At the moment, however, she had an added and entirely different reason to be grateful that her com, like theirs, was temporarily locked down. Since no one could hear her, she was able to give full and verbal vent to her fury—in a stream of profanity which, had it been broadcast, would have peeled the paint off a superdreadnought—when the final approach to the slaver turned into just the tangled-up mess she'd feared it would be.

But, finally, it was done. Not with grace, granted. *Thumpety-thump-thump-thump-thump-etc.,* ending with only Thandi herself landing on the *Felicia*'s hull with silent and springy ease. (Although she did note that Princess Ruth came surprisingly close.) Fortunately, it made no difference. The five-million-ton mass of the ship would have been impervious to collisions which smeared the bodies across the hull, instead of just leaving half of them sprawling. The tiny vibrations which resulted would simply go unnoticed inside the ship, in much the same way a mountain would ignore the clumsiness of inexperienced climbers on its flank with lofty indifference.

Done. Thank God. She'd even managed—somehow—to land them all within a short distance of the personnel hatch they'd selected. Ruth was already unhooking herself and moving toward it. As they'd agreed, the Manticoran princess would do all the code work.

Now that it was over, Thandi's exasperation vanished within seconds. All that was left was a deep regret. She'd been so preoccupied that she hadn't been able to keep an eye on the progress of the shuttle taking Victor and Berry to the ship. By now, it was too late. The shuttle would have docked already, somewhere out of sight around the curve of the gigantic hull.

So, she'd not gotten the glimpse of Victor she'd wanted. Her last glimpse, quite possibly. It would be typical of her life to have finally fallen in love—just in time to have her man killed a few hours later.

She shook off the dark thought firmly.

You'll have something to say about that, *woman. Not to mention—*

A grin finally came to her. A savage one, true. But it was enough to dispel all gloom and get her combat instincts back into their usual full and furious shape. When all was said and done, the new man in Thandi's life wasn't really all that easy to kill.

To put it mildly. There were advantages to having an alpha male for a boyfriend, after all—especially *that* one—even leaving aside Thandi's little kinks and foibles.

"That's her signal," said Watanapongse, sitting at one of the com stations in the control room of *The Wages of Sin*. "The strike force has landed."

He gave the display screen in front of him a look of grim satisfaction. "Fanatics, meet Thandi Palane. A Masadan's worst nightmare."

Standing by the shuttle's airlock, Betty Gohr gave Berry and Victor a last inspection. She held a pulse rifle, as did the Marines, in case the Masadans tried a last-minute double cross in the arrangement they'd negotiated. The deal had been simple: the Manticoran princess and one companion—both unarmed and wearing simple, tight clothing—in exchange for the Masadans holding off on their threat to blow up the *Felicia*. Further arrangements to be negotiated.

The Manticoran lieutenant was not happy about it, especially the clothing. Berry Zilwicki, like the real Princess Ruth she'd been transformed by nanotech to resemble, was not a beautiful girl by any stretch of the term. But she did have the kind of healthy, youthful prettiness which was perfectly capable of arousing any normal male's libido—the more so because her figure was set off quite well by the close-fitting jumpsuit she was wearing. The Masadans had insisted on clothing which couldn't possibly disguise any weapons. Unfortunately, the jumpsuit didn't do any better at disguising Berry's female characteristics. Given the Masadan reputation—a well-deserved one—for sexual predation . . .

"We can still call this off, Berry," she said abruptly, almost blurting out the words.

Serenely, the Zilwicki girl shook her head. "Don't be silly. I'm sure it'll all work out as well as possible." She shrugged. "And if it doesn't, it's just one or two lives measured against thousands. Please open the hatch, Lieutenant. Now, if you would."

For a moment, Gohr was disoriented. So were the Marines, judging from the alacrity with which they obeyed the girl's order.

And an *order* it was, however politely stated. No member of the House of Winton in its long centuries could have surpassed that regal assurance. The fact that Berry Zilwicki was an impostor simply didn't seem to matter.

Gohr's own reflex was automatic. "Princess," she replied, coming to attention. The Marines did likewise, as the hatch opened, bringing their pulse rifles halfway to the present arms salute.

Only halfway there, of course, because this was a possible combat situation. But the first in-person view the Masadans at the other end of the short connecting boarding tube got of Berry was of young woman they'd been told was Princess Ruth, with her Manticoran escort showing all the respect and deference you'd expect them to provide a member of their royal family.

It never once crossed their minds that it was all an act. How could it? In that moment, it was no act at all.

A princess came across. Somehow, she even managed the awkward transition from the boarding tube's weightlessness to the ship's internal gravity without losing her royal composure for an instant. Even the Masadans stepped half a pace back.

"She's in," Lieutenant Gohr said softly into her com, as soon as the hatch closed. The shuttle's pilot was already beginning to disengage from the *Felicia.* The lieutenant, like the House of Winton itself, belonged to the Second Reformation Catholic Church. "May the Virgin in Heaven watch over her."

Receiving the signal, Watanapongse grunted. Like most officers in the Solarian Navy, he was a hardboiled agnostic. "The 'virgin' be damned, and 'heaven' is in another universe. That girl's got something way better, in the here and now. Hell's Pure Bitch is coming—and she's not more than a kilometer distant."

"A kilometer full of corridors and compartments like a maze,"

Imbesi cautioned, "not to mention a spider's web worth of security barriers."

Watanapongse didn't seem impressed. "Hell's Pure Bitch, I said. There's a reason, you know, that Captain Rozsak wanted that Marine officer on his staff, once Colonel Huang brought her to his attention. She's not even thirty years old, but with her record—and decorations—she'd have been put on the fastest possible track and probably even been a major by now, if she didn't come from an OFS planet. You watch."

At the moment, as it happened, Berry Zilwicki's fate *was* in the hands of a young woman who, if not a virgin, wasn't really all that far from it. Like most young people in most royal families in history, Ruth had labored under a degree of chaperonage she'd often found exasperating. The fact that the Winton dynasty put all its youngsters through extensive sexual education and training made it downright frustrating—because the dynasty was just as careful to keep an eye on their children avoiding premature emotional entanglements. A lot of theory, and . . . not all that much in the way of practice. In a modern society whose members were usually sexually active by the age of sixteen, the fact that she was twenty-three and as inexperienced as she was—though not in the least bit naïve—was a source of considerable disgruntlement.

"And I'll be just as easy," she muttered, as she broke the security code on the entry hatch within fifteen seconds, "when the right young fellow comes along." Sourly: "Assuming I can get away from the eagle eyes of my mother and aunt."

She watched the hatch swing smoothly open. Pleased, by her easy success in the actual deed at hand; frustrated, by the symbolism of it all.

"What was that?" asked Thandi. There was a trace of amusement in her voice. Ruth had forgotten that Lieutenant Palane had restored the com circuits.

"Nothing," she said, flushing a little.

Her embarrassment increased when one of the Amazons chimed in.

"Must be man trouble. You want help, girl? Just say the word, and I'll hold him down for you. Help you get him up, too, if he's pretty enough."

Thandi led the way, gliding into the entry with a gracefulness that the Manticoran princess still found a little shocking, coupled to such a large and powerful body. Even in a skinsuit, in deep space maneuvers, Thandi Palane reminded Ruth of a two-legged tigress.

"This is no time for sexual fantasies," the commander of the strike force stated firmly. Sternly, even.

An odd little gurgle seemed to echo in the com circuits, as if several voices at once had just managed—barely—to suppress laughter.

Ruth was one of them. She'd *seen* Thandi at her fantasies, after all. And while she hadn't watched for the three minutes Berry had accused her of, she'd certainly not watched for a mere three seconds, either.

It had been . . . impressive.

And now, in its own way, also reassuring. Ruth made the transition from weightlessness to the ship's gravity field with the grace of someone who'd participated in deep space sports since she was a young girl. But since she'd followed directly behind Thandi, she'd watched the Solarian Marine officer make the same transition with something that went far beyond "grace." The sight, coupled with the one Ruth had gotten of Thandi at play, brought a different predator to mind.

If she's skilled and experienced enough, a human can be graceful passing through an airlock on her way to an assignment with violence. An anaconda simply pours herself through.

CHAPTER 35

"I STRONGLY SUGGEST YOU KEEP your eyes on *me*."

Another man might have hissed the words, or half-shouted them, or . . . somehow, tried to make them emphatic. But Victor Cachat simply stated them. In the same cold and empty way in which Berry had seen him, the day before, state to three men shackled to chairs that he was going to kill them if they didn't do exactly what he wanted. *Now.*

The voice had pretty much the same effect on the Masadans assembled on the *Felicia*'s bridge. Their gaze, which had been focused on Berry herself, was now firmly riveted on Cachat.

"Ignore the girl," he continued, in that same tone of voice. "She is now irrelevant to you—provided she isn't harmed in any way. Have her taken out of here and put in with the cargo. She'll keep there, well enough, while you and I discuss whether or not we can reach a suitable arrangement. Your lives—and your purpose—now depend entirely on my good will. My purpose, I should say. My 'good will' is nonexistent."

Some part of Berry's brain which remained capable of calculation registered Victor's use of the callous word "cargo." That was a term which only Mesans and their underlings used to refer to the shipment of human slaves. Very subtly, it was a signal to the Masadans that, in some way or other, the grim man staring at them through flat and dark eyes shared at least some of their attitudes and thought processes.

Mostly, though, she was just fascinated. Mesmerized, even—as the Masadans now seemed to be. They'd only been brought onto the bridge half a minute since by the three Masadans who'd taken them into custody. And, already—despite being unarmed and to all appearances at their mercy—Cachat was wrapping the Masadans around him. It was as if a human black hole had entered the room.

On a purely personal level, Berry was immensely relieved. The last thing she wanted was to have Masadans focusing their attention on *her.* The Masadan version of the Church of Humanity Unchained was indeed, as the Graysons claimed it to be, a heresy. Not so much in terms of religious doctrine, as simple human morality. Patriarchal religions were nothing new in the universe, after all. Most of the human race's major religions had contained a great deal of patriarchal attitudes—and still did, as witness the fact that almost all of them routinely referred to God as if "He" were naturally male. (She and Ruth had once enjoyed a pleasant few minutes of ribaldry, trying to visualize the size of The Almighty's penis and testicles.)

But the Masadans had twisted patriarchy into what could only be called a sick perversion. However stern and autocratic they might be, "fathers" were not rapists. And it was essentially impossible to describe Masadan doctrines—and practice—toward women as anything other than sanctified rape. A bizarre and bastard concoction, made of equal parts lust and misogyny, all of it dressed up in theological gibberish.

Until Victor spoke, every Masadan's eyes had been on her, not him. And that wasn't half as bad as the "weapons inspection" one of them had put her through almost as soon as she came aboard the *Felicia.* The man's hands groping her body—as if that skin-tight outfit could have concealed so much as a penknife—had left her feeling half-sick and clammy.

"And who are *you* to be giving orders here?" demanded one of the Masadans. Hosea Kubler, that was, one of the two pilots and the one whom Watanapongse guessed was now the leader of the small number of survivors in Templeton's gang. Kubler was red-faced with anger, but his voice had a slight tremor in it—as if the man was deliberately trying to work up a rage in order to overcome his own intimidation.

Cachat bestowed the flat-eyed stare upon him. "I'll show you who I am. More precisely, what I am."

He glanced around the bridge. Other than the Masadans, there were four other men on the bridge. All of them, unlike most of the Masadans standing near the center, were seated at various control stations. From their uniforms, members of the *Felicia's* actual crew. Only one of them, judging from the uniform, was an officer.

They all looked petrified, as, indeed, Berry was sure they were. Cachat was bad enough—but he came on top of having had their ship taken over by religious maniacs who were announcing to the galaxy that they were quite prepared to blow it up if their demands were not met.

"Where's the control for destroying the ship?" Cachat demanded. As if guided by a single will, the eyes of all four crew members went to the one Masadan seated at a station. More precisely, to a large button on one side of the panel in front of him. The button had the vague appearance of being something jury-rigged, not to mention—Berry almost giggled at the absurdity of the melodrama—having been painted bright red. A very recent and rather sloppy paint job, in fact.

"That's it? Fine. Push the button."

Kubler's mouth was open again, as if to begin a tirade. But Victor's last three words caused it to snap shut.

The Masadan seated at the control, on the other hand, was almost gaping. "What did you say?"

"You heard me clearly, you imbecile. I said: *Push the button.*"

Now, the Masadan *was* gaping.

Cachat didn't move a muscle, but somehow he seemed to be almost looming over the man by the red button. His spirit, rather. Like some dark and terrifying hawk stooping down on a rabbit.

"Are you deaf? Or simply a coward? Push the button. *Do it now, you self-proclaimed zealot!*"

The Masadan's hand began to lift, involuntarily, as if he were falling under Cachat's spell. Finally, Kubler found his voice—but his face was no longer red with fury. It was quite pale, in fact.

"Don't touch that button, Jedediah! Remove your hand!"

Jedediah shook his head, half-gasped, and snatched the hand away.

Cachat turned back to Kubler. His lips were not actually twisted into a sneer, but somehow he managed to project one simply with his eyes.

"Zealots. How pitiful. Don't think for a moment that you can possibly intimidate *me* with a threat of death. You know who Oscar Saint-Just was, I presume?"

Kubler nodded.

"Delightful. An educated zealot. Let me further your education, then. I was one of Saint-Just's closest associates. Secretly hand-picked by him—one of only five such—to serve at moments when any sacrifice was called for. And I was the first to volunteer, when the traitor McQueen launched her insurrection, to take the codes into her headquarters and blow it up myself if the remote controls failed in the purpose."

He made a minimal shrug. "As it happened, the remotes worked. But don't think for a moment I wouldn't have done it."

He swiveled his head to bring the large red button back under his gaze. This time, his lips did twist in a slight sneer.

"How impressive. A big red button which can destroy eight thousand people. The button in Oscar Saint-Just's command center was a small white one. When I pushed it—yes, he allowed me that privilege, in light of my volunteering to go in—I destroyed perhaps a million and a half people in Nouveau Paris along with McQueen and her traitors. There was never an exact body count, of course. With numbers that high, it hardly seemed to matter."

He brought the gaze back to Kubler. The slight sneer was gone, but the dark eyes looked like bottomless pits.

"Ask me if I lost a moment's sleep over it."

Kubler swallowed.

"The answer is: no. Not so much as a second's sleep. Everyone dies sooner or later. All that matters is whether they die for a purpose or not. So I say again. Take the girl out of here so we can begin our negotiations, or match your zealotry against mine. Those are your only options. Obey me, or push the button."

There was silence, for a moment.

"Decide *now,* Masadan. Or I'll go over there and push the button myself." Cachat lifted his wrist-watch. "In exactly five seconds."

Less than two seconds later, Kubler snarled at one of his subordinates. "Get the slut out of here, Ukiah. Put her with the cargo. Take one of the heathen crew to show you the way."

Ukiah let out a sigh. He gave a hard glance at one of the crew, who rose from his station with alacrity. The man was clearly even more relieved than Ukiah.

Berry, on the other hand, was not relieved at all. Ukiah was the Masadan who'd subjected her to his leering "weapons inspection"—and she was sure it was a long way to the "cargo."

But Cachat stifled that instantly, also. His snake-cold eyes were now on Ukiah.

"You've already pawed the girl once, zealot, despite the fact that not even a cretin could believe she might be concealing a weapon—and despite the fact that you gave me no similar such 'inspection.' Do it again and you are a dead man. Lay so much as a finger on her, and the first demand I will advance in my negotiations will be your bowels fed to you. Yes, I know how to do it while still keeping a man alive. And you *will* eat your own colon, don't think you won't."

He shifted the cobra gaze to Kubler. "That demand will be nonnegotiable, of course. His bowels, shoved down his throat—or push the button."

Kubler's fear and rage finally had an outlet. He took three quick strides, drawing his pulser, and literally hammered Ukiah to the deck. The butt of the weapon opened a large gash on his forehead and left him completely dazed.

"I told you to keep your hands off!" Kubler shrieked. He aimed the pulser. For a moment, Berry thought he was going to shoot the man as well. But, barely, he managed to restrain himself.

Seething with rage—but still careful, Berry noted, not to aim directly at Cachat—Kubler turned on another Masadan. "You take the whore to the cargo, Ezekiel. And don't touch her."

Hastily, Ezekiel complied. Within seconds, Berry was being taken off the bridge.

"Ushered" off, rather. Again, she had to restrain a giggle. The Masadan and the crewman were being careful—oh, *very* careful—not to get within three feet of her.

She gave Victor a last glance over her shoulder. But she could read no expression at all in that face. It was like trying to scrutinize a plate of steel.

Berry gave him silent thanks, anyway. And, in the minutes which followed as she was led—ushered—to the slave compartments, found herself simply wondering at the mysteries of human nature.

She wondered, first, if Victor had been speaking the truth when he told Kubler he'd pushed the button which destroyed half the city of Nouveau Paris.

She didn't think so. Victor was certainly a good enough liar to be able to pass it off as the truth. On the other hand—

With Victor Cachat, you never know. If he thought it was called for by the demands of his duty . . .

She wondered, second, what Victor was going to do next. Berry had no idea—not a clue—what sort of "negotiations" he intended to conduct with the Masadans now that she was out of the way. Whatever it was, she was sure it would be a doozy, thought up on the spot. If Victor Cachat suddenly found himself cast down into the lowest pit of the Inferno, Berry had no doubt at all he'd be improvising a plot against the Devil before he'd finished brushing off the bone dust of sinners.

Mostly, though, she found herself wondering about Thandi Palane.

Not whether Thandi would get there in time. On that subject, she had no doubt at all. She just found herself, again, wondering at the quirks of human nature. *What does she see in him, anyway?*

She decided to ask her, when she got the chance. It was none of her business, true. But since Berry had decided that Thandi was another big sister, it was her simple obligation to help the woman sort out her own feelings.

The thought cheered her up. Berry was good at that.

Once Berry was off the bridge, Victor began to speak. The few short seconds had been enough for him to jury-rig the outlines of his scheme.

If you can call something this ramshackle a "scheme," that is. Pray to whatever might be holy, Victor, that these people are as stupid as they are maniacal.

"Your original purpose is null and void. Templeton is dead—both of them, Abraham as well as Gideon. The six of you here are all that survive of your group, other than two of you who were injured and are now in captivity."

Quickly, he scanned the little group of religious zealots, confirming his original assessment that all of them were Masadan.

"Both of them are Scrags, by the way. I leave it to you to decide whether you'll try to insist that they be released from custody and returned to you. Personally, I don't care in the least."

"Who *are* you?" demanded Kubler.

Victor smiled crookedly. "A good question—and one I've been trying to keep people from asking for some time now. My name is Victor Cachat. I'm an agent from the Republic of Haven's Federal Investigation Agency, supposedly here to determine what happened to a shipload of Havenite religious refugees who disappeared on their way to Tiberian. What I *really* am, however, is a loyal member of the revolution and someone determined to restore the principles of Rob Pierre and Oscar Saint-Just to my star nation. I had to leave Haven, because I knew that soon enough the investigators of the new traitorous regime would uncover my true loyalties. So when the chance came, I volunteered for this mission to get myself out of Havenite territory."

Shrugging: "I could care less what happened to a pack of social deviants, who would have been arrested sooner or later anyway under a sane regime. As it happens, I *do* know what befell them. You—or the Ringstorff sociopath you've been working for—had them all murdered."

He paused for a moment, giving them another quick inspection.

"The moment I realized what was happening here, I saw a way I could advance my own project. Since I'd already managed to work my way into the good graces of the Erewhonese authorities—ha! talk about a pack of carrion-eaters trying to avoid responsibility—I was able to convince them to let me accompany the Princess and negotiate for them."

What a lot of babble! A moron could spot the holes in the logic.

But he let no signs of his uneasiness show. And, as he pressed on with his nonsensical prattle, consoled himself with the thought that Masadan religious fanatics—other than their real expertise at mayhem—were fairly hard to distinguish from morons, when you got right down to it.

"I can get you out of here, Kubler. All of you. If you insist, I can probably get your two Scrags back also. But you'll have to agree to do it my way—and give up any plan of using the Manticoran princess for anything other than a hostage to ensure your safe passage."

"Safe passage to *where*?"

"The same place I imagine you were planning to take her in the first place—Congo." Victor scowled, looked around for a chair, and eased himself into a nearby control station. He didn't give the control panel itself so much as a glance, not wanting to make the Masadans nervous that he intended to meddle with the ship. He simply wanted to shift the discussion to one between seated people; which, in the nature of things, automatically defuses tension.

Once seated, he ran fingers through his stiff, coarse hair. "I imagine Templeton's plan was to blackmail the Mesans there into providing him with shelter. Frankly, I'm highly skeptical that would have worked under the best of circumstances. This whole affair is going to have Mesa—especially Manpower—shrieking with fury. Not even Manpower is arrogant enough to want to infuriate the Star Kingdom of Manticore. Certainly not in a way which will make it very difficult for their normal Solarian protectors to provide them with much of a shield."

Kubler, hesitantly, had taken a seat himself. Victor gave him a level gaze.

"That's the reason I insisted—and will continue to insist—that the girl be handled delicately. Harm her in any way, Kubler, and you're likely to bring down the Eighth Fleet on Congo—possibly even on Mesa itself."

One of the Masadans tried to sneer. "Be serious! No way—"

"Really?" demanded Cachat. "Were *you* there when White Haven cut half the way through the Republic of Haven?" After a silent pause. "I thought not. Well, I *was*—attached as a commissioner to one of the Republic's superdreadnoughts before our fleets were routed. So I wouldn't be too sure White Haven couldn't cut his way through a goodly portion of Solarian space in order to turn Mesa into a slag heap if the whim struck Elizabeth the Third. The Solarian Navy is vastly overrated, in my opinion. But it hardly matters—because you can be sure and certain that the Mesans themselves will have no desire to run the risk."

His expression became slightly derisive. "For what? *You?* What are the six of you—all that survive—to the Mesans, that they should accept that risk? Even if Templeton had survived, I doubt they would have agreed. With him dead . . ."

He left the thought hanging. To his relief, he saw that all the Masadans were too preoccupied with their own extremely dire predicament to be spending much thought on the contradictions and just plain silliness in Victor's prattle.

He glanced quickly at his watch. *Five minutes down. One hundred and fifteen to go, assuming Thandi can do it in two hours.* Glumly: *Which I doubt.*

His thoughts grew less glum, hearing one of the other Masadans suddenly blurt out some words. Solomon Farrow, that was, the second of the Masadan pilots.

"In the name of God, Hosea, he's right—and you know it. You've told me yourself, in private, you had doubts about Gideon's plan."

Kubler glared at him briefly; but, Victor noted, didn't argue the point. Instead, after a moment, Kubler shifted his eyes back to him.

"All right, Cachat. What's your proposal?"

Hallelujah. Just keep prattling, Victor.

CHAPTER 36

WITHIN TEN MINUTES AFTER ENTERING the *Felicia,* Thandi was thanking whatever gods there might be for the fact that Ruth was with her. Without her, the stealthy attack would have turned almost instantly into a straight-up boarding assault—with no possible end except the destruction of the ship. Thandi was still quite sure she could have defeated Templeton's gang—even had she been alone, much less with the Amazons at her side. But so what? The religious maniacs would have simply blown up the *Felicia* once they realized they were overmatched.

The problem was simple, and one which Thandi should probably have foreseen. Lieutenant Commander Watanapongse had, after all. Granted, Watanapongse had a lot more experience dealing with slavers than Thandi did. Marines simply weren't called for when dealing with slavers, except under rare circumstances. Slaver crews were too small to put up any significant resistance, once they were overtaken by a military vessel. So, they usually surrendered outright.

Although . . . that depended on the identity of the arresting vessel. The navies of most civilized powers subscribed to the theory that the slave trade constituted an offense against humanity. The Solarian League had certainly taken that position for centuries, and had pursued an official policy directed toward its eventual eradication for just as long. The Solarian approach was based on an entire network of interlocking bilateral treaty agreements with its independent neighbors, coupled with bureaucratic fiat within its own territory or that under the jurisdiction of the OFS. Since it would have been extremely difficult to get a significant number of independent systems (especially those already keeping an uneasy eye on Frontier Security) to agree to allow the SLN to police their space on *any* pretext, the treaties in question were negotiated on a basis which granted the SLN authority to intercept slavers flagged to the independent systems only outside the smaller nations' territorial space. And although League law equated slavery with piracy for its own citizens, which made it theoretically punishable by death, the fact was that the Solarian League had *never* executed a single slaver whose ship had been seized under one of the treaties. Solarian nationals had—on rare occasions—been sent to prison, sometimes for quite lengthy sentences. But the League as a whole was too "enlightened" to actually impose the death penalty, even in relatively extreme cases.

In the case of those who were not Solarian nationals, the options were even more limited. The ships themselves were impounded and destroyed, but since the other parties to many of the treaties didn't equate the two crimes in the same fashion (officially, at least), the most the League could often do was return "alleged" slavers to their systems of origin for trial.

Over the years, however, slavers had discovered that there were some exceptions to that nice, safe arrangement. Specifically, there were the Star Kingdom of Manticore and the Republic of Haven. Manticore's implacable hostility to the genetic slave trade had been a part of the Star Kingdom's foreign policy ever since the days of King Roger II, whose youthful infatuation with the Liberal Party of the day had left its mark in several ways even after he assumed the throne. The original Republic of Haven had been just as disgusted by the practice, and even the People's Republic, for all its myriad faults, had retained that disgust and a hostility which fully matched that of Manticore. In fact, the one solemn interstellar accord to which both star nations were signatories and which had remained in effect throughout all of the tension and even outright hostilities between them was the Cherwell Convention.

The provisions of the Cherwell Convention were quite simple. All signatories to it endorsed the equation of slavery with piracy . . . and prescribed the same punishment for both. It was the most stringent of all of the League's anti-slavery treaties, and, unlike any of the others, it was multilateral, not bilateral. All of its signatories agreed that the naval forces of *any* of its signatories had the right to stop, search, and confiscate merchant vessels transporting slaves while sailing under the protection of their flags. And, even more importantly, that they had the right to try the crews of those confiscated vessels for piracy.

Despite the official provisions of the Cherwell Convention, the rigor with which it was enforced in practice varied widely from one star nation to the next, even among those who had officially signed onto it. Both the Manticorans and the Havenites were ruthless about it, and the death penalty was often applied immediately to slavers caught in the act. Even if the slavers were not executed, they were invariably sentenced to much longer prison terms than was the Solarian norm.

By and large, the Andermani Empire tended to follow the same policies. On the other hand, the Silesian Confederacy's treatment of captured slavers and pirates was a sour joke in the starways. The Confederacy had signed the Cherwell Convention only under the threat of Manticoran military action during the reign of Queen Adrienne, and as often as not, the criminals were released almost immediately by a corrupt governor.

The Solarian League's practice varied a great deal, depending primarily on the specific unit which made the arrest. More precisely, on the political connections which that unit had with one or another of the various power blocs in the League. Some captains, those who were effectively in Mesa's political pocket, were as notorious as Silesians for releasing captured slavers. Others—Rozsak being one of them, especially since his assignment to work with Governor Barregos in Maya Sector—enforced the available penalties with as much harshness as possible.

At one time, the standard response of slavers about to be overhauled was to jettison their "cargo" into space and then try to use the absence of slaves as proof of their innocence. In order to put a stop to that practice, the star nations who had signed the Cherwell Convention had adopted the "equipment clause" first proposed by Roger II. In effect, the equipment clause stated that any ship equipped as a slaver *was* a slaver, whether she happened to have a "cargo" aboard at the moment or not.

Many of the Cherwell Convention signatories, including the Andermani Empire, simply seized the ship and sent its crew to prison when exercising the equipment clause in the absence of actual slaves. The Star Kingdom and the Republic, however, had adopted the official position that a slaver crew found *without* a living cargo would be immediately tried for mass murder and, if convicted, executed by the same method: ejection from an airlock without benefit of space suit. Death by decompression was . . . pretty horrible.

Nor was it possible to conceal the fact that a ship was a slaver. That was what the "equipment clause" was all about, because the nature of her "cargo" was such that any slaver *had* to be designed differently from a normal cargo hauler or legitimate passenger vessel. The old shackles and chains of the slave trade on Earth in pre-Diaspora days might no longer be needed, but the design of the ships themselves, with their multitude of security measures to forestall any slave revolt, was simply impossible to disguise.

That was true even leaving aside the peculiar design whereby hundreds—sometimes thousands—of unwilling human beings could be ejected into space. It would be impossible for a small slaver crew to physically manhandle thousands of people into airlocks. So, the ships were designed to flood the slave living compartments with powerful (but not lethal) gases, forcing the slaves into large cargo holds where the big bays could be opened to space.

That design was somewhat obsolete, now, at least anywhere near Manticoran or Havenite space. Too many Manticoran and Havenite captains had started the quiet practice of immediately executing *any* slavers found aboard a ship equipped for that kind of mass murder—whether the "cargo" was still alive or not. The official rules be damned. Even the occasional *Solarian* captain in those regions, barred from such direct and forceful action by his own government's policies, had adopted the policy of handing the crews of such ships over to the closest Manty or Havenite captain. After all, both the Star Kingdom and the Republic were treaty partners, weren't they? What happened to criminals after being duly delivered into the custody of one of the local governments was hardly the arresting captain's business, was it?

And, besides, the method of execution was such poetic justice.

As it happened, the *Felicia* did have the design which enabled the crew to jettison its cargo. That much was obvious to Thandi within five minutes. There could be no other explanation for the number of large cargo holds they passed through after entering the ship. *Empty* cargo holds, with very wide bays—and with no passageways connecting to them wide enough to move large items of cargo.

Clearly enough, Princess Ruth understood the purpose of the peculiar design. Her thin face was tight with anger.

"We'll fix *that,*" she muttered. A moment later, moving with the sureness of an expert, she had the panel removed from the nearest instrument console and had her own mini-computer plugged into it. Ignoring Thandi's hiss of warning, Ruth's fingers started working the keyboard.

Shortly thereafter, the princess unplugged her unit. She didn't bother replacing the panel.

"Those won't work any longer. The bastards can't jettison anybody. And I disconnected the controls to the gas units, while I was at it." She glanced at Thandi's skinsuit. "The gas wouldn't bother us, of course, but if the slavers released it—"

She didn't need to finish the thought. Wincing, Thandi nodded. The gases used to drive slaves into the jettison holds were only technically "nonlethal." More precisely, they were nonlethal so long as the victim could move away into cleaner air. Trapped in compartments with no way to escape, most of the victims would die eventually. And die horribly, too, in an even worse manner than being jettisoned into space. Slavers themselves wouldn't voluntarily kill anyone that way, because they'd have to clean up the multitude of corpses—not to mention vomit and other excreta left behind. But in these circumstances, if Templeton's gang got desperate enough, they might do it as part of their suicide pact.

"Can you disconnect whatever setup they've got to blow the ship?"

Ruth shook her head. "Not from here. I'm willing to bet that they've jury-rigged their own, independent system to do the job. Most slavers aren't real big on suicide, you know, so I doubt *Felicia* came equipped with a scuttling charge. If Templeton's thugs did rig their own system, it's certainly a stand-alone I can't access. And even if *Felicia* did have one already in place, getting to it from the outside would be virtually impossible. In a number of ways, slavers are built more like warships than cargo ships. That's especially true with their electronics. The ship control, security, and environmental systems are kept separate, instead of all being connected to a central computer. It's less efficient—much less—but it also gives you a lot more in the way of safety and internal security."

One of the Amazons shook her head. "Why here? On a slaver, I mean. They don't have large crews—it'd cut into their profits. It must be awkward as hell having to operate that way."

"You're forgetting the nature of the 'cargo,'" Thandi said with a frown. "Material objects don't resist their handlers with anything more than inertia. Livestock, not much more than that. But when you're trying to haul unwilling human beings somewhere, you've got the added problem of a 'cargo' that might revolt."

The Amazon still seemed a little puzzled, and the princess smiled crookedly at her.

"You're making a common mistake. Yana, isn't it? Most people think of Manpower slaves in terms of the types which are most notorious—sex objects, or heavy labor and combat types. But the truth is that modern slavery has to fit a modern economy. Even on a hellhole like Congo, most of the labor is highly mechanized. *And* computerized. Sure, the slaves designed for that work have been given a minimal education, and one which carefully steers clear of training them in any of the underlying principles. Still and all . . ."

Ruth pursed her lips. "You've all met Web Du Havel, I think—or know who he is, at least. He's a J-line, which is Manpower's most popular, uh, 'product.' Low-level technical workers, what you might call 'sub-engineers.' " The princess nodded at the panel she'd just been working on. "You think a man like that—some of them, anyway—would have any real problem figuring out how to crack into a ship's central control unit? Sure, they'd probably set off alarms doing it—that's really where all my extra training pays off—but so what? When people are desperate, they're not going to worry about the fine points. If nothing else, once they gained access to the central computer they could probably make sure the slaver crew went to Hell with them."

Yana's frown had been deepening as Ruth talked. "Damnation, Princess. If that's how it's set up, how do we disconnect the charge without taking the bridge, first?"

"We don't," Ruth said grimly. "And now that I've seen the setup, I'm pretty sure that *is* how they've done it. So." She gave Thandi an uncertain look. "Can we still manage it, Lieutenant?"

The Solarian officer gazed at her for a moment, then gave her a grin. Well, a widening of teeth, anyway. It was more like a shark's grin than a human's. That was all the answer she gave. All she needed to, really.

A moment later, Thandi and Ruth were moving down yet another passage, the Amazons in their wake.

Less than five minutes after leaving the bridge, Berry found herself ushered through a heavy—and heavily locked—entry hatch. "Ushered," in the sense that Ezekiel and the slaver crewman stepped back once the hatch was unlocked and slightly opened, and urgently motioned her to pass through it. Both of them seemed very nervous, and both of them had pulsers in their hands pointed in the direction of the hatch. To all intents and purposes, they looked like men ordering a sacrificial victim into a chamber full of demons.

Seeing no alternative, Berry pulled the hatch open a bit more and stooped through the opening. She had to stoop, because the hatch was unusually low. Obviously enough, it had been specifically designed to make it impossible for more than one human being at a time to pass through it—and then, not without some difficulty.

As soon as she passed through, the hatch was slammed shut behind her. An instant later, she heard the locks closing.

But she really wasn't paying much attention to what was behind her. She was far more concerned, at the moment, with what surrounded her.

She was in a smallish compartment, not more than five meters in any dimension. Which was crowded, at the moment. Eight men and five women, all of them armed with jury-rigged bludgeons—very primitive; torn strips of clothing weighted down with something—and all of them looking as if they were ready to tear her limb from limb.

Hurriedly, she tried to think of something to say to forestall her imminent destruction. But the effort proved needless. Not more than two seconds after she entered the chamber, one of the women gasped and exclaimed:

"It's the Princess! Herself!"

This was no time for complicated explanations. Berry drew herself up in as dignified a pose as her ridiculous skin-tight clothing permitted. She tried to put the same dignity—what a laugh!—into her voice.

"Yes. It is I."

Victor was getting desperate. Not at whether he could keep stringing along the Masadans—he was now quite confident of doing that, for at least another hour—but at how he was going to explain it all to Kevin Usher afterward.

Assuming he survived, of course.

Well, boss, then I broke another of your rules and made an already too-elaborate scheme still more elaborate by swearing to them that you were part of the conspiracy to overthrow Pritchart. But were hamstrung because you couldn't trust your own security people any longer and that—of course—is why you told me, when I got sent to Erewhon, to keep an eye out for the possibility of hiring Masadans. "Best wet work men in the galaxy," you said to me. "Look how they almost managed to nail that bitch Elizabeth and did *manage to nail her tame Prime Minister."*

Sure, they swallowed it. What do you expect? It wasn't even their vanity, just . . .

Dammit, boss, they're CRAZY. They really BELIEVE human affairs are all guided by deep and dark conspiracies. They see two dogs sniffing each other, they see Satan at work. So why shouldn't they believe in a deep and dark conspiracy which—just maybe, and with their backs to the wall—might save their own hides?

Gloomily, he could foresee Usher's sarcasm and ridicule. Still more gloomily, he tried to figure out how to respond to the next question.

"Yes, that makes sense," allowed Hosea Kubler. The leader of the surviving Masadans rubbed his chin. "But let's leave aside, for the moment, the manner in which we'd penetrate President Pritchart's security. First things first. How do you propose to get us free of *this* situation? As you said yourself, the Mesans won't be enthusiastic about providing us with asylum on Congo."

"To say the least," snorted Victor. "But that's only because they don't want the heat coming down on them. They'd be perfectly happy—delighted, in fact—to let Congo be used as the route through which to pass along an assassination team against Pritchart."

"Why?"

Victor took a deep breath. The way a man will, about to dive off a cliff into what he *hopes* is deep water.

"Well . . ." He put on his most ferocious glower. (Which, he had been told, was quite ferocious. And so it seemed, judging from the reaction of the Masadans around him.)

"I'll have to relax security a bit, here. I warn you, though—the slightest lapse on your part . . ."

The Masadans actually shrank back a little. It was all very odd. Victor had glowered at himself in the mirror, quite often, when he was displeased with his own lapses. But he'd never—alas—noticed himself shrinking back.

"Pritchart's a traitor, but she does have a few principles left. Theisman, now—the admiral who led the rebellion and is the real power today in Haven—his treachery has no bottom. The swine has agreed secretly to form an alliance with Mesa. Turn the whole Republic of Haven into a fertile new territory for Manpower slavery and exploitation. It was when my leader Kevin Usher made *that* discovery that he realized we could wait no longer—"

I'll never hear the end of this. "Wonderboy" was bad enough. Once

Kevin finds out—maybe I could lie—no, not a chance, Ginny'll weasel it out of me, she always does—

The thought of *Ginny's* sarcasm almost made him shudder. Still, he pressed on fearlessly. Not much else to do, really, once a man has taken the plunge and he's sailing through the air.

God, I hope that water's deep. Really deep.

"—set himself up like a Pharaoh of old, with Manpower's bribes filling his coffers. He'll make Nero look like a saint. Whatever's left of Haven's moral fiber will be gone within a few years, the whole population given over to idleness and debauchery. The Revolution has to be saved before—"

Working their way through the passages wasn't as bad as Thandi had feared. On this, at least, Watanapongse had been wrong. The simple logic of the slaver ship's semi-obsolescent mass jettisoning design precluded complex internal passageways. The slavers couldn't afford to have slaves being driven to their death by poison gases die along the way from simply becoming lost.

So, the passage layout was simple and straightforward. Nor was there any doubt where the slaves themselves were kept. Every corridor was lined with hatches which obviously opened into the slave quarters.

The problem was *opening* them.

More precisely, the problem was that Thandi had no choice but to do so. She'd have preferred—this had been the plan all along—to bypass the slave quarters altogether. From a purely military standpoint, the slaves would just get in the way. Better to leave them locked down and release them after it was all over. Even then, Thandi hadn't looked forward to handling the chaos which was sure to result.

But now—

"You're *sure* you can't open it?" Thandi glared at the hatch at the end of one of the passages. That hatch, clearly enough, did not lead to one of the slave chambers. It would, instead, allow them to penetrate closer to the areas of the ship restricted to the crew; and, eventually, to the bridge.

Ruth joined Thandi in glaring at the recalcitrant hatch.

"Can't," she grunted sourly. "There *is* no electronic control for that hatch, Lieutenant. It must have a purely manual mechanism for opening it—and the mechanism is on the other side."

Ruth's technical expertise didn't extend to metallurgy, and unlike Thandi, she was no Marine. But even she could tell that the hatch was made of battle steel. It would have taken forever to burn through that thing, even if they'd had the proper equipment. Which they didn't.

"This is taking paranoia to new limits," she growled. "Not even warships have purely manual hatches."

Thandi was almost grinding her own teeth, but she snorted in bitter amusement.

"Warships don't worry much about mutiny, Your Highness. Not enough, that's for sure, to do something like this."

"You're right." Ruth shook her head in disgust and closed her minicomputer. "I'm sorry, Lieutenant. But there's nothing for it. I don't think we've got any choice except to go through the slave quarters."

Ruth swiveled on her haunches and studied a hatch a few meters down the corridor. That one, unlike the one she and Thandi were squatting before, was of a standard design. Not very heavily built, for one thing. And, more important, with the tell-tale instrument panel not far away which would provide her with access to the locks.

"Weird design," she murmured. "But it all makes sense, in a way. At least, if you can think like a sociopath. They aren't worried about slaves breaking into most of the ship, after all. What can they do"—she nodded toward the manual hatch—"assuming they can't get access to the passages leading to the ship's control areas?"

She glanced up at the ceiling and spotted the vents immediately. "If the slaves do succeed in breaking out, they just get gassed and jettisoned. A big loss of profit, sure, but they really can't threaten the ship itself."

Thandi looked at her watch. "We've already used up an hour and half, most of it spent wandering these passages trying to find one that gives us access to the bridge. We can't delay any longer." She scowled at the hatch leading to the slave quarters. "As you say, 'nothing for it.' We'll have to go through the slave quarters, however much that delays us."

She sighed heavily. "I hadn't counted on this. And who's to say we won't face the same problem *there*?" She poked a stiff finger at the offending hatch. "Why wouldn't *all* the hatches leading to the bridge have the same manual-only design?"

Ruth shook her head. "That's possible, but . . . I'd be surprised. Keep in mind that these passages—and the hatches that lead to them from the control areas—are used very rarely. Except for emergencies, probably only twice each voyage. Once to load the 'cargo,' and once to unload it. Whereas the hatches—probably just one hatch—leading directly to the slave quarters would be used by the crew every day. Manual-only hatches are a real pain in the ass. It wouldn't be that hard to make a *single* electronically controlled hatch pretty much fool-proof."

She glanced down, with great satisfaction, at the mini-computer in her hands. "Fool-proof from slaves, at least. Who can't possibly afford the kind of equipment a princess can—and you don't want to know how loud and long my father howled when I told him what I wanted for my birthday. This thing is worth more than its weight in gold. Uh, *considerably* more."

Thandi was puzzled. "Why would the crew need regular access to the slave quarters? Once they're locked down—*oh*."

Ruth's faced was pinched and hostile. "Yeah. 'Oh.' You're dealing with the scum of the universe here, Lieutenant. It's one of the perks of being part of a slaver crew. All the sex you want—any way you want it, with anybody."

Angrily, she rose and stalked over to the other hatch. The Amazons, despite being much larger and more muscular women, gave way before her instantly. The expression on the princess' face was truly savage.

Ruth had the panel open and began working on her computer again. "Well, not exactly," she muttered. "They'd have no interest in most of the slaves. But a large shipment is bound to have some of the pleasure lines included. They'd be kept in a special quarters not far from the entry hatch."

Thandi squatted down next to her. "How do you know so much about it?" she asked.

Ruth kept working. "I hate slavery. Always have. Imbibed it from my mother's milk, probably. She was a slave too, you know. Not exactly the same kind as Manpower's, but close enough. And the two things I always study a lot are the things I love and the things I hate."

The quick fingers paused at the keyboard. "That's odd . . ."

She looked up at Thandi. "I was going to disconnect all the surveillance equipment in the slave quarters. More precisely, set the records to just keep recycling on a two-hour interval so we'd be able to move through there without anyone on the bridge knowing we've arrived. But—"

She looked back down at her computer. "The slaves must have already gotten loose. All the surveillance equipment in the slave quarters appears to be have been smashed."

Thandi pursed her lips. "That'll make our life easier in one respect—but it also means it'll be chaos in there. *Damn*."

"Well, it's all done except the last, then. It's your call." Ruth tapped one of the keys lightly. "Once I punch in this last command, the hatch opens and we're in the middle of them. A madhouse, probably, even if Manpower hadn't packed this ship with twice the number of slaves they'd normally be hauling."

Thandi didn't hesitate. "Do it."

The hatch slid aside. Thandi was through it in a combat crouch. Not wanting to inflict mayhem on panicky slaves, to be sure, but still prepared to do it if necessary. Time was running out for Victor and Berry.

She stayed in the crouch, for several seconds. But that was simply due to surprise.

"Welcome," said the smiling man who greeted her. He was wearing the very utilitarian garb provided for slaves in transport. Nothing much more than a jumpsuit with no pockets, and cheap sandals on his feet. A dozen other men and women were crammed into the same small chamber. Most of them were perched on the chamber's four cots, which were stacked two deep on either side. They must have been forced to share the beds.

Thandi stared. She was almost gaping. All of the slaves were smiling. And not one of them seemed even surprised—much less panicked.

"Greetings," he repeated. "The Princess told us you'd be coming. Let me take you to her."

CHAPTER 37

WITHIN HALF AN HOUR AFTER BEING FORCED into the slave quarters, Berry had managed to adjust to the . . .

Surreal situation.

There was no other word for it, really. By then, she'd discovered that the slaves had not only seized the slave quarters and held them for a day, but had even managed to jury-rig a government of sorts. They'd been able to do so, for two reasons:

First, the Masadans had killed over half the slaver crew, including most of the officers, in the course of seizing the ship. That, at least, was the best guess of the slaves' steering committee—based on admittedly sketchy evidence. But their estimate matched the number of crewmen Berry had seen on the bridge.

She did the arithmetic herself, and came up with the same basic conclusion. There'd been just four crewmen on the bridge, including only one officer. Allow for perhaps another officer and two or three crewmen still alive in the engineering compartments. There'd been only four Masadans on the bridge also, which left two unaccounted for. Assuming that Kubler would have put them to oversee the surviving crewmen in the engineering compartments, that meant that in the course of seizing the ship the Masadans had wound up killing about two-thirds of the crew. Including, presumably, the captain.

No wonder the Masadans aren't trying to control the slaves any longer! They CAN'T.

Nor, she realized grimly, did they really need to. There was no way for the slaves to break out into the rest of the vessel. And unless they could do so, they simply couldn't threaten the ship itself or the men running it. What they could do, they had done—taken control of the slave quarters and gotten themselves organized.

After that . . . nothing. Just wait, and probably die when the Masadans decided to blow the ship.

"How did you find out about me?" she asked, early on.

The slave named Kathryn, who seemed to be presiding over the steering committee, issued a harsh little laugh.

"They told us."

Kathryn gestured at a piece of surveillance equipment suspended on the wall of the compartment which the steering committee had seized for itself. A former mess compartment, judging from its accouterments. There wasn't much left of the surveillance gear, beyond smashed pieces hanging limply from brackets.

"We wrecked most of the surveillance equipment early on, so they couldn't monitor what we were doing any longer. But we left the equipment intact in a compartment not far from here so we'd still have a way to negotiate with them if we needed to. Not long after that, one of the new people—the 'Masadans,' you're calling them?—got in touch with us. We think he simply wanted to calm us down. The gist of what he told us was that they'd seized the ship, they weren't slavers themselves—and they'd either free us eventually or kill us all by blowing up the ship."

Juan, another member of the steering committee, snorted sarcastically. "Of course, we told him we didn't believe a word he was saying. Why should we? So, after a few minutes, another Masadan came on—said he was the leader, a guy named Kubler—and explained to us that he was going to use a Manticoran princess as a hostage. I guess in order to prove his point, he showed us some footage of you."

He gave her costume a quick, smiling scrutiny. "You were wearing a lot fancier clothes, then. Standing in front of some kind of mansion shaking hands with . . ."

The words trailed off. All nine members of the steering committee seated at the mess table in the center of the compartment were now staring at Berry. So were the dozen or so other slaves standing around nearby.

"Was that *really* the Countess of the Tor you were shaking hands with?" Kathryn asked quietly. Her tone was almost awestruck. "And was that *really* W.E.B. Du Havel standing next to you?"

Berry's eyes widened. "How do you know who—?"

She bit off the words. It was already obvious, just from the quickness and efficiency with which the slaves had organized themselves over the past day, that she'd drastically underestimated their sophistication. She really didn't know that much about the inner workings of Manpower's genetic slavery, she now realized, especially from the vantage point of the slaves themselves.

Juan smiled crookedly. "What? Did you think we were all foot-shuffling illiterates? Something out of the history books?" For all that he was obviously trying to keep any anger out of his voice, Berry could detect the traces of it.

"This is the modern galaxy, Princess," he elaborated, shaking his head. "Even the combat and heavy labor lines have to know how to read and write. And most of us are trained for fairly complex work. We *have* to be, whether the scorpions like it or not."

Scorpions. She'd now heard that term at least a dozen times. It was the way the slaves referred to their Manpower overlords.

Kathryn waved a hand, indicating the members of the steering committee. "Several of us belong to the Audubon Ballroom, Princess. The Ballroom's been organizing slaves for at least ten years now."

Seeing the unspoken question in Berry's face, Kathryn also smiled crookedly. "How do you think? Some of us—I'm one of them, so's Georg over there—volunteered to let ourselves be recaptured. So we could start organizing on the inside of the scorpion nest."

Berry tried to imagine the degree of courage involved. That . . . she could do. But she knew she could never—not in a lifetime measured in centuries—match the sheer hatred that lurked under the terms.

Scorpions. In their nest. God help Manpower if they ever fall into the hands of their slaves. They'll be as merciless as demons.

Can't say I blame them any, of course.

Berry cleared her throat. She had to remind herself not to tell them that "the Countess of the Tor" was, in point of fact, her *mother.*

"Yes, that was she. Except she's not a countess any longer. She gave up the title so she could run for a seat in the House of Commons. And, yes, that was Web Du Havel standing next to me."

"Good for her," grunted the one named Georg. "She's always been the best of the lot, in the Anti-Slavery League. My opinion, anyway. Not sure what I think of Du Havel. We're all proud of him, of course, but . . . I think he's something of an appeaser."

"Let's leave politics out of this, shall we?" suggested one of the other slaves, a stocky man somewhat older than the rest. Berry had been given his name, but couldn't quite remember it. Harry, or Harris—something like that. The man gave Kathryn and Georg a somewhat frosty look. "We're not *all* members of the Ballroom, I'll ask you to remember. Personally, I think very highly of Professor Du Havel."

Kathryn raised her hand in a pacific gesture. "Take it easy, Harrell. Georg wasn't trying to start a debate, I'm sure. We can leave that for another time."

"Assuming there is one," muttered Georg. He glanced at the shattered surveillance equipment. "Easy enough to break *that.* But unless we can figure out a way to break into the rest of the ship, we're so much meat waiting for the slaughter."

Berry cleared her throat. "Uh. Are you *sure* we can't be spied on, any longer?"

The response she got was a lot of rather unfriendly looks.

Right. Stupid question. "Scorpions," remember? They probably spent two hours crushing every little functioning piece they could find.

"Never mind," she said hastily. "The point is . . . well. I'm not *actually* a captive here. Well. I mean, yes, I am—right now. But there's an assault team on its way to deal with that. The real reason I came over was to serve as a decoy. Keep the Masadans preoccupied—me and Victor, that is—while Thandi and her women take them out."

She stopped, suspecting her account fell somewhat short of coherence.

"Who's 'Victor'?" Georg demanded immediately. Suspicion didn't exactly "drip" from the words. But it did seep noticeably.

"Victor Cachat. He's an agent—of some kind, I haven't figured out the details—for the Republic of Haven."

Kathryn's eyes widened. "I *know* him!"

The other slaves fixed their gazes on her. Kathryn shrugged. "Well, not exactly. I wasn't there myself—where it happened—but I was on Terra at the time. So I never met him personally, but Jeremy X told me about it afterward."

That was apparently enough. Most of the slaves sitting at the table had wide eyes, as did several of the ones standing about.

"*Him?*" asked Georg, a bit shakily. "The guy who massacred all those Scrags at the Artinstute?"

Berry had to bite her tongue. She *had* been there. Close by, anyway, even if she hadn't witnessed the killings herself. But her sister Helen had, and had given Berry a detailed description of it later. She hadn't realized that the incident had become so famous among Manpower's slaves—although, now that she thought about it, it was hardly surprising that it had. That day in Chicago—the so-called "Manpower Incident" which had begun with Victor Cachat's killing spree in the underground—had seen the wholesale destruction of Manpower's headquarters on Terra, as well as whatever Scrags the Ballroom had managed to get their hands on throughout the city. Which had been several dozen of them, by all accounts.

The butchery had been great enough, her father had told her a year or so later, to eliminate almost entirely the Scrag presence on Terra. Anton estimated that the survivors—which was most of them, he thought—had emigrated afterward to other planets. It had undoubtedly been one of the Audubon Ballroom's greatest triumphs—and a story which any Manpower slave would cherish.

But, again, Berry had to remind herself that she was "Princess Ruth"—who'd been several hundred light-years away at the time. So, she tried to act as innocent and naïve as she could.

"Yes, I believe that's correct. Him."

Whatever suspicions might have existed were clearly gone, now. It was as if the name "Victor Cachat" were a magic talisman. It was a bit disorienting, at first, until Berry realized that over the past few years she'd fallen into the habit of looking at the universe through Manticoran eyes. To her, more than anything, "Victor Cachat" was an agent of the Republic of Haven—and hence, basically, an enemy.

But the war between Manticore and Haven meant little to Manpower's slaves. And, even if they were inclined to take sides in the affair, she suspected they'd be more likely to incline toward Haven. True, the Star Kingdom had a better reputation than most, when it came to the issue of genetic slavery. In fact, Manticore had signed onto the Cherwell Convention almost forty T-years before the Republic had. It also had the prestige of being the homeland which had produced Catherine Montaigne, who was perhaps the Anti-Slavery League's most glamorous leader. But, against that, there was the fact that Manticore was ruled by an hereditary aristocracy—something which was bound to rub the wrong way against people yoked into a harsh caste system—whereas Haven had a reputation throughout the galaxy for being a bastion of egalitarianism.

The fact that the Havenite regime under the Legislaturalists had been even more dominated by its own hereditary elites than the Star Kingdom, or that under Pierre and Saint-Just it had also been a bastion of savage political repression . . . simply wouldn't register very much on most slaves. Nor, Berry admitted frankly to herself, would they have cared much anyway. She'd lived herself, all of her life until Anton and Helen rescued her, under the conditions of "personal freedom" which were supposedly enjoyed by Terrans. In the real world, what that meant if you didn't come from "the right people" was that your life was sheer misery. The only freedom she'd ever enjoyed had been the freedom to starve.

She understood more clearly, now, something Web Du Havel had said to her in the course of their long journey to Erewhon. Berry had no passionate interest in political theory, true—but, on the other hand, she found almost everything pretty interesting. So she'd been a willing enough participant in Web's discussions with Ruth. (The princess, of course, being a veritable addict when it came to politics.)

"It's just a fact, girls, like it or not. Make someone live under a yoke like an ox, then don't be shocked and surprised when he turns into a rampaging bull when he breaks free. You were expecting the milk of human kindness? You'll get the same charity and mercy you gave *him*. The lash repaid by the sword, or the noose, or the torch. That's the way it is. Study any slave rebellion in history, or any uprising of serfs against feudal lords. *Kill the master, kill his family, burn his house to the ground. Right off!*"

"You sound as if you approve," Ruth had said, half-accusingly.

"'Approval' has nothing to do with it, Princess, speaking professionally. That's like accusing a doctor of 'approving' of metabolism. Metabolism is what it is—and sometimes it can be downright horrendous. Learn to look truth in the face, Princess. Most of all, whatever else, learn not to avoid it with circumlocutions."

He shrugged. "As it happens—again, speaking professionally—I don't approve. But let there be no misunderstanding between us. My disapproval has nothing to do—*nothing*—with any qualms about the fate of the slaveowner." His eyes, normally warm, were icy. "Any man or woman in today's universe who participates voluntarily in the practice of slavery has thereby automatically forfeited any claim they had to life, liberty, or the pursuit of happiness. That's my attitude, and it's the attitude of every slave or ex-slave I ever met. You'll never see me shed a single tear over the killing of a slaver. Not one."

He drew a deep breath. "However, that's neither here nor there. The reason I disapprove is because of the effect on the *slaves*. Because there's another clear pattern in history, and one with precious few exceptions." Grimly: "Successful slave rebellions—or any kind of government set up by former slaves, even ones which didn't require an outright rebellion—almost always turn out badly, soon enough. Within a generation, you wind up with a new tyranny which, while it doesn't follow the same genetic lines, is every bit as brutal as what it overthrew."

"Why?" asked Berry.

"Because all the odds are against the slaves. The ex-slaves, I should say. They come into power ill-trained to use it, and accustomed to brute force as the only way to settle anything. And, usually, in conditions of extreme poverty and deprivation. All in all, just about the worst possible culture medium for the emergence of a tolerant and genuinely democratic polity. Not to mention that, nine times out of ten, the ex-slaves immediately find themselves under attack by hostile outsiders—which means they become a garrison state, almost at once, and a garrison state is inevitably going to be autocratic."

He ran fingers through his short, stubby hair. "It's one of the many little bitter ironies of political dynamics. What a slave rebellion needs most of all, right away, is the thing it's least likely to get: a breathing space. A period of a generation or two where the new state it sets up can relax a little. Work out its own customs and traditions for resolving disputes short of the knife—and feel enough in the way of stability that it can afford to do so. Instead of, almost at once, being compelled to surrender authority to an autocrat. Who is likely, mind you, to be quite an impressive leader—and, while he's alive, often does far more good than harm. But the problem is that after he dies . . ."

Ruth knew far more history than Berry did. "Toussaint l'Ouverture . . . and then you wind up with Duvalier and the Ton Ton Macoutes. Yeah, sure, Spartacus was a hell of guy. And since he wound up being executed, his historical legacy is untarnished. But what if he'd *triumphed*? What would Spartacus Junior have looked like?"

"Exactly," Web had replied, sighing. "It's a problem—as you can imagine—I've spent most of my life wrestling with."

"Come up with any answers?" Berry asked.

Web chuckled. "Oh, sure. I figured the answer out years ago. The problem is that the odds of ever getting it are . . . slim, to say the least."

Ruth and Berry tried to pry the answer out of him. But Web had refused, smiling. "Not a chance. You'd both think I was crazy."

Kathryn's voice brought Berry back to the present.

"Where's Victor Cachat now?"

Berry stared at her, suddenly realizing that her little sketch of the situation had been . . . yes. *Incoherent.*

"Oh, sorry. He's on the ship." She nodded in the direction that she thought—although wasn't sure—was the location of the bridge. "He's trying to keep the Masadans distracted while Thandi—uh, that's Lieutenant Palane of the Solarian Marines—leads a strike force into the ship through one of the entries."

The wide-eyed stares were back. "The *Solarians*?" Georg was squinting suspiciously again. "Solarians are all a bunch of two-faced—"

"No politics!" snapped Harrell. He was glaring at Georg. "I also happen to think quite highly of Hieronymus Stein, even if *you* don't. And what the hell gave *you* the right—"

" 'No politics,' you said, Harrell," growled Kathryn. "Good advice. Follow it yourself."

Harrell's mouth closed. After an instant, he grunted something halfway between an apology and a simple acknowledgment.

Kathryn was clearly the leader of the group. She now growled at Georg: "And I will remind *you*, Comrade, that the Ballroom has never officially denounced the Solarian League. Whatever you—or I—or Jeremy X, for that matter—might think in private."

When she turned back to Berry, she smiled. "Still and all, it *is* a bit odd."

Berry tried to figure out how to explain. That was hard to the point of impossible, for the simple reason that she herself had only the fuzziest notion of *exactly* what the Solarians were maneuvering for.

Get Web to give me some lessons, she told herself firmly. *Right after I start exercising. Oh, yuck.*

She fell back on simplicities. "Well . . . Thandi's from Ndebele. I don't think she's all that fond of the Solarian League herself, when you get right down to it, even if she is a lieutenant in their Marine Corps."

Again, a word proved to be a magic talisman. The name of a planet, this time, rather than a man.

"Oh. Ndebele." That was from Georg. Even he seemed mollified. "They get it almost as bad as we do."

One of the other slaves, who hadn't spoken yet and whose name Berry couldn't remember, barked a little laugh.

"What do you mean, 'they' and 'we'?" she demanded. She bowed her head and ran fingers through very blond, very kinky hair.

"Where do you think I got this pelt from, Georg? My upper-crust ancestors?"

Her laugh was echoed by others. Looking around, now that she knew what to look for, Berry could see Mfecane genetic traces in the faces—not to mention the size and musculature—of several of the slaves.

"How soon can we expect this Lieutenant Palane of yours?" asked Kathryn, bringing things back to the business at hand.

"Oh. Well . . . knowing Thandi, I'd say sooner than you think," she said, then paused, considering exactly how to broach the next little point it had suddenly occurred to her needed explaining in light of Mesa's personnel hiring practices.

"What is it, Princess?" Kathryn asked, gazing at her shrewdly, and Berry sighed.

"It's just . . . well, Thandi's assault team's members aren't Marines like she is."

"They're not?" Kathryn and Georg both frowned.

"No," Berry said, then shrugged. Best to take the hurdle in a rush, she told herself firmly. "She's got her own people—sort of her own, private little unit. Very much undercover and off the books, I think. But the point is that all of her other team members are, well, Scrags."

"*Scrags?!*" Kathryn hissed, and Berry saw her sudden fury mirrored in more than one face. She could literally feel the hatred rising about her, and she started to shrink back. But then, to her own surprise, her spine stiffened and she raised her chin.

"Yes," she said flatly. "It would be more accurate to call them *ex*-Scrags, actually. 'Amazons' is what Thandi is calling them now, and they're busy trying their best to grow into the new role she expects of them." The "Princess" chuckled suddenly. "Believe me—you *don't* want to disappoint Thandi. Not if you know what's good for you!"

Kathryn looked a bit more mollified, but not a lot, and Berry shrugged.

"You have my personal assurance that Thandi's Amazons will do exactly what she tells them to . . . and that they have their own personal reasons to hate Mesans and—especially—the Masadans aboard this ship every bit as much as you do. For that matter, they've already saved *my* life from other Scrags aboard the space station." She paused, considering that last sentence, then shrugged again. "Well, actually, they helped Thandi do it and sort of held her coat for her while she kicked the crap out of the Scrag in question barehanded."

Kathryn gazed at her for a few more moment, then barked a sharp, sudden laugh. It was not at all a pleasant sound, but it seemed to have banished any lingering reservations about the nature of the assault party, and she started giving orders. Within seconds, most of the onlookers were gone, hurrying to spread the word through the slave quarters.

"Okay," she said, turning back to Berry. "That'll avoid any possible immediate problems. But then what happens? Assuming that your Lieutenant Palane—and Victor Cachat—manage to take the ship back from the Masadans." She made a little sweeping hand gesture, indicating all the slaves. "What happens to *us*?"

Berry started to explain. Within seconds, the feeling of surrealism was back in full force.

Being a "princess" is weird enough. Being a "prophetess" is even weirder.

CHAPTER 38

"ALL RIGHT, PRIN—UH, BERRY," Thandi said, quietly but firmly. She rose from her squatting position in front of the hatch, where she'd been watching Ruth at her work. "Now you get your butt out of here."

For a moment, Ruth looked mulish. Smiling, Berry hauled her away from the hatch.

"Leave it be, '*Berry,*' " she whispered. "You are *not* trained as a commando."

As reluctant as she might be to break away from the action—it was obvious to Berry that, deny it however she might, Ruth had been having the time of her life—the Princess didn't really put up a struggle. The young royal was adventurous, true, but she wasn't downright insane. She'd already done what she needed to do: break the codes which would enable Thandi to open the hatch leading to the bridge without setting off any alarms. From here, it would be all mayhem and fast-moving havoc. As relatively athletic as she was, Princess Ruth had no chance at all of keeping up with Thandi Palane and her Amazons. She'd just get in their way, and she knew it.

Berry guided her toward the hatch on the opposite side of the small chamber, which led back into the slave quarters.

"Damn," Ruth muttered. "You know as well as I do that once my aunt finds out about this . . ." She made a face. "I'll be lucky if she ever lets me out of my own suite in Mount Royal Palace. Till I'm dead or she is."

"Hush," whispered Berry, nodding meaningfully toward the hatch she was starting to open. "And *don't* forget that you're still me and I'm still you."

Ruth nodded. She and Berry had managed a quick, whispered consultation after Thandi and her assault team had been welcomed into the slave quarters. They'd both agreed that it would be best to keep the masquerade going.

That had been Berry's suggestion, and she still felt weird about it. There was actually no reason to maintain the subterfuge, from the standpoint of the Masadan enemy. Those enemies would either be dead in a few minutes or they'd *all* be dead when the ship exploded. So why keep up the rigmarole?

But the simple fact was that—

Weird-weird-weird.

—by now, Berry had established a peculiar position among the slaves. The combination of the news she'd brought and her assumed identity as a "princess" seemed to settle their nerves. She'd noticed that the steering committee, which had been in continuous—and often raucous—session since they'd learned of the plans for Congo, was now often turning to her to serve as something in the way an informal court of final appeal.

Weird-weird-weird.

Still, it seemed to work. The steering committee's members were all strong-willed, were by no means all personally fond of each other, did not necessarily share the same political opinions, and had little experience working together—not to mention that the committee itself had been slapped together in the press of circumstances. Even with Kathryn's generally sure leadership, tempers had gotten frayed.

But, they'd never snapped—and not least of all because, very quickly, Kathryn had started using Berry as a calming agent. It didn't even matter so much what Berry said or didn't say in the disputes. As a rule, she said as little as possible, being mainly concerned simply with keeping everybody calm.

It was simply who she *was.* Or, rather, was supposed to be.

"Princess." What was it, Berry wondered, that gave that term—a fake term, as it happened—such a peculiar magic?

Ruth had seemed to understand it immediately, when Berry tried to explain.

"Oh, sure," Ruth whispered. "It's 'cause your authority doesn't derive from anything really legitimate. Might be better to say, from an arbitrary legitimacy that stands outside of the hurly-burly. Monarchy's really a silly business, when you get right down to it—but don't you dare tell Aunt Elizabeth I said so. I'm going to be in enough trouble as it is."

The two girls shared a conspiratorial glance around the mess compartment. Fortunately, all of the slaves were still completely preoccupied by the presence in their midst of Thandi Palane and her Amazons.

"Amazons." When Thandi and her women had first entered the mess compartment being used for the slave headquarters, Berry had been sure there'd be a brawl right then and there, despite her own efforts to prepare against it. Any slave of Manpower would have immediately recognized the tell-tale genetic traces on the faces of the "Amazons," and within two seconds, prepared or not, they'd been like so many dogs facing off in an alley with their hackles raised and their fangs bared.

Scrags. The self-proclaimed supermen who had, for several generations now, served Manpower as its bully boys. It was enough to be a "Scrag" to be under sentence of immediate death, so far as any member of the Audubon Ballroom was concerned.

Fortunately, Thandi's glower had intimidated everyone for just long enough. And a very intimidating glower it was, too, coupled to that fearsome physique. Berry had made an immediate private vow to make sure that Thandi remained her "big sister." Had given that priority, in fact, precedence over her vow to start exercising and taking political lessons from Web Du Havel.

(It had been an easy vow to make, of course. Being on close personal terms with Thandi Palane did not fall into Berry Zilwicki's definition of *oh, yuck.*)

Just long enough—for Berry to pitch in and capitalize on her own earlier spadework to settle it all down.

"Thandi!" she'd exclaimed, leaping from her seat and practically hurling herself into a embrace. Then, quickly, disengaging the embrace and hurling herself upon the nearest Amazon.

"Yana! S'great to see you again!" Disengage; embrace another—*quick, quick, quick.*

"Lara!"

"Hanna!"

"Inge!"

Lara even had the presence of mind to exclaim "Princess Ruth!" when she returned the embrace. Granted, the woman's grin tended to detract from the solemnity of the occasion.

Still, it was enough. By the time Berry resumed her seat, if nothing else, she'd muddled up the slaves' automatic reactions to the point where immediate mayhem was ruled out. And, thereafter, she was relieved to see that Kathryn had the good sense to continue using Berry as her combination sounding board and social relaxant.

Did it more than ever, in fact. Berry suspected that Kathryn was even more relieved than she was at the way things were remaining reasonably harmonious. And she was beginning to understand, concretely and not abstractly, what Web Du Havel had meant when he explained the political pitfalls awaiting newly liberated slaves.

Like open wounds, all of them, she thought. *Never being given enough time to heal before being lacerated open again. Be nice to each other, boys and girls. Oh, and here's another crisis. More salt to rub into your bleeding flesh.*

Too, there was this: Berry was by nature a very empathetic person. So, within a short time, happening almost like a gravitational attraction, she found herself emotionally identifying with the slaves and their predicament. Not the immediate one—Thandi Palane would either save their lives, or she wouldn't—but with the very uncertain future which faced them all.

"Freedom." A splendid word, especially in the abstract. A sanctified and hallowed one, even, when the person uttering it has no immediate prospect of escaping bondage. Like a mantra, or the name of a saint whispered in prayer. But once it loomed as an imminent reality . . .

Freedom to do *what*?

Starve? What does a slave do, when he or she gains her freedom—having been bred and trained to do nothing except a master's bidding?

Historically, the answer had generally been bleak. "Freedom" meant the freedom to fight over the scraps—or sell yourself back into another form of bondage, to someone who would give you the scraps from his table.

And so, in the time that followed, Berry was almost oblivious to her friend Ruth, perched nearby on a chair a little back from the central table where the deliberations and arguments took place. She was much too intent on the discussion itself, bending all her will and attention to the task of keeping it steady and as relaxed as possible.

Ruth, on the other hand, was not oblivious to her. She was fascinated, actually, watching Berry at the table. She'd come to cherish Berry's friendship, but realized now that—like everyone—she'd never really thought of Berry *except* in terms of friendship.

Now, studying her friend in action, "on her own" as it were, Ruth Winton applied to the task all the intent scrutiny and thought of which she was capable. Which was a great deal, indeed. Ruth had not been boasting when she told Thandi that she always studied the things she loved and the things she hated.

Here, she could do both at the same time. It did not take her long to reach a conclusion, and she resolved to raise it with Web Du Havel at the first opportunity.

The opportunity to do so would come, not long after. That didn't surprise Ruth, knowing Thandi as she did. Du Havel's reaction, on the other hand, did surprise her. Astonished her, in fact. She'd been expecting either a long lecture on girlish folly or a simple sneer of disdain.

But, he simply grinned. "Join the club, Ruth Winton. There are now two of us in the universe who are crazy."

This is crazy, thought Thandi. *Pure lunacy.*

She tried her very best glower on the Amazons.

"Are you all insane?" she hissed, hooking a thumb toward the bend in the corridor. She was trying to speak as quietly as possible while still being forceful—a difficult task, to say the least. "If the schematics Ruth pulled out of the ship's computer are accurate, we're less than fifteen meters from the bridge."

As she whispered, Thandi continued stripping off all of her gear except her armored skinsuit itself. Now that she had been able to size up the tactical situation concretely, she'd decided speed was the key. She'd make the assault armed only with a hand pulser. Thandi was an expert with just about any kind of handheld weapon, but she was particularly proficient with sidearms.

"There's only one hatch leading into it," she pointed out. "How in the hell do you think you're going to pull off a 'mass charge'? And what's the point, anyway, beyond giving the bastards a lot of targets? If it can be done at all, I can do it alone."

It was no good. Great Kaja or not, the Amazons seemed to think there was a matter of honor at stake. And they were making clear that they would stick to it. Grimly, Thandi realized that no matter what she said—even if she threatened them—they would just follow her anyway.

"All *right,*" she muttered. "But you will still do it *my* way, understood? You *follow* me onto the bridge. If a single one of you tries to push ahead of me . . . I'll break her neck, I swear I will."

The blood-curdling threat was met with grins.

"No problem, kaja." Lara nodded with exaggerated obeisance. "You may lead, so long as we may follow."

The last sentence had the flavor of ritual about it. Thandi realized that she knew very little, when all was said and done, of the strange subculture the Scrags had developed in their long centuries of social isolation. Given their obsessive preoccupation with "superiority," however, she suspected that they'd developed—to a very high degree—a sort of human equivalent to the dominance rituals of pack animals.

A wolfess will respect the preeminence of the alpha female in the pack, true enough—so long as her own canines are acknowledged. And nobody tries to suggest she's actually a rabbit with pointed teeth.

Thandi chuckled. "Maybe Berry can civilize the lot of you. I give up. All right, then. My plan is about as simple as it gets."

Thandi had already used a Marine spy-eye to peek around the bend—nothing more than a very thin and flexible optic cable attached to a tiny viewer. There was no guard stationed at the hatch, and the hatch itself was unlocked. So she assumed, anyway, since the tell-tale light above it was green. Unless slaver ships followed a different protocol than any other ships she'd ever encountered, she'd be able to get through it within a split-second.

"As soon as I start, Yana, you give the signal to Inge."

Yana nodded. She'd been appointed the one to stay in communication with Inge and the three Amazons who'd gone with her. Their job was to take out the men in the engineering compartments. Thandi had delegated that job, since she had the personnel to carry out both assaults simultaneously. The Masadans wouldn't have jury-rigged a blow-it-up-now switch in the engineering compartments in addition to the one she was sure they'd set up on the bridge. There would have been no reason to, and two switches more than doubled the chance of an accidental explosion. The Masadans were fanatics, but they weren't careless.

The men in the engineering compartment could still blow up the ship, true. But not quickly, with all the safeguards that would have to be removed. That was assuming the Masadans could even do it at all, without having to force the slaver crew to do most of the actual work. They certainly couldn't do it before Inge and her women had them all down and dead.

The real problem—the only problem, so far as Thandi was concerned—was the possibility that one of the Masadans on the bridge could reach the suicide switch before she killed them all. That was the reason she'd planned all along to lead the assault on the bridge. She could move faster than any of them.

Faster still, she thought sourly, *if I didn't have to worry about a bunch of honor-besotted cretins insisting on stepping all over my heels. Oh, well. Just move even faster, Thandi girl.*

The thought was sour enough to impart an acerbic edge to her final orders.

"As for the rest of you, just come after me and do what's needed. I warn you—even one of you steps on my heels and slows me down, I'll break her neck. See if I don't."

The only answer was so many grins. Thandi snorted, came out of her crouch like a tigress out of ambush, and was around the bend.

There never was any danger the Amazons would step on her heels. The point of honor having been satisfied, the women were sensible enough to understand that Thandi would just be hampered if they crowded her too close.

Which they couldn't have done, anyway. They hadn't witnessed the killings in Tube Epsilon, only the aftermath. So the Amazons had never really seen her moving at top speed.

They did now, and even they were astonished. The Amazons weren't halfway down the passage before Thandi was through the hatch leading onto the bridge. All that came crowding on her heels was a shrieking cry of adulation and triumph.

Great kaja! Kill them all!

For the past hour, Victor had been keeping an eye on that hatch. A corner of his eye, rather, since he couldn't afford to make his interest obvious.

By now, he was feeling bleary-eyed. Not so much from the strain of trying to watch something without actually doing so, but from the mental strain of keeping what had become a completely absurd concoction of lies and half-truths and sheer gibberish from collapsing under its own weight.

A collapse which, he was quite sure, was imminent. Even the Masadans, as prone as they were to conspiratorial paranoia, were now obviously suspicious.

"That does *not* make sense, Cachat," said Kubler, almost growling the words. He didn't quite heft the pulser in his hand, but the hand did twitch. "In fact, not much of anything you've said in the past—"

Kubler's head exploded.

Despite the watch he'd kept upon it, Victor never did see the powered hatch snap silently open. Neither did anyone else. All of their attention was focused on the obviously growing tension between him and the senior Masadan. Which made the sudden carnage erupting in their midst even more horrifying and stunning.

For a split second, like all the Masadans, Victor simply gaped at the demon flowing onto the bridge with a pulser in her hand. Then—he'd planned this all through, which they hadn't—Victor was up and moving.

There was no need to push Kubler aside. Thandi's first shot had done for that. First three shots, in fact. Somehow, she put them all into Kubler's head without so much as scratching Victor.

She was still firing, not from a marksman's crouch but striding forward onto the bridge and blazing away. She was moving so fast she seemed to flicker. *Stride-stride-stop-fire; stride-stride-stop-fire.* Three-round bursts, every time, as the pulser in her hand picked out targets like a machine, or one of the legendary gunfighters from ancient films Victor had seen.

Bad films. Silly ones, where the hero takes on a saloon full of cutthroats and never misses a single shot.

Victor almost cackled, as that absurd image flashed through his mind in the middle of his desperate lunge to do the one and only thing he was concerned about.

Get that bastard AWAY from the switch. Die in the doing, if need be—but GET HIM AWAY FROM IT.

Later, he would realize it all happened within a few seconds. At the time, his lunge toward the Masadan by the suicide switch seemed to take an eternity. Sailing through the air, at the last, his only purpose in life to tackle the man and take him down to the deck before he could destroy them all.

Victor felt a moment of elation, then. The Masadan had been as shocked as any, by Thandi's sudden and unexpected assault. Victor could see the determination beginning to congeal in the man's face, as realization replaced surprise. But even a Masadan does not commit suicide without a moment's hesitation—and he no longer had that moment. Victor would reach him in time, and no matter how he struggled, Victor was quite sure he could overpower the man. Certainly with the force of his lunge to give him the edge.

And so he did. But no overpowering was needed. By the time he brought the Masadan out of his seat and onto the deck, he'd tackled a corpse. In the final split-second, he saw a snarling fanatic face disappear in an explosion of blood, brains, and very tiny splinters of bone.

Yet another three-round burst, he realized, then grimaced as he drove headfirst into the expanding cloud of gore which had been a man's face. And then, as he sprawled onto the floor atop the dead man, Victor was mostly just puzzled. How had Thandi managed *that*—without, again, putting a scratch on him?

"Idiot," she muttered, hauling him to his feet by the scruff of the neck. "Biggest damn problem I had was trying not to kill *you.* Worse than the Amazons."

But he didn't miss the love in the voice, or in the smile that faced him when he finally saw it.

"I'll try to remember that," he croaked. Piously: "Never interfere with a professional at her work."

Then he smiled himself. He had no trouble doing so, despite the carnage on the bridge, or even the blood coating his own face. Other men might have quailed at the prospect of falling in love with a woman who could kill eight men in half as many seconds.

Not Victor Cachat. Perhaps oddly, he found it quite reassuring.

CHAPTER 39

WHEN WEB DU HAVEL FIRST ENTERED the former mess compartment which had become the semi-official headquarters of what the *Felicia*'s ex-slaves were now calling "the Liberation," he went unnoticed. Ruth had taken him there, with no other escort, since he'd insisted he wanted no fanfare. Web wanted to be able to observe the proceedings, for as long as possible, before his identity became known. Thereafter, he knew, he would inevitably be drawn into the center of things.

About *that,* Web had very mixed feelings. On the one hand, he knew full well that for the Liberation to have any chance for long-term success, he would have to play a leading role. In a very real way, he'd been preparing himself for it all his life since escaping from Manpower.

On the other hand . . .

The exercise of power, in itself, held no attraction for him. Rather the opposite, actually. By temperament, he was far more inclined toward a scholarly approach than an activist one. He enjoyed the detachment that position gave him, and knew he was about to lose it—probably for the rest of his life.

Still, duty was duty. From that same detached and scholarly viewpoint—almost a clinical one—Web understood that the same personal characteristics which made him shy away from a leading political role would also make him a valuable asset to the Liberation. More so, perhaps, than his actual expertise in the theory of political dynamics. Theory was one thing; practice, another. History was full of scholars who, risen to power, had made disastrous political leaders.

Web understood the reasons for that, also.

First, intellectuals usually tried to force things into their theoretical framework, reluctant to accept that no theory could possibly encompass all of reality. Certainly not when dealing with a phenomenon as inherently complex, contradictory and chaotic as human political affairs. Theory was, at best, a guide to practice, not a substitute for it. That was something which any experienced, practicing politician understood instinctively, but which came with difficulty for people whose lives had been spent in the cloisters of academia.

Second, because scholars attracted to power were as prone as politicians to all the vices of power, while sharing few of its virtues. From long experience, Web knew there was perhaps no form of politics which could be as petty, vicious, unrelenting and pointless as academic infighting. Fortunately for the universe, in the vast majority of instances, the scholars involved didn't have the power of star nations and modern weaponry at their disposal.

But *give* such a scholar that power . . .

Web's face twisted into a grimace. He had a well-integrated personality, and wasn't really worried that a brutal despot lurked beneath the affable surface of the man known as "W.E.B. Du Havel." But, as much as anything, that was because he'd planned for such an eventuality—in broad outlines, if not in detail—and had long since decided he would make sure he was never given the temptation in the first place. Or, more precisely, surrounded himself with checks and barriers which made the temptation a moot point.

He'd come here, quietly and with no fanfare, in order to study for himself the first—perhaps the most important—of those prospective checks and barriers. And was able to do so, for several minutes, before he was finally recognized. The compartment was so packed with ex-slaves observing the proceedings that Web was able to squeeze himself into the crowd with no notice. He was wearing better clothing than most of the slaves, true, but already a number of them had been able to exchange the pathetic garments provided by Manpower for the still-utilitarian but far superior jumpsuits being sent over quietly from the space station. Ruth was noticed, a bit, but by now—almost a full day after Cachat and Palane had seized the *Felicia*—she was a familiar figure to the ex-slaves.

He found the crowded conditions a bit amusing, actually. The members of the steering committee—now renamed the Liberation Committee—were barely able to fit themselves around the table at the center of the compartment. From the scowls on several of their faces, Web suspected they were none too happy about it, either.

Sooner or later, they'll have to start meeting in executive session.

No way to really conduct practical political affairs in the middle of a mob. But . . . not now. Now is a time for establishing legitimacy, pure and simple. That's Moses and the prophets. The rest can wait for the commentary of the scholars.

Besides—

Web chuckled. The one thing that made the press at the center manageable for the Committee was that the worst of the press wasn't surrounding them, in any event. The heaviest clustering of the crowd took place around a smaller table, located just a few meters away. Where sat a very young woman—not much more than a girl, really—listening carefully to something being said to her by five ex-slaves seated at the other chairs around the same table. As Web watched, Berry said something. He couldn't hear the words. But from the immediate looks of satisfaction which came over the faces of the five ex-slaves—and that of most of the ones hovering in the immediate vicinity—he was sure she'd made some small pronouncement regarding the logical handling of some immediate and probably petty problem. Not an *order,* but simply a calm, reasoned, practical suggestion.

Which, of course—coming from her—had all the force of a pronouncement by Solomon. All the better if it came from an open, young, warm girl's face instead of the face of a stern patriarch. Authority, still, but with all the lurking menace of authority leached away.

Ruth echoed his chuckle. "She's *perfect,*" she whispered.

Web exchanged a smile with the young Manticoran princess who had become, in effect, his co-conspirator. *Lunatics of the galaxy, unite—even if, so far, there are only two of us.*

So far.

It was Berry who spotted them first, and forced Web to surrender his life.

"Web!" She sprang from her chair, and was over to him in an instant. Managing, somehow, to clear a way through the crowd without actually pushing anyone aside. A moment later, he was enfolded in her embrace.

He made no attempt to stint that embrace. Quite the opposite. As Web Du Havel bade farewell to a scholar's existence, he embraced the new one with good cheer.

And why not? The girl in his arms was enough to bring good cheer to anyone.

"Your Highness," he intoned.

He could hear Berry's little laugh against his cheek. "So solemn!" she whispered. "Silly fakery, I'll be glad to be done with it. It's just *me,* Web."

Her embrace tightened. So did his. Like a man cast into the great ocean might embrace a flotation vest.

"Your Highness," he repeated.

He was surprised, at first, to find himself weeping. Then, the still-remaining intellectual's part of his mind—that part which would always remain—understood the phenomenon. Not so odd, really, that even a scholar should find his emotions swept into theory, when that theory takes on real flesh and blood. Truth and illusion, in politics, were not such distinct categories. More precisely, had a way of transforming into each other.

So he maintained the embrace, and let the tears flow freely. Knowing that, in the years to come, this moment—observed by all in the compartment—would enter the legends of the new star nation.

Soon enough, to be sure, scholars of the future would debunk the whole business and rambunctious youth would turn the debunking into criticism and even, here and there, outright scorn and rebellion.

So? By then, the generations would have done their work. A nation, once established and secure, can afford to laugh at itself—even jeer and ridicule. Must do so, in fact, from time to time, to retain its sanity. But it can only do so from the vantage point of maturity. Coming into birth, a new nation needed certainties as much as any infant. A mythology of its *own* creation, never mind that the bits and pieces were taken from anywhere.

Scrap metal, molded and beaten into plowshares and swords—and custom.

"*Your Highness,*" he repeated yet again.

In the hours that followed, as the Committee suspended its deliberations and the compartment was given over to what amounted to a seminar on political affairs, Web built upon that moment as best he could. The process was a bit difficult, given that he had to remain in the world of abstractions.

That, for the simplest of all reasons: authority without power is an abstraction, and Web had no illusions that any amount of symbolic manipulation could substitute for sheer force. Counterbalance it, yes—even complement it, where necessary. But substitute for it?

Not a chance. And he made that clear, very early on.

"I am not prepared to discuss—or even speculate—on what might be the best form of government for us to adopt," he said firmly, in response to a question raised by Harrell. "Nor will I be, until Jeremy X arrives. Which, as I told you, should be fairly soon. Jeremy, as it turns out, is currently residing on Smoking Frog—and word has already been sent there of the new developments, via one of Captain Rozsak's courier ships. So I expect Jeremy to arrive in Erewhon within ten days. Two weeks, at the outside."

He almost laughed, then. Out of the corner of his eye, Web could see the expressions on the faces of Berry Zilwicki and Ruth Winton, who were seated nearby. Anton Zilwicki was also on Smoking Frog, and he'd be getting the news too. Berry's face had all the apprehensiveness you'd expect of a teenager anticipating a truly volcanic reaction from her father when he learned of her latest escapade.

If anything, Ruth's expression was even more apprehensive. Anton Zilwicki, after all, was an even-tempered man. Ruth's aunt, Queen Elizabeth, on the other hand, had a truly ferocious temper—and she'd be getting the news not all that much later than Anton. A courier ship had also been dispatched to the Star Kingdom, bearing messages from both the Manticoran ambassador to Erewhon and Captain Oversteegen. Ginny Usher had left the system as well, returning on the Havenite courier ship to take a report to her husband and President Pritchart.

Oh, yes. Within a few weeks, both young women were going to find themselves at the center of an interstellar firestorm.

But, at the moment, Web had more pressing business to attend to. Squelching another firestorm, before it got started.

Of the nine members of the Committee, three were members of the Audubon Ballroom—Kathryn, Georg, and Juan. All three of them, hearing Web's words, visibly relaxed. They hadn't been precisely hostile at the reception given to Du Havel by most of the ex-slaves packed into the compartment, but they had been more than a little reserved. In the case of Georg, almost openly suspicious.

Web wasn't surprised. That was a predictable political reaction, and one which had occurred innumerable times in human history. The revolutionary grunts in the political trenches, who'd suffered most of the casualties, being unceremoniously pushed aside when the self-proclaimed Big Shots arrived.

Sometimes, they were forced to accept the situation. More often than not, however, what followed sooner or later was what Web himself had referred to several times in various of his writings as the "Kerensky Fallacy." Which could be summarized in the notion that power derived from position, legitimacy from titles; or, in philosophical terms, as the political variant of the Platonic delusion that reality was the shadow of abstractions.

To the same degree as the Ballroom members relaxed, others did not. The older man named Harrell, in particular—the one who'd raised the question—was visibly disturbed.

He began to speak, in a somewhat heated tone of voice. "Simply because Jeremy X is the best-known—most notorious, rather—"

"That's beside the point," Web interrupted, forcefully. "It doesn't matter how well known Jeremy is. He could be a shadowy figure completely unknown to the public at large, and it would make no difference. What matters is the *reality.* And the reality is this: for at least two decades, it's been the Ballroom which has carried the brunt of the battle against Manpower. Disagree as much as you want with their tactics. I've often disagreed myself, and in public. So has the countess—Catherine Montaigne, I should say, since she's given up her title. So have any number of individuals and organizations prominent in the struggle against genetic slavery. That doesn't change the equation of power. No government of former Manpower slaves set up against the will of the Audubon Ballroom has any chance at all of remaining stable. *None.* You might as well ask me to make you a snowman in Hell."

Harrell was still glowering. Web pressed forward. "Nor is it simply a matter of raw power. It's also a matter of legitimacy—as *we* define that term. Whatever disagreements or reservations any slave has with the Ballroom—whether freed or still in captivity—all of them must acknowledge the Ballroom's courage and dedication. *Must* acknowledge it, even if at the same time you criticize their tactics. To do otherwise is to accept the slavemaster's limits—to accept, tacitly, the *master's* definition of what is and is not 'acceptable' and 'legitimate.' Which is nothing but a *yoke.*"

When he needed it, Web had quite a fearsome glower of his own. He used it now, stinting nothing.

"*Under no circumstances.* Not so long as I breathe. Whatever government is set up by ex-slaves *must* have the acceptance—the publicly *visible* acceptance—of the Ballroom. Not simply to reassure the Ballroom, but—perhaps even more!—to assure the universe that we will accept *no slavemaster's limits*!"

A cheer filled the compartment. No small cheer, either—nor was it by any means confined to those members of the Ballroom present. Even Harrell himself, hearing the matter put in such a manner, nodded his head.

"No limits," Web repeated, "set by anyone except ourselves. Allow an outsider to tell you what is and isn't acceptable, and you have sold your birthright."

Again, a cheer, and louder still. Web allowed it to ring through the compartment for a moment. Then, his glower faded and was replaced by his usual affable expression.

"Mind you, that doesn't mean we can afford to ignore tactics. I imagine I'll be having plenty of sharp exchanges with Jeremy once he arrives." He shrugged. "No matter. He and I have had them before, plenty of times. But that's just a family quarrel. All families have them, and get through them well enough. But woe unto the family that allows one of its members to become labeled a 'black sheep' by outsiders, and tries to obtain legitimacy by denying its own blood. 'Legitimacy' gained at such a price isn't worth it—nor will it last, in any event."

Harrell still seemed uncertain, but it was clear most of his outright hostility was gone. Fading, at least. He turned to look at Berry.

"What's your opinion, Princess?"

Berry was startled. "Mine?" She looked around, confused. "Well . . . I really don't think it's my place to tell you—any of you—what you should do."

Kathryn burst into laughter. "What *else* have you been doing, since you got here?"

Berry looked embarrassed. But Kathryn's laugh hadn't been sarcastic, as she immediately made clear with a smile. "I'm not complaining, Princess. At least half the people who've been coming to you to settle a dispute were sent over to you by us in the first place. Just to get them out of our hair, if nothing else. And the truth is . . ."

Kathryn glanced at Harrell. "The truth is, I'd like to know myself. What *is* your opinion?"

Berry gave Web a look of appeal. He understood at once that the appeal had far more to do with the girl's identity than her opinion.

Why not? It's going to have to come out sooner or later. I'd intended to wait, but . . .

He cleared his throat. "For reasons which will soon be obvious—tactical reasons—what I'm about to say is not for public consumption. By which I mean the public *outside* of the thousands of us on this ship."

He saw no reason to rub their noses in the fact that control over the *Felicia* itself—including the communication equipment—was still in the hands of Cachat and Palane, so the ex-slaves had no way of using the coms anyway. Everybody knew it, even though all the lockdowns had been ended. Many of the ex-slaves had visited the bridge, by now, and had been greeted cordially. Some of them had even begun to fraternize with the Amazons, especially after Saburo and Donald and the other Ballroom members from the space station had come over on the first sled and they saw the obviously intimate relations which they'd established with the former Scrag women.

That had been . . . a bit shocking to them, at first. But, like most oppressed subcultures in history, Manpower's genetic slaves were not given to hoity-toity fussiness about such things. Soon enough, the Amazons had moved from the category of *enemy* to that of simply *exotic.*

"The fact is," Web continued, nodding first at Berry and then at Ruth, seated next to her, "that we've been engaged in a subterfuge here. For complex reasons of state which I don't feel at liberty to discuss at the moment"—*that oughta to do it,* he thought smugly—"the woman you know as 'Princess Ruth' is actually Berry Zilwicki. And the real Ruth Winton has been passing as Berry Zilwicki."

Everyone in the compartment was now ogling the two women. Most of them looked a bit cross-eyed.

So did Berry and Ruth, for that matter.

"Oh, yes, it's quite true." Du Havel chuckled as heartily as he could manage. "It's quite confusing, really. I find it almost impossible myself to keep them straight any longer."

Ruth—bless her heart!—chimed right in. "That's because Berry really makes a much more believable princess than I do. I don't have the temperament. Really, I don't. Not at all."

Kathryn was the first to speak. To Web's relief, her tone seemed more curious than anything else. It certainly wasn't hostile.

"Berry Zilwicki. I realize now that I hadn't given that much thought. You're *Anton* Zilwicki's daughter, correct? Not his natural daughter. That's 'Helen,' as I recall. But the girl he found in the Loop? The one who'd been surviving in the underground with her little brother?"

Berry nodded. She seemed a bit pale, but otherwise composed.

"A mutt from Terra's slums, in other words." Kathryn's smile was an odd thing. *Wintry,* it might have been called—except there was no coldness in it at all. "I rather like that, now that I think about it."

Juan grunted. "Yeah, me too. Besides, it doesn't matter. Whichever is which, these are the two young women who risked their lives to give us our freedom. You can't ask for more than that, not from mutt or princess or anyone in between."

He gave the packed compartment a gaze which was something of a challenge. But, clearly enough, not a challenge which anyone was inclined to take up.

"Good enough," he said. He brought his eyes back to Berry Zilwicki and studied her a moment. "Yeah. Anton Zilwicki's daughter—Catherine Montaigne's, too—and a mutt from the warrens. And, sure as hell, no slouch herself. Good enough."

Later that night, as they relaxed in the quarters of one of the former crew which had been given over to them, Berry expressed her relief to Ruth.

"That went better than I thought."

Ruth tried not to look smug. It was difficult. "Yup."

"'Course, the real hell to pay is going to come when Daddy and your aunt find out what we've been up to."

Ruth didn't have any trouble not looking smug, now. None at all.

"We're dead," she moaned. "Dead."

"Don't be silly," Berry countered. "It's much worse than that. We'll both be confined to a cloister somewhere. You watch. Chateau d'If, I'm talking about."

"It's the modern universe!" Ruth tried to protest.

"Sure is," agreed Berry, gloomily. "Makes it even worse. Prolong will keep us alive for centuries. You watch. Chateau d'If, if we're lucky. Probably be something like Devil's Island. For *centuries.*"

PART IV: *FELICIA III*

CHAPTER 40

IT WAS A GOOD THING, Admiral Lady Dame Honor Harrington, Duchess and Steadholder Harrington, reflected, that the modern universe had abandoned the practice of blaming the messenger. Or else the captain of the courier vessel which had brought the news to Landing would have expired. Queen Elizabeth's glare alone would have been enough to immolate him on the spot. As it was, the poor man was doing his best to appear as inconspicuous as possible.

That was difficult, given that there were only eight other people in Queen Elizabeth's private chamber. None of whom were standing on the carpet in front of her. And none of whom were people whom the very junior officer would have much reason to hope would intercede on his behalf when the Queen summoned the headsman.

Two of them were the Errant Royal Daughter's parents—Michael and Judith Winton. They were glaring at the officer not much less ferociously than the Queen. The next was Ariel, the Queen's treecat, who crouched on the back of his adopted person's chair with his ears flattened and fangs half-bared as her fury flooded through their empathic link. Then there was William Alexander, whom everyone knew was the person the Queen *wanted* for her Prime Minister. His glare . . . about the same as the Queen's. Standing next to him was his older brother Hamish, the Earl of White Haven, and his treecat Samantha—and *his* glare was notorious throughout the Star Kingdom's Navy.

That left Honor herself, and, Nimitz, Samantha's mate. Neither of whom was glaring at the poor fellow, granted, but whom he also did not know personally. All he knew about Honor was the fearsome and (in her opinion) grossly over-inflated reputation the Star Kingdom's newsies had given her along with the nickname of "the Salamander." And all he knew about Nimitz was that he looked less enraged than Ariel . . . for whatever that was worth. Unless he were an expert on 'cat body language, he would never have guessed that what Nimitz actually felt was more amusement than anything else. But, then, Nimitz always had had an odd sense of humor.

All in all, however, and whatever Nimitz—or Honor—might be feeling at the moment, it was a very poor place for a mere lieutenant in command of an insignificant little courier boat to find himself. And from the taste of his emotions through the empathic sense Honor shared with Nimitz, she knew the lieutenant in question felt very much like a Sphinxian chipmunk face to face with a hexapuma.

Despite the seriousness of the occasion, Honor found herself forced to stifle a laugh. She did so by turning it into a small cough.

"Perhaps—"

That was enough to draw Elizabeth's eye. A moment later, the Queen waved her hand.

"Thank you, Lieutenant Ajax. You may leave us. Please place the record chips on the table next to you. If we have further questions, we'll summon you."

The officer did as he was told, very hastily, giving Honor a quick glance of thanks on his way out.

The moment the door closed behind him, Elizabeth's temper boiled to the surface. Not in a volcanic burst, but in a hissing, bubbling snarl.

"Which room in this entire palace has the thickest walls, no windows—or steel-barred ones—the heaviest door, and the best locks? *Real* locks, I'm talking about, not electronic ones which that—that—that—"

The glare was now fixed on her younger brother. "—that *precocious daughter* of yours could hack her way out of!"

She didn't wait for an answer. "And Zilwicki! I'll kill him! What did he think he was *doing,* flying off to Maya and leaving the two of them—those *hoydens! I wouldn't leave them alone in a sandbox!* Who in their right mind—"

Michael Winton didn't have his older sister's explosive temper, and he might no longer technically be a prince, since his nephew had officially succeeded to the position of Heir. But the present Duke of Winton-Serisburg *had* been a prince . . . and was still a Winton. So Honor wasn't surprised at all to see the Queen's rebuke serve the purpose of raising his hackles and shifting his anger from his daughter to his sister.

Not surprised, no, but very relieved. So, from what Honor could tell by a quick glance at Willie and Hamish Alexander, were they. Elizabeth's temper was often a political liability—and, if she couldn't control it, it might all too well become so again in this newest crisis. The Alexander brothers had been glaring also, true. But that was because there were far greater things at stake here than the suitable punishment for perhaps-reckless young women.

Perhaps reckless. Honor wasn't at all sure about that. She'd been accused herself of recklessness any number of times. Enough, certainly, to know it was an easy term for people to throw around . . . when they weren't the ones in the cauldron.

Winton-Serisburg's words were spoken in a tone very few of the Queen's vassals would ever have dared to use to her, and his eyes were unflinching as he glared at her. "I will remind my esteemed sister that while she is the monarch of the Star Kingdom, she is *not* Ruth Winton's parent. That happens to be—that *honor and privilege* happen to be—mine and my wife Judith's. And ours *alone.*"

Younger brother and older sister matched glare for glare. "So if there is going to be any room chosen with heavy doors and manual locks—*if*—that will be up to me and Judith. *Not you.*"

Suddenly, Elizabeth broke off the mutual glaring match. She even seemed a bit embarrassed. "Still," she said lamely.

Michael wasn't going to relent. "I will also point out to my esteemed older sister that whatever criticism she—or I myself, or Judith, or anyone—might have of my daughter's judgment, no one can question her courage. Nor that of her companion, Berry Zilwicki. Which is no small thing in this universe, Elizabeth *Winton.*"

Judith spoke up. Her eyes were moist. "Whatever else, Elizabeth, they seem to have saved the lives of several thousand people."

"Aboard a ship full of exiles," Honor took the opportunity to murmur, and smiled faintly as aunt and parents both looked at her quickly. "Seems like something of a family tradition to me," she pointed out. No one spoke for a moment, and then Winton-Serisburg chuckled and gave her an appreciative nod.

The air of tension eased still further, and Honor felt a distinct sense of relief as the emotional tempest receded. She reached up and stroked Nimitz's ears gently, and he pressed back against her palm, sharing her relief.

Then Willie Alexander cleared his throat.

"While we're looking at the bright side—such as it is, and what there is of it—I suppose I should point out that, from what little

I can tell at this distance, they've also managed to salvage something from what's obviously a disastrous situation. And by 'disastrous,' I'm *not* referring to the episode on the slave ship. I'm talking about the very real damage our relationship with Erewhon has obviously suffered."

He gave Michael and Judith an apologetic glance. "Fortunately, Ruth survived. But, to be blunt, the damage we could suffer if Erewhon opts to withdraw from the Alliance is far worse than even the killing of a Manticoran royal daughter would have been. Especially if that idiot High Ridge keeps right on screwing around until we're back at war and need every ally we can find!"

Elizabeth looked at him, then nodded curtly and drew a deep breath. Ariel flowed down from her chair back, and she folded her arms about him, her dark eyes darker than ever as she hugged him. Her anger was fading, replaced by concern and calculation, as she finally began to consider the reports brought back by the courier ship as a monarch instead of a furious aunt whose rage had stemmed far more from fear for her niece than actual analysis of the situation. Famous as her temper might be, her political acumen was equally well known, especially in foreign affairs, and as she brought that acumen to bear now the political implications and possible ramifications of those reports she'd managed to evade, however briefly, leapt out at her. They were . . .

Not good. Not good at all.

"How likely do you think that is, Willie?" asked Hamish. Of the two Alexander brothers, Willie was the recognized expert on foreign relations. Hamish was very knowledgeable himself, of course. But, like Honor, his career had been entirely in the Navy.

Willie shrugged.

"That's hard to say, Ham. The imponderable factor is that touchy Erewhonese sense of honor. That was something Allen was always very careful to treat with kid gloves," he said, referring to Allen Summervale, the assassinated Duke of Cromarty who'd been Manticore's prime minister for so long. Then he went on gloomily. "Whereas if High Ridge and his people were *deliberately* trying to provoke it, they couldn't have done a better job—or a worse one—than what they have done."

He shook his head. "That statement from Countess Fraser! Was the woman *insane*?"

Now that the Queen's anger had a different target—and a far more legitimate one—it came back in focus. Fortunately, an actual focus rather than a shriek of quasi-parental fury.

"No, 'insane' is being too charitable. She's a *coward,* Willie, like they all are. Passing the buck and shifting the blame comes as naturally to that High Ridge crowd as gorging does to a hog."

She laughed, harshly, upper lip curled in a snarl which would have done Ariel proud. One which mingled contempt for "her" ambassador with something else. Something suspiciously like naked pride. "I take it all back, Michael. And I apologize, to you and Judith, both. Say what you will about the good sense of our girls"—proudly, that last, and no suspicion about it now—"they were no cowards, that's for sure."

The Queen shook her head. "And now what do we do? Not that I suppose it matters. Any suggestion I send over to the Government will just be shrugged off. Nor do I have anyone on the spot in Erewhon I can use as a private channel. Except those—ah, how to put it delicately?—not-too-cautious girls."

Willie cleared his throat. "Actually, Elizabeth, I disagree." With a little wave of the hand: "Not about the likely response from High Ridge, of course. I have no doubt at all he'll take the same tack Fraser took on the spot. Pass the buck, shift the blame, and do everything conceivable to aggravate the Erewhonese still further. But I do disagree—have reservations, let's say—about your assessment of the rest of it."

Elizabeth cocked an eyebrow. It was an invitation to continue, not a reproof. The Queen's hot temper was never inflicted on someone for simply questioning her judgment, unless it was done in a disrespectful manner.

"The thing is that now that I've had a bit of time to digest the reports, I'm not at all sure your niece and the Zilwicki girl *were* reckless. I suspect the opposite may well prove to be true—that, faced with a very bad situation, they did exactly the best thing they could have done. Very boldly, to be sure. But 'boldness' and 'recklessness' are not the same, even if they often appear to be from a safe distance."

Honor nodded. She'd already come to the same tentative conclusion.

Elizabeth spotted the nod. "*Et tu,* Honor?" she half-chuckled.

Honor hesitated. She had far more experience gauging military situations than she did the forms of combat involved in this episode. She might have operated on the periphery of a few black ops during her career, but never one this . . . fraught with potential disaster, and she was acutely aware of her own lack of expertise.

Yet for all that, her instincts were leading her to the same conclusion Alexander had just stated.

"I think so, yes. The key thing that strikes me, taking the reports as a whole, is the role the girls are playing in the *future.* By which I mean this Congo strategy."

"I don't necessarily disagree, Honor," White Haven interjected, "but I would point out that the report also indicates that the strategy seems to have been proposed and shaped by a Havenite agent. That Cachat fellow, whoever he may be. *Both* reports, in fact, Ruth's as well as Captain Oversteegen's." He smiled crookedly and shrugged the shoulder not encumbered by a treecat. "Even though the Princess obviously did her best to minimize his role in the affair. For what you might call 'home consumption,' I suspect."

Honor matched the smile. She'd noticed that herself. If they'd had only Ruth Winton's report, without the far more dispassionate one from Oversteegen which had accompanied it, the name "Victor Cachat" would have been mentioned exactly once—and almost in passing.

"True enough, Hamish. But so what? On *that* score, I have to say I agree with Princess Ruth and Captain Oversteegen. Regardless of who first advanced the strategy—or who's playing the major role in shaping it—the strategy itself is impossible for us to oppose." She considered what she'd just said, then frowned slightly. "Actually, that's not putting it strongly enough. Under the circumstances, at least from what I can see at a distance, it sounds like a very good strategy. Taking away one of Manpower's most notorious hellholes and handing it over to their slaves for a homeland strikes me as a dandy proposition."

"I agree with Honor," Alexander said firmly. "Elizabeth—Hamish—we *can't* oppose it. Not now, for a certainty. I suppose, being completely cold-blooded, we could have tried to sabotage the scheme before it got off the ground. But it *is* off the ground. Or, rather, sailing forth soon enough in a merchant ship packed with thousands of former slaves. So do we support it, as best we can, or try to . . . try to do *what*? We can't stop it anyway. Nor, to be honest, do I even want to. As Honor said, this would be a splendid hammer stroke at those stinking slavers, if they can pull it off."

Elizabeth literally growled. The Queen hated Manpower. "Me neither. The truth is that if my so-called 'Government' was worth a damn, I'd urge them to send a task force to ride shotgun for them."

Honor sighed. That *would* be the best response Manticore could make, at this point. And the chance that Baron High Ridge would order it done . . .

Started at "Hell freezes over" and went downhill from there.

But there was no point wasting time over impossibilities. Honor's mind was made up.

"Do the best possible, then. Elizabeth, I strongly urge you to send a private message—two messages—no, three—to the people you have on the spot. Urging them—since you can't give any orders, unfortunately, except to your niece—to throw their weight behind it as best they can. If the worst happens, I think we can at least salvage the dynasty's reputation from this mess. That may not shield us from the immediate damage, but it could help us—quite a bit, in fact—at some point in the future."

The Queen was frowning. Not in disagreement, simply in puzzlement. "*Three* messages? To whom? My niece—and the Zilwicki girl, I suppose, I'm sure the two of them are thick as thieves, by now. That's one. Then—oh. You're thinking of Captain Oversteegen."

She looked at White Haven. "What's your opinion of him, Hamish?"

There was just a slight moment of hesitation. Honor smiled and Hamish, seeing the smile, smiled back. A bit ruefully.

"I'll admit the man tends to rub me the wrong way. But I'll also admit that's probably my own prejudices at work. As a naval officer . . ."

The earl twitched his head, as a man flicks off a fly. Then, spoke very firmly. "He's a brilliant ship's captain, Your Majesty—probably as good in a single-ship action as any the Manticoran Navy's ever had. Very decisive; very gutsy. And he's got moral courage, too, not just physical bravery. If the Lords of Admiralty had any sense—which they don't, under the present management—they'd already have given him a commodore's slot. Made one for him out of whole cloth, if they had to, just to push his career along. I don't have as clear a sense yet of his overall command capability. But that's not a criticism of the man, simply a recognition of reality. You can't really gauge a prospective flag officer's judgment until you try him in action. Conclusion? This is as good a time and place as any to find out. To be sure, he'll still command only a single ship. But, given the political complexity of the situation there, he'll be functioning as if he were leading an independent task force. Let's give him the reins and see how he does."

"I agree," Honor said. "Oversteegen's mannerisms can rub me the wrong way, too, but he's every bit as good in action as Hamish says, Elizabeth. And he's also demonstrated a surprisingly sensitive ear where the need to create mutual respect between the Star Kingdom and our allies are concerned. Even—or especially—Grayson, which I happen to know irritated Janacek no end. And if he can tick Janacek off that thoroughly, he can't possibly be all bad!" She smiled slightly, and Nimitz bleeked with amusement on her shoulder.

White Haven's younger brother spoke mildly. "I would remind you, Hamish—and you, too, Honor—that this is the Star Kingdom and not the Protectorship of Grayson. Which means that, unlike Benjamin Mayhew, the Queen cannot directly issue orders to a Naval unit. Not to mention that it's quite possible Oversteegen will now be relieved of his command for having overstepped his orders."

White Haven smiled thinly. "Teach your grandmother—well, ours, I suppose—how to suck eggs. In the first place, Elizabeth *could* give him a direct order if she chose to. Technically speaking, the Crown's direct line authority in the military has never been revoked, whatever the unwritten part of the Constitution says, you know."

Alexander groaned, and White Haven chuckled.

"Don't worry, Willie! I'm not proposing that we add a fresh constitutional crisis to the mix, as well. On the other hand, there's no need to, because 'suggestions' from the Queen should push things along quite nicely in this instance."

"And just how do you figure that?" his brother demanded.

"Well, unless my estimate of the situation is entirely off the mark, two things are going to happen." White Haven spoke with the confidence of a man who'd spent his own time as a Space Lord. "And one thing isn't. What is *not* going to happen is Oversteegen being relieved of command. I'm sure they're furious with him, but he's too well-connected, to begin with, and he also gives them someone to blame when everything goes to hell. So here's what *will* happen. First, the Admiralty will send Captain Oversteegen a set of orders whose murkiness would shame the thickest fog, and whose sole purpose will be to cover Janacek's ass and set Oversteegen up for the patsy. Second—especially if he receives some private words of support from the Queen—Captain Oversteegen will cheerfully interpret those orders any way he sees fit, and the hell with the consequences to his career."

The Queen clapped her hands, gaily. "Another beachcomber, is it? That was just what I told—"

She broke off, her mouth open with surprise, and stared at Honor. "Is *that* the third message you referred to? A message to Anton Zilwicki?"

Honor nodded. "Yes. Who else are you going to use as your political agent on the spot, Elizabeth? Countess Fraser? Hardly. Nor can Oversteegen serve the purpose, given the limits of his position. And while I share Willie's assessment of the judgment of your niece and the Zilwicki girl, they *are* still very young women. One of them's literally a teenager. I don't care how bright they are, a youngster is still a youngster. I've met Anton Zilwicki personally several times, you know, to discuss that information about Mesa he, ah . . . happened across on Old Earth. And the contact I've had with him, like everything else I've ever heard about the man, suggests that he's as canny as they come."

Honor started to add something more, then decided against it. There was no need to burden the Queen with just how closely she, Zilwicki, and her senior armsman Andrew LaFollet, had discussed the information Zilwicki—and Catherine Montaigne—hadn't gotten around to handing to the Crown officially, for some reason.

The Queen was back to glowering, however. "If he's so canny, why did he disappear?"

But the glower was gone by the time she finished the sentence. "Hm. Actually, now that I think about it, that *is* an interesting question. Why *did* the man hare off to Smoking Frog? Captain Oversteegen's report gave no explanation, and Ruth's version was so murky it would put High Ridge to shame."

By now, Elizabeth was actually smiling. "Hm. Hm. Well, now that I've calmed down . . . I'll make you all a bet. I've met the man, too, you know. So I think we'll eventually find he had a good reason to do so. One which probably bodes ill for someone I'd very much enjoy seeing experience some ill-boding. Whoever that may turn out to be."

The Queen looked to each of her human guests, in turn. "We're all agreed, then? I'll send private messages to the girls, Captain Oversteegen, and Anton Zilwicki. Assuring them all of my private support and my confidence in their judgment."

Five heads nodded. Judith added: "And Michael and I will want to include a private message to our daughter." Tears still glimmered behind her eyes, but her voice was clear and strong. "Telling her how much we love her—and how proud of her we are."

"Indeed," Michael chimed in, his own voice husky.

Elizabeth eyed them for a moment. "You are aware, I suppose, that such a message from you, on top of the one from me, will make it impossible to restrain her from further adventures. She'll insist on accompanying the expedition to Congo."

"Of course," Michael rasped. He reached out a hand and squeezed his wife's. "And so what? She's a *Winton,* Elizabeth, doing her service. If she were regular Navy, she'd be getting ready for her middie cruise by now, so how is this any different? And after all these centuries, I see absolutely no reason why we should suddenly begin shielding the scions of our dynasty from the risks of such duty."

There was no answer, beyond a nod.

A few minutes later, the audience broke up. The Queen asked the Alexander brothers to remain behind, to discuss the newsfaxes' latest reports of the Pritchart Administration's increasingly harsh rhetoric, and Honor found herself walking down the corridor, Nimitz on her shoulder, with Michael and Judith Winton.

She could taste their deep concern, and she tried to think of something reassuring to say to the parents of a twenty-three-year-old woman who had been—and would be soon again going into—harm's way. Alas, she could think of nothing. Honor had been in harm's way herself far too often to have any illusions. Royal blood meant precious little, matched against the vagaries of fate and chance.

But she was spared the necessity of scraping up some ridiculous platitude. As it turned out, Michael had a purpose of his own in choosing to walk with her.

"There is one thing, Admiral Harrington," he said, with unusual formality, "which I will ask you to remember in the years ahead. In case my daughter does not survive."

He stopped, and Honor faced him squarely. "Yes, Your Grace?" she asked with matching formality,

Michael's voice was hard and low. "My sister, as much as I love and respect her, is not entirely rational on the subject of the Republic of Haven." He held up a hand. "Don't say anything, Honor. I don't expect you to agree with me—certainly not to say so aloud. But I'll tell you that it's true. And the day may come when the damage that irrationality will do to our people needs to be contained, as best as possible."

Honor didn't know what to say. *How* to say it to the Queen's brother, rather. But she understood what Michael was saying. Had understood it for some time now.

She decided a nod was enough. It could be a nod of agreement—or simply one which acknowledged that the duke had spoken.

Michael smiled thinly. "You've gotten *so* much better at diplomacy, Honor. Have I mentioned that to you lately?"

Thin to begin with, the smile faded almost at once. "Just remember this, Admiral. If and when that day ever comes, the existence of a neutral planet where Manticore and Haven have been able to maintain informal liaisons may save a lot of lives. Even if creating such a planet came at the cost of our daughter's life."

Honor heard Judith inhale sharply as her husband said the words. Not in surprise, or even disagreement, Honor knew. The woman who'd led an entire shipload of women to escape their hellish existence on Masada when she was younger than her daughter was now would never flinch from confronting such a bitter prospect. But that didn't mean she was able to blind herself to the very real risks that daughter had already run . . . or the ones yet to come.

"I understand, Your Grace." Honor said quietly, meeting Winton-Serisburg's eyes levelly and speaking in the tone of someone swearing a formal oath. Which she was, she realized. "And I won't forget."

Michael nodded. Then, he and Judith turned and walked away, holding hands, leaving Honor standing alone with Nimitz.

It was all she could do, as she watched them leave, not to call out some stupid, idiotic reassurance.

I'm sure she'll be fine! Honestly!

But, she managed to retain her dignity and theirs. Seconds later, the royal couple rounded a bend and were gone from sight. Honor took a deep breath and let it out.

"Oh, sure," she muttered. " 'She'll be fine.' Maybe—and maybe not. A pulser dart is no respecter of persons."

Nimitz made a soft sound on her shoulder, and she looked at him. His grass-green eyes were dark with shared memory of the hard lessons which had taught them both that bitter fact. But she tasted his support and love . . . and his acceptance of the harsh truth that sometimes one had no choice but to surrender hostages to fortune. It came with the responsibility not to stand cravenly by, like a High Ridge or a Fraser, and do nothing in hopes that the blame for whatever disaster ensued fell elsewhere.

She shook her head and resumed walking. Striding, rather, because she had a lot of work to finish in a very short time. Her task force was scheduled to leave orbit for Sidemore in three days, and there were always a million details to crowd a departure date. Especially under the Janacek Admiralty.

Honor would be long gone from Manticore by the time the next reports came back from Erewhon, and there was nothing further she could do about that situation anyway. So she put it out of her mind, after taking a brief moment for a private salutation.

Here's to you, Ruth Winton. And you too, Berry Zilwicki. I hope you both make it. But if you don't . . . the universe needs princesses, too. Real ones, even if they die in the making.

CHAPTER 41

ANTON ZILWICKI ARRIVED AT THE *FELICIA* with no fanfare or advance notice of any kind. That was the way he would have wanted it, anyway. But the real reason for the secrecy was the man sitting next to him on the sled which carried them over from *The Wages of Sin.*

It might be better to say: strapped in, and very securely, rather than simply "sitting." Anton, from his years as a yard dog in the Manticoran Navy, was qualified High Expert with virtually every kind of vacuum gear, from skinsuits to self-contained, modular hardsuit yard craft. All of which meant that he was quite comfortable and at ease.

Jeremy X wasn't. The galaxy's most notorious terrorist—or "freedom fighter," take your pick—might very well also be the galaxy's best pistolero. But what he knew about extravehicular activity in a spacesuit could be inscribed on the head of a pin.

That would have been true under any circumstances. Under these, riding in a stripped down, pure reaction-drive yard sled chosen primarily because it was so tiny—and unsophisticated—as to be undetectable by any except very good military grade sensors at very close range, he was visibly nervous. Given that Jeremy generally had the proverbial "nerves of steel," Anton found the whole thing rather amusing.

"Where did they find this piece of crap?" Anton heard him mutter. "A toy store?"

Anton grinned, secure in the knowledge that Jeremy wouldn't be able to see the expression since he was sitting behind him. Jeremy would be peeved, if he did. As it was, he was going to be peeved enough when he discovered that Anton had overheard the remark. Jeremy's lack of expertise when it came to EVA also extended to his lack of expertise with space communication gear. Apparently, the head of the Ballroom had failed to grasp the fact that although their coms had been stepped down to levels which precluded long-range communication—for security reasons—that didn't mean they'd been taken totally off-line. Since safety concerns made it far better for the passengers of the sled to be able to communicate with each other in an emergency, they'd retained their short-range capability.

"As a matter of fact," he said, slandering the standard yard sled with cheery mendacity for his passenger's benefit, "I believe a lot of these jury-rigged sleds of the casino's *were* put together from stuff found in the space station's toy stores. The framework itself looks like plumbing supplies to me—non-metallic, of course—but the seats and handlebars are taken from children's tricycles. I'm quite sure of it."

He glanced down at the dinky little handlebar upon which the gloved fingers of his right hand rested lightly. It really *did* look like something from a kid's bike which had been glued, solely as an afterthought, to the flimsy-looking (but incredibly light and strong) composite tubing which made up the main shell of the sled. "In fact," he added, "this looks a lot like the kid's model—the VacuGlide, I think they called it—I bought for Helen, oh, maybe fourteen years ago."

He heard what sounded like a choking noise coming from Jeremy. Anton's grin widened and he proceeded on with great cheer. "Oh, yes. No reason to use anything heftier, of course. If we were in a gravity field or under any kind of real acceleration, it'd be different. But in the here and now, the principal concern is to have sleds which can transport people back and forth without being detected. In order to keep this masquerade going, of course. It'd be hard to convince the galaxy my daughter—sorry, 'the Princess'—was still in dire captivity if it became known that the *Felicia* had as much traffic coming and going as a small spaceport."

With very great cheer: "Oh, yes, it all makes perfect sense. Nice to see somebody's thinking clearly for a change. Of course, I admit it makes for flimsy transportation." He glanced back at the rear of the sled. "Propulsion, ha! That gadget back there is just an aerosol can with delusions of grandeur. Don't want anything big or powerful enough to push our radar signature too high, now do we?"

Anton could see the Manticoran rating from the *Gauntlet* who was serving as the sled's pilot sitting ahead of both of them, at the very front of the sled. The woman's shoulders were shaking a little, from suppressed laughter at the breezy mendaciousness of Anton's remarks.

Jeremy's helmet swiveled, to bring his face toward Anton's. The motion was a very gingerly one, as if he were afraid even a head movement might fling him off the sled.

"I am *not* amused, Captain Zilwicki."

"My, what a majestic pronouncement—although I think that's supposed to be 'we are not amused.' The royal plural, you know." Anton clucked. "Surprising, really, coming from such a rabid egalitarian."

Jeremy started to make a testy response. But Anton could now see his face through the turned helmet, and saw the man bite it off. Then, his usual puckish humor returned.

"I won't argue the point, given the role your daughter is playing in this mad affair. But I'll be interested to see if you retain your good humor when the holovids go berserk. Which they will, you know, once the news gets out. Ah, yes. *Captain Zilwicki, Rogue of the Spaceways.* I can see it now, splattered all over every display screen within five hundred light-years. A month from now—two, at the outside—your face will be the best known in the inhabited galaxy." Jeremy was almost cooing, now: "*Do* try to smile into the recorders, Captain."

Anton scowled. And reminded himself, not for the first time, that needling Jeremy X was a risky proposition. The man's tongue was as quick and accurate as his gunhand.

They were almost at the *Felicia* by then, however, and Anton set aside his gloomy prognostications concerning the future prospects for his much-cherished anonymity. His only thoughts now were for his daughter.

He'd been furious with her, at first, when Jeremy X and his comrade Donald brought him the news on Smoking Frog. All of Anton's smug self-satisfaction at the successful conclusion of his little expedition had vanished instantly. (Oh, yes, it had been quite successful. For about the hundredth time since, Anton contemplated with great pleasure the prospect of ruining Georgia Young with the information about her he'd uncovered on Smoking Frog. More precisely—destroying her completely, as a political factor in the Star Kingdom.)

But the anger hadn't lasted long. Before Donald X, who'd brought the news on the courier ship, had gotten halfway through his explanation, Anton had realized the truth. Yes, granted, he could still chide his daughter for the minor recklessness of going to *The*

Wages of Sin in the first place. But Anton knew perfectly well that a maniac like Templeton would simply have struck elsewhere. If there was anyone to blame, it was Anton himself, not Berry. *He* was supposed to be the superspy, not her. Which meant *he* should have been the one to discover that the Masadans were lurking on Erewhon—in which case, he never would have made the trip to Maya Sector in the first place.

But all of that was hindsight, and Anton Zilwicki had never been a man given to pointless recriminations. Not even pointless self-blame, much less shifting the blame elsewhere. What mattered—*all* that mattered—was the courage and determination his daughter had displayed thereafter. Which had been great enough that even such hard-bitten revolutionists as Jeremy and Donald had clearly been in something approaching a state of awe.

So was Anton himself, for that matter. It was obvious to him that the waif he had rescued years earlier on Terra was . . .

Hard to say, what she was now. But certainly no longer a waif.

"Welcome," the ex-slave in charge of the docking bay said as Anton and Jeremy swung out of the boarding tube and into *Felicia*'s internal gravity field. She motioned toward another ex-slave, standing nearby and smiling. "Eduard will take you to the Princess. I assume that's who you'd like to see first, Captain Zilwicki."

One of the things Anton had been told was that the ex-slaves on the *Felicia* had been made aware of the true identity of the two girls. He finished removing his helmet and shook his head. "No, actually. I'd like to see my daughter first."

Both ex-slaves seemed confused. "Yes, of course," said the one named Eduard. "That's why I'm taking you to her. The Princess."

Then, understanding, Eduard chuckled. "Oh, I see. A mismatch of perceptions, here. By 'Princess,' you refer to the real one. As the galaxy sees such things. But you're among us now, Captain, and we have our own attitudes. Please follow me. Berry doesn't know you've arrived, so she'll still be in the audience chamber."

Anton followed, shaking his head. *Princess. Audience chamber.* He was trying to sort it all out.

Following right behind him, he heard Jeremy chortle. "Remember, Captain! Remain of good cheer! Ah, yes. I can see it now. All over the holovids. *Captain Zilwicki, Scourge of the Spaceways—and now! Introducing his daughter! Princess Berry, She Who Makes Slavers Howl!* Do try to make sure she wears modest apparel, though. I've always found those scantily-clad sword-wielding princesses of the fantasies rather gauche. Don't you?"

The so-called "audience chamber" appeared to have been, at one time, a large mess compartment. But after entering it, and observing for a few seconds, Anton understood the peculiar terminology.

Berry was seated on a chair not far from one of the walls. She was surrounded by people, some of them sitting on chairs, others standing, and was engaged in some sort of convivial conversation with all of them. Anton couldn't hear the words, but he didn't need to. He'd known Berry for years, and had met few if any people in his life who could converse so easily and comfortably. Part banter, part friendliness, part advice, part comfort—and, most of all, the girl's superb capacity for *listening.* Talking with Berry was a genuine pleasure.

As for the rest . . .

Yes, he could see it now. As an "audience," it bore no resemblance to any royal audience you'd have found anywhere else in the galaxy. Leaving aside the fact that Berry's chair was neither elevated nor any larger or fancier than any other, she was comporting herself far too casually and unpretentiously. But he had no difficulty—none at all—understanding how completely the ex-slaves would have taken her into their hearts, in the two weeks since she'd arrived on the *Felicia* and rescued them.

Anton didn't have Web Du Havel's encyclopedic knowledge of history, but he knew more than enough to recognize the pattern. This wouldn't be the first time that a scorned and despised people, finding a glamorous champion, adopted him—or her—for their own. If Berry wasn't actually a princess, she was close enough. Close enough, after all, to consort with princesses and pass for one—not to mention being the adopted child of Anton Zilwicki and Catherine Montaigne. Cathy had given up the Tor title, true, but that would be irrelevant to the ex-slaves. For them, she was and would always remain *the Countess*—the wealthy, powerful aristocrat who had made their cause her own. Who'd committed herself to the liberation of the most despised, abused, *forgotten* victims of the galaxy not because she'd had to, but because she'd *chosen* to. And who'd given those same victims, and the "terrorists" who fought for them, her unstinting support for so long and so fiercely, even at the cost of exile and the voluntary renunciation of her title when it got in the way of her work. Her adopted daughter would have basked in that stature alone, among these people, even if she hadn't played a central role in their rescue. Combine the two . . .

Then, he caught sight of Web Du Havel, sitting a bit aside from the conversation. Web was not participating, simply watching. And he had a very smug smile on his face.

In that lightning way that everything could suddenly make sense to Anton, after he'd chewed on it for a while, he understood what Du Havel was scheming for. He even remembered Du Havel once using a term to describe the strategy. *The Bernadotte Option,* he'd called it.

"I'll kill him," he growled. "W.E.B. Du Havel, you are lunch. No. Dog food. No. I wouldn't feed a dog—"

Jeremy was standing next to him, by then. He frowned slightly. "Why the sudden animosity, Captain? I'd have thought Professor Du Havel far more congenial to you than I am—and you've never threatened to make *me* the main course for dinner."

Anton set his jaw and glanced at Jeremy. Then, managed a chuckle.

Brace yourself, Jeremy. You're in for a shock.

Du Havel didn't waste any time. Two hours later, as the ship's wild celebration over the arrival of the famous Jeremy X and the almost equally famous Captain Zilwicki was well underway, Du Havel drew the two of them aside.

"We need to talk. Now. Come to the necessary agreements while everyone's good will is at a peak."

Jeremy nodded. "Agreed, Professor. Your compartment?"

Du Havel shook his head. "No, I think the compartment of the two princesses would be best. And with both of them present."

Jeremy cocked a quizzical eyebrow. Then, shrugged. "I've no problem with that. What I've got to say in private will be no different from what I'll say in public."

It took a few minutes to round up Berry and Ruth and retire to their compartment. Then, with everyone seated except Jeremy, who remained standing, the leader of the Ballroom opened the discussion. The negotiations, to use the proper term.

"Whatever you and I decide here, Professor Du Havel, it'll all have to be ratified by a popular vote after the liberation. That goes without saying. But I don't foresee any problems so long as you and I can reach agreement. So I'll begin by laying down my first two conditions.

"One. You will be the first head of state of our new star nation.

You're the only one who could give us the necessary interstellar legitimacy. I'm the only other one with sufficient authority among our people, and I'm simply too notorious. For the moment, let's call it the presidency.

"Two. There will be no restrictions whatsoever on the movement or actions of the Audubon Ballroom. I'm willing to discuss tactics with you—and I'll abide by any agreement—but there will be no presumed limits. Not one."

Web nodded his head. "I've no problem with the second provision, Jeremy, provided you accept one of my own. *You* will accept a position in my Cabinet. Specifically, as Secretary of War. And that's exactly what I insist the position be titled. No stupid nonsense about a 'Secretary of Defense.' We're at war with Manpower and Mesa, we'll make no pretense otherwise—and I can think of no better way to make that clear than for you to hold the position."

Jeremy smiled thinly. "You're such an *odd* sort of 'conservative,' Professor, if you'll pardon me saying so."

"I'm not a 'conservative' at all," Web countered, "as most people understand the term. Except in the broadest sense—which goes all the way back to Edmund Burke—of recognizing that societies are analogous to organisms, not machines. And that you must therefore understand that changing laws and customs is equivalent to medicine—or, sometimes, surgery—and isn't so simple a matter as swapping parts in a motor." His normally pleasant face was almost tight with anger. "That does *not* prevent me from undertaking surgery, when surgery is needed."

Jeremy studied him for a moment. "You're a shrewd one, too. Which, in itself, is fine with me. You're assuming that if I become Secretary of War I'll have to forego my previous tactics."

"I don't 'assume' it, Jeremy. I'll *insist* on it." He began talking a bit faster, trying to head off a collision. "I make no condemnation of what you've done in the past. I never have—not publicly, at least—and I won't do so here in private. But I will tell you that it *must* change. Whether or not the tactics of individual killings and other such dramatic gestures is effective for an outlaw group can be argued till the heat death of the universe. But it's completely ineffective as a tactic used by an independent star nation. Worse than ineffective. The reasons are—"

Jeremy waved his hand. "Skip the lecture, Professor. I won't argue the point, since I agree with you anyway. About the future, if not the past." His jaws tightened a moment. "So long, that is, as you understand that I *will* be waging war. I'm not quite sure how yet—

yes, yes, I'll give up the pleasure of shooting the occasional swine—but I *will* do it. War to the knife, until genetic slavery is erased from the universe."

Du Havel leaned back in his chair, smiled widely, and gestured to the empty chair next to him. "By all means, Mr. Secretary of War. Your Pres—ah, head of government, will give you his full support. You have my promise on that. I'll be more precise. There will be nothing 'covert' about *this* war. I propose to make the first act of the new government of the new star nation a formal and official declaration of war against the planet of Mesa. To hell with restricting it to an informal struggle against Manpower Unlimited. The entire planet of Mesa is our mortal enemy—and let's name them so before the entire human race."

Jeremy grinned, very savagely. Then, strode over, shook Du Havel's hand, and flung himself into the empty chair with an acrobat's ease. "Splendid! Professor Du Havel, I believe this is the beginning of a long friendship."

Now that he was returning to his usual impish self, Jeremy's thought processes were also returning to their normal quicksilver pattern. "But what's this hemming and hawing about the 'presidency' business? Surely you're not going to go all modest on me?"

Du Havel cleared his throat, and gave Anton a nervous glance. "As it happens, I'd much prefer the title of 'Prime Minister.' And I'd prefer to think of myself as the 'head of government' rather than the 'head of state.' My reasoning is as follows—"

He paused, glancing quickly at Ruth. She returned it with what was obviously an expression of support—an expression which bordered on being conspiratorial, in fact.

So, thought Anton. *She's in on it, too. The treacherous lass. Sharp as a serpent's tooth is the ingratitude of children.*

Anton looked at Berry. There was no expression on his daughter's face beyond simple interest in the discussion. Clearly enough, Berry herself had no idea at all what Du Havel was scheming for.

In the next few minutes, Du Havel explained. Long before he was done, Berry's mouth was wide open with stunned surprise.

Anton had that much in the way of satisfaction. At least his own daughter wasn't trying to manipulate him.

Jeremy, clearly, was almost as shocked as Berry. It was the only time Anton had ever seen the man at a loss for words.

Which, alas, meant it was time for Anton to speak. He took a deep breath, and bade a sad farewell to the pleasures of fatherhood. Then spoke, in as even a tone of voice as he could manage.

"It's entirely your decision, Berry. For whatever my advice is worth, here it is. First, it will often be very hard on you. It will certainly be dangerous, and—" His deep voice grew even huskier. "And there's a good chance it will kill you. Possibly at a very early age."

Hearing her father speak had cut through Berry's sheer paralysis. Her mouth finally closed. "What's the second thing?"

"The second thing is that Professor Du Havel's right. On both counts. It's a hell of a good idea—and, like him, I can't think of anybody who'd be better than you."

With some difficulty, he managed to restrain himself from saying the next sentence. *But it's the last thing in the world I want you to do!*

Jeremy was staring at him. "You're daft! Well, I suppose I should expect that, coming from you. A Crown Loyalist. Idiots." He turned the stare on Du Havel. "But from *you*—"

Web smiled. "I'm not a Crown Loyalist, Jeremy. Nor, by the way, do I think that label fits Captain Zilwicki all that well, either. Not today, at any rate. But that's because 'crown loyalism' makes a fetish out of the matter. Hereditary monarchies have advantages and disadvantages—and, taking history as a whole, the disadvantages usually outweigh the rest. By quite a margin, actually. But it's just as much of an error to make a fetish out of republicanism, too. There *are* times and places where an hereditary monarchy's advantages come to the fore. And this is one of them."

Jeremy started to argue, but Ruth Winton interrupted.

"He's right, Mr. X—uh—"

Jeremy winced. "'Mister X' is ludicrous. The name is Jeremy, if you please."

Ruth gave him her nervous smile. "Okay, then. Please call me Ruth. I don't much like formalities, either." In a rush: "But that's not surprising, since you and I are much alike. Oh, yes, we are! Not every way, of course. I can't shoot worth a damn and I can't imagine being as ruthless as you are. Well, maybe. Sometimes. But, still—"

She, too, seemed at a loss for words. Which, for Ruth as for Jeremy, was a most unusual state of affairs.

It didn't last long, naturally. "What I mean is that we're both sort of, well, compulsive. High-strung. Nervous. Very capable, too—sorry, I'm no good at false modesty, either. But the thing is . . ."

The next words came almost in a wail. "She'll calm you down, Jeremy! She *will.* That's why I like being around Berry so much.

Well, one of the reasons. She's good for me. Kind of like, I don't know—those rods they use in old-style fission power plants, to keep the chain reaction from getting out of control."

Du Havel chimed in. "As it happens, Jeremy, that's quite a good analogy—and one which I could show you in the mathematics of political dynamics." Before Jeremy's look of suspicion could congeal, Web waved his hand. "But the analogy may be even better. Truth is—don't ever tell my colleagues I said this—those fancy equations aren't what they're cracked up to be. Politics is still more of an art than a science, don't let anybody tell you otherwise."

Jeremy, clearly, was still not convinced. Du Havel tried a different tack.

"I'll predict the following, Jeremy. Initially, our new government will be a marvelous 'government of national unity.' That will last not more than a few years. Soon enough—it always happens—our new nation will become politically factionalized. And that will be the most dangerous moment. Period, rather. Those years after the factions form, but before we've had time to develop our own customs for keeping factionalism harnessed and under control. Berry Zilwicki—Queen Berry, of the House of Zilwicki—will buy us that time. She'll be our anchor—or stabilizer—when we need it most."

Web ran fingers through his hair, and glanced back and forth between Berry and Jeremy.

"Let me put it this way, Jeremy. The day will come—I'm certain of it—when our current accord collapses. You and I will then be in political opposition, and perhaps quite sharp opposition. At some point in the course of that, the day will come—I'm sure of it, again—when you'll begin considering the use of armed violence to resolve the dispute. Or, if you don't, some of your supporters will urge it upon you. The same dynamic will be at work within my camp, of course. But for reasons which are blindingly obvious to both of us, it will always be your camp which controls the balance of sheer force." With a wry smile: "I'll have most of the old farts and the professors, and you'll have the experienced fighters and the young firebrands."

Jeremy chuckled and nodded his head. "Go on."

"Easy enough, really, to ponder my overthrow—or suppression, if you happen to be holding the reins of government at the time instead of me. By then, I'll be a tiresome old fart to you myself. Someone who'd look damn good with a pulser dart in the head."

Quite dramatically, Web pointed a finger at Berry. "But how easy will it be for you to ponder killing *her*?"

"And consider the risks," growled Anton. He was looking at Jeremy through eyes which were almost slitted. "You're not the only one in the galaxy who knows how to organize an assassination."

He was expecting to see Jeremy match that look of menace with one of his own. That same flat-eyed, deadly stare Jeremy had once bestowed upon him on Terra. But, not for the first time, Jeremy surprised him.

True enough, the head of the Audubon Ballroom was perhaps the galaxy's most cold-blooded killer. But he'd been bred and raised by Manpower to be something of a court jester—and, in this if nothing else, Manpower's plans had not gone awry.

Jeremy's eyes widened, his mouth made a perfect "O" of shock and surprise. Then, springing out of his seat, he flung himself on one knee before Berry. One hand outstretched to the girl, as if pleading for mercy, the other waving about dramatically.

"Your Majesty! Pay no attention to these foul calumnies! My accuser is a professor, an academic, a pedant and a scholar—which is to say, a scoundrel and a rogue! 'Tis all lies and traducement! I swear it on my sacred honor!"

Berry burst out laughing. So, a moment later, did everyone else.

Jeremy rose lithely, grinning. But he wasn't finished yet. He was in full court jester mode now, and—Anton had seen it before—managed the affair not only with panache but that odd combination of drollery and insight which was his hallmark.

"All right, Professor. I'll agree to it. But—but!" He capered about gleefully. "Oh, yes—but! I'll have no half measures here! I won't stand for it! If there's to be a crown of slaves, then a slave's crown I insist it be! Which is to say—shiftless, goes without saying, but also cunning. I demand a queen who can pilfer the pantry with the best of 'em!"

For a moment, he stooped and gave Berry a narrow-eyed examination which was half-glower, half-assessment. Then he rose, seeming satisfied with what he saw.

"She starts well, mind. Oh, very well indeed. A scamp from the Terran warrens, scurrying like a mouse through the underground. A good sign, that—and I shall have to insist that a rodent be included in the House crest."

"Done!" cried Berry, clapping her hands. "But it's got to be a cute little mouse. No nasty big rats. I hate rats—and I speak from experience."

"By all means. A mouse it is." Jeremy now managed the feat of stroking his genetically determined hairless face as if he were an elder stroking a wise beard. "So much for cunning. We also need caprice. Hm . . . I have it!"

This time, it was Du Havel who was the recipient of Jeremy's glower. "I'm afraid I shall have to insist that the Queen retain some whimsical powers, Professor. Your equations be damned! I'll have no prissy constitutional monarchy for slaves! Damn me before I'll agree! I want a crown with some teeth!"

Before Du Havel could argue the point, Jeremy waved his hand. The gesture was histrionic, of course. "No, no, nothing preposterous. Ruling queens are usually a dull lot, after all. Tsarinas, even worse. Far better to leave government in the hands of politicians, who can at least entertain the populace with their knaveries. But I shall insist that the Queen has the right to have one person a year executed at her whimsy, just to keep the politicians unsettled. One every T-year, mind you, no slouching—I understand Congo's years are almost three T-years in duration."

Berry grimaced. Jeremy eyed her, still stroking his non-existent bead, and shrugged regretfully.

"Well, I suppose not. Alas, a tender-hearted queen. Pity. Catherine the Great was so much more colorful. Very well, then—a compromise! The queen gets to *banish* one person a year from the kingdom! No debates, no argument, no appeal. Out you go, lout! You've irked Her Majesty! Or—worse!—you've bored her."

Berry chuckled. So did Web. "Be careful, Jeremy," he cautioned. "She might banish *you*, you know."

"I'll take my chances," replied Jeremy smugly. "A sprightly young lass? Far more likely she'd banish a tiresome old fart of a professor who kept telling her 'don't do this, don't do that.' Whereas *I* am a lively, droll sort of fellow."

Du Havel looked a bit startled. Anton laughed. "He's got a point, Web. And what else, Jeremy?"

The Ballroom's leader continued that ridiculous "beard" stroking. "Well . . . there's the matter of an armed force responsible to the crown, of course. I think that'd be a good idea. Something in the way of a Praetorian Guard to serve as a counterbalance to us bloodthirsty Ballroom types. We'll have to form the core of the new army, of course."

Web frowned, pondering the pros and cons of that idea. But before he could reach any conclusion, Berry settled the matter.

"No," she said. "Under no conditions. Absolutely not."

She turned to Anton. "Tell me true, father."

"I'll miss you," he said, almost choking on the words. "More than I can tell you. Although . . ."

Anton was still catching up with things, and a new thought suddenly came to him. "Maybe not as much as we think. It occurs to me that an independent star nation of ex-slaves would make the ideal headquarters—central location, at the very least—for the Anti-Slavery League. Of which—" He made a modest cough. "—I think it's fair to say I'm the organizer of the muscle. So I might be seeing you quite often, now that I think about it."

That thought obviously cheered Berry up as much as it did him. Anton chewed on it a bit longer.

"Do it, girl, if you've a mind. You're an adult now, so far as I'm concerned, so the decision is entirely yours. But, leaving aside everything else . . ."

The conclusion, so hard to make, flowed through him easily and naturally once made. "You'd be awfully good at it, Berry, you really would. And I think you'd enjoy your life. However long it lasted."

She thought about it, for a moment, in that simple, translucent way she had about her. Then, nodded.

"Okay. That makes sense to me. But—"

She gave Jeremy the same look which she had so often bestowed upon Anton, over the years. Simple, translucent—sanity in springtime, he often thought it.

"I'll neither reign nor rule—to whatever extent, that last—except on two conditions."

"Name them," stated Jeremy.

"First, it has to be voted on by the people, and approved by them. I won't be foisted on them by a clique, no matter how prestigious."

"Done." Jeremy glanced at Du Havel, who nodded. "And the second?"

"I'll have no bodyguards. Not even one, much less a whole damn Praetorian Guard."

Both Jeremy and Du Havel winced. So did Anton. Ruth, on the other hand, nodded.

"None of you are thinking right," Berry said firmly. "The only point to this—only point at all, so far as I can see—is to give a new people a chance. *My* new people. And, that being so, let them also understand that their new Queen will place her safety in their hands alone. I haven't had a bodyguard since I came aboard this ship. Why should I start now? I'll share their life—perils and triumphs both—and move among them freely with no shield between me and them." She shrugged. "If that leads to my death at someone's hand, so be it. It's one life, measured against building a nation's hope and self-confidence. No contest, the way I look at things."

Before Jeremy or Web—or Anton—could say anything, Berry shook her head. "That's how it is. I'll insist on that. If you don't agree, fine. But find yourself another monarch, because it won't be me."

The words were spoken in Berry's normal tone of voice. Easily, almost gently—but with all the solidity and sureness of a continent moving across an ocean floor.

Oh, my, thought Anton. *If she lives long enough . . . these fine gentlemen are in for some surprises, I think.*

Not Web, perhaps. "Illusion becomes truth," Anton heard him murmur. "So does true custom arise." Then, more loudly: "Very well, Your Majesty. I won't argue the point."

Jeremy hesitated no more than a second longer. "Me, neither. You're quite insane, of course. But I find the idea of Mad Queen Berry rather charming, now that I think about it."

Web smiled. "That leaves, however, the problem of the armed forces. Not to put too fine a point on it, Berry—uh, Your Majesty—"

"Keep it 'Berry,' if you would. I foresee that I'll also be establishing probably the most informal customs of any monarchy in history. Which suits me just fine. I wouldn't know one end of proper royal protocol from the other, anyway."

"Berry, then. As I was saying, that still leaves the problem of the armed forces. Whether he intended it that way or not, Jeremy's proposal of a Praetorian Guard does have the advantage of giving us a certain balance of power in the new nation. Which is important in all things, but especially so with the armed forces." He cleared his throat. "Meaning no offense, but I have to speak bluntly here. I am not happy at the thought of the Ballroom having an effective monopoly over control of the military. Which, between Jeremy being Secretary of War and some other Ballroom member being head of the military—there's no one else with the experience—is what we'd wind up with. That's not a statement of suspicion toward the Ballroom, on my part. It's just a cold-blooded and objective assessment of a political problem."

Anton saw Berry and Ruth exchange a glance; accompanied, a moment later, by two rather self-satisfied looking smiles. He didn't understand the glance, or the smiles. But knowing both of them, he was sure a scheme had just been hatched.

He thought about it, for a moment. And then decided that he'd stay out of it. All things considered—given those two young women—it would probably be a pretty good scheme.

"I propose that we defer that issue for the moment," said Berry, almost brightly. "Let me think about it, for a bit. Since I'm apparently going to be the new Queen, I ought to do *something* useful for a living. I've gotten to know quite a few people over the past few weeks. Maybe I can think of someone."

Jeremy and Du Havel gave her a look which bordered on suspicion.

"Please," she said, in that winsome voice with which, over the years, Berry had managed to cajole damn near anything she wanted out of Anton.

He watched the future head of government and his bloodthirsty secretary of war cave in just as fast. And tried—it was *so* hard—not to smirk.

Try to use MY girl as your tool, will you? Good luck, you chumps.

CHAPTER 42

THANDI PALANE STARED AT THE TWO young women perched on the bed in the crew compartment Thandi and Victor had taken for their own. Berry and Ruth were trying to maintain, as best they could, an air of casual relaxation. Almost nonchalance, as if they advanced such proposals every day of the week.

They weren't pulling it off, though. Not even close. Both of them—especially Berry—were obviously tense.

"You're nuts," Thandi pronounced. "Let me explain some realities to you. I'm a *lieutenant.* Okay, a first lieutenant with as much experience as you'll find anywhere. But I still have neither the training nor the experience to do what you're asking of me. I'd probably blow it, and . . ."

The words trailed off, as Thandi fought down a surge of anger. *Not that I don't think I* could *do it—if those snotty bastards who run the SLN had ever given me the opportunities they give their pets. Until Captain Rozsak came along, anyway.*

She shook it off. Her resentments at the class elitism of the Solarian League were neither here nor there, as far as the immediate issue at hand was concerned. Facts were facts, whether they should be or not.

"I'm not what you need, Berry. It's as simple as that."

Berry looked distressed—very—and looked away. Thandi saw tears coming to her eyes, and felt a sudden and profound pang of guilt. The kind of sharp pain that a big sister feels when she realizes she's let down her little sister.

Ruth, on the other hand, seemed to perk up. However close she and Berry had become, the two had very different temperaments. Berry was essentially a problem-resolver; Ruth, a woman who loved a challenge. Put both of them in front of a cliff, and Berry would start trying to find a way around it—while Ruth would start scrutinizing the face, looking for handholds.

"You're quite mistaken, Lieutenant Palane. You're *exactly* what Berry needs. Queen Berry, founder of the House of Zilwicki, monarch of a small, newly created nation, I should say—because that's the concrete situation we're dealing with. And that's what you're overlooking."

Thandi started to argue, but broke off. "Explain," she said curtly.

"Nobody's proposing that you suddenly become elevated to lead the armed forces of a major star nation in the middle of a war, Lieutenant. Yes, that would be insane, even if you were the reincarnation of Napoleon or Alexander the Great. Although I *will* point out that both men were very young when they arose as great commanders." She held up a hand, forestalling Thandi's response. "But, yes, even at the start of their careers of conquest, neither of them had been restricted to the training and experience of a small unit commander. So what?"

Ruth couldn't contain her energy any longer. She rose and began pacing. It was a bit comical, given that the compartment was small and her paces were energetic. She reminded Thandi of a pensive hamster in a cage, scuttling back and forth as she tried to cohere her thoughts.

"Look, Lieutenant. It's obvious that the foreign policy of Berry's new nation is going to be simple, when it comes to war. Congo—whatever name they pick for it—will be scrupulously neutral toward everybody except Mesa. So, as commander of the armed forces, your task will *not* be that of leading large forces in a sprawling multi-sided war. Your task will be quite different. First, preparing and then leading a war against a planet of scumbags and adventurers—"

Thandi laughed. It was something of a caw. "Will I now? Don't you think Jeremy X will have something to say about that?"

Ruth shook her head, very firmly. Still pacing—scuttling, rather. "Of course he will. So what? *He'll* he perched to the side, as Secretary of War. Your immediate boss, sure—but *not* part of the military. Besides, Jeremy strikes me as a man who cares about results a lot more than he does the perks and petty privileges of being a big shot. Do you really think he'll meddle that much—especially after you start handing him some Mesan heads on a platter?" She paused in her pacing. "Speaking figuratively, of course."

Not all that figuratively, thought Thandi savagely. A memory came to her, of a Mesan outpost she'd passed through once as she was reporting to a new assignment. The planet was named Kuy, and wasn't much more than a large mining operation run by one of Mesa's major combines, using Manpower slaves as the primary work force. Thandi had been traveling via civilian transport, paid for by the Marine Corps. She'd spent two days there, after being dropped off, waiting for a connection to take her to her final destiny.

It had been a grim experience. Not a surprising one, of course, for someone born and raised on Ndebele.

Kuy's not far from here, now that I think about it.

For a few moments, images flashed through her mind. How she'd plan and lead an assault on the planet. To do it properly would require a battalion-sized force, but she was quite sure she could manage that. A few warships—small ones would do—to clear away any pickets and capture any Mesan commercial vessels in orbit.

I'd need to start building a Navy. Get someone to do it, rather, since I don't know squat about naval stuff. Zilwicki's been using the Anti-Slavery League's frigates as a training force . . . there ought to be somebody *there by now. . . .*

She pictured the control center of the mining operations, with the guard unit's barracks next to it. *Flatten those, right off. Hard and fast. There'd be some slaves killed too, but that's the way it goes. There aren't many located there anyway. The slaves are kept mainly in their own compounds—and in the mines, of course. But once the control center and the guards are taken out . . .*

She could do it. She *knew* it. Easily, in fact. And that was a major mining operation, no dog hole. It'd *hurt* Mesa. And—still better—free at least two thousand slaves in the process.

Need to start thinking about transports, too.

She shook her head, throwing off the fierce little reverie. Ruth was back to her pacing, throwing off words like a hamster scattering wood chips in a cage.

"Piece of cake, that kind of war—for *you.* What you didn't know, you'd grow into. And if you need or want advice, Manticore can send you advisers. I'll make sure of that, if you ask for them. My aunt'll listen to me, too—you watch."

Berry choked. "Is that before or after she tosses you into the Chateau d'If?"

Ruth Winton, going full bore, was not someone to be stymied by petty obstacles. She waved her hand, as if shooing away flies.

"Not a problem. She'll listen to me through a keyhole, if she has to—especially after I point out that the alternative is for Congo to get Havenite advisers. Or Andermani advisers. Or Solarian advisers." Ruth looked triumphant. "Not that I'll have to point it out, anyway, because my aunt is no dummy and she'll have figured that much out already. Although I will toss in the little tidbit that Thandi's boyfriend is a Havenite secret agent, so it's not like she'd have any trouble getting in touch with the Republic."

It was Thandi's turn to choke. "Uh . . . Ruth, I hate to tell you this . . . I'm not positive, because Victor's very close-mouthed about it. But I'm pretty sure he's been operating on his own, out here, and bending whatever orders he had into a pretzel. So Victor's just as likely to be talking to whoever's running the show in Haven through a keyhole too, once he returns."

Ruth still wasn't fazed. "So what? Politics can be greased by personal influence, but it still runs according to its own logic. You're not *thinking*. An independent planet of ex-slaves fighting a war with Mesa can call in a lot of favors, Thandi. And, where favors won't do it, can play one end off against the middle. Manticore will send you advisers just to keep Haven—or the Andermani, or the Solarians—from doing it. Besides . . ."

The young woman paused again, her eyes growing a little unfocused. "It's hard to figure yet, but . . . I don't think you understand—not sure any of us do—just what an impact this is going to have on the Manticoran public. *Especially* the Liberals. And there are a lot of Liberals in the Star Kingdom, Thandi. Forget New Kiev and that crowd, I'm talking about the rank and filers, the average voter. The ones who're starting to gravitate toward—"

She pointed a dramatic finger at Berry. "Her *mother.* Goddamit, Thandi, *think* about it! New Kiev's been dragging the Liberals through mud for years. Now—suddenly—something bright and sharp and clean comes along. A *cause.* The kind of cause any Liberal—and plenty of other people, too—can get excited about." She was almost cackling, now. "I wouldn't be surprised to see volunteers start showing up on Congo. That's happened before in history, you know, plenty of times. And some of them will have military experience. Not to mention that High Ridge's policies have left plenty of officers on the beach—good ones, too. Some of them will come too, just from being bored if nothing else."

"That's assuming the truce between Manticore and Haven lasts. If war breaks out again, forget it."

"So? In that case, the pressure on either star nation to out-influence the other on Congo just increases. Either way, Thandi, there are so many angles you've *got* to be able to play one of them."

She shook her head. "But all that's something of a side issue, because the *main* reason Berry needs you as the head of her armed forces has nothing do with foreign affairs. She needs somebody she can *trust.* And whatever else you might or might not be capable of, the one thing Berry won't have to worry about is that you'll carry out a *coup d'état.*"

Thandi grunted. "Why should she assume that?" She gave Berry as hard a look as she could manage. Which . . . was not easy, meeting those open, limpid young eyes. "I'm ambitious, girls. That's why I left Ndebele—whored myself to do it, when I had to. That's why I jumped at the chance to join Rozsak's staff, even though . . . Well, let's just say that not every assignment the captain's given me tastes all that good. But I swallow it anyway. And I'll do it again."

But, even as she spoke the words, she could feel the harshness in her tone fading away. Till, at the end, there was nothing left except . . .

A very bad taste. Not the taste left by any specific act or deed in her past, but simply the sour, acrid taste of ambition itself. It came to Thandi Palane, with something of a jolt, that she really didn't *like* ambition. She'd latched onto it simply as a tool to escape her past—and, since then, because she had no idea what else to do with her life.

She was still staring into Berry's eyes. The tears in those eyes were gone, now. All that was left was that clear gaze which Thandi realized—with the same jolt—she would miss desperately once it was gone.

"I got curious once," Berry said softly, "so I did a little research of my own. Names on Ndebele usually mean something, I found out. Yours does. 'Thandi' means 'I love this girl.' "

Thandi swallowed, remembering a father—briefly, before he died—who'd been drunk most of the time, but had never been cruel to her. And who'd always tried, when he could, to give her presents on her birthday. And a mother . . . tired, beaten down, who had just seemed to finally fade away.

"Just a romantic moment," she rasped. "It didn't last, I assure you."

"You don't believe that, Thandi, any more than I do. There was a time of hope. Not just a moment. That it didn't last is no excuse for surrendering hope itself. Only cowards do that, and you're no coward."

Thandi tried to look away, but couldn't. Berry's calm eyes seemed to have her fixed. Before the girl's next sentence was even spoken,

Thandi knew what it would be—and that it would pin her like a butterfly.

"I love this woman. And I want her—no one else—to be my shield and my sword arm, and my boon companion."

Thandi's own eyes were watery. "I'll have to think about it."

"Sure," said Berry, smiling like a cherub.

"I'll need to talk to some people," Thandi added. "Victor. And . . . I've got to talk to the captain, too. I owe him that much. He should be arriving today, back from Smoking Frog. And Jeremy. And Professor Du Havel."

"Sure," echoed Ruth, smiling like Machiavelli.

Her conversation with Victor on the subject was brief. He heard what she had to say. Then replied, very softly:

"You'll have to decide for yourself, Thandi. Frankly, I wouldn't trust my own advice, if I were you. The reason is probably obvious."

She swallowed, and nodded. It was obvious to her, also. Victor Cachat, whatever else might change about him, would always remain a partisan and a fighter for his own people. A Havenite, through and through. If Thandi gave her allegiance to the new star nation being born . . . a scrupulously *neutral* nation, except for its war with Mesa . . .

Whatever else, Victor and I would never find ourselves on opposite sides. And—I could keep seeing him!

She tried to suppress the sheer joy that thought gave her. Her life had trained her to be cold-blooded, after all. Even if she was sick and tired of it—as much as she was of ambition.

Still . . .

"Would you come and visit me?"

"Every chance I got," he said huskily. "I love this woman, too."

Her discussion with Jeremy X and Web Du Havel was lengthier, but not much. That also took place in her own compartment. This time, with Thandi perched on the bed, Du Havel sitting on the chair she'd occupied earlier, and Jeremy lounging easily against the door.

"I'd insist on incorporating my Amazons into the new army," she stated, as soon as the preliminaries were over. Firmly, almost harshly. "As well as any other former Scrags—or anybody else—who emigrates and wants to enlist. And not in their own separate unit, either. Take it or leave it. That condition is nonnegotiable. Assuming I decide to agree."

Jeremy shrugged. "No argument."

"From me, either," said Du Havel. "In fact, I support the idea. It'll cause us plenty of rough moments, of course, integration always does. But . . ." He eyed the very large and imposing woman sitting across from him, and smiled. "On the other hand, I dare say you'll manage to handle the disciplinary problems involved."

"You'll need someone else in charge of naval forces. I'm not trained for that. Wouldn't even know where to start."

"I'll check with Anton Zilwicki," said Jeremy. "I know he's been training at least three Ballroom people. One of them could probably do it—on the scale we're talking about, anyway." He paused for a moment, frowning, then shrugged. "I could be wrong, too. But if he doesn't have one of our people he thinks is ready now, he and Cathy certainly have the contacts to find us someone who's up for the job. And who we can trust. It's not as if our new 'navy' is going to amount to much, anyway, so we should certainly have the time to grow our own officer corps from within, I'd think. Privateers, in all but name—and that's not going to change all that fast. Warships—real ones—are fiendishly expensive, and we're going to start off the way freed slaves always do. Flat broke."

"It might change faster than you think," demurred Du Havel. "I've been studying the economic figures available for Congo, as many as I've been able to track down. Which isn't much—and that's significant in itself, because it means it's been a gold mine for Mesa and they're keeping it hidden. That planet is potentially *rich,* Jeremy. The market for pharmaceutical products isn't going to go away. And I don't believe for one minute that Mesa's brutal methods for extracting the wealth are necessary. They just use up people because it's easy for them, and it's their way of doing business. Give us a few years—fewer than you think—and we can start producing more wealth using civilized methods than Mesa ever did with whips and chains. We'll be able to afford warships, be sure of it. Enough to match Mesa, anyway."

He looked at Thandi. "Not immediately, of course, so that's a problem you simply don't have to worry about. And as Jeremy just suggested, by the time you do, you'll have grown into the job."

Thandi cocked a quizzical eyebrow. "And why are you so sure I can? You barely know me, Professor."

Du Havel shrugged. "I know more about you than you think, Lieutenant Palane. False modesty aside, I *am* an excellent scholar. And there's about as much information available on you as there is on Congo—and, likewise, what's most intriguing is what's absent."

Thandi's eyes were wide. "How the hell did you find out *anything* about me? I'm quite sure that SLN Marine Corps records aren't being made available to the public."

"Of course not. But you're forgetting that Watanapongse's personal computer *does* contain that information, and that it's been hooked into the *Felicia*'s network for weeks now." He cleared his throat, delicately. "Ruth Winton tells me that the lieutenant commander's security is very good. But not, of course, up to snuff. Not with her around."

"She hacked into *his* data banks? That girl is crazy!"

"Crazy or not, she'd undoubtedly be a contender if hacking were an Olympic event. I spoke with Anton about it recently, and he thinks she'd bring in the silver medal. He'd take the gold, of course."

Du Havel cleared his throat again, less delicately. "The point being, Lieutenant Palane, that I know a great deal about you—insofar as records can tell you anything, at least. But what's blindingly obvious is that if you didn't suffer from the handicap of being born on Ndebele, you'd be much farther along in your career. As it is, Captain Rozsak has you tagged in the records for—this is a quote—'agreed; advancement as rapid as possible.' That's in response to a recommendation from Lieutenant Colonel Huang, the commander of Rozsak's Marine forces. Who, by the way, has one of the most impressive records there is in the entire SLN Marine Corps. Between Rozsak's opinion and Huang's, I don't see any reason for me—or Jeremy—to have many doubts. The only real issue, frankly, is your lack of higher command experience. But, there, I agree completely with Ruth—yes, we've talked about it."

Du Havel glanced at Jeremy. "And so have Jeremy and I. The overriding question here, Lieutenant Palane, is simple. Your loyalties are really all that matter. Neither I nor Jeremy—certainly not Berry—is in the least concerned about your experience."

"That—loyalty, I'm speaking of—and your detachment from politics." That came from Jeremy, who was giving her a stare which was not hostile, but so flat-eyed that Thandi could understand the man's reputation for ruthlessness. Only Victor Cachat, in her experience, could match that empty-eyed manner of gazing at someone.

"I shall be blunt, Lieutenant Palane. The one and only concern of mine is that you not meddle in the internal politics of the new nation we'll be creating. Professor Du Havel and I—God knows how many others—will be mucking up those waters quite sufficiently, thank you. The one thing we cannot afford, in the middle of it, is an armed force whose commander is doing the same."

Thandi set her teeth, mulishly. "I'm not taking my distance from Berry. Anything else, fine. Politics doesn't much interest me, anyway. But don't ever think for a moment that you'll be able to separate me from her."

Jeremy grinned, the flat-eyed killer's look vanishing like the dew. "I should hope not!" he exclaimed. "Or else this whole silly business of setting up a queen is a waste of everybody's time."

"He's right, Thandi," agreed Du Havel. "If you were familiar with the math, I could even prove it to you. *Those* equations are about as well-established and accepted as any in political science. There's nothing that gives stability to a nation—especially, keeps its military in line—than a solidly established pole of loyalty which stands above and apart from the fray of politics. It can be a royal house, or a revered constitution—anything, really, as long as it's *solid* in custom and tradition. In law, too, of course. But law is just custom and tradition congealed into code, and ultimately derives its strength from them."

"You—we—wouldn't have such customs," Thandi observed.

"No, we wouldn't. Not for a time—and you and Berry, together, will buy us that time. You'll do much more than that. The two of you, together, will *establish* traditions and customs, which will become those of the new star nation."

He smiled, gently. "Trust my judgment on this, will you, Thandi? The close personal bond which has grown between you and Berry Zilwicki may well be the single factor which works most in favor of the long-term success of our project. It's still too early—too many variables, yet—for me to translate that into mathematical calculation. But I suspect that's true."

"So do I." Jeremy's smile was not gentle at all. "It might interest you to know, Thandi Palane, that my Ballroom gunfighters are beginning to adopt some foreign customs of their own. From Scrags, no less—excuse me, 'Amazons.' I've now heard several of them—ones newly arrived on the *Felicia,* mind you, not the ones who came with you—refer to you simply as 'the kaja.' It seems your reputation is spreading."

"Indeed," said Web. "It all bodes quite well, Lieutenant. Difficult enough for anyone—even ruthless killers like Jeremy or scheming maneuverers like myself—to seriously contemplate the overthrow and murder of a girl like Berry Zilwicki. Add to the mix a commander of the armed forces who is her big sister and goes by the nickname of 'great kaja' . . ."

Du Havel's smile was now the oddest one Thandi had ever seen. That of a cherub and a Machiavelli combined. "I dare say that, whatever else in the years to come, we won't have to worry about a coup d'etat."

"Don't even *think* about it," Thandi grated.

"You see?" demanded Jeremy. He shuddered, histrionically. "Look! I'm already purging the evil thought!"

CHAPTER 43

THANDI WASN'T ABLE TO MEET WITH Captain Rozsak until the following day. By the time he arrived back in Erewhon system from Smoking Frog, managed the lengthy surreptitious transfer to the *Felicia*—and got some sleep—almost twenty-four hours had passed.

So, by the time she was ushered into the compartment which she'd managed to squeeze out for the captain and his immediate staff on the increasingly jam-packed slaver ship, she'd already made up her mind. She wasn't going to be consulting with Rozsak, simply extending him her resignation.

She felt a bit guilty, given all that she owed the captain. Guiltier still, when she saw how crowded he and his staff were. Rozsak had apparently shared a bed with Colonel Huang, the night before, with the two female members of his staff who had accompanied him to the *Felicia*—his XO Edie Habib and Lieutenant Karen Georgos—sharing the other. Watanapongse, she knew, had shared a bed with Lieutenant Manson in his own, even tinier, compartment.

Watanapongse was present, along with Habib and Huang, when Thandi came in. Manson was not—and, as soon as she'd ushered Thandi into the compartment, Lieutenant Georgos closed the hatch behind her, not entering herself. The two junior staff members were not, apparently, going to be invited to join. Thandi was almost sure that the reason was because Rozsak—or Watanapongse, more likely—had already figured out the reason she'd requested an interview.

Rozsak confirmed it immediately. "I have a bad feeling you want to offer me your resignation, Lieutenant Palane." The captain was sitting on a chair against the far wall, his hands laced over his belly. He nodded politely toward the bed next to him, the only vacant place left in the compartment. "Please, have a seat. Let's talk about it."

Thandi was standing at attention, wearing her SLN uniform

rather than the simple jumpsuit she'd been wearing most of the time since she came to the *Felicia.* She'd had that uniform brought over just the day before, anticipating this moment. Her beret was tucked under her armpit, her hands clasped behind her back.

"I'd prefer not to, Sir. Yes, that is why I came. And I've already made up my mind."

Rozsak studied her for a moment. "Sit anyway, Thandi," he said abruptly. "There are other things to talk about. Other aspects of the matter, let's say. I'm not going to tell you that I'm happy about this. I'm not, and I'd be delighted if you reconsidered. But I'm not planning to give you a hard time about it, I promise." He glanced at his staff members. "None of us will."

Put that way, Thandi thought it would be sheer rudeness to refuse. She moved over and, somewhat gingerly, lowered herself to the bed. The very edge of it, sitting ramrod straight.

Seeing her pose, Rozsak smiled. "For God's sake, Thandi, relax. I'm not going to bite you. Sure as hell not after hearing Jiri's report of the mayhem you've been passing out around here. 'Great kaja,' no less."

A little chuckle went around the room, which Thandi found herself joining. Whatever else, Luiz Rozsak was a genuinely charming man. Charismatic, in fact, in the way that relaxed and good-humored and supremely self-confident people can be.

When the chuckle died away, Rozsak's expression was solemn. Just this side of grim, actually.

"I'm wondering how much of your decision was determined by the last assignment I gave you. More precisely—I'm sure you didn't shed any tears over killing Masadans and Scrags—by what lay behind it." His voice was flat, harsh. "And I'm not going to pretend that we don't all know what I'm talking about. Yes, I was responsible for the murder of Hieronymus Stein. As well as a number of innocent people who were taken out at the same time, including, I discovered later, two kids. That was not part of the plan, by the way. That was the Masadans' doing. But—such things happen, especially when you employ maniacs like them, which doesn't relieve me of the responsibility for it."

He cocked his head, waiting for her reply.

Thandi hesitated, before giving it. Not from caution, simply in order to put the words as precisely as possible. She wasn't going to lie, she decided—not even fudge the truth—but, on the other hand, she also wasn't going to evade behind any false pretenses.

"Some, Sir. But it's not the killings themselves, so much—not even the dead kids." She thought of her growing plans to assault Kuy. Plans which she would carry through, when and if the time came, knowing full well that innocent people—probably some kids, too—would be among the fatalities.

"It's . . . all the ruthless manipulation and maneuvering. And for what? No offense, Sir, but I just can't see anything in it except the worst kind of power politics. And I've discovered that I don't enjoy any more being on the top of the pile—fairly high up, anyway—than being on the bottom."

"A lieutenant is hardly 'high up,' Thandi," observed Edie Habib.

"It is when you come from Ndebele, XO. *Way* high up."

Habib nodded, acknowledging the point. Watanapongse smiled serenely. Huang's smile—the burly lieutenant colonel had been born and raised on an OFS planet himself—was not serene in the least.

Throughout, Rozsak had not smiled at all. "I can understand that, Thandi. But I would ask you to consider—just for a moment—that maybe my willingness to play power politics might work out for the best. I'm not about to deny my own ambitions, but . . . the same could be said for just about any significant figure in history. Including, for that matter, Hieronymus Stein. He was not the saint he was made out to be, you know—and, sure as hell, his daughter isn't. That man never missed a single chance—not one—to increase his influence and prestige."

Thandi said nothing. She tried to keep an expressionless face, but suspected she was just looking mulish.

Rozsak sighed. "I'm really not a monster, Thandi."

That, she could answer. "I've never once thought you were, Sir." Seeing his quizzical eyebrow, she shook her head firmly. "I don't. I understand what you're doing—even why you're doing it. And if you want to know the truth, I think you'll probably make a hell of a good ruler as well as conqueror. Way better than the swine we've got running the show in the Solarian League nowadays, that's for sure."

Seeing the stiffness those last words brought to everyone in the room—it was a subtle thing, but Thandi didn't miss it—she sniffed. "I am not stupid. Not even uneducated, any longer. I figured out some time ago what you—this inner circle, here—were up to. I knew it even before I figured out the truth about the Stein business. You're figuring the Solarian League is about to come apart at the seams—and you intend to grab as big a chunk of it as you can. Who knows? Maybe all of it."

Rozsak was now giving her a flat-eyed look which, if it didn't quite match the one Victor and Jeremy X could manage, came awfully close. "And what would you say if I offered to bring you into that 'inner circle,' Thandi?" He unlaced his hands and sat up straight. "Piss on the subjunctive tense. I *will* offer you a place in it. Along with an immediate promotion to captain and—I guarantee it—as fast a promotion track as I can manage. Which—you're right—I intend to eventually include the modern equivalent of a marshal's baton."

So, there it was. Spread out before her, wide open—dreams greater than any girl from Ndebele could have even imagined. Nor did Thandi doubt for a moment that Rozsak was being perfectly sincere. This was no ploy. This was for real.

She felt calmness settling over her, and knew that she would never lose it for a lifetime. Whatever else happened in the years ahead, she would always be grateful to the captain for that. Not the offer, but the fact that only that offer could have finally reassured her. Thandi Palane had compromised a lot, in her life, given much away. Traded it away, rather. But she'd never traded herself.

"No, thank you, Sir. I appreciate the offer, believe me I do. But . . . how to say it? I've got no hard feelings at all, Sir. You have my word on it. I just want a different life, that's all."

She met Rozsak's eyes, levelly and evenly. Trying, as best she could, to match Berry's sort of gaze. Rozsak seemed to examine her, for a while, before he finally looked down and nodded.

"Fair enough, Thandi. Your resignation is accepted, and—my word on this—there's no hard feelings on my part, either."

"Thank you, Sir." She rose and started to turn away. Rozsak's hand on her sleeve halted her.

"Come back again tomorrow, Thandi. Better yet, arrange a meeting in some larger compartment, big enough for my staff and whoever else you think should attend. There's still the matter—ha! to put it mildly—of planning the assault on Congo. I've got some news to report, from Maya, which you'll all want to hear. And let me suggest that we keep your resignation a private matter, for the moment."

Thandi saw the captain and his staff members exchange a meaningful glance. Huang cleared his throat. "There's an option you'll want to think about, Thandi. We could—just for a time, and just for the record—keep you on the Marine Corps rolls. With an immediate promotion to whatever rank it'd take to make it plausible that you were leading a rather large unit of Marines in the assault."

The lieutenant colonel grinned, rather evilly. "I'd be your adviser. Staying in the shadows while you get the limelight. It'd give you a chance to lead a large unit in action, for the first time, under ideal circumstances. It's pretty much what we were planning to do, anyway. The only difference is that your public resignation comes afterward."

Thandi looked from him to Rozsak. "All I'm suggesting, Thandi," the captain said, "—now that you've settled your nerves by resigning—is that you start thinking about the situation from a tactical and political viewpoint. Get some advice from the people you've grown close to. I'm talking about Professor Du Havel and Jeremy X. Your friend Victor Cachat also. There *would* be advantages to the way we're proposing to do it. Advantages to you as well as to us."

He made a little waving motion. "But you don't have to give me an answer right now. Just set up the meeting I requested, would you?"

Thandi nodded, saluted, and left the compartment.

Out in the corridor, Thandi exchanged a polite nod with Lieutenant Karen Georgos and went on her way. She had to struggle a bit to keep her steps at a normal pace, instead of striding. Some part of her wanted to get away from that compartment as fast as possible.

Not from shame, or guilt—or even fear. It was simply the reaction of a human being who crosses paths with a behemoth, and survives the encounter. Unscathed, as it happened—but still eager to put some distance between them.

Once she was around a bend and out of sight, Thandi stopped and leaned against the bulkhead. Her arms crossed over her chest, and she took a few breaths.

She hadn't been lying. She *didn't* think Captain Luiz Rozsak was a monster. He was not an evil man. Neither cruel nor even deliberately callous. An amoral man, certainly. But Thandi was not a hypocrite, and knew perfectly well that she herself could be called "amoral." Not in all things, perhaps. And so what? Captain Rozsak was not amoral in all things, either. Just . . . in those things which touched on his ambition.

That great, sweeping, behemoth ambition. That ambition whose appetite reminded Thandi, more than anything else, of the great predators which roamed the oceans of her home planet.

Those creatures were not monsters, either. Just giant predators, doing what predators do. A beneficent force, even, if you could step back and consider the planet's ecology as a whole. They not only kept the population of Ndebele's other sea life in balance, they also provided immediate sustenance for a multitude of symbiotes and scavengers.

None of which kept an encounter with one in the open sea from being a terrifying experience. And Thandi now knew—for a certainty—that whatever else she wanted from her life, being a scavenger or a predator's symbiote was not included.

She relaxed then, bringing up the image of her newly acquired "little sister" to purge the vast frightening image of a sea beast swimming through the deeps. She held the image, as tightly as a drowning woman would clasp a lifevest.

I love this girl.

After Thandi left, there was silence in the compartment, for perhaps half a minute. Then Edie Habib's face grew tight.

"Dammit, *somebody's* going to have to come out and say it. I guess the XO always gets the really crappy assignments. So here it is: *She knows too much.*"

Rozsak glanced quickly at Huang, and then at Watanapongse. The Marine officer's face was stony. Watanapongse's . . . serene, oddly enough.

Huang's reaction was predictable. Understanding the importance of it—the last thing he could ever afford was losing the trust and loyalty of his combat leaders—Rozsak gave voice to the stone. "I gave my word, Edie. To one of my own officers."

But Habib was an excellent XO; which meant, among other things, that she was persistent in probing for error. "Yes, Captain, that's true. And I will tell you what else is true—and everybody here, including Kao, knows it damn good and well. It's not going to be the last time you went back on your word, in the years ahead. Not where we're going, if we ever expect to get there."

That, too, was the simple truth. But hearing it just made Huang's face grow stonier.

"Still," Rozsak demurred, "it's not a thing to do lightly. Having a name for having a word is worth . . . maybe not its weight in gold, but damn close. Which we will *also* need, where we're going. If there's any bigger pitfall in the path of ambition than being too clever for your own good, I don't know what it is."

Watanapongse's expression had remained serene throughout. Rozsak found himself curious.

"Why are you so blasé about the matter, Jiri?"

"Because it's a moot point, that's why. Unless everybody here suddenly develops the intelligence of a vegetable—no offense, XO, you're just doing your job—then it ought to be obvious why the idea of assassinating Thandi Palane is just plain dumb. Not even that. 'Insane' comes closer."

"Why?" demanded Habib. But there was more relief than anything else in her tone. Edie hadn't proposed the idea because she liked it. She'd be as glad as Rozsak to be convinced otherwise.

Watanapongse levered himself up, from his relaxed slump. "Let's start with the fact that trying to assassinate Palane is a bit like trying to assassinate a tiger. Easier said than done. Who, after all, would we normally have given the assignment?"

Huang rasped a little laugh. "Thandi Palane."

"Exactly. But leave that aside. The woman's not superhuman, after all. With our resources, I'm sure we could figure out a way to do it. Which . . . might even work. And then what?"

Watanapongse shook his head. "Oh, yeah. A really bright idea. In order to protect ourselves—from a very remote threat, since Thandi Palane is almost certain to keep her mouth shut—we kill a woman who is simultaneously—"

He began counting off on his fingers. "The girlfriend of the Republic of Haven's best secret agent; a man who is—I've seen him in action—one of the deadliest men you'll ever meet.

"The protector and close friend of Berry Zilwicki, whose father Anton would probably be Manticore's best spy if the idiots hadn't fired him—and, whether in or out of uniform, has demonstrated several times just how dangerous it is to cross him.

"And—oh, perfect!—we'd also be assassinating a woman one of whose close associates now is a certain individual by the name of Jeremy X. You *have* heard of him? If you want more character references, just check with Manpower. Ask for their body count department."

He slumped back in his chair, the serene smile returning. "Just forget it, Captain. This is one time when doing the right thing and the smart thing happen to coincide. There is absolutely nothing I can think of you doing in this situation which would be stupider than killing Thandi Palane. Unless you want to spend the rest of your life—probably a short one—looking over your shoulder."

By the time Jiri had finished, Edie Habib was looking very rueful.

"Never mind," she said, in a little voice. "I never even raised the idea. Honest."

Rozsak chuckled. "Just doing your job, XO, as always. But I think Jiri's pretty well settled the issue. And I can't say I'm unhappy about it. Not at all. I can handle a bad taste, but that one would have been *really* foul."

Rozsak expected that to be the end of it, but, to his surprise, Watanapongse spoke again.

"Besides, it's probably a moot point from another angle, anyway. I'm quite sure that, by now, some other people have figured out the truth about the Stein killing."

"Who?" demanded Habib. "Our security's been tight as a drum, I'm sure of it."

"Victor Cachat, for one. About him, I'm positive." Catching Habib's quick angry glance at the compartment door, Watanapongse shook his head. "No, no, XO—he didn't get it from Thandi's pillow talk. He's *smart,* that's all. Better, being honest, at this kind of black ops than we'll ever be. And he was right in the middle of it, remember. He'll have figured it all out by now, don't think he hasn't."

"Who else?" grunted Huang.

"Hard to say. But I wouldn't be at all surprised if that too-damn-smart Manticoran princess does—the real one, I mean, Ruth Winton. Anton Zilwicki certainly will. So will some of the Erewhonese. It's not as if it's all *that* hard to figure out. Not for someone who's good at this kind of work, and takes a look at the determination with which Thandi saw to it that no witnesses survived."

Rozsak wasn't really surprised, nor was he upset. He'd calculated on this possibility from the beginning.

"Okay," he said. "It's fallback time, then. Speaking of which"—smiling, now—"I have good news from Smoking Frog. I had my meeting with the governor, and he was most deeply upset at what I had to tell him. Confess to him, rather. Oh, yes. Shocked and distressed, he was. But he also agreed that this Congo situation provides us with a perfect way to sweep the dirt under a shiny public rug."

Everybody in the compartment was now looking cheerful. "Indeed so," said Jiri. "There are always conspiracy theories floating around, whenever somebody gets assassinated. Who but a handful of malcontents is going to believe them—when they see the glorious role played by Captain Rozsak's flotilla in the liberation of Congo? Especially when the people in the know—all of them—have every reason to keep their mouth shut. Given that, to a considerable degree, the liberation's success depends on maintaining the good will of Maya Sector and its governor."

Rozsak cleared his throat. It was a harsh sound. "And given, as well—the governor made a point of this—that Cassetti will have to take the fall. Quietly, of course. But that should be enough to satisfy everyone who knows the truth and wants a sacrificial lamb. Goat, rather. Cassetti was too nakedly in love with power to have been a popular man. He'll do very nicely, and it clears him out of the way."

He chuckled. "Odd, isn't it? The way things sometimes work out. Thandi Palane's the one I would have given that assignment to. And I don't think it would have bothered her at all."

Huang made a little noise, as if he'd started to say something and then choked it off. Rozsak glanced at him. Then, seeing the meaning in his eyes, looked away.

Oh, that's good, Kao. "Black ops" with a vengeance. And the truth is, I really don't think Palane would *mind doing us that last little service.*

"Perhaps . . ." he mused aloud, "—he's still here, you know, staying at the Suds—Cassetti will want to accompany the expedition to Congo. I'm sure he will, once I suggest it to him. That'd add luster to his name, after all . . . which could certainly use some help, as black as it's become in so many quarters."

PART V: CONGO

CHAPTER 44

"YOU'RE TELLING *ME* THEY'RE a bunch of fanatics?" Unser Diem was practically shrieking. He jerked his head sideways, in the direction of the man standing not far from him on the bridge of the *Felicia III*. "He'll *do* it, Lassiter! Don't think for a minute he won't."

The Manpower official whose image was displayed in the screen glanced at the man being indicated. Then, glanced just as quickly away. The image he saw matched the holopics of Abraham Templeton—as closely as the bandages permitted, and making allowances for the way the Masadan's face was distorted by a ferocious scowl. The General Manager of Operations, Verdant Vista, was clearly having no difficulty at all imagining the maniac blowing up a ship carrying thousands of people.

"And if that isn't enough," Diem continued, snarling, "then take another good look at that Manty cruiser. That's the *Gauntlet*, you—you—"

He managed to bite off the epithet. As angry and terrified as Diem was, he didn't want to offend Manpower's top official in the Congo system. Kamal Lassiter was fairly notorious for letting petty personal issues get in the way of his decisions.

But the name of the ship was enough, it seemed. Lassiter swallowed, and Diem saw him look away—presumably at another screen in the com room of Congo's central headquarters. A tactical display screen, that would be, which would show the General Manager all the vessels within the Congo system.

"Is—ah—?"

"Yes," Diem bit off. "He *is* still in command. Captain Michael Oversteegen. You may recall that he has something of a reputation. And if you're wondering if the reputation is overblown, I can personally assure you that it isn't. He spoke to me less than twenty hours ago over this same com, promising me that if the Princess comes to harm he's holding Manpower responsible. He was *not* pleasant about it, to put it mildly. And he took pains to remind me that the Eridani Edict does *not* apply to strictly commercial operations on privately owned planets."

Diem could feel the sweat on his forehead, as he waited for Lassiter to finally make a decision. The sweat was real enough, even if almost everything else was fakery. The reason it was real—and Diem *was* on the edge of panic—was because the "fakery" was only technically such. If anything, the reality being disguised was even worse than the illusion.

He hadn't spoken to Oversteegen over the com, as it happened; he'd spoken to him in person. And it had been six days ago instead of less than twenty hours. So what? In person, the Manticoran officer had been an icy aristocrat. He'd made it crystal clear to Diem that he *would* see to it that Manpower's installations on Congo would be so much slag if anything went wrong. Diem hadn't doubted him in the least.

Not that Diem really cared that much. Long before *Gauntlet* could start taking Congo apart, Diem himself would be a dead man. Of that he had no doubt at all. The man standing near him on the bridge of the *Felicia* was not the religious maniac Abraham Templeton, even though Erewhon's nanotech engineers had done a good job with the physical resemblance. He was something a lot worse.

Victor Cachat. A man whom Unser Diem had had nightmares about—real ones, no poetic license here—since he first met him.

Cachat spoke up, right then. "Decide, Lassiter," he said, glancing at his chrono. His voice was hoarse, presumably due to the injuries he'd suffered in the course of abducting the Manticoran princess.

"I will give you two minutes, exactly," he rasped. "Then I will shoot Diem. Then, at fifteen second intervals"—the Havenite agent masquerading as Abraham Templeton nodded toward the people shackled to a console behind him—"I will kill the rest of them. Ringstorff first, then Lithgow, then the whore. Fifteen seconds after that, I will destroy the *Felicia.* Three minutes from now, if you continue to quibble, eight thousand people will be dead—including Ruth Winton, of the royal house of Manticore."

"Abraham Templeton" glanced at the tac display on the bridge of the *Felicia* and smiled sardonically. A half-smile, rather. The apparently severe injuries to his throat and jaw made the expression as distorted as his rasping voice. "All of it in front of every news media in the inhabited galaxy, from what I can see. I count at least eighteen media vessels somewhere in this system. Most of them in orbit nearby."

From the very sour expression on his face, it was obvious that Lassiter would have liked to curse. Not so much at the situation as at the media presence. Normally, Manpower would have forbidden those ships to remain in the Congo System, but with *Gauntlet* present . . .

That was something else Oversteegen had been emphatic about, in his terse discussions with the Manpower officials on Congo. Any move toward the media ships by any of the light attack craft which Manpower had in orbit around the planet would be met with instant force. Nobody doubted for a minute that Oversteegen would make good the threat—and a Manty heavy cruiser was perfectly capable of destroying twice the number of LACs Manpower had on the spot.

There were undoubtedly heavier warships nearby, upon which Manpower intended to rely for support if needed, Victor knew. They were not, however, part of Manpower's private fleet, which posed its own problems for Lassiter and his masters.

"Verdant Vista" was the private property of Manpower Unlimited, duly registered as such under interstellar law on the planet Mesa. As an independent and sovereign star nation, Mesa was empowered to recognize the claims of its citizens or business entities and, under existing interstellar law, Manpower had the right to appeal to the Mesan Navy for protection of its private property rights. But other star nations were *not* required to respect those rights as they would have been required to if Verdant Vista had, itself, been a sovereign star system.

Admittedly, it was something of a gray area, with competing interpretations of the precedents. What it boiled down to, however, was that a private corporation's claim to interstellar property rights was only as good as the naval strength which backed that claim. That was why Solarian trans-stellar corporations seldom had any problems (aside from the occasional raid by outright pirates). No star nation in its right mind wanted to provoke the SLN, so they tended to sit on their own potential troublemakers—hard—when there was a Solly corporation involved.

But while Mesa maintained a navy, it was nowhere near so grand as the SLN. Indeed, it was on the small side even by the standards of single-system star nations, although its individual units had excellent hardware. Despite its nationhood Mesa was, after all, essentially a conglomerate of business interests, and navies, by their nature, are expensive propositions which do not normally show a positive cash flow.

That was why some Mesa-based corporations, like Manpower, maintained private fleets. And another reason for Manpower, in particular, to do so was that the council which governed Mesa was hesitant to use military power too openly in Manpower's special interests. There was no point actively courting negative news coverage, after all.

In this instance, however, thanks to Michael Oversteegen and Her Majesty's Starship *Gauntlet*, the cruiser force Manpower had assembled to back up its LACs in Congo had suffered a mischief. A rather terminal one, in fact. That was one of the odd little facts Ringstorff had been willing to confirm for them . . . along with the fact that Manpower had not replaced the destroyed ships. Which had become another factor in the planning of the unusual alliance of interests now moving in on Congo. If there were heavy ships in the vicinity at all, they were regular Mesan naval units, and they would be doing their dead level best to maintain a low profile, particularly in the face of such massive news coverage. That meant they would be somewhere else—close enough to reach Congo fairly rapidly, but not right on top of the system.

So there was an automatic delay built into the response loop. Lassiter would have to send a courier to summon them, and that offered a window in which the "forces of liberation" would be free to act. Better yet, it meant that when (or if) those units did turn up, they would be commanded by someone whose primary loyalty was to *Mesa,* not simply to Manpower.

"I need at least ten minutes just to discuss the situation with my people," Lassiter complained.

Cachat, masquerading as Abraham Templeton, did not bother to look up from his chrono. "You have one minute and forty seconds before I start the killing. You've had weeks to decide what to do, Lassiter. There's no point in any further delay."

"One moment." Lassiter reached out a finger and the display screen went blank.

Diem heaved a little sigh. "What are you going to do if he goes past your deadline?" he asked nervously.

The answer, somehow, didn't surprise him. Cachat was still looking down at his chrono. "In one minute and twenty-five seconds, I'm going to kill you. Then, at fifteen-second intervals, Ringstorff and Lithgow." He glanced at the pale-faced young woman shackled to the console next to the Mesans. "I will not, of course, shoot Berry Zilwicki. Her father is likely to take umbrage." Cachat sounded vaguely miffed about it, the way a craftsman will when he is not permitted to do his finest work.

Off to the side of the bridge, sitting where he was out of sight of the screens, Anton Zilwicki snorted. But he didn't bother looking up from the console where he and Ruth Winton were busily cracking into Manpower's secure communications systems.

"Pray to whatever gods you hold dear, Diem," Zilwicki murmured, just loudly enough to be heard. "If Lassiter's as careless and sloppy as his security, you're a dead man." He snorted again, as a new screen came up. "Bingo. We're in. And there's not even any internal encryption. God, I love carrier signals, especially when the people on the other end are idiots. Take it from here, would you, Ruth?"

Eagerly, the young princess' fingers began flying over the keyboard, and Zilwicki looked up and grinned at Diem. There was no humor at all in the expression.

"Personally, I remain to be convinced that Lassiter can even tell time."

Lassiter could tell time, of course. But, for almost a minute, he wasted it in a fit of screaming invective aimed at his subordinates in the control center of Congo's headquarters. There was no point to the shrieking, as, once it began tapering down, Lassiter's chief subordinate Homer Takashi pointed out. Sullenly:

"It wasn't *our* idea to hire those crazy Masadans, boss. In all fairness, it wasn't even Diem's—and Ringstorff tried to talk them out of it. If you want to blame somebody, kick it upstairs. It was the Council that made the decision."

Lassiter ground his teeth. Everything Takashi said was true. But Lassiter was the type of supervisor who fawned over his superiors and lorded it over his subordinates. He wasn't about to send a blistering message to the three Manpower top executives who were part of the Mesan task force lurking in the barren, unnamed star system thirty-six hours away through hyper-space.

"And we're almost out of time," Takashi pointed out. None of Lassiter's other subordinates would have been that bold. But Takashi had his own patrons in Manpower's hierarchy, and beyond a certain point didn't have to put up with Lassiter's temper.

Fortunately, Lassiter's tantrum had calmed him down a bit. He was still angry, but was able to think more or less clearly.

"I don't have any choice, do I?"

Takashi shook his head. "Not unless you want the big shots to hand your head on a platter to the Star Kingdom. And the Manticorans *will* demand it, if their princess gets killed, don't think they won't."

Lassiter had already come to the same conclusion. If *Gauntlet* had been commanded by some other officer . . .

But, she wasn't. Oversteegen, no less!

Scowling, Lassiter brought the display back on. The image of Abraham Templeton returned. The maniac was still studying his chrono, with an intentness that made Lassiter's blood run cold.

"All right, all right," Lassiter said hastily. "We agree. You can dock alongside the space station and we'll do the transfers there. Although I still think—"

"Forget it, Lassiter," rasped the religious fanatic. "There is no way I'll agree to a transfer using shuttles. That would give you too many opportunities for an 'unfortunate lapse.' You can still try to double-cross us once we're docked, of course. But I can guarantee you that I'll take out your very expensive space station as well as the *Felicia,* if you try it."

Lassiter *had,* in fact, planned to take out the Masadans during a shuttle transfer, if he could manage it without killing the princess. His security crew on the space station might not be quite up to the best professional military standards, but the technicians manning the space station's close-defense weapons were more than capable of swatting shuttles with ease.

On the other hand, it had been a long shot anyway, given the need to keep the Manticoran royal alive. So, he mentally shrugged and made the best of a bad situation. A really bad situation.

"We'll be waiting for you," he said curtly. "We'll indicate the docking bay as you approach. Remember: just you and the Princess, that's all. Leave the cargo under lockdown."

A bit lamely, he added: "When I say 'you,' that means all of you."

Templeton didn't even bother to sneer. "Do I look like an idiot? I'll leave two of my men here, Lassiter, until the transfer is complete, the Princess is handed over to you, and we've got control of the ship we'll be leaving the system in. Then—I warn you—even after those two are transferred there'll still be both a remote-controlled detonator as well as a delayed-action detonator left on board the *Felicia*. You can probably block the remote-controlled one, once we're out of orbit, but I can guarantee you that you won't find the hidden one for at least several hours. Long enough for us to reach hyper-space, at any rate. I'll send you a message letting you know where it is, once I'm sure we're safe from ambush."

"How do I know you'll keep your word?"

Templeton bestowed on him a look which combined fury and contempt. "I swore on the name of the Lord, heathen. Do you doubt me?"

As it happened, Lassiter didn't. He found it hard to imagine himself, but on this subject his briefings had been clear. Crazed they might be, but the religious maniacs could be trusted to keep their word, if they took a holy vow.

"All right. Let's do it, then."

As soon as the contact was broken, Victor Cachat heaved a little sigh of relief and massaged his throat. "That damn rasp is going to give me a permanent sore throat," he grumbled.

From her seat, without looking up, Ruth said cheerfully: "Can't be helped, Victor. Nanotech will change your appearance or even adjust your vocal cords for the right timbre, but changing accents is harder. And—it's a bit shocking, really, for a secret agent—you've got a really thick Havenite accent and your attempts to mimic a Masadan one were pathetic. So, the rasp it is. Ah, the joys of combat injuries. Explains everything."

Victor would have scowled at her, but there was no point. Everything she'd said was true, after all. He'd tried for hours to get a Masadan accent down, and had failed just as miserably as he'd always failed at attempts to disguise his own. That had been one of the few subjects on which he'd been given a barely passing grade in StateSec's academy.

The other option would have been to let someone else undergo the nanotech procedures and try to pass himself off as the now-dead Templeton. But . . . everyone had agreed that, voice aside, Victor had been the ideal candidate. He more than anyone could *act* like a Masadan, as Anton Zilwicki had pointed out. Victor still wasn't sure if that was praise or insult. Probably both at the same time.

"Are you ready to support Thandi?" he asked Ruth now, and the princess nodded.

"Well, almost," she qualified. "We're still accessing, and the main security system looks like a stand-alone. But the com hierarchy ties it all together, and I've got access to the main system. And I've located the internal communications and surveillance systems. I'll be into them by the time she can get aboard the station, and I've already tapped the net between the station and Torch."

Cachat grimaced. The ex-slaves had settled on a new name for Congo, after the liberation: "Torch," the planet would be called thenceforth. The debate had come down to a final decision between "Beacon" and "Torch," and Jeremy had carried the day. A beacon of hope was all very well, he'd agreed, but their world was going to generate more than just light. It was going to ignite the conflagration which would finally reduce Manpower and all of its works to ashes and dust. From the perspective of an agent accustomed to operating in the shadows, Victor found the name a bit overly flamboyant, but the servant of the revolution inside him was firmly on Jeremy's side.

"So notify Thandi that Operation Spartacus is ready to roll," he said almost curtly.

"Just did it," replied Ruth cheerfully. "God, is this fun or what?"

Thandi acknowledged the message from Ruth, then checked her chrono and nodded in satisfaction. She still had a few minutes—long enough for a quick last inspection of her troops. "Quick" was the right word, too. She was now in command of a battalion-sized unit of troops, divided into four companies. Each of those companies was positioned in one of *Felicia*'s large bays, so Thandi had to visit each of them in her inspection tour.

For all that the dispersal of her troops was a bit of a headache, Thandi found a grim satisfaction in the situation. It was ironic that the large bays Manpower had intended to permit the rapid murder of hundreds of slaves would also permit people wearing battle armor and Marine-issue armored skinsuits to launch a lightning mass assault on Manpower's space station. Anton Zilwicki called it "being hoist on their own petard," an archaic expression which Thandi understood once he explained, but still found a little silly.

She was a bit nervous at the prospect of leading such a large unit into battle, but not much. First, because she had the experience and steadying influence of Lieutenant Colonel Kao Huang at her side. Second, because although Thandi had never herself commanded anything larger than a company before, she'd been an assiduous student since she first joined the Marine Corps. So she'd observed the process at first hand—which, for the past year working with Huang, had put her in close proximity to one of the SLN Marine Corps' premier combat commanders.

But, finally—and probably most importantly—because this entire operation was so far outside normal Marine Corps practice that *any* amount of prior experience would have still left her jury-rigging almost everything. And, in practice if not in theory, she'd really only be leading a company-sized unit anyway. Her own company, as it happened. Bravo Company, Second Battalion, 877th Solarian Marine Regiment, which she'd been leading for months since its former commandant, Captain Chatterji, had been placed on indefinite medical furlough for the treatment of severe combat injuries.

Bravo Company had been divided into its four platoons, and those platoons would be spearheading the assault on Congo's space station. In theory, they would do so as private volunteers acting as an integral part of company-sized units of the new "Torch Liberation Army."

It was a threadbare mask, perhaps, but not unheard of by any means. OFS frequently used the practice of "granting leave" to entire units which then "volunteered" to "assist" some out-planet regime in the suppression of dissent. Or, more rarely, even in the outright conquest of someone else. The regular SLN and Marines did not, perhaps, but the precedent was there.

Besides, it was *supposed* to be threadbare, she reminded herself. At the proper time, everyone in the civilized galaxy was supposed to see right through it . . . although, naturally, no one would officially admit that they had.

So "the Torch Liberation Army" it was. In theory. In practice—as Thandi had made crystal clear to the Ballroom gunfighters and Amazons who filled out the ranks of the battalion—her regular platoons would do all of the fighting. That was true for the assault on the space station, at least, whatever might wind up happening later when the assault on the planet itself occurred. The "friendly fire" casualties and indiscriminate damage which would be sure to occur with a mob of amateurs storming a space station were enough to give her nightmares. The Ballroom and Amazon troops could tag along behind—and get most of the glory—but she wanted them in the back and effectively out of the action.

She'd expected a ferocious argument, but there hadn't been one. For the first time, she and Jeremy X had faced a potential clash—and Jeremy, to her relief, had sidestepped it neatly. She was beginning to realize that a very shrewd mind was at work beneath the superficial appearance of a maniacal terrorist. Jeremy was no fool, and understood himself that a military assault on a gigantic space station was a different matter than an assassination carried out by a small unit of killers. All the more so, since they wanted to *capture* the space station—as intact as possible—rather than destroy it. This would become *Torch*'s critical space station, after all, which would be useless if it had been gutted in the taking.

So, in effect, she was leading a company-sized unit of Solarian Marines. Granted, in an operation which was hardly being done by The Book.

The memory of the expressions on her Marines' faces when they were informed they had all "volunteered" to participate in the splendid project of liberating genetic slaves from Manpower could still bring a chuckle to her. Like all Solarian Marines, Bravo Company's people were hard-bitten professionals—the majority of them mercenaries, in all but name—with about as much in the way of idealistic impulses as so many Old Earth barracuda. But, they'd seemed more amused by the subterfuge than anything else. They certainly weren't going to argue the point—not with Lieutenant Colonel Huang scowling at them, and with their own several months' experience with Thandi in command. True, her Marines called her "the Old Lady" instead of "Great Kaja." But they said the words in a tone of voice which her Amazons would have recognized.

That had been Captain Rozsak's proposal, which he'd advanced the day after Thandi's resignation at a meeting of all the central figures involved. Easily and smoothly, Rozsak had explained all the advantages to the ploy. Not the least of them being the mutual benefits to Torch and the Solarian League's Maya Sector of establishing a publicly close relationship from the outset. A benefit to Torch, because Maya Sector would provide the new nation with the safe and powerful neutral base which gave any liberation movement an invaluable reservoir.

From the other side, covering themselves with a thinly veiled halo of moral glory from their participation in the liberation of Congo would be of inestimable benefit to the Solarian political and military forces associated with Governor Barregos. Leaving aside the need to cover up the truth about Stein's murder—which only a few people knew about, after all—things were about to get very turbulent within the Solarian League. Barregos intended to stake out the moral high ground for himself, right from the beginning—and Congo was to be the proof of it.

Thandi had been a bit dubious, but Du Havel had agreed immediately. And then later, in private conversation after Rozsak and his Solarian staff were gone, had elaborated on the logic.

✧ ✧ ✧

"It's a very smart move, on their part. Whatever else he might be, Barregos is as canny a politician as any in the Solarian League. That means, among other things, that while he doesn't fetishize public opinion, he also doesn't make the more common mistake of seasoned politicians of underestimating it either."

Thandi's expression must have been cynical. Catching sight of it, Du Havel shook his head. "Don't read the reality of the OFS planets onto the entire League. Yes, to be sure, actual *control* of the League—in the sense of day-to-day operations—rests in the hands of its bureaucrats and combines. But that's only true above the level of the great star systems in the Old League—and then, only on sufferance. The one thing which the powers-that-be in the League have always been careful about is not to get the huge inner populations stirred up about anything. Their luck is about to run out, however, unless I miss my guess. The liberation of Congo, followed immediately thereafter by the foundation of a star nation of ex-slaves and its declaration of war on Mesa, is going to shake everything up. That's why—"

He smiled cheerfully, glancing at Anton Zilwicki. "—I'm so pleased that Anton called in every favor the Anti-Slavery League has piled up with the media over the past few decades. This flamboyant military operation is going to be happening in front of the galaxy's holorecorders, not in some obscure frontier outpost where the bureaucrats can keep the media away until the cover story is in place. I guarantee you that it will be headline news all over the Solarian League—and wildly popular with a significant proportion of the population. For years, every Solarian official has clucked his tongue at the iniquities of genetic slavery, while making sure that absolutely nothing was done about it. Now, their hands will be forced—with Governor Barregos standing out as the dynamic League leader who played a key role in the affair. They'll want to cut his throat, of course. But . . . he'll have made that ten times harder to do."

"Especially after the Renaissance Association jumps into the act," added Anton. "They have even better connections with the Solarian media than the Anti-Slavery League, and they'll pull out all the stops as soon as I notify Jessica Stein of what's happening." He cleared his throat. "Which I will, the moment it's too late for her to meddle with it."

Her last-minute inspection tour done, Thandi returned to the bay where she'd be leading First Platoon. To her surprise, Berry was there. The Queen-to-be was making a last-minute inspection of the troops herself. Insofar, at least, as Berry's informal way of mingling with soldiers could be called an "inspection." Even those hard-boiled Marines seemed rather charmed. It was like getting a send-off from everybody's favorite kid sister.

"What are you doing here?" Thandi demanded quietly, almost hissing. "The balloon's about to go up. Get yourself out of here, girl. We can't afford to lose you."

Berry smiled. She took Thandi by the arm and led her to the hatch which led out of the great bay. "I'm leaving, I'm leaving. I really came just to make the same point to *you.* Don't forget that you're now our new Supreme Commander-in-Chief, Thandi Palane. So none of your hair-raising personal charges, d'you hear? We can't afford to lose you, either."

Thandi didn't quite know what to say.

Berry did. "Your monarch has spoken," the girl said. With considerable royal loftiness, in fact, marred only by her stumble as she passed through the hatch.

CHAPTER 45

LIKE MOST SPACE STATIONS of its size and type, Manpower's installation in Congo boasted modestly respectable space-to-space defenses. There was no point trying to build something which could hope to stand off an attack by regular fleet units, but out in the back of beyond, people had to look after themselves. More than one unarmed station had been overwhelmed and looted by the equivalent of barbarian raiders in space-going rowboats, so it was generally considered a good idea to provide valuable pieces of real estate with sufficient defensive capability to at least make them unattractive targets for low-budget pirates.

In addition, however, Lassiter's station served as not just the command center and freight transshipment point for the entire system, but also provided the primary defensive node for the planet of Congo itself, as well. Just as the guards in a prison were unarmed in order to prevent the inmates from seizing their weapons, the administrators and overseers on the surface of the planet had very few heavy weapons at their command. They scarcely needed them, with the equivalent of a battalion or so of Marines ready to drop on their heads at a moment's notice . . . supported by kinetic strikes from orbit. And especially not when Manpower had made it crystal clear that they would punish *any* rebellion attempt with a brutal ferocity that beggared the imagination.

While it would have been impossible for anything which happened on the surface of the planet to directly threaten the space station, it was always theoretically possible that, despite everything, a desperate slave uprising might succeed in capturing some of the system's heavy-lift cargo shuttles while they were planeted and using them to attack it. If that happened as the *first* stage in an insurrection, then the lightly armed enclaves on the planet would be essentially at the mercy of the slaves who hated their inhabitants with a blazing passion. So, remote though the threat might be,

Manpower's planners had provided the space station with sufficient light weaponry to annihilate any such attempt.

Then there were Manpower's LACs. By the standards of the Royal Manticoran Navy, they were hopelessly obsolete, but there were fifteen of them. Theoretically, they were simply Verdant Vista's "customs patrol," with a secondary legitimate function as additional pirate discouragers. They, too, could be used at need to suppress any insurrection by Congo's enslaved labor force, however. They could also have made mincemeat out of the *Felicia* if they'd chosen to do so. Of course, their commanders had also been informed of precisely what HMS *Gauntlet* would do to any LAC stupid enough to open fire on a merchant vessel whose passengers included a member of the House of Winton.

All those factors had played their part in the planning for Operation Spartacus. While it was extremely unlikely that any of Manpower's forces currently in the star system would be foolish enough to challenge *Gauntlet* or attack *Felicia* directly with "Ruth Winton" on board, it was only too likely that they *would* attempt to beat off any attack craft *Felicia* launched, and they had more than sufficient firepower for that. At worst, that would result in a blood bath for the attackers. At best, it would create a standoff which would force the abandonment of the attack or else require *Gauntlet* to engage the defenders in an obvious act of aggression.

That was the reason all of Thandi's personnel were assembled in the slaver's "cargo bays" as the big merchant ship crept slowly into her designated mooring position off Space Dock Eleven. Thandi watched the tiny holo display projected against the visor of her battle armor, the relayed imagery from *Felicia*'s external visual pickups as the big ship maneuvered cautiously under reactor thrusters alone. It was impossible for any vessel to approach this closely to another one under impeller drive, and her lips thinned in a hungry smile as she saw the bright light shining through the docking bay gallery's transparent armorplast. She could actually make out a handful of moving figures on the far side of that armorplast, and her smile grew still hungrier as she contemplated the surprise they were about to receive.

Felicia's tractors reached out and locked on to the space station as she killed the last of her relative movement and the boarding tube reached out to nuzzle against her main personnel hatch. Normally, the station would have supplied the necessary tractor lock, but "Templeton" had contemptuously dismissed Lassiter's offer to do so this time. Not that it really made any difference at this point, Thandi reminded herself, and reconfigured her visor's HUD. The imagery of the illuminated bay gallery vanished, replaced by her command and control schematic. The lieutenants commanding her platoons glowed as golden triangles in the schematic, with their platoon sergeants and squad leaders shown as golden and silver chevrons, respectively.

"Tango-Lima-Alpha leaders, this is Kaja," she said, remotely surprised, as always, to hear how calm her voice sounded over her own com. "Prepare to execute Alpha One on my command. Acknowledge."

Four gold triangles flashed brightly in obedient response, and she suppressed a grunt of satisfaction. Then—

"Now, Thandi," Ruth's voice said quietly in her ear bug.

"Tango-Lima-Foxtrot, execute now!" she said instantly. "I repeat, execute now, now, now!"

"Arnold wants to know what you want him to do," Takashi said over Lassiter's private com channel.

"I already *told* him what to do!" the general manager snapped back, never taking his eyes from the mobile mountain of alloy as it eased to a stop relative to his space station. He'd come down to the dock gallery from his command center. Not because he wanted to, but because he already knew that whatever happened here, and however little choice he'd had but to agree to it, his career was about to take a major hit. Under the circumstances, it was imperative that he be able to present himself as having been hands-on at every stage of the disaster. It might not do much good, but it would certainly look better than cowering safely in Command Central.

"I'm only telling you what he said," Takashi replied.

"Goddamned idiot," Lassiter growled in a deliberately ambiguous tone which might equally well have applied to his senior assistant or to the commander of Verdant Vista's security force. Then he drew a deep breath.

"Tell him," he said in a dangerously patient voice, "that he will do nothing—repeat, *nothing*—except stand by in the positions he and I already discussed unless and until I tell him differently. This situation is fucked up enough already without him deciding to play goddamned Preston of the Spaceways on his own!"

"I'll tell him," Takashi acknowledged, and Lassiter half-growled and half-snorted in satisfaction. Or as close to satisfaction as he could reasonably expect to feel at a moment like this. He'd allowed

Arnold to issue weapons and put his heavy combat teams into their battle armor, but not without some severe misgivings. Major Jonathan Arnold was basically competent, if not particularly imaginative. Not all of his personnel were, however. In fact, in Lassiter's considered opinion, at least half of them would have been incapable of organizing a bottle party in a brewery without direction. They were a blunt instrument in Manpower's hands—adequate when it came to keeping an iron boot planted on the necks of Congo's slave laborers, but not much more than that. Indeed, Manpower hadn't *wanted* them to be much more, and that was why the current situation was far enough beyond the parameters of their capabilities to give Lassiter nightmares every time he thought about the potentially dire consequences of a single itchy trigger finger.

Unfortunately, it was a case of damned if he did, and damned if he didn't. If one of his security people screwed the pooch, he'd be blamed. But if he ordered Arnold to stand his people down and something went wrong anyway, someone on the Council was absolutely certain to suggest that it was all Lassiter's fault for not having made proper use of his resources. As if anything he did at this point—

That was odd. Why were they opening the—?

The docking tube had just touched *Felicia*'s main personnel hatch when the huge doors of her specially designed "cargo bays" snapped open. Kamal Lassiter's eyes widened, but consternation turned almost instantly into panic as human beings began to spill through the gaping openings. Not the unprotected bodies of slaves, but armed and armored figures shooting across the gap between them and the gallery with bulletlike speed.

Surprise was total. Despite all the tension and anxious precautions *Felicia*'s arrival had engendered, no one aboard the space station had even contemplated the possibility of an actual attack. Not after the way Victor Cachat's strategy had misdirected everyone's attention to the "terrorist Templeton's" demands. Lassiter's brain was still fumbling with the new data, trying to force it into some sort of coherency, when the first Marine breaching teams hit the gallery's armorplast.

The operations manager stumbled back a step or two as the Marines touched down on tractor-soled boots. They landed and clung as naturally as so many houseflies, and Kamal Lassiter's face went paper-white as he finally realized what he was seeing. He spun away from the sight, dashing madly for the gallery lifts, but it was far too late for that.

Six three-man teams of Marines slapped breaching rings on to the armorplast. Each of those rings was approximately three-meters in diameter. They adhered almost instantly, and the Marines stepped back and hit their detonators. Precisely shaped and directed jets of plasma sliced six perfect circles through the tough, refractory armorplast as easily if it had been no tougher than old-fashioned glass.

The consequences for the personnel inside the gallery, none of whom were in spacesuits, were as ghastly as they were predictable.

Thandi watched the hurricanes of atmosphere explode out of the breaches her teams had blasted. Computer chips, loose furniture, sheets of paper, and human beings came with them, sucked out by the hungry vacuum before interior blast doors and emergency hatches slammed shut, sealing off the air-gushing wounds.

"All Tango-Lima-Alpha units, this is Kaja. Phase One accomplished. Move to Phase Two."

The golden triangles on her display blinked fresh acknowledgment, and her assault teams began swarming through the openings as the space station's emergency procedures conveniently shut down the torrents of atmosphere pouring out of them.

Thandi, obedient to Berry's admonishment (and Lieutenant Colonel Huang's silent but pointed example), was in the third wave, not the first. But she was the first person to reach the control console at the center of the gallery. She studied the console for a dozen blazingly intense seconds, then grunted in satisfaction. Ruth and Colonel Huang had been correct during the planning sessions; it was a standard Solarian design. She looked back up, waiting impatiently as the last of her Audubon Ballroom personnel came through the breaches, then stabbed a button.

Alloy panels slid slowly downward, locking across the armorplast. The system was designed to protect against collision with minor debris, but it served a secondary function by sealing off the holes her Marines had blown. She waited, wishing she could tap her toe impatiently (not exactly practical for someone in battle armor), until the panels locked down. Then she punched another series of commands into the console and bared her teeth in truly wolfish delight as the gallery began to repressurize.

✧ ✧ ✧

Homer Takashi wasn't cursing, but only because he didn't have the time.

He also didn't have any better idea what was happening than the late, unlamented Lassiter had had, but he did know that it wasn't what the entire galaxy had been led to expect. Whoever those people were, they weren't Templeton's Masadan terrorists. There were far too many of them, and they were moving with a trained precision and ferocity possible only for elite combat troops. Worse, before the interior visual pickups in the space dock gallery went out, they'd given him an excellent view of the attackers' equipment.

Which appeared to be first-line Solarian Marine issue.

"Who the fuck *are* these people?!" Jonathan Arnold's voice sounded on the brink of hysteria over Takashi's earbug.

"How the hell do I know?" Takashi shot back.

"Those are goddamned Solly Marine plasma and pulse rifles they're carrying!"

"Oh, *really*?" Takashi's response dripped vitriolic irony. He started to add something even more bitingly sarcastic, then made himself draw a deep breath, instead.

"Yes, they've got Marine-issue equipment," he said. "It doesn't make them Marines. Hell, *you've* got Marine pulse rifles and tribarrels! Besides, what would Solly Marines be doing attacking us?"

"What the hell is anyone *else* doing attacking us?" Arnold demanded. Which, Takashi admitted to himself, was a perfectly reasonable question. Unfortunately, it was one he had no answer for.

"Who they are doesn't matter," he said instead. "What matters is that you and your people get your asses in gear and stop whatever it is they think they're doing!"

Arnold grunted something which might have been an affirmative, and then Takashi heard him begin giving his first coherent orders to his own personnel. The security man's voice still didn't sound anything remotely like calm, but at least he sounded as if he was beginning to think, not simply dither, and that had to be an improvement.

Didn't it?

"Okay, Thandi," Ruth Winton's voice said in Thandi's ear. "Their military commander—his name's Arnold, if it matters—is starting to get his act together. Do you want a direct feed from his com link?"

Thandi managed not to roll her eyes. Anything less like proper military procedure than Ruth's idea of communications protocol would have been impossible to imagine. On the other hand, how often did a tactical commander have the opportunity to actually listen in on her opponent's instructions to her troops? Still . . .

"Not a raw feed," she decided. "I don't know enough about the station's internal layout to be able to interpret movement orders. It'd only confuse me if I tried. Captain Zilwicki?"

"Here, Lieutenant," a deep voice rumbled.

"Please monitor the op force communications. Don't worry about the details. Just keep me informed of anything you think I should know."

"Check," Zilwicki acknowledged, but then he continued. "Ruth's done a little better than you know, Lieutenant. She's not just into their communications net now. She's managed to tap into the visual pickups of their internal security systems." Thandi could almost hear the savage smile in his voice. "We can actually see their troops moving into position."

"Can we, now?" Thandi murmured, and she had no doubt at all what Zilwicki heard in *her* voice.

"Indeed we can," Zilwicki assured her. "In fact, Ruth is still pulling in information, and it looks like she's just found the master schematic for the entire station. We're integrating now against the visual input from their security cameras. Give us another couple of minutes, and we ought to be able to begin giving you the other side's positions and movements."

"Like fish in a barrel," Thandi heard Lieutenant Colonel Huang murmur over the command net, and she nodded, not that anyone could tell from outside her armor.

"Yeah," Zilwicki agreed. "Pity, isn't it?"

Major Arnold, unlike Thandi Palane, didn't believe in leading his troops from the front. To be fair, it wasn't out of any particular cowardice. He simply saw no reason to leave his own command post. All of the space station's security systems reported to him there, which meant it was the best place from which to monitor the battle. And it wasn't as if his troops were the sort to inspire a commanding officer with the kind of mutual loyalty which led to nonsense like commanding by example.

"—sorry ass up to Level Twelve," he said, glaring at the anxious face on his com screen. "I've got Maguire's team covering the lifts on Ten and Eleven. But so far, it looks like these bastards have a pretty damned good idea where they're going and how to get there. So if you don't get up there in time to block Axial Three, the sorry sons of bitches are going to march straight past you into Command Central. Now *move,* dammit!"

The woman on his screen gave a nod somewhere between curt and spastic, and Arnold punched for a fresh connection to another of his team commanders.

Captain Zenas Maguire decided he'd been an idiot to ever sign up with Manpower, however good the money had been. Of course, it was beginning to look as if it were a bit late for second thoughts, but still—

He took one last look at the schematic of his units' positions and nodded to himself. It was the best he could do, and at least his teams of plasma gunners were positioned to make it suicidal for the attackers to approach along any of the main passageways. He hadn't actually seen any of the imagery of the initial break-in into the dock gallery, but he hadn't had to see it to realize that whoever was coming after him was a hell of a lot better trained than *his* people were. But at least the defenders were intimately familiar with the vast, labyrinthine maze of the space station's confusing internal passageways.

"What d' you think's going on?"

Maguire turned to look at Lieutenant Annette Kawana, his second-in-command. Kawana had once been a Solarian Marine sergeant, herself, although she hadn't exactly left the Corps on the best of terms.

"I think Manpower is about to get buggered," he said flatly. "And unfortunately, it looks like we're going to get the same, only harder."

"What the fuck do they *want*?" Kawana demanded, and Maguire managed not to throttle her by telling himself that the question was obviously rhetorical.

"I don't know," he told her with massive restraint. "On the other hand, I think it might be good idea for someone to ask *them* that question. Don't you?"

"All right, Lieutenant. They're in position and settling down." Anton Zilwicki's voice was a rumbling murmur, almost as if he were afraid the Manpower security goons might overhear him, Thandi thought with a flicker of amusement.

Of course, he's busy listening to them, *so maybe it isn't quite as silly as it seems. Not that keeping his voice down is going to make any difference!*

"Acknowledged," she said, keeping any trace of humor out of her reply. "Wait one."

She checked her tactical display. Colonel Huang had been right about the fish and the barrel, she thought. Of course, it helped that the other side obviously couldn't have poured piss out of a boot without printed instructions on the heel. Thandi's Marines had been systematically knocking out the security scanners as they advanced, but by now it should have occurred to at least one of the Manpower morons that certain of her people had been dropping steadily out of sight.

Ruth Winton's penetration of the space station's surveillance net allowed her to do more than simply spy on the enemy. She'd also managed to compare the master schematic for the station to the surveillance coverage, and she'd discovered that the central ventilation system wasn't monitored at all. The access points were, but once the cameras in any given section of corridor had been knocked out, there was no way for anyone on the other side to know who—or what—might be slipping quietly into the ventilation shafts.

Seems like I end up crawling around the guts of every space station I go aboard, she thought sardonically. *Maybe my lunatic ancestors included a little rodent DNA in the mix?* She snorted. *Not that I'm about to complain.*

"Decoy One," she said.

"Yes, Kaja?" It was Donald, in charge of the Ballroom gunmen who continued ostentatiously, if slowly, advancing down the direct route towards the Manpower blocking position. She'd left a half dozen Marines to keep an eye on things, but it was Donald's command.

"We're just about ready," she told him, "but Lara's team is about four minutes behind, and you're only two hatches from contact. Slow down just a bit. We want them looking your way, not spooked, and she needs to catch up."

"Understood, Kaja."

"Kaja, clear."

Surely by now someone on the other side should have noticed that over three-quarters of her battle-armored personnel had disappeared. *She* certainly would have. But maybe she was being a bit harder on them than was fair. They were getting only glimpses of the front of Donald's column before their visual sensors were knocked out, after all.

She watched her display, suppressing any sign of impatience, while she waited for Decoy Two to get into position. It wasn't Lara's fault that her group had fallen a bit behind the others, and the ex-Scrag was working hard to make up the differential.

There!

"All Tango-Lima-Alpha units, this is Kaja. Standby to execute on my command."

She waited two more heartbeats, then—

"All units, execute!"

Zenas Maguire settled deeper into his selected position. There wasn't any such thing as a *good* position from which to direct the defense of such a complicated tangle of passageways and corridors, so he'd had to select the best one he could find. At least it was more or less centrally located in his area of responsibility.

Unfortunately, it appeared that the attackers were headed directly for the same position, almost as if they knew that it lay at the center of his dispositions. Which was impossible, of course.

He watched the imagery from the cameras covering the last hatch between his people and them, and his belly was a hollow, singing void. He'd never expected to face serious combat as one of Manpower's hired guns. That was one reason he'd taken the job. He was tired of getting shot at for the miserly pay of a Silesian Army lieutenant, and making sure that a bunch of slaves didn't get uppity had seemed a beguiling change of pace. Not to mention how much better the money was.

Well, I guess what goes around, comes around. Whoever these people are, they obviously don't much like Manpower, which means they aren't going to like anyone who works for it, either. So the only way to save my *ass is to save Arnold's and Takashi's. The sorry bastards. If they'd done their jobs properly in the first place, none of us would—*

Something clanged behind him. Metal on metal, his mind reported, but what *kind* of metal? He started to turn towards the sound, and a blur of motion caught at the corner of his eye.

His attention flicked towards it, and both eyes began to widen in disbelief as he saw the deck-to-ceiling ventilation grate lying on the deck and the Solarian Marine, battle armor in heavy-assault configuration, striding out of the opening.

Zenas Maguire's eyes never finished widening all the way, and his brain never quite completed the identification of what he saw, because the trigger finger of Corporal Jane Borkai, Company Bravo,

Second Battalion, 877th Solarian Marines, closed the circuit on her plasma rifle first. That "rifle" was a cannon in all but name—the sort of weapon only someone in battle armor could carry—and the ravening packet of plasma it sent screaming across the compartment wiped out Maguire, Kawana, six more of Maguire's personnel, eight bulkheads, two blast doors, three main power conduits, a sanitation main, two fire suppression control points . . . and all trace of central command among the defenders.

Five other ventilation grates were kicked open almost simultaneously, and five other Marines—two of them armed "only" with heavy tribarrels—bounded through the sudden openings and opened fire. They appeared in the midst of Maguire's carefully chosen defensive positions, like demon djinn conjured out of nothingness, and their fire was devastatingly accurate. Maguire's troopers outnumbered their attackers by at least three-to-one, and it didn't matter at all. Not when Ruth had been able to steer Thandi and her Marines into positions of such crushing advantage. Almost half the defenders were killed in the first four seconds of Thandi's attack, and the sudden, totally unexpected savagery was too much for the traumatized survivors. Their stomach for combat died with their commanders, and weapons thudded to the deck amid frantic offers of surrender.

Homer Takashi watched in gray-faced shock as the green icons of friendly units vanished from his display with sudden and terrifying finality. How? How could anyone *do* that? It was impossible! Unless—?

The ventilation system! That was the only possible avenue, the only way people in something as bulky as battle armor could have avoided the main corridors. But that was still impossible! For it to work, the attackers would have to have known the internal layout of the space station better than people who'd lived and worked aboard it literally for T-years!

Not that it mattered. However they'd managed it, they'd also timed it perfectly. Arnold had divided his available strength into four well chosen blocking positions . . . and the attackers had maneuvered into position to take all four of them out simultaneously. In the space of less than ten minutes, effectively every defender, aside from the single platoon Arnold had held out as a tactical reserve, had been eliminated. And even as Takashi watched the illuminated schematic of the station, whole sectors were turning from green to bloody crimson as the invaders fanned out towards the fusion rooms, life-support, the com section . . . and Central Command.

And then the illuminated schematic disappeared, and Takashi swallowed hard as a beardless face replaced it. *He* certainly hadn't ordered the display reconfigured for communications, and a cold, numb suspicion of just how the enemy had become so intimately familiar with the internal geography of his space station filled him.

Not that he had much opportunity to digest the thought. Even as he stared at the screen, the cold-eyed man on it opened his mouth . . . and stuck out his tongue.

Takashi's breathing stopped. Every voice in the command center fell instantly still. The only sound was the subdued beeping of com channels and emergency alarms. Then the face on the screen spoke.

"My name," it said, in a voice of liquid helium, "is Jeremy X."

"*Oh my God,*" someone whimpered into the sudden, ice-cold silence. The galaxy's most notorious terrorist allowed that silence to linger for what seemed a small, deadly eternity. Then his lips moved in a smile which held no slightest trace of humor.

"Surrender, and you'll live," he said flatly. "Choose not to surrender, and you won't. Personally, I'd prefer for you to take the second option, but it's up to you. And you have precisely ninety seconds to make up your mind."

CHAPTER 46

"CIC CONFIRMS THE OUTER PLATFORMS' reports, Sir." Commander Blumenthal's quiet voice only seemed loud in the quiet of *Gauntlet*'s command deck. "Three light cruisers, two heavy cruisers, one battlecruiser, and fourteen destroyers."

"Still nothin' from them, Lieutenant Cheney?" Michael Oversteegen asked calmly.

"Not a word, Sir," the com officer confirmed.

"But they're not exactly makin' a secret of their identity, now are they?" Oversteegen murmured rhetorically.

"You could put it that way, I suppose, Sir," Commander Watson agreed with a slight, sardonic smile.

The twenty incoming ships hadn't transmitted any messages or challenges—not yet. Except for one. Their com sections might not be saying anything, but they were making absolutely no attempt to hide their approach, and every one of them was squawking the transponder code of the Mesan Space Navy.

"Now, I wonder just what they could want?" Oversteegen responded to his XO, and several people surprised themselves with chuckles. It was the first time any of them had felt a great deal like chuckling over the last three standard days.

"Well," the captain continued after a moment, "I suppose that if they're not goin' t' be courteous enough t' open communications, then it's up t' us. Be kind enough t' put me on mike, Lieutenant."

"Aye, aye, Sir," Cheney responded, and tapped a stud at her console. "Live mike, Sir."

"Unknown vessels," Oversteegen said calmly, "this is Captain Michael Oversteegen, Royal Manticoran Navy, commandin' Her Majesty's Starship *Gauntlet*. Please identify yourselves and state your purpose and intentions."

The transmission went out at light speed, and Oversteegen leaned back in his command chair, waiting while it crossed the four light-minutes still lying between the newcomers and *Gauntlet.* Nine minutes later, a square-jawed, strong-nosed male face appeared on his communications display.

"Captain Oversteegen," the face's owner said harshly, "I am Commodore Aikawa Navarre, Mesan Space Navy, and I find it difficult to believe that you are not perfectly well aware of the reason for my units' presence in this system."

Cold hazel eyes narrowed, and Navarre allowed several seconds of silence to linger. Then he continued.

"Before Mr. Takashi was forced to surrender his space station to the notorious terrorist Jeremy X, a dispatch boat had already been sent to summon assistance. Fortunately, the boat was still in communications range of the space station at the time of its surrender. Equally fortunately, the system authorities had been informed of the presence of my task group in the vicinity, conducting routine exercises."

The hazel eyes didn't even flicker at the straight-faced phrase "routine exercises," Oversteegen noticed.

"Because of that, I was able to respond immediately. And also because of that, Captain Oversteegen, I am quite well informed on what had occurred prior to the dispatch boat's departure. Which means, Captain, that I am aware that the entire 'crisis' in which the supposed 'terrorists' kidnaped a member of your kingdom's royal family, was obviously a pure invention. A carefully engineered deception whose sole purpose was to permit an organization outlawed by every major star nation—*including your own*—to seize the property of a Mesan corporation and to murder scores of its employees.

"Not content with that, *Captain,*" Navarre's voice went even colder, "your ship has seen fit to sit here in orbit while those same terrorists carried out systematic, brutal atrocities and the massacre of men, women, and children on the surface of the planet Verdant Vista!"

Navarre might not have spent any effort on opening communications with *Gauntlet,* Oversteegen reflected, but he had obviously taken time to download a complete news report from the media ships still covering the story of the liberation of Congo.

And what a spectacularly bloody story it had become, he thought grimly. Much though it galled him to his soul to admit it, there was more than a faint echo of truth to Navarre's last accusation.

"Under the circumstances, Captain Oversteegen," the Mesan

continued, "and given that you yourself have completely failed in your obvious responsibility to prevent the brutal and savage shedding of innocent blood, *I* intend to put a stop to it. I would not advise you to further try my patience by attempting to impede me in the performance of my duty."

"I don't believe you accurately apprehend the circumstances obtainin' on this planet," Oversteegen replied in an equally cold voice. "I give you my solemn word, as a Queen's officer, that not a single 'terrorist'—or anyone else—landed from the space station orbiting the planet *Torch*—" he emphasized the planet's new name deliberately "—participated in any of the bloodshed you just described. If you so desire, you may check with the officers and news personnel aboard any of the four media vessels which, at my suggestion, were invited t' monitor events aboard the space station following its surrender t' the forces of the Torch Liberation Army."

"*Torch Liberation Army!*" Navarre's face twisted in a sneer as he repeated the phrase. "What a *respectable* name for a pack of cowardly, murderous vermin. I am shocked—no, Captain, *sickened*—to hear anyone calling himself a naval officer, even of a backwater, neobarb '*star kingdom,*' acting as a mouthpiece for the scum of the galaxy. I suppose they expected to be in a position to pay you a handsome bribe for your services after they got done looting *Verdant Vista*."

"How fortunate for you, Commodore," Oversteegen said calmly, "that you're in a position t' bandy your accusations from the security of your command deck. I, of course, as a benighted subject of my 'neobarb' monarch, far too uncivilized t' appreciate the splendor of your civilized turn of phrase, might be tempted t' react t' them with unseemly violence. Particularly when they come from a man who chooses to wear the uniform of the single so-called 'navy' which has, for the past nine T-centuries, *protected* the systematic trade in human bein's. And which, I might take this opportunity t' observe, since you have just so rightly condemned the massacre of women and children on Torch, has connived at and cooperated with the systematic sale, torture, degradation, and casual murder of literally millions of those same human bein's durin' that period. At least, Sir, the uniform of the Queen of Manticore has never been sold t' the service of whoremasters, murderers, pedophiles, sadists, and perverts. I suppose, however, that those of you who choose t' serve in the navy of Mesa feel comfortable amid such company."

Navarre's face flushed and his square jaw quivered as Oversteegen's cold, cutting words struck home. Then his upper lip drew back.

"I do, indeed, feel comfortable in the service of my star nation," he said, softly. "And I am looking forward to the opportunity to deal with you and your ship in the fashion you so amply deserve, Captain. In the interest of demonstrating respect for interstellar law, however, I will give you one last opportunity to avoid the consequences of your arrogance and criminal activities in this system. You will release any surviving Mesan citizens in your custody. And you will turn over to me the terrorist butchers responsible for the outrages and murders committed on the surface of Verdant Vista."

"There are no citizens of Mesa in my custody, Commodore," Oversteegen replied. "All such prisoners are in the custody of the provisional government of the independent planet Torch. And, I repeat, none of the personnel involved in the capture of the space station in orbit around Torch participated in acts of violence against any civilian, regardless of age or gender, on that planet's surface. The actions to which you refer, and which the provisional government deeply regrets and deplores, were committed by the citizens of Torch in the course of liberatin' themselves from the brutality and systematic abuse, starvation, torture, and, yes, murder, of the institution of genetic slavery of which your star nation thinks so highly."

"*Citizens!*" Navarre spat. "Rabble! Scum! Cat—!"

He chopped himself off before the word "cattle" slipped fully out, and Oversteegen smiled thinly. The encrypted communications channel between *Gauntlet* and Navarre's flagship was theoretically totally secure. Theory, however, had a habit of sometimes coming up short against reality, and Navarre was clearly conscious of the watching—and possibly listening—news ships still camped out in the Congo System. For that matter, he had to realize that Oversteegen was recording the entire exchange, so a certain discretion was undoubtedly called for.

The Mesan commodore drew a deep breath, then squared his shoulders and glowered at Oversteegen.

"Very well, Captain," he said icily. "Since you decline to discharge your responsibilities, I will discharge them *for* you. I suggest that you stand aside, because my task group is about to put an end to the bloodshed and atrocities being committed on Verdant Vista."

"I regret, Sir," Oversteegen replied, not sounding as if he regretted anything in the least, "that I can't do that. The provisional government of Torch has appealed t' the Star Kingdom of Manticore for protection and assistance in establishin' and maintainin' public order on their planet. As Her Majesty's senior officer in this sector, I have provisionally agreed in her name t' extend that assistance t' the government and citizens of Torch."

"Stand aside," Navarre grated. "I won't warn you again, Captain. And while I am aware of your somewhat exaggerated reputation, I suggest that you consider the odds carefully. If you attempt to hinder me in the performance of my duty, I will not hesitate to engage and destroy your vessel. Do you really wish to kill your entire crew and risk open war between your star nation and mine over a planet full of outlaws?"

"Well," Oversteegen said with a cold, hungry smile, "defendin' other people's planets against unprovoked attack by murderous scum seems t' have become something of a tradition for my Queen's Navy over the past few decades. Under the circumstances, I'm sure she'll forgive me for followin' that tradition."

"Are you totally insane?" Navarre asked in a tone which had become almost conversational. "You have one cruiser, Oversteegen. I have five, plus a battlecruiser and screen. Are you really stupid enough to take on that much tonnage all by yourself?"

"Oh, not quite *all* by himself," another voice said coolly, and Navarre stiffened as his com screen split and an officer in the uniform of a captain in the Solarian League Navy suddenly appeared upon it beside Michael Oversteegen.

"Captain Luis Rozsak, SLN," the newcomer said, "and this is my command," he added, as the units of his destroyer flotilla disengaged their stealth systems and brought their impeller wedges to full power in a perfectly synchronized maneuver. Eighteen destroyers and Rozsak's light cruiser flagship suddenly appeared on Navarre's sensors.

"Who the hell are you?" Navarre demanded, shocked out of his easy assumption of superiority by the abrupt appearance of so many more ships.

"I am the senior naval officer assigned by the Solarian Navy to the Maya Sector," Rozsak said calmly. "And, as Captain Oversteegen, the Solarian League, in the form of the Maya Sector, has also been appealed to by the provisional government of Torch for assistance and protection."

"And?" Navarre snarled.

"And the sector has decided to extend that assistance and protection," Rozsak told him.

"Barregos has *agreed* to this lunacy?" Navarre shook his head, his expression incredulous.

"The actual decision was made by Lieutenant Governor Cassetti," Rozsak said. "The lieutenant governor has initialed a commercial and mutual defense treaty with the provisional government."

"There *is* no provisional government!" Navarre half-shouted. "There can't be!" He clenched his fists, obviously fighting for self-control. "The planet is the property of a Mesan corporation."

"The planet, like any other planet, belongs to its citizens," Roszak corrected. "That, Commodore, has been the official policy of the Solarian League from its inception."

Navarre stared at him, and Oversteegen was hard pressed not to laugh outright at the Mesan's expression. True, the policy Rozsak had just enunciated—with, Oversteegen noted, a completely straight face—had indeed been the official one of the Solarian League from the beginning. It was also one the Office of Frontier Security had ignored for centuries . . . when it hadn't actively conspired to fold, twist, and mutilate it with the connivance of powerful corporations and business combines.

Corporations and combines headquartered, quite often, on Mesa, as it happened.

"The 'citizens' to whom you refer," Navarre said, after a long, silent pause, "were transported to this planet, housed, and fed by Manpower. They are, in effect, the employees of the corporation. As such, they have no legal standing as 'citizens,' and certainly no legal right to . . . expropriate the company's property."

"The citizens of Torch," Roszak said, and this time his voice was just as cold as Oversteegen's had been, "were transported to this planet by Manpower not as employees, Commodore, but as *property*. And I would remind you that the Constitution of the Solarian League specifically rejects and outlaws the institution of slavery, whether genetically based or not, and that the League has steadfastly refused *ever* to recognize any legal standing for the institution or its practice. As such, the League views the present inhabitants of Torch as its legal citizens and owners and has negotiated in good faith with the provisional government which they have established."

"And that's your final position, is it?" Navarre's hazel eyes glittered with fury and hatred, and Roszak smiled.

"Like Captain Oversteegen, I'm only a naval officer, Commodore, not a diplomat, and certainly not a sector governor. I am obviously not in any position to tell you what Governor Barregos' final official position will be. At the moment, however, Lieutenant Governor Cassetti, as Governor Barregos' personal representative, has provisionally recognized Torch's independence and entered binding treaty relationships with it. I suppose that it's always possible Governor Barregos will determine that the lieutenant governor exceeded his authority in taking those actions and repudiate them, but until such time as he does so, I remain bound by the existing treaties." His smile disappeared. "And I *will* enforce them, Commodore," he added in a very cold voice, indeed.

"The two of you together wouldn't stand a chance against my task group," Navarre said flatly.

"You might be surprised by how much of a chance we'd stand," Roszak replied. "And while you might very probably win in the end, the cost would be . . . considerable. I rather doubt that your admiralty would be very happy about that."

"And speakin' purely as a backward and benighted neobarb," Oversteegen observed with deadly affability, "I really suspect, Commodore, that your government would be most unhappy with the officer who managed, in one afternoon, t' get them into a shootin' war with both the Solarian League and the Star Kingdom of Manticore."

Navarre deflated visibly. It was rather like watching the air flow out of a punctured balloon, Oversteegen thought. The commodore was clearly picturing what a squadron or two of modern Manticoran ships-of-the-wall could do to the entire Mesan Navy. Especially if the Solarian League wasn't simply giving them free passage to reach Mesa but actually acting as a cobelligerent.

Rozsak saw the same thoughts flow across Navarre's face and smiled once more, ever so slightly.

"I think, Commodore," he suggested gently, "that it might be best, all things considered, if you left the sovereign star system of Torch.

"Now."

CHAPTER 47

BERRY FOUND IT DIFFICULT NOT TO WINCE, watching the Mesan personnel filing past her into the building which served Congo—*no, Torch, now*—as the assembly area for its shuttle grounds. The faces of the children, of which there were more than she'd expected, were especially hard to watch. Their expressions were a combination of exhaustion, terror, shock—in some cases, what looked like borderline psychosis.

Those people were the survivors of the savage slave rebellion which had erupted on Congo as soon as word began to spread that the space station had been seized by . . .

Whoever. It didn't matter, really, as long as they were anti-Mesan. Congo had been a prison planet, in essence. Once all of the really powerful military forces at the disposal of Mesa, including the kinetic missiles with which the planet could be bombarded in case of extreme necessity, had been taken out of the equation, the Mesan personnel on the planet had been, for all practical purposes, in the same position as British clerks had been when the Sepoy Mutiny swept over them. Dead meat, if they didn't get to an enclave quick enough. The light weaponry in the hands of the overseers, by itself, was simply not enough to cow slaves filled with the fury of generations of oppression and exploitation.

Not even close. Those overseers who did try to stand their ground had been overwhelmed—and their weapons turned to the use of killing other overseers. Not just "overseers," either. *Anyone*—even a child—associated with "Mesa" or especially "Manpower" had been under sentence of death, everywhere on the planet's surface. A sentence which had been imposed immediately, mercilessly, and in some cases accompanied by the most horrible atrocities.

There had been some exceptions, here and there. Mesans whose duties had not involved discipline over the slaves, especially those who had established a reputation for being at least decent, had been spared in a number of cases. There was even one instance where an entire settlement of Mesan scientists and pharmaceutical technicians and their families had been protected by an improvised slave defense guard against slaves coming in from the outside.

But, for the most part, any Mesan who hadn't gotten himself quickly enough to one of the enclaves where armed Mesans had been able to fort up and hold off the slaves until the surrender was negotiated had simply been slaughtered. The entire surface of the planet had been engulfed, for two days, in a wave of pure murder.

And it hadn't taken long for the word to spread, either—nor the further word that the space station was now in the hands of the Audubon Ballroom, which had simply poured fuel on an already spreading conflagration. *Death to Mesa. Death to Manpower. Now.*

Once again, Berry realized, the economic reality of slavery based on a high level of technical advancement had manifested itself. There were simply too many ways for literate slaves, in a modern technical society, to gain access to information once the opportunity arose. Which it had, in most cases, when dumbfounded slaves suddenly saw Mesan overseers and staff personnel piling into vehicles and abandoning the area—their faces making their own panic obvious. The slaves, after an initial hesitation, had simply walked into the communications centers and discovered the information on the computer screens—computers which many of them knew perfectly well how to operate.

Death. Death. Death. All of them! Now!

In some cases, the departing Mesans had had the foresight to destroy the equipment. But, more often than not, in their panicky haste to simply flee for a refuge, they had neglected to do so. And, once the com centers had started falling into the hands of the slaves, the slaves had rapidly begun establishing their own communication network across the planet. This was a rebellion which had all the pitiless rage of Nat Turner's—but whose slaves were very far from illiterate field hands. They had organized themselves just about as quickly and readily as the slaves on *Felicia* had done, after Templeton's seizure of the ship. And, like the slaves on *Felicia,* there had been enough undercover agents of the Ballroom to serve as an organizing and directing catalyst.

Berry drew a long and shaky breath. It was over now, at least—and, at least, she could remind herself that she had been the central figure in ending the slaughter. Before the second of

Congo's twenty-seven-hour days had passed, she'd been able to establish contact with all the remaining Mesan enclaves, as well as the major slave organizing centers, and negotiate a surrender. Her terms had been simple: In exchange for their lives and whatever personal possessions they could carry, provided they surrendered immediately and made no attempt at sabotage, any Mesan who wanted to leave the planet would be allowed to do so with no further harm. Under Solarian Navy escort, and into the safekeeping of the Solarian Navy. She'd even offered to place the *Felicia* at the disposal of the Solarian Navy, to provide the needed transport.

That last decision had been one she'd made with some reluctance. As with everyone involved during those long weeks, *Felicia* had come to occupy a special place in her heart. She'd even been the one to give the ship her new name: *Hope,* she'd called her, repeating the name until she simply drove under all the competing names. Of which *Vengeance* had been the most popular.

She'd had to drive over even sharper opposition to get everyone's agreement to her proposal to use *Hope* as the transport for the departing Mesan personnel. Web Du Havel had sided with her immediately, but Jeremy had dug in his heels.

Let the swine make the trip in cubbyholes aboard Solarian warships.

The children, too?

Those are not children. Those are young vipers.

No. NO. There isn't enough room for all of them. Leave any behind . . .

Vipers.

Damn you, Jeremy! I will not be crowned standing in a lake of blood and vomit! End the slaughter now! NOW, do you hear!

It had been the first clash of wills between her and Jeremy. And . . .

She'd won, to her surprise. Mostly because, she decided afterward, even Jeremy had been a little shaken by the horror. Especially after one particularly savage group of slaves had gleefully broadcast a transmission which recorded for posterity the execution of three overseers. Insofar as the antiseptic term "execution" could be applied to death by torture.

Web had helped, adding his quiet and calm reasoning to her own stubborn fury.

"We must end it now, Jeremy—as quickly as possible, whatever it takes—or we will suffer a monumental disaster in public relations.

Bad enough that recording will be used by Manpower from now on, every chance they get. If we can at least demonstrate that the new government did everything in its power to bring the butchery to a halt, we can contain the damage. In the end, most people will accept the spontaneous fury of rebelling slaves. They will *not* accept the cold-blooded callousness of established power. Let them have the *Hope*."

Rozsak had even helped. "I'll see to it you get the ship back, after we've transported the survivors."

Whether the Solarian captain would make good on the promise, remained to be seen. But now, as she watched the last survivors filing toward the waiting shuttles, Berry found herself not caring any longer. The *Hope* was a small price to pay, to end *this.*

Even worse than the expressions on the faces of the survivors, in some ways, were the expressions on the faces of the Ballroom members—any ex-slave, really—who stood near her watching them leave.

Pitiless. Utterly, completely pitiless.

Berry understood the reasons for that, true enough. There were many recordings in their possession now, which the triumphant slaves had seized. Some of them official recordings made by the Mesan authorities, but many of them private recordings left behind by now-dead or evacuating Mesan personnel. A number of the overseers had been particularly fond of keeping mementos of the atrocities they had visited on slaves, over the long years. Recordings which ranged from nauseating depictions of personal brutalities to the—in some ways even more nauseating—depictions of slave bodies being used as raw material for Mesan chemical vats.

Let Mesa try to use their few recordings of slave atrocities. Now that it was over—had been ended, as all could attest, as quickly as the new government could manage it—Mesa's propaganda campaign would be buried under an avalanche of *their own* recordings. Already, Berry knew, the galactic media's representatives in-system were practically salivating over the material. It was all . . . disgusting, really. But she could accept "disgusting," for the sake of the future.

That same future, moreover, was clear as crystal to her. She understood now, deep in her belly, everything that Web Du Havel had once explained to her and Ruth about the dangers which faced a successful slave rebellion. Fury and rage and hatred might be necessary to create a nation and drag it screaming and fighting out of the womb of oppression and cruelty, but they could not serve as its foundation. Those emotions, for a society as much as an individual person, needed to be leached away. Lest they become toxic, over time, and lead to madness.

It was odd, in a way. Berry herself had once had to go through that experience, after Anton had taken her from Terra's underground and brought her to Manticore. At Anton and Cathy's insistence—though Berry herself had protested it was an unnecessary expense—she'd gone through an extensive therapy program. Where she'd discovered, to her surprise, that her own horrendous experiences—especially the protracted beating and gang rape she'd suffered just at the end, before Helen rescued her—had left far greater wounds on her psyche than she'd realized.

She knew that her therapist had told Anton, after it was over, that Berry was perhaps intrinsically the sanest individual she'd ever treated. But "sanity" was not a magic shield against the universe's cruelties. It was simply a tool. The same tool she would now spend decades using, to do what she could to heal a new nation.

She turned her head and looked up at Jeremy, standing to her right. He avoided her eyes, for a few seconds. Then, sighing, looked down at her.

"All right, lass. You were right. Although if that damn Solarian captain doesn't return the *Hope* . . ."

"You'll do nothing," she said. Proclaimed, rather.

"Blast it, you're getting far too good at this proclamation business," he muttered.

Berry restrained her smile. Indeed, she even managed to keep her face stern and solemn. "You *still* haven't agreed to the other. I know you, Jeremy. You don't forget things. You also keep your word. So the only reason you haven't given me an answer is because you're stalling. You've stalled enough. I want an answer. Now."

He made an exasperated little gesture. "*Will* you cease and desist with this Catherine the Great imitation? I wouldn't mind, if it were a bad one."

This time, she couldn't help but smile a little. But all she said was: "*Now.*"

"All right!" he said, throwing up his hands. "You have my agreement. My word, if you will. Any stinking lousy Mesans who choose to remain on the planet can do so. No repercussions, no discrimination against them, nothing."

"You have to stop calling them 'stinking lousy Mesans,' too. Those who remain behind are now simply Torches."

Jeremy's lips quirked. "I still think 'Torches' is a silly expression."

"It's better than 'Torchese,' which sounds like a breed of dog," she replied firmly. "And stop changing the subject."

"A tyrant! A veritable tsarina!" He glared at Web Du Havel, standing to her left. "It's your fault. You created this Frankenstein's monster."

Web smiled, but made no reply. Berry decided that she'd probably been imperious enough, and it was time for royal wheedling. Teenage queen style.

"Oh, come on, Jeremy. There aren't that many, first off. And almost half of them live in that one settlement that the slaves themselves protected. They're nothing but *biologists,* for pity's sake. According to the reports I've heard, they didn't even realize where their contract was going to wind up placing them. And, after they got here, they were too engrossed in the fascination of their work to pay much attention to anything else. If nothing else, we can use their talents. They brought their whole families with them, they've now been here for years, and this is their *home.* That's enough. The same's true, one way or another, for all the others who want to stay. Which, as I said, isn't more than a few hundred anyway."

Now, imperiously again: "So the issue is settled. You agreed."

Jeremy took a deep breath, then nodded. Then, after glancing at the assembly building and seeing the last of the survivors passing through the doors, he shrugged. "As you say, it's settled. And now—Your Majesty—I need to be off. Cassetti's coming down tomorrow for his precious little 'victory tour' and I need to make sure my, ah, not-entirely-respectful Ballroom detachment has a proper attitude about their duties."

"I though the Solarians were providing Cassetti's bodyguard?" asked Du Havel.

Jeremy's lips quirked. "Oh, they are. Quite a sizeable one, in fact, with none less than *Major* Thandi Palane in charge of it. Her last assignment, before her resignation takes effect. But it seems the honorable Ingemar Cassetti feels that a native contingent is needed as well. Apparently the man has firm opinions on the subject of his own security and prestige."

After Jeremy was gone, Berry smiled up at Du Havel. "What do you think, Web? Is my 'Catherine the Great' impersonation really all that good?"

"It's pretty impressive, as a matter of fact. But . . ."

He studied her for a moment. "I'm glad it's just an act."

She made a face. "So am I. Even leaving aside what Ruth told me about the rumors concerning her sexual habits."

Web grimaced. "The famous horse? That's almost certainly a legend invented by her enemies. Not that Catherine was exactly what you'd call fastidious in her personal habits. But that wasn't really what I meant. I'm not worried about *you,* actually. I'm concerned about how your new people decide to look upon you. Especially in light of the poll taken yesterday."

The proposal to make the new star nation of Torch a constitutional monarchy, with Berry as the founding queen, hadn't been voted on by the populace yet. Nor would it be, for several more weeks, to allow everyone scattered across the planet time to ponder the matter. But Web had taken an initial poll the day before, using standard techniques which usually gave good results. He'd been a bit shocked when he saw the results. *Eighty-seven percent in favor, with a margin of error of plus-or-minus four percent.*

He hadn't expected better than seventy percent, he'd told Berry. He wasn't sure yet, but he thought two factors had made the difference. First, the enthusiastic recommendation of the thousands of ex-slaves from the *Felicia*, who were quickly spreading across the planet as the new government's informal organizing cadre. Second—perhaps even more importantly, and certainly something he *hoped* was true—because now that the slaves had sated their initial bloodlust, they were a little shaken themselves at the experience. Berry's holo image had been broadcast widely across the planet's com web. Her *real* one, since the weeks aboard *Felicia* had also been used by Erewhonese biotechs to reverse the nanotech disguise. And if there was any human image Web could imagine that might help people claw their way out of a pit of rage and hatred, it was that calm, intelligent-looking, pretty young girl's face. It was simply impossible to look at Berry and think her a threat or a menace, to *anyone.*

"What do you mean by that?" she asked.

"Let's put it this way. There will be a strong impulse—especially given your own capabilities, which are becoming increasingly clear to me—for your new nation to want to call you, as time goes by, 'Berry the Great.'"

She made a face, as if she'd bitten into something sour. "Oh, *yuck*. Between exercise and taking lessons from you—and trying to stagger along under the weight of 'the Great'?" She practically whined the next words: "How am I supposed to get a *boyfriend*, in all that? And what kind of screwball would he be, anyway?"

Web grinned. "Oh, you'd manage, I don't doubt that. But—being honest—that's the least of my worries. Mainly, you need to be careful about it because the truth is, judging from the historical record, that monarchs who go down as 'the Great' are usually a mixed blessing for their nations. As a rule, so obsessed with what they considered 'victories' and 'triumphs' that they left a pretty impressive butcher's bill behind."

"Not my style at all," Berry said firmly, shaking her head. "So what *should* I shoot for, Web?" With a half-giggle: " 'Berry the Sweet'?"

Web almost seemed to giggle himself. "Hardly that! A good monarch can't afford to be *too* gentle, either. No . . ."

His eyes ranged the landing field, looking beyond the first shuttles starting to take off to examine the lush, green terrain of Torch beyond. It was a rich landscape, almost steaming with potential wealth.

"I'll tell you what to shoot for, girl. Mind you, it'll take decades to get there. Long, slow decades, where a new people has time to settle into itself. Relax, if you will. And part of that relaxation—no small part—simply coming from steadiness and stability. Shoot for that. Aim *that* high. Aim for the day to come when they call you something which precious few monarchs in the long history of the human race have ever been called. Far fewer, when you get down to it, than have been called 'the Great.' "

He brought his eyes back to her. "Nothing complicated, nothing fancy. Just . . . 'Good Queen Berry.' That's all. And that'll be enough."

She thought about it, for a while. "I can do that," she pronounced.

"Oh, yes, dear one. I know you can."

CHAPTER 48

"DON'T EVEN *TRY* FEEDING ME THAT CRAP, Kevin," hissed the President of the Republic of Haven. Eloise Pritchart leaned so far forward in her chair that she was almost standing in a half-crouch. The palms of hands were planted flat on the desk, supporting much of her weight. Her eyes were slitted, her face pale with anger.

"You planned this from the very start! Don't try telling me that Cachat just—what did you call it?—'accidentally stumbled into an unforeseen situation.' Bullshit!"

Kevin Usher tried to snort derisively. The sound was . . . feeble.

"C'mon, Eloise! You're an experienced op yourself. You know damn good and well nobody could have 'planned' something like—"

"*Cut it out, damn you!*" Now, Pritchart was fully on her feet, leaning still farther over the desk. "I *know* you didn't 'plan' it that way. So what? I also know that you told Cachat from the get-go to see what he could stir up on Erewhon—and then run with it."

She glanced angrily at Ginny Usher, who was seated on a chair next to her husband. "*That's* why you wanted Cachat. All that stuff about Ginny was a smokescreen. Cachat is your gunslinger—your damn shoot-from-hip specialist. I *know* his record, Kevin! That lunatic can and will improvise anything on his feet. This stunt he pulled on Erewhon was even hairier than what he did in La Martine!"

Her eyes fell on the now-empty display screen on her desk, where she'd spent several hours studying the report Virginia Usher had brought back from Erewhon the day before. "Hairy?" she demanded. "Say better—'furry,' as in grizzly bear. For God's sake, he *deliberately* set up the killing of an entire unit of the Queen's Own Regiment!"

"That's not true!" burst out Ginny.

Pritchart glared at her, but Ginny stood her ground. Sat up straight, at least.

"Well, it *isn't,*" she insisted. "The attack was launched by Templeton and his fanatics. Victor had nothing to do with it."

Pritchart's snort wasn't feeble in the least. "Oh, splendid. But he *knew* about it, before it happened. Didn't he? He could have warned them—in which case dozens of people wouldn't have been slaughtered, half of them completely innocent civilians."

Ginny's expression was mulish, but she said nothing. Eloise continued her tirade.

"Not to mention the possible murder of a member of the Star Kingdom's royal house—whom he left right smack in the middle of a gunfight! Do you—*either* of you—have any idea what an unholy mess you'd have landed me in if it ever became known to the Manticorans that a Havenite agent . . . "

Her words trailed off, ending in a groan. She slumped back into her chair.

"Oh, I forgot that, didn't I? The Manticorans *do* know about it. Cachat—*that maniac!*—dragged the princess herself into the scheme afterward."

"He didn't *drag* her," Ginny muttered. "It'd be better to say, she jumped at the chance."

Before Pritchart could respond, the fourth person in the room cleared his throat and said: "You're really *not* being fair, Ms. President."

She swiveled her head and stared at Wilhelm Trajan, the director of the Federal Intelligence System. Her lips quirked into a half-grimace.

"*Et tu,* Wilhelm? I'd think you—of all people—would be even more pissed than I am. Among other things, this whole shaggy operation was a complete slap in the face to *you*."

Trajan shifted uncomfortably in his chair, his shoulders moving in a little shrug. "Yes. On the other hand, who's to say it wasn't a deserved one?" He gave Usher, seated across from him in the President's office, a none-too-friendly glance. "I can't say I appreciate it personally, of course. But the truth is—"

He planted his hands on his knees and leaned forward. "Madam President, let's start from what is in fact the key point. However he did it, Victor Cachat seems to have laid the basis—helped it along, anyway—for a break between Erewhon and Manticore. And, possibly, the beginning of an alliance between them and us."

He paused, cocking his head, waiting to see if she chose to

dispute the point. Pritchart's expression was sour, but . . . she said nothing.

"Right," Trajan continued. "And I'd point out that, if push comes to shove, I'm a lot more impressed by the possibly tens of thousands of Republican soldiers' lives which may be saved as a result of what he did, than I am with the death of some Erewhonese civilians and some Manticoran soldiers. With whom, by the way, we are still officially at war. Sorry, I know that's ruthless, but it's a cold universe."

Pritchart's face was very sour. But, still, she said nothing.

"Right," repeated the FIS Director. "So I think that before we climb all over Cachat, we at least need to give the devil his due."

"'Devil's' the word, too," hissed Eloise. "Or demon."

Trajan smiled thinly. "Well . . . what's that old saying? 'He's a bastard, sure—but he's *our* bastard.' Face it, Ms. President. Cachat is brilliant at this kind of thing. The real problem we've got here—the reason, being blunt, that he *had* to use what you call 'furry tactics'—is because FIS is still such a shuffling mess. If I'd been able to get this outfit turned around fast enough . . . if we hadn't had such an incompetent FIS staff on Erewhon . . ."

The FIS Director's face sagged wearily, and he lapsed from his usual formality. "Look, Eloise, face it. I'm not really cut out for this. You know—I know—Kevin knows—that Kevin would be ten times better at it. And, on the flip side, if we didn't face such a delicate political situation, I'd do a lot better as the head of the police force. I'm just not cut out for this work. I'm not incompetent, and I'm honest. But, other than that . . ."

He shrugged. "I don't have what it takes to give a foreign intelligence service the kind of panache and self-confidence it needs. It's as simple as that. And with so many of the real experts from the old Saint-Just regime now tossed out, that means I'm left with a cadre that's prone to sluggishness and excessive caution. And I just can't turn it around."

Eloise rubbed her face, which, in that moment, looked as tired as Trajan's. "Wilhelm, I can't afford to lose Kevin as the head of the FIS. Whatever else, I've got to make sure there aren't any more coup d'etats. And I don't know anyone except him who'd really do any better than you running the FIS."

Trajan smiled crookedly. "Of course you do. It ought to be blindingly obvious by now."

She frowned with puzzlement, for a moment. Then, when his meaning penetrated, gasped. Partly with shock, partly from outrage.

"You can't be serious! *Cachat?*"

Trajan's smile remained on his face. And his gaze remained level. "Yes, Eloise. The 'demon' himself. Again—start with the key point. He's *loyal.* Whatever else about him irritates you, I know you don't have any doubts about that. And he *is* a wizard at this work."

"He's a maniac!"

Ginny shot to her feet. "He is *not*!" Then, as if realizing who she was talking to, she flushed a little. "Okay, maybe a little. But he's not a 'maniac.' That just isn't fair." She plopped back into her chair. "It *isn't,*" she insisted.

"I'm not proposing to replace me with Cachat immediately, Madam President," Trajan said softly. "I agree with Ms. Usher that he's not a 'maniac,' but . . . ah . . . there's no question he could use some . . . ah . . ."

"Civilization?" Eloise demanded sarcastically. "Massive anti-testosterone treatments?"

Hearing a suspicious choking sound from Usher, she moved her eyes to him. "What are you trying not to laugh about?"

Usher waved a large hand. "Ah, never mind. Someday, after you've calmed down, Ginny can fill you in on some of the more private details of Cachat's, ah, operation on Erewhon."

Pritchart rolled her eyes. "Oh, marvelous. I had a *hunch* there was more to that renegade Solarian Marine officer than the reports said."

"She's *not* a renegade," Ginny growled.

Kevin sat up, discarding any traces of his previous—and very atypical—abashment. "No, she isn't. And cut the crap yourself, Eloise. You know the reality of the Solarian League. The woman's from *Ndebele,* for Pete's sake. Even if she were a 'renegade' from the SLN, so what? More power to her."

Pritchart rubbed her face again. "All right, all right," she grumbled. "Forget I said it. So Cachat's finally got a girlfriend, huh? Yes, yes—I'm sure she's a paragon of virtue."

Finally, the President's underlying sense of humor surfaced. Her shoulders rippled with a little laugh. "Figures, though. Who else but an Mfecane superwoman wouldn't be intimidated by the maniac? Ah, sorry, Ginny. 'Excessively irrepressible agent of, God help us, the Republic of Haven.' How's that?"

Ginny chuckled. "I can live with that."

Eloise studied Trajan. "Are you really serious about this? And, if you are, how do you propose to train him properly? I warn you, there is no way—*no way,* Wilhelm—that I'd agree to promoting

Cachat to that extent until I'm satisfied he's under some kind of control. Self-control or otherwise."

Trajan looked at Usher, his eyes not quite hard, but . . . close.

After a moment, Kevin nodded. "I'll give him up, Wilhelm. And no tricks. I'll make clear to him you're his boss from now on."

"Good enough." Trajan looked back at Eloise. "This doesn't have to be done all *that* quickly, Madam President. For the moment, I think what's probably needed most is to give Cachat a major and important assignment. An *official* one. I'll go out there myself, as soon as possible, to spend some time with him. But let's give the young man a chance—for once—to show what he can do when he isn't being forced to circumvent authority at the same time. He'll *be* the authority."

Eloise frowned. "Go out there yourself? What 'there' are you talking—oh."

Her eyes widened. Then, a cool smile came to her face. "Hm. Hm. You know, I think I *like* that idea. Victor Cachat, chief of station on . . . Erewhon? Or Torch?"

"Both, I think," replied Wilhelm. He cocked his head at Usher, soliciting his opinion.

Kevin nodded. "Yes, both. We'd be crazy—I'm just being blunt, Eloise—to yank him out of Erewhon now. From everything I can tell, he's got an inside track with the Erewhonese. If we yanked him, that would certainly send them exactly the wrong message."

"True," agreed Eloise. "But why add Torch to the mix?"

Ginny started to say something, but choked off the words. Pritchart glanced at her. "Should I take it that he'd be visiting Torch every chance he got anyway?"

Ginny nodded. Pritchart's smile remained cool, but spread a little. "Not a casual girlfriend then, I gather. Well . . . who knows? That might help things, too."

"Besides," Kevin interjected, "Victor's got the inside track with the Torches also. If you send anybody else out there, he'll just—ah—"

"Run rings around them?" Eloise jibed. "Leave them lying flat on their back in a cloud of dust?"

"Something like that."

The President of the Republic of Haven moved her eyes to a blank spot on the far wall, which she examined for a minute or so. Then, leaning forward, she planted her hands on the desk again and spread her fingers.

"All right, we'll do it. And since we need to send someone official to attend the coronation of the new Queen of Torch in a few weeks—Kevin, you're it. I'll let you break the news to your protégé that he's now an Official Maniac. Which means if he pulls a stunt like this again, I'll flay him alive."

Usher nodded, looking as innocent as a lamb.

"You're not fooling me, Kevin," growled Pritchart. "Your lamb imitation wouldn't fool Little Red Riding Hood."

But she was laughing softly when she said it. And then added: "I'd love to be there myself, actually. Just to watch you and Ginny having to act like a respectable married couple, for a change."

It was Ginny's turn to look innocent. She managed it about as well as Kevin. "You mean I can't wear that sari I bought on *The Wages of Sin*, the day before I left?"

As they got up to leave, Pritchart said: "You stay behind, Kevin."

Once Ginny and Trajan had left the room, Pritchart gestured at the display screen. "I didn't see any reason to bring this up in front of Wilhelm, since I'm sure he missed it. There's still a loose end here, Kevin. A big one."

"Stein's killing?" Usher shrugged. "Yeah, sure. But I'm also sure it's being taken care of."

The President of Haven rolled her eyes. "Oh, wonderful. Cachat's Hairy Ride of Death and Destruction is about to get underway again."

Usher shook his head. "It won't be Victor's operation. I'm sure of that."

"Who's, then?"

"How am I supposed to know?" complained Kevin. "I'm umpteen light-years away! But it won't be Victor. No reason for it to be, really."

Eloise stared at the empty screen, bringing up in her mind various tantalizing bits and scraps of the reports. Reports which had been, she was quite certain, carefully edited in some respects.

But there was no great anger in the thought. She was experienced in black ops herself, and knew perfectly well that Victor Cachat had been careful to provide her with "plausible deniability." Now that her fury had faded, Eloise was willing to admit—to herself alone—that Trajan had been right. Cachat *was* brilliant at this kind of work. If he could be brought under some kind of control . . .

She leaned back in her chair, mollified at the thought—the possibility, at least—that in a few years Haven might have an excellent foreign intelligence service again. One with a different ethos than Saint-Just's, but every bit as capable. Not even in her angriest moments did Eloise think Cachat was cut from the same cloth as Saint-Just. Every bit as ruthless, yes. But she didn't misunderstand the moral code that lay beneath that ruthlessness. That was as different from Saint Just's as a grizzly bear from a cobra.

"I guess I can live with 'furry,'" she said, half-smiling. "So what's your guess, Kevin?"

"The girlfriend," he said promptly.

Eloise had come to the same tentative conclusion herself. Again, she rolled her eyes. "Too much to ask, I suppose, that Victor Cachat would get the hots for a prim and proper debutante."

The impulse came as a surprise, but Rozsak wasn't in the habit of arguing with himself. He too, he realized, had come a bit under the spell of a teenaged queen-about-to-be. So, he turned toward Berry just at the moment when he estimated Thandi would strike.

One of her Amazons, rather. Thandi herself was standing next to Cassetti, as he addressed the crowd gathered in the closest thing Torch's main city had to a central square, with Rozsak and Berry a meter or so away on Cassetti's other side.

There was no one behind Cassetti now, who might get hit by a dart passing through his body. Rozsak had no idea how Thandi had managed that. He suspected Anton Zilwicki's hand was involved, somehow—Berry's father was also standing on the administration center's terrace. Which, if so, underscored Watanapongse's warning that the whole operation was no longer "covert" to at least some people outside their own ranks.

No one standing behind Cassetti . . . It would happen now. Rozsak wouldn't have bothered with that curlicue, but he was more ruthless than Palane.

The Solarian captain turned to face Berry, his back toward Cassetti, shielding the girl, as Thandi reached out and touched the lieutenant governor on the upper arm.

"So, Ms. Zilwicki," Rozsak said, and smiled, even as he felt a shiver of respect for Palane. He knew what she was doing . . . even though Cassetti himself didn't. "When should I start calling you . . . what *did* you decide upon, anyway, for a suitable cognomen?"

Her smile was almost a grin. "We're still arguing about it. It doesn't look as if I'll be able to get away with 'Your Modesty,' so now I'm angling for—"

Rozsak heard the pulse rifle dart's impact. From the solid *WHAP!* of it, a good center impact shot. He had Berry by the shoulders and was pulling her down to the terrace a split-second later. It was not quite a "tackle," but . . . close.

Only then did he turn his head and actually look at the lieutenant governor. Not that he'd really needed the confirmation.

The marksman had hit the sniper's triangle dead center, and the hyper-velocity dart had smashed squarely into the man's spinal column on its way through him. The transfer of kinetic energy had been, quite literally, explosive, blasting a twenty-centimeter chunk of Cassetti's neck and shoulders into a finely divided spray of blood, tissue, and pulverized bone even as it flung the instantly dead body back and out of Palane's iron-fingered grip.

No one, Rozsak knew—not even the newsies, some of them standing less than fifty meters away—would ever realize just what Palane had done. They might remark on the freak coincidence which had led the major to tap the lieutenant governor on the arm, undoubtedly to remind him of something, in the very instant before the shot was fired. But none of them would realize that her touching him had been the signal to the person behind that pulser dart. That she had deliberately stood less than a meter from him, holding him motionless to guarantee her chosen shooter a perfect shot and eliminate the possibility that a moving target might change her carefully planned trajectory and put someone else in the line of fire.

Which was a pity, in many ways, he reflected. Because since no one would ever guess, none of them would appreciate the steel-nerved courage—and total confidence in her chosen marksman—required for someone to do what she had just done.

Even as the thought flashed through his mind and the corpse catapulted away, Palane dove to the floor of the terrace herself. Her com was in her hand before she landed, already barking out orders.

Rozsak's eyes ranged the terrace. Everybody was now on the floor, shielded by the terrace's low retaining wall, except for one particularly determined holorecorder crew. His eyes met the hard gaze of Anton Zilwicki.

Rozsak didn't have any trouble at all interpreting that gaze. *That's it, Rozsak. Don't even THINK about taking it any further.*

The Solarian Captain gave Zilwicki a minute little nod. Then, a second later, found himself matching gazes with Jeremy X. The head of the Ballroom was on the terrace floor not far from Zilwicki, his hand pulser gripped in his hand.

To the holorecorder viewers, it would simply look like the natural reaction of an experienced gunman. But Rozsak didn't misunderstand the meaning of that flat-eyed stare—nor the fact that while Jeremy's weapon wasn't directly pointed at him, it wasn't pointed all that far away, either.

He gave Jeremy the same tiny nod. *Yes, yes, yes. That's it. This black op is over.*

In truth, he was glad of it himself. As cold-blooded as he was, even Rozsak would have found it difficult to order Palane's murder. But it was all a moot point, anyway. Watanapongse had been correct: Palane was by no means the only person who had figured out the truth behind Stein's killing. Only a lunatic would start a private war with the likes of Anton Zilwicki and Jeremy X—even leaving aside Victor Cachat.

Cachat wasn't there. Rozsak hadn't expected him to be, since the Havenite agent was doing his best to keep his own involvement in the affair as much of a secret as possible.

He was startled to hear Berry speak calmly. He'd expected the girl to be in something of a state of shock. He was even more startled by the half-whispered words themselves. They carried to his ear quite clearly, even under the shouts of the crowd and the cries of alarm rising from the media crews.

"Victor's keeping guard over the former Mesans who decided to stay. Not the settlement—they're safe enough—but the ones who came in to surrender individually. For the moment, they're all being kept in the old barracks."

Half-propped on an elbow, Rozsak looked down at her. The back of Berry's head was resting on the terrace floor, her eyes fixed on him. It was a gaze far more hostile than he'd ever have expected to encounter from the girl.

"Didn't think of that, did you?" she whispered, icily. "The retaliation that angry ex-slaves might visit, after the killing of someone they think is a liberator of sorts."

He *hadn't* thought of it. Startled, he glanced at Palane, still on the floor barking commands into her com. It was an act, he knew—by now, the Scrags would be dead and the cover-up well under way—but it was a very good one. He had no doubt at all that the media would be fooled. To all appearances, Palane was organizing a manhunt.

"Thandi thought of it, though," Berry whispered. The underlying contempt in her tone was not disguised at all.

And even the girl knows. Rozsak realized in that moment that a teenaged queen-to-be already had what amounted to a staff as good as his own—and probably even more trusting. Odd, really, given the disparate elements it was made of.

He sighed softly. "I'm glad to be done with it," he whispered, trusting in his scrambling equipment to keep the words from being recorded by anyone. Half-protesting: "Damnation, Your Highness, *somebody* had to pay for Stein."

She said nothing. He forced himself to meet her eyes again. Berry's gaze was no longer hostile so much as . . .

Royal. Imperious, even.

"You and Thandi Palane are *quits,* Captain Rozsak," she commanded.

"—got them, kaja. They put up a fight, so there's not much left. Scrags, by the look of the remains. Two of them."

"Don't touch anything," Palane snapped into the com. "We don't have much of a forensic capability, but I want the media to get recordings while the scene of the crime is still undisturbed by investigators."

She rose to her feet, glanced down at Cassetti's corpse, and stalked toward the crowd of reporters.

"It's over," she announced.

"Who was it?" cried out one of them. "Mesan agents?"

"Don't know. I doubt if we ever will. There were two assassins and they put up a fight. The unit who took them out are special commandos, not cops. They didn't leave much, it seems." Thandi shook her head. "You'll be allowed to record whatever there is. The unit commander tells me she thinks they were holdovers from Templeton's gang. Whether they were operating on orders or just trying to get revenge . . . who knows?"

And nobody ever will, Rozsak thought with satisfaction. The Erewhonese, he was quite sure, had already erased any evidence that two Scrags had been captured on the space station. The same two Scrags that Thandi's Amazons had just blown away, after one of the Amazons shot Cassetti. It was a nicely planned, well-executed operation.

Nobody? Well . . . except for the ones who mattered.

"Quits, Captain," Berry repeated.

"Yes. My word on it."

He meant it too. Very, very sincerely. Everybody on the terrace was rising to their feet, holstering whatever weapons they might have drawn. Everybody except Jeremy X, who was still prone on the floor and still had his hand pulser in his grip.

True, it was not pointed at Rozsak. Not exactly. But the Ballroom leader's gaze was pinpointed on the captain. That flat-eyed, empty, killer's stare.

"My word on it," he said again.

EPILOGUE

MICHAEL WINTON-SERISBURG SMILED. "So she lost, huh?"

His daughter Ruth nodded. "'Lost' is hardly the word. She got smeared. Flattened. *Nobody* agreed with her—not even me. But I will say she put up one hell of a fight. And—Berry's a lot slyer than most people think—she got what she wanted out of it in the end, I'm pretty sure."

Judith, Ruth's mother, had a smile on her face also. But it was a distracted sort of smile, since she was preoccupied examining the thousands of ex-slaves spilling through all the streets in Torch's main city to watch the coronation. "I assume she made sure the whole populace knew about the brawl."

Her daughter gave her a *hey, no kidding* sort of a look. "That was my job," she said, a bit smugly. "Well. Captain Zilwicki helped."

Her father's smile widened. "Indeed. That was before the vote, yes? So by the time the entire populace was able to express their opinion on whether they wanted a constitutional monarchy, they all knew that their prospective Queen had been waging a battle royal to have herself referred to as 'Your Mousety.' With 'Your Incisorship" as"—he choked down a laugh—"the 'compromise' she was willing to settle for."

"Yup," said Ruth. "Like I said, she got smeared. But the vote in favor of the constitutional monarchy was ninety-three percent—and she did manage to hold the line on the royal 'We.' She just flat refused, pointing out that nobody could make *her* use the expression. And since she's the only one who can, that made it a moot point. She said it made her feel fat already, with her eighteenth birthday just behind her."

Ruth's mother didn't try to choke down her own laugh. "Probably just as well she lost. The Andermani Emperor would have had a fit. He's got precious little use for 'constitutional' monarchism in the first place, much less kings and queens being likened to mice."

"Your aunt would have been none too pleased either, for that matter," commented Michael idly. He was now examining the crowd closely himself; but, in his case, concentrating on the notables gathered on the terrace where the coronation was finally getting underway. The same terrace that he and his wife and daughter were standing on, as the official representatives of the Star Kingdom.

"No reason to irk your neighbors unnecessarily—especially when, for the moment at least, you're awash in official goodwill." He made a discreet little swivel of his head, indicating by the gesture everyone gathered on the terrace. "This is quite an assemblage, when you get down to it. Official representatives from every star nation on this side of the Solarian League. And even if the League itself didn't send anybody . . ."

His eyes settled on the figure of Oravil Barregos. The governor of Maya Sector was standing almost right next to the rabbi who would be officiating over the ceremony. Close enough that he was almost crowding him, in fact. The governor was smiling widely and waving at the crowd gathered below; the rabbi was clearly trying not to scowl.

Michael's gaze shifted to the man next to Barregos. The new top military officer of the SLN in Maya Sector—formerly Captain, now Rear Admiral Luiz Rozsak—was standing just a little to one side, and just a little farther back. Not much. Clearly enough, Maya Sector felt it had a certain "special relationship" with the new star nation of Torch.

Which, in truth, they did. But Michael didn't miss the importance of the position which had been given to the Erewhonese representatives. Jack Fuentes, the President of Erewhon and in fact its central leader—never automatically the same thing with Erewhonese—was standing on the *other* side of the rabbi. Just as close as Barregos, had he chosen to crowd his way forward the way the governor of Maya was doing.

Of course, Fuentes wasn't. That was not the way of Erewhonese leaders. If anything, the Erewhonese President was doing his best to remain inconspicuous. As inconspicuous as possible, that is, for a man standing very close to the center of the crowd's attention—and the small horde of media people who were recording the event.

Not such a small horde, actually. The dramatic events on *The Wages of Sin* followed by the equally dramatic liberation of Congo had riveted the galaxy's attention and interest. The Mesans had taken a tremendous body blow, here. There were not down and out, certainly—not with the connections they had with the real powers in the Solarian League. But the shadows in which Mesa and the Office of Frontier Security preferred to operate had been obliterated by a blinding glare of public scrutiny. The Mesans and the Solarian bureaucrats and combines had been caught like cockroaches when the lights go on. Too busy frantically scurrying for cover to really be able to do much to prevent the final unfolding of the drama.

"Final" unfolding? he asked himself. *Hardly that.*

Hardly. Michael was now certain that the Solarian League, center of the human race, was in for that ancient curse: *interesting times.* Governor Barregos' popularity in Maya Sector itself had soared to stratospheric heights. For that matter, Web Du Havel had told Michael yesterday that the most recent poll indicated that Barregos was now the best-known and most popular political figure in the *entire* Solarian League. Which wasn't perhaps saying much, looked at from one angle, since the huge population of the League tended to be oblivious to most political affairs outside of their own systems. There was certainly no chance that Barregos could parlay that new popularity into a real challenge for wresting control of the entire League away from its established ruling interests.

Still . . .

Rear Admiral Rozsak, the same poll indicated, was now quite a well-known and popular figure himself. Michael knew that, for all practical purposes, Maya Sector now had its own independent naval force—and Barregos and Rozsak were quietly launching a massive armament program. If civil war did erupt in the League, Maya Sector would be a very tough nut to crack.

But that was a problem for a later day. Michael shook his head slightly, reminding himself that he had far more immediate concerns to deal with.

Again, his gaze moved to Fuentes. For a moment, the eyes of the Erewhonese President met Michael's. Fuentes gave him a cordial, polite little nod—and then looked away.

Michael stifled a sigh. Erewhon, he was almost sure, was lost to Manticore, though nothing formal had been said or done. The most he could do, now, was contain the damage.

His hand rose, his fingers closing around the hilt of the new ceremonial sword he'd chosen to bring to the ceremony.

It was not a sword, really; the weapon was much too short for that term. The blade scabbarded to his hip was more in the way of a very big knife. The same kind of knife which, tradition had it, had figured prominently in the ancient clashes of the gangster families who had founded Erewhon centuries earlier.

Walter Imbesi had presented it to Michael, the day he'd arrived at Erewhon on his way to Torch. When Michael had looked at inscription etched on the blade, he'd felt his heart sink.

To the House of Winton, with our compliments and thanks. It had been signed: *Fuentes. Hall. Havlicek. Imbesi.* The new quadrumvirate-in-all-but-name which ruled Erewhon.

"To the House of Winton." *Not* "to the Star Kingdom of Manticore." The Erewhonese were making clear, in their own way, that the back door would always remain open for Manticore's dynasty. But the front door was closing on the Star Kingdom.

The coronation ceremony was about to begin. All eyes were now on the figure of Berry Zilwicki, coming toward the terrace through the crowd below. She was wearing very fine apparel, but—another of the girl's subtle touches—had no escort at all. She was relying on the crowd itself to make way for her.

Since no one was looking at him, for the moment, Michael allowed the sigh to emerge. He tried to look on the bright side. Given Erewhonese custom, the back door was actually a prestigious entrance. Close friends as well as servants always came into the house of an Erewhonese grandee through the back door, never using the front door. In fact, the very closest of friends were given the combination of the lock on that back door.

Translated into diplomatic terms—Michael glanced sideways at his adopted daughter—that "combination" was Ruth Winton.

Judith had already made clear she was in favor of Ruth's proposal. Michael had been the one to hesitate.

"Okay," he murmured. "If that's your desire, Ruth, I don't object. You can stay here, for as long as you want. With my blessing."

Ruth's smile was almost a grin. "Thanks, Dad."

Berry was making slow progress through the crowd. Not because people weren't giving way for her and clearing a space, but simply because she was chatting with them as she came. Since he still had some time before the ceremony began, Michael chewed on the matter further. And, after a while, discovered himself agreeing more and more with his wife's assessment, despite his own misgivings.

Judith had expressed herself bluntly. That very morning.

"Leave diplomacy out of it, Michael! This place is *good* for Ruth. And I'm not talking about the spy business!" Judith had chuckled, then. "Of course, being trained by such as Anton Zilwicki and

Jeremy X—not to mention those Erewhonese not-all-that-far-from-gangsters—she'll become more of a holy terror than she is already. What's more important is that it's finally something that is *hers*, Michael. And for the first time in her life she has real *friends.* One, especially."

Indeed, so. One, especially. And as Michael Winton-Serisburg watched that special friend start to climb the staircase up to the terrace, he found all his doubts fading away.

"You'll have to accept a guard detachment from the Queen's Own, though," he murmured. "I'll leave the same unit behind that escorted me here, since Judith and I won't need them on the trip back."

He saw Ruth wince.

"Don't even try to argue the matter, daughter. My sister would kill me if I didn't leave them behind."

Ruth didn't argue the point, at the moment. It would have been impossible anyway, since Berry was now on the terrace and approaching the rabbi. The ceremony was finally about to get underway. But Michael knew she would argue it later. And he also understood the true reason, which had nothing to do with the diplomatic folderol she'd advance—her own feelings of guilt over the fate of her former guardsmen. Not so much their death in the line of duty, but the fact that she'd immediately allied herself thereafter with the man who had done nothing to prevent those deaths, even if he wasn't personally responsible for them.

But Michael wasn't worried about it. He understood the mentality of the Queen's Own far better than his adopted daughter did. Or ever would, in truth. Despite her upbringing, Ruth would never really *think* like royalty—or their closest retainers. Michael was quite sure that the soldiers of the Queen's Own had already made their own assessment of his adopted daughter. Royal ruthlessness for purposes of state, even at the cost of their own lives, would not bother them in the least. Such was the nature of the game they had chosen to play. What they *did* care about was that the royal person they served and protected knew how to play the game—play it well, for a real purpose, with courage and panache. They would lay down their lives with no complaint, so long as they thought those lives weren't simply being thrown away by a fool or a poltroon.

"I won't tell them to do it," he murmured. "I'll ask for volunteers. They will *all* volunteer, Ruth. Each and every one. You watch."

Struck by a related thought, Michael's eyes scanned the notables gathered on the terrace. The official representatives of the Republic of Haven, Kevin and Virginia Usher, were standing near the front. But . . .

"Where *is* this mysterious Victor Cachat, by the way? I still haven't met the fellow."

Ruth looked a bit uncomfortable. "Ah. He's not here, I don't think. Well, maybe he is. Hard to know. And if he is, you won't see him anyway. Thandi—uh, General Palane—asked him to oversee the security arrangements. She couldn't do it herself, since she's part of the ceremony. It's a little irregular, of course, but Torch doesn't have a security apparatus really in place yet."

"Irregular" was putting it mildly. Michael chewed on the thought of his own security—and his wife and daughter's—being in the hands of a Havenite secret agent. It was certainly an odd taste.

Ruth smiled thinly. "Relax, Dad. For the moment, he's on our side. Or, at least, the same side we are, if not exactly 'ours.' So long as that's true, we're as safe as can be. Trust me on this one."

Michael spoke only once, during the ceremony itself. "This is very shrewd," he whispered. "Whose idea was it?"

"Web's," Ruth whispered in response. Her eyes flicked toward the figure of Jessica Stein, standing in the crowd of notables on the terrace. "Rabbi Hideyoshi was probably her father's closest friend, even if he was never officially part of the Renaissance Association."

Michael suspected that Ruth was missing some of the equation. He resolved to discuss it with Du Havel himself, later, in private. Granted, choosing a rabbi from Hieronymus Stein's own branch of Judaism to officiate at the ceremony was a smooth way of furthering ties with the Renaissance Association. It also neatly sidestepped the awkwardness of creating a new royal house without the blessing of any organized religious body.

Still, he thought those were secondary concerns, in Du Havel's political calculations. Michael himself did not know as much as he wished he did, concerning the history and theology of Autentico Judaism. He'd have to do some studying on the matter. But he did know two things:

First, it was easily the fastest-growing branch of that ancient faith, even if some of the most orthodox branches of Judaism refused to accept the Autenticos as a legitimate part of galactic Jewry. If for no other reason, because they choked at the notion of the "Chosen People" as a self-selected body rather than a hereditary one, and the proselytizing that went with it.

Second, it met a particularly favorable reception from the galaxy's most downtrodden peoples. He'd heard, though he wasn't sure it was true, that it was by far the most popular religion among Manpower's ex-slaves—not least of all because the Autenticos, like the Audubon Ballroom, were willing to send organizers back into slavery to proselytize from within. He'd also heard—though, again, he'd have to check the accuracy—that there had been some trouble on the Mfecane worlds because of Autentico activity. He did know, for a fact, that the religion was officially banned on Mesa.

"Shrewd," he murmured again.

The murmur was loud enough to be heard by his wife. "Yes. It's not a militant or intolerant creed—blessedly"—Judith had her own very good reasons for being hostile toward fundamentalist religions—"but . . . how to say it? Autentico Judaism lends itself well to rebellion, leave it at that. Which is fine with me."

Michael delicately cleared his throat. "Fine with me, as well, dear. But *do* try to find a more diplomatic way of putting that, should you ever happen to discuss it with my sister."

Judith smiled serenely. Berry Zilwicki was now kneeling and Rabbi Hideyoshi was placing the crown on her head. It was a simple tiara. Berry had insisted on that, and, this time, won the argument. She'd even managed to win the argument over the decorations: nothing more than a golden mouse, with pearls for its eyes. Looking a bit startled, as if it had been caught while stealing cheese.

"Oh, bah," she murmured back. "*There's* a queen who won't have trouble embracing rebellion, where it's needed."

The crown was securely placed. Berry rose, turned, and moved to the front of the terrace to face the throng. On her way—this was quite impromptu, Michael was sure of it—she took the hand of her adopted father and mother and brought them forward with her.

Queen Berry, of the House of Zilwicki, faced her new subjects—using the term loosely—flanked by a former countess of Manticore and . . .

Cap'n Zilwicki, Scourge of the Spaceways.

Michael winced, even before the crowd's erupting applause smote his ears like a hammer. *Oh, Lord. Interesting times, indeed.*

The thunder of applause rolled over him like a waterfall. The sound continued as Berry, like the star of a just-concluded drama, cheerfully dove back into the little mob of notables and started hauling some of them forward to share in the applause.

She began, diplomatically enough, by escorting Governor Barregos and Admiral Rozsak to the fore. Then, the Erewhonese representatives. Then—it was very well done, with a simultaneous wave of her hands, avoiding any favoritism—she brought forward Michael and Judith themselves, with Kevin and Virginia Usher advancing on her other side. (Michael was amused to see the slick way in which Ruth managed to stay behind, avoiding the limelight.) Then, the notables from the Andermani Empire and the Silesian Confederacy; Jessica Stein; any number of others.

But Michael didn't miss the significance of the sequence. Berry saved three for the last.

First, the two central figures in the new government of Torch: Web Du Havel and Jeremy X, whom she brought forward together.

The crowd's applause was now almost deafening. Michael wished he'd had the foresight to bring ear protectors.

When Du Havel and Jeremy stepped back, the roar of the crowd eased a bit. Michael thought the worst of it was over.

Then, as Berry brought forward a tall and very powerful looking woman wearing a uniform Michael was not familiar with, and he heard the crowd almost sucking in a collective breath . . .

He knew who she was. Thandi Palane, the newly appointed commander-in-chief of Torch's brand new military in creation. But he hadn't had a chance to meet her yet.

The next wave of applause hit like a tidal wave. Michael couldn't help but flinch a little. Not even so much at the sheer volume of the sound, but at its timber. This was no longer simply applause. This was a snarl of pure fury. The new star nation might have adopted—cheerfully, with good humor, even gleefully—a queen with a mouse on her coat of arms. But no one would ever confuse that nation's fangs with those of a rodent.

The applause soon crystallized into two slogans, chanted over and over again, like a collective blacksmith hammering out a sword.

One of them he understood. *Death to Mesa!* was a given.

The other had him puzzled.

After the ceremony was finally done, he asked his daughter. "What does 'Great Kaja' mean?"

Ruth managed to look ferocious and smug at the same time. "It means Mesa is history. They just don't know it yet."